FIRST A
TORCH

A NOVEL OF DIEN BIEN PHU

BY
RICHARD BAKER

second printing

Library of Congress Control Number: 2011927362

ISBN: 978-0-9705148-6-8

Ink & Lens, Ltd.
8012 14th Ave. Court East
Tacoma, WA 98404

To Nev Tickner and Herman Gollob for their belief in the book

Forward

In what is really a timeless story, "First a Torch", Richard Baker has captured the essence of ordinary people in extraordinary times... weaving together the strands of humanity that appeal to us all, and despite any impression it is just another book about war, it is as much a love story as it is an adventure.

Vietnam was the jewel in the crown of the great house of French colonialism... a torch that lit the way to a new world... IT was, in a sense, the flames that brought western ideals into the lives of the people of what, for almost 200 years, was quaintly called Indochina. Sometimes for the better, sometimes for the worse... never with permission.

The French stand in an isolated valley 200 miles from Hanoi was a demonstration of both their arrogance and their desperation... the greater good of their colonizing endeavor in the Far-East had begin to crumble, and in the fog of a humble people's desire for freedom and self determination... the torch was extinguished in a vain attempt to defend what was not theirs in the first place.

But destiny never drives us to where we want to go, it pushes us along a path that is determined by the choices we make, the chances we take, and the circumstance of particular moments along the way...such is this story.

In his own inimitable style, Baker works to his crescendo with great care. The earlier lives of the main characters are meticulously re-constructed step by step as the logic and reason behind their unfolding lives develops into a climax as unpredictable as it is inevitable.

With the passion of someone who has lived through it all, Baker has created an amazing sense of the real and terrifying experience of the individual in life and in war... In so doing his brilliant command of the English language breathes insight into the rarest of opportunities... to understand the thoughts, fears, prejudices, hopes, and aspirations of the unfortunate souls upon whom the burden of circumstance and sacrifice had been thrust.

This is a story for people who seek more than entertainment in a book... it is for people who seek the truth behind the history.

Nev Tickner

By 1953 the French Colonial War in Vietnam is going badly. General Navarre, newly arrived military commander for French Indochina, devises a bold plan to capture major Vietnamese opium fields, stop Viet Minh incursions into Laos, and to defeat the communists in a decisive battle. On November 20, 1953, French forces parachute into the valley of Dien Bien Phu.

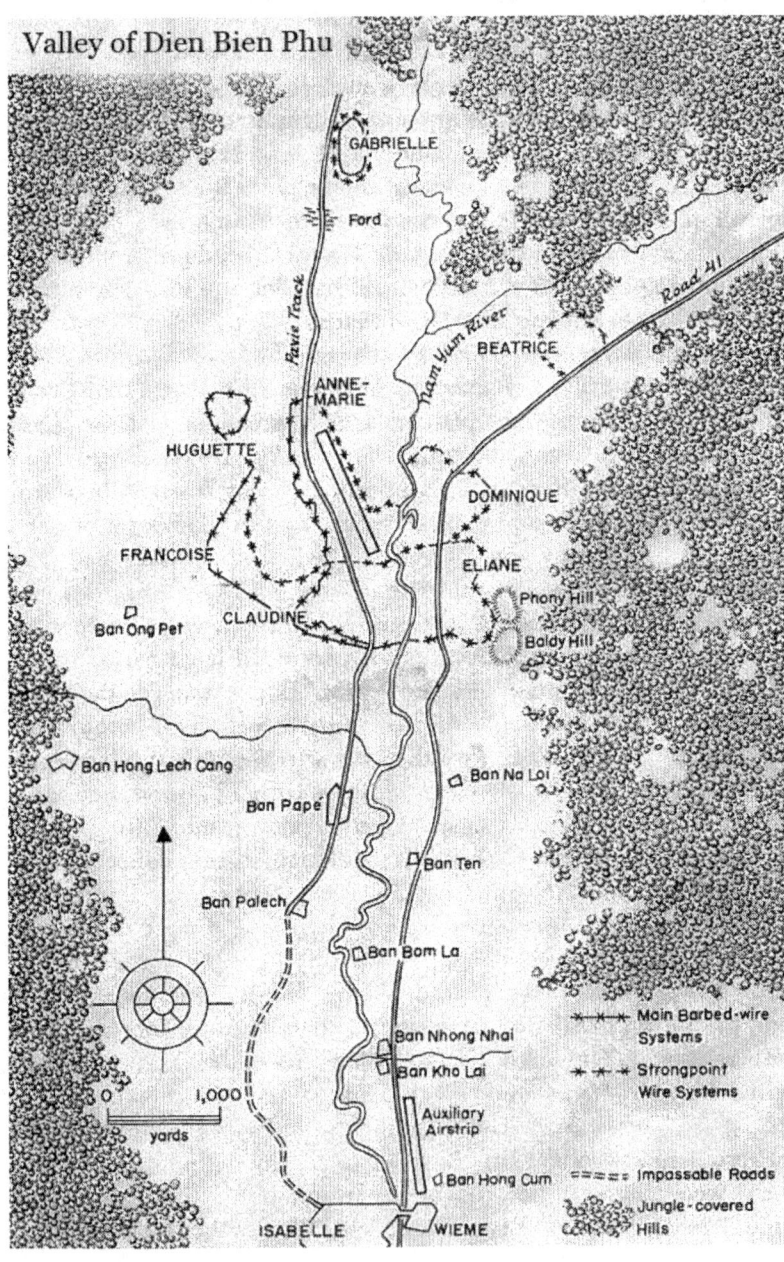

Valley of Dien Bien Phu

FIRST A TORCH

The house is first a torch, and then a ruin,
And then a sweetening field, quiet after storm,
Songs flower in the night by whose light we dance
And go up.

Alan Grossman

ACT 1 - Chance Encounters

Chapter 1

Bix knew that retaining the severed head of Smith was a mistake. The rotting skull became an obsession with his friend, the old Nazi, Henrich Knowles and he later watched the Frenchman, deJohn, peer into the empty black eye sockets as he sank in a nebulous sea of insanity. Only Nicole, the French prostitute, devoted to a single man, had remained unaffected. Her capacity for compassion, mixed with the hard resolve of detachment, stayed consistent until the end, until nothing mattered except love, when not even survival counted. But what most fascinated Bix was Smith's truncated head riding high above the Center of Resistance on a bamboo pole; the head, unwavering like an iron flag under the enemy Viet Minh shell-bursts; the head who, Bix was convinced, partly instigated the events of his history. But all that came later, during the siege at Dien Bien Phu, when Bix exchanged the loyalty and duty of a French Foreign Legionnaire, for the insight and understanding of a man.

He was born William Bloomfield in the farming town of Woolsey, South Dakota, but his friends called him Bix after the early jazz cornet player, Bix Beiderbecke, not because he played cornet – he had no musical ability - but because he read everything he could about the jazzman and constantly listened to all his surviving recordings. A man needed to make a mark in the world to vindicate himself from the unnoticed lives of others plodding through the dust of anonymity. If he could have been anyone in history he would have been Bix Beiderbecke, tortured soul, romantic, musical innovator, legend, genius, drunk and dead at the age of 31. Bix left school in his junior year knowing he was not university material and saw no reason to delay his entry into the world of men and a chance to become a romantic tortured soul and make his own history. Great things awaited him and, like Odysseus, he had only to find them. He gathered his savings from many summers working fields bucking hay and went on the road, at first lonely and timid, waiting to grow into a manhood he had not yet known. He passed the empty swimming pool where he felt Nora Buchamp's breasts, the restaurant crowded with farmers sipping coffee, the high school proud of its championship basketball team on which he never played, and watched the water tower grow shorter as he drove southeast. Days later, around midnight and inside Georgia's border, depression and frustration set in. After two weeks of travel he recognized his inability to find his own history or an adventure that would cut him, like a prize bull, from the common herd of men. With the depression came frustration and the embarrassment of not even knowing where to look. He had seen winding blacktop, miles and miles of corn, flatland, clear rivers that had turned brown the further south he had driven, cheap hotels and restaurants plastered together with cooking grease, but nothing remarkable, nothing that drew him in, no Cyclops, no tempting Sirens luring him to rocky shores. Grendel slept refusing to exit his lair and play. Not even the Holy Grail left hints of discovery. Bix had found no giants or golden goose, no Goliaths.

The road sign, black lettering on a chipped white background, indicated the next town as Shell Bluff. He needed to stop and sleep before arriving there. Since leaving South Dakota he had slept on the back seat of his car, a 1941 Studebaker with plenty of room, and had nestled into the gray felt, breathing the moist evening air smelling of burnt engine oil. Eating a breakfast of sausage gravy and biscuits one morning at a truck stop in Pennsylvania a driver called out asking if anyone wanted work unloading his rig. Bix joined the man, who drove a furniture moving van, and spent four hours carrying boxes into a house. The work proved easy for a boy who had been bucking hay his entire life and he earned ten dollars, enough to keep him in gas and food for two days. Since then he ate breakfast at truck stops whenever possible, often yelling to truckers that he was available for work, and landed several more jobs assuring his continued travel. He learned early that the nicer the truck - west coast rigs like Kenworths, Freightliners, and Peterbuilts - the smaller the pay. The truckers who paid best drove east coast beater Fords, GMCs, Macks billowing heaps of diesel smoke, and Internationals.

Earlier in the evening, rain had fallen and the oncoming headlights of an occasional passing vehicle had made stars of the raindrops outside the wipers and the greasy streaks under the frayed wiper blades had annoyed him to tiredness. He slowed before driving down a pitted dirt road for about a half-mile, and bumped along between wayward tobacco cans, broken beer bottles, and clods of paper and cardboard, the headlights of the car flashing between the trees and the ground. Distance from the main road helped him sleep easier and he needed a wide place to park so he could turn around in the morning. Dim light shown ahead making a flat glow of mist in the tree leaves. Cautiously he doused his own lights and turned onto a matt of pine needles, stopping under a canopy of foliage and pinecones. The interior light was broken and the only notice he made of his arrival was the dry creak in the hinges of the door. Carefully he closed the door without pushing it completely shut. Bent over like a thief he crept toward the lights and the increasing sound of drunken laughter, a flashlight in his hand but not turned on. Twice he fought off spider webs that wrapped around his face. He knelt before a small clearing. In the headlights of a rotted Ford pickup, one back fender missing, the other bent almost flat, two men in coveralls were beating a small boy. Two other men in faded and ripped bib overalls, holding sticks and bottles of whisky, yelled encouragement, their yellow and black teeth barely visible.

"Beat the shit out of that yellow bastard!" "Jab his eyes out!" "Ain't no Chinaman fucking our whores, even if they is black. Besides she done got hers already."

Bix looked in the shadows for anyone else and saw what seemed to be a dress of yellow and blue with one dark leg cocked at the knee in an awkward inverted V. He was no match for the drunken men. He had to act to save the boy, but how? He moved quickly back into the woods. Perhaps this was his great adventure? At a distance, he yelled into his cupped hands.

"Over here, Sheriff, I think they're over here!" He listened for a moment. Still the men laughed. Slightly opening his hands he yelled again. "Sheriff, Sheriff, I think they're over here!" He started tramping on twigs, flipped on the flashlight and shone it through the trees to get their attention. The laughing stopped and all the men looked in his direction like deer aware of danger, motionless, eyes bright, ears up.

"Come on, Sheriff. Bring the boys! We can still catch them!" He started running toward the opening as the last man jumped onto the running board and the truck spit out clods of mud from the tires that mixed with a cloud of blue smoke.

Bix broke into the clearing, pointed toward the truck, and frantically yelled, "They're getting away! Come on. They're getting away!"

A wet blanket of black air fell to the dirt behind the disappearing headlights. Bix cautiously moved toward a dark shape kneeling face down on the dirt. The boy seemed small, undernourished. Bix knelt beside him and said, "You OK?" feeling embarrassed at such a ridiculous question but not knowing what else to say. How could someone beaten half to death be OK? Tentatively he touched the boy's quivering shoulder. Practically no meat covered his body and Bix felt the bones under his fingers. The boy lifted up his head, his face covered with blood as if it were a Halloween mask. Bix looked past the blood and the swelling and saw that he was not a boy at all but rather a young man, probably older than himself, a tiny creature looking innocent and afraid. He could not tell if he were Chinese, because he had never seen a Chinese, had never seen any kind of Orientals before, except the ones on the movie screens: round glasses, buck teeth, always bleeding from their mouths after some American hero had shot them to death in a effort to save the world for democracy and freedom. He did not look like that at all. In fact, he looked rather pleasant even with the blood and the swelling.

"Here, buddy. Can you lay on your back?" Bix lowered him to the ground then bent up his knees to keep the blood running to his head to prevent shock, like his Uncle Alvin had taught him after returning from the war. "I've got some water in my car, maybe a cloth." He knew of nothing else to do except make him as comfortable as possible.

"Thank you," the man said, cupping his hands together as if in prayer and attempting to nod his head. "Just leave me here for now. I think I have a cracked rib." His voice was quiet and jagged, a whisper emerging through the blood.

He spoke perfect English with just a hint of something else, something European like Italian or French. Bix motioned that he was going to look at the other person and would return. He moved toward the bright dress, dim in the dark. A woman lay motionless, her shoes knocked off and lying on their sides, her hands bent strangely at the wrists. She might have been attractive except her black face had been crushed, maybe with a tire iron or a large tree limb. The repeated blows had flattened her nose; one eye clung, by tendons or muscles, to the side of her face while the other gaped in surprise toward the sky; her lips, like two fat sausages, were almost torn off and bits of teeth had embedded themselves into her cheeks. Bix felt both sick and fascinated. Dead animals on the farm were one thing he had witnessed many times but this was completely different, a person, a complete human being who just a short while ago was living breathing flesh. She did not repulse him as much as she surprised and fascinated him. He wanted to touch her but something about it seemed sacrilegious. He touched her anyway, first her arm then her thigh then up into her blouse to feel her heart, running his hand over her breasts on the way. She was cold to the touch, colder than anything living. He felt a little ashamed at feeling her breasts and resisted the temptation to feel them again.

"I'll get the car," he said, as he passed the man.

"And her?" He waved his hand toward the woman.

"Dead," Bix said. "I didn't touch her. Couldn't. She's dead and we need to get out of here and get you to a hospital before they get back."

He lit the man with car lights as he drove up, brought him water to drink from an army canteen. He used a wet T-shirt to clean his face.

"I wish to see her," he said.

"Not a good idea," said Bix. "She's pretty torn up."

"I must."

Bix helped him stumble to her side. He knelt beside her, ran a finger through her hair, held her hand, and said nothing.

The car bounced back to highway 80, a narrow strip of two-lane highway. Bix wanted to get another look but the dash lights fell short of illuminating the man. He turned left toward the town.

"I think I remember a hospital sign for Waynesboro. We're not stopping until we get there." He thought the man might ask him how far it was but he said nothing, just sat there quietly breathing in a steady rhythm. "You OK?"

"Yes," he said.

They drove slowly through Shell Bluff: a restaurant, two taverns, several barns of unpainted and weathered wood, a tobacco shed. Under the moonlight Bix noticed the Ford pick-up truck beside one of the barns. He saw no police station and would not have stopped had it been the only building in town. He heard too many rumors about Southern crooked cops, mean ignorant residents. People not from the south attempted to avoid the area. They were still pissed about losing the Civil War and took too much pride in ignorance to be forgiving or in recognizing their own faults as a people. The men did not speak until they left the town.

"I'm Bix." The dash lights cast a glow in the car and slightly against the side of the man's face when he leaned near.

"Ho Van Chau."

"Ho what?"

"Van Chau. Ho Van Chau." The words sounded strange. He had heard about Chinatown in San Francisco. Maybe he was Chinese.

"Are you a Jap?"

"Annamite."

"You hurt bad?"

"I feel better." Bix had never heard of an Annamite. Maybe it was some kind of a Chinaman.

"You're not a Jap?"

"I'm from Annam, the city of Hue."

"In South Dakota, where I was born, we don't hear much about other countries. I thought maybe you were Chinese. I've never heard of an Annem-what-ever."

"The Corn Palace," said Chau.

"You know about the Corn Palace? Even Americans don't know about it. It's not really made of corn, just the outside plastered on to make it pretty."

"Will they find the woman?"

"We'll tell them at the hospital." The image of the woman flashed into his mind. He had slaughtered many animals but had never seen anything like her. "Maybe we should forget about her."

"Sometimes people call my country Vietnam. We belong to France."

"You're not in trouble, are you?" He almost hoped he was, then he would not have to inform the cops. This was the South. Everything he heard said the cops were suspicious of strangers. Besides, if Chau were on the run then his big adventure, his mark in the world, might have already started.

"I came here after finishing from university in Paris. This trip is a gift from my

5

family, from my father."

"I don't know Vietnam, either," said Bix. He cleared his throat. "I don't mean to be disrespectful. Lots of places I don't know."

"Learning about the places of the world help determine the fate of poor countries like mine," said Chau. They both went silent as the feint lights of Waynesboro came into view.

The hospital, a single story white building, sat back from the road. Bix drove to the entrance and helped lift Chau to his feet. Chau bent over and spit up a mouthful of blackish red blood. A nurse, seeing the two, opened the door and helped get Chau into a seat. The room smelled of bleach. Scuff marks had scarred the tile floor. A wheelchair sat beside the door, light from the red exit sign mirrored in the chrome. A radio quietly played something by Hank Williams.

"What's happened?" she said. Her face wrinkled up as if she had never seen anything more dramatic than a sore throat. She started reaching toward his battered eye but drew back her thin hand when it got close.

"He's been beat up and needs help."

"Looks like he's been in a fight."

"Just beat up by a bunch of guys."

"What for? They hit him pretty hard."

"Maybe we can get some help?"

"You hurt in other places?" she yelled, like people do at foreigners as if the noise helped them to better understand the language.

"He speaks English fine."

She rather huffed and called several people. Another nurse emerged, wiping the sleep from her eyes as she pushed a gurney.

"What's the problem?"

"He's been beat up," said the nurse.

"You take his vitals?"

"Not yet."

They placed Chau on the gurney and a black man wheeled him into the back.

"We'll need some information," said the nurse.

"I don't know much." Bix was starting to feel tired. "I just found him. His name is Bo Dan Chau, something like that, and he's here from Paris. He's an Anamonk. That's someplace in Vietnam."

"How do you spell that?"

"What?"

"Vietnam…"

"I don't know."

"How do you spell that other, his name?"

"I don't know. CHOW, maybe – or CHU. You'll have to ask him. Can I sit down?"

She pointed to a chair where tufts of hair emerged from a tear. "Maybe we should call the sheriff. I think a woman's been killed."

"Oh dear." She slapped her chin and her eyes glistened as if the news was the first excitement she had ever experienced. She immediately called the sheriff. Bix was asleep when he arrived.

"Young fella," he said, shaking Bix's shoulder. "Wake up there, buddy."

Bix looked up. The sheriff was not what he had expected of a Southern sheriff, fat, inarticulate, sloppy with a long Southern drawl. His face seemed chiseled with tones of kindness, and he was slim, neat, and with no discernable accent. "Yes, sir," said Bix. He started to rise but the sheriff motioned him back down and slid over another chair.

"I'm Sheriff Waters. What's been going on?"

"I'm not sure," said Bix. "I've been driving around the country and sleeping in my car to save money. I pulled down a dirt road some miles back just before a town called…" He had to think for a moment. "Something Bluff."

"Shell Bluff?"

"Yes. I saw these guys beating up this guy. They drove off when they saw me coming."

"Why are you driving around the country?"

"Just wanted to see it."

"You've got no job?"

"No, not yet. I've just been driving and sleeping in my car to save money."

"Any description of the men? Take a minute and think." He dropped some change in a coffee machine and watched the thin brown water partially fill the cup. "It's the best we've got," he said, handing the cup to Bix.

"I didn't get much of a look. They were facing the other way. One was wearing a red -checkered shirt. They were regular looking, not too fat or too thin. It was the truck I noticed, an old gray rusted Ford. Pretty beat up. One of the back fenders was torn off. They got out pretty fast when they saw me."

The sheriff nodded several times as he wrote on his notepad. "What about the woman?"

"She was off to the side, near the trees, wearing a pretty dress. I didn't touch her. I've never seen a dead person before and I hope I don't see another one."

"You knew she was dead?"

"Her face was all beat in and she didn't seem to be breathing. No one could live with a face crushed like that. Nothing on her moved."

"Anything else about her?"

"She was a black woman."

"Black, huh?"

"Sure."

"How did you see her in the dark?"

"What do you mean?"

"Where is the road?"

"I guess it's about the second one outside that town. Yes, the second one. I remember passing one other one before we got to town. Going in this direction it runs off to the right. I thought it wasn't used much when I saw a pile of oil cans beside the main road."

The sheriff stood and offered a hand to lift Bix up. "I'd like you to stick around at least until tomorrow, until we can run an investigation. You probably don't want to leave your friend, anyway."

"I don't even know him," said Bix.

"You know him better than anyone else." He smiled. "He might be needing some help."

"Can I just pull my car around the parking lot and sleep there. I don't want to break any laws."

"Go down the road here about four blocks. Marsha owns the motel. Tell her to give you a room and charge it to the county. She'll be grumpy getting up this time of morning. The same with the food at the restaurant next door, on the county."

The sheriff guided him to the door. "Guess I forgot to ask. What's your name?"

Chapter 2

The first thing Steve Johnson did after his release from prison for drug possession was buy a few joints, a quart of Kentucky mash, then pass out under the shade of a Kentucky sycamore tree, his pants around his ankles and his penis, red and badly beaten, waving limply in surrender under the fading afternoon light. He often joked that he was twenty before he discovered he could have sex with another person. Eventually he awoke, aggravated by the ants starting to nest in the crack of his ass. He was not sure if the incarceration had taught him any lessons about the law or rehabilitation but he thought, probably not. As a free spirit and true American he believed people were entitled to engage in the pursuit of happiness as long as it did not interfere with others and, every time he was drunk or high, he was about as happy as a man could get.

Steve picked out the ants, pulled up his pants, and counted his money: six dollars and seventy-one cents, a meager amount on which to carry on life, yet more than he needed for financial success. He still had a half-filled carton of Old Gold smokes in a smashed pack, a plus in his line of work. He retrieved one of the bent cigarettes and lit it with a Strike Anywhere match snapped to life with two drags across his pant leg. The smoke swirled around his pockmarked face, covered with two days' stubble, and gravitated to his eyes, the lids blinking at the irritation. Tobacco had colored his fingers tan and one side of his lips from a habit learned at the age of five when he worked in the tobacco fields, something he later preferred to school where he often sneaked snakes into the classroom and, because the teacher knew he was not afraid of them, was asked to remove them back to the woods, which he did gladly without returning to class. He remembered there being a bar with a pool table someplace nearby and decided to return to the woods to sleep after a visit, a meal, and some conversation.

He liked people, especially their stupidity, and used his own hillbilly antics to make them resemble fools without them knowing it.

The early evening brought with it a layer of moisture heavily scented with livestock and foliage: the green scent of newly mown grass and alfalfa, corn and tobacco leaves, the rich sweet odor of milk cows and the sharp smell of pigs, trees, and dirt. Even the heavy air carried the aroma of molasses. Dust from the road curled over the toes of his scabbed shoes and he walked carefully like a man who had spent many years trying to balance himself at sea. As he reached to his lips for his cigarette his hand quivered, an affliction he had carried since birth. He released the smoke in small swirls, replaced the cigarette and adjusted his bent brown fedora worn to gray at the creases with a black sweat ring where it fit his head. He had a talent for music and started to sing an old spiritual. Completely lost in thought, he hardly noticed the car pull up beside him. The cracked window rolled down in jerks and he tried to peer toward the voice coming from the darkness.

"Need a ride, buddy?" Except for being rather deep the voice seemed undistinguished.

"Don't mind," said Steve, twisting the door handle. The door came away stiffly and with painful groans as if the hinges had been rusted shut. He never refused a ride, out of politeness if for no other reason. He slid onto the torn cushion. Dust covered the dash and several wounds had cracked across the paint.

"Name's Myron T. Welliver," said the man, holding out a hand of bones patched together with thin layers of dried wrinkled skin colored like agate.

"Steve Johnson, but I answer to any four letter word," he said, responding with his own hand.

"Where you headed?"

"Heard there's a tavern up ahead. Thought I might shoot some pool." Welliver seemed so thin as to be almost invisible and his coveralls resembled a clown's costume in which he was poured. "Live around here, do ya?"

"Bancroft, 'bout ten miles back. There's some good hunting over near Smithtown, a liberal sort of place. Going to talk to a friend 'bout it. He got no phone so I usually drive over and he puts me up. How about you?"

Steve glanced over his shoulder and in the evening light saw a shovel and pick on the back seat. "Just traveling," he said. "Done some time in Donnorsville and just got out."

The car engine rumbled under low revs and heat grilled the floorboards.

"Didn't ruin you, did it?'

"Naw." Steve offered Welliver a cigarette. He shook his head. "I needed the rest, anyway. Got some good fellas there done fell on hard times. Be pleased to buy you a drink at the tavern or give you a dollar for some gas. Going to do some digging?"

"Looking for flowers. Clean living, I say." Welliver slapped the steering wheel. "Never been in a tavern in my life. Don't drink, don't smoke, don't do anything but work. Course I try to eradicate the world of vermin through hunting while at the same time filling the cooking pot. I sometimes use the shovel to bury the carcasses when I just take the skins. Only vice is religion, if that's a vice? But thanks for the offer. Shows you're a decent fella."

"Don't read too much into it. Reckon I couldn't handle a life like yours, just not tough enough. I never met a vice I didn't like and one that didn't like me. Trouble is, anything that feels good is against the law. I'm a god-fearing man but I don't think we ought to be punished for feeling good."

"There are all kinds of thoughts on it. Country used to be Democratic," he said, "but they seemed to lose their way, no direction, just confusion. I turned Republican a few years back. They want to clean up the trash, the confusion, of the world. Don't know if that's a direction or if it's even a good idea but at least it's a plan and I figure any kind of a plan is better than no plan."

"Politics ain't for me," said Steve. "I got enough trouble just minding my own business and it don't seem to make no difference who's in charge, anyway. The rich folks will always be rich and the poor ones 'ill always be poor. The folks with money is the folks that win. Just wish they'd leave me alone while they're doing it but they just ain't happy unless they can tell other folks how to live."

"Isn't much of a town, but there it is," said Welliver, pointing toward the windshield. "A tavern, grocery store, and a gas station." He held out his hand. "They feed in the tavern if you're hungry and it's always full of folks, farm folks and do-nothings."

"Sounds like my kind of place. Good luck with your hunting," said Steve, grabbing the hand and squeezing the forearm with his other hand.

"I got a feeling I'll be getting something, sure as all get-out," said Welliver.

Steve stood outside the tavern and watched Welliver drive away in the Humpmobile, his left taillight blinking like code. The grocery store looked abandoned and the gas station, a skinned-up white box, held two Texaco pumps, the white glass bulbs on top dripping green with wear and one of them cracked. A Hudson with run-away tires gathered rust on one side of the building and out back he could just barely make out a Kaiser with no hood and a door-less Henry J leaving the indication that the town had died, rather than sprang to life, with the homecoming of troops from World War Two. A cacophony of laughter, yelling and the voice of a scratchy country-western singer attempting to escape his incarceration through the music-box speaker, emerged from the tavern. The parking lot was filled, mostly with pick-up trucks. A flickering neon sign reading "Amanda's" hissed and crackled above the door. Budweiser, Miller and Rolling Rock posters were plastered over the cracks in the windows. Steve drew a breath and entered.

Boots had worked the grain from the wood floor leaving it smooth and dark like a newly tanned hide. The floor had not been swept for some time. A dance floor, sprinkled with sand, stood before a small stage empty of musicians. Only a single guitar leaned against the back wall. The teak bar carried hand carved images of lizards on the corners and a brass rail ran the length eight inches above the floor cradling an assortment of shoes: scuffed brogans, work boots (dirt folded up over the soles), a woman's shoes strangled with straps around the ankles and "fuck me" heels three inches high; a pair of army boots, shoelaces untied and dangling limply like the arms of an exhausted runner. More men than women milled around, tall ones worked and sweated to bone and wearing blue work shirts; fat ones with bellies stretching buttons and watermeloned between suspenders and over belts; a biker, something new since the war, in his confederate kepi cap stretching for a shot at the pool table while his companion in a union cavalry hat with gold tassels leaned on his cue and blew smoke from a blown out stogie; a scrawny man with a misshapen leg, twisted arm, shuffling in bedroom slippers, and wearing shorts sagging around his waist, his knees like two astonished faces and a cigar filling his whole mouth; fat women in tight jeans and ski-slopped waists jutting to the sides like wings with thick hams stuffed into cowboy boots; small women with badly painted faces strangling beer bottles by the necks; and one woman in a short tight dress, braless, her nipples pushing through the thin material like two stubby fingers pointing accusingly yet invitingly.

Most eyes turned to Steve as he stepped toward the bar. He tipped his hat to everyone and said, "Howdy" followed with a large grin as if to show he was unarmed and not the least bit dangerous. The misshapen man in shorts ambushed him and leaned over like a wrecking ball crane and hovered too close. "I'm Gary. Do you like cigars? I don't know how long I'm going to live. They gave me another kidney but it went bad. I don't pee anymore because it comes out through my blood. Can't screw either but I got a wife just the same. I'll show you the cigar room. Anything you want is back there." He placed his arm over Steve's shoulder and guided him toward a door through the back wall. He limped on his thin leg and his slippers dusted the floor.

Steve stood inside the cool room and felt the moisture, a relief from the heat Gary emitted. Boxes of cigars lined shelves in the humidor and the thick tobacco aroma brought a smile to his face.

"What kind do you like?" said Gary, "Mild medium or strong? The governor of Huston is a friend of mine and I often stay at his house to help him out. These are pretty mild with a decent taste. Give it a smell. I was into sports in high school and ran on track and played basketball. I'm a cigar slut and smoke anything anyone gives me. All the jocks gave me crap and I hate them. I've been playing wheelchair basketball lately. I'm related to Daniel Boone. There are a lot of soldiers here whining because their legs were blown off by the Germans. I don't feel sorry for them, not after the way they treated me in high school. They got what they deserved. Try one of these maduros. The company quit making them but we still have some."

"Rain falls like rocks," said Steve, to see if Gary listened to anyone.

"My dad was a drunk and drove truck. I handled all the money and kept track of him. I drove the truck on level ground where I didn't have to shift. Women just won't leave me alone. I don't know why. All they want to do is take me to bed. My wife died and the women were all over me so I got married again so they would leave me alone. What's your name? Did I say mine is Gary? I bowl twice a week and am the league champion." He threw back his head and gave out a high octave laugh like a mistuned calliope. "I taught some professional ballplayers how to pitch. Some of them didn't want to try for the big time but I set it up and look at them now. These smokes are pretty pricey. They smoke great. Now, these others, wow! Easy on the pocket book and a good smoke. We've got short ones and long ones. I was going to go pro in basketball but it didn't work out."

"Why, did they shoot the donkeys?" said Steve.

"I really like ballet and studied as a kid but I decided to concentrate on square dancing. There's more skill to it than people think, maybe more than ballet. In ballet you jump all over the place but in square dancing you have to stay in a square. People read me books because I can't read. I might write a book someday. It can't be too hard. A friend of mine, Wrigley Brogan, writes them and he's dumb as a rock. He just sits down and taps them out with no effort. How hard is that? A cigar slut, that's what I am. Did I say I don't know how long I'm going to live? What kind of cigar do you think I should smoke?"

"A short one," said Steve, as he backed toward the door.

"I have my blood cleaned three times a week. I hit the second longest ball in the home run contest back home. The nurses are always trying to squeeze my dick and they rub their tits on me when I show up…"

Steve backed out the door, leaned against the wall and drew a deep breath. He could still hear Gary's voice screeching like a cat dumped in a lake. "…Cindy comes to buy cigars. She's got it bad for me and what a looker. Sure, I know the governor of Kentucky but I don't like to tell people about it. I hate people who always talk abut themselves…"

"How about a beer?" said Steve, finally reaching the bar.

"Got nothing special here," said the bartender. "Weren't sure you'd get out alive. Gary'll talk a man to death in short order.

"Anything'll do," said Steve. "Had a hankering for one since I got out of the can. Something wet and on tap will do, I ain't particular."

"What were you in for?" said the bartender, pulling the tap. "It couldn't be any worse than being trapped in the cigar room with Gary. He means well, just got no life."

"Having fun's all I can make out. Seems the government don't cotton to men having a good time." The bartender wiped the bar before setting down the beer. "If ole' Bob Lee and his reb boys woulda' fought harder we might not be in this predicament."

"My great granddaddy gave it his all," said the bartender. "He fought with the Tennessee boys."

"Mine too; but I heard he couldn't hit a barn with a baseball bat. He might'a been better used as a barricade. My granddaddy said he sure could make some hooch, though, pure lightning leave a man blind drunk after one shot. What you got to eat?"

"Only sandwiches this time of night. Got a good beef tongue on rye."

"I ain't partial to food that comes from an animal's mouth. How about an egg sandwich?"

"LuLinda!" he yelled to the woman in the dress. "Get this man a egg sandwich." He leaned closer to Steve and spoke quietly. "This is a full service bar, if you get my drift." He smiled and nodded to LuLinda. "We got a room in back and the rates are down right reasonable."

Steve watched her walk toward the kitchen, her butt fighting like two pigs in a gunnysack. She had high cheekbones from Cherokee descent and, through the rouged wrinkles and painted lips she might have been attractive a while back, a long while back. A mole near her nose looked dark rough and cancerous.

"Why, that gal's just a light-switch away from beautiful," said Steve, "but I ain't in the market. Money comes pretty hard in the can, besides; I like them on the dark side. The meat's always sweeter there and more tasty. I love that ebony color."

"We can get you that too."

"How's the pool table here?"

"Those boys won't bother you. LuLinda will bring over the sandwich."

"Can I run it on a tab?"

Steve worked the crowd as he walked to the pool table tipping his hat, giving a "Howdy" to everyone and offering his hand as introduction. He twisted a chair backward and sat with his arms over the back holding the beer. He knocked his hat back and watched the game. "Nice shot," he said to the rebel in his confederate kepi. The man glanced his way and nodded as if he already knew it and didn't need any affirmation. "Nothing I like better than a good game."

"You want in?" said the man, looking Steve square in the eye as if to size him up. "We could make it interesting."

Steve fought back his elation. He knew he could beat them both; the tall one was not even a challenge. "You good for nine ball?" he said. He had the man hooked, now he had to reel him in. "I just don't want any hard feelings. I can shoot a little pool and I don't want anyone complaining I'm a pool shark."

"We don't live in a world of fear," he said. His leather jacket was worn to the suppleness of glove leather, the cuffs scuffed to their original brown color. He obviously meant business since he removed his jacket and tossed it over a chair revealing arms sinuously muscled from his T-shirt like twisted bread rolls baked golden brown. His arm held a tattoo and a stanza from one of Blake's poems sat in a square on his left forearm: "Tiger tiger burning bright…" "Fearful semmetry," misspelled, barely fit and

14

the "y" was smudged from a runaway needle.

Steve ran his hands over the row of cue sticks, the maple smooth and alive, more ornate than most tavern cues, but warped and bent like an English longbow. He clipped one out, sighted along the shaft, rolled it in his hands like a wad of bills. For him, the game now became mental. "My name's Steve."

"That's BoBilly," he said, pointing to his friend. BoBilly nodded. "I'm Jacks."

They lagged for break. Jacks' ball rolled a half-inch from the rail. BoBilly landed near the center and Steve's ball came an inch from Jacks', just like he had planned. Steve laid down his six dollars. "How about a buck on the three, two on the six, and three on the nine?" They put down the money and BoBilly wadded it up and placed it in his pocket, strictly against pool etiquette but a sheer sign of supremacy. Steve felt pool was still a gentleman's game and the money should have gone to an impartial by-stander or stayed in everyone's pocket and paid after the game. Jacks tried to hold back his smile after the break, a lovely scattering of balls with the one ball rolling into a side pocket. "Nice break," said Steve. With his next shot Jacks dropped the two ball, then the three. He missed his third shot but left the cue ball behind the five and block-ing the four. Steve took a walkabout around the table. He shot quickly knocking the cue off the rail to the four and rolled it into the end pocket. Jacks and BoBilly tapped their cues on the floor, a good sign. Two more difficult shots followed, both good. He now had his six bucks back. The next shot seemed easy, straight in but this was the only shot Steve took his time with, a narrow miss. BoBilly smacked the ball as hard as he could probably hoping something would roll in. Jacks, with a smile, finally sank the nine. Steve offered them both a cigarette but took none for himself. They squinted through the smoke for the other games. After about two hours of play, Steve was up eighty-four dollars. BoBilly was broke and they decided to quit.

"Hope there's no hard feelings," said Steve, feigning guilt at having been the big win-ner.

"We like a good player," said Jacks. "Yes," said BoBilly, the only word he ever spoke.

"Listen, anything you boys want tonight put it on my tab."

"That's pretty decent."

"Greed ain't my thing. I don't think anyone needs more money than he can use."

As he walked away he stepped on the cowboy boots of a heavyweight. "Sorry," he said.

"Sorry isn't going to do it," said the man, grabbing Steve by the shirt. "I just spent one hundred dollars on the boots, custom made." Steve looked at the boots, red leather with a blue and white eagle spread across the front.

"I didn't mean nothing," he said. "I expect the best a man can do is treat everyone with decency and respect and not bother anyone." He saw Gary peering through the gathering crowd leaning forward from under his silly flowered bucket hat, the cigar boiling like a furnace and spewing out smoke and gasses. The big guy wore a black cowboy shirt decorated with red horseshoes and the snaps strained across his stomach. His short-cropped beard had obviously been dyed an unnatural brown, the white roots pushing from his chin. His breath smelled of Bourbon and one front tooth had been broken in half, the rest yellow-brown from tobacco. The crowd inched in closer and laid down a warm front of anticipated breath. Steve saw the glowing eyes of hungry jackals between the startled faces of fear and anticipation and loathing. One woman held her hands to her face while another clenched her mouth and fists, knuckles stretched white and ready to split. "I don't know what to do except shine your boots and apologize. I think all folks ought to get along." Then, he noticed the guitar on the stage. "How about I dedicate a song to you?"

"What kind of crap is that?" He stepped closer to Steve.

"A song, man. You probably kick a man's ass every weekend. It's got no meaning and I ain't even a challenge. All it takes to kick my ass is a phone call. But a song – man, there's nothing like a song. You won't soon forget it and folks will talk about it for years."

The big guy started laughing at the absurdity of it, grabbed Steve by the front of his shirt and threw him onto the stage. He sprawled across the rough wood like a bowling ball hunting the nine pin. "I'm supplying the entertainment tonight," the big guy said. "And if the bastard can't sing I'm kicking his ass."

Steve brushed off his knees and gave a wave to the crowd. The guitar felt good in his hands and he plucked each string into tune. He turned to the crowd and said, "This song's going out to the big fat bastard with the red fairy shoes. He's a good friend of mine and I'm letting him put all his drinks on my tab."

Steve broke into a rendition of "Under the Double Eagle." Before the song had finished the crowd had gathered around yelling and clapping and the big cowboy danced in a circle, his arms raised in jubilation and yelling, "That's my boy! That's my boy!"

Steve played to the adulation of the crowd until closing time. People could not wait to congratulate him, the women pecking him half to death with kisses and licking him clean, the men beating him across the back as if just to touch him brought glory. He reciprocated with shyness, self-deprecation and a tipped hat. When he went to pay his tab the bartender shook his hand and said, "Don't worry about it. We haven't had that kind of show in years." Truly it was one of the best days of his life and he knew he would die a happy man.

After stepping outside he sat on a bench and savored the night letting the bugs buzz around him. A perfect day. Not many men ever had a perfect day and he imagined a good night's sleep under the tree in the field; not that he had to return to the field. LuLinda had squeezed him between the legs and given him a wink indicating a free ride but he was too new to the world and was not sure he could hang on without puking.

"Steve!" The elation had so blinded him that he had not seen the car parked outside.

It was Welliver.

"What ya doing?" said Steve, walking to the window.

"My friend wasn't home. Since I was passing this way about closing time I thought I would stop and give you a ride."

"That's right neighborly of you. It's been one hell of a night."

Steve told him all about his night, the drinking, the pool, the cigars, the singing, and LuLinda. When they arrived at Steve's tree Welliver said, "You've got some nice flowers by that tree there. I wouldn't mind having some." The flowers glowed in the yellow headlights and doused the blinking fireflies.

"Let me dig some up for you, said Steve. "It's the least I can do for a new friend." He pulled the shovel from the back seat. Welliver turned off the headlights and watched him. Steve dug up a nice clump, handed the shovel to Welliver who laid it over his shoulder, and placed the flowers in the trunk. He lit a Camel and drew in the smoke slowly thinking how great life was. A perfect night hung on his arms like a mistress and the smoke warmed him. He closed his eyes and felt he would live forever. He remembered seeing Welliver grabbing the handle of the shovel but did not remember it swinging toward his head and knocking him to the ground. Blood ran over his face and he tried to work his arms and legs. Welliver swung again but Steve blocked the blow with his arm.

"What?' Steve managed to mumble as Welliver drew back the shovel.

"I am God's servant here to rid the world of vermin." He raised the shovel high over his head. Steve rolled away from the blow and the shovel sliced his arm as he rose to his feet. He grabbed the shovel before Welliver could draw it back and strike again. Steve swung the shovel in a wide arch. The blade slit Welliver's throat, the blood spewing in a gush. His arms and hands twitched as Steve stood over him. When the blood stopped, he rolled Welliver over.

"Damn," he said. The man was dead. Steve looked around then walked to the road and looked both ways. He knew no one would believe him, not any hick sheriff, not the words of a newly released con. He tore several strips of cloth from Welliver's shirt then dragged Welliver into the brush and covered him with limbs. He sat on a fallen log and bandaged his arm and wiped the blood from his forehead. With some reluctance the car started and Steve drove away. He did not care where he went so he just followed the headlights. He decided to drive as far as possible then ditch the car in a field before continuing to hitch-hike to the West Coast, maybe even leave the country, someplace the law could never find him.

Chapter 3

Bix tossed all night, the images of the black woman stuck in his mind, the beating of Chau, the hicks swilling whisky. Feeling uncomfortable in hotels did not help - too confining, too dirty, too comfortable for a farm boy used to fields of grass. He much preferred sleeping in his car, the felt seats warming his face, or under a tree in a field covered with the fresh smells of the outdoors and waking with a layer of dew across his face. The room was painted dull yellow spotted with brown stains, a hole in the ceiling above the tiny table ringed with cigarette burns. Years of bare feet had mashed a trail in the carpet to the bathroom matching the dirty isthmus inside the front door. The linoleum had cracked on the bathroom floor making a road map leading to nowhere. Yellow-orange stains covered the inside of the bathtub and sink with brown streaks behind the faucets. Looking into the toilet was like looking into the bowl of a well-smoked pipe left in the rain. Shaking the toilet handle had no effect on the dripping water. The room smelled moldy, old, with a mixture of wet soil, burnt engine oil and sweat so thick it could not be removed. Cigarettes had burnt two holes in the top sheet of the bed and smoke had colored the pillowcases light tan. Water stains on the ceiling melded into an abstract puzzle of Yugoslavia. His head turned and caused him to rise from the knock on the door. Morning sun backlit the sheriff.

"You look like hell," he said. "Worried about your friend?"

"Motels." Bix flipped his head. "They're not for me. Want to come in?"

"No need. You always sleep in your clothes?" He held a note pad under his arm. "She's fine. The woman. The woman is fine." A slight grin curled up his face. "She was just unconscious. Her face was beat in pretty good, though. You were right about that. She came around after about an hour."

"What?" The morning had already started to warm and the sun half closed his eyes with soft fingers.

"The woman. She was beat up a little but she wasn't dead." He fiddled with the top button on his shirt and looked from side to side.

"The one I saw was dead," said Bix. "I've seen enough dead animals on the farm to know when something is dead." He moved outside and crossed his arms. The sun caused him to squint.

"Must have been unconscious, like I said. You said you didn't touch her. Her eyes were in place; she was just a little beat up. Sometimes when you get excited things look different. We haven't found your friend's car."

"Is she in the hospital? I want to see her." A glow of light surrounded the sheriff leaving his face in the dark.

"It's been taken care of." His grin faded. "She's being taken care of, had to take her to a bigger hospital because of the injuries. We'll get her home in no time, just don't you worry."

"I'd like to see her just the same, maybe drive over there to see if she needs anything."

"You need to mind your own business." The sheriff started to sound harsh and he poked a finger at Bix. "She's been taken to another hospital, like I said. Go get your half-nigger

midget friend and move on. If I see you this afternoon…well, just don't be here."

"Something doesn't seem right." Bix had not learned the advantages of keeping silent. The woman's image had stayed in his head. She was dead, all right.

"I won't be telling you again. Now get the hell out."

Bix watched him climb into the Buick police car and speed away. He had certainly changed, certainly had something on his mind. He appeared more like the Southern sheriffs of reputation. The woman was dead, no doubt it. Bix took the opportunity to shower and shave before going to the hospital. Maybe the nasty ignorant South of myth was too true to be anything else. That woman was dead, he knew that much, and, from her face, had hung an eye. He had never seen anything so dead, so cold, so lifeless, so completely gone from this earth. Why should he get Chung or Chau, or whatever his name was. He didn't know him, nothing about him except he had graduated from a university in France and his parents were wealthy. Someone with cash might come in handy on a long trip, providing the attackers hadn't taken it from him, and he could probably use a friend.

The hospital inside seemed as hot as outside and a medicinal aroma permeated the air: iodine, medicinal alcohol, various unguents and overtones of puke and urine. "I brought in a guy last night that was beat-up. Can he leave?"

The nurse looked from side to side and leaned over the counter. "Has to," she said. "We left him in the room as long as we could but he has to go, for his own protection. Take him as far away from here as you can. Don't ever come back, never. Here…" She handed Bix some medicine containing notes for their use. She directed him to Chau's room. He was dressed and leaning back over his pillow, his shoes off and his knees bent up. He appeared to be sleeping. Bruises covered his face and several bandages had been taped to his face.

"You OK?"

Chau moved slowly, his head rolling to one side. He raised his hands and felt his face. He was still groggy and looked physically ill. Bix tried to help him sit, pulling his legs off the bed. The nurse moved to help. Together they helped Chau stand. Unable to straighten up, his legs shook. They moved him slowly outside into the car. He moaned slightly as they placed him onto the seat folding him in the cab like dough into an oven.

"Wait just a minute." She went back inside then returned and placed an ice bag into his hands. "You go on, now. Don't you come back. Don't never come back."

Bix watched the nurse in the rear view mirror growing smaller and smaller. The brick buildings were on fire, the sun's flames in every window. The theater marquee featured "The Sound of Music" with some actor named Yule Brenner. He noticed the sheriff in his car beside the Bank of Georgia. He seemed to be watching Bix and Chau making sure they left. The town turned to countryside, miles of okra, tobacco, corn. Limping tobacco sheds and barns sank in the soil from age. In one field a mule plowed the soil, a black man in coveralls walking behind; in another a Farmall tractor spit black smoke. Cotton wagons circled the edges of cotton fields waiting for their puffy loads. A dirty white boy, bare-footed and freckled carried a rifle and walked beside his tall friend who wore pants whose legs went half-way up his calves, his brogans scuffed brown, and flicking a switch with one black hand and, with the other, attempting to wipe the sun from his black face, both unaware as children that they would be unequal as adults. The empty road pulled the Studebaker west. Bix glanced at Chau.

"You OK?" he said. "Someplace I can drop you?"

"My head is cloudy. I'm going to San Francisco in the state of California in the United States. I must catch a ship for home. Can you take me there?" He held his ribs and groaned when he coughed.

"You know how far that is?" Chau shook his head. "It's way across the country. I've never been there so I don't know how long it will take but it's a long way."

"I will pay."

"It's not that, although I'll need some money to get there. I'm going around the country, you know, see what it's like. I've not been out of the Midwest. Was going to take my time, give me a chance to meet some people and see if they are any different than the ones I know. I want to find out something about the world."

"There is no hurry. I am also looking for the country. Sometimes a chance meeting can make a lasting friendship." He smiled and offered his hand.

"Deal," said Bix. He was curious about the woman and asked, "Anything strange about the woman you were with? I know she was dead but the sheriff said she was ok."

"I met her in a club in New York. I wanted to know about black people because I have heard they are not treated well here. There are few in my country and they are regarded as good luck. The French have them in my country from their other colonies but they are treated the same as anyone. They say they fight even better than the Legion, the French Foreign Legion. In a jazz club in Harlem I was listening to a saxophone player named Charlie Parker. He was playing some new kind of jazz that I did not understand. Many notes were played. They sounded like a nest of ants, the notes all jumbled together." He jiggled his fingers together and made noise. "Our music is simpler although in France they like American jazz. I heard a trumpet player there named Billy Butterfield that I liked and a saxophone player they called Prez. Two women walked into the club looking for a place to sit so I invited them to my table. They were working on some kind of equality thing - is that the word? - some equality thing for blacks. Melba, the woman with me, wanted to go Alabama to recruit new members for this equality. She thought a bunch of them had their names on a list throughout the south. I offered her a ride. She talked about the ill treatment blacks had received in the south. She said white people still hang black people there for no reason. It's a very confusing place. In this country aren't all men created equal?"

"We don't hear much about it in South Dakota. Of course, I have never read much news, anyway. It doesn't seem to make any difference." Bix swerved to miss a squirrel running across the road. Chau explained all of Melba's concerns and how things must be changed before there was a revolution. She loved her country but thought it a fraud. Blacks mostly had no rights, especially in the south. They were taught to live in fear and when that fear lessened, the whites hanged one of them as a reminder.

"That is all I know," said Chau. "We stopped to eat. They would not let her in, said 'they don't serve no niggers' so I protested because I did not understand. She went to the car and I ordered something to take with us. They said they weren't serving no half nigger either. Outside I fumbled for some nickels to put into the Coke machine. These men drove up in a truck, shoved me into my car and someone got in to drive it. They took us to that place. The man drove off with the car."

"Do you think she's alive?"

Chau did not answer and they drove on in silence. Chau attempted to disassociate himself from his pain. He let the rumbling of the car comfort him as the wind from the open window blew over him.

Conversation eventually infiltrated the car, a word or two at first, then another and another as the breach widened with tiredness, the language acting as Benzedrine. Bix was curious about Chau's country thinking it might be the place he could find his great adventure. As an educated man, Chau was very knowledgeable and slowly the history rolled out almost like a university lecture.

The area, consisting of Vietnam, Cambodia and Laos were historically connected by similar people, similar vegetation, and through repelling invasions. In 1887, the French occupiers named the area the Indochinese Union or, by most nations, French Indochina. Vietnam was traditionally divided into three sections: Bac Bo or Tonkin in the north, Nam Bo or Cochinchina in the south, and Chau's home area, Trung Bo or Annam, in the middle. Together the three parts of Vietnam are slightly larger than Italy and is called the Three Ky. Annam only measures 31 miles wide at its narrowest point while the largest width at Tonkin is 350 miles.

The country is vastly different in various sections from hot marshy lowlands to chilly hills and mountains, (almost three-quarters of the area is mountainous) averaging over 4,900 feet above the sea with some high ranges, in Tonkin, standing at 10,300 feet. Not long ago half of the country was covered in tropical forests. Animals are plentiful and various. Wild boars, elephants, tigers and panthers make certain areas extremely dangerous. Even Asian rhinoceros, gaur buffalo, bear, deer, monkeys, birds, and an abundance of snakes, poisonous and otherwise, live with various reptiles, giant insects, roaches, beetles, and ravenous mosquito-carrying malaria. Towering Elephant grass in the highlands cuts like straight razors. Interspersed with grassy savannah rolling into bamboo forests in the valleys, parasitic plants and undergrowth cling to trunks and limbs of trees. High triple jungle canopy often blots out the sun leaving the soil wet and musty, the aroma of mud and rotting vegetation filling the air. The mountains on the western border are nothing less than primeval, sheer cliffs and gorges tumbling to rushing streams where, especially the area known as the Central Highlands, ancient tribes and primitive peoples live in shadows, often roam naked, and live off snakes and insects.

Three rivers run through the area of Tonkin and rice paddies are plentiful near the coast. Caves used by various defenders and invaders, sprinkle limestone buttes throughout the country with many along the coast. Chau said the Viet Minh, a guerrilla force and Communist political movement attempting to disrupt French order and their effort to move the Vietnamese into the twentieth century, use the caves for protection and to launch attacks against the peaceful population who only wish to live in peace.

Twenty-three thousand square miles of wetlands soak the southern areas where the great Mekong River spews, through hundreds of tributaries, pouring tons of sediment into the South China Sea. The area is one of the most productive rice producing areas in the world.

Two thousand years of warfare has washed over Vietnam leaving in its wake a varied mixture of peoples. The country was first inhabited by Australo-Asiatic probably drifting in from Indonesia. Khmers, Chams and Chinese soon pushed their way in. Mongoloid Chinese set up government in the Red River delta and flourished for many centuries but always in conflict with the surrounding feudal society. A national language eventually formed between the Thai, the resident Chinese and Indonesian peoples who eventually considered themselves Vietnamese. As a unified people they rebelled against the Chinese to the north. The Trung sisters merged into legend because of their fight against the Han Dynasty and further solidified Vietnamese nationalism. The Chinese crushed other uprisings, but the Vietnamese continued to fight them until they agreed to independence but with an allegiance to China. The Vietnamese persisted in waring with the Chinese in an effort to become totally independent from their influence. They also fought the Chams, Khmers and remarkably repelled three Mongolian invasions. During the Ming Dynasty, that attempted to destroy the Vietnamese culture through cruelty, the Vietnamese were again beaten. Yet, no one could ever discourage them from being their own people and, after regaining their strength, they fought again. In 1428, through savage guerrilla warfare, General Le Loi restored independence from the Chinese. The next invasion came from the west as Dutch and Portuguese set up trade centers taking out rice and bringing in weapons. French missionaries soon stormed the beaches. Chau thought of them as a civilizing force attempting to wrench out the godless religions of Buddhism, Confucianism and hundreds of ancestor forms of worship, from the ignorant farming population. The Tay Son Rebellion barred another Chinese rebellion – they seemed to be slow learners – and Emperor Gai Long unified the nation and announced the city of Hue as the capitol.

French missionaries had difficulties with the local populations who found no interest in a cannibalistic religion where flesh of the savior was eaten and his blood drunk at ceremonies. They were not inclined to overthrow religions of peace and nature for one of brutality and a vengeful god who wiped out entire civilizations or families at his unsteady whim. They did not find the missionaries a civilizing presence, as did Chau. Rescuing the missionaries became the excuse for invasion by a confused France. The French people found colonialism distasteful and tended to view it as a way to enrich the already wealthy. Not the government who sent in the military. The French military first landed in 1858, without success. They made another attempt in 1861 and the Vietnamese, armed with archaic arms, including many spears and clubs, were defeated at Chi Hoa. Emperor Tu Duc offered generous dispensation to the French enraging local populations to form guerrilla armies and continue the fight. They were now the most prolific resisters in the world. Of course, the resistance gave the French reason to import more soldiers and capture more territory. They declared Cochinchina a French colony in 1867. Cambodia became a French protectorate. The Vietnamese continued to fight, refusing to attend French schools and learn the ways of civilized society. Chau said they preferred ignorance to culture. Here was their chance to move into an enlightened society, yet they refused. Thai highlanders, renegade Chinese troops, pirates and bandits formed an army called the "Black Flags." Soon the whole country was at war with various factions fighting one another and the French. When the French attempted to destroy the Black Flags, French Captain

Riviere found his head on the end of a local spear, along with many of his men. In 1883 the French placed a puppet government on the throne and brought in the legendary and feared Foreign Legion, in part to placate French citizens tired of French soldiers being killed. Events turned in their favor and they formed the Indochinese Union and declared Laos a protectorate. Yet fighting continued.

Farming remained the main industry of the people of French Indochina, mostly rice in self-sufficient villages with their own form of village government built along Confucian ideas of respect. A plow, often fashioned from wood, a flail to beat out the rice, and a water buffalo was all they required. Coveting possessions or working more land than they needed to feed their families was discouraged by their religions, mostly Buddhism, animism, ancestor worship and Taoism. They usually brought in two rice crops a year, difficult work during planting and harvesting, but rather leisurely the rest of the year.

Chau welcomed the French and had never known a Vietnam without them. He had gone to French schools and, with his father, had worked with them exporting Vietnamese goods and importing French ones giving them wealth and status. The French had improved the roads, refined many buildings in the city and had built modern structures on a European design. Without them there had been virtually no law and order. Medicine had been abysmal, mostly folk remedies, strange poultices, teas, herbs, administered in smoky bamboo huts with opium for a relaxant, until the French brought in western medicine and built sanitary hospitals. Schools had been built and new jobs were abundant. Artists, craftsmen, government functionaries, servants, and many laborers were needed everywhere.

"But the French are constantly bogged down fighting the Viet Minh," said Chau. "They spring up everywhere, like a poisonous weed, to cause trouble, kill our people, destroy the roads and bridges, ambush the French soldiers, blow up restaurants and businesses."

The sun had started to drip into the west leaving a hazy egg-yolk hovering over the road and warming the greens of the fields.

"Who are they? said Bix. "Who are the Viet Minh?"

"Pirates and ruffians. Communists mostly, lead by Ho Chi Minh. He says the country is his and belongs to the Vietnamese and would like to take us back to the Stone Age. The French will not let it happen. They have the might of Europe with them: tanks, trucks, boats, airplanes, paratroops, Foreign Legionnaires, Colonial troops, mighty cannons. The Viet Minh have nothing: a few weapons taken from the French dead, some antiquated rifles. They even make some of their own guns in villages. The head of their military is a schoolteacher, not a soldier. Why they continue to fight is beyond me."

The more Bix listened the more fascinated he became. Vietnam seemed a place for adventure; more adventure than in the United States, exotic, a strange culture with many types of people, and most of all, a war. A man could prove himself in war. Only in war could a man make his passage to manhood.

Steve, still on the run for killing the old man, drove the old car as far back into the woods as he could and covered it with limbs after breaking out all the windows, tearing up the seats, smashing the dash, and releasing the air from the tires. It was bound to be found. He was careful to find a little-used road to drive down and if someone discovered it, they would probably consider it an abandoned wreck that had been sitting for years. He used only old limbs for disguise so it did not look as if it were being hidden. He remembered about fingerprints, removed some limbs and his shirt, and wiped down everything he remembered touching. He thought of the steering wheel and removed his underwear and ran it around the wheel leaving a dirty line in the crotch, something that looked natural in case he was searched. When he finished, he walked down a side road and turned at an intersection that took him to the main road. There he sat on an old tin bucket, his hat tilted to the side, his thumb waving in mock distress. A cigarette dangled from between his lips. He counted the passing cars that did not even slow to get a better look at him and he never became upset, content to enjoy his smoke. Prison taught a man patience, if nothing else. In the distance a Studebaker drove his way. It slowed, as it got closer to him then drove past, came to a stop and backed up.

"This is right kind of you," he said, to the window being rolled down. "Don't reckon I would-of froze out here but I might of starved."

"Where you going?" The voice came from the driver's side and pushed itself through the passenger window. He noticed a Chinaman in the passenger seat leaning back as if to let the words pass unobstructed.

"Don't rightly know. Wherever you folks are going, I guess." He held the cigarette behind his back. "I'm just out to see the country."

"Us too. Climb in."

He flicked the cigarette away with the accuracy of a man who had practiced for many years. The door squeaked as he entered the back seat.

"What about you fellas? Where you headed?"

"Same as you," said Bix. He reached over his shoulder to shake hands. "Just trying to see the country too. This is Chau. He's a Vietnamese." Chau turned and offered his hand, a small kid's hand soft from lack of labor.

"I don't rightly know what a Vietnamoose is, but you look like a regular fella to me," said Steve, taking the hand. The car started down the road. The sun was almost down.

"It is in Asia," said Chau. "Just south of China. Do you know where China is?"

"Just cause I'm a Kentucky boy don't mean I'm stupid." Steve laughed. "China's smashed up against Russia and has more people than a whorehouse on payday." The car felt warm and comfortable, the hum of the engine, the slight vibration of the driveshaft under his feet. He instantly felt comfortable with the men and did not have the inside jitters that often accompanied a free ride with strangers. "I want to be square with you folks. I just been let out of prison for having too much fun and I don't want that to come as a surprise down the road."

"Didn't let yourself out, did you?" said Bix. "Looks like you've been banged up."

"Three meals a day and a roof over my head. Tell the truth, I weren't too anxious to leave. I tried to take a short cut through the woods and fell over a downed tree. It kind of cut me up. I don't have much money but I'll be right happy to contribute what I can."

Bix started to smile. A little extra money would be a help. If Steve and Chau paid for everything he could drive a long way and see a lot of country.

As they continued to talk their friendship grew at a rapid rate as if they were old buddies and had met again after a long absence: Bix, young, slightly naive, looking for adventure or a defining moment in his life; Chau, educated, wealthy, a foreigner bringing into play his exotic life; Steve, not much older in age but long past middle-age in experience with prison stories and tales of his upbringing on a poor Kentucky tobacco farm.

The Studebaker rolled through the streets of Arkadelphia, Arkansas in the early evening. Chau had agreed to rent them a room, an inexpensive one to save on money. A hotel of bones and dried membranes stood at one end of town, white paint curled like soft wood from a woodworking plane. Trapped dim lights pushed against dirty windows, unable to escape and hanging from the glass as if from exhaustion.

"This is my kind of place," said Steve, excitedly peering over the front seat. The parking space out front was made of dirt and tracks criss-crossed from tires that had visited during a rain.

"I'm not sure," said Bix. "It doesn't look very safe or very clean." He realized too late that a man looking for adventure would have kept quiet.

"That's the point. You can't find no experiences in a decent place where respectable white folks come and go in mystery, never talking, just in and out. A joint like this offers mountains of opportunities: gambling, whoring, drinking, maybe some tea for sell so's we can get high. Don't suppose you've ever had any pot?"

"I've heard about it," said Bix. "It's supposed to be dangerous and people on the coasts, like writers and musicians, smoke it."

"It's only dangerous if you don't have enough." A decent looking green Buick was parked beside several dented and rusted derelicts. "Lookie there, someone with class is here, someone looking for a good time. A person with that car is up to no good and this is the place to find it."

They walked across the porch and pushed through the front door. Cardboard from one of the door's window panes fell to the floor. Chau picked it up and placed it on a stuffed chair. A rather handsome young man was leaning over the counter talking to the clerk. Warped planks covered the floor of the lobby and held up several wicker chairs and a sofa with scars that had been sewn up. A fan twirled unevenly over head, the whitewashed walls carried their own injuries of cuts and gouges, replicated paintings had crucified themselves to the plaster, and a Confederate flag drooped in surrender beside the stairs. Bix watched the young man.

"Three hundred bucks and it's yours," he said. "You can't go wrong for three hundred bucks, even without the title. Three hundred and a room, that is and it runs smooth as a dove on the breeze, an evening breeze as the sun dips into the cornfield."

"Let me take carin these boys while I think about it," said the clerk. He scratched at his undershirt. "What can I do for you-all?"

"We need a room," said Bix.

"Just one?"

"Sure."

"Three fellas in one room cost extra. If we didn't do it a hundred folks would only rent one room."

"How much extra?" Bix attempted to sound authoritative, like a leader, and cautious, giving the impression he was not new at this kind of swindle.

"The same as two rooms. Only one bed in a room."

"We're going to use the floor." He could hear music from upstairs.

"Same thing. We rent rooms by the square feet of folks."

"Hold on," said Steve. "You dumb bastard don't even know what a square foot is, probably think it's some kind of childhood illness that causes folks to limp." He leaned across the counter. "You got music up there. That means you got whores, whisky – no doubt watered down – and anything else a man might want including chickens that lay golden eggs. If we got to pay extra we won't be inclined to party all night so you won't get your cut and you're going to lose money. The boss ain't gonna like that. What we spend up there will be a sight more than the extra for the room."

"OK. Five bucks for the three of you but when I come up later I expect to find you boys having a good time. We even got an oxymoron dancing up there."

"I expect you're a little light on the oxy and heavy on the moron," said Steve, laughing.

The man at the counter also laughed and said, "That's pretty good, I'll have to remember it when I get to Frisco."

"It's true about the dancer," said the clerk. "You'll see, right out of Barnum and Billies circus." He handed them the keys and watched them walk up the stairs, then turned back to the man.

"Three hundred bucks for a stolen car is mighty steep."

"I never said it's stolen, and three hundred's cheap for a beauty like that, stolen or just on vacation. You know what a Buick costs, a fine one like that that runs like a golden ticker and floats down the road like it was on the high seas? Man, I just don't have the title is all. You're a smart man, a real cool dude from the wide wide world that knows how to get a title for a few coins. Stolen, you must be crazy to think that, a fine person like me stealing cars and trying to sell them. I'm insulted, hurt, bowled over with such bodaciousness."

"Three hundred dollars is hard to scratch up but I could know someone who might be interested. Why'nt you go up to the club with the other fellas and I'll send for him? He got money and plenty of it."

The hotel room smelled of bourbon, sweat, nights of feigned emotions on dirty sheets between biting mosquitoes, soiled panties, the deflowering of innocent farm girls imagining themselves as sexy women before the pain and weight of grunting penetrating men ground into them leaving a mattress covered in blood, the aroma of soiled work boots covered with mud or oil and gasoline, or slick brogans broken at the sides and held together with shoe grease slapped on in layers by some boot black, his hands covered with polish and earning a nickel to buy a Coca Cola. Even the walls smelled faintly of coal oil before electricity snaked itself in wires stapled to the baseboard under the peeling paint refusing to stick to the plaster. Discolored rectangles marked wall spaces where pictures had once hung, and a bare low-watt bulb bubbled from the ceiling to balance with the yellow-shaded lamp sitting on the nightstand, dimples of cigarette burns having burrowed into the veneer. The springs of the single double bed had long ago gone swayback making the mattress resemble a shallow tub. One overstuffed chair with slick arms suffered interrogation under an accusing floor lamp. Red flowers on the linoleum floor had worn to asphalt in traveled areas and the mirror on the dresser, one drawer missing, held two jagged scars in a hotel that even new never rose above low class.

"Do we flip for the bed?" said Bix.

"That's the way," said Steve. "The winners sleep on the floor."

"Many people in my country would welcome such opulence," said Chau. "Perhaps someday…"

Music rattled the room from the club at the other end of the hotel making it impossible to sleep or even to rest. "This is the time to howl," said Steve, slapping his hands together. "I've got the first round of drinks. If we don't stay up and party we'll never get any sleep."

The club felt like an empty barn, all wood, a small dance floor, a stage about one foot off the floor, five feet deep and eight feet wide. A red light shown partly on the stage and partly on the wall. About ten tables were scattered about, all with different wooden chairs. A bar clung to a nearby wall in the shadows. The men grabbed a table and sat. The tabletop was sticky with beer and Bix wobbled on an uneven chair. A waitress in a g-string and pasties strolled over.

"What you boys want?" she said. She brushed her breasts against Bix's head, licked her lips. "You can have just about anything."

"Just about? Thought this was a full service establishment. How's about running a wet rag over this table," said Steve. "And not the one between your legs. We want to leave a fresh mess and see if we can get your ass to stick to it."

"You're the feisty one," she cooed. "The feisty ones never come through, never have any cash or meat to go with it." She prodded him, tried to embarrass him until he would eventually take her to the back room to redeem his manhood, a manhood he neither felt inclined to redeem nor defend.

"Whisky?" he nodded to his friends. "Three whiskys straight up and don't forget to wipe the table when you get back. I just won't do you on a dirty table." He slapped his hands together. "Yahoo," he said. "I reckon we'll be rolling tonight." Chau sat uncomfortable and adjusted himself several times on the chair. Bix appeared confused and a little embarrassed.

"Don't worry," said Steve. "This'n is my country and the women needs some tough talk to keep them spry."

Only two other tables were occupied, two older men in coveralls at one and four well-dressed young men, probably university students who had talked themselves into manhood before they were ready for it and attempted to convince one another who the best man was, the most worldly. The biggest liar always won at this game although none of the other players ever believed him but were wowed just the same.

"Just wait," Steve continued. "Women'll be coming out the woodwork in a few minutes."

Music started again and a beautiful sensual body knocked dust from the side curtain as she emerged onto the stage, her front facing away from the men. "Hot damn," Steve yelled. "Turn round and give it all to us." Her calves would just fit into a man's hands and her thighs tapered like those of a goddess under her firm buttocks. Above that stood a perfectly muscled back gently creased in the middle. She folded her arms over her shoulders and with shapely supple fingers pulled her long hair over her face as she turned slowly to the rhythm on the musical beat. Leisurely she turned, supple breasts high on her chest, her face still covered with the hair. Since she was totally naked she was not performing a strip-tease and her movements invited everyone in, flesh against perfect flesh all in one easy payment. Her hands came apart as she tilted her head back as strands of hair fluttered down as if in a mild breeze. Her falling hair revealed an ancient and hideous face, one tortured by demons, claws scraping across her face, her skin baked to desert alkali, trod on by the countless wandering of those lost and searching for something that did not exist.

The men gaped unable to speak. Never had they seen two people in one body, not in the physical sense. Bix started to feel sick. Chau, who had seen many deformities in his lifetime, especially in the country, the small villages where ghosts still lived, watched curiously. Steve had witnessed a two-headed pig, and a legless duck that looked a lot like his cousin, Slim. He felt more fascinated and curious than anything else. What evil spell could have enjoyed such a joke?"

"Damn," he finally said. "That's a face that done sunk a thousand ships."

Slowly the woman continued to turn around and around. Each time Bix expected her to emerge with a different face, as if it had all been part of an act, that perhaps each frontal appearance might reveal her ten or twenty years younger slowly twirling up youth, beautiful vibrant youth to match her body.

The man having trouble in the lobby slid up a chair and scooted to the table as if they had all been great friends. "Neal Cassidy," he said, parking his hand from one man to another. "Can you believe that cat downstairs doesn't want to buy that Buick? Man, that baby glides down the road at one hundred miles per, wheels that purr, radio cranked up to Diz and his big band, be-bop in its truest. Hope you don't mind me sitting here but I'm working my way across the country from New York and a man becomes anonymous too soon while by himself. It takes a bunch of cats like you to build a legend."

"Look at that gal." Steve pointed his chin toward the stage. "Her puss done got caught in a time machine."

"Meat grinder," said Neal. "You can take some real trips with the right dope and never see anything like that." Steve perked up with the word "dope." Bix felt even more uncomfortable and Chau, a man from a country that grew more opium than almost any other in the area, never flinched. "It's all happening in New York. Those jazz cats are turning music inside out, bop mostly, Bird, Diz, Miles, and that new cat on sax, Coltrane blowing notes from here to forever, wild man, wild. He takes the stars from the night, pulls them into his gut and blows them through that reed, the entire universe coming across that sliver of bamboo."

The maniacal talk from Neal was difficult to follow, the words flying everywhere and at great speed.

The four young men started hooting at the woman on stage. If one comes out naked there is no strip-tease, nothing to tantalize, just the horrible reality of vulnerability, exposed to the world as some beautiful demon, the makings of a cynical god snickering in the heavens.

"Why did you leave?" said Bix, the fascination about the woman having cooled, gone to his memory for stories to skeptical listeners over drinks at a later date.

"The words are in Frisco, the docks, the bars and clubs, the coffee houses. When we get there I'll take you to some righteous cats, groovy intellectuals wrestling with words and society in a provocative way. And the dope." He leaned close to them and spoke quietly. "Nembies, goof-balls, coke, marijuana, heroin caps, barbiturates, Benzedrine, Yage, Morphine, scopolamine, peyote, and a hundred others, anything you want, any time. You don't even have to live on this world. Take a trip and pack your bags because you ain't never coming back."

"Most of those is a circus I ain't never been to," said Steve.

"The rides are on me. I've got a little something that will make an elephant laugh."

"I've never heard about most of those," said Bix.

"I can fix you up too," said Neal.

"I'd rather do without. I'm used to beer and whisky."

No one seemed upset, or even thought about the fact that Neal had invited himself along on the trip, had become part of the team: some stray dog that had hopped into the car and panted his way to friendship expecting never to leave until he wanted to leave.

The table of young men started to stand and to dance and to pretend to masturbate and push one another across the table in fake sex. The clerk ambushed Neal, tapping him on the shoulder and nodded with his head, as if it were a fishing line, to follow him downstairs.

"Be back in a minute," he said.

As he left two scantily dressed women moved to the young boys. They knew that if they offered sex, regardless of how much the boys did not want it, they would not refuse; they would decline to be ridiculed by their peers, declined to protect themselves from disease, would step into the back room in a mock imitation of men and emerge minutes later, the cash in their wallets replaced with experience, an experience they would now push onto future conquests, as if they were all whores. After the first boy succumbed to a woman the other two would follow feigning that they had to take sloppy seconds without realizing that second was so far down the numerical system with these women as to not even register as a percentage.

Downstairs Neal stood before a big man.

"Neal's the name," he said, offering his hand in warm greeting, the only kind of greeting he knew.

"This is Waterson," said the clerk. "He's the mayor."

"You talk too much," he said to the clerk. He placed his hands over his stomach and glanced around to see if the sheriff was still standing just outside the open door. "Hear you've got a car for sale."

"That Buick right outside, a smooth machine almost like new, the kind of vehicle a mayor should drive. I'm giving it away cause I need some traveling money, trying to make my way up north where the air is cool and clean." Waterson pulled fifty dollars from his wallet.

"I'll give you fifty."

"Fifty! Man, it's worth a thousand if it's worth anything. Three hundred, and that's it and that's a steal, a downright bargain."

"Not worth fifty to me, boy," said Waterson. Again he looked at the sheriff. "You come to my town and expect to sell me a hot car. It's only because of my good nature I don't have you arrested. I ought to have Joey-Jean outside run you in and take the car."

Neal glanced out the door and saw the sheriff smiling. The sheriff nodded.

"We're not that way in this town. We understand that sometimes a man's just down on his luck. I'm a liberal man by nature and understand that everyone occasionally makes a mistake. I'm willing to help you out with fifty bucks in hopes that you walk the straight and narrow in the future. I won't leave you with nothing, no, not with nothing. Make a decision. I've got places to go. Whatever you decide, you're not leaving with the car however and fifty is a lot better than nothing."

The sheriff stepped inside, leaned against the doorframe, and skated his finger across his black leather gun-belt. Neal fumbled in his pockets and retrieved the keys.

"Man, you cats are something," he said. "You're just as slick as can be in this town, something I admire. I take my hat off to you as the new owner of that fine machine. Don't think I don't appreciate the break. It's the straight and narrow for me all the way, no more bopping through life, no ad-libbing, it's straight off the charts from here on."

Neal never lost his smile, didn't even become angry because there was no anger in him, just a sense of cool relaxation. Besides he could pick up a car any time he needed more cash and the fifty bucks was pure profit. He folded the cash into his pocket, nodded, and walked to the Buick, smiling at the sheriff and nodding, picked up a small pack.

"By the way, boy, you in this area again and need some cash you just let me know."

Neal smiled, pointed at the mayor with his index finger like a gun, and walked upstairs. He met the rest of the men returning to the room and followed them in. They all flopped around looking tired.

"Man, check this out," he said, pulling a bottle, void of a label, a label that might have condemned the contents as dangerous, from the pack. "Pure rotgut straight from the hills of one of the finest distilleries in the county, LeMour's Juice in a Can, the best boiled mash a dollar can buy, carefully aged for almost two hours and bottled hot to retain the subtle nuances of pine, corn, okra, and yesterday's washing including socks and underwear."

"That's almost a gallon," said Steve, his eyes glowing like some night beast that has spotted his next defenseless kill.

Neal popped the cork releasing the fragrant essence of turpentine, cleaning solution, and brake fluid, an aroma that continued to bulk up in the air the longer it lingered, building an incredible set of muscles anxious to fight.

"Woo," said Neal, curling up his nose and turning his head away from the bottle. "We have to join it, become one with the juice, the world, before it destroys us. Reluctance will only make it angry."

Steve lifted the bottle to his lips and forced down a stream of poison, twigs, pig crap, and all. He choked slightly before his throat burst into flame creating such a firestorm that it would not die to embers until the following morning. The bottle putted from man to man like a tugboat pulling smiles, laughter, and ever-increasing unguarded joviality. Although Chau drank as much as the rest, he did not lose his composure. He seldom spoke and appeared content to guard himself behind a large smile. Neal had a never-ending bag of words, articulate and snappy words meant to impress, to show he was more than a human yo-yo bouncing from coast to coast. His mother had died when he was a child and his father fell into a whisky bottle, never able to climb out. It seemed Neal had always been on his own, often stealing to eat, occasionally in the custody of social organizations, and, as he grew old enough to see over the steering wheel, becoming a first-rate car thief until that one unlucky day when he was caught and incarcerated in reform school. He hit the road upon his release and had been traveling every since. He relished telling stories and tossed in bits of humor with the drama.

"I've been checking the scene in New York," he said. "A mad city built on graft and creation, a high rise of emotion tugging at the stars. The jazz joints are hopping with new sounds and writing is being turned inside out. Cats like Ginsberg, Corso, Ferlinghetti, and Burroughs lay down words like musical scores, wild musical scores played with sticks, metal rods, wheat shafts, jungle drums and eerie banshee voices that sound just above the muck and goo of swamps. And a new pal of mine, Jack Kerouac, is helping to define a new generation that people do not even know is here and might never even know it until it is gone. And drugs. Man, there are drugs that will tunnel new rooms in your mind, make the okra turn blue and cause cats to swim. Asia is full of drugs, isn't it Chau?" Chau nodded.

"That boy ain't much on talking," said Steve. "But he's a right nice feller. Give us some words, Chau."

Bix seemed content to listen to the words, muffled by the whisky, and let them pillow in his brain, waiting for him to sleep.

"I am learning about your country," he grinned. "My father says the United States is a great supporter of the French. Almost all of the French military equipment is from your government. They even pay much of the salary of the French troops. He thinks we will be friends for a long time. Since I speak French and English I am required to learn much about this country. I understand the French, perhaps because I have always lived with them, but I am having difficulty understanding the American. I mean understanding the Americans."

"Hell," said Steve, rocking forward and touching Chau in the chest with his finger. His face resembled a glowing setting sun. "We're all just fellers, all come from different places. Each of us mostly have our own thoughts but we pretty much take all them idears in and get along, anyway." He looked at Neal. "You ain't got some of them drugs with you that you been talking about?"

"Just weed, man, just weed. Let me break it out."

The men partied, produced serious discussions, probed one another for insight, laughed uproarishly when Steve farted then held a five minute farting contest where they got too close to the bed sheets and lit them on fire and, in a complete marijuana fog, including Bix, drifted off to sleep just before daylight.

Chapter 4

The following morning Bix rose first. The marijuana had had little effect on him or, maybe he had been too drunk to notice. A grove of saguaro cactus had grown in his mouth during the night, dry and prickly. He attempted to spit them out but the barbs held tightly and only dust emerged. In the bathroom he brushed his teeth and doused his face in cold water. He sat on the toilet and felt the dam break gurgling and spitting in chunks. The smell caused his eyes to water and his stomach pushed through his colon and fell into the bowl.

The others suffered a like fate so they passed the remainder of the whisky around, as a cure, to be licked clean before stumbling out of the hotel and piling onto the seats of the Studebaker like sacks of grain. Dust rose from the seats and sparkled in the morning light and a slight aroma of motor oil floated in the air. All windows were immediately rolled down for ventilation, some small breeze, a hope for the least bit of wavy atmosphere. Everyone insisted that Chau sit in front with Bix while Neal and Steve placed their butts together and leaned their heads out the windows like two drowning cows attempting to catch one last breath before going under. Bix listened to the engine turn over, cough, choke to life under a fog of tail pipe smoke that engulfed the car. He adjusted the choke as the engine smoothed and the smoke died out under the choking exhaust. His stomach continued to revolt and he burped several times tasting the sweetness of the moonshine over again.

"We're eating down the road, away from this town," he said. "Isn't that what we decided, just to play it safe and get out?" Only grunts answered his question. Chau, for the sake of dignity, tried to keep his eyes open but was having difficulty staying awake. What a strange country, he thought: parties, roads, lawless police, odd languages or accents, people beside the roads gathered up like old friends then dumped someplace else to become a friend to someone else, and the miles – endless miles of roads chasing sunsets or sunrises. He had never traveled more than thirty miles in his own country and thought, at the time, he had journeyed a great distance, had been pleased to broaden his view of his own land. And yet, until leaving home, he had gone no place, had learned nothing. Even in France he had not ventured beyond the borders of Paris. The edges of the United States appeared limitless, endless roads and country bounded by more country. He understood that Russia was many times larger. There always seemed to be someplace larger if one just searched long enough.

Bix drove slowly toward the edge of town keeping the car in second. Neal's eyes watched the brick buildings pass, weathered wood, naked wood, bricks, one after the other. His head jerked and he yelled out. "Stop the car!" Bix hit the brakes. "Sono-fabitch," he said, opening the door. "Man, can you believe it, look at what that crooked bastard did, that dirty bastard all high and mighty and full of it." They all looked except Steve, who was already asleep, drool dripping from his mouth and pooling on the felt armrest. Neal pointed to the Buick sitting on the car lot of "Waterson's Motors." "I'll be damned. It's just as beautiful as ever sitting like a star in the galaxy, newly washed and begging to be driven. Look at the price on my car - $1500." He circled around it twice before slumping back into the Studebaker. "When these cats steal they steal big picking your pockets all the way down to your socks and $1500 - $1500 for a car this beautiful is a crime. I think too small, too much like a side-man, to ever get rich, not that money means anything to me, the love of it being the root of all evil and having the ability to corrupt even a saint. Man, I can hate money and still be rich just as long as I'm disgusted every time I make a hundred." Neal started laughing as they drove away.

They decided to stop in Smition for breakfast. On the way Bix pulled into a lonely gas station between towns, a small affair of warped and tattered slats, quart bottles of oil frowning through the greasy windows, their tin spouts pointing toward the ceiling. A green and white Bardahl sign hung at an angle beside the door, next to that an advertisement for Phillip Morris cigarettes. A bench built of planks, with inverted V legs on each end, rested beside the door, the seat worn smooth. Leaning against one bench was a tin Pepsi sign – a raised bottle cap - that had fallen off the wall. The single gasoline pump sprouted a head holding a faded star. The station had no garage so work was done outside and a wooden ramp three feet off the ground appeared to be used for oil changes. Rusted hulks of Detroit's finest sat scattered about the back, derelicts washed up on the dirt and picked mostly clean by scavengers or vandalized with rocks and bullets. A flat head straight eight Pontiac engine rested on its side while the pistons and connecting rods pitted and froze inside. Someone had started to dismantle a Ford flathead V-8 probably to put it into a stock car for weekend races at the track advertised several miles back.

The attendant wandered aimlessly toward the pump, a rag hanging from his front pocket, as if uncertain of his destination but taking the path of least resistance. "Help you fellas?' he said.

Bix popped the hood and said, "Fill her up. We might need a quart of oil. Bathroom?"

"Round back. Ain't but one and that don't always work. Piss anywhere you like. Everyone else does but if you're gonna crap take it out into the woods cause I don't like stepping in it."

Everyone stumbled around back, leaned against the wall and pissed on the dirt. Steve sighed relief and Bix said, "Shake it more than twice and you are playing with yourself." Big breaths of air filled all their lungs, enough oxygen to stagger them back to the car.

"You sure needed that quart of oil," said the attendant. Bix followed him inside. He pulled out a note pad. "Let's see. That was four dollars for the gas and thirty cents for the oil." He wrote the numbers on the pad and made fists with his hands as his lips squelched up. Bix wasn't sure what he was doing. He kept jotting down numbers and scratching them off. "I never was no good with rythmatic," he said. Bix finally realized he could not add the numbers. "I'm not rightly sure what to charge. I don't want to cheat you."

"How about this," said Bix. "The gas was four dollars, right? Let me pay you for that first." He handed him four wrinkled one-dollar bills careful not to hand him the five. If he could not add, subtraction might put him in the state mental hospital. "That's right, isn't it?" The attendant nodded his head, his greasy cracked fingers holding the bills. "Now I owe you thirty cents. Here it is. Now we're square." The man grinned as if he had learned a treasured business secret, one that might make ease his imagined troubled life. "See, if you take the money for each thing you won't have to do any calculus."

"I don't know what that calc stuff is but I never thought of that. One thing at a time. That sure makes it easy."

"It's the secret of life," said Bix.

Bix left him standing there in amazement and he realized how fortunate he was to have been educated in South Dakota. He wanted to tell everyone about the exchange but decided not to. Steve might be offended but he doubted it.

"Let's divvy up some money for the gas, get a small pot going, maybe ten bucks apiece and we will refill when it's exhausted." said Neal.

Smition was little more than a tavern with a cracked window, a dry goods store, a farm supply building, a stand-alone restaurant, and a phone booth. Again they tumbled from the car, a group of living dead staggering across the dirt. Steve grabbed Neal by the shoulder and nodded toward the phone booth. "We'll be along directly," he said. He spoke quietly to Neal until they both started laughing. "You up for it," he said.

"That's about the coolest thing I ever heard, a whopper, more fun than a barrel of junkies and it will turn the town on its head," said Neal. "I can't pull off the accent so you make the call, if you would be so kind."

"Batesville?" Steve said to Neal making sure he got the right town. Neal nodded and handed him several coins. "Operator, operator, get me the sheriff over to Batesville. Yes, that's Batesville. How much?" he fed the machine several coins. "This be the Sheriff over to Batesville? Yessir, the sheriff. Eyes got to let yous know about sumpin going on. Ids dear a Buick missing over your way? Yous must know the one. That's right; da one dats belongs to Mr. Buckingham. Eyes was passing through Arkadelphia last night and I heerd some fellas talking outside the hotel. Eyes was sitting beside the building and I heerd these fellas talking about theis purdy Buick. One of does fellers done tolt the otheren he could have the Buick for one hundert dollars. When des broke up I see the one feller is the clerk at the hotel. Next morning eyes was walking out of town and I sees the Buick for sale at a place called Waterson's car lot. Yessir, I knows it's the one. I done seen Mr. Buckingham in it on several occasions while lookin' fer pickup work and I gosta wash it once. No, I don't recon I'd give my name seeing as how I don't want no trouble. I just wanted to let you know. Over to Arkadelphia. The only car lot in town. Yes sir, I done hope eyes helped some." He hung up the phone and they broke into uncontrollable laughter. "Bunch of pricks," said Steve. "Let's see how they like it now."

"You sound more like a black man than a black man," said Neal. "A Southern black man, the ones up north remain articulate especially the ones on the jazz scene with minds like a calculus knocking wooden balls from east to west."

Bix started reading a paper that had been left at the table. He continued to reach around the paper to gulp copious amounts of coffee and paid little attention to Steve and Neal laughing over their joke on the phone and rolling through several possible scenarios of the outcome of their trick after the police arrived. They wanted to be there but decided that the imagining was just as good. Bix shook the paper and laid it across the table running his finger over a column.

"Chau, listen to this headline," he said. "'Woman found murdered outside Shell Bluff, Georgia.'" Chau folded his hands together on the table. "'A woman, identified as Melba Theran, was discovered beaten to death in the trunk of her car. Two local boys discovered the overturned vehicle down Mud Creek Road. Sheriff Waters has learned that Theran belonged to a radical Communist organization, 'Freedom for All' and had previously participated in disrupting the cotton industry through union organizing. Little else has been uncovered. Waters vows to stay on the case until solved.'"

"What does it mean?" said Chau. Knowing what Chau thought was difficult. His expression seldom changed and he spoke little.

"It means that rascal sheriff is full of crap," Steve answered for Bix. "He was probably part of the killing. That's the way things is done down here. No one ever knows the truth cause they don't know what the truth is until they make it up themselves."

"Should I do something?" Chau's expression remained the same, unconcerned and relaxed.

"Better to stay out of it," said Bix. "There's nothing to be done, anyway."

Back on the road, Neal passed around a tube of Benzedrine. "Dig on this," he said. "Shove it up your nose and take a big whiff and see how far we travel today, how the sting opens your eyes and gets your heart running up hill. We'll be balling the jack in no time, wide-awake and smiling, clear roads ahead calling us on to the promised land, full steam ahead, smoke rising with the sun. Sleep is a thing of the past, something for the old, not for hip-cats like us who have living to do and places to see and need twenty-four hours of every day to fit it all in. We are Odysseus and we'll know the sea, the land sea, before the trip is over."

Even the Studebaker seemed to take on new life as it gathered speed effortlessly, the men laughing and hanging from the windows singing Hank Williams songs. Only Chau, looking toward the west, sat quietly in the front seat dreaming of a brighter future for his country.

Chapter 5

Heat loosened the oil in the shocks, the brake shoes, the door and hood hinges, and the door handles; it caused the seats to dry out, draw up and shed dust; it rattled the dome light into nervous flicker, all while drawing the Studebaker toward Arizona. With windows down, air whistling in, the group leaked sweat from under arms, on upper lips and foreheads, feet hanging from the car windows, their socks flapping and pants legs snapping against the wind, as beer, the bottles strangled by slimy hands, warmed between thighs.

"This country is interesting," said Chau. "I have never seen such an expanse of dirt and rocks. Still, it seems to have a certain beauty, an appealing quality I don't understand."

"The southwest is mostly barren," said Bix. "I've never been here but I've seen plenty of pictures. We have cold, mountains, trees that never die and plenty of wild animals in the northwest; flat lands with unpredictable weather in the middle where most of our grain is grown; more cold green country in the northeast where the trees die each fall; hot humid weather down the east coast becoming worse at the southern end; then hot dry land with little water in the southwest."

"And California?" said Chau, feeling the dry hot wind on his hand and watching the cactus stand in surrender as the car passed. He had never known a place both hot and dry, a place not wringing with humidity.

"Neal would know most about that. A lot of strange stuff happens there, new things like in New York that I don't understand. I'm not sure what people do there – grow fruit, I guess. They grow lots of fruit like in Florida. Not much happens in South Dakota so I don't know a lot of stuff about other places." He glanced toward Chau and smiled.

40

Chau liked Bix and this strange country with its even stranger people. Buttes appeared in the distance and a thunderhead jabbed the sky with a trident of lightning. Occasionally he glimpsed a jackrabbit jagging it's way through the mesquite. Dry creeks and rivers snaked toward the horizon.

"Is your family happy," said Chau.

"Happy?" Bix did not understand.

"Are they pleasant?" he said. "Do they live without complaint?"

"My dad, mostly." He scratched at his chin. "He works very hard and I've never heard him complain about anything. Work makes him happy."

"And your mother?"

"Once, maybe," said Bix. He looked far down the road, not a bend anywhere. "She doesn't complain either but there is a sadness about her, even about her smile. My sister, Joyce, was born seven years after me, the pride of Mom's life. She couldn't keep her hands off her, always dressing her up, playing patty-cake, and things like that." He realized that Chau would not understand patty-cake. "That's where you keep touching their little feet together and singing patty-cake, patty-cake, baker's man. Silly, I guess. Anyway, Mom watched her closely after she started walking but one day she toddled out the back door. Mom couldn't find her anywhere and she started to panic. She saw a lump of pink in the corral. Joyce had wandered in and Rusty, my horse, had kicked her in the head and killed her. I had been with Dad that day and we found Mom sitting against the fence holding Joyce in her arms and singing patty-cake. Dad's rifle sat on the dirt beside her. Rusty was dead, a bullet in his head. Mom never was happy after that. I think she blamed some of it on me because Rusty was my horse even though I was too young to ride him. Dad got some blame too for buying him. They didn't talk much after that and when Dad tried to put his arm around her she jerked it away with her shoulder."

"Life is often difficult," said Chau. He lit a cigarette and handed one to Bix. Bix breathed it in deeply, the loose ash flying in the wind.

"I think the fear of loss caused her not to have any more kids. She has continued with life like any other person but she is never really there. She goes through the motions. At first she spent a lot of time at the church but she slowly quit going and stopped seeing her friends."

"All misery lies in the past," said Chau. "There is only now. That is what the Buddha says."

"The Buddha?"

"A strange yet interesting religion, or philosophy about life, from my country. They have no God."

"Then how is it a religion?"

"I don't know," said Chau, and he shrugged his shoulders. "I think they don't care. If you ask them about God they don't answer because they don't talk about something that is not there."

A fart, loud enough to be heard through the rushing wind, came from the back seat. Neal started to wake. Steve still laid asleep, his head dropped to one side, his mouth again oozing drool, the beer bottle tipped in his lap.

"Hey, man," said Neal. He coughed and lit a cigarette. The smoke caused him to smoke even harder. "I heard you say Buddhism, the religion of all religions, the path to nirvana and enlightenment where all things are understood and nothing is understood, the spirit of compassion encompassing the soul, love to all and injury to none, where you know less and less about more and more. Peace is the word. Harm nothing. It's all the rage on the coast where salt-filled water spreads its fingers along the beach and licks away footprints showing the mutability of all things – there is no now because when the now happens it is already past, no past – just becoming. It's the way to go. All the cats are studying it. And converting. Christianity, the religions of hate and power and sadism and sexual repression are dead."

"I don't understand?" said Bix.

"Man, it's cool, like really cool. You see there's like nothing real or solid in the world, just illusion and delusion, the great falsity that we all see differently. There is but there isn't, you dig, maya, mist, the fog of lies? Everything real is moving, swirling around, never stopping, nothing ever at rest, nothing made up of anything solid, just things like atoms that are also moving, everything we think is a great fog unable to hold. Everything is impermanent, momentary, so we can't get a real grasp of anything. Even our minds are momentary, mutable, ephemeral, flitting from one thing to another, one idea to another idea. Who can touch a thought, an idea?" Neal leaned forward, crossed his arms on the back top of the front seat and rested his head on them. Bix had no idea what he was talking about. "Now dig this, everything is the same thing composed of the same ingredient, the same stuff, if you like, so there's like no difference between a man and a plant or a rock and a cow. Buddhists are very peaceful and attempt to not hurt anything because hurting something is like hurting some part of yourself. Squashing a bug is the same as squashing your mother. I've been following the Buddhist way for several years. All is peace and love, a world without hate or injury." He patted Chau on the shoulder. "You know, man. All Asians know. Say, pull over. I've got to piss."

Bix pulled to the side of the road. No vehicles moved on the highway in either direction. Everyone except Steve, bathing in his own drool, piled from the car. Bix suggested a pissing contest that gave him much enjoyment. Chau placed first with the longest shot and said he had never heard of such a game. Bix came in a close second, Neal a distant third, partially dribbling on his bare feet.

"Like," he said, "I got more hose for it to travel through so it's exhausted when it gets out." Something in the distance caught his eye.

"Look," he said. "By that bush. I think it's a snake, the serpent in the Garden of Eden calling us into temptation." The others saw nothing. Neal tossed a rock in that direction. "There he goes," he said, pointing at a brown swirl across the sand. "Come on, let's get him and smash his brains to bits before he draws the entire world toward destruction."

He gathered several rocks. Bix picked up a dried branch and pointed to an abandoned beer bottle for Chau. Cautiously they moved toward the bush. Neal winced several times, when he stepped on rocks, and shook his bare feet. The snake began to rattle and coil as they got closer and surrounded the bush.

"Wow! He's a fat one," said Neal, " like a Mexican at a chili-eating contest. He's some kind of evil rattlesnake waiting to strike out, to strike the world with his venom, fangs sinking deep into innocent unaccustomed flesh. We are one with it, one with the serpent, to kill it is to kill us. I might need bigger rocks."

His aim was good and the first rock hit the snake in the face drawing a string of blood. Bix whacked it with the branch and Chau tossed the bottle before picking up a rock. The snake fought its best but eventually resigned to its fate, shrinking down, its head lowering slowly until it offered no resistance and accepted its death. After a close inspection by the men, and some touching of the skin to exhibit their bravery, Bix slid the branch under it and flung it through the air. It twirled like a tossed stick landing on top another bush.

"Do you eat them?" asked Chau.

"No," said Bix. "We mostly leave them alone or kill them. About the only way to find one is by accident. They don't like company."

"Alan could write a great poem about this one," said Neal. "Like, it would have some tremendous symbolism – the snake being the human condition and how it is always being beaten down by society and it constantly fights back to no avail until it eventually gives up and accepts its proletariat death at the hands of the bourgeoisie."

"How come you're not a Buddhist?" said Neal to Chau, returning to the Studebaker.

"Most educated Annamites are Catholics." The car door squeaked as he opened it. He slammed it hard. "We do not believe in ghosts and all those rituals. Some things do not make sense and sound like fables."

"Like a man walking on water?" said Neal. "That's something you can sink your teeth into. It takes a hell of an imagination to picture that. But the cannibalism is a nice touch, eating the flesh and drinking the flesh of Christ. A lawyer friend of mine, three-piece suit kind of guy, wouldn't be caught dead on a motorcycle, says he always picks religious people for juries. He says that anyone that believes a man can walk on water can be talked into anything. No intellect. No reasoning capacity. A void waiting to be filled."

"Sometimes belief exceeds reason," said Chau.

"Yeh, it's out there, man – way out there. The church wants power and control and reason and logic just don't mesh with their beliefs. The fat cats say faith needs no explanation, no facts, that's how they avoid proof, how they keep the little man down so they can control him and pick his pocket. Keep him afraid of dying, convince him he can live forever in total bliss, and you have him by the balls. I don't mean to put you down for your beliefs but discussion is a good thing."

First gear groaned from exhaustion as they pulled away. Not until they got up to speed did the stifling heat start to crawl out the open windows.

"Aside from not hurting anything, is that all there is about the religion?" said Bix. He had always been naturally curious and took every opportunity to learn about something new. He rubbed his hand on his pants where he had touched the dead snake.

"Man, there's lots about the religion." Neal loved the chance to talk, to air his intelligence. He knew plenty about the world and read constantly. "I'm totally dedicated to it. You see they know people are all miserable because of all the crap we own, all the junk we want, because we crave wealth, power and pleasure, because we want to live forever and refuse to accept our deaths. They say 'just get over it.' We must surrender our wants, our greed, and be better people to find happiness. Like I said, they call it nirvana. You see, if all us cats adopted a moral type conduct and developed some mental discipline we would find true happiness instead of trying to buy it, which doesn't work. Simple stuff but pretty cool."

"So you're really a Buddhist?" said Bix.

"It's cool and a person can really dig it," said Neal. "It's the one true religion, if it is a religion, and if you start coming on with this stuff to chicks you'll get laid every time. That's my nirvana. Yeh man, I'm devoted to it unless something better comes along."

The men pulled into Emery for dinner. Finding a restaurant was easy since there was only one in town. A woman too old and fat to be a waitress, or maybe just old and fat enough, took their orders. A small pair of baby shoes was pinned to the waitress's apron. She gave Chau a cautionary look as she fiddled with the pen. Chau felt anxious for rice. Any kind of rice dish would suffice but there was none to be found. He had not found any rice for almost two weeks and it had become a craving that rested in his mind constantly. Vietnamese lived on rice, could not exist without it.

"Do you have rice?" he said.

"Rice? You can't grow rice in this country – too dry. We have potatoes."

"What's with the baby shoes?" said Steve.

The question caught her off guard and she looked down as if she had misplaced the shoes and was surprised to find them there. She lifted them, then carefully lowered them back down.

"Kind of nosy, aren't you?" she said.

"I don't mean nothing by it," he said. "Us hill folks is kind of forward. If we're curious, we ask, probably because we ain't smart enough to figure things out. Having shoes hanging around your neck is different."

The easy self-deprecatory talk seemed to ease her.

"They were never worn," she said. "So, what can I get you?"

"That ain't much of an explanation but it sure makes the point."

After they ordered they sat quietly refusing to mention the baby shoes as if to do so meant breaking into a great personal secret. The coffee went down freely and loosened the words.

"San Francisco is now the happinin' place," said Neal. "There's a jazz sax man there called Sam Sausage, red blazer, white fedora, white tie, red rimmed shades, who blows notes from outer and inner space and a woman I befriended who's so far out she can hardly be reached. The coke keeps her going for laughs but she's hooked on H, spends too much time with Burroughs and she can't quit, not because of the joy of the junk but because of the pain at quitting. No one stays on because they like it but because they can't get off. You have to quit before the dust gets you, before you get hooked. Someday she'll catch a hot-shot, a cap of strychnine that looks and tastes like junk, give it to her cause she's got no more purpose, gone to bone and leather her twat dried like overcooked meat and no longer able to turn tricks to pay for her dope and teeth wasted to uselessness chiseled by the artisan of time. All the interesting people are there and New York. I want to introduce you cats to everyone, to enlarge your world-view, expand your minds and emotions of what's to come."

There was no rice for Chau. He fiddled with the green and white-checkered cotton tablecloth rolling the edge around his fingers to calm his craving as he listened to Neal and waited for his chicken. Maybe rice was his addiction. He continued to watch Neal as he spouted off to Steve.

Something through the serving window caught Neal's attention. He kept his eye glued to the opening. Twice more he saw a flash, a glint of milky tan skin and flowing black hair. Then he saw her, possibly the most beautiful Mexican woman he had ever seen. She looked through the opening and smiled, an open invitation to pleasure he thought. "Back in a sec," he said.

"It ain't cooled down outside yet," said Steve, "but it don't feel so bad without the moisture, sort of like being in the oven instead of the steam room."

"We have wind in South Dakota. Dry heat also," said Bix. "This trip is the first time I realized the wind doesn't blow everywhere on the earth. It's been a surprise." He turned to Chau. "What's different in your country?"

"It is very different from this," he said. "We have thick jungles, even in the mountains, and flat lands beside the coast. Most of our rivers and streams flow with mud. I have seen clear water here. Ours are usually muddy like rivers I saw in the South. I think it is because we have few rocks."

"We drink the water anyway," said Steve. Chau nodded with understanding. Steve cracked a smile. He glanced at Neal standing at the counter. "Look at that pecker-head. He must be spitting out that Buddhist crap by the wheelbarrow-full."

Neal leaned over the counter toward the cook, one leg lifted, the cook grinning back through the order window. The waitress stood in the corner, her arms crossed, eyes glaring. Whenever Neal attempted to slide around the counter and get closer, she smacked his hand with her hand, her head tipping him in warning. The food finally brought him back to the table.

"Her name's Yolanda," he said. "What a beauty, a flower of the desert blooming under my eyes and calling me in, calling me to love forever in that moist mattress of eternal life. Comes from a little town named Aripe and she's trying to make some money to take back there, help out the family. I tried to explain that she can live free as a bird without any money and said we can discuss it later on after work, if you cats are ready to settle in for the night, and discuss the work of Weston because she wants to be a photographer and she likes the work he produced in Mexico. She says Mexico has its own great photographers like Alvarez Bravo. She's also a Communist, or Marxist, and thinks all creative people are Communists. All the ones I know are."

Neal continued to babble uncontrollably about the woman he had just met. Bix found it amusing and frustrating. He wanted to move on and stop at dusk. Staying here for the night seemed to be no problem for Steve and Chau so he said nothing and accepted the fact that they would all wait patiently while Neal reveled in the flesh.

"You boys looking for work?" The man, short and thin, his pants legs flowing over his dusty cowboy boots, had entered unnoticed. His shirt, faded to sunlight blue, had a dark ring of dirt around the inside of the collar where it folded over his shoulders and sweat stains showed under the armpits. He scratched at a mole beside his nose toward the end of the ravines of his skin that dropped and hung from under his chin. Blue veins throbbed below the skin of his hands and up his arms where the shirt-sleeves rolled up to his elbows. "Work," he said as if he expected them to say no.

"What kind of work?" said Steve. He did not mind being short of funds but he was down to nothing and if anything, he was no moocher.

"Bucking hay," the man said, as he flipped around a chair and sat with his arms folded over the back. "I own the Tilbury spread outside of town. The name's Oberlin. I've got the hay all baled and need it put up – about a week's work, maybe a bit more. Besides the pay you can stay in the bunkhouse and Mabel will keep you fed. The money you make is all yours and I know every whorehouse and bar in the area."

"We could probably use some cash," said Bix, thinking it would use up time while waiting for Neal. "I humped bales in South Dakota. We have no equipment."

"I've got it all at the spread: haying chaps, hooks, even a stack of used boots in the storehouse." Chewing tobacco had yellowed his teeth and a small dribble of brown juice crept from between the corner of his lips. He dabbed it with the back of his hand. The waitress placed a paper cup on the table.

"Hiram Oberlin," she said. "Don't be spitting on the floor." He reached up and placed his hand on the baby shoes.

"Can you vouch for these boys?" he said.

"I don't know anything about them, except maybe that one," she said, pointing to Neal. "I've seen way too many like him."

"Good enough. How about it boys?" He flashed a wide grin.

"What do you say?" said Bix.

"I got nothing to do," said Steve. "A little hard work might put some energy back in this body and I could use some cash. How about it?" he said to Chau.

Chau nodded and said, "I am here to learn about your country. I have to sail home from San Francisco and cannot miss the date. There is time."

"I'll have to catch up to you," said Neal. "Business awaits and once I get things squared way, provided I'm not exhausted, I'll come by. Until then I propose to swim up to my neck in sweet glorious flesh, take in all that's owed a person and give back the same. That be OK?" he said to Oberlin.

Oberlin closely eyed them all. He had always been a man of good judgment and felt suspicious of Neal. Chau seemed much too small and delicate for heavy lifting. Yet he exuded an inner strength that showed that what he lacked in size he would compensate for with enthusiasm and determination. Steve carried a peculiar Southern humor about him that would come in handy under the hot sun and he seemed to be no stranger to hard work if given the right incentives. He might tell more jokes than do any actual work but he would do as much as he could. Bix seemed to be just what he said he was, a hard-working farm boy not afraid of work.

"I imagine you will drop by and do some work if you have time," he said to Neal, knowing he would not show up except to say goodbye. "The spread is easy to find." He drew a map on a napkin. "Come out whenever you like tonight. Remember we start early before the sun beats us too far down." He walked to the counter, talked to the waitress, kissed her on the cheek, and left without looking at the men.

After dinner the men walked outside and sat on a slatted bench facing the street. A gray Henry-J rattled past and pulled into the Skelly gas station at the end of town. An Indian man wearing an army campaign hat, staggered from the driver's side and wobbled to the side of the building. Two Indian women emerged from the other side, both wrapped in blankets in spite of the heat. One removed a bottle of beer and started to drink. The other one leaned against the rumpled front fender.

"I reckon you're seeing an example of folks who refuse to change," Steve said to Chau. "Just about every creature on earth will adapt except an Indian. If he can't hunt and make the women do all the real work, he won't do anything except drink."

"We have a lot of good Sioux back home," said Bix. "They want it like the old days too, but some of them are coming around. I give them rides into town whenever I see one walking along the road. What about the French Foreign Legion?" Bix said to Chau. The idea had rested in the back of his mind ever since Chau had mentioned them. "How do you join?"

"Just join," said Chau, tapping out an Old Gold cigarette from the pack then passing the pack around.

"Not much happening here," said Bix. "Gas is up to nineteen, twenty cents a gallon. It's getting tough to earn a decent living – thirty or forty bucks a week is good pay but that's hard to find. Someone like me doing farm work can't earn that much. You have to be special to earn more, a sports guy maybe."

"Didn't Joe DiMaggio get some big money a few years back?" said Steve.

"Joltin' Joe signed for $100,000 or more and that was just for one year."

"Reckon we could save all the money we earn from the French, if we join," said Steve. "It won't be $100,000 but they give us room and board. Every army does that. The vittles have to be decent from what I hear about French cooking. That's right, isn't it?"

"The blend of French and Vietnamese food is excellent," said Chau. "Perhaps it will be so in the Legion."

"Ain't they got whores on call, army whores?" said Steve. His eyebrows tickled the air as he smiled in anticipation. Chau nodded. "Woo! Is that part of the deal or do we has to pay?"

"The French are helping us," said Chau.

"If we has to pay I'll come home broke. I hear you can join under any name. I want to join as Crème Broulet. Whyent we just join our own army instead of running off?"

"You want to be part of an imperialist army?" said Neal. "Lackeys, they're just lackeys, puppets of the state destined to be used to suppress the masses of this country and all other countries. MacArthur did it to the bonus marchers after the First World War, run right through their camps hacking them up with sabers and burning them out, women and children too just because they wanted to be paid early because all of them were out of work and starving. Doug-out Doug didn't care although he wasn't Doug-out Doug then, a lackey of the government ordering lesser lackeys to trample the real soldiers. It won't last. Greed, arrogance, and the military will bury this country now that they're hooked up with industry and the people will just let it happen, sit in houses of apathy clinging to their last silver spoon. Someday we'll be nothing and people like the Chinese will be everything."

Bix asked for another cigarette and watched the Indians climb back into the car and drive off in a cloud of smoke and the aroma of burnt clutch. "It has to be the Foreign Legion if we want an adventure," he said. "No one cares about our army. Being in the Legion will turn some heads."

Neal moved to the railing and sat. The setting sun had started to pull down a drapery of yellow and red sky painting the wispy clouds pink against the horizon.

"I sing of Olaf glad and big – whose warmest heart recoiled at war," said Neal. "Cummings said it best in that poem and got right to the point with lines like I will not kiss your fucking flag, and there is some shit I will not eat." He blew a string of smoke into the evening. "Man, you dudes need to know that war is a bad thing, folks killing one another for no reason except to satisfy the greedy and arrogant in power telling them to, praising them, building the small man's ego until he thinks killing makes him important and not realizing he's taking all a man has or ever will have, a wife, a girlfriend, a father, a family, and for what? Hardy said how quaint and curious war is you'd shoot a fellow down – you'd treat where any bar is or help to half a crown. Of course if you don't go you don't have the ultimate adventure, that ridiculous passage to manhood that takes the place of those not having a circumcision, a physical indication of manhood unlike girls who become women one night as a teenager when they awake to find blood in their panties, blood that says today I am a woman and now understands she can never turn back. The blood of man's adulthood springs from another man, a confrontation, even a losing one, or a killing."

"And we don't wear no panties," said Steve. "Least not all the time. My Uncle Joey-D was my inspiration and give the best advice a man could want. I'd listen to him for hours as he sobered up after limping home from the bar. When I visited him at the jailhouse he said prison time marked a man's moving toward manhood, something he could be proud of. Some of the folks around town didn't think much of him after he got caught naked with them two Jemkins boys but he was the smartest man I ever knew. He did some time for that after he got caught a second time with the four-year old Mavis girl. He claimed that she seduced him but the judge didn't see it that way. He still stays active teaching the kids in Sunday school."

They all chuckled, especially Bix who thought that Steve and Neal were very bright or at least very clever, each in his own way. Steve liked to play the hick but seemed mentally quick. For Neal a few choice quotes could go a long way to someone like Bix who had never heard of Cummings or Hardy and did not know if the lines were real or not, but were certainly impressive.

"Maybe we should go," said Bix. He watched a scruffy yellow dog roll on the dirt in the middle of the road kicking up dust like an explosion.

Traveling by night was something they all seemed to enjoy, the cooling air, smells of the desert, high plains and mountain air, heavy bugs mushing against the windshield, the moisture on the wind creeping through one window and out the other, the quietness of talk in all its muffled tones, the orange glow of the overhead light reflecting Steve's image against the windshield while deciphering the map to the ranch. Bix turned down a gravel road under the Tilbury Ranch sign and listened to the small stones from the tires flipping against the undercarriage. The houses appeared almost a mile down the road. The car lights flashed against a large white two story building surrounded by a covered porch, then swung left past the lone tree toward a faded red bunkhouse in the distance. He parked the car in front of the bunkhouse hitching post. Dim lights, weak and unable to push through the night, shown from the windows.

"I reckon this must be it," said Steve, peering through the windshield. "I don't care to get shot going into someone's house."

From the backseat, Chau looked all around trying to see through the dark. He felt a tinge of excitement. The west. The Wild West. And he was about to be a part of it as they all walked quietly to the door. Bix tapped lightly, then harder after getting no response. A tall thin man opened it and stood fixed in place. He pulled at one side of his moustache.

"We've been hired to buck hay," said Bix. "I think this is where we are supposed to stay. Is this the bunkhouse?"

"Nobody knocks here unless they're working," said the man, as he walked away leaving the door open.

The men entered and stood just inside as the man returned to his seat beside a table under a bare light bulb. He picked up his cards then tossed one onto the pile. Two other men fingered their cards and eyed the newcomers.

"There are supposed to be beds," said Bix.

"Christ," said the man. "Are you going to be those kinds that have to be told everything and taken by the hand like a kid? You notice Chuck Dinknow is in that bed? Three more are messed up so you can't use them. I guess that means you can have any of the other ones. Figure it out. Hay hands, that's what you must be, simple-minded hay hands."

"I'm Bix and this is Steve and Chau. We're just here to work, not to cause any trouble."

They all looked up with the name Chau. Chuck Dinknow rustled in his bunk and looked over the side. His feet seemed enormous as they caught in the blanket when he tried to throw them over and sit up. He scratched at the stubble on his face. The whiskers outlined a scar shaped like the number seven and brown yellow teeth bit the bottom of his lip. Dirt clung to his arms.

"What's with the damn Coolie?" he said. "The yellow bastards are taking over the west and moving this way. Keep away from me, you hear. You sonsofbitches killed my brother in Korea and my uncle in the Pacific."

Chau barely tipped his head as he walked to a bunk across the room. The others followed and Bix repeated, "We're just here to work, no trouble, just work."

Chuck groaned as he rolled back onto his bed. "Don't mind him," said another cowboy. "Don't mind any of us. Dinknow never met his uncle and his brother was a half-breed he never spoke to. If he can't find something to upset him, he makes it up." He rose from the table and shook Chau's hand followed by the others. "There's a shitter out back and a sink on the wall. We got tin cups on the wall beside it for drinks. What you drink is your business. Everything you do will be your business except the work. You'll be wanting a bath after being covered with dust and hay. We use the creek. It's got a deep spot just beside the bridge. I'm Seth Hanson, that's Tiny Slim with the pot-belly and the other crabby one is Mink Parsons. He's not nearly as mean as he seems."

Bits of tobacco snuff stuck to Seth's lower teeth. His skin had the color and shape of wrinkled dried soil and he appeared to be near sixty years old although it was difficult to tell as it is with anyone who has lived under the sun.

"Just inside the barn is a room with boots, hay hooks, and such. Take what you need in the morning. Animals are nervous with other animals at first but they get to settling in soon enough. Come and go as you please just be here at working time. Doing the job is all anyone cares about."

"We right appreciate it, Mr. Hanson," said Steve.

"Seth," he said, returning to the card game.

"Well, we appreciate it and we're lookin' forward to some honest hard work."

The bunks, made of wood slats, were neatly covered with clean sheets and a wool army blanket. Rough wood, adorned with horseshoes, a hat and coat rack, a dried and rumpled cowboy boot, several pin-up posters, and a dirty mirror above a seldom used peeling white painted table, covered the walls of the bunkhouse. A small thin rug lay inside the door. A rocking chair, an overstuffed chair attempting to thin down by bleeding horsehair stuffing between cracks, and a swayback sofa completed the furnishings along with an end table holding a light with a burnt tan shade, and a box covered in magazines acting as a coffee table. Each bunk had a small footlocker for storage. Several deer and sheep horns hung from the rafters.

Chau slept fretfully, anxious to get in some work and just as anxious to return home. He missed his people, his language, his customs. Above all else he was still an Anna-mite, a Vietnamese who loved his country. He enjoyed the traveling but he never felt comfortable, never felt he could live in foreign lands for long periods of time. The world seemed cold compared to Vietnam where people, mostly women, hugged and walked arm-in-arm and slept curled up together like puppies. The ridicule he often felt outside the country did not bother him. All people wanted to be in their own groups, their own tribes, and viewed others suspiciously, a threat to the organization and safety of the unit. The feeling of unity started with the immediate family and branched out to the extended family, the village or town, the province then the country, Annamites with Annamites, Vietnamese with Vietnamese, Thai with Thai, Ho-mung with Homung. The organization remained consistent throughout the world, whites with whites, blacks with blacks, yellow with yellow, educated with educated, ignorant with ignorant. Something more base caused him to be uncomfortable, to feel alone. Perhaps it was as simple as the respect and care the young of his country gave to the old, the storehouse of wisdom the old held and their willingness to share and to teach, the sense of unity often abandoned in other countries along with respect for the wisdom of the old who were often scorned and ridiculed into silence. They seemed to be individually concerned rather than the people of a country unified. He thought of his position as the son of a wealthy businessman and the great advantages it gave him over others yet he still felt close with the poor and struggling people because his father felt that way. He was not fighting to bring Europe to Vietnam for his personal benefit but for the advantage of all his people. The cowboys and the work the following day bothered him not at all.

"This is the room," said Seth, the following morning and pushing open a wooden door to a room inside the barn. "Take whatever you need. Breakfast is in thirty minutes on the screened outside porch in back of the house. I shouldn't have to say anything but stay away from the farmer's daughter, in this case, the rancher's daughter, Burpee." He released the door and stepped into the gray light from a dawn that had not yet broken.

"The farmer's daughter," said Steve. "Woo-wee! Looks like we're in for the real thing. It's kind of a joke, a myth sorta," he said to Chau.

"We have this same myth," Chau said, sitting on a bale of hay and trying on the various cowboy boots, boots good for riding but not for walking. They all appeared to be too large.

"What about the preacher's daughter?" said Bix. He swung a pair of hay hooks.

"The French have that one," he said. "I have heard them telling it many times over glasses of wine. They always laugh. Because the humor is divergent from ours, I sometimes do not understand the jokes."

"They're all stupid," said Bix. "Have you ever used these?" He clicked the hay hooks together. "It's how we grab the hay – like this." He drove a hook into a bale and lifted it on end before rolling it over and hooking it on both sides, lifting it, tossing it through the air while releasing the hooks. "The more you do it the easier it gets."

Chau had spied a small pair of dust-covered boots near a corner. He smacked them together. Clouds of dirt burst in the air. They fit fine and he admired them by twisting one boot to the side, then the other. The boot-maker had inlaid white starbursts in the front and pounded swirls and leaves into the leather sides.

"Morning," said Bix, as they sat at the table. Tin cups and plates covered the wooden table top along with butter knives and three-pronged forks.

The cowboys sat on one side drinking coffee. "Worst coffee I ever had," said Mink Parsons. "Tastes like grounds and sewer water."

"Get some sleep, did ya?" said Seth.

"We're doing fine," said Bix. "Looking forward to some breakfast."

"I see you found some baby boots," said Chuck Dinknow, leaning over and spitting on the porch floor near Chau. "They don't have no yellow on the outside but I see they got plenty of yellow inside." He chuckled at his own cleverness and pushed out his chest and looked around for affirmation. No one looked his way. Their indifference jabbed him like a pin and he quickly deflated.

"I have the coffee ready for you boys," said Ms. Oberlin, walking through the double doors and carrying a big pot.

"Just in time. You make the best coffee in the state," said Mink Parsons, lifting up his empty tin cup.

"Wait your turn," said Ms. Oberlin. Without asking if they wanted any she poured coffee for the three new men, then Mink Parsons. "Burpee, come out here with the eggs and bacon." She turned to the new men. "She's rather shy around new people. Come out here now. No one's going to bite you."

Steve tingled with anticipation. The farmer's daughter. A job, breakfast, and the farmer's daughter; life could not get any better. The platters of eggs and bacon almost rested on her enormous breasts, breasts that matched her enormous size. She barely squeezed through the two doors. She resembled an elephant's butt, round and thick and with the same stump-like legs thumping from under her dress where her ankles folded over her shoes. Even her skin color seemed slightly gray except where the rouge and lipstick shown through.

"Good morning to yah," said Steve. She was better than he had imagined and the tingling became an outright vibration that started from his neck and toes before centering between his legs. She was better than a tub of pork fat and he felt like rolling around in the grease. "Aren't you a right lovely girl? No offense Ms. Oberlin." He tipped his head.

"We couldn't get along without her," she said. "Strangers take right to her."

Ms. Oberlin went inside for more coffee as Burpee placed the food on the table. She leaned over Steve, her breasts covering his head like earmuffs.

"Excuse me," she said.

"It don't mean nothing," said Steve, his smile zipped completely around his head.

"I'm pleased to meet all of you," she said. "I understand you're Vietnamese." She looked at Chau. "Isn't Annum a big part of Vietnam?" Chau looked surprised.

"I'm Annamite," he said. "I am surprised you know my country."

"I read a great deal," she said. "There isn't much else to do on a ranch, read and eat."

"I like a woman with some meat on her," said Steve, fidgeting and trying to get back into the conversation. He watched her waddle back inside.

"She don't know a damn Coolie when she sees one," said Dinknow.

"Whyent you shut up," said Mink Parsons.

"I don't have to shut up," said Dinknow. "I'll take some more of that coffee, if you please," he said, half standing, a grin across his face, and offering the cup to Ms. Oberlin as she placed the pitcher on the table.

"I'll leave you boys to your breakfast," she said. "Need anything, just yell out."

"Where are you headed?" said Seth.

"We're taking Chau to San Francisco to catch a boat back home," said Bix. "We had some extra time and needed a money boost."

"They don't come better than Oberlin. As fair as anyone."

Dinknow stood and farted in Chau's direction before leaving.

"Good thing we ain't smoking," said Steve. "Would'f sent up a hellava blast."

"What's with him, anyway?" said Bix. He buttered a piece of toast.

"He won't pick on anyone his own size," said Seth. "Notice he doesn't bother you boys?"

"Just a bully on the playground," said Tiny Slim, adjusting his stomach and trying to tuck in his shirt.

"He takes real pride on being a cowboy." Seth wiped his lips on his cuff. "Thinks we're the last of them. Being the last makes him arrogant and nasty. There's nothing lower than a hay-bucker in his mind. We go through this every year depending on the size of the help. If a bunch of big men show up for work he's nothing but a kitten. He swells up around the small ones. Best thing to do is to give it back."

Chau nodded thanks at the advice but Bix sensed that Chau did not have the personality to even act belligerent and he knew that everyone else knew, even Dinknow.

A rusted red flatbed Ford truck stopped in a cloud of dust and blew its horn. Oberlin stuck his head over the cab and shouted, "You boys come on. There's work to be done."

Chapter 6

Bales of hay lay like toppled dominoes all arranged in straight lines down a long wide valley beside which ran a thin river. It looked all too familiar to Bix, one more field of hay waiting to soak up his sweat and energy and leaving scratched and bloody forearms, dust dried lungs, blistered hands and feet, scratchy eyes, muddy nostrils, and small monetary reward, the only real satisfaction coming from having the fortitude and stamina to finish the job and, therefore, call himself a man. Chau had never seen anything like it. Americans produced so much. Vietnamese seldom planted more than they needed with just a small surplus to earn a pittance of cash. Most of them had no desire to have more than they had. What good was a large house when a small one would do? Why buy a vehicle if you planned no trips? Who needed more than one set of ceremonial clothes? He watched Oberlin hook a flatbed trailer to a tractor then drive to one end of the field and point the truck between the rows of hay. Dust covered the trailer concealing most of the red paint and rust with a fine powder. Steve and Chau jumped off the truck bed. Oberlin pulled far enough ahead to hear Bix give instructions over the popping of the John Deere's two-cylinder engine.

"As we go down the rows of hay one of you get on each side of the trailer and hoist up a bale. You don't have to get it all the way on. If you just get the end up I'll hook it and put it in on the stack. I have to stack bales from both of you but it evens out because I don't have to do as much carrying and lifting or walking. We can take turns switching around for something different to do. No position is sacred so yell if you need a change. It's not tough up here until the stack starts to get high and you have to do lots of climbing. When the trailer's full we'll ride on the hay to the barn and stack it. The ride makes a nice rest."

"I'll be," said Oberlin, to Bix. "I like a man with a take charge attitude. You're a natural leader."

The Jon Deere puffed slowly ahead, the transmission groaning under submission, and work commenced. Bix knew morning was the best time to work. A tinge of coolness lay in the air that would soon be eaten by a snarling tiger of heat, the green smells of alfalfa softly soaking through the nostrils, a hint of cattle in the air, two hawks hovering overhead riding the thermals and looking for exposed mice and rabbits attempting to hide in the cut stubble before hunger brought them out. He watched Steve, not built for work, struggle with the first bale and clumsily lift it to the bed where Bix inoculated the packed alfalfa with his hay hook, swung it to the wood, stabbed it on the other end, and lifted it to the front of the bed. Little Chau appeared to have no trouble. He disappeared under the bale as it rolled on to the bed. Bix waited for Steve's next package. He already looked exhausted.

Steve stumbled slightly to the next bale, his breath hissing through his lips. By the third bale he needed a cigarette to fire up his lungs and gain some energy. Lying around in prison had not helped his stamina. From what he remembered of work, it did not seem to be this strenuous. He never cared much for it, anyway nor did most of the hill people. They often mentioned having a hard life, that had more to do with making a living than anything else and earning a living was always difficult if one did not work to produce anything. His mind raced as he attempted the best and easiest way to lift the bales, the cigarette stuck between his lips, his eyes squinting from the tobacco smoke. Maybe he should trade with Bix? No, Bix did not need to walk but he had to drag in twice the number of bales, stack and arrange them just like he said. Maybe he was in the best place. Falling face down dead was the worst that could happen to him. Besides, Chau seemed to be just fine strolling along and tossing the bales up like balsa wood.

Even though he was the son of a rich man Chau had no difficulty lifting the bales. He enjoyed the stretching of muscles; his arms legs and back felt renewed as the blood pushed through his veins. Although the sharp alfalfa stems cut into his forearms leaving them scratched, raw, and bleeding, he took pleasure in suffering the pain, an obstacle that must be overcome like all pain must be overcome, disregarded, ignored. Surrendering to pain was never acceptable, either physical or mental. He threw another bale to Bix.

Bix smiled back. Chau appeared to be a machine, a small efficient machine puffing effortlessly down the rows while John Henry, on the other side, had driven his last spike into a pile of puke. Steve's rods were knocking, his valves starting to leak as he occasionally backfired. As he stumbled from bale to bale his compass had broken, his tires going flat. Bix suppressed his laughter. Steve was a one-man demolition derby, his body denting and rattling for no other reason than that it was his body. As the only entrant, his chances of crossing the finish line remained slim. In no other race could a bettor lose his shirt on the projected winner.

Bix stacked the bales six high - tremendously over loading the trailer as did all farmers and ranchers. As he reached the end of the bed he felt the tractor slow, then stop, the engine rattling down. Mr. Oberlin stepped down carrying a milk can filled with ice and water.

"Let's take a break, boys," he said. Icy sweat meandered down the tin cups as he handed them out. Bix jumped onto the trailer and sat with his legs dangling over the edge. Chau hopped up beside him. Steve staggered to what shade he could find near the trailer and twirled down like an extinguished witch, lighting a cigarette on the way.

"You boys are doing a fine job," said Mr. Oberlin, filling the cups again and passing them out. He paid no attention to Steve, hacking on the grass and watching his life pass before him, except to hand him the water.

The cool tin felt good against Bix's lips and he tasted the metal mixed with the water. Nothing tasted better and for a moment he remembered how much he enjoyed farm life. Maybe that was all the adventure he needed? He splashed some water on his forehead. "It does a man good to work," said Bix. The sun beat against his head and he leaned it back to catch even more.

"How you doing, young fella," Mr. Oberlin said to Chau. "Looks like you can keep up with the best of them. My worrying about you being too small was all for nothing. You're a right go-getter." Chau grinned at the compliment.

"I also enjoy work," he said. "It is good for the body and opens the mind." He took just a small drink before handing back the cup.

"You going to live, buddy?" Mr. Oberlin tapped his foot against Steve's thigh.

"Work don't bother me none," he said. "I can watch you fellers do it all day. I been cautious so to pace myself. My Uncle Billy-Jay did it once, worked too hard. Worked up a terrible sweat, caught pu-monia and died. Ever since, the family takes a fright when the first sign any moisture creeps outen the skin but I'll carry on just the same, maybe break the cycle."

"Do you want to switch with me?" said Bix. "We're half done with this load."

Steve looked at the size of the trailer, thought of dragging and stacking twice as many bales, and said, "I just need to get my feet under me. They're a bit like baby ducks whats lost their mama."

The alfalfa bales continued to pile onto the trailer. Only the leather hay chaps protected Bix's legs from being torn up. Hay and dust clung to his face, itched into his eyes, ears, mouth, down the front of his shirt. The sun shone hot and good and several times he closed his eyes and watched its reddish-yellow glow push through his eyelids. He saw Steve stumble along in drunken stupor using his chest more than his arms to push the bales onto the trailer. He had determination or the kind of pride that makes a man forge ahead rather than lose face before his buddies. Bix thought he might die from exhaustion yet he refused to surrender. Chau hardly worked up a sweat. Bix felt pride in the sweat dripping from his face. They loaded the trailer then all worked their way to the top to lay on the spiked bales as the trailer lurched and swayed toward the barn. Even the slightest motion of air felt refreshing.

"I think your legs are quivering," said Bix. "I heard you gag several times and I thought you would throw up."

"Just thinking about women," said Steve. He blew smoke from another cigarette into the air. The ash fell to his face. "These are just knee tremblers, something a man get when laying a woman up against a wall. Happens when I thinks about em."

"I wouldn't know much about it," said Bix.

"So, yourn not acquainted with the sexual arts? I started about the age of thirteen. I had done just about everything sexual a man can do by time I turned seventeen and decided I ought to try it with a person, preferably with a woman although I didn't know nothin' about pleasuring them. They got no handle on the pump so's you don't know when she's full. When you go looking fer it your pail usually gets kicked over and spills out before she's willing to spit up her juice. What's it like for you, Chau?"

"Perhaps it is the same the world over. We have educated sophisticated people who conduct themselves accordingly. The common man use prostitutes."

Bix enjoyed the swaying trailer, the sharp hay under him, the conversation between friends.

"Doesn't that make it tough on you rich guys?" said Steve. "You got to be one of the upper-crust, a man with standing and money. It must make you frustrated to see them common folk getting some relaxin' and not you."

"This does not present a problem for the wealthy. Like all educated sophisticated men of standing I also use prostitutes." When Bix and Steve started to laugh, Chau realized he had inadvertently made a joke, perhaps his first one. It felt good and satisfying to make others laugh.

Mr. Oberlin pulled parallel to the barn parking the tractor under the hayloft door. He and Bix dragged out a gasoline engine conveyer built on aluminum pipes. A metal spiked chain snatched the bales and carried them to the loft. Bix lifted several bales from the truck making himself a narrow trench to place the bottom of the conveyer. Steve and Chau crawled up the conveyer and Bix told them how and where to stack the bales. Bix choked the Clinton engine and garroted it to life before dropping the alfalfa bales onto the chain. The bales rose one after the other as Steve and Chau scrambled to get them stacked in the suffocating heat. When they attempted to blow their aggravated noses, black snot filled their handkerchiefs or, if they had no time to use them, splattered onto the floor of the loft when they held one nostril and blew snot through the other.

Finally they emptied the trailer. Steve and Chau fell against several bales panting like hot wolfhounds. Steve never felt so good. He had muddled through like any man would have, had refused to give in to exhaustion. The job was over and the sweat pooling onto his chest felt like a reward..

"I reckon we did it," he said, hanging his head out from the loft.

"Well done," said Mr. Oberlin, returning from the house. "Climb up on the trailer. Another three or four loads and we'll call it a day."

Steve felt rather light-headed as they rolled him onto the trailer bed. He might have gone kicking and screaming all the way back to the field had he not been in shock. Mud ran down his face from the tears but kept his face moist. By the end of the day all three of them felt beat, Steve no worse than the rest. They staggered to the bunkhouse porch.

"You boys look done in," said Seth stepping from the bunkhouse. "It's almost dark. Ms. Oberlin's held up dinner."

"That's more work than I've ever done in South Dakota," said Bix.

"Mr. Oberlin's like that. He gets an idea in his head about what needs to be done in a day and doesn't stop until it's completed. You better get washed up for dinner. The boys are mad enough as it is."

As they walked through the bunkhouse, Dinknow arrowed out his foot causing Chau to trip and sprawl across the floor.

"Oh, EXCUSE ME," he said. "Since I'm dying of starvation because you boys are late I just don't have the strength to hold in my feet in." He smiled broadly from down the rabbit hole. "It wern't because you're a stinking coolie, no, not that."

Bix lifted Chau up and they continued to the back. After dinner they returned to the porch, reluctant to go inside and face Dinknow.

"Do you have many people in Vietnam like Dinknow?" said Bix.

"The world holds all kinds of people. I think there is only one of him."

"He won't leave you alone until you do something."

"What should I do? I have not been injured."

"We call them school yard bullies. They won't quit unless you stand up to them. That makes it tough for you since you are so small."

"I'm going for a bath," said Steve, a slight grin on his face.

"You've got a fatty on your mind," said Bix. "No energy one minute, filled with electricity the next. We saw the way she rubbed up against you with that little smile. She whispered something in your ear, didn't she?"

"I don't spect I rember."

As Steve left, Bix continued to question Chau about his country and about the Foreign Legion. The mystique had grabbed him: blue uniforms, white cap dangling a shade from the back, marching across rolling sands to distant outposts. He had no idea how they presently looked. Chau said they resembled any other army and mostly used uniforms and equipment supplied by the United States.

Chau went inside when Bix decided to take a bath. The cowboys were playing cards, including Dinknow. Dinknow looked up when Chau sat on his bed and started to read a magazine. Bix gathered his towel, a pair of clean socks and underwear.

"You lover-boys going out for a diddle?" said Dinknow.

"What you got?" said Seth. "Either play cards or go to bed."

"Come on, Chau," said Bix. "It will feel good to get into that cold water." He did not want to leave him alone with Dinknow. The other cowboys would protect him but it was better if he left.

A chill bit the air but the thought of the cold water seemed exciting. They decided to sneak up on Steve. As they walked quietly toward the water they heard a rustling in the nearby grass. Bix and Chau exchanged glances and moved toward the noise. A moan and squeak caused them to move faster. When they got closer, gently pushing aside the grass and kneeing the ground carefully they stopped with surprise and confusion. What they saw was not the thick meaty ankles of Burpee swinging in the air in surrender and wonder but the shapely ankles, calves, and continued firmness of Ms. Oberlin's thighs. The two bare feet and legs slashed the air above the grass and Steve's pounding butt added torque that transferred to Ms. Oberlin lying beneath him. What Bix and Chau imagined to be a great laugh became an embarrassment as they moved quietly back to the water.

"Ms. Oberlin?" said Bix. "Who would have thought?"

"Old women must take love when they can," said Chau. "Sometimes they need it even more than young women since it does not appear often."

"Race you in," said Bix, throwing his clothes on the ground and splashing into the water, the cold sucking out his breath and kicking him between the legs. Chau followed, his voice coming in stutters.

"We have no such cold water," said Chau. "I have heard there is water like this in the highlands toward Laos but I have never been there. This water is clear and cool, not warm and muddy like in the delta."

Bix felt his body start to warm when Steve came splashing in and howling at the cold.

"I didn't think you'd have the energy," said Bix.

"Thought I felt someone behind me. I was too busy to give a look. She be humpin' like a rabbit in heat. I figured the girl would be waiting for me but it wern't her. She never said nothing, just started driving her lips on my body from the top down like they was an old joloppy. I started to say no, just couldn't get my lips to squeeze past the yes. The blanket was already laid out and we just fell into it. When twas over she wrapped the blanket round her and left like it was nothing. Never said a word. So I came over here to try and figure it out."

"I'll guess you'll be down for a bath every night?"

"I'm a bit curious," he said. "I don't know ifen she liked it or not. All the motions was there, the moves and the passion. Felt like an act to me, not that I care."

"You crazy Kentucky fool," said Bix. "Of course it was an act. Any woman except a blind one would have to be crazy to want sex with you. What do you think Chau?"

Chau thought for a moment then said, "I also think it was an act. You Americans call it a sex act." Bix and Steve burst out laughing. Chau liked telling jokes, making other people happy with laughter. A warm and satisfying feeling came over him and he was starting to experience the sensation of breaking the bounds of seriousness. They were still laughing as they walked back to the bunkhouse, arm in arm, Chau in the middle, a grin from ear to ear. He hoped he would see them again in Vietnam.

Chapter 7

Chau crawled his shoulders from under the covers and felt the morning's cold sit on them. Rather than pull the covers up for warmth he cocooned deeper inside the blankets. He had folded up several times during the night so he now slept on the middle of the bunk. He liked this place, this United States. It was so diversified that a man could travel until he found a place he liked and could stay there forever or leave it if he wanted to. If the enjoyment in another place dwindled down, he could simply move again. A person might spend his whole life in a different area and not live in it all. Vietnam seemed so much different, almost foreign since he had been gone so long. The coast was similar; more islands in the north than the south, but most of the people near the water were fishermen. Inland sat the farms, rubber tree plantations owned by the French, and the sunken squares and rectangles of rice farmers. Native tribes, often warring against one another, roamed the highlands, determined to remain primitive, to retain their own culture. He knew little about the people of the highlands except that many of the tribes were aligned with the French and fought with them against the Viet Minh.

Others had started rising in the bunkhouse and Seth had brought in a fresh pot of coffee and kept it warm on an electric coil.

"You up?" said Bix.

"Yes," answered Chau.

"I must be up, too," said Steve. "I hear something coming outen my mouth besides wind. The wind's escaping a bit lower."

Chau rolled his feet to the floor and felt the cold creep through the floorboards and work its way up. He quickly put on his socks and attempted to shake himself awake. Mink Parsons nodded a good morning as did Tiny Slim, his belly rolling over his belt and held from completely escaping to the floor by his stretched T-shirt. Dinknow still slept.

"Get your ass up," said Mink Parsons, banging the side of his bunk with the boots he held in his hands. "You're making us cowboys look bad."

Dinknow stirred, first his head wobbling from side to side, then his body slowly rising and tipping to the side. He attempted to focus his eyes until finally spying Chau.

"I had cow work to do last night while you all slept," he said.

"You ain't hardly done no cow work since you been here," said Mink Parsons. "Come on, breakfast will be up soon, that is if Ms. Oberlin has any strength left." He looked at Steve and winked. Steve shrugged his shoulders as if to say. "Who, me?"

As he dressed Dinknow continued to watch Chau. Chau finished belting his pants then slid into his boots. His face started to sour as he jumped back and started to force off the boot.

"Looks like he got the hot-foot," said Dinknow, laughing. "Is that what they call hopping mad?"

Chau's sock emerged wet, brown and green, and emitted a mist of stink. He turned over the boot and tapped out the remaining cow shit.

"Can't you never behave?" said Tiny Slim. He walked over to Chau and checked his other boot, then took the tampered one out back to wash it.

"What makes you mean?" said Bix.

"Oh, tough guy," said Dinknow. "You wanta fight? You wanta fight?" He danced around the room holding up his hands as would a bare-knuckles fighter, almost straight out and pumping them in and out like pistons. He moved his head and danced up and down and pretended he had been rocked by a punch. He enjoyed his skit.

"Grow up." said Bix. "We all have work here."

"Get dressed," said Seth. "You'll be exhausted before we hit the fields and we can't get any work out of you as it is." He turned to Chau. "It's nothing personal. The stupid bastard does it to everyone new. Sometimes it's a snake he puts in their beds sometimes a mouse, but it's always something. It's tough for illiterate people to find amusement."

"Who says it was me?" said Dinknow, getting dressed. "A man ought to check his boots before putting them on."

He shoved a foot into his boot then pulled it out cussing. Cow shit covered his sock.

"Who's the dirty bastard…" he started to say.

"Someone has a sense of humor," said Bix.

"I'll get you guys for this," said Dinknow, limping toward the back door.

Steve noticed nothing unusual about Ms. Oberlin that morning, no special glances at him, no tender touch on his shoulders, no extra food no lilt in her voice when she spoke to him. She served the coffee then left the food serving to Burpee.

"We're going to town tonight," said Seth. "You boys want to come along? We still have to work tomorrow so we won't be late. But a night out does a man good."

The three friends eyed one another. Bix knew they were thinking about Dinknow. If they did not go, he would think them cowards. If they did go, what might he do after several drinks? He was bad enough sober. One punch from him would probably kill Chau.

"I would like that," said Chau, surprising Bix and Steve. "Sure," said Bix, "Us too. We stick together."

"You got a mouse in your pocket?" Steve whispered to Bix. "Us? Us? We'll get our asses kicked if-in that moose gets liquored up."

"I might not be very smart," said Bix. "Any animal will bite if you show fear. We have no choice."

"That's just some old story," said Steve. "If it were true I'd be nothing but a bleedin' mass of scar tissue."

That evening they all piled into the pick-up, the cowboys in the cab, they boys in the back. None of them appeared to be in a good mood. At the tavern the truck pulled between two saddled horses and a Humpmobile all at the hitching rail. Consumption abounded in the various other bits of wounded vehicles piled outside: a Farmall tractor suffering oil incontinence, a Ford station wagon - the front and back passenger doors tied together through the missing windows, two inter-bred cars patched together from dead relatives, and a Mack truck loaded with hay out back. Honky-tonk music drifted from inside. Dinknow, careful not to muss his swirled blue and white cowboy shirt, pushed through the door. The floor had not been swept in months and scuff marks cutting across the wood spelled out words in some unintelligible language. Most of the mismatched tables had mismatched chairs and a pool table wounded in a knife fight lifted up its torn green skin in surrender to the bulb overhead. On life support, its lights fibrillating, the Juke Box oozed with guitar and fiddle music. The men formed a line at one end of the bar.

"Sally, where's Buff tonight?" said Seth.

"He's on a beer run," she said. "Be back in a while. This must be the hay crew? The little one getting paid half price?" she said, nodding toward Chau.

"Don't let his looks fool you," said Seth. "Oberlin says he's the toughest one on the crew. He don't usually say much about hay-hands unless he's found a really good one."

"Piss on him," said Dinknow, "and all the other yellow bastards in the world. He feels sorry for him cause he ain't yet a man. Bring on the beer."

"I don't think there's any humor in you," said Sally. "I'd almost hump you out back if I thought it would put a smile on your face."

"Then why don't you?"

"You wouldn't appreciate it and it wouldn't put a smile on my face," she grinned. "You all want beer?"

"I'm right sour myself," said Steve. "No one appreciates some cheering up like I do." After no response he said, "I believe I'll have a fine Chablis." His attempt to sound suave and sophisticated drew no laughter.

"You can put a tux on a muskrat but he's still some kind of rat," she said.

"I reckon the pig shit still shows," said Steve. "Some things just don't wash off over night."

"It's the walk," she said. "Kind of a stagger like you've been attempting not to step in it all your life only to land in a bigger pile every time your foot comes down."

Tiny Slim slapped the bar. "Bring us all beer," he said. "I'm buying the first round."

"Even for moose fart?" said Seth.

"You've never seen him with any money. If he had to pay for a glass of water he would rather die from thirst."

The conversation droned into the steady mix from the other men in the bar. Except for Sally there were no other women inside. Bix asked about it and Seth said they only came in on the weekends. About an hour later a voice boomed from the door.

"Well, well," it said. "If it ain't our old pal, Dinky Dick Dinknow come to pay us a little visit in town."

Everyone turned to look except Dinknow who peered into his beer glass as if the foam were a bundle of tea leaves predicting his future. Trouble was all he saw, gloom, despair, pain and blood.

"He doesn't want any trouble from you boys, especially you, Keys," said Seth. "We just came in for a beer. We'll be leaving soon."

"I don't think I was talking to you," said Keys. "You'll be leaving sooner than you think." Two men stood with him. His eyes surveyed the bar, landing on Chau. Chau thought he was the biggest man he had ever seen and stared back. "Our business is with Dinky Dick there, the coward refusing to turn around and face us like a man."

"Your sister was willing enough to do it with him," said Seth. "He didn't do anything she didn't want. Every woman is someone's sister or daughter or mother. You've done the same plenty of times with plenty of women. She's so damn horse-faced I suppose he did her a favor."

"I don't care what every woman is." Keys took a step forward and started to draw back his hand. "I don't even care if she goes whoring around with a Mex long as she keeps some pride and respect about her. Pride ends with Dinky Dick Dinknow. She just as well be doing the donkey act in Juarez as to lay with him."

Dinknow ran his finger over the bar counter. Pockmarks covered the wood. The rough craters made their own universe and appeared to stretch from one end of infinity to the other. He was nothing in this universe but a speck of a speck of a speck. Smiling, he turned just as Keys hit him flush in the face. His head twisted back and blood spewed from his mouth as he started to slump to the floor. Everyone moved away from the bar and Bix felt confused. He looked at the others who seemed just as confused. Is this a personal matter? Should we help? Is it our business? Do we get involved? He had no idea what to do, what was proper. Had Dinknow been a friend of his there would have been no confusion but he had not exactly endeared himself to any of the hay crew. His chest had difficulty filling with anger. Even his breath had not worked itself into short fluttery puffs nor did his hands and body shake with anger.

The two other men with Keys punched their fists into Dinknow's stomach as he crumpled then they lifted him and held his arms against the bar. Keys tapped him on his face with his left hand as he readied to strike with his right.

"Right here, boy," he said. "My five little friends are-a coming…."

Bix caught a flash of tan flesh fly past him as Chau vaulted from the floor and shot like an arrow through the air, his foot striking Keys on the temple and knocking him to the ground. Chau spun around kicking one of the men on the throat with his heel and smacking the other with the back of his hand on the nose. A geyser of blood spewed into the air as Chau, a sense of mad calmness about him, dropped his knee onto Key's throat and popped him twice in the face before cupping his hands and smashing them against his ears.

"I can't…" said Keys, rolling to his side, screaming and holding his bleeding ears as his legs jerked straight out then back. "I can't hear! I can't hear!" His friends knelt beside him, always watching Chau, and slowly lifted him up where he swayed on trembling legs. Bix, Steve, and the cowboys stood beside Chau, ready to defend him. Dinknow stood behind them leaning on the bar, blood running from his mouth, and watching Keys.

"I can't hear," Keys yelled again, cupping his ears. "Take me out of here and over to the hospital in Jefferson."

Chau stood quietly as if nothing unusual had happened. He seemed perfectly calm except for a twitter behind his eyes as if any mayhem had been temporarily caged yet capable of breaking through at any time.

"I froze," said Bix, ashamed to look at Chau. "I didn't know if it was part of my fight, or not."

"I never seen nothing like it," said Steve, shaking his head. "Imagine a man able to fly like that. Reckon it's almost as impressive as a man walking on water."

"I didn't know what to do," said Bix, again. "I kept trying to decide the right thing."

"Action requires no thought," said Chau, his breathing steady and even. "The body works on its own and needs no mind to direct it."

He moved back to his end of the bar, and it was now certainly, HIS end of the bar. Everyone in the bar crowded around him, offering congratulations, patting him on the back, shaking his hand, asking him how he learned to fight like that. Dinknow pushed through and said, "Why?" His face carried more confusion than hurt, a confusion that needed answers to be well again.

"Families in the same house often have difficulties yet they are still a family," said Chau, embarrassed by the attention. Dinknow scratched his head trying to understand. He had an answer but he was not sure it did him any good. He started to turn away when Bix said, "Come on, I'll buy you a drink."

Like a dying candle the crowd drifted away as the Oberlin boys walked down the soggy road into joviality. Talk and beer flowed freely and various life stories (everyone seemed to remember one) grew to enormous sizes. Buff, the bar owner, finally returned from his errands.

"There's been some real excitement here tonight," said Sally. Buff placed his grocery bag on the counter and looked toward the boys. The bag tipped to the side and a bottle of pop rolled out.

"I shoulda known you cowboys had something to do with it," he said. "Every time Dinknow comes in here it's bad news." He walked their way, then saw Chau. "What's the chink doing in here?"

"Everyone we meet down here says the same thing," said Bix, finally working up some courage.

"His mom got scared by an egg noodle before he was born," said Dinknow.

"You're defending him?" said Buff. "He must be something. I don't mind what a man is but you got to call him something to point him out till you get to know him - kike, coon, wop, blanket-butt, spick - something."

"He's a friend of mine," said Dinknow, holding Chau by the shoulder. "When he goes back to his own country, these two fellas are going with him to join the French Foreign Legion."

"I'll be," said Buff. "The Foreign Legion. There's no fighting force in the world tougher. The next round's on me. I appreciate men that can fight."

Steve slapped the bar. "I reckon we won't be going yet," he said. "We want to do some fishing in Alaska first to bring in some money. Bucking hay just ain't doing it. Then, if things is still going strong, we'll swim over to straighten things out."

"There're all Germans," said Seth.

"Who?" said Bix, listening carefully, "The fishermen?"

"The Foreign Legion. I heard they joined the French after the Krauts got their butts kicked in the big one and didn't know anything else to do except fight."

"That right?" said Steve, to Chau.

"German legionnaires are legend," said Chau. "They are fearless and fight as if they welcome death. They attack and attack and act like bullets cannot hurt them. They are the soul of the Legion."

"Who cares?" said Bix, a little annoyed. "How much different can this war be than the last one? People kill one another and a South Dakota farm boy is as tough as any beaten army from Nazi Germany."

Chapter 8

Bix was looking under the hood of the Studebaker and checking the oil. Laughter rolled from the bunkhouse with Dinknow's voice the loudest, big guffaws and snorts. Every minute or so he interjected "My little buddy here." He had been good company since the incident at the bar and almost as funny and witty as Steve but with less sarcasm. The engine was a half-quart low on oil, nothing to worry about, at least for another hundred miles. He topped off the radiator and the battery with water from a canteen. The car started easily but idled hesitantly kicking and spitting as it warmed up. He tapped the horn to bring out his friends. All the ranch hands emerged and opened the car doors for Steve and Chau. Seth leaned into Bix's window and handed him an envelope.

"The boys all pitched in a few dollars for gas," he said. "Even the boss threw in a ten, something he's never done before."

"Where is he?"

"He's never been one to say goodbye, gets too choked up. He said you boys could come back any time. We say the same."

Bix placed the envelope in the glove box. "Thanks for the extra cash. You have all been great."

As they started to drive away he watched the ranch hands herd in a bunch like cattle and waving. Ms. Oberlin stood on the porch watching as the car drove down the dusty road. She showed no expression as if she had been a granite ornament guarding a palace.

"I enjoyed that very much," said Chau. "Perhaps I have learned more about your people from this experience, that even the bad ones are good inside if given a chance."

"Don't take too much from it," said Steve, lighting a joint. "I reckon there's more good ones who are bad inside than the other way round." Chau and Bix passed on the joint. Steve smiled and leaned back to enjoy his good luck. He always enjoyed a declined offering.

A cloud of dust shown in the distance and grew like a prairie fire as it came closer. A pink Hudson Hornet coupe slid to a halt and Neal jumped out to wave down the Studebaker. He poked at a hole in his T-shirt, a large grin on his face. He attempted to see inside the Studebaker to see if Bix was there. The car stopped and the boys piled out. Neal hugged them all.

"I didn't make the farm labor team with all of you guys covered in dust and capitalism," he said. "Mexico is my destination, high desert and cactus between the mountains offering a harsh climate and tanned ass, inviting a man to love and sucking up joints and smack and goofballs in an effort to reach across the nations in friendship and where a dollar buys a weeks' rent and all the mescal a man can drink."

"Where did you get the car?" said Bix, running his hand over a fender. "And pink, no less."

"On sale for the man willing to drive it," said Neal. "The pink caught my eye, reminded me of love, and I'll do anything for love."

"Is that the same woman inside yall had before?" said Steve, noticing the dark figure in the shadow.

"A keeper," said Neal, taking a drag from Steve's joint. "She's on me like a fly on a doughnut, the best I've ever had and snakes around me every minute, her beauty, her personality, her intelligence, are like overwhelming and she comes from way out there beyond the cosmos where the light of dead stars still shine down on us revealing both our lives and our eventual deaths, our souls to travel forever the emptiness of space seeking nirvana. I couldn't depart without leaving you a guide to San Francisco, names and numbers of the cool ones, the hip ones with unbelievable minds, the ones that will enlighten you to the happening scene, the bars, the music, the dope, the sex. Women feel entitled to be screwed just like a man does and they will throw you on top of them as fast as possible and get up the same way to have a smoke. Leave my name and you will be treated like kings, wined dined and fucked out of your minds and you will depart with new visions and insight to spread on your world adventures."

Neal backed the Hudson into the shallow ditch as he turned around and sped off, a cigarette dangling from between his lips, an arm around his girl. Bix held the note containing the names, phone numbers and addresses in his hand.

"That boy's like a streak of lightning," said Steve. "He strikes everywhere leaving ash and smoke in his wake. I thought he'd have a different woman by now, maybe several of them. Is San Francisco our destination?"

"What do you think, Chau?"

"I have no choice. That is where I catch my ship for home."

"Staying with these folks will save us some coin so's we'll have plenty to get us to Alaska," said Steve.

Although the drive went faster than he expected, Bix could smell the cold salt air long before reaching San Francisco. California was a country of aromas: the dry heat smell of desert and sage; the perfume of grapes, apricots, olives, sweet potatoes, melons; the scent of trees on the coastal range and garlic in the valley beyond followed by the sea with its heavy salt air, fish, decaying algae, vehicles, oil, and construction. The glowing constellation before him turned into separate stars then street and building lights. Chau and Steve awoke when he pulled into a filling station. He watched Steve break through the cocoon of sleep his eyes fighting through the silk.

"We here?" he said, stretching and leaning his head back and forward then from side to side. He placed his chin on his arms on the back of the front seat. The attendant, in his white uniform, walked through the dim glow of the station lights toward Bix. Bix rolled down the window and said, "Gets cold here."

"Sure does," said the attendant, wiping his hands with a red rag. "Regular?"

Bix nodded and pulled the latch on the hood. Chau always awoke cleanly as if he had not really been asleep. He bumped Steve's elbow when he tried to turn.

"So this is it?" said Steve. "Ain't too hot. You going to call someone?"

"It's pretty late." Bix unfolded the paper with the names and phone numbers. The hood of the Studebaker screeched as the attendant opened it and checked the oil.

"Neal said they're a wild bunch of folks," said Steve. "Don't reckon yous can be wild by going to bed early."

"I'll pay for a room," said Chau.

The attendant returned to the open window carrying the dipstick, his thumb on the high mark the oil had left.

"It's about a quart and a half low."

"Sure," said Bix. "A quart will do it."

The attendant replaced the dipstick and took a glass jar of oil with a tin spout from a rack beside the pump.

"Can't hurt to call," said Steve. "If it don't sound right they don't have to know who you are. There ain't never going to be a phone made that shows your picture."

Bix walked to a phone booth near the station building. Inside he flattened out the paper on the little shelf. He had several numbers to choose from. He picked Deborah, dropped a coin into the machine and listened to it clang into the pocket of the phone corporation. He was surprised to hear the phone answered on the first ring.

"Hello," the voice said.

"I am sorry to bother you at such a late hour but I am a friend of Neal's."

"Are you Bix? Neal called about you. He never calls about anyone so you must be special."

"Yes. Well, he said to call."

"Neal phoned me so I wouldn't be surprised. He's usually such a conceited prick, seldom so thoughtful. Where are you now?"

"At a filling station."

"I mean where? The address, street corner, something so I can give you directions to get here."

"We can stay at a motel."

"Don't be silly. Everything you need is right here."

"Give a minute and I will find out." Bix let the phone dangle from its cord as he jogged back to the car. "Do you have a pencil?"

"I told-ya theyd be up," said Steve. "I got a tingle all over my body."

Chau handed him a pencil and paper and Bix wrote the address from the building. The attendant had finished washing the windows. "That will be three dollars and twenty-seven cents."

"These guys will get it," he said, as he scrambled back to the phone booth.

He held the phone to his ear without speaking. Music and laughter sounded softly through the receiver. He imagined Deborah anxiously waiting to hear his voice, waiting to fall in love with him, waiting to take him in her arms and to her bedroom.

"Hello," he said. "I'm back."

"Yes?"

"The address. I have the address."

"You want Deborah. I'm Ben. Tell me where you cats are and I will give you directions."

The voice sounded like a girl's voice, soft and gentle. It is California. Maybe Ben was a girl's voice in California. Bix offered his information and directions were returned. He wrote them carefully and handed them to Steve when he returned to the car. Within twenty minutes they had arrived outside a section of row houses on a slight hill.

"I'm not sure this is right," said Bix.

"There's the address," said Steve, pointing toward the green and blue house. "What could be wrong?"

"Not that; I'm not sure we should be staying here. It seems funny."

"You seem funny. Chau and me's looking for adventure and this rightly seems the place to find it. How you spect us to join the Foreign Legion ifin you're afraid to knock on a door?"

Bix opened the car door and waited for the others. The street appeared quiet, drab and treeless. Paint had chipped from the fire hydrant and cracks veined the sidewalk. Dim light glowed from the building as Bix knocked on the door. A woman, a cigarette dangling from between her dry lips, opened the door. The tight leotards she wore revealed her slim body.

"Come on in, dear," she said. She leaned down, hugged and kissed Bix. "We're having ever such a good time. We have plenty of relaxants so you can unwind after the long drive."

Steve rubbed his hands together and winked at Chau. "We're in the right place, all right," he said. "Relaxants is my favorite things."

The room was dim and people lounged on the furniture or lay on their sides on the floor. The sounds of Howard Magee came from a hi-fi in the corner surrounded by plants. A picture of a man playing piano hung on the wall next to a travel poster for Mexico. Deborah slouched on the couch and, as Bix came close, pulled him to the floor and rubbed his head. He liked the feel of her hands, warm and soft as they curled around his neck. Steve and Chau found spots on the floor and sat cross-legged.

"They call me Steve, but I answer to any four-letter word," he said, to a small man next to him lying heavy on a joint. "This is Chau."

"Ben," the man said. "Steve has five letters."

"Only if you spell it right. What yall got there?"

Ben handed Steve the joint. "Right obliged," said Steve, drawing in deeply. He started to hand the joint back. Steve handed it to Chau when Ben nodded toward him.

"You'll want to meet Bix," said Deborah. "He's the cat that leads the pack. I'm going to do him tonight. Neal says he needs it and I'm going to do him over and over again until he cries for mercy, until he gets the crazy notion about going to war out of his head. It's no good for anyone. Isn't he the cutest thing?"

"How about me?" said Bettina. Her sweater had several burn holes, neat charred little circles like bullet punctures.

"Bettina likes a good man," said Deborah. "Ben's no good. We love him dearly but I think he's been fucking Corso. He's a poet too." She picked a joint off the end table beside the two empty liquor bottles. "Cornelius makes movies." A man wearing a beret and dark glasses nodded. "Florence has been hookin' for caps. When you get down that far it is difficult to get up. We have to look out for her." Florence appeared to be nothing but bones and dried skin. Even her hair seemed dry, like sagebrush, and she looked tawdry and unclean. "We've got to get her in the tub tonight and wash her down. Junkies develop sensitive skin. Even water hurts them. She needs the cure to get straight again. Anton blows sax. He got off early tonight."

"Man, I was cooking, too," he said. "Them notes was everywhere and nowhere. You cats dig jazz, man?"

Bix nodded, his nod revealing a subtle lie. It made no sense to him and appeared to be nothing but a bunch of Chinese music all caught up in confusion. The music sounded all the same. The band started together then someone played a while followed by someone else then everyone else in order until they all came together and ended. No, it was not for him.

"Reckon I don't know much about jazz," said Steve. "I pay some bluegrass guitar and banjo but we ain't got no jazz back in the hills. Chau likes the music. I think Chau likes everything. He don't rightly want to offend anyone."

"It is a very interesting music," said Chau.

"I'm going to cook up," said Ben. He placed his hand on Steve's leg. "Want to join me?"

"I kindah like women," he said. "No offense, just don't want to lead you on, get things straight from the start. What is this cooking up stuff?"

"You're not that cute," said Ben "and I'm not that desperate." They both laughed and Steve realized he had made a new friend. "A little joy bang will do you good," said Ben. "I'll show you."

Anton was playing an imaginary sax, moving his fingers and nodding his head to a beat only he could hear. Betlina leaned over toward Ben. She recently had a fix and was hazy living in a kind of dream world. The heroin had become a habit too painful for her to break. That's how it was, creeping up on a person putting them into a mellow mood time after time until the pain of not having the dope overcame the joy. Paranoia soon entered and the fear of the pain, always the fear of the pain, consumed her. Junk is the apple in the garden. Gradually it gets into the system as a pyramid of dependence builds. She had become a danger to others. She would do anything for a fix: cheat, lie, rat on others, prostitute herself, maybe even kill. She was due a hot-shot, death from poison powder, because she had become dangerous to others, especially to dealers. At least a hot-shot would put her out of her misery. Deborah had plunged her hands down Bix's shirt. She nipped at his ears. He looked embarrassed.

"A square," said Cornelius, looking at the ceiling. "A square is nothing, emptiness, a void. I could use a square to show nothing."

"A square is not empty," said Chau.

"What?"

"A square is a frame or a fence or a wall. Inside of any square is something."

"That's deep," said Cornelius, "Real deep." He continued to look up watching the smoke from his joint curl skyward. "What's in it, what kind of thing?"

"It makes no difference, air maybe or atoms or wind. A frame has no use except to hold something in, to reveal the prison in which we all reside."

Ben had lit a candle. He spilled a small amount of ether into a spoon and mixed it with the white heroin powder. He placed the spoon over the candle and waited for the powder to dissolve and the mixture to boil.

" A square will not work to show nothing," said Chau. "Only nothing can show nothing."

"Wow! That theory is out there," said Cornelius. He tried to imagine nothing. Every nothing became something. "I can dig it but I don't know that I get it. Man, it's deep." He leaned toward Steve. "Give me your arm."

Steve skeptically offered his arm. Ben had carefully balanced the spoon on the carpet. He removed an eyedropper from his small silver case. He wrapped a strip of paper around a hypodermic needle and twisted it tightly into the eyedropper. He wrapped an elastic band around Steve's arm and smacked the crotch of his forearm.

"See," he said. "You've got to cook the horse, get it liquefied. Then you put a collar around the needle to make it tight when it plugs into the eyedropper. You tie up your arm and slap up a vein. Now, we ease the needle into the juice, pinch the rubber end of the dropper to suck up the sauce. Now, in she goes." Steve jerked his arm.

"That hurts," he said. "You sure this is safe?"

Before Ben could reassure him he felt the moon course through his veins pulling a string of stars. The numbness started in his legs as if they were going to sleep and flowed up his neck and into his skull lifting each body part toward the ceiling. Skin pulled away from muscle, muscle from bones, leaving nothing except lungs. He watched the room from the height. Chau became a squatting cat with an enormous head and saber-like teeth dripping with blood. A fear crept into Steve's body where the skin muscle had left. Ben spun in circles, sparks flying from his sides. Deborah's tits crawled like fat snakes striking toward him as Bix became liquid and puddled onto the carpet as a purple mud-pot. Anton became a giant pink prick that Cornelius hugged and kissed. Betlina's dry skin cracked, turned inside out revealing a body of gray and yellow pus that dripped onto the carpet. She pulled him down, eased his pants around his ankles as Chau clawed his way behind the sofa to sleep.

Bix felt embarrassed, swigged more whisky as he felt Deborah curl around him. He pretended to pass out from drunkenness and rolled face down. From the corner of his eye he watched Cornelius and Anton peel the leotards from Deborah. She mounted Anton and Cornelius mounted her from behind. Bix closed his eyes and ejaculated, the hot juice squirting through his shorts. He thought of the French soldiers in Vietnam and what it felt like to face danger and death. What was it like in the last war; what was it like fighting the Germans. Had anything changed? One war was as good as the next and he imagined the bravery of the Germans as they fought the Russians.

Chapter 9

"I hope to God I never see another fish," said Steve, tossing a mangled fish across the floor of the cannery. "Whose idea was this and if it was mine whyid I listen to myself?"

Bix pushed another fish his way. The cold cut through him, deep and to the bone. Not even in South Dakota had the weather seemed so cold. The wet air blew up from the water and washed between the slats of the building. Lately, Steve had gotten more and more surly. It was time to move on. The money had been good as had the whisky but Steve always complained about the lack of dope in Alaska. He needed it more and more, seemed to be unable to do without it.

"What next," said Bix? His hands hurt and he was tired of always smelling like fish. The oil appeared to sink into his flesh and he could never wash it out.

"I recon I'm ready fer something warmer. Maybe it's time to move on to Vietnam"

"We don't pay you to sit around," said Maurice, the foreman, as he passed. He limped slightly and his rough red hands shown brightly from his sleeves.

"You ain't paying me no more, anyway," said Steve. "I quit." He removed his apron and squatted in the corner like a pouting kid. The other workers laughed.

"This is the second time this week you've quit," said Maurice. "You want your pay check now or wait until you start back to work?"

"I mean it this time," said Steve. "I'm full of fish up to the gills."

Maurice looked at Bix. Bix shrugged his shoulders.

"If he goes," said Maurice "I imagine you'll be leaving with him?"

"We've been thinking about a warmer climate," said Bix. "Let's face it, Maurice, the work is boring and there must more to life than flinging fish about."

"That Foreign Legion thing, again?" he said.

"It's something to do," said Bix.

"Funny to think that I came from the Legion to work here, and you want to leave here to join the Legion," said Maurice. "It's tough life. You might make it but not numb-nuts there."

"There's got to be a right bit more sun and heat where they are," said Steve. He stretched out his legs across the floor.

"Try Florida," said Maurice. "It's always hot when people are trying to kill you and in the Legion someone's always trying to kill you. Florida is hot and safe. The Legion is no place for anyone looking for a long life."

"It's got to be betern dying of boredom," said Steve. "I don't mid smelling of fish from a woman but I don't take kindly of smelling like fish from a fish."

"Maybe it's time we go for real," said Bix. "You have treated us really well, Maurice, and we have made some good money. We don't want to stay until we're too old to fight. Bix shrugged his shoulders. "Were you fighting the Viet Minh?"

"Just at the end, in '47," said Maurice. "That was enough for me. They're like a bunch of fleas, they're everywhere. Let them have the place, I say. It's nothing but heat and jungle and bugs and snakes." He leaned against the table. "It was a big pincer operation. They dropped us from some old Junker's tri-motors. Caught them with their pants down at Bac-Kan, we did. Came in so fast Ho's mail was still on his table and the tea was hot. Of course he and Giap got away like they always do." He straightened up and said, "Well, you going to finish the day or not?"

That night Steve held his sprained wrist with his other hand. The bandage felt too tight and his fingers had started to swell. He had slipped on some fish oil while leaving the cannery and sprained the wrist when he fell. He went into the kitchen to make a sandwich. Bix was out. A chill filled the air. He thought he would never again be warm. Sections of white pint had peeled from the cabinets revealing cracked wood. All he found were cans of tuna fish. He spread catsup and mayonnaise onto some bread. And ate it. His bare arms stuck to the red and black plastic tablecloth. There had to be more to life than this? People in trouble always wanted more. He wanted a joint to calm his nerves, just a bit of weed, something difficult to find in Alaska. He pulled down his pants and masturbated, the juice squirting onto the tablecloth. He wiped it up with the washcloth.

Outside the cold appeared like a second skin covering everything with ice. Lights from the buildings lay yellow across the snow. He walked through one stage of lights to another as he wandered the streets. The Barnacle Tavern was as dirty as ever, peanut husks across the floor, red plastic bar stool covers split and sprouting tufts of white cotton, wooden tables etched with carvings, purple eggs drowning in glass bottles on the bar. He sat behind a row of cigarette burns and punched out two cylindrical papers from the punch card in an effort to win a toy tin fire truck. He rolled them flat on the bar then swiped them onto the floor.

"Usual?" said Wendover. He placed a tall draft on the bar before Steve could answer.

"What do you reckon life's about?" said Steve.

"Not tonight," said Wendover, moving to the end of the bar. "That's all you ever want to know. It's about nothing, nothing. Get it through your head," he said as he left.

Foam ran over the top of the glass and squeezed between Steve's fingers. He slowly twisted the bar stool completely around. Dead. The whole place was dead. Not even a whore or a toothless fat Eskimo woman willing to blow him for a beer. The bar felt sticky.

Three men entered the bar. Two sat at a table while the other one retrieved three draft beers and brought them back.

"Don't reckon she'll ever warm up," said Steve. He tipped his beer toward them, a grin on his face, an effort to relieve his loneliness.

"Colder than a witch's tit," said the big one. He started to slip out of his wool plaid overcoat. He adjusted the flaps on the cap folding them over the crown. Heavy knuckles rose from his fists and his hands were lumpy with calluses. "Any women in this town?"

"Naw." Steve sat on the empty chair at the table. "Don't mind?"

"Go ahead," said the smaller man. "Name's Jacks. This is Bradbury and Dillman." Dillman was the big man. "Barkeep, bring us a pitcher."

"I'll get it," said Steve. He poured from the pitcher. "Eskies come in sometime, Eskimos, you know. They ain't much for looks but they put up a nice fight in the sack like they actually enjoy a screwing."

"That's something," said Jacks.

"They all look good when the light's is out," said Steve. "Hump a fish, hump an Eskie. No difference."

"I hear it's polite for a man to offer his woman to a visitor," said Jacks.

"It's more a punishment," said Steve.

"We've been fishing," said Jacks. He seemed to be the talkative one. "Just be in town a day or two before going to Fairbanks. Thought there might be some women here. Nothing goes with fishing like women."

"I work packing fish," said Steve. "There's women there but they're toughern most men, the kind that wants to be on top all the time. Hard to get your spurs into them when theys riddin' so high."

"Makes no difference to me," said Dillman. "I've been without so long even the crack of dawn gets me horny."

"Any fish in Fairbanks?" said Bradbury. He pulled on his beard. "How about hunting? It's a long way up here without doing anything. We're going to Fairbanks after this."

"There ought not be a fish left anywhere in the world the way we packim in at the cannery." He filled the glasses with beer and finished the pitcher. He ordered another one. "Bring us sum of them peanuts, too."

Two men from the cannery, Charlie and Tom, entered slapping their arms around their chests as if to scare away the cold. Charlie's goatee had started to turn gray. He had a sharp wit and a dull mind, an unusual combination in any person. Often generous to a fault he was not adverse telling everyone about it or holding it against anyone who might have borrowed money during a time of need. Essentially, lazy Charlie kept his job because of his humor.

Tom, deaf in one ear, constantly spoke of his mother as if she were a saint. She managed to fit into every conversation until she became the center of conversation, at least with him, as the others moved on. Tattoos covered his arms and he was seldom seen without a cigar wrapped into his fist like a hot dog in a bun.

"You ain't quit, yet?" said Charlie when he saw Steve.

"Tomorrow," said Steve. "Come on over n party."

After introductions another table was pulled in and they sat and commented about the weather.

"Steve's joining the Foreign Legion," said Charlie. "From fish to Frogs, I say. What's the difference?"

"A turn in the navy was enough for me," said Jacks.

"There in Vietnam," said Steve. "Fightin' someone called the Viet Minks."

"A real weasely enemy," said Charlie. He always laughed at his own jokes.

"I've heard abut them," said Jacks. "I don't know why the French are having so much trouble beating them. All you have to do is have the navy throw up a blockade around the country to stop the weapons from getting in. Problem solved – war over."

"Reckon you're some kinda admiral," said Steve.

"Any women in this town?" said Dillman.

"Five fingered widows," said Charlie. "I used to hang sheetrock."

"You used to hang everything except your prick," said Tom.

"Any food in this place?" said Bradbury.

"Chili and sandwiches," said Steve. "There's a restaurant a block down. Decent country fried steak."

Jacks looked at his friends.

"Chili's fine," he said.

"How 'bout a round of chili?" Steve shouted to Wendover.

"Cheese and onions?"

"The works," said Steve.

"I only know we're going to get us some ass before the night is over," said Jacks. "We didn't come all this way for nothing."

"Where you fellers from?"

"California," said Jacks. "We came up for some fishing. We didn't know it would be so cold and dead this early."

"Any of y'all get to San Francisco?"

"Not this," said Charlie.

Steve shot him a short sharp look.

"What do you care?" he said.

Charlie looked at the Californians and chuckled.

"He's looking for dope. He's always looking for dope," said Charlie. "He hates it here because he can't find any dope."

"For sucha open-minded bunch of folks you'd think they was more progressive up here," said Steve. "There's folks like you boys wants some ass. Me, I like a good smoke. With a good smoke you don't need no ass."

The chili came in a large cast iron pot accompanied by bowls of cheese and onions. The bowls were wooden. The men ate and drank for almost two hours. After Charlie and Tom finally left, Steve walked the other men to the door. Jacks stopped just outside the entrance.

"Maybe we can help you," he said. He looked cautiously around. "We've got a bit of weed we might share. Just didn't want to say anything in front of your friends because we don't have much."

"Yes," said Steve actually rubbing his hands together. "I reckoned anyone from California has got some. Ain't no other reason to come from California."

"It's strictly on the hush-hush."

"I don't know nothing," said Steve. "Let's go."

"Not so fast," said Jacks. "Meet us in about an hour down by the pier. We'll give you just what you need. And we'll all go away happy."

Steve watched them walk away. Finally, he thought. A joint or two could change a man's entire perspective. He wanted to tell Bix but decided to keep quiet. Lately he seemed to be always on his ass about the dope.

Bix held Holga's hand. Her small hand refused to relinquish enough heat to keep his fingers warm. They were almost blue with cold, blue and dry and rough and the cold seemed to flow through his blood, up his arm and into his chest. He held her close to him, less from affection than for survival. He had been too long from South Dakota to remember the ice storms and brittle cold there. He only knew he was cold now and he needed a way to tell Holga he was leaving. They were lovers but he was not in love although he suspected she was. Many women needed love to have sex and were unable to enjoy a man simply for the pleasure of it. Attachment triggered orgasm and with attachment orgasm was not needed. There was never a clever way to abandon a woman's affection. Telling her she would survive the isolation was a slap in the face as if her love was not strong enough to hold the relationship together in the first place, as if she had just been fucking and not making love, as if she were a common whore, a tart, the local strumpet ruined for good and deserving men.

Bix was new with relationships but he understood enough to recognize that a man will stick his penis in anything that will hold it and not be concerned with having a relationship with his fist, a toilet paper holder, a folded over pillow, a cow's or chicken's ass, a bar of soap, or a person's mouth. He could rub his member between two greased breasts until the juice flowed and feel no guilt about not calling the twins in the morning.

Holga was a small woman, built more for the tropics, petite for an Alaskan woman where bulk fought off the cold. She did not think that Bix was "the one" to complete her; she needed no completion from anyone and felt complete enough as she was. He was fun, although a bit dour, and took great and selfish pleasure in sex with small regard for her enjoyment. She felt as much comfort from the warmth of his body on the outside of her as she did with it on the inside. He was the handsomest man she had ever seen and envy oozed from all the other women in town. From the beginning she had hoped he was not looking for any long-term relationship since she still carried on such a relationship with Elderman, a trapper from a small town outside Juno. Once a week she made a delivery of frozen fish there and once a week, all fingers and tongue, he drove her to sexual ecstasy. She enjoyed the company of Bix and his fumbling lovemaking but having driven a Packard she could never be complete in a Renault. She knew Bix was ready to leave and attempted to prepare a soup of tepid disappointment. He leaned her against the side of a building and kissed her.

"There's no other way to say this but Steve and I are leaving soon," he said. "We're going to France to fight."

"I knew it would not last," she said. "A deep love like ours never does. Will you be back?"

When he tried to kiss her again she turned her lips away and offered only her cheek. Kissing on the lips in such cold left a soon frozen rim of frost on her mouth. She turned back without looking at him.

Bix could feel her hurt and disappointment at the realization that she would once again be thrust into the world of loneliness. Fortunately she would be making her weekly delivery to Juno in the morning and she would have time to sort things out, to work out her grief.

"I would like to hold you one last time," said Bix. He wanted to show her that he was just as disappointed to say goodbye as she was to hear it, that it hurt just as much but mostly he wanted to get her into the sack once more and would have promised her the moon if that is what it took to get her there.

"Yes," she said. She would have said anything to get out of the cold and having his warm body next to hers was a start.

Steve was not at the house. He seldom was anymore. He seemed restless, aloof, in search of something. Bix had never witnessed such a contradiction in a person, the most relaxed jumble of nerves he had ever seen. Holga started a pot of coffee. She used a match to light the stove because it had no pilot light. Porcelain had chipped off the coffee pot in several places. She let the water run from red to clear before filling the pot.

"I suppose it was bound to happen," she said.

"We were never going to stay," said Bix. "I said that from the beginning. When I return maybe we can start up again." He moved the firewood axe from beside the stove to beside the door. He never planned to return. The country was beautiful but too cold, too harsh.

"Promises mean nothing." She adjusted the pot over the flame.

"We'll let it ride, then," said Bix. "I don't know how long I have to be in the Legion but if I don't go now, I never will. You know how it is? People spend their lives wishing to do something but they never do it and on their death bed they mumble 'I wish...' I don't need any 'I wish I's...' when I go. I want to travel around the world; I want to ride a motorcycle; I want to race cars or be a professional boxer; those sorts of things. People are all talk, more wishing than action. They are afraid to admit that they don't really intend to do anything, afraid to admit that they are just ordinary. They work at a job they hate, marry a woman they never really loved and if they did love someone, and it has gone sour, they are afraid to leave because misery beats uncertainty and they prefer the mundane over speculative action. Not that you aren't the right woman..."

"So you think you are going to make your mark in the world?" she said. She watched steam rise from the coffee spout. "What about dying?"

"That won't happen to me."

Dying never occurred to Bix. It never occurred to any young man. If it did there would be no armies, no wars. Every young man was invincible, able to kill without being killed. Dying was something that happened to someone else. Young men lived forever and he would be one of them, have an adventure and live forever; that was not too much to ask a lifetime, not much of a strain for a man who asked for so little. He would not mind a little wound, just to prove his manhood, but nothing more.

"I must leave early for my deliveries," said Holga. "Maybe I should go, just leave it at this, a simple goodbye."

"Once more, for old time's sake," said Bix, not wanting her to get away without leaving a piece behind.

Holga knew what he wanted. It seemed like too much effort to dress and undress. She decided to leave him with a blowjob, something that required little effort and she could keep the taste of coffee in her mouth while she performed and had only to spit the juice in the sink as she left and take another cup of coffee.

"Where is Steve?" She had once tried to get him into an affair but he refused claiming a man did not cheat on his friends, some unwritten code with men. Cheating on a wife or a girl friend was acceptable but not on a friend.

"I never know half what he's up to," said Bix "Probably looking for some dope. He gets more heavily into it every day."

"There's little in this part of the country," said Holga. "People don't need it up here with all the clean air and water to get them high. Only people running from something need dope. What's he running from?"

"Himself, maybe. I don't know. He likes to feel good, that's all, and he's not much of a drinker."

She kissed him passionately and dropped between his legs.

"Let me leave you with something special," she said, taking a drink of coffee.

Bix awoke early, cold from the empty bed and the blankets covering him. He knew that Holga could not take the separation and had decided to leave after sucking him off. A complete night with him would have torn her emotions apart. He could still feel the warmth of her head under his hands and he decided to carry that gesture of love for as long as possible.

He and Steve had never discussed exactly when they would leave, not the day or the hour but this day seemed as good as any day. He staggered into the bathroom. Sleep had masked his face in the mirror. He ran his hands over his cheeks and chin. There was not much there to shave but he decided to shave anyway. As the water from the spigot ran from cold to hot he took his morning crap, sitting carefully on the cold toilet seat and unable to void until the seat warmed. Each morning was the same ritual: turn on the water and wait on the toilet as they both warmed, pick the seep from his eyes and nose, bend over and check for smudge between his toes, turn off the hot water and brush his teeth, turn it back on and shave, masturbate in the shower if necessary, curl back in bed for a few minutes to get warm, then get dressed and go to work.

The general plan was to drive to Seattle, sell the car, then catch a boat or plane to France. If they took a boat they might be able to work their way over. They did not even know where to enlist. They knew the Legion had their headquarters in another country but they were not sure where. France would be the place to start looking and they might even take some time before enlistment to look around.

Bix heated the remaining coffee from last night and decided to chop some firewood to enjoy one last sit by the fireplace. The firewood axe was missing. He looked throughout the kitchen, then the rest of the house, although it never left the kitchen, either beside the stove or the door. Giving up on the idea he went to wake Steve. He had heard him come in just hours before. He never needed much sleep, or he needed too much sleep.

Steve was not in the room. Patches of blood dotted his pillow. On the floor was a pair of his underwear, a blood stain on the crotch. Bix sat on the edge of the bed. What now? he thought. Trouble followed Steve like dingle-berries on the ass of a long-haired dog. A note had been scribbled on a napkin and left beside the pillow.

"Went to Fairbanks to settle some business. Took the car and the axe. Be back in several days."

It's always something with him, thought Bix. We're ready to start a great adventure and he's off cutting up something.

Chapter 10

Heinrich Knowles grew concerned about his partly mangled leg and arm. As a young German Panzer tank officer he had been wounded on the drive toward Belgorod on the Russian front. They were nasty wounds sustained when a shell drove through the tank's side spraying metal fragments throughout the cabin and killing the driver and severely wounding the remaining crew. He had helped everyone from the burning tank and into a shell crater where they waited too long for medical help to arrive. The wounds filled with dirt when they snuggled low for protection and another of the crew member, hacking, spitting up blood, red bubbles popping as they emerged from his chest, died as they waited. Knowles knew his wounds would get infected and the doctors might have to amputate the limbs. Now, outside the hospital, in France, he was extremely worried. The wounds seemed to be healing, something that rather frightened him or, at the least, made him uneasy. Healed wounds meant a return to the front and he might not be so lucky next time. While recovering in Metz, he did not fancy a return trip to Russia, Germany's largest cemetery. Fighting the British or the Americans, civilized people adhering to some kind of rules, was not a problem. They almost seemed human, almost sophisticated. Hitler, supported by his top generals, thought so little of the British, French, and Americans' fighting ability that he only sent a little more than ten percent of his forces to oppose them, just enough to hold them off. The real war was with Russia. The Russians were mad raging animals, filthy inhuman beasts who gave no quarter. They attacked over and over again bashing themselves against the German machine guns, armor, and artillery, foaming at the mouth, tromping over their own dead comrades on the way to piling up German bodies. Because they had no fear nothing could stop them. They almost welcomed death, viewed dying as a grand sacrifice for the Mother Country. Anyone not at least wounded felt inferior, a coward, a slacker. Each man fought to be more badly injured than the next, and, once wounded, still move forward knowing that a life was brief but a granite statue lasted forever. They were filthy, they stank, they laughed and sneered with rotten teeth, black and green, they never washed themselves or their clothes, they tortured every German and, after interrogation, were unmerciful usually gutting every captive. A German prisoner who confessed extended his life only for as long as the confession. It was to be expected, Knowles realized, after what the Germans had done to them, but they seemed so much more vicious combined with an abundance of joy and verve as they killed. Regardless of German brutality they still seemed more civilized than the Russian barbarians.

Knowles might have been sent to Poland or Germany to recover. Although annexed by Germany, Metz remained French: a different look, different food, different clothes, a refreshing break from the war. The women, especially, looked and acted differently than organized, regimented, Arian women, mechanical, spotless, and cold. Moans and groans delivered in the heat of passion from German women sounded more like orders than sugar.

The French had odors, not stink like the Russians, gentle fragrances clinging to skin and armpit hair. Every woman had her own fragrance: earthiness, the bouquet of poppies, the aroma of onions, truffles or mushrooms, hay in the hair, smoke, wine, grapes, hedges, trees, cheese, pigs, geese, milk and cream. All the scents of France nested in her women.

Knowles looked for his favorite bench under the tree where he could admire the stained glass windows of St. Etienne cathedral. He loved and hated war but today he dreamed of peace. Everything existed in opposites and he reveled in both equally. Now was the time of peace within the war, away from the noise, the trembling earth, the night's falling stars tied to parachutes and drifting down from the sky before burning out. He was careful not to wear his uniform, not today, not when meeting Nicole Vaillant, his new love. He was not afraid to call her his love for he loved as diligently as he fought, with all the emotion and force needed to conquer any obstacle. Since she was French, even though Metz was under the control of Germany, she suffered danger dating a German so he never wore his uniform when with her and attempted not to speak within earshot of others, not because he could not speak French, but because he retained his German accent when he did.

He moved to a nearby tree and lighted a cigarette. The leaves made shadow patterns on the ground around him. He, like most of his fellow soldiers, knew the war was lost. The English and Americans caused scant attention and were easily beaten when equally opposed. But the Russians? That was the real war, not a sideline like the Western Front. Russians took the war seriously and played without rules. The people grew from a rough, harsh, unforgiving country. No ten Germanys could beat them. They refused to accept death except gladly and seemed to fight even after being mauled or buried. He imagined what damage and mayhem they might have accomplished had they any capable military leaders. As it was their generals only understood straight ahead slaughter, no nuance, no strategy, no finesse, just straight ahead charging like an angry bull.

The French cigarette, although putrid, still relaxed Knowles. He watched the clouds, a piece of newspaper floating on the water; the colored dresses of women on the opposite bank. In the distance a small delicate woman, like a holy apparition, walked toward him. Her shoes left no impression on the walkway. She turned to him, seemed anxious and eager to be near. She brushed at her long brown hair and ran a finger under her beret. Her deep eyes glowed with happiness as she stepped closer.

"Yes," said Knowles. "I love you too but we must be careful."

She looked up and down the street and found it mostly empty, threw her arms around Knowles and kissed him hard and violently letting the kisses diminish to passion and gentleness. Knowles felt peace and youth in her lips. They tasted slightly of peaches.

"I cannot help myself," she said. "Let them find us. I no longer care. We are no danger to anyone and I need you to touch me. To feel your hands against my flesh."

Knowles placed his hands against her cheeks and kissed her again.

"You're very dangerous," said Knowles. "Let's sit and pretend we are discussing the cathedral." He pointed to St. Etienne as if showing her some minute detail. Nicole moved her hand to capture his. "The Russians are on us and we'll not be able to hold on much longer. When the war is over we will be free to have each other." He felt her hand squeeze his.

"It will never end," she said. "Germans are too pragmatic, too proud, and stubborn. The French fight or not fight, as they please. Surrender is often our first choice so long as it is not inconvenient."

"Then why this fascination with me, a German?" He enjoyed prodding her and making subtle reminders about their different nationalities. "In war, one's country makes all the difference regarding love."

"Your injuries have made you softer, more French. The idea of you being a killer is beyond me. Are you hurting?" She glanced at him, some concern in her eyes.

"They'll be returning me to the lines soon," said Knowles. "The doctors doubt my complaints about pain and constantly remind that every soldier is required to fight, to do his duty for the Fatherland. It's a matter of choice. When the Russians get to Germany they will destroy everything, the industries, the towns, the people, especially the women. Nothing will remain whether we needlessly fight on or not. Resistance in a lost cause only makes the enemy more angry and destructive. We were lost the moment we entered Russia."

"You will remain," she said. "You will be with me, my soft gentle German, my lover.

We will always be together. If we are separated we will find each other again. Nothing binds like love; nothing lasts so long. When we are old and fat our love will remain."

"It's a pleasant thought," he said. "Of course if you are old and fat I should be forced to take another lover. Let's find a remote café for lunch. Perhaps you know of one?"

"And then we will go to my room and make love all through the night so you will be too decrepit to take a lover in old age. I love your body against mine. It fees so natural."

"You mustn't believe the German propaganda," he said. "I am no superman. With any luck I will be injured again in town and I can stay longer. The war can't last forever, not at this rate."

"The right woman can always bring a man to attention," she giggled. She could almost feel the heat from his blush. He was such a gentle man and so sensitive, so, un-German, far different than the granite features of his beautiful face and chiseled body. Only the eyes gave him away and even then she imagined that they could turn to ice and that he was capable of killing a man without any loss of sleep, in cold blood, no remorse. How else could he be so gentle, so loving without its murderous opposite? "Come, let's go where we can be alone, where no one can bother us." She placed her hand into his.

Laurent Tone held the automatic pistol in his hand, felt the weight, ran a finger over the metal showing through the worn bluing. The shabby barrel rifling, flat and chipped, still had enough grip to spin lead. Besides, if he held it to a person's temple and fired it was bound to drill a nice broken hole just large enough to let the gray pudding run out. He liked the feel of the pistol, the feel of any weapon with which to kill Germans. He wanted the world to know that there were Frenchmen who did not capitulate to the Bosh, who had vowed to kill every German they met. After looking around the room, he placed the weapon back inside the fireplace and slid the brick cover over the opening. He locked the door and walked downstairs.

"Going out Monsieur Tone?" the proprietor said, sipping at coffee that darkened the stains on the ends of his moustache.

"Lunch," he replied. The door rattled behind him and the bell tinkled from above the door casing.

"Ah yes, lunch," said the proprietor, used to conversing with himself. "You go to lunch and another German ends up dead. That's well enough for you, but what about the rest of us? If you get caught we'll all get hanged, especially me. For once think about someone else. Let the Russians kill them. They have a knack for such things."

Except for occupying Germans - mostly recovering patients who felt they were in France and should not have considered themselves occupiers, since they were not - (the town having been annexed) the city had been mostly spared the ravages of war. Most of the inhabitants considered themselves French even though their ownership seemed to change almost yearly. Metz seemed more comfortable and relaxed than Paris, where Tone had left two months ago, although less exciting. Cobblestone streets covered many areas, brick buildings rose to no great heights and balconies sprouted plants above street restaurants and cafes serving slightly chilled wines, cheeses, fruits and vegetables. Most food seemed plentiful and bubbling soups of cheese, onions, and beef broth, remained affordable and all the rage. Pork and chickens could be had at any shop, for a price. Tone expected more action in the area, especially with all the Germans, and he felt rather ill-used and anxious. Working with the resistance should be more exciting, more daring. His next meeting, safe enough to be held in daylight rather than midnight under smoky oil lamps in cellars, like meetings in Paris, was later that afternoon.

Tone walked to his favorite café, the eave covered with bright canvas, near the river. France had the best cafés in the world, each one unique. This one held more history than many - old, a bit shabby, dust occasionally on a wine bottle, tables and chairs of dinged dark wood. He sat in a corner so he could observe everyone, ordered cheese and wine, and eyed the young couple holding hands across their table. He had seen them before, several times, even followed them without much stealth knowing they were too preoccupied with one another to notice him even though the man, limping and obviously cradling an injured arm, appeared skittish, uncomfortable, and seemed reluctant to return her kisses, his affection showing in short snaps often in an attempt to make her stop and followed with an uneasy laugh and anxious words Tone never heard beyond the muffled sounds hanging on the air. The man seemed more relaxed today perhaps because the café sat away from any main streets and was sparsely occupied.

Knowles watched the garçon arrange the cheese on their table and pour the wine then wipe his hands on his dingy apron. He glanced toward Tone. Obviously French with his large nose, he appeared rather slight and delicate with a woman's hands presently adjusting his sweater, small ears, and an odd birthmark on his forehead that resembled Scotland. Tone, noticing Knowles watching him, raised his class and nodded with a smile. Knowles nodded back as Nicole turned to look and also nodded.

"I think you are too suspicious," she said. "Everyone is a danger to you. You must believe in the goodness of people even during a war."

"A soldier learns to be careful. An old soldier, almost paranoid." Knowles eased his hand from hers. "Eventually caution becomes instinct and with instinct one survives."

"He is a mouse in an old sweater," she whispered. She reached for his hand but he moved it to pour more wine. The wine was cheap, cloudy, greasy. Germany produced some very decent wines but he had not had any since the war. The French appeared to hide their best wines.

"Sometimes a mouse is more dangerous than a lion," he said. With a finger he lifted a drip of wine from the bottle and let her quickly place it in her mouth. "You worry me. I am a German soldier and immune from the French, but you? Your own people might harm you for associating with me."

"If Germany owns my town, then I too am German therefore not fraternizing with the enemy. People are all the same, it's the governments that cause trouble."

"You are mistaken. It's angry people that are all the same and they get the kind of government they allow."

"Pardon," said Tone. They had not seen him approach the table. "I am always pleased to see young lovers in this time of turbulence." He nodded politely. "My name is Laurent Tone." He offered his hand to Knowles and tipped his head toward Nicole again.

Knowles stood and reluctantly presented his hand ashamed he had not even noticed the man walk up. He was too long out of the war and a woman, or love, makes a man dizzy, giddy, unsure of himself as if he were drunk, his awareness narrowed to just her eyes. What did the man want?

"I, too, was a soldier," said Tone. "May I?" He motioned to the empty chair and sat, not waiting for an answer. "I don't mean to be forward. Although I served in the French Army, I hold no hard feelings, just respect for all soldiers because they have no interest in war but are forced to go, anyway." He rubbed the birthmark on his forehead. "This often happens with soldiers, a respect for the enemy as men in a complicated position and the German Army is certainly the best. One can't help but admire them. French generals, like French artists, are repeatedly confused and without any kind of plan. The soldiers fight hard but are often perplexed by conflicting orders and suffer from outdated weapons. Do you agree?" He looked carefully at Knowles, the Arian good looks, the firmness of jaw, the determined look. Knowles was fuming inside yet showed nothing except the tight jaw. Tone liked that. Knowles would be a difficult adversary.

"Why do you think I am a soldier?" said Knowles. Tone motioned for the waiter to bring his wine and cheese to the new table.

"I have seen you before with the mademoiselle, the other day when you came here. I was just leaving. Your limp caught my eye, and the way you favor your arm. Only recovering soldiers come here. I understand most Germans are preoccupied at the moment trying to repair their cities from the Allied bombs. But no matter. Love is my interest, so little of it is around these days. Sex, yes, but not love, not true love." He poured wine for everyone.

"I have never been here before."

"But of course. Lovers never remember where they have been and are only interested in where they are going. A simple mistake."

"Why should we be of interest to anyone?' said Knowles, taking a small drink and looking at Nicole. Her annoyance clearly showed.

"In war the French accept sex, a natural instinct and often profitable. We are fond of commerce." He tapped Knowles on the forearm. "Even rape seldom raises an eye. We feel it justified as punishment for letting us go to war in the first place. Odd that we should think of it as punishment, yet at other times as pleasure. In dangerous situations people want to procreate, advance their kind should they die in the war. We often have difficulty tolerating love with the enemy, however. Love is beyond sex, you understand, beyond countries, and represents a commitment between two people. You must be careful. Not everyone is as liberal as me. One need not have sex to have love. Not me, of course." He winked at Nicole. "I say, let people alone. We are, after all, one family; one group of human beings and it is refreshing to see people in love, especially two such handsome people. I just wanted to express the joy you have given me, some hope for the future, a reassurance that life will continue, that someday we will all be normal again, fall in love, have families, grow old together without the hardships of conflicts." He raised his glass. "And so, a toast to the future, peace, and to normalcy."

Knowles raised his glass and watched Nicole raising hers. She had started to like Tone; a small man of innocence filled with kindness and clinked her glass against his.

"I must be off," he said. "I hope I have not disturbed your afternoon."

"Not at all," she said. "Perhaps we'll meet again?" He again nodded to each of them.

"I'll make a point of it. Bring a few friends with my views, if you don't mind, and we'll have a celebration. I know a café where American jazz is played. Until then…"

He spoke to the waiter at the counter then moved down the street, turned for a moment to light a cigarette, nodded and walked on.

"What a strange fellow," said Nicole, reaching for Knowles' hand. "The birthmark on his head is rather interesting."

"I wonder?" he said. "He seems right enough yet there is something unnerving about him, something deep and false."

"A lost love. It must be a lost love. All French have a lost love, a melancholy about them because they love so easily and so hard."

"And you? I've noticed no sadness." She leaned across the table and kissed him.

"You have drowned my misery. Let's go so I can show you my appreciation."

Knowles waved for the bill. He looked at it very closely, slightly confused. He showed it to the waiter as if he had not seen it or had made a mistake. "And this extra charge?"

"Yes, monsieur," he smiled. "The charge is for your friend. He said you would take care of it." Knowles took back the bill and started to laugh.

"You have restored my faith in humanity." He continued to laugh as he threw his arm around Nicole. "All that work for a free meal. He might have asked and I would have gladly paid." Together, past the everyday traffic of people not concerned with war, they walked to her apartment for an afternoon of lovemaking.

Three weeks later Knowles entered the hospital, a dim brick building scrubbed spotless, as is the German habit. Because fresh cases were not treated here, it lacked the hustle, filth and noise of the combat hospitals he had visited on the Eastern Front. Order reined as solders entered back rooms and emerged again. Those facing more convalescence exited with smiles because they were safe a while longer and had difficulty holding back small twists of the lips as if any display of pleasure might cause a reversal of diagnosis. Soldiers ready for combat appeared beaten and lifeless, a blank stare, trembling hands, feet dragging across the floor unprepared to make the long trip back to the Russian cemetery. Not even the joy of being alive energized them since life seemed a temporary event, another spin on the roulette table, all the odds against them. The chances of future wounds resulting in another convalescence diminished with each day on the line, with each visit to the aid station or hospital until one day there remained no uncharted places to go except into the ground.

Knowles entered the examining room and sat on a wooden table. No propaganda adorned the walls, no slogans of the mighty German Army rolling over new territory, no pictures or posters of a grim-faced Hitler. The doctor entered carrying no paperwork, no medical records.

"How are you feeling today?" he said, not looking at Knowles. He sat on a chair and drank from a coffee cup he had left there.

"I am still stiff and in pain. Neither my leg nor my arm work correctly."

"Perhaps you are getting soft?" he said. "Too many days in the cafés, too much time with the women, too much good food."

"Perhaps, but still a concern," said Knowles. "A soldier must be in top shape to fight well. Would you like to examine the wounds?" Knowles started to unfasten his tunic.

"Never mind." The doctor waved him off, leaned back and ran a hand through his hair. "Things are tight at the front. Every soldier is necessary, especially officers. I understand you are a good officer, respected and liked by your men. We need such men for a future Germany. For you it's time to return to the line." Knowles stiffened. He was not ready and needed more time with Nicole, more time to enjoy life, just more time.

"Between us, and every other German soldier in Russia, the war is lost," said the doctor. "No one knows that better than you." The doctor drank slowly and looked at the floor. "It's because we need men like you to rebuild Germany that I am transferring you to the Western Front where your chances of survival are greater. You must attempt to stay alive. There is nothing else I can do for you." Knowles did not know how to react - with surprise, perhaps? Of course he was surprised. The Western Front was a joke. Hitler had never ordered more than a small percent of his efforts there. What about his men to the east? He could do little for them. Why not take a chance and go to the west? The war was between Germany and Russia with the Western Front just an annoying sideline. "Return for your new orders in two days." The doctor shook Knowles' hand and walked out with the cup.

Knowles remained confused. Yes, he had to leave; yet, he had a chance to live. The British and Americans were not animals. One might even surrender to them without being executed and even be treated humanly or kindly. America was full of Germans; even his uncle had emigrated there. His elation and sadness mixed together and emerged as indifference. One must accept his fate without question or go mad attempting to change it. It was best to tell Nicole as quickly as possible, no procrastination, get the words out tonight so she might prepare for a less than certain future. But at least some hope for the future, a possibility he might return to her and they might live happily after like is said in the fairy tales.

Because it might be the last one he ate for some time, the duck at dinner tasted better than usual. The French enjoyed cooking with butter and garlic. He kept his eyes on Nicole as if painting her face onto his mind. As beautiful as she was, she seemed to glow in the candlelight, her delicate features soft and tender, her smile touched with innocence. Warmth filled the café and the tinkles of glasses and cutlery, the murmuring fog of drifting voices, seemed subduely staged for his enjoyment, a kind farewell from old friends.

"It's best to tell you now," he said.

"Don't," Nicole said. "I'd rather pretend that you and I would be together forever. Leave when you must but don't tell me. One day I will awake and you will be gone and I will picture you working at your new job in the museum. I will go about my duties thinking of you and smiling, knowing you will be home soon."

Outside, Knowles placed his arm over her shoulder no longer concerned about the danger. One last time he wanted to treat her with the love he felt, to show her to the world as his woman, his true love, proud, unashamed and unafraid. On the way to her apartment they often leaned into a doorway or alley and kissed.

She was so much more than the war, the death, the mangled bodies, the freezing and screaming, nights bursting into light, the grumbling of his tank as the heat rose through the metal during the summer and froze solid in the winter, soldiers burrowing into the earth for safety, cold soup and moldy bread, the crunch and slime of Russian soldiers under the tank treads, the dull hammer knock of rounds against the metal sides, the smell of leaking diesel fuel from the engine, the tank drowning in mud during the rains, skating on ice during the winter, choking with tons of dust and dirt in the summer. Images flashed in and out of his mind, images he could not erase. How would peace torture the old soldiers who no longer knew how to work after all the years of battle? Their lives were over the moment they dressed in uniforms. All they knew was war and the images of war and the hollow despair and cold indifference it brought, the blank stares and confusion others saw in their faces unaware of the momentary madness projecting death and love and hate and anger behind the soldier's look, a private sold-out showing on the big screen of the entire mind of the self, tickets unavailable to the uninitiated. Only she could erase the memories, the images, if only for a moment.

After closing the door to her apartment, they relied on the moonlight to let their bodies see, simply through its sense, one another. Knowles slipped off her clothes a piece at a time letting them fall to her feet where the edges touched his feet. The clothes would have felt like silk even if they were burlap. Her flesh seemed to tremble giving off the aroma of freshly baked apples. He slipped off his own clothes and felt the warmth of her body drawing him in. Like butterfly wings her hands fluttered across his chest and face picking out small bits of sweetness before moving on. Together they warmed the bed sheets. Quietly Knowles whispered mass between her breasts as she kneaded his temples. Tenderness accompanied their lovemaking and slowly the juices of two lives mixed, never to be separated. Later they lay together, her head across his chest, his injured arm under her neck and over her shoulder.

The door burst open as the armed men entered and stood at the foot of the bed. Knowles sat up and partially covered Nicole. "What is this?" he said, attempting to make out faces in the dark. No one spoke. He had let down his guard because he had believed there was a small section of peace in the world, a place he might relax and breathe in the deep aroma of safety. A small man entered the doorway and stood quietly before moving forward.

"I see you have found the love you so much desired," he said. It was Tone, looking down at them. Nicole tried to peek from between Knowles arm and chest. She had never heard a voice so cold. "A little wine?" he said. "You disgust me. Not you, soldier boy. Her! All soldiers have the same things in mind: killing, survival, a bit of food, and sex, lots of sex. But she is French and such games are not for her. Perhaps she has forgotten that the true French are at war with Germany. Perhaps she needs a reminder."

"We've done nothing." Knowles tried to remain calm. He should not have said anything, not have responded to this puny clove of French garlic. A man must remain calm and keep his head, to think out a solution to his dilemma. Talking interrupts that process. "She's just a girl. There were supposed to be no hard feelings." The men moved to each side of the bed. Two of them held lengths of rope, another a straight razor.

"It's a matter of national pride, nothing personal," said Tone. "I actually like you but, as you might understand, we'll have no bastard Hun children running around France. You are not the only ones desiring a pure race." The moonlight cast strange shadows on his face and his birthmark, resembling Scotland, seemed to glow with yellow flames.

"Someone will hear you," said Knowles. "The police will be on their way." It was the voice of desperation, the voice of fear, not fear for himself (a soldier should die with honor) but fear for Nicole who would not understand such violence, the voice of surrender, of defeat, and he saw himself like an animal that, lying calmly in the jaws of a predator, has accepted his fate.

"Police? You must be mad to think anyone in this fine French building would call the police. Scream, if you like. Bang on the walls. Break the washbasin. No one will come to your rescue." Tone's face soured and he said quietly, "Take him," as he jerked his head to the side.

The men jumped on Knowles as he tried briefly to fight back, yet understanding all was lost. His punches went wild and landed without effect from his sitting position. The men grabbed him by the hair and his injured arm and threw him to the floor. He continued to struggle, trying to strike like a snake, as the men spread his arms, tied the rope to his wrists, dragged him to the foot of the bed lifting his head over the top railing and tying his arms to the bedposts. Except for groaning while reaching out for him, Nicole said nothing, too frightened to squeak out the slightest sound, her chest too tight to even breathe. Tone patted Knowles on the head.

"There, there," he said. "Spread wide like a German eagle with no place to fly." He leaned close to Knowles' ear. "It appears we have the little French whore to ourselves," Tone whispered. "I didn't want you to miss the fun we're going to have with her. I am sure you will enjoy this."

The men took turns holding her down as they continually raped her. It was not necessary. She just laid there, tears dropping to the mattress, also accepting her fate. Rape was not love, not even sex, but a cruel act of barbarism and she thought of the minuscule margin between love and hate, between tenderness and brutality, how the act of inviting someone into her body so differed from the act of someone uninvited bursting in. She realized then that love was not part of the physical world but an emotion far beyond the flesh.

The men took turns holding up Knowles' head so he could not look away. When they had finished, Tone sat on the edge of the bed and patted her on the head. He ran his fingers through her long hair.

"Such a lovely girl," he said, smiling. "So moist and juicy." He started to laugh. The others joined in with deep growls. "Surely you didn't think we would stop with that bit of fun?" he said. "All the city must know what she is, all the decent French men and women." He held out his hand for the razor. Nicole pulled away but he pulled her back. "No reason to fight. It's going to happen, anyway. Save your strength. You didn't seem to fight that hard for your little Nazi or for our little fun. Perhaps you enjoyed it? Sit back and enjoy this too."

Nicole fought to pull away but Tone held her tightly around the neck and sliced at her hair. Spots of blood appeared on her scalp as the hair fell away and the razor constantly cut into her scalp. After he had finished, she held her bloody bald head and sobbed quietly as if watching her baby die. Tone slapped the side of the razor against his palm.

"So," he said. "What to do with you?" He moved to the back of Knowles and ran the razor over his shoulders. "I understand the needs of men, the animal in them that must be satisfied. You will be back to the same tricks in no time. This cannot happen. You must be an example to others." He nodded to the other men. "Pull his knees apart." Tone ran his hand over Knowles' buttocks and between his legs. "What have we here?" he said, holding his testicals. Knowles lowered his head and waited. Tone placed his head on Knowles' neck as he slid the razor between his legs. "I do apologize," he whispered, "but, you will be back to your old ways. I mustn't be too hasty. You need to think through the pain."

Knowles was determined not to cry out or to whimper as the razor drew slowly across the bottom of his sack. The skin opened as the testacies dropped, hanging from the cords. Tone pulled each one slowly and gently as Knowles felt the cords tear away before he passed out.

Chapter 11

Tone held the testicals for Nicole to see. "Look," he said. "It seems the Karut is not the man you thought he was." He rolled the slimy bloody eggs around his hand like marbles before dropping them to the floor. He wiped his hand on her cheek and slapped her.

He grabbed her arm, pulling her from the bed, and kicked her out the door. She fell to the floor, still in shock, before running naked down the stairs, past the front desk where the clerk looked up briefly before returning to his paper, and, the tears finally starting to flow as if attempting to wash her face, stumbling onto the street. She needed clothes, some kind of covering, and help for Heinrich, but where? She crouched near the buildings as she moved, stopping then scurrying to the next pit of protection like a frightened mouse. She knew someone would eventually see her, cry out, strike up the band to announce the latest sideshow attraction: the bald-headed lady, the turncoat, the French whore, come one, come all, bring your bricks, stones, rotten fruit to toss, your slangs and ridicule; prove that love might have a place in the world but that place is not in the heart during times of war. She tried to convince herself that it was no more than a naked dream, that she could walk upright through the town and no one would notice she was naked except her and she would soon wake in the arms of Heinrich.

An old woman in a torn brown coat started flapping her arms like a wounded condor, her plaid scarf blowing over her shoulder, and yelled "Traitor! There is a traitor here! Just there – look!"

"Where?" a man cried, trotting to her side and squinting across the street.

"There, there in the shadow," she pointed, her crooked finger like a dried twig in winter.

"Bitch!" he cried. "German whore!"

A crowd gathered at the excitement, a woman pulling her daughter by the hand, two men walking arm-in-arm, a butcher from a nearby shop in a bloody apron and holding a bone. Others joined the group forming a pool of distrust, evil, a crawling maggot-infested meat. They became ranting dogs, snarling and salivating; she became frightened and quivering; they became snakes, spitting venom, curling and crawling; she became exposed and innocently vulnerable; they became iron hammers bashing against stone and razors against flesh; she became stoic yet supple; they became harsh and putrid, all ignorance, a pack of animals clawing and snarling; she became upright and dignified; they became murderous, jaundiced, and all too human; she became weak, loving, tearful, and all so human.

"Whore – Karut lover – stinking bitch – have you no pride? – kick her out – expel her." Several men shouted in hopeful anticipation "Let's rape her – drag her into the alley and rape her – show what a good Frenchman is like – "

Nicole stepped into the light, stood quietly on the street, for all to see. No use hiding now. She raised her head and let her mind go blank. Only white light entered her eyes and the noise of the crowd became a muffled distant stream flowing over smooth rocks. But the events around her were not a dream and waking into another world, another life, was not possible. Only scorn and ridicule remained on the street. She lifted her hands over her face and attempted to cover her shame but she drew them back for their love is never shame; love is honor, a binding of two people, an unbroken chain of caring, and protection. Without Heinrich, who would protect her now?

An older man walked firmly toward her clenching his cane, his steps hard and deliberate, each one a crushing indictment. People tentatively moved forward, lips curled at the edges, in anticipation of beating Nicole. "Knock her a good one," said a man wearing a scarf around his head. The old man continued to walk toward her. At his age he had seen plenty of traitors, plenty of women denouncing country for love. The man's face contorted like an ancient burl and the knuckles on his burlap hands glowed white. He stopped before Nicole, staring into her frightened eyes peering from between her trembling hands that now held her cheeks. He raised his arm then dropped the cane and slid off his trench coat. Yes, that was it. Strip down, lighten the load to get a good swing with the cane, a hammer against the face, knock her teeth out, leave her welted like a red striped Zebra. He looked at her again, pulled her hands away from her face, and placed the coat around her shoulders. She pulled the coat tightly and looked into his eyes. The ancient eyes resembled two clouded pools of former hatred that had melted through years into compassion and understanding as if a clenched fist thrown in anger had become an open palm offering aid and assistance when it had reached its destination. He kissed her on the cheek before retrieving his cane and placing a tired look of shame and disgust onto the crowd. Nicole slid her arms into the coat, gathered her senses and ran down the street, the cold wind against her bald scalp.

Panting, she stepped into her father's house for safety. The room was dark and musty with only a band of light cutting through a closed curtain on the far wall. Her father looked up from his bowl of potato soup; his eyes cold and soggy liked the limp carrots and onions in the broth.

"Papa," she said, as if the word was all the passport she needed to enter into his land of sympathy and understanding. The idea remained false. He had never shown any sympathy or understanding before.

He started to smile, not knowing who had entered, the odor of gin rising from the corners of his cracked lips. He was no common drunk, just a man whose dreams had never reached fruition, not the actuality of the dreams but the dreams themselves. He had not the imagination to form any real dreams, only clouds hinting at something lying beyond, another indistinguishable mist behind which stood another and another. He had always wanted the feelings of love and compassion and tenderness. He carried them once, before the First World War had taken them along with his leg, his humor, his focus, leaving only bitterness, confusion, and the realization that his life had ended on the Western Front so many years ago and could not be resurrected, could not be raised from the mud of the trenches and a world of stench, flares, gas, artillery, and body parts. He saw Nicole's cropped head, her bare legs and dirty feet.

"You?" he said, in response to her single cry for help, his word filled with condemnation, shame, spite, a betrayal of family, of blood. "You, coupling with the Huns. I warned you for your own safety but you would not listen. Shame is what you have brought me. You're no daughter of mine! A whore, a filthy whore!" He tried to stand, to give her a mighty slap to knock out the love in her head, but the liquor's road ran at angles tipping him off balance, his hand, in an attempt to steady himself, caught the edge of the bowl and betrayed him with a vomit of mush spilling to the floor.

"What am I to do?" She reached out for his arm.

"You cannot stay here," he said, placing his hand over hers. He had seldom touched her and he noticed the tender skin of her hand, the warmth. "When you assume the responsibility of love and sex you assume your life, make your own decisions and live in the world as best you can. What you cannot do is stay here and bring your shame on me."

Nicole ran upstairs, dressed, placed a scarf around her head, gathered what money she had, and returned to the street leaving her father cursing at a single potato he had retrieved from the floor. There was no hiding now, even with the scarf as holy relic. People would discover her. She returned to the hotel to find Heinrich. The clerk watched her enter, remained silent, let her walk upstairs. She might be dangerous or even insane, might have a gun. Better to let her go about her business, dip her hands into the blood escaping through the floorboards. The door was slightly open. She pushed it with her hand and looked inside, afraid of what she might see. Heinrich had gone. She stood over the blood. His clothes were also gone. She looked at the clerk on her way out but said nothing. Let her find out for herself how fleeting love is, he thought. She'll find another rod to fit between her legs soon enough. A man is his testacies, even a German, and he is no man now.

She staggered toward the street looking pale and distant. She looked a last time toward the clerk and started to re-enter the hotel. Her mouth started to open, to question him. She closed it again knowing he would not answer except to be cynical, to make crude jokes and accusatory comments.

For over a week she sought employment and Heinrich. Nothing. Everyone knew she sin and no one knew anything about the German officer. Bad news is the wind while good news limps along like a cripple. Her money started to dwindle. Moving to another town was no solution until her hair returned. She sat at a café, whose patriotism lay in cash, and sipped her wine. She sat in many cafés hoping to see Heinrich walk past. Her love for him lay beyond sex, beyond anything physical aside from touching and holding.

"A difficult time?" said a woman, neatly dressed as she sat beside Nicole. "You don't mind?"

"It's dangerous," said Nicole, holding back the excitement of conversation.

"One can think everything is dangerous," she said. She ordered a bottle of wine and tray of cheese and cucumbers. "Everything is simply everything. It goes on day after day. If you are French, making you an outcast over the love of a German love is good. It's the others who are bad, the others who do not understand love. Incidents of love are always the same only the perceptions are different. I'm sure you understand." She filled Nicole's glass and pushed the tray of food her way. "Of course, I am a practical business woman able to separate my mind from my body. My body earns me a living yet I have a husband I love terribly and he loves me. He was wounded during the invasion and lost his legs and an arm. There is no work for such a man so I bring in the money, a very good living I might add. He is not his body as I am not my body. What makes us what we are lies beyond the physical. All emotions, all thought, all love, lives there. And this?" She ran her hands up and down her body. "This is nothing more than transportation, a way to earn a living, a receptacle for food and other goods."

At first Nicole noticed others watching them, eyes condemning and hurtful. They soon disappeared into the background.

"How rude of me," the woman said. "I am Rita and you are Nicole?"

"How…" Nicole started to say.

"Of course everyone knows you in this neighborhood. The whore that will not leave, that is what they say. Deep down they admire your resolve at staying but they will not say it. Your reputation for stubbornness is growing. You have been looking for a German officer named Heinrich Knowles. The hospitals will offer no information and others will not talk to you. Never mind. He is no longer here. The doctors sewed him up. In an act of kindness they recommended he be assigned to a unit on the Western Front saying he is incapable of the hardships of the real war against the Russians. He will be safe. The Germans rather trust the English, French, and Americans, and will not resist with much vigor. They know they are finished and can expect better treatment from them while those on the Russian front are already in their graves. Anyone unlucky enough to be taken prisoner there faces a short and torturous life sentence."

She pushed more food toward Nicole. Nicole took another bite. She liked this woman, her straight and practical talk. She knew what Rita wanted. Practical? Maybe? But whoring was not for her. The wine started to warm her and Rita ordered another bottle.

"You'll not last long on the streets," said Rita. "Your money is about gone along with your options. A pretty woman can always earn a living, a decent living, without consequences as long as she remembers it is a business. When is happiness a crime? You will spread joy to others while earning a decent rental fee for your body. A doctor checks you weekly to keep you healthy and Bruno, a dear man whose body has outgrown his clothes and his mind, handles any other problems. You don't even have to be present, just your body. You'll be working the streets in time anyway. Hunger has a way of doing that. Only dirty unscrupulous creatures rent from the streets. Our customers are screened and most are regulars, most are German officers with too much money, too much arrogance, and extremely clean as are most Germans. The sex is brief, the stories they relate to their friends about it, long stories about the lasting sexual impressions they have left on the women who have barely noticed their comings and goings. Many of them are happily married because of us. A change of pace makes a wife more exciting and there is no fighting because he wants sex more than three times a week and she? Less than three times a month."

"You're very kind," said Nicole. The wine was making her slightly drunk and she felt flushed. "I don't think I am capable."

"Of course." She reached across and held Nicole's hand. "Remember, we are always paid for sex. Sometime the payment is in emotion, sometimes in francs. Living demands a price. In any case, I won't let you starve. Come to my place of business to stay. You can cook and clean a bit, get to know the girls. You need a change of clothes, a hot douche and a chance to think it over. Nothing will be forced on you and you will find that everything is run like any business. The way most girls go astray is not with the sex but by spending all their money. They are then stuck in the profession, fall into drink and drugs and eventually die as hags on the streets. I protect my girls. Their drink is limited and anyone suspected of drugs is dismissed immediately. They receive an allowance. I place the remainder of their earnings into savings or small investments. They are allowed to see the books and may leave at any time with all their funds, a chance to start a business, to take a vacation, to move to another town, get married, live a happy life as if nothing has happened. Sex leaves no signs of frequency. You might even wish to run your own bordello and, if done correctly, have a successful business with decent girls and reputable clients. Finish up now and let's be on our way." She tossed some money onto the table and led Nicole down the road, her arm through hers, laughing and patting her along the way.

The building looked innocuous enough, three floors of brick, stone and a freshly painted door. Flowers lined the walkway and the porch, something seldom seen on French houses. Nicole had only seen them in American magazines. The first floor inside resembled a small club. Sofas, plush chairs and several tables with chairs were arranged around a small dance floor. Drums sat near one corner of a bandstand. Work was accomplished on the second floor, very plain rooms to hold the beds, a table for the washbasins and a rack for towels. The women had their personal rooms upstairs decorated to their tastes. Light from the balcony shown across the Oriental rug in a common sitting room. The kitchen sat in the basement where the women ate and meals and drinks were prepared for customers. The house seemed rather cheerful and not as Nicole had imagined: a dungeon of horrors, dim, moldy, shabby red curtains and painted, worn, women with leering smiles and constantly wet, lubricated crotches.

The women she met appeared nervously nice and welcomed her with warmth, and kindness, as they avoided her eyes. If she needed anything, just ask them. Two of them took her arms and escorted her for a hot bath. She sat on a stool as they filled the tub. "You'll like it here," one of them said. "Rita insists we stay clean so we are required to bathe every day." Nicole lay up to her chin in bubbles and perfume yet felt uncomfortable with the care as they scrubbed her down and washed her hair, only accepting their touch as a kindness to them, as if they needed more console then she. Two other women brought clean decent clothes as might be had in any respectable shop in town, dressed and powdered her as if she were a delicate and precious doll. They all gathered around, checked her carefully, made suggestions before adjusting a strap here or there, all very mechanical and cautious of speech. She felt very special and, without even knowing them, already thought of them as friends, friends she did not quite understand. They showed her to her room, undressed her, arranged her clothes, turned down the covers and tucked her in after sliding her into a sleeping gown. "We know you are tired but we wanted to see you in the dress before we put you to bed. This will help you sleep. Put this piece of sugar cube into your mouth and drink it quickly." The green alcohol tasted bitter. One by one they kissed her on the forehead as they left. By morning she thought she had slept more soundly than she ever had.

She awoke to find Rita sitting in a chair beside the bed. "Good sleep?"

"Yes, thank you," said Nicole. Rita motioned for her to sit up and turn around. She started massaging her shoulders and neck.

"You're very tight," said Rita. "Breakfast will fix you up. Angela will know just what to fix. She makes the most insignificant ingredients taste wonderful. Some mushrooms, onions, whipped eggs, and bread." She worked her hands over Nicole's shoulders, down her waist, leaned forward to push on her thighs, then back up again before brushing her bald head. The bristles felt good scratching her scalp. "Come now, put on your new clothes, this wig, and we'll go down. Most of the girls are still sleeping. They are required to clean their rooms and the servicing areas, nothing more difficult than that. I don't allow lazy girls who consider themselves common whores who have no respect for themselves. Most of them take an afternoon walk or visit the cinema or café."

Rita introduced Nicole to Angela Rimbaud, an old stick dressed in sloppy clothes, bent over the washbasin, sloped at the shoulders, her gray hair escaping her bun causing her head to resemble a fuzzy muffin covered with powdered sugar. A dent shown from the side of her head. The basement was musty and dark.

"Madam Rimbaud," said Nicole, slightly tipping her head. Madam Rimbaud grinned. Her eyes seemed to be alight with some past fear mixed with the delight at meeting Nicole.

"We're not so formal here," said Rita, after introducing them. "Calling her Angela is fine. She doesn't talk, in fact, can't talk – a victim of the last war with the Germans when they rolled across the country for one of their visits. This was at the start, before they started living like rats in holes and traveled through towns on their way to Paris, destroying everything they found. They took her from her home, killed her children, bashed in her skull with a rifle butt, then raped her. Uncontrolled men are mostly beasts, especially in packs. They could have killed her but perhaps they thought they were being kind. Instead they cut out her tongue, for sport I suppose, another trait of men, as is war itself. As you can see, part of her lived. She is an excellent cook and mixes tremendous drinks although most of our customers have their liquor straight. We couldn't be without her. We call her Angela because she thinks she is a little girl and we sometimes buy her dolls. Her room is filled with them." She hugged Angela who curled tightly under her arms like a little girl, her eyes looking up with the innocence and love of a child.

Slowly the girls started to drift down, each one giving Rita a slight bow: Sophie Hentouille, short, big breasted, long dark hair drifting over her shoulder; Bettina Schagin, not yet twenty, a crooked nose and a slight limp; Molly Cologne, Irish, red cropped hair and freckles, still wearing her lipstick; and Iziz Gilot Bretstein, a round German, white doughy skin, her hair an explosion of blond sprouting red ribbons dangling down her neck and shoulders. The girls often called her Ball of Fat after a famous French character in a short story. As they sat their conversation slowly warmed from a rough idle to a purr as they shifted through all the verbal gears until they hit the open highway.

"Nicole, you must join us - this is a wonderful place if you ignore the men – Pabst has the cutest little willie – and that Adolf, what a hulk, he almost crushed my ribs – I never made so much in tips as last night, the war must be winding down to spend so freely – I wouldn't say it on the streets but Rita has a house several blocks over for the French boys willing to sneak in. Most are very handsome, and clean, they never cause trouble and are always polite – Rita must clear them to enter and she is very strict. The men attempt to be brave about the war but they are really frightened children. Try it Nicole, you will have earned a fortune in months – it hurts no one and if there was more of it there would be no wars."

"You talk too much," said Sophie.

"Don't be silly," said someone next to Nicole.

"How is it outside?" said Sophie.

"Outside?" Nicole did not understand the question.

"Yes, outside this house." All noise ceased.

"Don't you go for walks in the afternoon?"

"That will be enough chit-chat," said Rita. "Nicole is still tired and you will have plenty of time to talk later." They girls lowered their heads in agreement.

A rough scraping sounded from the stairs. "That will be Oskar, Oskar Eckener the guard, bringing down Anton," said Molly, tapping Nicole on the arm. "Anton is Rita's husband, what's left of him. Oskar is so big he scrapes the wall."

Oskar's back emerged first, a solid sheet of armor plate, followed by his trunk-like arms, then his bent head pointed towards a smaller head that pulled through the channel next. He carried a small piece of man in a strange boxed wheelchair, no legs, only one visible arm, the shape of another under his shirt, a leather mask covering part of his face and skull. Oskar gently placed his chair at the head of the table, nodded to the ladies and left.

"I understand you are Nicole," said Anton, extending his good arm. I am sorry, but you see I am blind and can't find your hand. I understand you are quite beautiful."

"It's my honor," said Nicole, softly taking his hand.

"None of that. I feel the sympathy in your voice but it's not needed for me. I am out of it now and have no more fears. Good morning ladies." He grinned and turned his head from side to side. They all stood, walked stiffly to his side, and kissed him on the cheeks as he patted the sides of their heads. "You see, no man should be so lucky. I live in a house filled with beautiful ladies and a wife who approves. My legs, wheels now, take me wherever I like to go." The wheels had been attached to the box under him. He patted the box fondly. "I can still feed and clean myself and as for my eyes, I see better without them. I wear the mask so not to offend people with the hideous carving given me from a steel sculptor too eager to do his work. Rita says I wasn't much to look at in the first place. Of course the ladies are willing to service me because they know Rita doesn't mind, but I don't use them. I won't have it. A man in love has no need of other liaisons although I do enjoy them kissing me." He blew a kiss to them all and smiled. "Their lips and smell tell me who they are. One would think Iziz has the fullest lips but they are rather thinly packed, so much so one can almost feel the teeth underneath. She smells constantly of soap. The aroma of clover drifts from Molly and her lips are the fullest while Sophie smells like a Frenchman, fresh bread and onions. Her lips lack passion and are more like a friendly handshake. I don't think she really likes men." Sophie blushed. "Bettina, ah, there's a woman. Bettina cannot get enough of men and would probably work here for free just to have a night of them. We must keep an eye on her or she would be around town ruining our business. She smells of sex and passion and her lips are always parted by her tongue as it seeks copulation with yours. The man that marries her must be wealthy because a working man would have no energy to do his job. And you, Nicole, what about you?"

"I was hungry and Rita has offered me food and shelter." Nicole felt something sly behind his dark glasses and smiling face, a joke, maybe, or something more twisted. She did not know if she liked him or not.

"Ah," said Anton. "She is very kind but remember she is first of all a business woman. She will soon expect you to earn your keep. Come, let me feel your face."

He reached out his hands as Nicole leaned in. His hands were rough and his fingers roamed over every hill and valley on her face. She pulled back when he had finished.

"I don't know if I can sleep with other men." Her voice started to quiver. "I have…"

"Yes, another man. Posh," said Anton. "Just lay there and dream of your man. You are French and sex is our greatest game. We know the difference between fun, work, and love. As a pretty woman I am sure you had lovers before this last one. Do the same thing here, just don't consider them lovers. Strictly business, that's all. Besides, with the love and comfort you get around here from the help, the ladies will have you on your back in no time." They all laughed nervously except Nicole who quietly lowered her head.

That night, Nicole ventured into the greeting room as customers started arriving. Lights glowed low and warm, casting a blanket of yellow about the room. She recognized the song on the phonograph as something by Glenn Miller, a sweet big band sound less raucous than Benny Goodman or Chick Webb. American jazz music had been spreading across Europe for many years, both big bands and small groups. Something untamed lived in the music, something new and exciting, wild, animal-like, unknown to older European societies, a sound of freedom spiraling from a new and uncomplicated country not tainted by culture or superiority, a sound broken from the chains of sophistication and propriety, a guttural cry of individual recognition, an emotional referendum of spirit, soul, longing and laughter.

Civilian customers strutted in dressed in suits and polished shoes, most of them older pusillanimous men retaining the remnants of slight paunches in spite of difficult times. Alluvial chins flowed over shirt collars from the ones profiting from the war through outside arrangements, pasty chins and pasty faces, under-nose brushes glowing from grease and framing crooked teeth, yellow and black cinders burnt from smoke, and thick sausage lips sweet with whisky. Fat crowded their many rings as they picked at their fingers and imagined their own sophistication. Yet, they appeared harmless enough, jovial, animated in a rolling dough kind of way, and rather nontoxic. The German officers looked quite different, impeccably dressed in starched uniforms, walking upright and stiffly, everything quite formal including their talk. Their boots resembled black mirrors and many of them carried leather riding crops.

The customers had made their choices in women, although not always their final choices as they occasionally tossed back a thin one to hook a fat one or a young one for an older one, not as moist but more knowledgeable. No one seemed impolite, not the men nor the women. Oskar Eckener, standing with crossed arms near the door, had a calming effect on everyone. The nasty smell of French and Turkish cigarettes mixed with the sweet aroma of perfume and powder. Couples traveled up the stairs and usually returned within a very short time although the men probably imagined it to be most of the night.

"Nicole," Rita called. "Come and meet my friend Herman Henle. Nicole stepped slowly, careful not to trip, her head down. "This is Heir Henle, our party boy. Ordinarily he would be just another filthy Hun but he has always lived in France and has proven himself a decent fellow."

Henle clicked his heels together and tipped his head as he offered his thin warm hand. His gray handlebar moustache drooped like two flags of surrender. He looked older than he was and bones pushed against the skin from the inside of his face. If he were prosperous it was not in food.

"Herman is one of my oldest friends," said Rita, squeezing his arm and almost spilling his drink. "He is a gentle man, a good man, unfortunately a lonely man since the loss of his wife. No one will treat you better. Come, have a drink with him." She pulled the two closer together and walked away.

"My apologies," said Herman. "Rita can be forceful."

"I don't work here," said Nicole. "I mean, just below, in the kitchen, and upstairs cleaning up."

"Everyone works here," said Herman. "They don't always know it, or admit it, but they do eventually." He smiled at her rather shyly and innocently. "I don't mean to be rude. Truth is a rare commodity in war, almost as much as in peacetime. It certainly saves time, however. Let's sit and have a drink together. You have nothing to fear from me. With the death of my wife, typhus, you know, I can no longer be aroused. Perhaps one love was all I had in me. Maybe later we can go upstairs to your room and lie together. I still enjoy the feel of a woman beside me and you can be assured nothing will happen unless the sound of contentment bothers you." He led her to an empty table and ordered drinks.

Nicole awoke before daylight. Only the impression of Herman's body remained on the mattress. True to his word he had not requested anything more than to lay next to her, completely clothed and contented. His arm curled under her head and he held her close. Because she drifted off quickly, she did not know if he ever fell asleep. She placed her hands on the cold impression on the sheet.

She was the first one to arrive at breakfast and ate quickly. With her wig securely fastened, she hoped to take a morning walk before the other girls arrived. Angela seemed nervous with only her there and twice made an attempt to talk after looking toward the stairs. The kitchen looked more dingy this time. Perhaps she had not gotten a good look the first day. Dirty floors, unwashed pots and pans, grease and flour on the counter shown under the foggy light pressed against the small window cut through the concrete foundation. Smoke lingered in the lounge as she passed causing the room to stink of moisture, mold, whisky, and a hint of puke. A broken bottle of absinthe lay under a table, a hint of the green and potent liquor lifeless at the bottom of a glass surrounded with sugar cubes.

When she tried the door, it was locked. She shook the handle, pushed and pulled the door. Oskar Eckener grabbed her wrist from behind, pulling it away. She turned to face his expressionless face.

"I want to go out," she said. Oskar placed himself between her and the door and folded his arms. "Why can't I leave?"

Chapter 12

Nicole sat in her room combing what hair remained. It was growing, slowly, but growing and soon she would be better, able to venture outside without ridicule from others, able to conduct her life in quiet solitude. Perhaps, after turmoil, everything returned to normal in the world, even Heinrich and love, given enough time. He was out there, somewhere. Time was what she did not have. She would not have minded being a prostitute had it been her choice. She understood the mind and the body were two different entities easily separated. Men could do as they pleased with her body while her mind might choose to participate, or not to participate. Men were not easily separated from their minds. Their minds and bodies seemed riveted together. If this were not so, they could not have sex, could not enjoy the pleasures of the flesh. The mind and body must remain as one in order to have sex. As long as they remained joined they could have sex with anyone. They seemed to feel physical pain more deeply than women and love appeared to affect their bodies. A love gone bad ripped at their chests, caused them to be irrational, to swell like a mighty storm and crash against the shore with fists and even death. Yet, love is just a simple mental condition. Their minds had to link with their bodies to have sex but did not have to link with the person with which they had sex. If it did, they were insufferable. Knowing this inseparable connection in men, she thought of her next move and paid special atten-tion to her looks for the evening. All she had to do was to convince Herman to take her home, who then had to convince Rita to agree.

Business seemed especially good, and Rita, was especially pleased. She appeared to have her own secrets as she worked the room pouring drinks to the patrons, compli-menting the girls on their good looks and their choices on being with such handsome and brave German soldiers and French businessmen. The drunken soldiers, tunics partially undone and mussed, tipped their glasses in congratulations to themselves and toasted the Reich, usually sarcastically and tossing in phrases like, "the little paper hanger has gotten us into a fine fix" or "let's see him fart his way out of this one," the words rolling through tunnels reeking of puke and whisky.

Herman entered through the back before midnight looking for Nicole. He handed his coat and hat to Oskar as Rita greeted him, arms outstretched, a smile on her painted lips and thick mascara covering the bruises around her eyes.

"Oh Herman," she said, throwing her arms around him and kissing his cheek. "Back so soon?" Herman, placing a finger on her lower lip, nodded and smiled, something he seldom did even during the best of times. "What would you like to drink? Cognac? Some champagne? You're not the beer type. How about a whisky?"

"A glass of water, if you please," he said. "I would like to rest a few moments. Perhaps a drink later, when I've caught my breath. Is Nicole here tonight?" he said, knowing she could not leave. His fingers played with one another then tapped out a rhythm on his knees.

"I have just the easy chair for you, plush and warm and in a subdued corner. I'll get you settled then call for Nicole."

"That is a fine bruise you have on your face. Anton should not be so cruel, especially with the one he loves."

"Life is not without its problems," she said, through her cheek as she walked away.

Nicole seemed willing enough to be with Herman. She carried something interesting about her, some kind of mystique, an air of desirability on which he could not quite place his fingers. From the darkness he watched the German soldiers, wrinkled uniforms, several unshaven, others boisterous and drooling spittle from the edges of their lips. How different they were than at the start of the war, starched and proper uniforms on starched and proper soldiers, men on top of the world willing to exchange pride for death. No pride or arrogance remained, just enough polluted energy to savor each hour before the final losing battle. Pride did not goeth before a fall; pride dribbled from the neck down in fear induced sweat, the sharp smells of cordite and earth lifted through the air, tracers slicing the night like bloody razor cuts, screaming and splattered guts, hunger, thirst, pants filled with piss and shit, freezing limbs, filthy men and ruins, armies of lice crawling up a man's ass and sleeping in his armpits before pride leaked over his boot-tops to puddle onto the torn earth, then scurry safely away to stiffen the backs of the winning side before the losing armies fell forever, planting themselves on, or under, the mud.

Nicole was not built of pride. She was sensitivity and sensuality, her touch like rose petals across a cheek, her breath the mint of eternal spring. And looks? Her beauty was just beauty made even more so by her personality and warmth. Having a woman required sacrifice. What would it take to possess her, what part of him must he surrender? By the doorway near the steps he saw her emerge, slowly, an apparition of balmy sexuality. She wore nothing slutty, no garter belts holding silk stockings or tight bras where breasts reached over the tops to breathe. She walked quietly straight to Herman.

"You've come again," she said. "I was hoping." She offered no sloppy inviting kiss but rather a gentle handshake. Herman raised the delicate hand to his lips as he half stood.

"I'll bring another chair," he said, suddenly annoyed that Rita had not seen to that before. Lately she had seemed pre-occupied.

Nicole sat and placed her arm over his, both feet on the floor, knees together, not tangled vines wrapped around tree trunks like the other girls did with men.

"I have been thinking of you," he said, almost afraid to look into her eyes, or maybe not afraid, maybe just embarrassed or shy. He worked them up slowly pushed by longing.

"You should have a drink," she said. "You're uncomfortable." Nicole knew he needed to be drinking or she would be drawn elsewhere for the sake of business. Rita wanted her to work, to spread her legs and earn her keep. No longer would she tolerate a virgin bordello whore. Either she earned her keep tonight or face a night with Oskar only to be tied to the bed the following night and offered as a rape fantasy to Germans far too eager to comply and willing to pay extra for the privilege of once again feeling supreme and dominant. She motioned toward a corner and a whisky, the most easily watered down drink in the business, appeared. He was her ticket out. She had to play it carefully. The slightest mistake might ruin her plan indefinitely. Be friendly, not overly friendly; keep a hint of sexuality and vulnerability, yet no weakness in her voice; touch him only in appropriate places and always on his face, his neck, his hands; be honest, admit that you will always love Heinrich and you will go to him when you can after the war but that you are willing to stay with Herman until then, stay as a wife, a loyal faithful and caring woman who will never do anything to embarrass him. He needed to take her away but do not say it abruptly; slide it in as a hint, then decide how to proceed depending upon his reaction.

They talked quietly revealing the little secrets people are willing to concede as they grow closer. They watched the girls travel up and down the stairs with disheveled laughing officers who returned minutes later, embarrassed and quiet.

"Nicole," said Herman, looking into the room. "Would you consider living with me, being my companion? I will never sexually betray my wife but I enjoy your company and I sleep better with you by my side."

Nicole was shocked. All the planning she had done was for nothing. How to play it now was the problem.

"I am flattered," she said, needing time to think.

"I have a little money although I am not exactly a wealthy man. I am certainly well off and able to meet your financial needs."

She pulled back her hands to see if, without any physical connection, Herman would feel differently. Physical human connection clouds the mind.

"I don't believe Rita will release me," she said, seeing how far Herman would go to have her.

If Rita was willing then what about Anton? or Oskar?

"The arrangements have already been made."

"What?"

"We have already spoken. You can leave tonight. I know you love another man. In return for your companionship I will do my best to find him."

"Must you pay a lot?' she said, embarrassed after saying it and not sure why she mentioned anything except out of nervousness.

"Pay?" He turned to look at her. "Pay what?"

"For me," she said. "I know Rita is a business woman and is reluctant to part with an asset."

"Nothing, I paid nothing." He said, looking confused. "People are not bought and sold like chickens or cheese. On the contrary, she seemed pleased at my request and said she would have your belongings packed when you are ready to go. "

Nicole was also confused. Why could she leave and not the others? A tinge of guilt hit her mixed with the elation of freedom.

"Let's go now," she said. "I want to get away from the dark, the smoke, the soldiers." She looked around the one room for one last time, the girls busy at work, Oskar guarding the door, Rita, at a motion from Herman, coming their way.

"Are you ready?" she asked, smiling at them both then drifting a glance toward Oskar. Oskar nodded before walking upstairs. "We must go upstairs with Oskar and leave out the back."

"But Oskar?" said Nicole, suspecting trouble.

"We must go now before it's too late."

They followed her up the stairs as she laughed and acted nonchalantly as if she were going to get them settled into a room. Oskar put his ear to Rita's door then nodded to her. She placed a finger to her lips to indicate silence and they walked quietly to the rear exit. She did not follow them out, just kissed them both and handed Nicole a small wad of francs. In the alley waited a suitcase for Nicole. Herman picked it up and they left for his home to wait for the war to finish.

Chapter 13

Anton lay stretched out on the bed smoking a cigar, his perfectly intact legs crossed at the ankles, one hand across his stomach, the other clipped to the cigar. He felt the elastic in each muscle tingle. Soon he would never have to slither into the box again and pretend to be crippled. It had been a good disguise, a valuable deception, useful in his line of work. His eyes remained sharper than the eyes of younger men and he watched the smoke rise from the cigar and change from a thick cloudy stream to a thin white disappearing parachute slowly falling about the room. He seldom received as much money as he would this time from the underground. Even Herr Seydlitz, local Gestapo head, never paid so much for information on the underground. Something big must be in the wind, he thought, something big enough to make another sale if he could find a bit more information. Rita's girls would have to get busy and squeeze every last drop of information from between German legs to sell to the underground. Then, he would gather what he could from the underground and sell the information to the Gestapo.

The war had been good for him and the safe in the cellar had gone from empty to bursting, deutschmarks and franks co-habiting in harmony and insulating the gold and silver piled in stacks. Diamonds, precious stones and jewelry he kept in a hole under several bricks. The damp increased their luster making them drip with beauty. He had more money than he had ever imagined, more than he could spend in a lifetime or, several lifetimes. Of course, Rita would want her share but he easily managed her. To the brains of the outfit go the major spoils. Give her a few trinkets; she would not know the difference. Women remained dim creatures, carried no business sense, had little ability to plan anything clandestine or devious. Even the capacity to lie convincingly was beyond them and only an idiot was blinded by their schemes. Only the

Germans, the world's greatest buffoons, willingly gave them information. The only facility women had for lying concerned sex. They could have sex in the yard with several men then enter the house carrying a basket of potatoes without any hint of mendacity or deception. Not even a kiss on her lover's mouth, fresh juice dribbling from between her legs, left any impression more sinister than complete loyalty and devotion.

But a man! He could lie convincingly about anything except sex. Simply touching another woman's hand appeared as a poster across his face advertising infidelity. Anything more than a touch and God started laughing at his ignorance. Man's problem was not eating the apple but attempting to gorge on the whole fruit bowl, then quietly spread the seeds hoping Eve would not notice the vines growing from his ass.

What a good boy am I, thought Anton; what a clever boy; what a rich boy. How easy it was to play both ends of stupid people and let the cash flow to the middle and into his pocket. He heard Rita opening the door.

"Have the girls come up with anything more?' he said. Rita appeared tired as she dragged herself to the chair and looked into the mirror. "Answer me!" said Anton, in no mood for her to break his happiness. "Information, I want information. This night could make us or break us."

Rita picked up a brush and pulled it through her hair. She looked tired, very tired and she noticed several strands of gray hair in the bristles. Crows had etched their tracks around her eyes and for a moment, just a moment, (for she was never one to linger on the past and did not possess the capability of fiction,) she remembered the beauty she had once held, then shrugged her shoulders and remembered what was troubling her.

"I'm worried for you," she said. "Perhaps you are going too far. Everyone is frantic these days, uncertain about the future."

"Not my future," he said. He had difficulty controlling his smile. "It's secure and you'll be with me so long as you behave. I don't want to drop you but I will."

"Both sides are anxious." She picked the gray hairs from the brush and turned to face him. "When people get desperate they find excuses for mischief. The Gestapo is never your friend, never anyone's friend. If you have information to sell to the underground, Seydlitz will find out and that will be the end."

"Forget that Nazi prick," said Anton. The Gestapo is the most ignorant and ineffectual organization in the whole German government, in any government. They couldn't even find the invasion plans for Normandy! As always, I have made sure no one knows about this information. Besides, tomorrow it will be over. I'll have a few trinkets of information on the underground to sell to Seydlitz. He will lap them up with pleasure and never be suspicious. The Gestapo recruits from the bottom up with the only requirements being the ability to light a fire and snapping a whip. Ignorance is their strong point. Even the girls laugh because they must be physically directed to their destination or they lose their way." He blew out another cloud of smoke. "And what about the girls? Information, I said, information!"

Rita knelt beside the bed and rubbed Anton's chest. He did not react or acknowledge her presence. She turned her head to the side to prevent the blow she suspected might come.

"They are working on something. They will have it by tomorrow night." She flinched and tightened her jaws expecting a blow when she saw his arm move. He patted her on the head.

"We'll not worry about it right now," he said, a smile coming over his face. "Today is too good to be interrupted with disappointment. Tomorrow is another story. And the new girl? Is she at work?"

Rita thought quickly. News of her leaving would throw Anton into a rage from which no one would be safe.

"She is the one gathering the information."

"Her?" he threw his legs over the bed and sat. "And how can that pretend virgin get any information?"

"I thought it was a risk worth taking," said Rita, looking into his eyes for understanding.

"What are you up to? What kind of risk?" His hand tightened around her arm.

"She went with Herman – just for a day or two."

"You stupid…" He lifted her to her feet.

"He paid in advance," she said.

"How much?"

"Paid for two whole days plus some extra," said Rita. "He promised to return her. He knows something and I think she can get the information. She will have it in a day or two but it will cost."

"What do you mean?"

"You were right, as always, to think she is not so stupid. She said she will get the information but we must let her go and stay with Herman."

"Maybe you're not so stupid, after all." He drew her close and kissed her. She responded. "You're my woman, all right. The hottest thing I have ever seen." He bent her over the bed and started pumping, one hand on her back, the other holding the cigar to his lips as he started to laugh. "What difference does it make where she goes so long as she gets the information."

Anton left early the following morning as Rita slept. She awoke at the tapping from the door.

"Yes," she said, curling from the warm covers. She could not remember when she had slept so well. "Come in."

Oskar entered carrying a tray. He placed it onto a table and slid it beside the bed. Cheese, a fluffy plain omelet, cold slices of duck, butter and jam, rested on the plate, surrounded by two warm croissants, the brown skins flaking over their sides. He poured tea and coffee into the porcelain cups.

"You've always been good to me," said Rita. She kissed his forehead. "Has it all been arranged?" He nodded. "Of course," she said. "How could I have doubted. Such tasks are dangerous yet you have always come through. Tomorrow is another day, a brighter day. I worry about you. Such is the burden a sister carries for her brother. Anton would be surprised. He has never known, will never know, not now. A new peace will reside in this place and we shall make it the best and the most respected brothel in all of France. Men will come from around the world just to say they have been here. They will be treated like royalty and charged like royalty. Women will beg for employment. One must think big in order to become big. The sex is always the same, just a slippery receptacle, but think small and one will soon be turning tricks in the alleys for wine money. The more we charge the better they think the sex is. Nothing is more difficult to believe than the excitement a man gets over an object through which a woman pisses and bleeds. And Nicole?"

"A comfortable night," said Oscar.

"Send up the girls in an hour to help get me dressed. Tell them to wear their best walking clothes. We're going outside to have lunch with Nicole and Herman."

Herman's house, a moderate sized three-story stone affair beside an avenue of other stone houses, felt quite comfortable to Nicole. She had slept with Herman, wearing a large night-shirt, on a bed so filled with feathers she thought she might drown. He had held her for some time before rolling over and drifting off to sleep. In the morning, he was gone so she placed her toy feet onto the cold floor and balanced her way to the vanity to comb her hair. The hair was now longer than twigs above her scalp. It appeared to be growing back even fuller than before. She drew into a robe and slippers before going downstairs for toast, jelly and tea. She looked through the cabinets and took inventory: cups, plates, teapot, etc. The entire house appeared to be spotless and she discovered why when the maid entered and frightened her.

"I'm so sorry," said the maid. "I have a key and Herr Henle has instructed me to enter to do my work. He is seldom here."

The maid was small and underfed, her face covered with pockmarks under her white scarf. She rubbed her rough hands together against the apron and kept her face low and appeared to be embarrassed by the scruffy brown shoes that she tried to hide by pinching the toes together.

"Just a small fright," said Nicole. "Herr Henle said nothing about a maid."

"I hope it is not a problem," she said. "I can return later, whenever is convenient."

"Don't be silly," said Nicole, offering her some tea. She declined and nodded.

"I should be off to work." She started to turn.

"Not yet," said Nicole. "Have you worked for Herr Henle long?"

"About two years. Before that my mother worked here. This is the family house."

Nicole sipped the tea. "Where are they now, the family, I mean?"

"Still in Germany, I suppose. His mother is French and his father is a German officer. They moved there at the beginning of the war. Herr Henle says little about them. He is a very fragile and quiet man, a good man. It would not be my place to say he is lonely but he misses his wife, Rivka. You never saw two people more in love." She placed her hand to her mouth as if trying to shut herself up. "I must go. Always I talk too much."

"Of course," said Nicole. "I'll not bother you, and do come and go as you please. Let me know if you need anything."

Nicole was not sure of her place, her job. Could she leave as she pleased? Go out with friends? Ask people in? Did she cook and help clean? These questions needed to be answered before she could start to be comfortable. What about money, if she wanted a drink or a lunch in a restaurant? Was she allowed at a bistro? Was there a curfew? She returned to the bedroom to think and to get dressed. Opening the suitcase she was surprised to find it filled with new clothes and a small tobacco can containing an amount of money. She rolled the bills in her hands.

From the street she felt a rumbling. She held a new dress to her chest as she twirled toward the window. Below, a worn Panzer III tank clattered by blowing up a cloud of black exhaust, followed by a Tiger tank squeezing between the buildings and sinking into the cobblestone road. Soldiers had piled onto the tanks and held on to any protrusions. Those nearest the turrets were able to sit and lean against the steel plate. An armored radio car followed then two trucks stuffed with soldiers, standing room only. Nicole briefly watched them pass. She had seen many German Wermacht vehicles over the last years but seldom in town and never down narrow streets. She saw Herman pass behind the last truck and walk toward the house. Quickly she slipped into the dress and started downstairs. He had already entered when she arrived, panting and still adjusting the dress.

"You're back," she said, as if his return was a surprise.

He looked at her in confusion. He placed his greatcoat on the post and adjusted the hat on the peg above. He placed his arms around her and kissed her on the cheek. In the kitchen, Nicole started to heat a kettle of water containing tea leaves.

"Is the maid here?" said Herman.

"She's working on the next floor. She seems a nice young lady although she frightened me. I did not expect her."

"There is much I have not told you." He pulled off a piece of black bread and nibbled at the edges. "We have always known her family. Has she said anything about the situation?" Nicole fiddled with the kettle and pretended to see if the water was boiling. "Don't worry," he said. "She has always been a talker and it is no bother. From her mother you could get nothing, seldom even an answer to a direct question. Minou has an answer for everything even if she does not know the answer."

Nicole poured the tea into a cup.

"She said that your father is in the German Army and that you loved your wife very much." Herman motioned Nicole to sit.

"Her name was Rivka Klajnbort," he said. "A Jew, so you can understand the problem for my family, especially the General. He stayed here as long as possible."

"They did not approve?"

"Nothing like that. The General is a professional soldier and never discusses politics. He is also a good father in spite of his son's frailty. The whole family loved her, her kindness, her compassion, her simple beauty. Her family, who owned a sausage business, tolerated us. She was not a practicing Jew but an atheist. They suspected I was to blame but that is what drew me to her in the beginning. I had never met a Jewish atheist. Her family were also gracious people and never said anything derogatory or unkind about my father's profession. He had always been known as a fair man. It was the feeling they emitted, one of disgust and distain – always too polite like an over-eager actor playing a part he detests. The General protected them from the Gestapo for as long as possible. Herr Seydlitz eventually had them removed along with the other Jews, homosexuals and Gypsies. My father could only protect Rivka, and at great risk to himself and his position."

Nicole poured another cup of tea for Herman and one for herself. It was good to hear him talk and she placed crackers, cheese, and a knife on the table in hopes he would continue.

"The General was never a man of prejudice, unusual in a staunch German general. I think my mother added to that. Being French, she accepted, or at least tolerated everyone and their ideas. I know he felt some disappointment in me but he never showed it. I was not fit enough to be a soldier and was not inclined to be one anyway, although I would have to save him any disgrace. Removing Rivka's family killed her. She lost all interest in life, seldom left her room. One morning I rolled over to wake her and she was dead. Not a mark on her, just dead."

"I am so sorry," said Nicole. She placed her hand on his arm. "Soon the war will be finished and you will find another wife."

"No," he said. "I will remain true to her in body and in spirit. It's just that I sometimes get so lonely. I thought of having Minou, the maid, stay with me but it is difficult for her to remain quiet about anything and, let's be honest, she is not quite an intellectual. One occasionally needs talk as well as a warm body."

"I am no thinker," said Nicole.

"Perhaps not. But you have an innate intelligence and seem to know something about the world, the way to act and dress in different situations, to understand the difference between right and wrong as you see it."

"I am flattered," she said, sipping at the tea. "You think too much of me for having known me for such a short time."

"I want you to live here as you would in any house, to be comfortable, to come and go as you please, visit others and have them visit you. I have made a list of businesses where you need only to give my name to get what you want. I have also placed some extra spending money in that porcelain jar on the far left of that shelf. I have invited Rita and her girls over this evening for a small party. She did not mind closing for one day and said the girls need a rest to be at their best for when the Americans arrive. She hears they are sexual brutes with members like those of a horse that will not be deigned. Most importantly, they have money."

"I already miss the girls although I am still confused at why Rita released me."

"You are different than the others," he said. "She did not want Anton to ruin you for the sake of business." He sliced off a bit of cheese and placed it onto the bread. "Another thing – I have found your lover…"

As if she had been punched in the stomach, Nicole bent slightly, the breath running from her. She felt sick, excited, empty, joyous, depressed, thrilled, disheartened, energized, tired, every emotion bumping against one another in confusion not knowing or understanding their place in the queue just soaking up what oxygen remained in her lungs. Her hands held her face then covered her eyes as she started to cry, then laugh.

"Where! Where?" she blurted. "I must know."

"He is with the 9th Panzer Division," said Herman, quietly. In the west. Somehow he has escaped the Eastern Front so there is hope of him surviving."

Nicole threw her arms around Herman and kissed him over and over. He did not respond, just took her kisses and affection with grace.

"Can I go to him; can I see him?"

"This is not possible," said Herman, lowering her back into her seat. "The General, my father, found him almost immediately. You may write, nothing more until the Germans surrender. Even if you write there is little chance he will receive the letters. The entire army is in confusion and mail is not a priority."

Nicole threw her head back, covered her face, and continued to sob.

"How is it possible that I have found such a good man as you?" she said. "How can I repay you."

"You have only to stay with me until the war ends. Already the last of the German troops are leaving for the front and you must prepare for Christmas. The General – and I call him that because of my love and respect for him - says it will not be long now, not more than a year or possibly less. The Wermacht is on its knees, the Luftwaf is destroyed. The Allied bombing has prolonged the war by destroying cities, killing women and children, thus raising the resistance of the people and the soldiers. Had they left the cities alone it would probably be all over by now. Although equipment is being produced at a record pace there are no men left to use it, and no fuel to keep it running. Stay here and we will see what the end brings." He drank the last of the tea. It was cold.

For Nicole, life seemed almost worth living again. How different things looked than as if Anton had gotten hold of her.

Anton, thoroughly enjoying the day, a smile on his face, spring to his walk, had also not felt so good in years. The information in his briefcase would finally seal his fate and make him truly rich for the first time in his life. Yes, he would get more information from Nicole, but he had enough already. He did not want Rita to know, wanted to keep her off the track, create doubt having enough. The money might not last a lifetime, as he had thought, but to have it in his hands, no matter how briefly, would make him a happy man, make all his scheming worthwhile. He could leave and make a home anywhere, someplace sunny, on the coast so he could watch the sea endlessly battle the shore, in the mountains sitting by the fireplace with a brandy in his hand while studying the giant snowflakes fall onto his estate, a woman under each arm. He might not even take Rita. She was, after all, starting to sag and wrinkle. She never minded him with other women but he did not need any unsightly decorations hanging about when he could have new.

He sat on a bench and lighted a cigarette, keeping the briefcase close but not so close that people might think it was important or valuable. He rolled the cigarette, cheap French Gauloises, with his fingers. No more of these, he thought; American cigs all the way, Lucky Strike, Old Gold, Camel, all the best all the time.

Ordinarily he was not anxious to arrive anywhere on time. Today time dragged and regardless of how hard he tried – his heart racing, his chest pumping in short breaths, his muscles tensing - he could not push time along fast enough. The second hands on his watch appeared to drag, restraining himself from the grand prize. Only money and personality equaled power and he had no driving personality. Hitler, always a poor man, had personality, personality and charisma, an iron will that had taken a beaten country and, through personality and words, built it into a mighty nation. Yet even his personality could not continue the farce forever, just like money would not last forever. What a fine time, regardless of how short, to be on top of the world. Of course, with the right investments, the money might linger, even after his death. What good was that to him? No, spend it all, burn up the night with a mighty flame and die in the ashes.

Anton smoked another cigarette and then another. He was earlier than he had imagined. The café was down another block and he stayed far enough away so that no one would be suspicious of his sitting for so long. There was not much work for anyone these days and, even in the best of times, people refused to do anything at a rapid pace, anyway. They were used to people sitting for long periods but it was best to be safe. The people continued to shuffle past him paying no attention. Most of the women dressed very well, some conservatively, some provocatively. Many wore shoes with higher heels. Silk stockings were rare so some of the women had drawn a seam line down the backs of their legs with eyebrow pencils to give the illusion of stockings. They all wore dresses, no pants. Even the women who wore coveralls for factory work always wore dresses on the streets. They took pride in being women.

Anton stood, glanced up and down the street, and started toward the encounter. He looked straight ahead, a single mission that needed to be accomplished. He walked slowly into the café and saw his contact drinking a glass of wine. He placed the briefcase at his feet and folded his hands on the table.

"Is everything in place?" he said, looking from side to side.

"It's a nice day," said Toan, placing a wrapped package tied with thick brown twine onto the table between the wine glass and the bottle.

"Not yet," said Anton. "I would like a look."

"That's rather dangerous in here, isn't it?"

"We're out of the way," said Anton. He reached for the package and untied the string carefully folding back the paper, just enough to see the francs and deutschmarks inside, the fantasy colors of street fairs or the circus. He quickly snapped the paper together and retied the string. Toan tapped the table with his fingers.

"Come on," he said. "This works two ways." He looked over Anton's shoulder and nodded that everything was clear.

Anton unfastened the leather straps to the briefcase. He cracked the lid an inch and slid the case toward him. Toan lifted it high enough to get a better look.

"It's all here?" he said. "Everything about the German attack?"

"Yes, yes. Everything. All the troop movements now taking place in the west and the placements of every division. I may be able to gather a bit more. Of course it will cost."

"Greed is never a good thing," said Toan. He nodded and Anton reached inside the briefcase to slide the papers inside a tan folder that he handed to Toan. He placed the package of money inside the briefcase and fastened the straps.

"I may have something else by next week."

"Yes, of course," said Toan. I will be here on Thursday for lunch. I don't trust that you will be."

"Don't be silly. This can be good for both of us," said Anton. "I know you are a patriot but I suspect you are also selling this information to the Allies. You would be a fool not to."

Anton turned to leave as Herr Seydlitz pushed through the door. Two more Gestapo followed him, guns pulled. Three more regular soldiers pushed inside, rifles at the ready.

"I see you have come for lunch," said Seydlitz. "Something nourishing, I hope." He crossed his arms across his leather sleeves.

"Herr Seydlitz," said Anton, his lips shaking. He managed a chuckle. "I didn't know you were in the area or I would have invited you." He looked around. Toan had disappeared. "I may have something for you, something very important."

"Of course. You always have something for us. Very loyal, yes, very loyal. I know I have something for you," he said. He reached out for the briefcase, lay it across a table rapidly evacuated by a young couple, and opened it. He peeled back the paper revealing the money. "I see business is good."

"I was buying some information, something you could use. Of course the information was so valuable I needed to bring everything I had. It could change the outcome of the war."

"Something like troop movements from the Allies?" he smiled, as the men surrounded Anton. "No; perhaps you were selling, not buying – selling troop information about the Germans."

"How silly. You could not be more mistaken. I would never betray you. Sit down and let me explain…"

"Stupid French fool." He slapped Anton across the face. "Do you think I would actually let you get your hands on any real troop movements? I am not, after all, some kind of an idiot."

"You don't understand," said Anton, taking a step backwards. A rifle in his back pushed him forward. Seydlitz kicked him between the legs. All the patrons had lined the walls, motionless, afraid to move, all wanting to leave but not stepping toward the door. Anton groaned, cupped his hands, started to beg.

"Please, please," he said. "It is for you I am working." Seydlitz kicked him in the face. Blood gushed from his nose. Seydlitz sat, leaning over and talking quietly, his elbows resting on his knees.

"We have much to talk about," he said. "I hope you last longer than most. Few men live long without their skin. Don't worry, however; we'll just take a strip at a time." He lifted his head and said, "Take him away." The men kicked him through the door before picking him up.

Seydlitz snapped his fingers. The waiter quickly poured him a glass of wine and left the bottle. Seydlitz lit a cigarette and waited for Oskar. Oskar did not sit when he entered, just stood over Seydlitz. Seydlitz handed him the briefcase. "Tell Rita everything went as planned. She is quite the spy. Say it was good working with her and say thanks to her French friend, the one pretending to be with the underground. He has considerable acting skills. I trust he will return the information to the usual spot? He was so convincing I almost mistook him for a member of the underground, myself."

Act III - The Mirror Reflects Itself

Chapter 14

Chau, already missing his American friends Bix and Steve, yet anxious to return home, had smelled Vietnam a day before the ship's arrival from San Francisco. The aroma of ancient soil, years of rotted foliage packed tight by monsoons, fresh vegetation of entwined trees and jungle, the thick scent of rice paddies, all had lain subtle on the air. Even the sea had taken on a heavier oily flavor of salt and humidity. As the ship pulled into Haiphong Harbor the tang of cooking fires carried the taste of smoked fish, rice, banana leaves, bubbling pho, French bread, sewage, sweating bodies, a layer of perfume from prostitutes, and exhaust smoke clouding the air from the pipes of ring-worn vehicles. The smells of war also lingered: diesel fuel, airplane fuel, cordite, rotted bodies, and canned food. Ships from many nations crowded the docks as white French passenger liners, red and blue Japanese and Australian cargo ships, gray French warships for transporting troops, supplies, and equipment, fought for space to be unloaded before traveling back to sea loaded with rice, tea, and rubber. As he walked down the gangplank, Chau thought how good it was to be home among his own people, in his own land, his own food, a country he understood. The servant Ling met him on the dock.

Ling bowed low when he saw Chau. "It is with much pleasure that I welcome you home," he said. Chau dipped his head and offered his hand, a western custom Ling had never felt familiar with, and gave him a brief hug causing Ling even more discomfort.

"Ling, my friend," he said, "I am pleased to see you. Having my feet on my own country is like rising from the dead to again walk upon the earth. I hope you are well? You look good, firm and healthy." He stopped a moment. "Uncle, the other servants?"

"Retrieving your luggage. They will deliver them to the house. All is in order, as it should be."

Chau had been gone long enough to feel slightly uncomfortable being waited on and pampered. What had once felt natural now felt slightly ostentatious. He hoped he would not soon become complacent. Taking care of himself away from home had been good training, had made him stronger and more confident in his own abilities, more European and independent. The training had been small since he always knew he had his father and the family money to fall back on but he had never gotten used to excess. In a daring move in France he had even ironed his own shirts although it had been easy enough to have them done. He understood class distinctions as a fact of life yet also understood it was his father who had raised the family to a higher level. Some people had no desire to rise above coolie status. If everyone in the world strove to rise higher in the world, who would carry the luggage? He enjoyed thinking for himself, contemplating subjects deeper than arranging the day for servants and making lists of dinner guests, not for enjoyment but because they might prove useful to the business. His father had taught him the stealth, trickery, and deceit needed for a successful capitalist in order to increase wealth. Thinking of the good of the people, as did most Vietnamese, had lost its humor early, outdistanced by more individualistic thoughts while traveling the road to personal gain and success. One could take pride in his country, even attempt to advance it in a national society, without actually joining the people. As the Americans understood, greed makes nations great. Caring for an entire population required time and money, time and money better spent elsewhere. No country, including his own, became eminent while caring about others. The need to surge ahead, leaving some classes in the dust of progress, was necessary for success. He wanted that success, wanted to move his country ahead, and the French were leading the way.

Workers crowded the docks shuffling crates, pallets, barrels, barbed wire, artillery pieces, sacks of grain and boxes of foodstuffs. The Vietnamese, supervised by French civilians or French soldiers in slouch hats, short-sleeved tunics, shorts and scuffed boots, supervised the workers. French soldiers often confused the locals by wearing shorts. Shorts were for children; men wore pants regardless of the heat or humidity. Chau realized that through his travels many Europeans wore shorts in hot weather, the German civilians, British soldiers, and French soldiers. He understood Australians did also but not Americans, at least not U.S. soldiers.

Ling opened the back door of the Citron as Chau, who had started to enter the driver's door, climbed in and tweaked his body to sit comfortably. Having Ling drive him, a skill he had mastered, seemed silly. Bix drove him most of the time in the U.S. but having Ling drive somehow seemed different. Being driven in other countries was an act of equals, two or more people moving toward a destination and all willing to drive. Equality was an individual act and Americans lived it - if not always in practice at least in rhetoric. They were not however, as independent as the French. Americans often joined together on common beliefs and attempted to subjugate those who opposed the common trends. Not the French. Every Frenchman was his own person with his own opinions, his own voice, and accepted by all, even those with opposing ideas. Freedom often caused difficulties for finding common ground and making uniform decisions. The French preferred chaos to unanimity as witness of freedom and individuality. Each person had his own accepted ideas and opposing ideas rarely interrupted a friendship.

Ling threaded his way between crowds, scooters, bicycles, cars, army trucks, rickshaws, food stands, old ladies, old men, kids, beautiful spotless women dressed in traditional aoi dai. Vietnamese remained an eagerly clean people who often bathed four of five times a day. The French never understood that and occasionally held classes, especially in the villages, on cleanliness, to the confused farmers. Did the French want them to bathe just once every few days or weeks as they did? The villagers refused to go unclean and had no desire to smell of sweat, dirty clothes, greasy hair, with breath of garlic and onions, like the French. Such requests were unthinkable so they listened quietly waiting for various treats offered after the speeches. With the French, rewards often followed torment. Chau admired the French yet he preferred the bathing habits of the Vietnamese and Paris offered a constant offensive barrage of foul aromas to his nose.

His father's house, designed by a prominent French architect, was built in the old French quarter off Nguyen Sieu street and surrounded by many French-built two story buildings. They towered over Vietnamese buildings but appeared small against buildings of commerce. Chau learned to read the importance of buildings in a society. The group that controlled a country always built the tallest buildings: castles with the kings, European churches with the clergy, powerful government buildings, and now towering structures of business. Workers on bamboo scaffolding continued to erect French buildings built of stone and mortar. The spidery bamboo encased the buildings in a crazy, ever-tightening web. Ling drove through the gates of the family home and stopped beside the fishpond. Lazy fish were free to live out their lives in slippery comfort, fed daily and never eaten, unlike village ponds where people crapped into the water to feed the fish then, in the circle of life, later ate the fish. In villages life was a constant cycle: life and death, young and old, hot and cold, season following season, generation following generation, light and dark, plenty and famine, eat and be eaten throughout eternity. Europeans refused to believe such ideas. Generation followed generation yet there was often no connection or respect between them. The old were discarded and younger people never asked their advice. When things died they died and refused to return. Each garden crop was a new crop not a continuation of the old crop. Light did not follow dark, the sun chasing the moon as the pagans believed. Progress proved they were both always there, always occupying the same sky. Backward thinking remained redundant: forward thinking always advanced. The French thought forward and were the best thing for the country. Don't accept that dark followed light – turn on a light bulb, supply your own light.

Chau's father met him in the garden, a short handsome man resembling a successful European male where rotundness equaled wealth. Not overly round he maintained a respectful girth equal to his position, clean shaven given most Vietnamese had few whiskers, dressed in a fine silk suit of French cut, a black tie, and wearing fine brown leather shoes handmade in Europe. Everything about him appeared immaculate, not a black hair out of place, perfect teeth slightly dimmed from smoking, and beautifully manicured fingernails. Chau welcomed the smells of aftershave and Scottish Rattray pipe tobacco as his father hugged him vigorously patting him constantly on the back. Although they had always been close the amount of affection startled him. As an only child he always received much attention from him yet his father was careful not to spoil him, a talent many doting parents avoided. Chau had virtually anything he ever wanted yet, because of his father, he seldom wanted much. He understood that knowledge weighed more than possessions, decency and kindness bought more than arrogance and greed. The greatest wealth a man could have was the respect of others. Although all people should be treated equally, the ambitious, lucky, and resourceful ones managed to exceed the pack. Few people succeeded without the help of others and a person's success often depended on those working under him. Such thoughts kept Chau Asian. He believed in success without orphaning respect for those less successful. A truly gifted man remained comfortable conversing with the poor and uneducated as well as with the enlightened rich. Yet he understood a servant must be treated like a servant and a governor like a governor. Everything in the world had its place.

"My heart soars," said his father.

"Mine too, Father," said Chau. "It is good to be home in your house." His father looked smaller than he had remembered and with a concern behind his eyes.

"Home in our house," he said, stressing the word our. "You must tell me all about your travels, what you have learned of the world, how the Europeans and the Americans think and act – especially what they think of us or if they think of us at all. But there is plenty of time for that later. Let's have a cool drink and some food. A party has been planned for tomorrow night in honor of your return. Ling has worked very diligently on the details. Many French and Vietnamese dignitaries will attend to show their respect."

He placed his arm around Chau's shoulders as they walked into the garden. They sat beside the fishpond, the water looking slightly green, under an awning covered with cooling vines and pink flowers. Ling brought the drinks and a tray of bread, cheese, cucumbers and tomatoes. The Scotch burned Chau's throat as it wandered down and smoldered in his stomach. He enjoyed the slight alcohol taste of the burnt wood. He tipped the glass toward his father.

"And what have you learned my son?" His father smiled with the bright eyes of a child awaiting a tale of wonder.

"I thank you for the trip, Father, and for the education," he said. "There is so much to tell that a great deal remains a jumble waiting to be sorted." Chau nervously twitched his fingers together.

"Let me help with questions. How was France, their attitude about the world and about us? Are they very concerned about the Viet Minh?"

"I found the French to be the most interesting and the most confusing people on my journeys. They believe in freedom more than any others. What I mean is they do not just talk about it, they practice it to the fullest. The people are obstinate and opinionated yet kind loving and sensitive, often at the same time. They agree on nothing and argue constantly like bitter enemies, then drink, laugh and agree to meet and argue the following day. Very strange, very rewarding."

"Yes," said his father. "They have always been bewildering and unique." He nodded for Chau to continue. Chau attempted to corral more thoughts.

"The country is populated with Communists. All unions are under the directions of the Communists. It is perfectly acceptable to hold Communist meetings, or any other kinds of meetings and to march unmolested in the streets. The war there is much on everyone's mind. The older class, the rich and higher classes, appear to favor the war while the younger, middle class and poor peoples, are against it. Of course, like I said of the French, all classes and ages are represented on all sides. Any kind of consensus is impossible." He reached for the food tray; stopped and slid the tray toward his father, not taking a slice of cucumber until his father pinched a piece of cheese.

"That is how I have often remembered them because of my visits there. Here, we just see the political side," said his father. "They are admired and hated everywhere yet they care not either way. They are arrogant although accepting of all things. What are they saying about the war?" He tore off a slice of bread and placed cheese onto the corner of it. His hands seemed delicate and daintily nervous. "Too much cheese. It makes us fat and lazy," he said, patting his stomach.

"Many of those who are against the war are not against the war." Chau tried to think of how to explain the situation. "They are a group inside a group. They claim that all the allies in the last war had agreed to relinquish their colonies as a sign of freedom and democracy, the reason they were fighting. President Roosevelt, of the United States, attempted to hold them to the agreement fearing they would break their word after victory and hold their colonies. When he died and the war was won that is what happened. One French group feels, in the name of freedom, that no country can colonize another and view such behavior as a form of slavery, a disgrace to France. War is fine. Just not this war. Another faction is against the war for financial reasons. The cost of the war far outweighs the benefits. It has placed a burden on all French citizens and only a few of the rich benefit. There are also those who believe that all war and killing is wrong, that no Frenchman's life is worth giving for the wealth of others or that no invaded country should lose a life attempting to defend itself." He looked to his father for an expression but saw none. "Making something of their attitudes is difficult, something that represents them as a whole."

"Ling!" His father clapped hands. "Bring the bottle." He crossed his arms and said, "An interesting statement considering that no French soldiers serve in foreign wars unless they volunteer. Their military is only for defense. The Legion does as it pleases, fights anywhere, but only the Legion, volunteers, or Colonial troops, many Vietnamese."

"I didn't know that." Chau pondered the new knowledge.

"Only the officers, because they do not believe colonial troops are capable of being leaders, and the volunteers are French. The Vietnamese fight with them mostly because of money or because they want to be on the winning side. Some Vietnamese are made to fight as are the troops from their other colonies like Algeria and Morocco."

"No one can best the French," said Chau, smiling. He downed his whisky in one gulp causing him to choke. "They have the best of everything, the weapons and equipment, the airplanes. The Viet Minh must scrounge for everything, use whatever cast-offs they are given."

"Ho Chi Minh says 'we will beat them with their own weapons,'" said Chau's father. He motioned for more cheese and vegetables. Ling already had a tray ready. "You're a good man, Ling," he said. "My trusted friend. How long have we been together? Since before Chau's birth, I think. Pleased I was to have you here after his mother died. You have helped raise my son as if he were your son and taught him all the finer things in society."

"You are very kind," said Ling. He bowed and started to speak more but Chau's father motioned him away. He bowed again and backed from the room.

"His mannerisms are very Japanese," he said. "They always have been." He thought a moment, drifted away, painted a sour face, then drifted back. "What the French may lack is determination and courage, a market the Viet Minh have cornered."

"Without respect, father," said Chau, "I am surprised to hear you say such things." Chau knew no soldiers more brave than the French. "The French are fearless and non-stoppable. They have often stood their ground to the last man, not a step backwards."

"So it is said." Chau's father leaned over his knees. "Perhaps it is my age. An enlightened man must view all situations without bias. Anyone who cannot be objective cannot know the truth. Perhaps I am the one confused." He sat back and appeared to look through his son. "What of the other countries?" he said.

Chau was not sure what he meant. Was he being admonished for narrow thinking?

Perhaps his father was criticizing him for having learned so little. He tried to form his thoughts carefully to impress his father.

"The English are also arrogant," he said. "They stand straight and proper and are well spoken. Laughter comes to them without my understanding. They are direct and do not talk of one thing while meaning something else. They do not speak kindly of others, especially the Welsh. On the other hand the Welsh people appear generous and carefree. They work much harder than the English and do it without complaints. The English live off the backs of the Welsh, also the Hindus, but are annoyed that they will not bow to them. The Scots, difficult to understand, are also friendly and live as if the English do not exist. I still do not understand if they, like the Canadians and Australians, are part of Great Britain, or not. What is their relationship?"

His father shrugged his shoulders. The sun had started to lower, casting a pink glow to the sky. The mosquitoes would soon appear for dinner.

"I was not there long enough to learn much, just a week," said Chau. "My short time in Germany was much the same. The country had been almost destroyed in the war and people are building everywhere. Entire cities flattened to dust now rise higher than ever, thanks to the United States who is supplying all the finances."

"Yes," laughed his father. "The best any impoverished country can do is lose a war with the United States. And what about them? It is one place I have yet to travel and know little about them."

"There is not enough time to describe them," said Chau. "The nation, as a whole, is so confused it is a wonder it functions at all. The hatred between different groups is palpable. The Irish hate the Italians, the Italians hate the Jews, the Germans hate the English, and they all hate the Negroes. Almost all the native peoples have been killed or driven to worthless land. Traveling through the country is like traveling through Europe; every section a different country. They are obstinate, greedy, spiteful, ignorant and opinionated. Yet there is another side to them, a curious side. All the nationalities there, willing to annoy one another, are often the first to help one another during times of crisis. They are free thinkers, generous to a fault, intelligent, creative, and will help anyone they can, except – and I never learned why - the Negroes. They hate Communism yet know nothing about it, and, have no desire to learn anything about it. They are often willing to accept what is told to them. It is not against the law to be a Communist, but they find ways to prosecute them. To sum them up, the country is so large and so diverse that they represent all people and ideas from all the world. They preach freedom as long as it does not interfere with their general views on capitalism. Probably the people least represented are the Annamites or Vietnamese. I never saw a single one."

"Interesting," said Chau's father, rising slowly from his chair. "You should sleep now. Tomorrow I wish to hear more about the land and about your adventures. I understand they were many and exciting. Tomorrow we shall take a walk through the city and then, in the evening, the homecoming party."

"The party?"

"In your honor as the eventual head of the Chau family. As a special surprise I have invited General Salan. He has assumed command of all French forces here."

Chau looked surprised. "Not General de Tassigny?"

"A tragic story that we will discuss tomorrow. For now - rest. I too have much to say tomorrow, some of which may be depressing or confusing to you. Know only this, that I love you and, that as a man, you must decide your own way in the world and do not make decisions on what you believe to be true, but what you know to be true."

Chau stepped closer and touched his father on the shoulder. "Father, you're not ill?"

"Not at all. Tomorrow we will continue."

He suddenly looked older as Chau watched him walk away, slightly stooped, his shoulders sagging. Maybe he was concerned about General de Tassigny. They had all placed so much hope on him to defeat the Viet Minh and now something was wrong.

Chapter 15

Ling awoke Chau early to a blanket of humidity. Chau peeled open his eyes by stretching his arms. "Your father has planned a big day," said Ling, laying out the day's clothes. "A tour of the city, reliving history, lunch and tea, then the welcome home party tonight. All is in order for a blissful day."

Chau could not believe how well, or how long he had slept as he nestled back down onto the feather mattress, unable to rise. He reached out his arms again, yawned, and stretched his legs pointing his toes toward the wall and a painting of Ngo Quyen, an early Vietnamese hero who defeated the Chinese at Bach Dang in 939 B.C. He watched the picture and waited for his morning erection to deflate. It usually rose before he did but soon flattened at the sight of sunshine.

"Does he think I am a tourist?" he said. He drank a glass of water Ling had placed beside the bed. "I have lived here since birth; I probably know the city better than he does. He was born in a small village in the highlands."

"You are his number one son and he continues to teach you about the country. No man can know enough to be safe in these difficult times."

"I am his only son, Uncle. Why, are we not safe with the French defending us?"

"Of course. There is no need to worry. He has raised a fine son. Perhaps he has trouble realizing you are a man." Ling poured a cup of tea and handed it to Chau. "It can be difficult to admit. He is proud of you."

"The boy or the man," said Chau, placing the hot liquid to his lips.

"Regardless of how old you grow, you will always be his boy. I am sure he has great plans for you, a good wife, a glorious future. With good comes bad, with joy comes sorrow, with wealth comes poverty, with intelligence comes stupidity. Everything has its opposite."

"Has he always treated you well, Ling?" He looked over the cup to see Ling's expression. "Has he been fair? Are you happy here?"

"Such questions." Ling looked surprised. "I have never met a better or more decent man. I look after him as he has looked after me. He is the most respected man in the city by both the Vietnamese and the French."

Chau handed Ling back the empty cup and worked his legs over the bed placing his elbows on his knees and supporting for his head with his hands.

"And the French?" he said. "Do they really get along with him or do they just pretend to like him?"

"The French?"

"Do they respect him, as a man?"

"They constantly seek his advice. When trouble arises with the people he is often called to quell the disturbances. Of course he is respected by the French. No one in this country could throw a party and have so many dignitaries, especially French, attend."

"The French are the future of Annan," said Chau. "Without them we will be lost, ploughing fields with buffalos, not tractors, treating illness with leeches, not medicine, learning only to survive but not to live. I do not understand why so many of the people oppose them."

After dressing, Chau stood outside on the sidewalk, leaning against the building and smoking a cigarette while waiting for his father. His country seemed small and crowded after traveling the United States and Europe. Most of the enterprises in Vietnam concerned food. People hustled here and there carrying baskets of vegetables or sacks of rice over their shoulders, and riding bicycles stacked with cages of cackling chickens, feathers sticking through the wire. With ropes, men pulled reluctant potbellied pigs to slaughter and fresh fish still flopped in baskets waiting for the boiling oil. The outside food stands seemed endless.

"You are looking well, Father," said Chau, when his father arrived.

"Let us start at the beginning, Ngoc Son pagoda," he said. "A good walk clears the lungs and a receptive and logical mind soon follows."

Chau's father asked questions about the trip to get Chau talking. Once started, Chau could hardly fit in the adventures and the things he had learned. They soon reached Hoan Kiem Lake, crossed the Bridge of the Rising Sun, and stood before the Pagoda. The bridge seemed as stunning as ever: a long red arch built by the Chinese and typical of their temple compounds. Beside the pagoda, old men played Chinese chess and dominoes. The voices of chanting monks emanated from inside. Willows drooped over the edge of the lake.

"It is here peace came to Vietnam," said Chau's father. "A giant tortoise rose from the lake and snatched a magical sword from Emperor Le Thai To and brought peace to the land."

"I remember," said Chau. "Such silly myths. They hold back progress."

"Many times I brought you here to play. Then, you loved the stories."

"Children love many things," said Chau. He watched two ducks paddle through the shade crossing the water. "When reason arrives, myths become lies. Perhaps it is better to tell the truth from the beginning."

"How would you grow?"

"I don't understand?"

"Growing is casting off a former truth, found false, to be replaced by a newer one. The more that is cast off the more one grows. Eventually all knowledge must be discarded to reach the final truth. W cannot grow without the little lies that lead us in the correct direction and truth remains elusive."

"And what is the truth?" said Chau. "What is truth and do we know when it arrives?"

His father said nothing and they continued to walk. They followed the path east and stopped at an ancient banyan tree.

"Nowhere on earth is there such a tree," said Chau's father. "Look how it spreads and has lifted some stones and grown around others."

Chau did not understand. Yes, it was a nice tree and very beautiful but the world was filled with many fine trees, some more beautiful and many much larger. For centuries masons had built walls around the tree and people continued to stuff incense into its cracks and between its limbs. Offerings of wine circled the base.

"It resembles a living temple," said Chau's father. "Merchants once made ropes here but most of that business is gone. And look there, where we passed. The area is known to the Vietnamese as Dong Kinh Nghai Thuc Square."

"I remember it," said Chau. "They talked of it in the French school. The nationalist movement started here in the beginning of the century. It grew into Communism and Ho Chi Minh and the Viet Minh."

"They are a dedicated and committed group of men, regardless of which side you choose."

"Honoring the brave is old thinking. Intellect and education is what counts today," said Chau. He crossed his arms. "Do you think the French will win? They are smarter than the Viet Minh."

"So they tell us," said Chau's father. "They are also very brave. Does that not count?"

"If combined with intellect it should be a winning combination."

"Are not the Viet Minh also brave?" Chau's father looked into Chau's eyes making him uncomfortable.

"The Viet Minh want to hold us back, to keep us in pajamas bent under the hot sun to root around in the mud. That makes them stupid. They cannot win even if they are brave. How much smarter it is to work less by using a tractor than to slop in the mud behind a water buffalo."

"Yes, one man can do the work of an entire village. What happens to the rest of the men? What do they do?"

They started down an alley and past the Yen Thai Communal House, a long low roof stretching to a courtyard. People were busy cooking on the sidewalks. Not far along they entered an open-air market. Customers fingered fruits and vegetables, clothes, hats, and trinkets. Past another, larger market, Chau's father stopped to peer into a raft of bamboo bird cages and stick his fingers inside to get the birds to bite. Tobacco and pipe sellers lined Hang Dieu Street. Chau's father bought a classic French pipe and some tobacco.

"I only smoke Scottish tobacco," said his father. "They soak it in whisky."

"This is what I mean," said Chau, pointing to the buildings ahead. "Look at the beautiful filigreed French Colonial buildings. We could never build anything like that."

"But we did build them." Chau's father chuckled. "People are often blind to the obvious. We are capable of building anything. The question is, do we want to build as the French request or do we build as the Vietnamese like. Regardless of your respect for the French, we cannot stop being Vietnamese. The French show us respect as long as they can use us but underneath they still view us as half-wit coolies."

Chau felt as if he had been subtly chastised. Had not his father made his fortune from the French? Did he not respect the French, speak French beautifully, dress in European clothes, send Chau to French schools?

They walked past busy merchants selling clay bowls and teapots on Bat Dan Street, some turned in plain earthly colors for practical use, others brightly painted and fired. Workers made the bowls in shops beside the Red River and carried them into town after completion. Near number 52 Bat Su Street, they stopped for coffee by a low tile roofed traditional house.

"What of General de Tassigny?" said Chau, sipping his coffee. De Tassigny had been one of Chau's great hopes for the future.

"Very sad," said Chau's father. "A man respected by all, even the Viet Minh." He slowly shook his head and looked toward the street. A legless man begged on the corner as two Buddhist monks passed.

"He came in our hour of need," said Chau. "Without him we might have forever been a third world and backward country. He brought pride to the country and to the French soldiers."

"Yes," said his father. "He was a great man to many."

Chau remembered the parade honoring his arrival as his father related the General's history. Just his name inspired confidence, European sophistication and professionalism – General Jean de Lattre de Tassigny, soldier extraordinaire. He had represented France at the German surrender and may have been France's most admired soldier. Totally charismatic and an immaculate leader, he inspired soldiers everywhere. At the age of 61 he had enough stamina remaining to rebuild the confidence of the soldiers and the people of Vietnam. Although autocratic he instantly motivated his men.

Soon after his arrival, he staged a removal of inefficient French stall officers returning them in disgrace to Europe. He required total loyalty and refused to have anyone on his staff he did not know or trust. Realizing his soldiers had been badly led by cowardly officers, he sent the troops a message: "I promise you that from this point on, you will be led!" His deputy, General Salan, carried out the plans. General de Tassigny remained absolutely fearless and once, after flying into the front lines to take command of an operation, he responded to his headquarters personnel, who pleaded for him to return because of the danger, "…then come and get me out." He quickly had General Giap and the Viet Minh on the run. He placed rear echelon soldiers into mobile units, convinced Vietnamese to join the French Army, and won support, finance and material, from the United States. He built a series of concrete forts across the delta as everything started to go his way.

Chau's father completed his tale saying it all ended in depression when his only son, Lieutenant Bernard de Lattre died while leading his troops against Regiment 88 near Ninh Binh. The general continued as best he could and remained upbeat and positive around the men, continuing to win victories and reclaim land. But inside he was beaten. Then, doctors diagnosed him with advanced cancer. He fought both battles relentlessly until the last minute, dying within a few weeks after leaving Vietnam.

"A great man," said Chau. "I should have paid more attention to the European papers while I was away." He felt embarrassed at his lack of knowledge concerning recent events but the rest of the world had little interest in the problems of France or Vietnam. Occasionally something might appear in European newspapers. He had never seen anything about the two countries in the United States."

"And his replacement, Salan?"

"General de Tassigny's principal fighting general. Always first into a battle, he understands the policies and the tactics yet he does not inspire the men as did the General. The Viet Minh will have an easier time with him."

They continued to walk to the Hanoi Citadel, built by the Nguyen dynasty in the 1800s. Chau's father pointed at the structure and again mentioned that the Vietnamese could build anything. Walking through the ethnic Chinese district, they passed many bins and pots of herbs and natural medicines stuffed into small drawers in dark wood cabinets: bear gall bladders and monkey paws. The combined aromas felt intoxicating. Houses and buildings dating from the 17th century with narrow entries and low moss-covered tiled roofs seemed endless. They walked into a dark smoky communal house on Hang Dong Street to view the banyan tree in the courtyard. Chau's father talked of Vietnam's history and how they had tossed out all invaders. Now the invaders were the Viet Minh and Chau knew the French would cast out.

Buildings became more French as they passed Quan Chuong Gate and Chau's father spoke of the great scholar Nguyen Sieu, and of many important Vietnamese teachers. They entered the Bach Ma Temple to view Buddhist statues and altars and the massive red pillars. The temple was built to honor a legendary white horse that helped King Ly understand where and how to defend the city from invaders. Not much of Vietnam's history was taught in local French schools, and very few legends told. What Chau had learned was European history.

"I am getting older," said Chau's father. "Perhaps we should talk seriously before going home. We will need our energy to impress tonight's guests."

Chau was also tired and concerned. There appeared to be something somber happening with his father. Chau enjoyed the walk but the hint at intrigue disturbed him. His father always retained a level calm never losing his temper, never depressed, the most evenly tempered man Chau knew. That made it difficult to know what concerned him.

The Sofitel Metropole Hanoi Hotel looked as gallant and sensuous as when it was built in 1901. It remained a showcase of French sophistication. Invading, civil, and liberating armies had hoisted their flags from the roof. Dignitaries stayed there in opulence and luxury catered by Hanoi's finest servants, cooks, prostitutes, and bartenders. Rich oiled wood covered the floor; cane furniture filled the lobby and classic crystal fixtures practically dripped from the high ceiling and down the walls. The men passed the pool and entered the Bamboo lounge. Two French Foreign Legion officers in shorts sipped whisky at a table. Officers often frequented the bars of the hotel, slinky dark Vietnamese women under their arms. Chau's father found a quiet table in a secluded corner. He was careful to look for eavesdroppers before sitting. He ordered whisky for them both.

"This whisky is from Scotland," he said. "Oban, very rare here." He placed the glass to his lips letting the liquid slightly sting the flesh. "With just a touch I can taste the wood and fire."

"I ask for forgiveness father, but there is something on your mind," said Chau. "I can clearly feel it."

"We are often too formal in our society," said Chau's father. "A son should not have to ask for forgiveness to ask what is on his mind." His smile at Chau revealed the love he held for his son. "What have you learned about capitalism in your travels?"

"Capitalism?" Chau had not expected the question and did not believe that was what was bothering him. His father nodded and waited for the answer. "It is a good system for those willing to work. People who work hard will rise to the upper level of earnings and respect. Everyone has a chance to succeed."

"Is that true?" said his father. "Does everyone have the same chance to thrive?"

"Of course. Schooling is free for young people and the finest of them advance to higher and better schools."

"I wonder?"

The two legionnaires started laughing as another joined them. They hugged and kissed and slapped one another on the back before sitting as a humble and bent Vietnamese scurried to the table to take another order. Dressed all in white he looked immaculate.

"You have doubts?" said Chau. "Everyone has an equal chance if they want an equal chance. Many people do not. They refuse to learn even if the schooling is provided free." He thought of the countless street people he had seen in the cities of the United States or of the ignorant trash who had killed the woman in the South. Of course everyone had a chance if they would take it. It all seemed so obvious yet he knew his father seldom believed in the obvious.

"The world is often more complicated than we think," said his father.

Chau looked toward the French officers. They had switched from laughter to seriousness then back again. More drinks were brought to them.

"It is possible but I do not assume it is true. One may still move on to a better life," said Chau. He downed his drink and ordered another one. The questions, not his father's demeanor, sounded like an interrogation.

"If a person starts a successful business that requires employees, is he entitled to earn the greatest amount of profit by paying the employees as little as possible?" said his father. Chau did not understand what that had to do with a better life or with an education.

"If he owns the business, he may take what he can," said Chau. "Without him there would be no business so, no profit. He had the initiative and the funds to start the business."

"And the money...?"

"Of course the money. What's his is his."

"Suppose a person started a business and no one would work for him. Would the business be a success?"

The question placed Chau on overload. The words rattled around in his brain. His father wanted something but what? What was his point?

"He needs people to work unless he has a business he can operate himself," Chau finally said.

"Then, who makes the business a success?"

Chau thought capitalism seemed so simple, especially if he did not think about it and just accepted it as the good thing he was taught.

"I suppose the workers make the business a success. But they cannot do it without the owners."

"Since workers make a business a success, should they not share in greater profits?"

"I suppose," said Chau.

"If the owner takes all the profits, does he not keep it within his family so his family has the money to start other business until a few people have most of the money?"

"I suppose," said Chau.

"The French are the businessmen, the Viet Minh, the workers who want the wealth to be more evenly distributed and they want a say in the business. It is just an example," said Chau's father. "For a truly intelligent man, anything that is important, anything that affects others, must be thoroughly explored. Even something as important or simple as religion is seldom thought out by most people. They will research a new vehicle, compare many of them, before making a choice. Why not religion? This has always puzzled me."

"I have never thought about it," said Chau. "Still I get the feeling that something deeper is troubling you. Perhaps it is not my place to ask."

Chau's father ordered another drink and cheese, for both of them. Two French officers replaced the three soldiers who had left.

"There will come a time when you will want to judge me. I ask that you consider everything before making a decision."

"I will always love you, father."

"I fear I have placed your life in danger." He reached across the table and grasped his son's hand. "I am giving you a small envelope. It contains an address and some money. If anything happens to me, you are to leave Hanoi immediately. Take nothing. Do not inquire about me. Talk to no one, understand – no one. Do not ask for help or advice. Leave as quickly as possible and never return. When you arrive at the address, state you have come for the mountain package. Do not open it until you are out of the city and alone."

"Father, I must know…"

"Nothing more will be said of this. Understand that you are my life and I had no right to place you in danger. Let us go and prepare for the party. There are many important people you must meet."

Chapter 16

Ling had laid out Chau's best suit - a hand-tailored white cotton double-breasted - and a blue striped tie. The supple brown leather shoes and belt had also been made by hand. Ling helped him dress before a full-length mirror. Chau turned from side to side and stared into the glassy pond thinking he was quite a handsome man, a man in his prime, virile, strong and intelligent. Self-indulgence was not flattering to a Vietnamese but, except for his skin, he had never been a Vietnamese.

"I expect a grand entrance," said Ling.

"Something is troubling my father?"

Ling brushed the shoulders of the coat and said nothing, as if he had not heard, as if straightening the coat was the most important thing in the world.

"You know him better than anyone." Chau tried to see the expression on Ling's face but he showed none. Emotions seldom rose to the surface on a yellow face as they did on those of Europeans. "You must tell me!"

"He has said nothing to me," said Ling. "No one ever knows what he is thinking, no one."

Chau opened his top dresser drawer and looked under his socks. The small envelope was still there, folded in half. It held an address and some French francs. The address was at the edge of the city and he had been tempted to visit there, to see what kind of place it was. Perhaps it would give him an idea of the trouble. The other drawers contained casual shirts and sweaters. Chau looked in the chiffrobe – all suits, slacks, and sports coats, formal shirts, ties hanging from the door, leather shoes for daily wear and brogans worn in the warehouse, and two brown fedoras on the top shelf. He had not noticed before but he had no traditional Vietnamese clothes, not even slippers.

The smells of the food hit Chau before he entered the room. He stopped to straighten his suit and breathed in the sweet odors of fish, the aroma of steamed vegetables and rice in various sauces, the scents of powder and perfume from the women. He heard the subdued clatter of metal and porcelain, passive voices, the hint of western music, something by Tommy Dorsey. It sounded dated but pleasant after his experiences with the itch of new jazz in New York and San Francisco. He opened the door to his premiere as the only son from the house of Chau, educated, sophisticated, world traveler and bon vivant. Upon his entrance one clap sounded in the distance and gathered other hands together as the applause grew to polite exuberance. Chau dipped twice at the waist and started moving toward his father who was standing with several French officers on the other side of the room.

Chau worked his way around tables of food that ran into the courtyard and were lit by paper-covered lamps, a concession to the Chinese in attendance. He had never seen such an abundance of food: bubbling pho noodle soup; sea bass wrapped in banana leaf and dashed with vanilla; peanut crusted shrimps; green mango salad; grilled fish tikka in pandanus leaves; coconut covered beef; bun cha; rice noodles; banh khoi, the doughy pancakes filled with vegetables, herbs, and shrimp that he so liked; live prawns soon to be sizzling in flaming rice whisky; seven different curries of various colors from red to green; tomato covered with imported mozzarella; nicoise chicken salad in crème sauce; steak tartare; dessert glaces; crème caramels; fresh fruit; pizza; roasted salmon; wasabi mashed potatoes; green tea; smoked duck; tempura soft-shelled crabs; sautéed eel mixed with chili and lemon grass; and many dishes he did not recognize. Whisky spiked with cobra venom was available for those who wished to carry on the party later into the night with sexual liaisons until the morning.

Guests had dressed immaculately: the men in clean pressed suits of fine silk, the women in the latest Paris fashions, dresses and wraps in subdued or raging colors from red to black, colors crying to break free. The clothes seemed rather odd on the oriental women, something Chau had not noticed before. Only servants wore traditional dress.

"Father," said Chau, offering his hand. His father grabbed his hand with a firm European grip unknown by most Vietnamese and placed his arm around his shoulder as he pushed him forward.

"Let me introduce you to General Salan," said his father.

General Salan stood stiffly without a hair out of place. The creases on his pants could cut steel. Rows of ribbons covered his tan tunic.

"My son," said Chau's father, Bo Dan Chau.

"I am honored," said Chau, knowing he should have bowed slightly but too European to even try. "I have heard of your exploits for many years and welcome this opportunity to meet you."

"My aides, Major Raffray and Lieutenant Sahraoul," said General Salan, indicating the men at his sides.

General Salan and his aides also had firm handshakes, grips the Vietnamese did not possess, grips indicating power and dominance. Their eyes exhibited intelligence and a countenance of courage emanated from their presence.

"I have read about your exploits, under General de Lattre," said Chau.

"He can never be replaced as a leader or as a man," said Salan. "How unfortunate things ended up so badly for him. The fortunes of war? I think not; just bad luck."

"How do you feel the war is going?" said Chau.

His father broke in and said, "Enough of that for now. This is a night of celebration. We must save any serious talk for later. After much alcohol has been consumed. Let us eat."

After dinner and social mingling in which older women hopefully introduced their daughters to Chau, the men retired to the den. Ling brought in drinks and additional snacks and placed them on a carved table surrounded by plush chairs. The constant humidity had dropped slightly. Bookshelves covered the walls containing a large selection of volumes from philosophy to fiction: Hume, Kant, Rousseau, Shakespeare, de Maupassant, Voltaire, Hemmingway, Faulkner, and Steinbeck. The room appeared like the den of any wealthy European.

"We are pushing back the Viet Minh in most places," said Salan. "It's only a matter of time. Even a defeated boxer needs time to understand his fate. Of course the highlands have always been a problem, too many mountains and valleys, too many villages supporting the Viet Minh. If we could get them to fight it would all be over in weeks but the little cowards always run. Asians haven't the guts for fighting."

"I am not a military man," said Chau's father, pouring whisky for Salan. "I should think they would want to fight, a chance to show themselves as men."

"Cowards. All yellow peoples of the world are all cowards… Of course I mean no offense to you and your family."

Chau's father nodded. "Of course not." Chau felt offended.

"The Viet Minh tap us on the nose and then run away. They are very courageous when they do fight and that makes them easy to kill. It is more annoying than anything else. New arms and equipment are coming in daily from across the Chinese border. Most of the artillery has come from captured American guns in Korea."

"It is a wonder they beat you so often," said Chau's father.

"Stupid people always fight hard," said Major Raffray. "The more stupid they are the harder they fight."

"A toast to the French and their fighting efforts," said Chau's father, raising his glass.

"I have recently returned from the United States," said Chau. "They, like the French, believe in freedom. Perhaps they will help us defeat the Viet Minh."

"They are sympathetic to our cause. They have recently increased their aid to 60 million dollars a year." They all lifted their glasses in another toast. "To freedom-loving Americans," said the lieutenant.

"The General is quite the hero," said Chau's father. "He graduated from the military academy of Saint-Cyr and has won the Croix de Guerre."

"Many years ago," said Salan. "Such things are of no importance and not worth mentioning." He sucked on a piece of cheese. "In the first world war my father was a doctor and he wanted me to follow in his footsteps but there was adventure in my blood."

"The General has been here so long he is called an ancein d'Indochine," said the major, without enthusiasm.

"All the years I have spent in intelligence have been a great help," said Salan. "If I do not know about something, I discover it very quickly." He turned to Chau's father. "I understand you know Ho Chi Minh?"

"Hardly a secret," said Chau's father, without so much as a quiver. "I met him briefly in Paris many years ago. He was attending some conference and attempting to get recognition for Vietnam. He was not allowed to talk nor was he recognized as Vietnam's envoy. I went with a group to meet him at a bistro. An interesting man."

"Now he is a great Communist," said the major.

"A nationalist, I should say," said Chau's father. "The Communists have given him recognition, while he has been ignored by the rest of the world, but I think he cares little for them."

"Certainly you are not defending him?" said Salan.

"It would be a lie to say he is not charismatic. He also had hoped the United States would come to his aid."

"How stupid! The United States!" said the major. "Why in the world would he think the United States would support him?"

Chau's father laughed. "Of course, it is ridiculous. Since the United States supports freedom, rather than domination, he felt they might help a nation struggling against French Colonialism. He simply does not recognize the French as our friends."

"The Vietnamese are too stupid backward and incapable of governing themselves," said the major.

"That is why we so appreciate the French," said Chau's father. "We can never be a success on our own. And what do you think, General?"

"I think the Major fancies himself a politician. I am a soldier and I do not think beyond that. If France asked me to fight for the Viet Minh then I would fight for the Viet Minh. Soldiers who think beyond their duty are poor soldiers and I fancy myself a very good soldier."

Chau spoke little as the evening wore on. He had not known his father knew Ho Chi Minh. Why had he kept it a secret? It seemed he knew almost nothing about his father.

Chau did not see his father again for almost a week when they again walked to the lake. The weather looked bad and they waited for the downpour that was sure to come. He watched the reflections of the trees on the green water.

"What I am to do?" said Chau. "What is my station in life?"

"You have been neglected," said his father, touching him on the knee. He looked toward the couples walking near the lake. "Such a beautiful place…"

"I have my education – what do I to do with it?" Chau's voice cracked quietly. "Am I to work in the business, find my own job, get a job in France or the United States, or just be a rich person spending your money?" He felt reluctant to bring it up but did anyway. "The envelope. What does it mean?

"I have a place for you," said his father, "a place we can sit in private and talk like two intelligent men; a place I wish you to stay from now on."

They walked back toward home. Chau watched the sky. The rain would not announce itself in sprinkles like in other countries. Here the sky opened in a jagged slash and the water poured in tons, suddenly, weighty, drowning everything low to the ground. The fury passed quickly and often the sun shown afterward. Chau's father took him to an empty house, beside his home, one he owned and planned to remodel and give to Chau as a wedding gift. He unlocked the door, they entered, and he locked it again from the inside. They walked upstairs to a comfortable den overlooking the old house across the street. They sat in the two leather chairs. Chau looked at the sofa, the shelves of books, the teak desk and chair, the carpet in the center of the room, and noticed a door to a bathroom.

"This is your house," said his father. He lifted a bottle of wine from beside his chair and poured it before giving Chau an Old Gold cigarette. He stuffed his pipe with Rat Ray tobacco. "It was for your wedding but you have not taken any particular woman so perhaps you should have it now."

"I have been busy and many things are on my mind. Women take time, too much time at the moment. I am content with what I have. I thank you for the house."

"Ling says you have visited the brothel several times."

"I still have needs."

"That is good," said his father. "A woman is a large part of a man. If allowed, she often helps him to think wisely and carefully. I suspect the women you visit at the brothels are not scholars?"

"Warmth is what they have, and a sense of joviality," said Chau. "They are very pleasant and ask very little."

"Their knowledge in some areas must be unquestioned. When you find warmth and intelligence in a woman you will have found a wife. The joviality comes in the beginning of a relationship, but soon fades. That is the nature of women. The warmth will be there on your death bed."

Chau looked over the street. He could clearly see the side of his father's house. A food vendor mixed meat and vegetables over a coal fire on the street. People in Hanoi practically lived beside the streets, cooking, selling, drinking, gaming with friends. Steam rose above the pan. He had never seen a vendor there before. They seldom worked in the richer areas of town.

"We are going to have a serious discussion," said his father, "and I know, as my son, there will be no emotional outbursts, just quiet and thoughtful reasoning." He nodded toward Chau and looked into his eyes, a western trait they both carried. "I supply information to the Viet Minh."

The statement kicked Chau in the stomach and emptied his breath. Had he heard correctly? His ribs started to tumble around his lungs. His brain expanded to bursting causing a terrible pain as if a vehicle were slowly rolling over his head, then collapsed as his thoughts tumbled into the cavity and filling it again. He attempted to suppress his voice yet words pried their way through.

"…the Communists?"

"Listen completely," said his father. Chau forced his mouth shut. Air plugged his ears and his father's words floated through miles of water. "I have helped you to receive half your education. Perhaps I should have included parts of the other half to keep your life balanced. The balance will come all at once as if you have caught yourself at the last minute from falling over a cliff. Don't let it tip you over. All good contains bad; all bad contains good. There is no right nor wrong in the world, just decisions and choices. Make a decision and stick with it. The decision will be correct and incorrect and you must make the best of it."

Chau saw someone lean over the vendor and hand him something. The man was Ling. He moved to the side of the building, squatted and lit a cigarette.

"You have forgotten your heritage, forgotten you are Vietnamese. That is your choice and perhaps I gave you no other. If you wish to become French, go to France and make your way in the world as a Frenchman. Your choice is your choice and does not affect our relationship. You will always have my support. I am Vietnamese and have always been Vietnamese. One must befriend his enemy to defeat his enemy. He must know his enemy, empathize with his enemy, see the world from his enemy's eyes. Only then can the enemy be defeated. Arrogance will defeat the French as all arrogant peoples are defeated."

Chau's father remained calm and spoke kindly as a teacher might to a confused child or to a favorite student. He poured more wine and re-lighted his pipe.

"You have seen the French as civilizers and they have been very good to you. They have built hospitals and European schools, improved infrastructure, and, for those in the correct class, people like us, brought some law and order. They have offered opportunities for me to amass a fortune, to rise above the common Vietnamese by using them for their, for our, purposes. Others have become petty functionaries for the government, laborers, servants, and craftsmen. The church has turned out a force of literary foremen to increase the wealth of the church. Everything has been done for the benefit of France, not for Vietnam. People in the cities are mostly content with the French, which is why the Viet Minh have made few inroads here. The people have work and money. Corruption, prostitution, and moneylenders, have joined the French. We have always had these problems, if they are problems, but not to this extent. The French are not bad people they simply want whatever they do not have. They are easily satisfied by having everything."

Chau looked back to the street. Ling was on his second cigarette. He looked up at Chau and stared briefly, then nodded his head. Chau nodded back.

"Villages have been most affected. You have never lived in a village, also my mistake. The villages have always been self-supporting. Because of the people's beliefs about living in the world, living with nature, they seldom grow more than needed. An elder sits at the head of the village and there is peace in their world. Many people want no more. Then bureaucrats and Chinese entrepreneurs moved in on this system and instituted new rules. Some Vietnamese, learning the ways of greed, bought up more and more land, made the villages plant two crops of rice a year then bought it cheap and sold it dear and used the money to expand. The villagers could not afford to buy their own rice. Moneylenders flourished. Peasants went deeply into debt and lost more and more of their land to the growing class of landlords. Not even France benefited from this arrangement. The Vietnamese cannot afford French goods arriving into the country and the money made from the land goes to a few private companies." Chau's father stopped for a moment and watched his son. "Perhaps this is too much for you. We should continue at a later date."

Chau stood and placed his hands into his pockets. He wandered to a bookshelf and ran a finger along the spines.

"I have been living a lie," he said. "Without knowing it, I have been living a lie – all because of you." He turned and pointed at his father. "You have taught me what you do not believe. "I am no longer Vietnamese nor am I French. I am a bastard in the world."

"You are my son; and because you are my son you will find your own way in the world, your own truth. Anything you choose now is your own decision."

Chau leaned his forehead against the wall, unable to face his father. What was to happen to him now? Where would he go?

"What of the good things the French have brought," he said. "The schools, education, medicine? What of all those, Father? What of their efforts to drag us from the mud of the earth and push into the twentieth century?"

"You assume, as do they, that peaceful and contented people need more in their lives than happiness. Most attempts to modernize culture are little more than an effort to sell them goods, for more people to earn more money. If one is happy and contented being a farmer, should he not be left alone to be a farmer? Will he be happier with a radio, a vehicle, a tractor perhaps? Anything modern removes people from the land, from the natural way of being, from friends and family."

"Would you be happier, Father, working the land?" Chau returned slowly to his chair.

From the window he no longer saw Ling or the peasant.

"It is difficult to give up anything when you have everything. Only the rich can have everything and that is the problem. The rich want it all and they take it from the backs of the poor. The idea of possessions is the evil that upsets the balance of the world. When a peasant gets a new plow most of the village is happy. Others, however, also want a new plow and will do whatever it takes to get one. These are the world's entrepreneurs. Someone then wants a tractor and then someone else wants a larger tractor. A man marries a pretty woman so another man wants her. It goes on and on until one village sees that another village has many things and so it attacks to take the meaningless stuff. Then nations go after nations. A diamond has no value until someone else says it has value. These things have no value except in words. The way of nature is the way of the land."

"What have the Viet Minh done for their people except get them killed?"

"They are nationalists, not Communists. They have always preferred the help of France and of the United States. The Viet Minh can do little because they have little. The French have only one doctor for every 50 or 60,000 people and they seldom leave the cities and mostly treat the French. Ho Chi Minh continues to send out what few medical people he has to the villages. When he realized that most Vietnamese were illiterate he sent an army to teach the peasants how to read and had the teachers teach other teachers. He is the world's greatest patriot, gives everything for his country and takes nothing for himself. The decisions of Vietnam must be made by the people of Vietnam."

Chau shook his head. "It is too much for me and too fast."

"I am only concerned with your life," said Chau's father. "When you are not about town I ask that you spend most of your time here. I have told no one you are here. You must do the same. Should something happen to me you must follow the instructions I have given you. General Salan is a master at intrigue and intelligence work. Things will get tougher. Always use the back entrance and make sure no one sees you. In this place you can start to think about the world objectively."

Chapter 17

Chau met with his father every morning. Chau had regained his composure, attempted to be logical, and had been reading about all of Asia, a history ignored in the French schools. Often he ate at the Neuyen Sinh Restaurant Fiancais, sometimes for a strong coffee, at other times for fresh bread or a baguette with cheese and paté. He occasionally went to work with his father, in his export business, although his father said it was dangerous to be with him, or walked alone around the city. The One Pillar Pagoda became a good place to think. Ly Thai Thong King had it built in 1049 after a dream. The goddess of mercy, Bodhisattva Avalokitesvara, presented him with a lotus flower so he had the pagoda built on stilts on a lake to represent a lotus rising from the water. Chau became more and more drawn to pagodas and temples as he started to realize how ancient his country was, ancient and beautiful. He sat in the Tran Quoc pagoda, Vietnam's oldest, built in the 6th century, and listened to the Zen Buddhist monks pray, study, and perform rituals for the dead. Monks never prayed for "things" as did Christians, but for thanks to the Buddha for showing them the correct way to live. One did not pray for a person to get well. The only thing that could help a sick person get better was a doctor; nor did one pray for something like world peace, only people could solve that problem. The Buddha did not answer prayers; he only offered directions on how to live. Everything else was left up to man to figure out. Man was capable of solving all his own problems. The god Huyen Thien Tran Vo, of the temple, reigned over Vietnam's north for protection and happiness and a temple with a triple gate and courtyard was built for him in 1015.

The temples and pagodas offered quiet and coolness and several times Chau inquired into the different religions there, so different and difficult to understand compared to his Catholic upbringing.

During one of his walks he took an eager young woman to the Hanoi Opera house and, decorum cast aside, laid her against a tree in the park after the performance. He had heard that the French made love with their faces but he had not acquired the technique, or even understood the saying. His foreplay started and stopped with insertion and the woman was more than happy to have it considering the prize that might eventually be gained. The women always seemed willing. If she was telling a story and was asked to kiss you, she did, then resumed her story. Ask for sex and she would remove her pants, consummate the act, pull her pants back on and again resume the story as if nothing had happened. They seemed very childlike to Chau, as did many Vietnamese; no deep thought, no contemplation, perform, eat, sleep, crap, live, and little else.

At Hoa Lo Prison he watched the French drag Vietnamese political prisoners in and out of the brick and stone compound and remembered the 100 Vietnamese revolutionaries who had tunneled out in 1945. Many of them were now top revolutionaries with the Viet Minh. Over the years the French had executed so many Vietnamese that they installed a second guillotine.

He took a short vacation to the remote French hill station of Sapa, high in the mountains near the Chinese border where the air remained cool and the humidity low. H'mong, Tay, and Dao tribespeople went about their daily lives working crops on the terraced hillsides or selling trinkets in town on market days. Chau enjoyed walking deep into the valleys to the rivers below and through the Red Dao villages where vats of indigo cloth were being dyed. Balls of hemp piled outside doors and boys chased dogs as water buffalo lounged in pools of mud. Women, smelling of smoke and wearing red headdresses, nursed babies, wearing red and blue beanies atop their tiny heads. During the mornings blankets of fog and mist covered the valleys and he often drank coffee for long hours as he thought about Europe, about his own future although he was still unable to think collectively about the future of his country.

One evening, as Chau walked the back streets near the lake in Hanoi, he pulled up a chair before an open-air bar and ordered the house bia hoi, home brew mixed in the back rooms of most street bars. A liter glass jug, foaming over the top, wobbled on top of the table. Three more men pulled up chairs and ordered more bia hoi. Two teeth had fallen from between the lips of one man and two other crooked teeth framed the space. Chau never noticed how bad the teeth of most Vietnamese were. Black cavities had eaten into the teeth of the other men. The aroma of steamed rice and noodles fell from the building onto the street.

"The best bia hoi is here," said the man, with the missing teeth. "We drink all night, have good time."

"I can not stay long," said Chau, nervousness in his voice. He was not yet comfortable with peasants or with people in his personal space, a space not required by most Vietnamese.

"I think you have money," said the man, with a scar running up his arm.

"I have never been here," said Chau.

"Bia hoi in front, boom-boom in back," said the man, wearing a red French beret. "One loose, one tight, both good. You try?"

"Are you with the French?" said Chau. He nodded toward the beret.

"Spit on the French," he said. "If they ask I say I was badly wounded in the highlands. Sometimes they buy me bia hoi. Sometimes not. You buy me bia hoi?"

"And you too?" said Chau.

"The French make us beggars," said the one with the scars. "We come from a farm near Bac Can to find work. Our families are starving. The landowners take everything. Maybe they should just kill us and be finished. That is too easy. They like us to suffer."

"Maybe we should just kill the French," said Mr. Beret. "It might be easier."

"That is dangerous talk," said Chau. Another bottle of bia hoi was brought, this time by a young woman who placed her hand on Chau's shoulder.

"Maybe you are French in yellow skin?" said Mr. Beret.

"You French, rich boy?" said Mr. Scar. He poked a finger into Chau's chest and grinned, his yellow teeth the color of infected piss.

"I think he French boy," said Mr. Open tooth. "Maybe we tell the Viet Minh. They like French boys."

"I'm just having a beer," said Chau. "I did not invite you to my table." They all started to laugh.

"Tough guy," said Mr. Beret. "We no need invitation. At bia hoi bar everyone is friends, everyone drink together."

"Why are you being unfriendly?" said Chau.

"We want to know, are you French boy?"

"I never had bia hoi and I heard it is good, that's all. Look at me? Does my yellow skin look French?"

"Only French boys have money," said Mr. Beret. "You have money."

"My father owns a Vietnamese business. He is all Vietnamese and takes money from the French."

"Oh?" said Mr. Open Tooth. The three men looked at one another and shrugged their shoulders. "Then you will spend French money on bia hoi and on Vietnamese peasants?"

"Yes," said Chau. "I admit I have led a privileged life. I want to learn about my own people. Perhaps you can help?" He felt slightly afraid, nervous, confused as to how to make friends.

"We teach," said Mr. Beret. "Lesson number one, you pay for bia hoi. A good idea for both. Farms in the hills is the best life. Not too much work all the time. Lots of work for short times, planting and harvesting but not too much all the time. Plenty of time for a good woman." He winked and grinned.

"I have never been to a farm," said Chau.

"Baa - farms are everywhere," said Mr. Beret, swilling a large glass of beer. "The city is no good. More money, yes, but very difficult to find. Money makes people want more money. For what? To buy more things that makes them unhappy. There is no sunrise or sunset, no talking with friends or family. We must retake our farms, throw out the French and return to our good lives. Maybe you will help. You have money."

"Why do you stay in the city?"

"Why? It is not difficult to …."

"Taulards – on a de pisser?" said a French legionnaire caporal chef, his French accented with an English accent. The Vietnamese had not noticed him or his two friends as they approached. "We need to piss."

"Taulars?" said Mr. Beret, outraged at being called a prisoner. He pointed to his red cap.

The corporal laughed and pointed out the cap to his companions.

"A piece of shit," he said. "You are all bits of yellow shit." He leaned over and knocked off the beret. "These can be bought anywhere, or stolen, more like it."

Mr. Beret unbuttoned his shirt showing a massive intersection of red and white scars. He puffed out his chest. "The battle of Hoa-Binh. The Viet Minh shattered us with recoilless cannon and bazookas and I fought as bravely as any French soldier. We were overrun at Tu-Vu on the Black River."

"I have heard of it," said the corporal. "A nasty bit of fighting." His voice quieted, hinted at reverence.

Mr. Beret picked up his hat and adjusted it on his head. "Several of us were fighting with two Moroccan rifle companies and a tank platoon in a southern and a northern position. The enemy lit us up with heavy mortars before launching human wave attacks." Mr. Beret spoke in perfect French as his hands acted out the attack. "I was in the southern position. As we became overrun we moved to the northern position. Five Viet Minh battalions attacked the 200 of us that remained. The tanks attempted to drive through them and became flaming balls of fire as all were destroyed. We retreated for one last time and swam to a small island in the river and awaited our deaths. My chest had been ripped opened by a shell and I barely survived. Yet I managed to pull a French soldier, injured worse than me, to safety on the island. He died in my arms as the Viet Minh withdrew without attacking. Because of my injuries, I was relieved of my position as a soldier."

Mr. Beret seemed exhausted as he slumped into his seat and, with shaky hands, buttoned his shirt.

"Vietnamese soldiers are still shit," said the corporal. "Perhaps a Frenchman visited your mother before you were born so you are an exception." He tossed a few francs onto the table. "We'll piss someplace else."

Quietly, the men watched the soldiers as they walked away. They started laughing as they pushed their way into another bar.

"Is that true?" said Chau.

"I will piss on their graves," said Mr. Beret, ordering more bia hoi. He tossed his beret onto the street and watched a bicycle mash it into the bricks. "I fought at Hoa-Binh – for the Viet Minh."

Extremely drunk, Chau wobbled back toward home. Every few steps he leaned against buildings to steady his head. Trees danced like shadows in the darkness. In the distance a burst of flame flew into the sky as an explosive, too remote to toss any sound, before it fell into a red glow on the street. Lately there seemed to be more Viet Minh attacks in the city. People were seldom hurt or killed and the blasts appeared more of a warning than anything sinister.

At one building, Chau leaned against the wall then staggered down the alley where he fell to his knees and puked. The bia hoi, warm and soaking pieces of rice cakes, did not taste as good the second time around. He rolled over to his back and was quite certain he had never been so sick. The ground undulated as his head floated rocking his eyes from side to side. Closing them was no better. Trying to roll to his side he felt the liquid slosh in his stomach rolling up one side then the other. His mouth, tasting of puke, seemed dry and his tongue refused to work as it stuck to his lips.

The sound of off-key singing dripped into the alley as the three Frenchmen Chau had met before staggered into the alley. They walked arms-over-shoulders, their white legionnaire kepis cocked to the sides of their heads. They staggered to a stop, separated and formed a fence on three sides around of Chau.

"It's the fucking wog," said the corporal, speaking in English and using a British derogatory term, "the high-class yellow wanker in the suit." He tipped his kepi back and spit when he knelt down.

"Oh…" Chau mumbled.

"Merdique," said the private with a red birthmark on his cheek. "Look at them shoes, custom French made they is and just my size. He ain't no low class coolie. I'm having them shoes." He pulled off the shoes and felt the soft leather. "These cost more than I make in a month. Give'em a feel." He handed them toward the corporal who brushed them aside.

"What about me?" said the other private.

The corporal knelt and fished out Chau's purse, lifted it up and down, whistled to indicate the weight. He fingered through the bills, stuffed them into his tunic, then poured out the coins.

"Take the coat, you bloody wanker." he said. "It's worth something."

"What do I want with a stinking wog coat?"

"Stupid Frog. Why do we even pal with you? It's worth nothing without the pants. Rip them off and together they're probably worth more than the shoes. The damn thing is custom made."

They rolled Chau from side to side and stripped him naked to humiliate him. The private attempted to slip on the coat but it was too small. When Chau started to snore the corporal kicked him in the thighs, the chest, and the head. The other two joined in.

"They'll think Zip hoods did it," said the private with the red birthmark.

"You'll never be promoted," said the corporal. "The natives never steal anything and they ain't likely to pound anyone, either. They'll kill Frenchies soon enough but they won't hit him."

Chau barely felt the blows but they awakened him for a few minutes, his bare skin cooling on the stones. Sitting was impossible as the pain set in and he heaved again, the bile mixed with blood, before lying back down and closing his eyes. He drifted into the maze of another world, a world of pink and blue where giant trees grew tall and red and misshapen animals walked on three legs and birds flew without wings and purple fish swam to the surface of the water and spoke in a strange Khmer mountain language. A part of Chau floated over the landscape (he could not see his body nor feel it) and let the warmth bathe him in gold. Soon the landscape and temperature changed. Colors melted away leaving everything a stark black and white and the air bit him with flakes of ice and all went white as a blizzard engulfed him and he fought to turn around, back to the warmth and the bright colors. He could not turn so he crouched down attempting to warm himself and he realized he was naked. Totally exhausted he fell to his back as the cold seeped in and started to fill his body.

A prostitute, working late, or early, lifted his head. "You want a woman?" she said. Chau moaned, tried to talk. He tasted the blood in his mouth and, through a haze, saw the woman. Through the layers of make-up she had once been pretty. "A woman is good for clearing the head and healing the body." He quit trying to talk so she started pulling his prick but he pushed her hand away. "I check to make sure no one took it," she said. "They take everything else. Your body says you need a woman. Your one-eyed snake is looking at me. I think the French do not like you." He released his grip as she attempted to lift him to his feet. "Your wife no like this?" she said attempting to gain information. "No? Then your girlfriend? Not that either? This your lucky day. I will take you and your snake home as pets until you get better." Chau offered little help as she tried to lift him and, because he was too heavy, she lowered him back down before walking off. She returned several minutes later dragging a bent twig with a scraggly beard and bowed legs. His hands were calloused with long spidery fingers and his feet slid around the tops of his sandals almost slipping through the straps holding them on. He bent over Chau and, along with the woman, slowly lifted him.

Chau felt them under his arms, one as sharp and hard as stones, the other like a small soft melon, as he stumbled forward. The farther they walked the darker and aromatic it became. Only the slightest tinge of pink from the rising sun could be seen above the cavern of shacks and newly started cooking fires. Many people had already stirred, preparing meals of rice with rat meat and wringing out wet laundry. They paid no attention to him as if dragging half-dead naked bodies through the alley were as common as a morning piss.

They took Chau to a home consisting of one room, at the end of a block, and placed him on a covered bamboo mat on the packed dirt floor. The woman placed a wool U.S. Army blanket over him. She squeezed the old man between the legs and said, "Quack, quack, quack," then directed him out the door. "I promise him a good duck if he help me," she said. "I will show my friends my new pet but you must be cleaned. You stink. The Frenchies call me Marie because I am beautiful or because they want my head." The large red flower on her dress had wilted and she looked worn down from the night or from life. "You are Snake Boy because your bird look like a snake."

She lighted a brazier of coal outside in front of the door and placed a pot of water on top. Chau could see very little through the door as she talked to passing people and pointed him out to them. He was often not sure if he had heard her correctly. Vietnamese is a tonal language, a poor language for communication. The monosyllabic words are expanded through various tones and often Vietnamese have difficulty understanding each other and must repeat a phrase more than once. Any kind of distracting noise makes the language impossible. Vietnamese doctors never wear masks while operating for fear they will be misunderstood. Hello and goodbye are the same word, there are no words for yes or no and six different words are used for black depending on the situation. The written language is no better. Traditionally Chinese characters were used but the French, unable to read it, developed a combination of French words to change it. A priest in 1650 used a combination of the French, Portuguese, and Italian alphabets combined with a bucket of diacritics to indicate the six different tones leaving a language of twelve vowels, seventeen consonants, and nineteen double consonants. Chau much preferred French to his own language and found English to be the easiest one of all to read and to speak.

"Marie, please come here," said Chau, quietly in French. She returned to his side and squatted then started to berate him.

"You no speak French here," she said, in French. "We all Vietnamese, everyone here speak some kind of Vietnamese. The French steal our country and make beggars of us all. I must spread my legs for them to survive but I no like them. Kiss them, rub them, pretend to love them, but I must always think of killing them."

"I must go home," said Chau. "You must get me home."

"You no go anywhere, You sick. I make you better. I feed you, clean you, make you happy, and you love me like any good pet. This makes you better than a dog because I will not eat you. You more like a monkey but even they can be tasty."

Marie slipped out of her red dress and laid it over the wooden table, the only piece of furniture in the room except for two rickety bamboo chairs just inches tall. A porcelain pot, probably the toilet, sat on the floor beside a pile of bamboo leaves and newspapers. An old poster of Betty Grable hung on the wall beside a crucifix. An altar for ancestor worship sat below that. A large movie poster with a painting of a bikini-clad woman wearing bunny ears and saying DAI NHAC HOI covered almost the whole of another wall.

"Now we both naked," she said, returning with the warm water and a cloth. She started to wash Chau, first his face before working her way down. She spent considerable time between his legs. "Your snake has awakened and tried to bite me. I must bite him back." He watched her head disappear and felt her warm lips between his legs. Never had he experienced such pleasure. He felt weaker than ever when she had finished but very warm and relaxed. "I must suck out all the poison for you to get better." She brought Chau tea that she had doctored with herbs and helped him drink it. "This help you sleep and will ease the pain." With the rag she started washing herself as Chau dozed off into a deep and balmy sleep.

Chau awoke to find his chest tightly bandaged. The room was cold and when he tried to sit the pain was excruciating so he lay back down and pulled the blanket tightly about his neck. Everyplace on his body hurt and, taking inventory, he felt a lump on his forehead, a cracked and swollen lip, his chest, legs, arms, even his feet, hurt. He needed to use the toilet but could not remember where it was. Looking around the room he spotted the pot beside the basket of leaves and newspapers. Never had the sophisticated French toilet looked so good, a nice sit-down, a good wash with the bidet sprinkling his behind. For the first time he realized how French he was. He dressed like a Frenchman, lived in a French house, spoke French so frequently his own language sounded foreign, attended French Catholic schools, graduated from a French university, and read books in French. He crawled to the pot to relieve himself then crawled back to the bamboo mat.

The smells of different Pho soups filled the air along with the stench of poverty: old clothes, cooking fires, rotten fish, and poor sanitation facilities. He heard the cackle of chickens and the bark of a small dog that had not learned to keep a low profile around the cooking pots. Through the door he saw a peasant walk past carrying a monkey tied to a stick and a woman with a basket of birds on her head. Dead snakes hung from the shoulder of another man. Chau always hated snakes, one reason he seldom ventured into the country. He noticed a pencil and paper beside the mat and realized Marie had probably placed it there so he could get a message to his father. He started to write when Marie entered with a bowl of hot noodles floating in chicken broth.

"The doctor said you have three broken ribs and you must stay here as my pet." Without the make-up and dressed in a black ao dai she looked rather attractive in a used sort of way. "You take these noodles, finish your letter later." She helped him to one arm and started feeding noodles into his mouth like a mama bird does worms to her chicks. Chau choked after three or four bites and held his chest. Marie started sniffing.

"Something stink," she said. She walked over to the pot. "Hey, someone crap in my cooking pot." She pulled the pot closer to her nose as she looked in. "I think tonight's salad is ruined."

"How could you afford a doctor?" he said, trying to change the subject.

"I don't understand 'afford'," she said.

"Money," he said.

"Ah yes, I do understand money. We help each other here," she said. "Harmony must be kept in the world, nothing out of balance. All of us are greater than one of us, greater even than Snake Boy. Besides, the doctor wanted to see my new pet."

Marie drew an army locker from under the table and pulled out another blanket. Gently she covered him.

"I bring help to take you out back to use the toilet," she said.

"Out back?" Chau lifted his head enough to see the pot in the corner.

"Snake Boys are so stupid. Where else does one go? We are not animals no matter what the French think."

"Why are you here?" said Chau.

"The toilet?"

"I am fine. What brought you here. Why are you a prostitute?"

She thought for a moment, a hand on her chin, and she seemed to drift to another time and place.

"I am from the village of Vinh Yen. We are very happy there. We all work together but we do not think of it as work. Villagers spend their entire lives never leaving their valleys or rice paddies. From the earliest times I remember wading in the mud with my mother and planting rice. We are born on the land and buried in it. We eat the rice that grows from the graves so we are always part of our family, part of the land."

She looked peaceful and contented as she spoke.

"Maybe your village should buy a tractor," said Chau. "A tractor can replace 100 people?"

Marie looked confused. "Then," she said, "what would we do?" She brushed her hair with her fingers. "One day French paratroopers come to our village. They are led by the evil one, Bigeard, the fiercest French soldier in all Vietnam, a man who enjoys killing. He is fearless and ruthless, always the first one into a village. They found my father teaching some peasants how to read. They think that only the Viet Minh teach people how to read so they took him and my mother into the center of the Village and chopped of their heads. I hid under a house and watched everything."

"Was he Viet-Minh?"

"He was a good man. He never said anything, just knelt down and lowered his head after touching my mother's hand."

The more she talked the softer and more endearing she became. Chau knew she was not quite right mentally but there was something very interesting about her.

"So you came here?"

"The village said we must fuck the French so I am here fucking the French. I must start some healing tea. Someone will deliver your letter." She picked up the pot. "Who would crap in my pot and ruin my salad?" Chau looked toward the ceiling. "Part of the propaganda newspaper is also in here." Chau tried to roll to his side and look at the wall. "The news is always shitty," she said.

Marie moved in and out of the house all day, feeding Chau, giving him tea, rubbing his feet legs and back. Friends came in and chatted with her and bowed to Chau as she introduced her new pet.

"Do you work today?" he asked her.

"I hate the French. I work when I need money." She spit on the floor. "I hate the French."

"How much money do you need?" Chau asked, thinking he might be able to repay her.

"Little," she said. "Money is dangerous. People want little, then more and more. Soon they prefer money to life. They are sad and the world gets out of balance and they don't understand their sadness. Possessions lead to misery and they drown by flapping their arms and trying to swim. Better to be still. Maybe you need the toilet now. The soup will taste better."

Marie had two friends carry Chau to the back of the house where he relieved himself in a trench. Peasants worked along the trench picking up the leavings and taking them away in a wheelbarrow. She gave Chau more tea then worked him into an erection, removing her pants and straddling him. She washed him again before bringing him supper. Chau realized this was his opportunity to learn about sex. It seemed very important in European countries.

"Am I big enough?" he said, pointing between his legs.

"Very good."

"Be honest with me. I wish to learn."

"Oh," she said, giggling like a girl. "You just a little bigger than just right."

Chau felt relieved. There was no greater compliment, or feeling of satisfaction, than being bigger than just right. Everyone else could be just right, a common size, but just a little bigger could not be discounted.

"Am I OK for women?

"You stink," she said. "All Vietnamese stink. A woman is just a place to spit and does not count. Enjoyable sex is only for a man. A woman's pleasure is in serving him."

"Are you happy?"

Marie stood and stomped her foot.

"Vietnamese men stink. They are as pleasurable as cleaning crap from a cooking pot. Women should teach them correctly."

"Will you teach me? I wish to learn how to make a woman happy. In Europe it is very important. I will pay you."

"Bah; you crazy. Pets have no money. I teach, you learn. When you learn you will leave so learn slowly." She knelt beside him and ran her fingers through his hair.

"I hear the French make love with their faces," he said. "What does that mean?"

"It means I am in for excitement tonight," she grinned.

The following day a saggy-faced old lady came and knelt on the floor. She handed Chau a letter and asked him if he needed anything. The letter was from his father. Marie was out gathering vegetables and nuc-mum, a black fermented sauce made from rotted fish, for supper. The old lady did not move as Chau read the letter.

"Dear son…"

Chapter 18

Each day Chau's health improved. Soon he was up and moving, still with pain, and started to meet many people, all peasants, all happy and pleasant: the wood man carrying stacks of fallen limbs across his shoulders and placing them into his kiln made of dried mud bricks so he could produce charcoal for the braziers of the street vendors; the vegetable vendors cleaning green stalks, choy, and ginger root; healers sorting hundreds of herbs and roots into stacks before mixing healthful blends; women weaving silk on ancient machines; children occasionally playing together when not working; ragged beggars crawling on hands and knees, (if they had any) on their way to work the more prosperous streets and sometimes leading the blind with them; old men playing Chinese chess or checkers, moving about their little cannons or mighty war elephants, bent cigarettes dangling from between their lips and drinking green tea that poured steam into the air they inhaled; women of all ages bent over cooking fires or washing clothes in bubbling water or dyeing garments hung on sticks, the smoke from the fires laying a fine layer of mottled silk over the area; shirtless men, with bones held together by sinews of muscles and canvas skin, tanning hides; spotlessly clean young women in glowing white ao dai carrying flowers of red, yellow and blue; and the old lady that watched him when Marie was gone. Never once did he hear a single person complain about anything, so he refused to complain about the awful appalling situation in which he was presently in, a situation that he refused to admit was growing appealing. People might explain their lives as history but not as something unfortunate.

He had grown very fond of crazy Marie and felt alone and uncomfortable when she was away. Her silly comments always caused him to smile and he could not tell if she were very dim or very bright. The old lady refused to speak to him about her and cowered when he drew near. He had never had a serious relationship with any woman and he imagined, even if she were a whore, that this was a serious relationship although he did not understand what kind. It might have been love or friendship or admiration. She had given him clothes of silk pajamas and sandals stating that a pet should have no less nor more than his master. Her attempts at making him appear less than educated or aristocratic proved impossible. His stance, straighter than the others who had grown into a perpetual stoop from lowering themselves over the towering French, revealed his upbringing. He carried an air of security and self-confidence about himself, typical of people brought up with an air of singular importance rather than group and community effort. He was truly more French than Vietnamese and he found it difficult not to feel like an outsider although the peope treated him no differently than anyone else, always with respect and kindness as they did everyone. His father had visited him twice and asked him to return home but Chau declined saying he was learning a great deal about the Vietnamese people and promised to return after his investigation had finished and he was again fit. His father had also sent the doctor who declared Chau in good hands and recovering nicely. As a precaution the doctor also checked Marie for venereal disease and found her remarkably clean.

One night Marie went to work and did not return. For three days the old woman stayed with Chau as he quizzed everyone he could as to her disappearance. They always looked at him blankly as they did at any Frenchman seeking information. They did not know her. He asked about the house and the young woman who lived there. They said the old woman lived there, no one else, just the old woman. He tried to get the old woman to talk but she would say nothing. Finally, out of frustration, he left a note with the old lady telling Marie where to find him, and he returned home.

He seemed more confused than ever as he walked home caught somewhere between worlds, no longer totally French, not yet Vietnamese, an empty-chested man bemoaning his lost love, if love was what it was rather than the apex of sexual desire, and therefore also empty-headed for the same reason. He formally considered himself an Annamite with a formal French education and weren't Annamites the true Vietnamese? That was a lie soon revealed. He knew nothing of Vietnam and its people except what he had recently read. Thinking of himself as French was equally frustrating. His skin and eyes proved that he was no Frenchman and, regardless of their outward expression of equality with him, he was nothing more to them than a coolie, a wog.

Marie had told him that desire was the cause of all sadness and must be eliminated. He thought it silly at the time but, because of desire, he was thoroughly depressed at her loss. How did one eliminate desire? Desire kept people alive, drove them on to want more and more. Life was desire and wanting and craving. Aspiration made people human, separated them from the animals making them unique in the world. Did not God create the world and everything in it for the use and profit of man? How could Marie claim that desire is not a part of the natural world, that man is a part of that world, not separate from it as the Christians believed, and when man forgets this, or perhaps never understood it, the world becomes unbalanced? According to the French what balanced the world was having everything possible on one side of it, then wanting to take everything else on the other side. The French believed that; why else did they have their own country on one side and need Vietnam on the other? Britain, Germany, the Dutch and Spanish, all needed colonies to balance their countries. How could the Vietnamese seek balance and harmony with only a single country? France helped to stabilize them. A country without colonies for balance was weak, indeed, although Marie attempted to tell Chau that balance was not in wanting but in not wanting. Not wanting required no objects. Without objects or weight all nature was in balance. They remained in balance by not wanting the country of France.

Ling met Chau at the entrance of his father's house. "I am so pleased at your return," he said. He bowed and offered Chau his hand. Chau responded. "You must give me all the information, all the details," said Ling. "Who could have beaten you up? To keep you safe I must know where you are at all times." He eyed Chau from top to bottom and pulled on his pajamas. "I should have sent you some decent clothes. These rags are humiliating for someone of your status."

"It was just an incident," said Chau. "I needed the rest and thought it best to stay where I was. My ribs were broken and needed healing."

"But such a place?" said Ling. "I understand you were in the deepest of slums – very dangerous, very very dangerous."

"Not so dangerous," said Chau.

"Your father is inside." Ling pointed his hand toward the door. Chau's father sat on a wicker chair pulled beside the koi pond tossing bits of bread to the fish. "He has arrived," said Ling, as if announcing a king.

"You look well, my son," said Chau's father. He embraced Chau and led him to a chair in the shade where they talked away the morning on superfluous topics.

"We are attending an important masquerade party on Friday," said his father. "I had hoped you would return before then. All the better businessmen from many countries will be there and it is a good place to meet contacts that may be useful to you in the future. I had Ling place a costume in your new room. The French are often like little children and frequently play dress up. Did you notice this in Paris?"

"Many times," he said. "I have heard that the English sometimes do this but I saw nothing of it in America."

"Perhaps they are too serious. To immediately announce your status as king of the Chau family, you are going as King Louis the 14th."

"Am I also to lose my head?" Chau chuckled.

"The French take great pride in losing and have elevated it to almost an art."

Chau decided a good night's rest was what he needed most. In his room he admired his costume for the party. The white shirt flowered with forests of ruffles down the front and on the cuffs; the powder blue coat and pantaloons had swirls of white inlay. The legs of the pantaloons buttoned tightly below the knees and around the tops of long white silk socks; buckle shoes on thick high heels would add an inch or two to his height. Of course his father would not forget the hat, large at the brim and fielding ferns of red, green, and blue feathers. The wig had no powder. He decided to try it on in the morning.

Chau's hopes for sleeping proved impossible. He had gotten used to a woman at his side. He rolled from side to side on the bed and, since he had adapted to a floor mat, the softness of the mattress hurt his back. He attempted to read something by Hugo, then de Maupassant then Zola. He paced, sat, paced, sat, rolled in the bed, sat and paced. All he could think of was Marie and her wonderful sex lessons, her warm body, her humor. He finally fell asleep, an hour before sun-up, an unlit cigarette between his lips,.

His eyes, swollen and painful, opened with the brightening room and his body felt like cold lead, difficult to mold and twist into any recognizable form. Twice he attempted to sit up and twice he fell back onto the bed, beaten by the remnants of night and the lack of sleep. His head ached and he started to dry heave. He gagged while brushing his teeth and his gums bled. The diarrhea hit especially hard, the small lumps running in stringy fluid turning to brown water that set his anus on fire. Only a shower, warm water running over his closed eyelids, started to return him to life. He sat naked in a chair with a cup of hot green tea he had made. Life slowly continued to flow back into him and in an hour he started to feel alive enough to try on his Louis 14th costume.

Everything fit perfectly, the buckle shoes, silk stockings, pantaloons, ruffled shirt, wig, and brocade jacket. He twirled before the mirror. He could have been the King himself or, with a few changes, a grand matador parading solemnly into the bullring and bowing to the cheering and adoring crowd. He found the white powder and rouge for his brown face. He powdered his face and rouged his cheeks and lips. The white wig flowed over his shoulders and the feathered hat dipped jauntily to the side of his head. There was even a sword foil. Chau thought it might be a foil, much different than deceptively simple Asian swords. Any sharp piece of metal capable of removing a head was good enough. Even the Montagnard machetes, crude, some with wooden handles, some with buffalo horn handles, were quick and effective. He paraded around the room stopping occasionally to draw his foil as the stories of Dumas rolled around his head. He lifted his arm and yelled out "All for one, one for all!" He felt alive again and started to laugh and thought of Bix and Steve and crazy Neal with his dope-filled world of strange ideas and free sex and a land liberated from rules and flowing with thoughts ideas and dreams, a world of peace, harmony and freedom. It was the first time he had thought of them since his return and he felt a tinge of empti-ness at the memory, so different, so unique. He wanted to see them again. He seemed to fit more in their world than he did in his own. He was not French, he was not Viet-namese, but in America no one was anything particular. Everyone, except blacks, seemed to be accepted although each group suffered ridicule from every other group.

He wanted to show his happiness to his father and he knelt beside the window to open the curtain and see if anything was stirring across the street. The air dripped with the moisture of early morning. He tipped back the curtain and saw only the street vendor, smoke from his brazier fingering the air. He continued to view the world, a distant park, buildings wrapped with vines of electrical wires, boa trees with roots twisted into the ground, when three jeeps, followed by a truck, slid to a halt in front of Chau's father's house. The vendor removed a revolver from under his pajamas and waved his arms toward the front door. Officers and soldiers jumped from the ve-hicles and broke through the front door as other soldiers surrounded the building. They quickly dragged out Chau's father bleeding from his mouth and above one eye. He wore one of his best cashmere suits, subdued silk tie, and custom leather shoes. Ling emerged and stood on the edge of the sidewalk as the vendor swung his pistol toward Chau's father. An officer punched Chau's father in the stomach causing him to fold over, his head dropping to the road execution style. The officer motioned the soldiers to lift him up as the other officer continued to argue with the vendor. The vendor angrily moved toward Chau's father, his arms clawing the air as the officer pushed him off. The first officer turned to talk to the other officer, pointing to Chau's father. The vendor pushed forward and, before the officer could deflect him, he shot Chau's father in the head. His head flew to one side bouncing off his shoulder, a mega-phone of blood screeching death into the morning. He dropped face forward onto the street. The officer knocked the vendor over as two soldiers wrestled the pistol from him, dragging him to the back of the truck. The two officers shook their heads and one of them motioned to some soldiers indicating that Chau's father should be lifted into a jeep.

Ling, who had been standing quietly during the ordeal, stepped forward and bowed slightly. The officer looked at him with disgust as Ling smiled. The officer removed a thick envelope from his tunic and threw it against Ling's chest. Ling picked it up and pulled out a stack of money, fanned the bills in front of his nose, then replaced it. He turned toward the building across the street. The officers followed his arm as it pointed toward Chau behind the window. It took a moment for Chau to respond, a moment he could not afford. He jumped from the window, grabbing his package, as the soldiers ran toward the building. He knocked open the door and ran the long way to the back of the building shoving open another door covered in cobwebs. He rushed down the rickety steps almost breaking an ankle as one step broke under his weight. Another door opened to the adjacent building, also empty, then another one filled with bags of dusty rice, before he broke into an alley. He threw his hat and wig onto the dirt as he continued to run. Breaking from the alley he shot across the street, without looking for any following soldiers, and into another alley. Faced with running down the next street Chau drew his sword and whipped it from side to side to clear a path through the peasants as he looked for another alley. He felt the people looking at him although no one stared or yelled or screamed or even became excited. Except for upsetting an old woman after stumbling over a basket of fish, everyone remained calm as if King Louis 14th ran madly down their streets every day.

Finally he stopped to look back. Nothing. People carried on business as usual - cooking, giving haircuts, selling fish, chickens, fruit and vegetables, washing and selling clothes, women strolling the streets in immaculate white ao dais and carrying parasols, two nuns bowing as they passed peddlers. There were no soldiers. Perhaps Chau had escaped for the moment. He caught his breath, removed his jacket and attempted to wipe the make-up from his face. He walked into a basket shop and spoke to two men sitting, playing Chinese chess and smoking pipes. He traded them his clothes and sword for black pajamas and sandals before continuing his journey. He had to get to the shop at the outskirts of town before nightfall and into the jungle for safety. Two armed jeeps filled with legionnaires drove rapidly past him when he hit the next street. He bought two buckets and a pole and balanced them across his shoulder. Although the buckets were empty the weight on the pole cut into his bones. He scurried as he had seen many peasants do, with no place to go.

A truck drove down the street and emptied at the next block as soldiers started to erect a barricade. Armed soldiers moved from the opposite direction. Chau noticed a motion in the alleyway across the street. He peered into the darkness. A figure stepped slightly into the light, a thin Vietnamese in ragged clothes. The man waved to him inviting him to come over. Chau looked both ways and knew he was trapped. He would soon meet the same fate as his father. He scurried across the street and into the alley, the pole on his shoulders biting into the flesh. The man knocked the pole and buckets off and pulled him by the shirt through the dark. Chau tripped over various bowls and baskets and limped along as fast as he could. As they entered the light of the next street he noticed a drearily painted cyclo, a two seated cart powered by a bicycle in the rear, waiting, a hand motioning him to enter. He jumped onto the seat.

"You big trouble, Frenchie," said Marie. "Someone always must take care of you." She laughed and kissed him hard and passionately on the lips. "Put on this coat of red and gold so you look like you can afford a ride with a beautiful woman of class. Your white face need to be washed, too much powder and paint." She spit on his face and wiped it with a scarf until he shown brown again.

Chau struggled in the cyclo to slip into the coat and a pair of pants. People stood in various places around him, always looking out but never moving, curious but unattached.

"You confused?" said Marie. "This is your army watching out for you, your Vietnamese army. We do not look effective but fighting is born in us. Your father always with you. He pay me to keep you safe, a lowly woman with sense and skills, because you have none, who can save your life and keep you warm at night. When you finish your trip, when you have become a man, you can throw me away. Money, like women, only shines bright so long." She turned slightly in her seat. "Take us down the other street," she told the driver.

Chau thought she meant the street away from which he had just escaped but the driver, void of expression, moved right back toward danger.

"Are you crazy?" he said. "Go the other way or I'll be killed. The French are looking for me everywhere."

"Ba! Yes I am crazy," said Marie. "I am crazy enough to keep a stupid boy like you alive. Traveling peacefully through danger will keep you safe. Run and you are finished. The soldiers expect you to run and hide, not tip your head as you pass with a beautiful woman."

The cyclo pulled onto the once busy street. The people had drifted slowly away. Rows of bamboo scaffolding poles leaned against one building. Stacks of red and gold Buddhist icons and banners hung from another wall. They drew nearer the blockade and he saw the soldiers looking at him, cigarettes dangling from between all their lips. A young soldier held out his hand and ordered them to stop.

"Where are you going?" he said. "Do you have anything else in there?" He poked his head into the cycle and looked around,

"That's Marie," said another soldier wearing a red beret. He walked up and placed his hands on the bicycle wheel. "I see you're working." He nodded and winked with a grin toward Chau.

"Business is good," she said. "This Chinaman pay good and he is easy on my behind unlike your big sausage that splits a tender young woman apart."

"This is the putain I've been telling you about." He puffed out his chest. The others started to move in closer. "You're not hiding anyone up your dress, are you, or up your ass?" He reached over, lifted her dress and stuck his hand between her legs then smelled his fingers. "Fresh as a cow's ass. And what's about this petit encule?"

"I think your finger the biggest thing on you," she said, pumping her hips up and down as if she were having sex. The soldiers laughed.

"Vas-y!" he said angrily, his attitude changing quickly as he motioned them ahead. He walked away, head down, kicking at the street. "Go find something to do," he said to the other soldiers who continued to laugh and to use their fingers as rulers measuring the air. "You'd let that bastard Giap walk right past here without even stopping him."

"Because they think they are smart, the French are stupid," said Marie. waving to them as they left. "Always we fool them, always know what they are doing, where they are going to fight. Say little but think much, always think to stay alive. Talk makes you weak; silence makes you strong." She held Chau's hand and placed her head on his shoulder. "Do you love me very much?" she sighed.

Because of the short time he had carried the buckets, his back felt crushed by the time he had reached his destination and his shoulder still drooped under the pain of the wood. The sandals hurt his feet and had rubbed the skin raw between his toes. Marie held a small bag that attached to her back as she followed him. He entered the building while Marie waited outside under the shade of the awning. He confronted the man inside, a bent man of indefinite age so twisted he could no longer stand straight and was only able to speak to the floor. "Please," the man said.

"I have come for the mountain package," said Chau, quietly as if the building were a holy place.

"I am sorry for your loss," said the man, knowing what he wanted without any farther information. He slipped between the beaded curtains and returned a moment later with a small leather pouch, the color of his hands and just as supple. "You must go quickly west, toward the mountains. Avoid towns." He looked around and lowered his head even farther like a horse trying to drink. "Travel only back-roads and stay in the smallest villages. Avoid the French military but if questioned speak only in Vietnamese or indicate you are mute. Use the language to confuse them, to sound stupid but listen to everything they say. Always plead ignorance; always pretend not to understand. Be humble. Show no pride. Keep your head bowed. They expect you to be stupid. Give them what they expect and you will be smart. Let all emotion vanish, all sadness and joy. Take this small pot, sack of rice, and these matches. If you know of no other way to light a small cooking fire, use them but do not let the matches get wet. Take the path to the right past the bridge. The trail soon branches in many directions." He became quiet as Chau waited.

"Which way then?"

"No one knows. Your future lies on the trail you choose. Remember, misery lives in the past. Your father, the life you knew, are no longer there. There is only becoming. Go quickly."

"But which trail?"

"Go now."

Chau attempted to organize and sort out everything the old man had said, to arrange it into some kind of cognitive sequence. In the distance he saw the small bridge surrounded by forest, limbs drooping sadly down. Placing the matches and rice in the pot and thanking Marie, he started on his journey toward the dark tunnel of jungle. She followed him.

"What are you doing?" he said. He saw the trailing edge of town behind her.

"I see he has given you a pot to crap in," she said, grinning broadly. "Someone must wash it."

Chau stood with his arms crossed and looked at her tiny face, her eyes bright, shining, filled with determination. Trying to stop her would be energy wasted. He tipped his head as she moved up beside him.

"Remember how important it is to keep silent," he said.

"I am like a peacock," she said.

"I was afraid of that."

At first, as they came to forks in the trail, he stopped to contemplate which way to walk. Sometimes he chose by selecting the path most worn thinking it might lead to a larger village, even though he had been warned to avoid them. Breaking ties with civilization too quickly was something that confused him. Just walking in the jungle frightened him and he was happy to have Marie there. Other times, as difficult as it seemed, he picked the lesser trail remembering a larger village was to be avoided. Preferring one path to the other caused him doubt and anxiety and he always felt he had made the wrong decision. Every right choice later felt wrong. He finally realized, because he had no information on which decision to make, the choices were meaningless so he followed trails that appeared to border water - a lake, stream or river, so they would have something to drink. The jungle smelled ancient and odors from the soil hinted at years of decayed foliage and mixed with fresh foliage that smelled of aged dirt and in turn smelled of flesh, the flesh of thousands and thousands of people all lying underneath. Light filtered in streaks through the leaves painting mosaics on the dirt with its fingers. Occasionally the jungle pinched out all daylight leaving them in the dark. Bugs and gnats swarmed in the darker areas but avoiding the light. Often so small they caused Chau to swat at what seemed to be nothing but the idea of annoyance. Mosquitoes came and went in the light with few biting him. Before night set in Chau decided to start a fire and cook a handful of rice using brown water from the stream he was following. Marie assumed the tasks since that appeared to be her job and he was happy to let her do it. She had changed her clothes from a small bag she carried. The leather pouch he carried contained more money, a necklace, and a letter from his father. He sat and, under the remaining light, started to read.

"My Dear son, know that I am with you even now. This is a time of growth and discovery. Be happy in the joy of learning. As you gather insight throughout your life you will look back and realize there was an order outside your intentions that guided your decisions. Events you had not planned seemed to be planned for you and, in the end, made perfect sense. The necklace, constructed from simple materials and made unique by a peasant artisan retains value, not from an economic marketplace, but by the value given by you. What we hold dear, is dear whether it be an ideal, a country, a family, or a piece of dirt deemed worthless by others. Find the things most valuable to you. Travel to the village of Khe Hieu in the highlands and seek the wisdom of Lac Long Quan."

The letter ended abruptly as if nothing more be said and giving no directions to Khe

Hieu or to the identity of Lac Long Quan. The highlands were huge and finding one tiny and insignificant village appeared impossible. Chau slid the necklace over his head and around his neck. No engravings marked it; no symbols had been pounded into the metal, no words of wisdom, no adornment at all, just bent and pounded bits of metal in no consistent pattern or shape.

"Your father is a good man," said Marie.

"Was a good man," he said.

"Our family is always with us," she said. "We must feed them and revere them in every way. Ask your father's advice and he will answer."

"You are a simple girl. What is to become of you?" he placed his head onto his hands and watched her work.

He realized, after finishing the rice, it was too dark to continue but without a tent or blankets he had no idea of what to do. The night had started to grow cool. Any fire large enough to warm him and frighten animals might gather unwanted human guests. Marie flattened some tall grass to make a bed and thought they would be well hidden there. The gnats seemed to multiply with the evening and their buzzing caused him great annoyance. He stiffened at any strange sounds and in the jungle all the sounds seemed strange. Whenever he moved, Marie comforted him with her tender hands. He tried to concentrate on the gentle trickling music of the creek and could almost feel the water sliding over the rocks and under the dripping roots of hanging plants. What was he doing? He had enough money to catch a ship to Europe or the United States. What did his father expect from him? And Ling. It was obvious that Ling, almost a member of the family, had known of his father's clandestine activities and had turned him in for money. The image of his father's brains being scattered into the air, and the look of Ling, one hand full of money, the other pointed toward the window to implicate Chau, refused to leave. He slept restlessly and seldom during the night, shivering with cold, annoyed and half eaten by bugs and occasionally watching the few stars he could see between the trees. He finally rose, soaked by the pre-dawn mist. Marie immediately fixed tea before they started off again. No tea had ever tasted better.

They walked for two more days always avoiding the villages. Once he made love to Marie and it actually seemed like love, not just sex. The feeling of love was different than any other kind of feeling and he could not explain it. He had no ideas of securing her, of keeping her within his boundaries, of totally possessing her. If she took on a client, he would not have minded, not much anyway. Maybe he had confused love with respect. In any case, he enjoyed the feeling and loved to hold her in his arms at night, so tough, so gentle. All the peasants they met along the trail seemed pleased and happy. They felt they were born with happiness and did not have to waste time looking for it. Toward the evening of the third day, out of rice, they chanced entering a small village looking for food.

"We are hungry and willing to buy food," he said to the first person he met, a man about his age. The man clasped his hands together and bowed, as did Chau.

"Please be a guest in my home," said the man. "I am Kuim and my wife is presently cooking dinner. The food is not much but you are welcome to eat as much as you like. Meeting travelers is always a pleasure. We will place a mat down for sleeping and my wife will prepare hot water for bathing."

Chau looked over his own muddy clothes and dirt-clogged toes. He had never been so disheveled or dirty. Red welts from insect bites looked serious along his arms and they burned his neck and itched and his pants continued to irritate the bites on his legs. Kuim's house sat on the ground, as did many others in the village, and held a lean-to on the side, unusual for most houses. Often houses, mostly in the higher elevations, were built on stilts with livestock living underneath.

"The houses outside Hanoi are low to the ground," said Chau, sitting cross-legged with the rest of the family around the food "I thought these would be raised." Marie sat beside him and placed food onto his plate.

"The valleys of the mountains are like that," said Kuim. "They receive much rainfall therefore much flooding. We do not have that problem here."

"The food is very good," Chau said to Kuim's wife, a plain and simple woman fat with child, and her grinning black-toothed mother. The vegetables steamed in the rice were sweetened with nuc mum. "Do you know the village of Khe Hieu?"

"The are many villages around here. I have never left this one but I will ask around while you wash. Is it near here?"

"Khe Hieu is in the mountains," said Chau. "I know nothing more and fear I will never find it."

"Ooh, the mountains can be deadly," said Kuim. "Very dangerous."

"The Viet Minh?"

"The natives, the Muong, the Thai, and all the Montagnards, are bitter enemies. They hate the Vietnamese and fight with the French against the Viet Minh."

"I did not know."

"We have always treated them badly so they fight with the French to kill the Vietnamese, to kill us. Perhaps we should have treated them better."

"Do they fight all the Viet Minh, all the Communists?"

"Yes, because the Viet Minh are Vietnamese; no other reason. It is important to remember that when we had our only free elections after the World War that we voted for the Communists. All they know about the Communists is that we voted for them and so they do not trust them. They feel we want to take away their ancestral lands."

"How do you feel?" said Marie, smiling.

"Little affects our lives," said Kuim. "We have always been farmers and will always be farmers. This government, that government, what difference is it to us? If the Viet Minh visit our village then we are Viet Minh. If the French come then we are loyal to them. Governments are only for those with money who want more money."

A bowl of hot water was placed behind the house and some clean clothes to wear while his were being washed. The water rinsed away the gummy sweat that had clung to his body causing his arms to stick to his body. Marie scrubbed him down gently and his face felt new, his hair clean and fresh, like the clothes in which he dressed. Marie squeezed his penis and winked. "I think you like this new life," she said. Chau washed her with equal pleasure rubbing his hands over her small breasts and wrapping his arms around her.

"I think I like you too much," he said.

"Do you think being the kind of woman I am is a problem?"

"I think you are the best kind of woman. How can that ever be a problem?"

Kuim had gone to other houses to ask about Khe Hieu. A mat and blankets had been placed in a corner for Chau and Marie. The old lady brought him an ointment to spread on his bites and a pipe. Marie lit the pipe for him and the weight of uncertainty drained from him. Not a single bug had bitten her.

"No one knows of this village," said Kuim, when he returned. The old lady also brought him a pipe and they smoked quietly together. "The only people who have ever left the village have never returned."

"Are many villages like this?"

"I think so," said Kuim. "What does a man need beyond this that he should travel?"

"The world is huge," said Chau, blowing out a puff of smoke. "I have tried to travel around it yet have only been to a few places. Great machines cover the world, enormous buildings, airplanes and restaurants, cars and trucks and tractors that can plow one hundred hectares a day to plant enormous crops and make much money and live comfortably."

"I have heard that," said Kuim. "Everything we need is here. There are not a hundred hectares among the entire village. People travel forever looking for this place and we are already here. Have you ever had a better or more peaceful smoke?"

Chau fell asleep quickly, Marie's head on his chest, and when he awoke he realized he had never had a better night's sleep. He kissed Marie on the forehead and watched her slowly come to life. After tea and soup they prepared to leave. Kuim insisted he keep the extra clothes saying they weighed little and would be a comfort. Marie gave Kuim's wife her red dress saying it was too bulky to carry and that she wanted her to wear it after the baby was born. Villagers greeted Chau outside wishing them both good luck on their travels. An old woman gave him a sleeping mat wrapped around a blanket and tied to fit over his shoulder. Others offered him a hat to keep off the sun, a walking stick, food, and more salve for his bites. The generosity from a people who seemed so poor both warmed and confused him. How could people with so little have so much? He bowed gratefully, held Marie's hand in an unchacteristic sign of public affection and they continued on their journey.

"It feels good," he said to Marie. "I am also embarrassed that I do not know my own people."

"Knowing them has always been inside of you," she said. "No baby knows his family until he is awakened."

"I think you are a secret philosopher," he said, "not just a prosti…." He stopped and looked at her.

"A whore," she said. "Do not be afraid of words. Even a hungry person will eat detestable food to survive."

"I did not mean it. I have grown very fond of you." His steps were not as unsteady along the trail as when he had started. The words seemed a confession of love and he felt slightly embarrassed at saying them but was pleased he had said them anyway. He could tell Marie anything. "How is it you seem so mystical one minute and so silly the next?"

"My trick has worked," she laughed. "I wash you, feed you, play with your snake, now you want me. All men are like this. We are together now; nothing else matters."

"What if I wanted just you and no other woman?"

"Then you a very big liar."

Chau stopped and placed his arms over her shoulders. "Marie," he said. "Do you love me?"

"I think you are a silly snake boy," she said, pushing him back and turning him around. "You have many kilometers to travel to find your destination. Maybe love is on the way but I don't think so."

They slept together in the jungle the next two nights and asked anyone they met if they had heard of the village of Khe Hieu. Only one man, walking with a crutch, had heard of it. He knew they had to continue walking toward Laos and that it was near the border at the top of the mountains.

"The mountains are very large," said Chau.

"The village is very small," said the man, as he walked away.

"What the hell did that mean?" thought Chau. Vietnamese spoke in strange and mysterious ways. They always sounded like they knew more than they actually did because they never really said anything, never came to the point, did not understand a simple declarative sentence nor could they speak one. If asked, "Is there a heaven?" they might answer, "A rock is hard." He was then required to mull over the answer, nod his head in understanding, even if he didn't, and reply, "Ummm" as if he had learned something significant from the exchange. Of course a rock is hard; if it wasn't it might be called a piece of cheese. And what the hell did a rock have to do with heaven?

"We need more food," said Chau, days later. "Perhaps a chance to dry our clothes and sleep in the comfort of a house." An unlikely rain continued to dribble down. Generally it fell hard and for short times but today it seemed to scrape the air like falling fingers.

"I think we must be careful," said Marie. "We continue to sink deeper into the hills where ghosts take souls."

"How can you be afraid with me to protect you?" Chau laughed and hugged her.

"I think you not much good," she said. "I think you run so fast from danger you forget me very quickly."

Chau was not sure she was joking. Except in Arizona, he had been in no fights and he had not felt in danger there. In the mountains people just kill you. Fierce tribes lurked everywhere and he heard headhunters lived in the forests.

A small trail drifted off to the left and he decided that it must lead to a small village. Every trail went somewhere. He had learned that larger trails led to larger villages and smaller ones to smaller villages. Roads indicated towns and several roads marked cities. Within minutes he spotted smoke rising over the trees.

"You stay here," he said to Marie. "I will creep up and see if it is safe."

"Do not forget me."

"I won't let anything happen to you, I promise."

Chau slipped to the side of the trail and pushed through the brush. A small village of eight or ten buildings sat before him. on the wet ground. A water buffalo wallowed in a puddle of mud, only his eyes and nose poking from the muck. Two older men, obviously not peasants, staggered from one of the buildings. Both wore suits, gray and tailored in silk. A cyclo waited for them, an odd piece of machinery so far from any town or city. The shorter man helped pour the taller man into the vehicle before he climbed in and waved his arm for the driver to leave. The driver, all sticks and dried flesh, peddled out a wider more used trail behind the houses. The village now appeared deserted and the sound of crickets chirped at the air. Smoke rose from several houses. The area gave him an uneasy feeling and he was unsure if it was the best place to stay. He watched for several minutes to see if anyone appeared. He heard Marie coming up behind him. As he started to turn he felt the club smash him on the side of the head followed by the taste of mud then blackness.

His mid and body lived in two worlds, one of shadows, one of light, and he could not wake. His head felt huge and he drew his hands to his forehead and attempted to focus his eyes, eyes like two wet and heavy overripe grapes. Shadows, then light, shadows, then light. Every attempt to open his eyelids ended in failure. Each time he pried them apart they drifted back into sleep, heavy and tight. Occasionally he managed to keep them half open for very short times, not long enough to place him back into the world, just long enough to see the shadows and light conjoin and separate. He thought he might puke and tried to roll to the side but, because his head felt like a large sack of uncooked rice, he was unable to toss it over his shoulder. Even with his eyes closed the world spun, stopped, then spun again. He saw lines, bars, roads, streaks. A flash of light crossed his eyes and he thought he saw a shadow fly past then the music of bamboo in the wind. He felt a pain in his side driving out the confusion as the world came into focus. In the corner, lying face down and quivering, huddled Maria.

"Hey you. Hey you," said a voice. More sharp jabs. Chau rolled toward the voice. A man squatted outside the cage and jabbed him with a bamboo stick. "Hey you." The stick poked his stomach. "Sit up."

Chau rolled to his knees. Three armed men stood beside the squatting man with the bamboo pole. Two other men, some kind of natives, black leggings up to their knees, black loin cloths, bare-chested, a crossbow in the hand of one, a spear in the hand of the other, black wraps around their heads, lingered in the distance. A cigarette dangled from between the lips of the squatting man. When he spoke the cigarette stuck on his lower lip and his mouth revealed jagged black and green teeth stumped from purple gums.

"Water," Chau managed to say.

"Water?" They all laughed and Thuy jabbed him again. "You want water? We want money. Give us money, we give you water."

Chau felt through his clothes. "My money is gone," he said. "Someone has taken it. Water please."

"Your money is our money. Our money is our money. Everything here belong to us. Where you from?" He jabbed Chau three quick times causing him to hunch over. "You have more money?"

"We are travelers," said Chau. "We are looking for the village of Khe Hieu."

"You spy on us." Thuy spit onto Chau's face. "I think you family has money. No peasant carries money like you. You too fat to work the land. We want money. You no go until your family give us money."

"Who are you?" said Chau. The man raised the pole between the bars and smacked Chau across the shoulder. He fell back to his side. "What have you done to the woman?" The man struck him again.

"You no learn," Thuy said. "No questions from you."

"May I please have water for the woman?"

"The woman big time boom-boom."

"Water for her, please." The pain in Chau's side became intense and he started to retch.

"Bah," the man said as they all walked away.

Chau pulled himself toward Marie and rolled her onto his arms. Her lips were swollen and her nose, dribbling blood, hooked to one side from the broken cartilage. She shivered as if she were cold and wet. She managed to utter several words.

"You not protect me much."

"I didn't know what happened?" said Chau, managing to rock her gently. "I didn't see them. What could I do?"

"A sleeping man no good in times of danger," she said. "These are dangerous men,

Black Flag Pirates from China."

"They knocked me out. See the blood running from my head? I just woke up. What could I do?" He professed innocence, attempted to show that he would have saved her if he had not been knocked out.

"A man awake cannot be hit on the head," she said. "There will be no love for you tonight. You might fall asleep, smother me with your weight. Black Flag Pirates - very dangerous." Her voice seemed to drift off and fade into quietness.

"Yes, yes, very dangerous, just be quiet and rest," said Chau. He rubbed the cold sweat from her forehead as her breathing became labored. He leaned against the bamboo bars and they both fell asleep.

When Chau awoke his head felt bigger than before and too heavy to lift. Even his neck felt stiff and streaks of pain shot through it when he tried to move. Marie's resting head had caused his shoulder to ache. She lay perfectly still beside him as he moved to kiss her awake. The lips were cold and lifeless. He clasped his hands around her head. She did not move. He placed his head on her dead body, arms wrapped around her tiny chest, and lay there until Thuy returned.

"Water!" said Thuy, holding a can of green water. He held the bamboo pole in his other hand. When Chau did not respond he slid it between the bars and jabbed him. He placed the can of putrid water into the cage. "Today you will tell us your family or we will remove your skin."

Chau sat up and moved toward Thuy. He felt every muscle in his body tighten. When he noticed that Thuy was alone he felt like throwing himself against the bamboo bars believing they might break from hatred alone. He would beat Thuy to death with his own pole. He took a deep breath. Anger served no purpose and often lead to a man's destruction. His anger must become cunning followed by revenge. He knelt down and gave a slight bow.

"The woman is dead," he said.

"Dead?" Thuy stomped a foot. "Dead! She worth much money between her legs! Now you must pay more!"

Chau looked at the green water filled with floating larva. He thought carefully. What he needed was time. It would take days for someone to return to Hanoi and several more to return. Sickness was not an option so he needed decent water and food.

"Bring me good water and food and I will tell you," he said. "Let me bury the woman and you will know my family."

"You no tell me. I tell you."

"There will be trouble," said Chau. "I will not talk. You can torture me for days but I will not talk. I will finish as the woman finished. I must remain in good health or my father will have you all killed. He is a very rich and powerful man."

"Bah," said Thuy, and walked away.

Chau moved Marie into the rising sunlight for a short time before placing her into the shade. He did not see the blood on her face, only what he thought was contentment. "There was not enough sunlight in her short life," he thought. He started to think of how his life might have been had she lived – a joy? – a burden? She was certainly the most pleasant woman he had ever known. He tossed away the threats living in his mind. Better not to think of things beyond his control. Only the present counted.

Thuy returned early that afternoon with his friends carrying a shovel and jug of fresh water and food. Thuy threw the shovel onto the ground.

"We want a name," he said. "No name and you will lie with the woman for one last time."

"I will tell you the name and write down the address. I must also write a note to my father saying that I am OK and the money must be paid within the week."

"Note?" He ground his teeth. "We don't need no stinking note."

"I know you are a smart man," said Chau, appealing to his ignorance and his arrogance. "My father will not give money to anyone who asks for it. Many people falsely say that his life, or the lives of his family, are in danger if they do not pay money. A rich man must be careful to remain rich. You can write the note but it is better if I write it so he will know my handwriting." Chau decided to assure Thuy by saying, "I will write it in Vietnamese on one side so you may read it and in French on the other because that is his language and he will know it's from me. You must read French?"

Thuy paced back and forth scratching his chin and looking from his friends to Chau. Finally he sent a man for a pencil and something on which to write. Chau drank the water and ate. The man did not return for some time.

"Ah!" said Thuy, to the returning man. "I wait all day. You drinking?"

"At first I could not find anything," said the man. "We looked everywhere before someone remembered the sack we took from the priest."

Thuy tossed the paper and pencil into the cage. On one side Chau wrote out the ransom letter in Vietnamese, in case Thuy could read, and on the other, in French. In French he explained the situation naming the last village he had visited and about how far he had walked from there and in what direction. He pointed the letter so he and Thuy could both see the Vietnamese side and read it out loud. He turned toward the French writing and attempted to read the same thing as he had done with the Vietnamese side.

"There," he said. "As you can see, everything is fine."

Thuy scrutinized the letter turning it from side to side. He held it up to the men and they all passed it between one another and nodded.

"On this small piece of paper I will also write where to deliver it. That place is the Pacific Shipping Line office on dock 29."

The French ran the company, as they did most of the business in Hanoi. With any luck he might be rescued. In any case, it gave him hope and a person needs hope to live, if only a false one.

A runner was dispatched to Hanoi as Chau, under guard, buried Marie. He lifted her tiny body carefully as if she might break and held her to his chest as he carried her to a spot beside a tree. He dug far enough from the tree to avoid most of the roots. Vietnamese bury their dead twice, the first time without much ceremony and void of protection from worms and rot. Several years later the bones are retrieved and placed into an altar. There was nothing to say, no soothing words, and he felt uncomfortable covering her body with dirt. The idea that everything is part of nature, that everything is a piece of everything else, that she would return again as a vibrant and exciting person, was little comfort. He wanted to drop into the hole and hold her for one last time, to lose his composure and weep uncontrollably. There was little to do now except wait.

A black Citron pulled in front of the buildings as Thuy crossed the street. A man in a gray suit stood beside the door and motioned to him. "We want a special day," he said. "One we can remember. I understand you can supply it."

Thuy looked inside where another five men sat, all in suits, all oozing with money and power, all in fedoras.

"Who tell you?" he said. Some of his men stood beside the buildings with weapons at the ready, anxious to strike.

"We were told to say, 'We are not Captain Riviere.'"

Thuy felt his anxiety disperse. The French Captain Riviere seized Hanoi in 1882. The Black Flags soon battled against him and paraded his head, along with 30 of his men, through the town and around the country. Thuy motioned to his men and they relaxed their weapons. He could feel the money weighing down his pockets, could even taste it. He wanted what everyone wants, power, and money bought power. Their reputation as a place of pleasure was growing, pleasure only money could buy. Little boys, little girls, no problem – beatings and rapes – no problem – torture – no problem. The perversions of people, especially men, were endless and he could supply as many as money could buy. Women, provocatively dressed, emerged from a building and stood beside the car.

"I believe we can accommodate you," said Thuy. "Do you want the total pleasure package?"

"Of course."

"It cost much money. Only the richest of men can afford such a night."

"Don't worry about that." He slapped his hand on the car's top and the other men emerged, all sharply dressed in black, brown and tan silk suits, calfskin shoes, tailored shirts tied up with jeweled cufflinks.

"The meal is not for cowards." Thuy looked each man in the eyes. "Necessary for the full effect. You will find yourselves filled with sexual power and ready for love after eating live cobra hearts and drinking their blood and venom." Thuy smiled, a slight curve running up each side of his face.

The girls led the men into a building before leaving them alone. They seemed confused.

"The women?" one asked.

"No women now," Thuy said. "All true delights need preparation."

He led them into a back room where a man with a long stick in one hand, and knife in the other, stood. He pointed into a pit with the stick. The men, tentative, fear in their eyes, looked in at the jumble of cobras. The pirate jabbed the snakes with the stick causing them to coil, lift their heads and spit. He stirred them up, spinning, rolling, and lifting up several of them as they coiled around the stick anxious to kill. After pointing out an especially aggressive one, one snarling and spitting, dancing on its tail, he snatched it up with the stick and jabbed it toward the trembling men backstepping through a cloud of obscenities and exploding eyes.

"Tit Ran," said the pirate. "Snake Meat. Very good. "

"You want this one?" said Thuy. "You can love with women all night with this one. Your joy will be great. Never forget. The power will last for weeks. This one, yes?" He jabbed at it with a knife. "See how much they fight before death."

The men looked at one another, all afraid, all wanting to go home, all knees trembling, all growing sick at the stomach, all of them terrified at the venom, all of them wanting to cry "NO" before shaking their heads "yes" and saying that that is truly the cobra they wanted, if not one even more terrifying.

"Who is the leader?" said the pirate. The man from outside the car raised his hand. The pirate nodded and Thuy led them into an austere room with plain hard tables and chairs. The men positioned themselves around the table, laughing nervously. Thuy mentioned the price of the event and services. They conversed quietly, tentatively piling their money into a plate snatched away by Thuy when it was filled.

The other pirate entered holding the dancing cobra around the neck. He thrust the snake at each of them before straightening it out. Thuy placed a large glass jar, filled with curled dead snakes floating in rice whisky, on the table. The pirate penetrated the snake with the knife on the belly side just behind the head, tipped it upside down and let the blood run into the whisky, the red slowly sinking to discolor the liquid. He turned it upright and split it from the slit to the anus. Picking out the still beating heart he tipped it into the open mouth of the leader who gagged twice before swallowing, nodding his head in bravery toward his friends, and wiping the tears from his eyes. The pirate removed the liver for cooking and continued to gut the snake. The leader was offered the first drink of bloody rice whisky. His friends all joined in according to rank letting the drink warm and deaden their bodies and minds. The feast soon began as several women brought in the fried snake-skins. The men enjoyed the crunchy coverings and found it a nice complement to the snake soup. The body of the snake, now a grilled filet, followed next with snake fried rice. No meal was complete without snake spring rolls that the men, now wobbly drunk and stupid, enjoyed and shouting compliments to the chief. The mixed snake dumplings were almost more delight than they could handle as they shoved the dumplings into their mouths, spreading juice onto their lips, chins and noses. Juice ran everywhere and mixed with the bloody spills of whisky. Fresh orange wedges finished the meal. Now, gorged with slithering aphrodisiac, the men followed the women into other rooms for sexual pain and pleasures only imagined by the poor.

Thuy sat contentedly enjoying a glass of whisky with the other pirate.

When the men finally emerged, bloated on sexual satisfaction yet deflated physically, unable to look one another in the eyes until the drive home when the exploits would expand to blubbering and boastful myth, they waited for the next pleasure.

"You like?" said Thuy. "I think you like very much. You must now relax in our special room. Then, more delights."

The women guided them through the rain and into another building, a darkened room lit with two dim candles. Each man was directed onto a bed and lay onto his side facing the opium pipes. The women rolled the black gum into small balls before placing them into the pipes and bringing them to life and handing them to the men. They lay near the men stroking their temples as they smoked. An eddy of misty dreams entered their minds and surged in a mottled rainbow about the cranium. Green skies, red mountains, purple trees melted onto the yellow sea and blue waves. Ancestors visited in smoke fanned by the bellows of tender fingers against temples and all of time drifted in and out under the sweet smell of the smoldering drug. As they drifted off into sleep, Thuy entered and cleaned out their pockets.

Chau did not know what was happening; all he could see was the vehicles arriving and departing each day. Thuy continued to treat him well, even gave him a blanket and a small jar of whisky. But as the days continued without the arrival of the messenger, he became more agitated. He attempted to claw at the vines holding the poles together. The means of escape were at hand but, because of his upbringing, the idea of breaking the jar and using the jagged edge of the glass, never occurred to him. One simply did not break things belonging to others. Had someone mentioned it to him, it would not have been a problem but Marie was no longer able to help him overcome his educated and non-practical status.

After four days, his head lying in sleep against the bamboo floor, he thought he felt a slight vibration as if another vehicle was arriving. More than one vibration clattered and he looked from the bars into a mist so gray and heavy he could not even make out the buildings across the way. He did not rise but remained on the ground. The outline of a jeep passed, then a truck. He heard the rumblings of possibly two other trucks then sharp commands in French: "Allez – Au sol," then shooting and more commands between the shots: "Au sol – Roulez vers l'avant – A droite – Ne vous inquietez."

Automatic weapons and a machine gun sounded through the fog, several explosions, a flickering reddish light followed by the smells of smoke and ash, all came his way. The attack lasted about fifteen minutes. He heard screams, shouts, an occasional round fired, much clattered conversation. Two legionnaires emerged from the haze, weapons at the ready. They threw them to their shoulders as they saw Chau hunched on his knees, arms raised. He had been thinking of what to do, how to handle the situation. It would be foolish to reveal he was well educated and spoke French for fear he might be discovered. He still thought he might be that important.

"Petit encul'e," said the legionnaire wearing the American helmet.

"Clochard?" said the other, in the cloth hat and asking if Chau was a tramp.

"Please help me," said Chau in Vietnamese. He pretended to fumble for an understandable French word. "Taulard, taulard," he said, pointing at his chest and saying "prisoner, prisoner."

The soldier in the helmet cocked his head toward the burning buildings. The fog had started to lift and Chau could barely make out moving figures. The soldier moved toward him, lowered his weapon, and offered him a drink from his canteen. Chau bowed politely and drank, the water dribbling from the sides of his lips. He had decided to say that the woman, Marie, had written the note because he could not speak in French, then tell them what had happened to her. A captain, with a Vietnamese legionnaire, appeared.

"Ask him if he speaks French," he said to the Vietnamese soldier.

Chau said several French words before shaking his head no. "Merdique, quoi fucking, faire l'amour, pisser."

The captain laughed at the gutter language most men learn in another language. "Get him out," he said.

The two original soldiers attempted to pry apart the bars and the door with their bayonets. It was more difficult than they had imagined and one of them ran off and returned with an axe. The captain shook Chau's hand before placing it on his shoulder and asking him to sit on the edge of the cage. He asked the men to bring him some food.

Through the interpreter he said, "Why are you here?"

"Did you come to rescue me?" said Chau.

"Rescue you? We knew nothing of you," said the captain. "Was this cage made for you?"

"It was here when they took me. A woman and I were on a trail but got lost. They knocked me out and beat the woman until she died. She is buried there..." He motioned with his head. "They put me in this cage; I don't know why. Except for knocking me out they did me no harm. I don't know why they killed the woman."

"She probably refused to become one of their whores. I am certain they had something special planned for you."

The soldiers returned with food and hot coffee for Chau and the captain. Chau now saw the bodies lying near the buildings. The living pirates were being loaded onto a truck.

"I am sorry about the woman," said the captain. "Where were you going? Perhaps we can help."

The English legionnaire and another soldier were tapping a small cross into Marie's grave. Another soldier placed several flowers he had found beside the cross. They crossed their chests with their fingers, one from right to left, the other from left to right.

"I don't know," said Chau, then realized his mistake after seeing the confusion on the captain's face. He had a gentle face and kind eyes, something he did not imagine from an officer. "I mean, I know. I just don't know where to find the village. It is called Khe Hieu and I was born there."

The captain nodded and told the men to stay with Chau until he had finished. They appeared to take great delight in this and offered him cigarettes and asked him many questions as if they had never met a Vietnamese. One very green soldier asked, "Is it true that the twats of Vietnamese women run across rather than up and down?"

"What a twit," said another. "Ask Zimmerm."

"He doesn't know," said another. "That wasn't her twat he was poking, it was her mouth." They all laughed.

"Show some kindness, boys," said a sergeant. "The man has just lost his woman."

They became quiet and uneasy.

Chau was very grateful for the food and water and when they had finished they escorted him to the captain. The captain had laid out a large map on the hood of the Jeep.

"It was very difficult to find. I think it's here," he said, pointing a finger toward a tiny dot. The name had been slightly smudged. "What do you think?" he said, to the others standing around including Chau. They all looked carefully before conferring and deciding that the dot must be the place. "Unfortunately we are not going that way, but come with us anyway. We are bound to find a unit moving in that direction and we will hand you over to them. I only hope it is the place."

"Your kindness is much appreciated," said Chau. "If it is not the right place I will be no more lost than I am now."

"Don't worry, we'll help you find your way."

Everyone laughed and again the captain almost apologized. "I am sorry they will not be able to drop you off at the village. It appears that no road goes there. You will have to walk about fifteen kilometers. This is very dangerous country; Viet Minh everywhere and they control the highlands. If you are not careful they will either kill you or make you fight in their army."

It was not long before the captain found a convoy moving west. As he talked to their captain the men all wished Chau the best of luck and gave him more gifts of cigarettes, food, and water in a French canteen. The men on the convoy were as equally friendly and together they shared a bottle of wine before he was left at the head of a trail.

Chau watched the trucks drive away, dust rolling up like an artillery blast. He stood before the trail looking down the long, dark, narrow, corridor. At the end of his vision he thought he saw a streak of light. He caught his breath and started to move.

Chapter 19

Chau walked slowly down the trail giving him a chance to think and to reflect. Too much had happened, and too quickly. His life had already changed dramatically and he felt there was more to come, a new life in a new place. He was more than a little anxious about the future and he felt the concerns in his chest. He did not understand his feelings toward the French. He both liked and detested them. They were cruel yet kind, intelligent yet stupid. They were everything right and wrong, and he found them confusing. Perhaps they were the same as any people. Governments make them different, he thought, bent them to their wills, their agendas. With a kindly government the people are kindly, with a brutal government the people are brutal. It was an interesting thought and helped him occupy the time as he walked.

And what of the Vietnamese? They were also kind and cruel, honest and treacherous. What difference did it make if they were governed by the French or the Vietnamese? Everyone is governed by something – a wife or husband, parents and grandparents, society. One simply carried on and did the best he could. Nothing would change for the typical farmer whether governed by France or the Viet Minh. The United States proved that. After rebelling against the British claiming taxation without representation, the new government imposed higher taxes than had Parliament. The hypocrisy was not just laughable but also sinister. The United States was not a nation of the people, by the people, and for the people. It was clearly a nation of the rich, by the rich, and for the rich. Government officials were some of the wealthiest people in the country and they catered to the wealthy people. Most politicians were lawyers who enacted laws to benefit themselves. Everyone got the joke except the average American citizen. Still, it seemed a great place to live and they appeared to be generous with their help around the world. What Chau wanted was black or white, yes or no, hot or cold. What he was finding on his quest was gray, sort-of, and tepid.

Chau eventually exited the corridor of foliage to see what he could only think of as Shambala. There, in a small valley, sat a village of perfectly constructed houses on stilts, bamboo sides, roofs of straw and leaves, well constructed front porches, pigs, chickens, water buffalo standing in the shade under the planks or grazing or scratching about for scraps. A stream rolled through the valley beside rice paddies. Terraced paddies climbed the hills from the bottoms to almost the tops. Black pajama-dressed people stood bent in the paddies and on the backs of water buffalo children rode laughing with their friends who swatted the plodding indifferent beasts. Cooking fires smoked outside several houses, people sat about working on projects that Chau could not see. More children played in the stream and an old man carried water in buckets across a pole on his shoulders, his feet scurrying like the back paws of a mouse. Chau had never witnessed such tranquility, such apparent serenity, a valley of total peace and calm and for a time he could only stand and stare, waiting for excruciating noise and chaos. That was bound to follow. He finally took a first step toward the village.

Pigs and chickens folded back like a mighty river to let him pass. He stopped and talked to an old woman, pipe hanging from between her lips, feet and toes knurled with age calluses and dirt.

"Chao co," he said, politely referring to an older lady. "Is this the village of Khe Hieu? I am looking for a man named Lac Long Quan.

The woman looked up and flashed a mostly toothless grin, the three visible teeth tilted at odd angles and betel nut had colored them solid black as they stuck like cracked tombstones from her bright red gums.

"You have come," she said. She folded her hands together and bowed, almost touching the ground with her head.

"I don't understand," said Chau. "Toai muoan xem, I want to see Lac Long Quan. Laom on, please."

"He said you were coming. Look just there –" she pointed to a house at the end of the other houses. "He is waiting." She placed her hands around his ankles before letting him leave.

It seemed very confusing to Chau. How would she know him? No one knew anything about him, especially about where he was going or about his arrival. Small children, mostly naked, watched him pass, the little boys absently holding their peckers, the older children smiling and curious at seeing a stranger. Many of them had never seen anyone new in the village their entire lives. Chau stood before the building not knowing what to say or not knowing how to act. A strong voice called out from inside. "Please enter. We have been waiting." Chau tentatively walked up the steps. The door was open and in the dark he barely made out two sitting figures. "Please come in." Embroidered blankets lined the walls. Cracks shown through the wood and blades of sun sliced across the floor.

Chau stepped inside and bent low waiting for his eyes to correct from the sunshine. As he lifted his head he saw the figure of an old man, his scraggily beard glowing in the dark. Beside him sat another man, vaguely familiar.

"We have worried," said the familiar man.

The voice – Chau knew it well. It was the servant Ling. His muscles tensed and his breath came in shallow strokes as his fists clenched. He cried out – "Ahhhhh, Ahhh-hhh!" and he bent his head and started to move forward. If he could just get his hands on Ling for one second he would make him suffer, leave him gurgling and quivering in his own blood. The old man stood in his way and offered his hand.

"We knew there would be confusion, young Chau," he said. "Do not be hasty. Hate is in you now but remember never to react to it without knowing the facts of a situation. Please sit and let me explain before you make a decision. Then act as you will, according to your conscience at the moment." He took Chau's trembling hand and, with his other kind and calming hand, lowered him to the floor. "Au," he said. "Please bring tea so that we can discuss the world like civilized men. For now, let us sit quietly for a few moments."

Chau's hatred toward Ling blinded him and he paid little attention to Au as she poured tea for everyone. He only noticed the ghost of the tiny figure taking instructions. Had he been perceptive he might have noticed a petite and beautiful young woman with beautiful hands like the wings of butterflies, with the face of the morning sun and hair like the flowing mane of a well-bred champion horse. She chanced a quick glance at him and love enveloped her like a warm monsoon rain. He resembled her idea of the perfect man, wiry build, handsome almost to a fault, and even filled with anger, kind and intelligent eyes.

"What we see is often at odds with what we think we understand," said Quan. "I imagine that you saw Ling commit a terrible act of betrayal against your father. Ling can better explain the circumstances so that you might better understand him, but please allow me to try because right now your ears will not hear him." He slowly and deliberately lifted the teacup and sipped before replacing it. "Your father understood that General Salan had uncovered his work with the Viet Minh and that he would soon be coming for him. His arrest would mean either a lifetime of pain in prison or, most likely, a public beheading as a warning to the Communists of the consequences of working against the French. He thought a better way to serve his people, to show the brutality of the enemy and to give the people an idea of what they were fighting for, would be to be brutally executed in the street."

He motioned for Chau to drink by placing the tips of his fingers against his cup. Chau watched Ling from the corners of his eyes. He sat stoically looking straight ahead as if in a trance.

"He informed Ling of the discovery, the one man, beside you, that he could trust. He asked Ling to inform the French that he had discovered a traitor, confirming what the General knew. He arranged a time for your father to be picked up and he wanted a reward. He said he also had some incriminating papers that he had found. Of course, Ling was burdened with grief and tried to refuse but your father was insistent. Ling could be trusted and he would be doing a great service to him and to his people. The French had already stationed a spy on the corner, the street vendor. Of course, you then know what happened." He again went quiet. "Au, more tea," he finally said.

Au, sitting to their side in a corner, was only too happy for another glance at Chau. She had not been mistaken. Chau was beautiful.

"Of course they needed a way to protect you. Had you been informed, your father thought you would not leave him and your death would serve no purpose. If you had seen what had happened, you also would not go. The only way was to run you out. He wanted you to stay in your room and he had hoped that you would look out of the window when you heard the commotion. It was a risky chance but the only one he thought you had. When Ling looked up, there you were. He went into great theatrics so you would understand that the Legionnaires were coming for you and that, perhaps, without you taking time to think, you would run. His people watched you the entire way until Marie placed you into the cylco and drove you to freedom. Now, let us sit for a while and enjoy the simple flavors of life: tea, a home, fields to work, food and good friends."

Chau stood and finally walked over to Ling. Ling threw himself at his feet and, uncharacteristically, started sobbing. Chau placed his hands on his head, then lifted him to his feet and wrapped his arms around him. "You are a good friend," he said, then returned to his seat.

"Au," said Quan. "Come and meet our guest."

Au knelt before them and, for the first time, Chau looked at her, her kindly attractive face, her delicate features, a fragile porcelain doll. A feeling of affection and longing covered him and he was tempted to touch her hand, her lips, her hair. This was the woman his father had told him about, the lover and companion to cherish for life. If it had been possible he would have married her that night. He felt no need to know her further or to spend time with her, all he needed to know he already knew; he had known her his entire life and would know her forever.

"I am honored," said Au. "Will you be staying?" Hope sounded in her tiny voice, hope longing and desire.

"My role is uncertain," he said. Quan tapped him on the knee.

"It is a necessity you be my guest. You will be seeing much of one another," he smiled, but they did not notice as they stared, most un-Vietnamese like, into one another's eyes. "You must excuse Ling and I, but we walk in silence every day at this time. Perhaps Au can show you about the village?"

Au walked to the edge of a rice paddy, green stalks pointing toward the blue-emerald sky, tufts of clouds hanging from sunlight, the rays warming the crooked people in the paddies.

"We have grown rice for over two thousand years," said Au. "But you know that. We have been fortunate to have a small valley. It makes life easier and we do not need as many terraces as some villages. See how beautiful are the ones we do have, like green hands holding the crops."

"I met a man along the trail who claimed he had never ventured beyond the village rice paddies," said Chau. "Is this common?"

"Perhaps. Like most of our village I only know this valley."

The people in the paddies appeared contented. Naked children played along the banks tossing dirt clods into the water or chasing one another with twigs. Two boys aggravated birds by tying string around their legs.

"Have you no curiosity, no desire to visit other places?"

"Is there something in other places different from this village or something for my family or for me that is not here?"

The answer caught Chau by surprise. What was out there for her? Possessions perhaps yet possessions seemed to offer no interest to the people he had met.

"What do you have here?"

"What do we not have here?"

Again, Chau had no response.

"How do you know Quan?" he said.

"He is the brother of my grandmother. Whenever possible I look after him although he has never asked me to nor has he ever asked me not to."

"Do you live with him?"

"I live with my family. I have no husband." She gave him a sly look.

"I only wondered," said Chau. "I have never lived in a village."

"I have been told that the villages are all the same. We are self-sufficient and self governed, totally autonomous, a self-contained unit. Yet we are bound to every other village as a partner in farming. And there…" She pointed to an area under bamboo trees. They started walking in that direction. "Here we bury our ancestors. Their spirit passes through them and into the soil then into the rice so we can inherit their souls." Chau held his chin.

"Yes," he said.

"I see you are skeptical. I understand in the European religions they eat the flesh and drink the blood of their savior. I don't understand the religion of cannibals. Perhaps you can explain?"

Chau said nothing. Au was very smart but he attempted no explanation. The rituals and dress of European spiritual leaders suddenly seemed ridiculous to him, high Hessian hats, adorned robes, walking sticks, attempting to drown people, preaching peace but causing war, believing that men could walk on water and part oceans and that a boat could hold all the animals of the earth built by a man who invents wine. These and one hundred other beliefs seemed childish and inane.

"I think you like me," said Au.

Again Chau was stunned. Vietnamese women were not forward. Vietnamese never asked a direct question, always talking around the subject.

"Your talk is odd," he said.

"But true. I think in several months we shall be married."

"You speak madness," he said. "What kind of woman are you?" Already he felt at ease with her as if he had known her all his life.

"The kind of woman who speaks your thoughts because you are afraid to speak them." She turned to look at him. "I do what you are afraid to do." She placed her hands behind his head and kissed him.

Nothing seemed forward about her, the speech perfectly reserved and natural, almost shy. It appeared as if they had known one another for years and were comfortable in their relationship, nothing timid or inhibited, nothing to hide or to reveal, contented and relaxed clothed or naked. Chau placed his finger against her lips feeling the warmth, fullness, the shape that covered his lips so well with gentleness like a chance encounter against a tender morning leaf.

"I love you," he said, not understanding why he said it, maybe need or compassion or a confession that he had experienced something beyond words outdistancing the physical known world into a place of mute and ceaseless comprehension.

When Quan entered his home he saw Chau and Au sitting side by side. He sat opposite them, his legs crossed.

"Ling has gone into the forest," he said.

"Chau has asked to marry me in two months," said Au, calmly.

"Why wait so long, or so soon?" said Quan. "Perhaps your family wants you to have the traditional six months engagement?"

"They understand love and not arranged marriages."

"Chau and I must talk. Please excuse us until later. We have much to cover and very little time."

Chau felt his chest empty as Au left, felt he might topple over if she did not soon return, wanted to follow her, to hold her again. The speed of his emotions for her twirled about his head.

"She said she would marry you before she had seen or even known about you," said Quan.

"How is that possible?"

"So little about women is known. Their intuition defies our comprehension. Even as a little girl she said you were coming for her. Last week she mentioned you were near and yesterday she started making preparations for your arrival. Best not to think about such things least you go mad. May I help you with something?"

"Why am I here," said Chau, glancing outside.

"Why are we anyplace?" said Quan, "And still at the same place? We can travel forever and never abandon ourselves. Any attempt to deceive, to believe what we are not, always ends in failure."

"How do I know what I am? Lately I have been constantly confused, unable to make decisions; am I rich or poor? for or against the French? for or against my own people?"

"Do not be confused into thinking you are what you are," said Quan. He poured tea for them both now that Au had left. "All that you think to be true is an illusion, an amusement for what we really are. We will discuss this farther at a later date. Too many thoughts about answers at one time can be overwhelming. The past must be forgotten because it holds uncorrectable sorrow and can no longer be manipulated. The future does not exist since it is not here. There is only now and decisions are made from now. It appears that you have decided to be Vietnamese, at least for a while. Perhaps during another time you will choose differently."

Chau watched the old teacher carefully. His black eyes seemed deeper and wetter than most eyes, even brighter because of the white tufts of contrasting eyebrows bursting in surprise from his forehead.

"The French are too strong to defeat. The Vietnamese will be overpowered, suppressed and punished because they fought," said Chau.

"And yet you have come to the mountains. Because of your European training you view war as something physical, not spiritual. Remember, bamboo bends under the wind and survives; the pine stands erect and is brought down. We seek harmony in our country, harmony through moderation in all things. Outbursts of anger have always been condemned."

"The French do not hold emotions inside and they believe in self-expression," said Chau. "All Europeans practice this way of feeling. They say suppressing feelings is not healthy."

Quan nodded his head.

"Because our lives are ones of personal suppression we have developed the habit of thoughtful introspection. The French are angry and forceful, unable to control themselves. They only know how to attack in anything they do. We condemn such actions and view them as inferior. Because of our quiet introspection we have never been conquered. Nations, believing in physical wealth, have invaded but left because we have nothing to rob and loot. Peace and contentment have no value to those seeking power. Some nations, like the Chinese, have attempted to win us over. We view these attempts as futile charades. Because we are militaristically a weak country our survival depends on great acting skills. We pretend to acquiesce to others. Sometimes we collaborate with the French without giving any useful information. If trapped, we surrender our bodies to live and fight again. We conceal hate, fury, and contempt. Even our prostitutes appear to gladly service the enemy they hate. Often they collect valuable information from self-delusional Frenchmen who believe the women love them." Quan sat quietly, eyeing Chau carefully. "There is no more for today except this. Each day you must try and clear your mind, throw out all thoughts, all ideas. Do not attempt to think of nothing for that is a thought. Rather, release all that is inside, without force. It will be difficult at first. Thoughts believe they live in the mind, do not understand they can leave at any time. Sit quietly and let them go. This exercise must be practiced each day. Only by not knowing can you know; only by being empty can you be full."

Chau pretended to sit and contemplate nothing but it was useless. His mind was full of Au. There was a forcefulness about her like that of Marie yet different, a deeper love perhaps, a tenderness Marie had not developed or had not had the opportunity to develop. Chau sat for about an hour before going outside to stroll about in hopes he might run into her. She had disappeared and did not return until the evening meal. She pretended not to know him, went about her work preparing the meal. Chau wondered if he had done something wrong. After the meal she cleaned up and on her way out, grabbed his hand and led him into the darkness.

"Are you angry with me?" he said.

"I love you," she said.

"But did I do something to anger you?"

"My care of Quan is a matter of honor. There is no room for him and you both in my small mind. Dedication is always to the elders, to the older family members, to those already gone to another world. When I am with you, only you exist." She squeezed his hand. "I will teach you the wedding ceremony so you will not feel foolish."

Each morning Chau worked in the fields, met Quan for study in the afternoons, and spent the evenings lying under a tree in Au's embrace. Only then did she acknowledge him, otherwise she worked quietly.

One afternoon he said to Quan, "I am not sure I understand the significance of emptying myself? What must I empty?"

"It is a way of thinking, a way without bounds," said Quan. He smoked his carved bone pipe. "People are raised to think only one way, from only one angle, one perspective. This cannot be done to be free, to truly think. What is the importance of a tea cup?"

Chau thought, tried to come up with something unusual. Of course, Quan might want just a simple answer. He did not want to be fooled or to resemble a common dupe. There was enough French in him to still be embarrassed and important. He decided to take his chances.

"A cup holds the tea."

"How does it do this?"

"The sides of the cup hold the liquid in. Without the sides the cup would be worthless."

"So having something solid, like the sides of the cup, is what makes it important?" Chau nodded. "Perhaps you are right." Chau grinned although Quan showed no emotion either for or against the answer.

"Perhaps the importance of the sides has no importance. Maybe they are not relevant in any way that can help the tea. The sides of a bowl are useful to a bowl holding rice. This is what we are taught, this is what we believe. To be empty is to be full. What is empty is useful."

"I don't understand."

"Perhaps there is another way the cup is helpful, another way it holds the tea?"

Chau thought as hard as he could. There was nothing about the cup except the sides and sometimes a handle to distance the heat like the Europeans did.

"I sense you are trying to think too hard," said Quan. "The answers to most of the world's problems sit before us yet we do not see them. Often the invisible, the simple, is the obvious."

He crossed his arms and sighed, not out of frustration but from thought. Many answers were simple once pointed out but were so difficult to find on one's own.

"Where does the tea go when poured from the teapot? Does it go into the cup's side? Is liquid soaked up there?" He rubbed his hands together. "Of course not, that would be silly. The tea goes nowhere."

"How can that be?" said Chau. He seemed more confused than ever. "Certainly it goes someplace."

"It is poured into the empty space inside the cup. It is poured into nothing yet this nothing is what makes the cup useful. Without the empty space the cup is worthless as a cup. We are not taught that nothing is something much less that it might be the most important thing. Without the empty places in our lungs, our mouths, our ears, we could not breathe, we could not eat, we could not hear. Without the emptiness between objects there would be no objects. The importance of physical love is the emptiness between a woman's legs. We enjoy the sensation not because something is there but because nothing is there. For us the world is an illusion because we cannot see nothing or even understand what sort of thing nothing is. Think of this for a while and you will learn that nothing is as important as something. Understand they both exist. Understand that life and death, male and female, black and white, everything and its opposite are the same thing. Think about everything you know to be true then find a way to think of it differently, a way you have not been taught. Even contradiction is possible."

Chau wanted to know how he knew about so many things.

"In the universe there are as many things as there are," said Quan. "Is that true?"

Chau nodded.

"So, the universe is then finite, yes?"

Chau nodded again knowing that something was to follow.

"Between everything that exists lies something between, even if it is air. If something lies between everything, then the universe is infinite. Is that true?"

"It would seem to be true," said Chau. "But no logical statement can hold a contradiction. Every philosopher knows that."

"And yet contradictions appear to exist," said Quan. "The universe is both finite yet infinite. But enough of today's lessons. You must forget such foolish ideas and think of your wedding. All learning is essentially useless, anyway. Even words and descriptions are lies and can never depict the truth."

When Quan left, Chau continued to contemplate, to sit and attempt to empty his mind. It was impossible. One could not think about emptying his mind since to think meant his mind was not empty. He focused on various parts of his body, his feet, his hands, and his fingers. He tried to be aware of their presence without thinking about them. Then there was Au. She appeared all over his thoughts and refused to leave. His lungs filled and emptied in slow rhythm, in and out – in and out. Becoming Vietnamese was proving difficult. Quan was right, worry about the upcoming wedding.

The morning of the wedding Chau twirled in his blue dress, a simpler form of the ao dai worn by women. The loose fit felt unusually free and the cold silk brushed against his body giving him an erection, a daily occurrence from his thoughts of Au. They had not made love and his best friend had become a palsied right hand with a tender grip. Quan had made the engagement offer to her parents in place of his father and a Buddhist monk had set the date. Because of the spiritual nature of the occasion the date and time were very important. In the past marriages were arranged by the parents and the couples often did not see each other until the wedding. Now it was just a formality, a lingering of times gone by since the couples chose themselves.

Also from the past was the permission to receive the bride. The groom's mother and her close friends would visit the bride's home bringing a gift of betel and ask the bride's family for official permission to receive the bride. A useful practice in the past, when the bride often eloped with her lover rather than marry one she did not love or had not even met. A friend of Au's performed the tradition for Chau.

That afternoon Chau took his place in the groom's procession, everyone carrying decorated umbrellas, to the bride's house where gifts from the groom's family were presented to the bride and her family. Usually a man of stature, the village intellectual and a good speaker led the procession. Quan handled this job. The groom's father followed, then immediate family and friends. Friends he had recently met formed this function. To show she would not interfere with the bride's place in the home, the mother seldom attended. They carried lacquered boxes covered in red cloth and filled with gifts: wine, tea, betel, fruit, cakes, fabric and jewelry. Two of his friends carried a roast pig for the family feast. Since Quan was a simple man void of possessions, Chau wondered where he got all the gifts. He decided to just accept it and not question him.

The procession spread out before the bride's house and lit a row of fireworks, spinning sparks and short flames shooting into the air. Firecrackers sounded from outside the bride's house to welcome them. An exchange of introductions took place with bowing, handshakes, and a great amount of smiling mouths revealing chipped brown and black teeth. Chau stepped forward and presented the gifts to Au's parents. Once satisfied, the family invited Chau to greet the bride. Au stepped outside, radiant in her elaborate red ao dai sometimes called the ao menh phu and patterned after the royal ao dai of the Nguyen Dynasty. Chau had never witnessed such beauty, such a perfect woman, so tiny, so fragile.

They knelt before the altar of her deceased ancestors and lit incense sticks before asking the ancestors to bless their marriage and their future family. Au turned to her family and Chau to Quan and gave them thanks for raising and protecting them. They faced each other and bowed out of respect.

Vietnamese generally have only one formal tea ceremony, just after the wedding. The affair was a quiet one full of grace and advice as Au and Chau poured tea for their parents. The parents offered guidance on the tasks and joys of a good marriage, ways to get along, to raise a family, to remain happy and content through work and respect. Candles were lit and combined to show the joining of bride and groom and of the two families. Chau enjoyed the advice and the ceremony but was anxious to return home and revel in Au's love. He was forced to wait. Quan had chosen a good friend to perform the next act because Chau had no mother. She opened the box of jewelry and placed the baubles on Au for good luck. Speeches followed. Chau, slightly embarrassed, asked her parents if he might take her to his home. His voice had quivered with anticipation as they nodded. The procession followed him home and launched more fireworks before they were taken to his ancestor's altar to repeat the request to be watched over and blessed. Au was then taken into the house and shown her wedding bed. What would it be like, she wondered, to have a man inside her? Although a virgin she had been thoroughly instructed by her mother as to what was expected of her – lay back with her legs apart and grit her teeth until he had finished then catch her breath and wait for the pain and joy to subside. There must be more to it than that? She felt the need to have him inside her, wanted him there.

The reception began amid much joy and laughter. Food and drink flowed freely, Chinese banquet dishes, seafood hot pots, seasoned lobster, vegetable dishes, wine, beer, Scottish whisky, the house filled with gaiety. Chau did not know how Quan had acquired so many fresh ocean dishes. He waited for Au who was not allowed to appear until the party was underway. The guests brought gifts of money all rolled into envelopes and offered them to Chau and Au when she arrived. They traveled from guest to guest to collect the gifts and to thank the guests for their kind blessings. Chau never knew how the people had gathered so much money for them. They must have been saving for years but that could not be true for several weddings took place every year.

The couple finally found themselves beside the wedding bed. Au was an awkward combination of anxious joy and embarrassed confusion. She understood that the night would take its natural course and she felt wet between her thighs. Should she turn away to undress? Should she let him enjoy her naked body by facing him? Chau made the decision for her as he threw his arms around her, his lips against hers, and undressed her. She eased herself under the covers as his clothes fell to the floor. His penis looked tremendous and deadly and she was not sure she could take it all in yet it fascinated her. Chau slid in beside her and tried to remember all the ways of love-making Marie had taught him but it was no good. He had wanted Au for so long that he immediately mounted her. She felt she would split at the encounter and the pain tore at her. She groaned and panted in an attempt to hold back the screams from pain. The pain pulled with it some pleasure, some desire to keep him in and yet an equal desire to push him out. Her hips started to rise and fall with his rhythm until she felt all his muscles tense and a rapid throbbing followed by a gush of warm liquid that flowed into her.

For a moment Chau let his weight crush her tiny body before remembering to roll to the side with her still in her arms. He felt her tears roll down his chest like a miniature rainsquall.

Act IV - Waking to Nightmare

Chapter 20

General Henri Navarre sat quietly and alone behind his desk in Saigon. His Persian cat lounged on the desk, its tail waving like a shaft of wheat in the wind. Navarre had recently assumed command of the French Expeditionary Corps in Vietnam from General Salan. A quiet, cold, reclusive man, Navarre and the cat were not dissimilar. He trusted no one, not even his generals, and seldom revealed his plans until the last minute. Part of that mistrust concerned the Viet Minh, who always seemed to know of any French military action, and part because of his natural mistrust of others. No one could be trusted. That had been part of the problem for the dismal lack of military success in Vietnam. Too many people knew too much. Unless plans could be concealed from his commanders until just prior to execution, surprise, therefore victory, was not possible. An arrogant man, he had a strong will, believed in himself and seldom listened to others unless they agreed with him. His intelligence and courage were not in dispute, just his knowledge of Vietnam. He had never been there.

Navarre had always wanted to be a soldier. Even as a young man he was a quiet and suspicious with a bright analytical mind. As a 19 year-old cadet in a dragoon unit, he fought with distinction in World War I. After the war he served many years in North Africa fighting Arab rebels before moving to France and enrolling at the Military Academy of Saint-Cyr. The country bored him and, restless to move on, he cut his stay short after graduation from the war college and spent the next four years campaigning in Morocco. French secret intelligence work followed and, after the Germans invaded, he escaped to England, joined the Free French, and commanded the 3rd Moroccan Spahis. After the war he was assigned to Field Marshall Juin as Chief of Staff at NATO Headquarters then given command of the Fifth French Armored Division in Germany. What he wanted was war, some kind of action to prove his brilliance. What difference if it was in the desert or the jungle? – war was war. Understanding Vietnam, its people, and especially the difficulties of the terrain, was not important.

He lifted the cat off the desk and placed it on his lap, stroked its head with affection, an affection not shown to others. Even in social situations he avoided personal contact, wanted no a friends, and planted nervousness in others. The cat purred rhythmically under his gentle stroke.

France, tired of the war, the expense (although the United States was paying most of the cost) the political unrest, the street protesters demanding peace and to bring the soldiers home, had chosen him to establish an "honorable political solution" to the dispute, something amiable to both nations so peace could finally be established. What the government did not want was any further military action that might delay their plans. His mission was to keep the status quo, no hostile actions, until a diplomatic solution could be found. Under no circumstances was he to antagonize the Viet Minh under Ho Chi Minh.

Navarre had a better idea, a plan to defeat the Viet Minh. The plan needed to be implemented as soon as possible so he could claim he had not received the orders from the government to remain calm and to restrain from any hostile action. His victory would eliminate any need for negotiations, therefore any embarrassment with such an inferior people. Dictatorial instructions would become the order of the day, restoring France to its rightful place on the world stage, his goal. Even though he had outlined his plan to the government, they still insisted that any military action be strictly defensive. Fight only if attacked and wait for an agreement at Geneva.

He leaned back in his chair and checked his tunic. Orderlies washed and pressed his uniforms each day and he never performed in public unless spotless. With smartly combed grey hair, he was neither tall nor graceful yet no one ever doubted that he was in command. He always listened intently to his officers' suggestions and opinions before disregarding everything they advised. They did, however, appreciate the fact that after given an order, he never bothered them again – no standing over them, no constant checking up – he left them alone to work, and he expected the job to be done professionally and on time.

He had been waiting for a call, since before sun-up in his air-conditioned office, from General Gilles, circling in a C-47 from above the valley of Dien Bien Phu. Everything about the drop into in the valley depended on the weather and on General Gilles' decision to commence Operation Castor, often called the Navarre Plan. Castor seemed simple enough to Navarre. In an effort to protect the highland areas from the Viet Minh and their eventual invasion into Laos and its capital city of Luang Prabang, he needed a military force in the area, some kind of blocking force. This force would also divert many Viet Minh from the Delta giving that area a much-needed rest. French troops there had been battered down to complacency. A major problem with the Viet Minh was getting them into a fight with enough troops to cause them any damage. They usually fought from ambush then ran away before any counterattack could be formed. In order to dislodge the French from the valley of Dien Bien Phu, thus clearing their way into Laos, they would be forced to fight in mass. The valley of Dien Bien Phu already had an airfield, it seemed the perfect place for a force of elite troops to establish a substantial airhead. Planes could supply the units by using the airfield and also from the air by parachute should the main road be destroyed, (everyone agreed that would happen) so the soldiers could carry out uninterrupted attacks in the hills causing the Viet Minh no end of trouble. Returning to the base camp for re-supply, the men could attack again and again until they had wiped out the enemy or caused them to attack the airhead with enough force that the French could defeat them in one swoop thus causing their capitulation. Either way, the plan was brilliant, harass them to death or wipe them out. Even the best United States Generals had approved of the plan and had agreed to pay for the entire cost of the operation. They guaranteed Navarre that, should something go wrong - very unlikely with such an air-tight plan - American planes from offshore aircraft carriers would swoop down and rescue them. Even the use of nuclear weapons had not been ruled out by the United States should the need to use them arise.

Not all his officers agreed with the plan. Differing opinions seldom swayed Navarre. The biggest worry, which he felt was his biggest asset, was the airfield. Supply ships carried just enough fuel to get to Dien Bien Phu, 185 miles from the Delta bases, and return to the coast. There might not be enough airplanes to carry in the supplies unless all the planes in the area were used, impossible since many were always under repair or needing maintenance. Still, French Air Force Colonel Nicot agreed that the estimated 80 tons of supplies needed each day was possible from his three squadrons so long as he kept every serviceable C-47 in the air and was not called upon to supply other units facing combat. They would have to wait. Should the tonnage requirements increase, he had no response. No other aircraft were available. Navarre had already solved the problem by agreeing to hire civilian aircraft from a company secretly established by the American C.I.A. Also, the F8F Bearcat fighters could not reach the area without belly-tanks. Several could, however, be stationed at Dien Bien Phu itself and even more on the Plain of Jars in Laos. The weather, always unpredictable in the highlands, was also a concern. The valleys were known for heavy morning fogs and when the monsoons hit, supplies might become spotty or impossible. Navarre felt the monsoons would cause more problems for the Viet Minh , who had to travel through the jungles, than for the French.

Another problem, hardly discussed by anyone, was keeping the runway open. What would happen if supplies could not be flown in? Because the Viet Minh controlled the country, nothing could travel by road. Navarre dismissed the possibility. Not enough Viet Minh guns, or ammunition, could be brought against the French, and besides, they were terrible artillerymen, slow and inaccurate.

Navarre had unlimited faith in his favorite officer, the one-eyed General, Gilles. After all, Gilles had been an unwilling catalyst for this type of operation. He had commanded a similar airhead at Na San. Three divisions of Viet Minh, the 308th, 312th, and 316th had attacked the base and were beaten off after twice overwhelming the outer defense line. The French defended the airhead for six months constantly fending off the Viet Minh. General Salan, Navarre's predecessor, marked it a great victory, an example of what a determined French force could accomplish when properly deployed and supplied. General Gilles thought otherwise. The story of the battle made glorious headlines but he knew they had barely escaped disaster. The French had been constantly pinned down and the airhead was eventually abandoned as too costly in men and supplies for such minute results. He claimed it was the worst six months of hell anyone could have imagined. General Gilles, commander of all French airborne forces in Indochina, pointed this out to General Navarre, who listened quietly, ignored everything he said, and placed him in charge of the paratrooper drop into the valley. It was now up to him, circling in a C-47 above Dien Bien Phu, along with Deputy Commander-in-Chief General Pierre Bodet, and General Jean Dechaux, commander of air operations in northern Indochina, to make the final decision, the favorable decision anticipated by General Navarre.

Navarre understood the decision would go first to General René Cogny, his commander of French forces in northern Vietnam, in Hanoi. Navarre, upon his arrival in Vietnam, had placed Cogny in command. Now he wondered why? Other officers had warned him about Cogny, a difficult man to control, as opinionated as Navarre and just as strong willed. At the time, Navarre felt Cogny was the best man for the job. In the beginning of their relationship, they worked well together. Cogny had agreed to Operation Castor as long as its primary function was offensive, not defensive, and only lasted for a short time. Legionnaires and paratroopers trained for attack and counterattack, not defense. Nothing more hampered their spirit than digging a hole in the ground and waiting to be attacked. They needed to attack, and attack relentlessly, to be effective. They understood nothing about defense and attempting to fight defensively would only demoralize them. Navarre, chuckling to himself, had convinced Cogny that to attack was the primary goal and the troops would not be in the valley long even though he had planned the mission for defense. All he had needed was for Cogny to agree to invade the valley.

He looked out the window. The sun was full up and it would not be long now before the final decision. He held the cat, tail snapping from side to side, and blew on its face watching his eyes pinch together and sneeze. Everything was going his way. He wondered what Gilles was thinking?

The specialized radio equipment stifled the engine noise inside of the C-47 as the three generals attempted to talk over the constant rumble of engines that seeped through. They all looked quite serious, heads nodding, hands clasped or sometimes placed on chins or through hair. They had left Bach-Mai airfield at 0500 in order to reach the valley by 0630. Heavy fog blanketed the valley obscuring everything. A soldier poured coffee into tin cups from a tumbler, occasionally slopping it onto the general's boots.

"If the fog doesn't clear soon it's off," said Gilles. "We still have time." His glass eye, below his paratrooper beret, refused to follow his good one. He sipped the coffee and brooded. General Dechaux pushed his face to the window. The decision to proceed was actually his, not Gilles, since everything depended on the aircraft filled with paratroopers and equipment finding the drop zones. Gilles needed only to call in the decision.

To steady himself, Gilles slid his hand along the inside of the fuselage as he walked to the crowd of resting airborne pathfinders ready to drop and secure the landing zones for the rest of the troops. He stopped to look them over. They seemed huge under all their equipment, arms, ammunition, grenades, and food, stuffed into large canvas bags that would dangle from a strap below them, and hit the ground first. Helmets tightly strapped under chins squeezed out their thin faces. Parachutes and safety chutes pushed on backs and stomachs and bent the men, like strange gargoyles, over weapons. Gilles caught the eyes of every man, said nothing, nodded his head before returning to his seat. He knew the Viet Minh would be in the valley, just not how many. The area produced many tons of rice and generated about three million dollars each year through opium sales, money used by the Viet Minh to secure arms,.

"I have never liked a fortress in a valley floor surrounded by higher ground," he said.

"You worry too much," said General Bodet, Navarre's strictest supporter, his hands forming a megaphone around his lips. "Na San proved that."

"Luck," said Gilles. "Besides, this set-up is different. We formed two defensive rings around the airstrip at Na San, all interconnected. Even then the outer ring was breached twice. The idea here is to build separate strongpoints. The strongpoints are too far apart to connect. They might get cut-off, then what - a disaster?"

"No scrawny Viet Minh can beat even the worst paratroopers." Bodet punched his fist into his hand to emphasize the point.

Gilles turned away. Arrogance had been beaten from him by fighting the Viet Minh over the years and his views were more realistic. They were no longer a rag-tag force of guerillas scrounging for weapons and equipment. General Giap, with the help of the Chinese, had turned them into a first-class fighting force, a fearless and dedicated army. With the end of the Korean War, the Chinese had shuffled weapons to the Viet Minh including much needed artillery, captured from the Americans, and they had trained the artillerymen, once relatively incompetent, into very skilled soldiers. Na San had taught him much about the new Viet Minh army and their newly acquired skills. He looked out the window. The fog was starting to thin and to lift. If it continued, and General Dechaux agreed, he would have to radio General Cogny in Hanoi.

Cogny's headquarters seemed like a party compared to Navarre's. He sat at his desk, coffee in his hand, and boasted of the coming battle. "We've got them now," he said. He toasted with the cup raising it high over his head. "Once we secure the airstrip we'll fan out through the hills like tentacles strangling every one of the them." Light glowed from his eyes and the smile that cut through his face brought everyone to laughter. General Masson, Cogny's deputy, looked glum and shook his head. "Ah, René, why so glum?" said Cogny, leaning over his desk.

"You know, I'm on record opposing this mission." He said. "So are Gilles and Dechaux."

"René, you worry too much. This is exactly what we want, a big battle to end it all, isn't that right?" He looked to the other officers. "I only hope they don't get away." They all grumbled agreement and raised their coffee cups. Masson slowly raised his cup and forced a grin as he shrugged his shoulders. "Sure, René, I've had some doubts but that's the way of an officer. Once the decision is made it's full steam ahead, eh?"

General Cogny was a soldier's soldier. Standing over six feet, rugged and handsome, his soldiers, officers, and women liked Cogny. The press especially enjoyed him for his inability to remain secretive about anything. He loved to talk, especially about himself. Every private fart was announced to the press or at parties. While General Navarre refused to disclose anything important to anyone, Cogny could never resist broadcasting even the most insignificant details. His mouth flapped like a flat tire on a motorcycle. He loved the press and seeing his name and photos in the papers caused him no end of pleasure. He was also fearless. Twice captured by the Germans in WWII he managed to escape the first time and join the resistance. His luck ran short a second time when the Gestapo captured him. After being beaten and interrogated for six solid months, he spent the remainder of the war in Buchenwald and Dora concentration camps. That was the last time he ever kept quiet about anything. Little more than a sickly, limping skeleton remained after liberation and it took years for him to regain his health and he had walked with a cane ever since. Before the war he was a brilliant scholar and graduated not only as an engineer from France's Ecole Polytechnique, also with degrees in political science and law. He eventually became an artilleryman and moved rapidly through the ranks.

An orderly entered the room and handed Cogny a dispatch from the radio operator. He smiled and banged his fist on the desk. "The fog is lifting," he read. "It's on, men. Make preparations for the departure. The grand show is about to begin. Even now the boys are anxious to jump."

Bix sat quietly and uncomfortably in the waiting C-47. Sixty-five aircraft, from two airfields, had been secured for the jump – not enough for everyone needed in a single jump so the aircraft would have to return to their bases for a second drop. Bix glanced up and down at the other twenty-three paratroopers to see if he recognized anyone.

Almost half of them were sleeping. Several talked quietly, but not many. Most of the men sat with their thoughts: the mission ahead, home, family or girlfriends, about the number of their comrades soon to be wounded or killed. Bix did not like fighting without friends. Even dying bothered him little as long as a friend was there. This was not his unit. He had been temporarily assigned to the 6th Colonial Parachute Battalion under the command of Major Marcel Bigeard. He was the finest commander in Vietnam, totally fearless, and always inspired his men. Bix belonged to the 1st Foreign Legion Parachute Battalion, known as le BEP, scheduled to drop the following day, November 21st. Several troops, from units arriving the following day, had been assigned to drop on the first day to learn something of the terrain and relay it to their own units when they arrived. He had no idea of the objective except 1st Company was to secure a bridgehead west of their drop zone. Objectives made no difference anyway. He had parachuted enough times to understand the men would be scattered for miles. A C-47, from the first man dropped to last, would sprinkle them almost three miles, an impossible distance from which to regroup for twenty-four lightly armed soldiers. Various units would tangle with one another and total chaos would reign for hours, sometimes days, as they attempted to find their units and get organized. Until then confusion and disorientation were paramount.

Not having his friend, Henrich Knowles, by his side worried him. After Bix joined the French Foreign Legion, Knowles, a career soldier and former Wermach Panzer Officer had taken him under his wing. Knowles seemed to understand everything about warfare much like the sergeant he had read about in a novel about World War I. "It's something one studies by losing," Knowles had said "I wouldn't want to lose a second time." Bix was content with the Legion. In their ranks he had found the adventure for which he sought. He even attempted to visit his old friend, Chau, and thank him for the advice, but had yet to find the time. None of the soldiers had known where they were going that morning but they expected it to be somewhere in the highlands because they had been told to prepare for the cold. Weather in the highlands sometimes dropped to below freezing. He heard the engines cough, fire to life, and rattle the plane. Waiting was the difficult part. The noise and shaking fuselage had calmed him.

He looked around again for anyone he knew. Vietnamese filled much of the plane. They consisted of almost half of the French Forces in Vietnam and looked barely strong enough to hold up their equipment. At the end of the plane he noticed a familiar figure. He tried to yell out. "Lachen! Lachen!" His voice quickly fell to the floor. He motioned to another soldier who looked his way and pointed to Lachen. Lachen peered toward Bix, laughed and flipped him the finger. Bix responded in similar fashion, feeling comfortable in finding a comrade. As the plane rumbled into the air, Bix leaned back and fell asleep, content that he was not alone.

Viet Minh Regiment 148 had erected operations in the valley to train new troops and protect the rice and opium. The paratroopers were to pinch together from north and south crushing the Viet Minh Regiment in the village Muong Thanh, sometimes called Dien Bien Phu, like a walnut shell, an easy operation on paper.

None of this concerned Bix as he awoke over the valley and waited to jump, with his friend Lachen and twenty-two other fully equipped paratroopers, from the side door of a rattling C-47. The sergeants knew what to do, that was all that mattered. He shivered as if the cold had crept between his bones. Cold crouched over the high-lands in the mornings and from the open door Bix saw the valley mist still rising. He expected to make an easy jump, gather with the parts of his unit he could find, and destroy the surprised Viet Minh soldiers. With any luck, he would get a scratch, a small wound, something to finally mark him as a soldier and complete his adventure. That was the final touch he needed to complete his grand adventure, something to show his friends back home and to impress the women. The C-47 idled down to 104 MPH, jump speed, as the engines quieted. A rush of air whisked into the plane as the door opened. Regrouping on the ground was the most difficult part of any jump. Jumping was just a matter of stepping outside, letting the air grab him.

Bix waited for the red jump light, felt an air pocket ripple the wings of the plane, breathed in the crisp atmosphere as it brushed in. He wanted to touch Lachen's hand but his hand shook too much and Lachen stood too far back. Soldiers did not admit to being afraid but they understood that inside they were all afraid. Although he had been in several skirmishes, this would be his first heavy combat, his first time drifting into a possible stream of bullets. His stomach ate into itself and he forced a tight grin. Jumps always warmed him and the rush of falling free for several moments, of having no weight pressing against anything solid, caused him to flush. He moved into posi-tion, secured the ripcord, hummed, because he knew no one could hear the vibrations of, "Begin the Begin" rattling in his throat. The light flashed and he tumbled out.

His stomach rose with the drop, then snapped into place with the swelling chute, his body pulling against the nylon cords. Heavy under packs, ammunition and equip-ment, he carouseled above the earth. Surprisingly, dropping faster than usual, Lachen drifted to his left, held out a thumb before disappearing under his chute. Below, through the lifting haze, Bix saw the valley: long, wide, and flat. High hills, black with vegetation, surrounded the several smaller hills pushing from the valley floor. As he descended the 4,000-foot dirt runway and over a hundred distinct houses, Dien Bien Phu appeared. Smaller villages dotted the area. Two roads traversed the valley and crossed the Nam Yum River just outside the town. Half dry rice paddies butted to-gether in irregular checkerboards of off-colored greens.

Bix looked carefully over the ground. Jumping was never a problem – landing was. An incorrect landing meant a broken ankle or leg, neither of which qualified as a wound. He had twisted an ankle before and the pain still troubled him. A small creek cut through the runway and the Viet Minh had pocked and trenched the landing strip rendering the field unusable. Bix felt his chest go hollow as he descended and finer details appeared. Below, the ground bubbled with Viet Minh. Bix twisted from side to side, aware of his vulnerability. The Viets ran in confusion. Machine gun emplacements and mortars stood directly under his feet. He looked for Lachen but he had joined the other paratroopers as they became so many drifting doves. The Viet Minh had apparently been training on the drop zone. No one had expected so many soldiers. Bix fumbled with his M-1 carbine, attempting to work the action.

Many of the Communists, quickly gathering their heads, positioned themselves and fired on the descending paratroopers, splatters of dust sprinkling the ground where empty cartridges flew. Bix forgot about getting wounded. His bowls loosened, sloshed against his insides. Only his pinched, frightened sphincter prevented him from crapping in mid-air. Stories about messing one's pants were false. Not even gas could escape such a tight seal. The crapping came later.

He pulled into himself, loaded and unlocked his weapon. Enemy bullets snapped the air, several ripping through his parachute. The ground rose quickly with his descent. He released two quick rounds, tapped back the safety on the weapon for protection, and twisted into a favorable landing position before cracking against a small incline and tumbling into the dirt. Dazed, dust powdering into his eyes, he fumbled for the harness release. Before unlatching the harness, the parachute jerked him back to his feet. He trotted behind the billowing kite, a stumbling target, trying to retain his balance. Like spinning tops, paratroopers tumbled to the ground around him and disappeared into clouds of dust. More bullets zipped through the nylon as he worked free, flopped to the dirt and jumped back against the bank waiting for the rest of the unit to assemble.

Above, blankets of white twirled, billowed, toward earth. Parachutes, a sudden pox, almost blocked the sun. The sky resembled a field of mushrooms, the new chutes white, the old ones a dirty gray. Viet Minh fired into the air. The few paratroopers who died during descent, arms at their sides, legs stiff, smacked against the soil like felled wood. One paratrooper's chute, spiraling like a torn rag, refused to open and he frantically clawed at the lines and attempted to fly before crashing against the dirt fifty yards from Bix. Lachen, breathing heavily after freeing his chute and running through the dust, tumbled to the dirt beside Bix.

Communists immediately pinned down the Airborne Artillery and the Engineers as the paratroopers landed directly in their midst. Bix and Lachen, keeping close to the ground, offered supporting fire. "I can't tell them apart," yelled Bix. The paratroopers and the Viet Minh both wore French camouflage uniforms. Lachen did not respond except to tip his head. Only the helmets of the opposing armies were different. Bix, shaky, confused, looked directly at the fighting as if he were not involved, just an observer at a parade. The fighting appeared unreal, mystical, the soldiers like puppets on an ethereal stage. If he blocked out the noise, moved his eyes from one side to the other, disregarded the smoke and fighting, the valley became beautiful and he could imagine swarms of butterflies sunning themselves in the air, lovers sneaking a kiss beside the river, an old man enjoying a bowl of tobacco as he watched the sun rise.

"It's going to be hell today," said Lachen, to several paratroopers who gathered near. His voice brought Bix back into the battle. "We all look alike," said Lachen, confirming Bix's confusion.

"They'll be the ones running," said a corporal, who bled from a wound across his forehead. He fired a shot toward the airfield with his MAS 36 then fought with the awkwardly designed bolt to feed another round.

"Maj. Bigeard is at the southern end of Natasha, our drop zone," said Lachen, who always seemed to know what was happening. "We had better follow the rule to work toward the start of the drop and fight our way there."

"What about the bridgehead?" said Bix. Lachen shrugged and started ahead.

The Viets, numbed by the number of paratroopers, fell back toward the village before regrouping and starting a counterattack. Bix quickly forgot about the bridgehead, did not even know where the bridge was. A battle was nothing more than mass confusion anyway, soldiers running this way and that, noise and explosions.

Major Bigeard, without regard to safety, stood in the line of fire on a small knoll issuing orders. Radio sets gathered at his feet, some apparently broken. Bigeard, affectionately called Bruno, always inspired his men and Bix, stopping a moment to admire him, had never seen anyone so fearless. A radioman, eyes like two headlights and aware of the danger, crouched at Bigeard's side. Bigeard, one hand on his hip, spoke to an aide. He rallied the nearby troops moving them toward the village of Muong Ten with his pointing hands. Bix stumbled along beside Lachen not wanting to leave the safety of Bigeard. The heat was becoming killing and he refused to show Lachen the effect it was having on him, that an American was not twice the man of a Frenchman. The forward push soon bogged down under heavy defensive fire from the Communists. The battle lines became more clearly drawn and Bix did not have to distinguish helmet shapes to know the targets anymore. The Viet Minh were on one side, he was on the other. His stomach had calmed and he had learned that waiting, not fighting, was always the difficult part of a battle. Bullets cleared the senses, left little room for pondering life's more difficult problems. But waiting, that was something else. Waiting was a sore inviting infection. He turned back to see Lt. Allaire talking to Bigeard.

Sweat ran from Lieutenant Allaire's face and his body itched. To prepare for the cold, he had worn his pajamas under his uniform. He dragged a mortar at his side.

"Where is our artillery support?" said Bigeard. They had crouched behind a pile of downed bamboo. He did not hear Allaire's response and instructed him to bring the artillery to fire ten rounds into the valley.

Bix pushed against the shafts of his own bamboo cover knowing they would not stop a bullet. Lachen offered the corporal, who had stayed close, a drink of water. The blood had dried on the corporal's forehead and started to chip off in small flakes.

"Look there, my friend," said Lachen. He pointed to several other mortars being dragged along. "We have the tubes but no one is firing them."

"That's a curious thing," said the corporal.

"Strange?" said Lachen. "And what about the big guns, the artillery? They were surrounded by the Viets but should be free by now."

The mortar crew moved without enthusiasm, dragging along, half bent at the waist. Their tubes appeared to be a great burden, like hollow crosses scraped across dusty ground. The smells of cordite and napalm, the sounds of aircraft engines, distant guns, and a solitary legionnaire singing a German fighting song, electrified the air. A bullet drilled the bamboo and Bix lowered his head. He wanted to offer an arm or a leg to an enemy bullet but they refused to move. Hands were not easily repaired and he clearly needed legs to get away or to slide forward. Receiving a minor wound was not always bad luck but he was not sure how much good luck he carried. A soldier, panting hard, ran past the mortar crew and joined the group.

"A rough day," said Lachen, nodding in welcome.

The corporal reloaded his MAS 36 with a five round stripper clip. "The sun is unbearable," the new man said, rows of cracking dirt clinging to his forehead.

"Things change quickly," said Lachen. Bix let him do all the talking a habit he had developed from being with Steve. "Only this morning I shivered wishing the day would heat up." He handed the new man his canteen.

"What's with the mortars?" Lachen pointed toward the mortar crew. "I saw you talking with them."

"It's a joke," said the man. "They have the tubes but can't find the ammunition. Someone else has the ammunition but no tubes."

"What?" said Bix, thinking he heard incorrectly. The corporal also appeared confused.

"They're lost someplace," said the man. "All the rounds. They have scouts out looking. Even Lieutenant Allaire, commander of the 81-MM mortar battery, could find only three rounds for his piece."

"Then there is nothing to do," said Lachen, "except look for better cover and wait until the artillery gets free. We can't do much without it."

The enemy, who appeared to have limitless ammunition, laid down a heavy field of mortar fire as the group, moving for new cover and crouching like beasts of burden, dove against the edge of a rice paddy embankment. The ground shook, dirt and smoking metal flying high into the air. Noon rapidly approached as they waited and nothing remained of the cool morning. The heat, unmerciful, windless, everything dry, the earth too hot to touch, shimmered up from the ground. Lachen drank the last of his water, fired another clip, then lay still, drawing tiny circles in the dirt. Without artillery they were stuck.

Bix rolled to his back, closed his eyes, watched the sun burn red and yellow through his eyelids. Sweat dripped into his mouth and he licked the salt from his lips.

Within the hour, word reached them that the Airborne Artillery, along with the Engineers, had been liberated from their encirclement; but the artillery, who had located all their ammunition, could not locate their cannons.

The new man, after recognizing a comrade, ran to new cover. Lachen dug a pack of crackers from his tunic. He had exhausted almost all his ammunition and he looked for a re-supply point. Enemy fire chipped at the embankment; he crouched low and covered the crackers, then offered the others a bite.

Bix took only one cracker. He had already emptied his canteen and without any liquid to wash it down, the cracker was a mistake and shingled the inside of his mouth. He tried spitting it out but the crust refused to move. The enemy mortar fire continued strong and through the dust and smoke both the 1st and 3rd companies had completely stalled. Bix rolled to the side and pissed, trying not to drag himself in the dirt and being thankful he did not have to crap.

"I need water and ammunition," said Lachen. Bix was also running short and he looked to the corporal who lay motionless in a prone firing position. "Supplies," Lachen said again, as if Bix had not heard. Mortar rounds continued to fall and Lachen hunched low covering his head, falling dirt sprinkling his shoulders.

Bix relayed the message to the corporal and touched his shoulder. When he did not move, Bix shook him. The corporal released the rifle and collapsed to his side. He looked almost asleep except for the dime-sized hole in his head that emitted no blood and looked like an ink spot above his left eye. Bix knew the bullet had killed him. Taking his pulse was little more than a reaction from Legion training. He wanted to feel the flesh, to touch the thing that was not there. Without reaction, he cradled the cold wrist. Bix thought he would be sick at seeing another dead man, although he had seen others without effect. Curiosity struck, not illness. Holding the wrist revealed to him that whatever constituted the man, the being of man, the thing that made flesh real, vital, even fundamental, had gone. Whatever the man was, he was no longer part of the body. Bix felt no sensation of death, just of another empty residence. Nothing more religious or spiritual came to mind than the idea that Bix had come to visit and the house was empty.

Bix released the wrist, peered into the tiny black hole where death had pushed in, and the man had leaked out. Not a single drop of blood emerged from the opening. No exit wound, no skull shattered out the back, no scalp flipped into the air like a blowing rag, nothing unusual or ghastly showed. The bullet had quietly entered, rattled around the skull, and decided to stay. A bandolier of ammunition sat beside him. The 7.5 French cartridges of the MAS would not fit Bix's carbine and, his curiosity now settling into wonder, he refused to search the corporal for other rounds.

"C'est la guerre," said Lachen. He tried to be flip, cold, show he was the stronger soldier, the old master. Bix new better. Lachen, who had seen many deaths, would have said nothing if he had not felt uneasy.

A Moraine observation aircraft circled overhead, and a lieutenant, behind another berm of dirt, motioned them down to cover up. Lachen had been babbling since the death, talking about home, women, liquor, all the good times they would have when this business was finished. Mortality had struck him hard. Bix lowered himself gently deeper into the dirt. The sound of B-26's droned from above. The ground around the village erupted in convulsions of torn earth as the bombers dropped heavy loads of explosives with devastating accuracy.

At 1530, still thirsty and hungry, they moved ahead with 1st Co. attempting to encircle the village from the north. Nothing lasts long in war and after the bombing the Viets had regrouped and soon pinned the French down again with automatic weapons. Another air strike was called and Bix watched the village of Muong Thanh burst into flames and dust. A French mortar company, having found several rounds, joined in the fight to dislodge the Communists. 1st Company moved into the village.

Lachen ducked behind a tilting house. Dust and smoke from the devastated houses stuck to his forehead. The remaining houses stood above the ground on posts. Bix crouched low, in the open. Sporadic fire sounded from the Company. A Viet, out of uniform wearing black pajamas rolled above his knees, dashed across the street. Bix fired three times and, watching through his rifle sights, saw the Viet Minh stumble into a ball, then roll onto his face, legs together, arms outstretched as if he had been crucified on the dirt. The killing was efficient, not personal, which always surprised Bix who, although knowing he could do the job, thought he might at least experience remorse or something like buck fever, the term used back home for frozen hunters. He tried to view the man as a target. Shooting men, human beings, was a personal act, not a military one yet and he felt nothing personal about it.

Lachen moved ahead cautiously, deliberately. The sun glared, devastatingly laying a thick layer of heat over the burning village. Smoke balled in the sky. Flames flickered, flared to waves of shimmering heat. Lachen stepped carefully, walked like a duck on rough pavement. Bix did not see who fired the bullet that hit Lachen or from which direction it came; he only remembered the force as if Lachen had been kicked in the shoulder. The power of the round knocked Lachen to his knees and his eyes showed faint nauseated confusion. When he reached for his arm, his hand came away bloody. Another bullet snapped at the dirt and Bix snagged Lachen by the collar and dashed for the safety of rubble, Lachen stumbling behind, his helmet strap drumming against his tin pot in frantic rhythm. Smoke, dust, heat reflecting from the earth, was all Bix saw when he looked for the Viet Minh that had fired.

Bix dressed Lachen's wound, nothing serious, a layer of skin peeled up leaving a flat red gash, and started him toward the rear. Bix's attempts to get a wound of his own remained a failure. Lachen had his wound. For a moment Bix was tempted to shoot himself. Instead, he jerked Lachen along by his good arm.

"It's a good wound," said Bix. "The mark of a hero."

"Don't despair," said Lachen. "There'll be time enough for you. Just don't get your legs blown off."

The walk back seemed a long one. The battle continued toward the village and the sounds of war slowly died in Bix's ears. Lachen, who said he felt flush, dizzy, twice dropped to his knees and lowered his head to regain his senses and keep from passing out. Bix tried to hold him up. If Lachen passed out, Bix could carry him and receive recognition as a savior, if not as a soldier.

The rear area had been secured and they stumbled into the medical bunker and learned from a Spaniard, whose ear was a bloody stub, that the Battalion doctor, Capt. André, had been shot in the forehead as he jumped into the valley. The makeshift hospital ran smoothly without him and Lachen was soon stitched together and placed in a covered trench where he fell asleep. The wound was Lachen's first and, unfortunately, not serious enough to keep him from the later siege and a horrid, venomous death.

Chapter 21

Before the French parachute drop into the valley, Chau sat in his quarters drinking tea and writing reports by candlelight for General Giap. Morning, usually before dawn when his head was clear, was the best time to work. He enjoyed his special assignment for General Giap and his officer's rank gave him much prestige. Although he was not a part of any unit, he was a part of every unit. He went where he liked, fought where he could, and supplied reports to General Giap about the capabilities of various units, their morale, their care, their treatment by officers, their supplies, and their fighting ability and dedication. Wherever he traveled he was well respected by the troops and word had quickly spread that he could be trusted not to condemn anyone for doubts about the conflict. For those who had lost heart, he was more apt to share a smoke and tea over swaying and encouraging conversation than any punishment or exposure to the Political Commissars.

Chau had awakened earlier than usual that morning, before sun-up, and strolled through the village, the mist, layered with several cooking fires, folding over his shoulders. Life was good in the valley, a rural life of farming, pig and chicken raising, and the rice fields. It seemed to him that the fewer possessions people had, the happier they were. Maybe they had no choice. The families and friends appeared tighter and life centered on conversation and rituals. Everything had an order, a natural order. The people looked after and cared for one another like one big family. They called one another uncle, aunt, grandfather, daughter and son, always some kind of family relationship for Vietnamese believed they were all descendants from a single family. That is not to say they did not fight among themselves and have squabbles as do all families. They knew little of crime and children were children of the village as well as a single family. Extended families lived together and respect traveled from the youngest to the oldest with the oldest having the final say. Decisions were seldom made individually but in groups bringing everyone even closer together. Every village had its own government with an elder usually at the head. Crime was rare not because of laws but out of respect for one another and respect for the family. To be shamed was the most severe punishment a person could receive, far more brutal than anything physical because shame was everlasting, a beating just temporary.

Chau thought of Au and the new baby, she so delicate, the baby so small and helpless. His father had been right after all. This was a country and a way of life worth fighting for, without outside intervention. It was not that it made much difference who ran the country (governments affected few lives and were, after all, just governments) but that a certain amount of pride came with having one's own government. Graft, thievery, prostitution, corruption, fraudulent justice, anxiety, depression, and more followed the Western powers. They always worried about what they did not have, not what they did have. Their wants were for the outside not the inside. Everything seemed geared toward money, power, and the individual, not toward the benefit and wellbeing of the people. A Vietnamese government would be no different but it would at least be a Vietnamese government. Chau understood that in the cities people without money starved, lived in shacks or on the streets and died from lack of medical attention and sanitary conditions. How different the villages were. They had exchanged money and arrogance for a few moderate possessions and for happiness. Perhaps there should be no cities; perhaps everyone should be a farmer. A silly thought but he enjoyed it anyway.

The village consisted of about 100 houses, modest affairs, most of them on pillars to keep them dry during the rainy months when torrential downpours caused flooding and animals could be stalled under the floors. During several months of the rainy season, 59 or 60 inches of rain were not uncommon. Chau strolled through the streets and alleys between most of the buildings. He decided to travel home to Au and the baby, then to the Delta region when the monsoons hit the highlands in March. In Vietnam, good and bad weather reigned simultaneously in different parts of the country and he had the freedom to travel to where he liked unless ordered otherwise. He felt like the freest man in all of Vietnam.

The rag-tag guerrilla force of the Viet Minh had grown into a real army and Chau thought how much had been done with so little. Men and officers were now trained in China, and Russia had been a big help by supplying trucks. Both countries supplied much of the equipment and arms for the Viet Minh. China, especially, since they had an overabundance of material resulting from the cease-fire in Korea. Artillery was the biggest help and captured American105's were in abundance. Even more useful was China's help in training artillerymen who had formerly been inept. The 675th artillery unit of the Heavy Division of the Vietnam People's Army, and Company 226 of Battalion 920 trained in the valley practicing with recoilless rifles and mortars.

How different they were than in the beginning of the conflict when Ho Chi Minh was informed there was simply no arms to supply the men, nothing except crossbows and black powder rifles. He had replied that they would "beat the French with their own weapons." Over the years, they had been doing just that. They had ambushed several French soldiers and had taken their rifles. With those guns they had killed more Frenchmen, taking their rifles and it had continued until they had gathered machine guns, grenades, mortars, artillery pieces. For a Vietnamese, much could be done with little.

Chau had been observing all the units, including an Infantry Company from the 148th Regiment of the 320th Infantry Division that was resting after being recently mangled by the French. Independent Regiment 148 of the Vietnam People's Army had made the valley its permanent base. Chau decided to watch the training near the airfield later that morning. Until then he enjoyed walking through the village. Besides Muon Thanh another 100 small villages lined the valley, little conclaves of peace and tranquility not interested in war or politics, only concerned with the everyday problems of survival.

The Viet Minh fought without wages. The government clothed and fed them, supplied the arms and medical care, what little medical care there was. Families survived as best they could, the women and children working the fields, the grandparents minding the houses. Remarkable, Chau thought. In the west no one worked for free, especially the soldiers. Perhaps that is why the Viet Minh fought so hard, so willingly gave up their lives, Chau thought, because they really believed in something: independence, freedom, and the right to govern their country. He chuckled at his own foolish thoughts. Yes, they wanted their own country but they also understood the repercussions if they refused to fight. Why they fought so hard, and so fearlessly, remained a mystery, even to him.

Chau squatted before a building and lit a cigarette. Peace and tranquility. He thought of the day the war would be over, the day the French were driven out. The days of invading and occupying countries were over. More could be accomplished with friendship than with war. Working out trade agreements with Vietnam, not attempting to rule them, would have been beneficial to both countries. "How silly governments are," Chau mumbled into the cigarette smoke. "How silly." He could not understand why the two countries refused to work together. Much might be accomplished through friendship and cooperation.

By the time he returned to his office, the troops had already eaten – thick bowls of pho soup. A bowl of Luath rau awaited his return. "I thought you might be hungry," said Luat, his orderly. "I know you enjoy vegetable soup." Chau nodded as he sat. Luat brought tea as Chau finished the soup. He drank it slowly, leaning against the doorway, as he watched the troops forming outside to prepare for the day's training. Luat walked with him as he leisurely strolled toward the airfield. Farmers were herding cows and water buffalos to pastures and groups of men, women, and children harvested rice from the paddies. Many of the peasants wore black silk pajamas, others, like the White Thai, in white. Although all from the same people, the Thai were known by the colors they wore, White Thai, Black Thai, Red Thai, etc.

Chau squatted on a small knoll and lit another cigarette, his last Old Gold, before switching to his French smokes. Various units surrounded the airstrip digging machine gun emplacements and leveling ground for the mortars. A squad continued to dig holes and trenches, as they had done for the last month, into the airstrip to make it unusable. Chau listened without concern to the engines of the airplane overhead. Airplanes constantly surveyed and photographed Viet Minh areas. It did seem unusual when the airplane refused to fly away. He knew it could not photograph through the fog.

"What do you make of that airplane?" he said to Luat.

"If you don't have an air force you're not worried about a single bird," said Luat.

"Airplanes have always been ineffective," said Chau. "They mostly kill civilians."

"Were they effective in Korea?"

"Propaganda, according to the Chinese," said Chau. "Every government lies, even ours. Every man must choose his own truth. The Chinese laugh at the American newspaper articles glorifying their air force. They never stopped any supply lines in Korea with their expensive flying artillery pieces. Even in the World War they were ineffective. After all that bombing by the Allies, Germany's military production was at its greatest the last months of the war. Having no air force, or ships, has never hampered us. Determination, faith, persistence and belief in a cause will always win over equipment."

"If Uncle Ho lies, why do the people follow him?" Luat looked confused.

"We understand his good heart. He is for his people and asks nothing for himself. Our hardships are his hardships. Even now he lives a simple life in the jungle, no frills, just a small bamboo house with no water or heat or electricity. Sometimes his subordinates twist his words to accomplish his tasks. Sometimes they are cruel, even unmerciful but without the love and devotion of the people we should always be ruled by others. Yet, we should still be cautious about any government. Eventually they all go bad."

"Yes." Luat chuckled. "I think they would not like us talking like this."

"And you?" said Chau.

"We all feel the same way but remain cautious with our language. You know the great leaders, not me."

"They fear for themselves," said Chau. "They are not stupid people. I have met Uncle Ho, a kind man, and have spoken with him freely. He does not care that people have negative thoughts, only that the thoughts should discourage others. All language must be positive to win this war; let them complain later."

"You are fortunate to be your own man. Look, the fog is lifting and we should see the airplane soon. Maybe some day we will have our own air force?"

"A waste of money almost as foolish as having a navy. You can not buy determination and that, along with a decent assault weapon, is all that is needed to win a war."

Chau clasped his hands in his lap, interlacing his fingers and dropping his head. Luat understood this as his sign to leave. He moved toward the airfield looking back just once as Chau sat quietly thinking about home.

Living in a family hut had, at first - since he had come from one of the finest homes in Hanoi - seemed foreign to him, a quiet life far from the intensity of the city, time to be with his thoughts through manual labor and simplicity. His thoughts of the present returned when he heard the sound of many airplane engines overhead. He did not know how long he sat there, but when he looked up, the fog had almost cleared.

He rose to his feet as the planes appeared through the clouds leaving parachutes in their wake. Such a sublime sight, he thought. Paratroopers blotted out the sky and drifted toward the airfield. Chau had no time to enjoy the spectacle and he ran to the troops to help direct fire toward the enemy, a difficult situation since the French appeared to be everywhere. Already the Viet Minh were filling the air with tracers and mortar shells burst onto the runway to keep the paratroopers and any possible landing aircraft away. He jumped beside a machine gun crew, the barrel of the weapon smoking.

"Keep up the fire on the airfield," he shouted. The three men continued to fire bursts of five to ten rounds. Several riflemen, using Japanese weapons, also fired. "Keep an eye out behind you. They're falling everywhere but it's the airfield they want. I'll be back." Chau worked his way to the west of the airfield encouraging troops to fight, even though he was not a military man. Paratroopers dropped too far north were moving cautiously back to the strip.

Luat, carrying two rifles, emerged from some brush. He handed Chau one of the weapons and a handful of cartridges. "They are trying to surround us, Lieutenant," he said. "The Colonel says to fall back on Muong Thanh, form a defense as our units attempt an escape."

Chau tapped him on the shoulder then started to run gathering soldiers on the way. He tried to pick up a fallen soldier, his face covered with blood. Luat looked at the soldier then helped place him back on the dirt. Chau nodded his head and continued back toward town, moving troops with him. They continued to turn, drop, and fire to cover the retreat. They ran through bits of elephant grass and brush whenever they could for protection. The French were slow in organizing and the Viet Minh constantly brought them to a halt as they attempted to bring up mortars. Without such artillery the paratroopers seemed helpless. Each time mortars released several rounds, they moved ahead but not far before the Viet Minh stopped them again. They had too few mortars or too few rounds. Chau reveled in his comrade's fighting spirit. Most of them remained calm and organized, a real army, a real fighting force, one capable of standing against any European army. Of course, the French were a cold calculating fighting force and, especially the Foreign Legion, often fought to the last man. They believed there was glory in defeat. Lately they had been getting the worst of it, yet still they fought, always advancing regardless of the causalities.

By time the Viet Minh reached the town, most of the residents had fled. Many of them had prepared ahead of time, always ready to flee. Almost all villagers had stashes of food and goods buried throught the country and jungle. Those slow to move remained caught in the town: old women, black teeth and red gums, huddled under hut posts with nervous shaggy Thai horses; round-faced children, eyes wide with confusion and new to war; and the newly permanent residents, misshapen and bloody lying face down in the red dirt.

A line of defense formed quickly and Chau offered advice and encouragement. He attempted to study military tactics although it was not required. A Major took command issuing orders to Chau who passed them to sergeants and corporals. Most of the non-coms and officers were elected by the regular troops for leadership and fighting ability. Anyone proven inefficient was quickly demoted, keeping everyone motivated. Two and three man machine gun positions interspersed between the riflemen. Mortar crews moved farther into town quickly mounting the tubes and firing. Bullets from the French zinged through the brush clipping grass from the huts. For hours the Viet Minh held off French attacks until the bombers arrived. There was no defense against them.

Bombs ripped the earth trampolining dirt and shrapnel high into the air. Two huts, with ignited roofs, teetered on broken legs. The bombs cut a swath from east to west through the town. Some Viets held as most of the Viet Minh soldiers made their way down the east side of the Nam Yung River, through the north end of the village and out the south to disappear into the brush and the hills.

The bombers returned, this time hitting the village directly. Cauldrons of smoke and flames rose toward the sky and dust filled the air in a choking cloak of powder. Chau ran to a toppled child, his hand blown off. He held the dazed and bewildered girl, wrapping her arm in torn garments, then passed her to an old woman leaning against a post and laughing in madness. Her laughing stopped when the weight of the child brought her to her senses, brought back fear and bewilderment, a mystification that brought her to the realization to save the girl, brought her to her feet, brought her to the memory of running as she headed to the south with the other soldiers.

As the sun started to lower, and additional parachute drops increased the French ranks, it was clear the Viet Minh could not hold. Chau stayed with the remaining units until the last minutes of the fight, proud they had embraced the French so tightly that their friends could escape to fight another day. They gathered as many wounded and dead as they could and left toward the hills. Chau congratulated the men. They had gotten away without being encircled. Again they had embarrassed the enemy. Chau looked at the dead and wounded. Among the pain and sadness there remained great joy.

Chapter 22

Bix remained in the center of camp near the makeshift hospital and airstrip in anticipation of the following day's drop of the First Foreign Legion Parachute Battalion. Gunfire still sounded in the south and burning buildings tossed red light into the sky. Considering such an operation, the mission had gone rather well: units had gathered quickly, assault lines formed, attacks moved ahead, casualties seemed acceptable. Before Bix had taken Lachen to the hospital, Major Jean Souquet's 1st BPC had been dropped and supported the 6th BPC in overrunning the town. They all fought well, even the little Vietnamese in the French units. Vietnamese filled almost half of every French unit. Not known as courageous soldiers, at least those serving with the French as opposed to those serving with the Viet Minh, they fought as well as they were lead. Good officers and sergeants raised the courage of the friendly Vietnamese. If poorly lead they quickly faded into the countryside leaving the French at half strength. Most of the colonial soldiers fighting for France had no faith in them and they were often shunned or mocked.

Shadows in the dark worked everywhere, digging shelters, spreading barbed wire, developing gun emplacements. Little red dots from cigarettes, small beacons of life, pocked the area. One unit had already started filling in the holes on the runway since keeping the runway open was the key to the valley operation and vital for support and supplies. Soup bubbled from cooking fires casting the smells of onions and beef broth into an air to mix with the odor of cordite and rotting vegetation. Bix helped retrieve supplies and stack them away from drop zone Natasha, to the west of the airfield. Natasha was a paratroop drop zone but some supplies had landed after being cleared of troops. Simone, to the southeast was the other paratroop drop zone and Octavia, southeast between the two, was reserved for equipment and supplies. Food went into one pile, ammunition into another, and medical supplies into a third. Various units retrieved supplies as needed from the piles and stored them beside anticipated dugouts.

Ammunition seemed to be most important at the moment since most medical units were not yet in place and if the troops had ammunition, they could always eat later and if they were careful and fought hard they would not need much medical help or more medical supplies than they personally carried. Soup was fine for now and their medics carried enough basic supplies to patch up all but the most serious wounds. As Bix piled another box onto the growing stack, he looked again to the south. The fires were burning down, as the gunfire quieted. Sporadic shots still sounded but only in spurts outside the town.

Bigeard had moved his headquarters into the village. The radio sets seemed to be tied to him as he continued contact with the other units. He wondered if he had been too hard earlier in dressing down his friend and superior, Lieutenant Colonel Fourcade, commander of the First Airborne Group. Fourcade was to order Brechignic and his units to the south of the town to cut off the Viet Minh retreat and to capture as many of them as possible. Fourcade, eager to get into the fight, had initiated battle with other Viet Minh units rather than moving on to the objective. The only officers left in Vietnam all appeared to be fighters, enthusiastic and impatient for battle. The passive ones had been driven out long ago to take up positions with the U.N. He liked a good fight and did not feel like standing by and letting others do it for him. Bigeard, never known for calmness, had torn into him on the knoll outside the town accusing him of failure of duty by not working with Brechignic and therefore letting the Viet Minh escape. "Your job isn't to play chief of commandos," he had said. He reminded him that his job was to stay by the radios and issue orders to his men otherwise everyone was in the dark and battle could not be coordinated. Lead the men, yes, but let them do the fighting. The two men had been friends for many years. Fourcade had not protested or pulled rank at the dressing-down. "He knew I was right," Bigeard thought. No need to apologize to him. Fourcade knew him all too well and of his temper. Under pressure Bigeard always carried that raging temper and it got him into trouble because he was outspoken with everyone, including superior officers. If he thought they acted stupidly, and he often did, he let them know it. Even generals suffered his wrath when he thought they made a mistake, especially when it caused injuries to his men. Concern for his men was paramount. He had no problem having them butchered if necessary, but not foolishly.

He had been just as feisty as an infantry warrant officer at the start of WWII. His father, a railway man from Toul, had a lesser temper, and it was claimed that his temper came from his mother. Bigeard fought hard from the beginning of the war and refused to retreat, resulting in his capture by the Germans in 1940. He spent his time as a P.O.W. devising ways to escape. When he found his opening he crossed the country at night, foraging for food and sleeping much of the day before joining the Free French forces in West Africa. He fought fiercely through the remainder of the war and so impressed the command he was promoted to the temporary rank of Major, skipping the ranks of Lieutenant and Captain on the way. Even the British noticed his flair for bravery and awarded him their Distinguished Service Order to complement his French decorations. His radio call sign was "Bruno", a nickname he held for the remainder of his life. He had a lust for adventure and was assigned Captain of the 23rd Colonial Infantry when he arrived in Vietnam in 1945 before again being promoted to Major. The unit saw little action so he volunteered for the Thai auxiliaries in the highlands, a place that better suited him. His second tour found him as a company commander in a paratroop unit and he finally felt he was really into the action, into the life he had imagined a soldier to have. He then formed the 6 BPC and took them to Tonkin for his third tour. There was no better combat leader in Vietnam, hardheaded, surly, often intolerable to other officers, compassionate to his men, humorless, serious, and quiet except when aroused. Officers who found him difficult to tolerate as a man, respected his bravery and insight as a leader.

Bigeard stepped outside and sat on an empty ammunition box. A full moon started to rise casting light on the town. Soldiers moving in and out of the moonlight continued to investigate houses. A small campfire glowed in the middle of the dirt street where soldiers burnt any Viet Minh banknotes they found, as was their custom. Lieutenant Renee Blanc kicked up another box and sat. He held a bottle of wine and two tin cups. A tall young man, wiry muscles shown through his forearms.

"You had better roll down your sleeves," said Bigeard, taking a cup of wine. "The mosquitoes are a thirsty lot."

"Always worrying," said Blanc. "It's been another fine day. Plenty of action."

"Not what I wanted but it will have to do." He drank the wine down and held the cup out for a refill.

"Brechignic radioed. He's finished setting up his battalion on the east bank of the river and on the lower hills. Everything appears set for the night."

"What about the 1st Colonial Paratroops?" said Bigeard, tapping out a cigarette and offering one to Blanc."

"All is well. They've entrenched around Natasha with a company of 120-mm mortars, two batteries of 75-mm guns." Blanc lit the cigarette, breathed deeply and blew out a billowing cloud of smoke. "Of course you heard the medical officer, André, was killed?" Bigeard nodded, stood, and motioned Blanc to follow him. Blanc ran a finger down a long jagged scar on his cheek and over his chin, a recent habit from a wound still tender.

"That was a close one," said Bigeard, noticing the scar.

"We almost didn't make it," said Blanc.

"Tu-Le might have been the end. I suppose another medical officer is on the way?"

he twisted the cigarette between his fingers.

"It's never the end with you," said Blanc. "The men would rather fight with you in a tight spot than with another officer in an easy one."

Bigeard thought of the battle of Tu-Le just a year ago. The Communist 308th Division had crossed the Red River destroying the small French outposts on their way toward the hills and a major French garrison at Nghia-Lo Hill. The hill fell in less than an hour but Nghia-Lo village offered stiff residence not falling until the following morning. The French knew that all their units in the Thai hills would fall unless something drastic was done. In order for the units to escape they decided to sacrifice one paratroop battalion to draw the Viet Minh into battle so the outposts could escape across the Black River. Everyone understood, including the paratroopers, the enemy would eliminate the battalion. The mission was strictly a suicide one and quite possibly not a single soldier would survive. If they held off the Communists for one night before succumbing, they would have done their job. Bigeard and his 6th Colonial Parachute were ordered for that mission. He accepted without complaint.

On October 16th, 1952, the paratroopers were dropped into Tu-Le, twenty miles from Nghia-Lo. Bigeard, as always, jumped unarmed with his men from the first plane. He refused to carry a weapon on any mission, revealing to his men the confidence he had in their protection. They floated into Tu-Le, nothing more than brush-covered hills surrounded by larger jungle-draped hills. A single belfry on the open plain marked the small garrison of five machine gun emplacements. Bigeard walked calmly through the path between ten rows of barbed wire surrounding the compound, taking in the layout of the area as he went. He ordered entrenchments dug around the post. He never considered himself or his men as sacrificial anything and he was determined to accomplish the task and surprise everyone by escaping. He laid out the retreat route over the hills to the river.

That evening he spent drinking wine with the men and offering cigarettes as they watched the night flicker with red from artillery near Nghia-Lo. The plan had worked to draw off the Viet Minh toward Bigeard and the following morning the first enemy elements had reached the crests of the surrounding hills. With the Communists moving toward Tu-Le, the French outposts started retreating to the river: the 17th Moroccan, and the 1st Thai Mountaineer battalions plus the 3rd battalion of the 1st Moroccan Rifle regiment. The plan had been successful without Bigeard's paratroops firing a shot. He received orders to pull out but a single rifle company radioed from Gai-Hoi saying they were trapped. Bigeard said he would stay without retreating and give them until the following morning to extricate themselves.

The Viet Minh struck about three A.M. the following morning, first with a mortar barrage before charging down the hillsides. The paratroopers knew it was the end but, with Bigeard walking calmly amongst them and offering encouragement, they held on against two massive attacks. Bigeard finally ordered the wounded be gathered together, including the stretcher cases, and prepare for their escape. They might leave other wounded soldiers behind, but almost never one of their own. Any paratroopers captured by the Viet Minh were in for a special kind of hell. Of all French forces, the Viet Minh hated them the most.

The retreat started off unusually quiet, a quiet that bothered Bigeard. The Communists never stopped a battle unless they were sure not to succeed, hardly the case here. They were up to something. Cautiously the paratroopers moved to the hills. Traversing hills required tremendous strength and stamina in the heat and moisture and few units except his could handle it. Two men carrying a stretcher lasted less than fifteen minutes before collapsing from exhaustion, the stretcher to be taken up by two others for another fifteen minutes. Paratroopers carrying radios, mortars, machine guns and extra ammo boxes suffered the same fate. Equipment passed from hand to hand. At least they were not harassed as they rested for several minutes on the top of the first hill. Bigeard refused to believe their luck and dispatched advance and rear guard units. They walked down the first hill and up the next when the Viet Minh struck with enough ferocity to stop them in their tracks. Rather than bash the French entrenchments with frontal charges at Tu-Le, the 312 had withdrawn into the hills to catch them strung out along the trail. The paratroopers fought valiantly, diving for cover yet still crawling ahead toward the river. Two of the rear guard companies, holding off the Viet Minh to allow the remainder of the battalion to escape, succumbed to the fire and were obliterated. Because of their action the paratroopers, fighting constantly, finally crossed the Black River to safety, a scraggly unit welted from leech bites, bent with hunger, dragging their feet and weapons from exhaustion. Everything had been taken from them except their esteem and fighting spirit. They were still a battling unit whose pride rose for having served under Bigeard.

He loved war, action, excitement, the tingle of knotted muscles clinging to bones, and his adrenaline addiction caused him to constantly look for battles. The thought of the Tu-Le adventure caused a slight smile to curl up his otherwise stoic face as he walked along with Lieutenant Blanc through Dien Bien Phu. Blanc again rubbed at his scar.

"Still bothers you?" said Bigeard.

"We'll be at them soon enough," said Blanc. Bigeard nodded. A group of paratroopers knelt in a semi-circle near a fire of burning money. They started to rise after seeing Bigeard. He motioned them back down.

"Look at this, Major," one of them said. He moved closer. One of the soldiers held a baby of several months old. "He's a cute little Red. His family must be dead." Bigeard knelt down and squeezed the baby's fat toes between his fingers.

"Don't attach yourself to a python," he said. "Eventually they all bite."

"We put some goat's milk in a canteen and tied a cloth to the end." The soldier held up the contraption like a trophy mug. "He sucks on the rag when we tip it over. I've one about this age at home."

"There are plenty of old black-toothed women still here. See that he gets handed to one of them before long. It's not a good idea to get attached."

"He's got nothing to do with the war?"

"You heard the Major," said Blanc. "It's not personal, just poor judgment."

"You'll view him differently once you have to clean up his crap." Again Bigeard squeezed the toes before walking back to his headquarters. A sergeant looked down at him from the door.

"The count's in," said the sergeant. "Ninety Viet Minh dead and four wounded. At least that's what they left behind. You know they always drag off their dead when they can so it must be at least twice that many."

"And us?"

"Eleven dead and fifty-two wounded," said the sergeant, looking anxiously at Lieutenant Blanc.

"We'll take that as a win," said Blanc, looking at the bright full moon. "More troops will be flying in at sun-up."

"Bring us some more wine," said Bigeard. "The airplanes will be here soon."

General Gilles leaned against the vibrating fuselage of the C-47 the following morning. Clouds drifted by the window rimmed with gold light from the rising sun, a light that glanced off the dull wings of the airplane. He flew with Airborne Battle Group 2, commanded by Lieutenant Colonel Pierre Langlais who, like Bigeard, loved the excitement of battle. Airborne Battle Group 1 had done its job the previous day and he was anxious to jump. As the plane entered the valley Gilles popped out his glass eye and buttoned it into his pocket, a precaution since a replacement might be long in coming. A man did good to keep what he had in this country.

The door opened and the blast of wind started to slow with the dying groan of the engines as the airplane dawdled to drop speed. Gilles looked to the rest of the paratroopers standing down the long tube, eager to jump. He gave them a nod then, at the jump master signal, pulled himself through the door, a one hundred mile an hour wind slapping him on the face, his stomach briefly rising as he fell, then the sharp snap of the opening chute followed by gentle drifting. During the descent he took careful inventory of the area, the flat valley smoking in thin lifting fog several miles wide and many more miles long, solitary hills dotting the valley and surrounded by much larger ones, the morning glow skipping off the meandering Nam Yum River, the long runway of the airstrip, the many tiny villages near the hills. The stubble piled on a harvested rice paddy cushioned his landing. He lay there and scouted the area before getting to his feet and neatly folding his chute before looking for his friend Bruno, Major Bigeard.

Lieutenant Colonel Pierre Langlais soon followed. He was the only paratrooper with a more violent temper than Bigeard, one that exploded with the slightest match and blew hotly for miles, a prairie fire eating up everything in its path. He also treated his men extremely well and visited them as often as possible. Because he understood the concept of war, he was made commander of GAP 2, including le BEP. His jump landing went badly and his foot twisted against a bank breaking his ankle. He refused to groan at the pain as he watched the soldiers falling around him.

Bix watched the sky fill with parachutes in anticipation of his friend Henrich Knowles. Of course Steve, known to the others as Crème Brulee, laughing and joking as always, would also be there. He seemed to take nothing seriously yet underneath the joviality lived a very intelligent and practical man. Bix knew of no other human being who would have joined the French Foreign Legion simply to use a joke name. They knew to assemble at what would become the Center of Resistance near the west of the airstrip. The morning sounded peaceful except for occasional distant gunfire from units pursuing lagging Viet Minh. Several paratroopers, carrying a man between them, motioned him over. Moving closer he recognized the injured man as Colonel Langlais. Crème Brulee was one of the men carrying him.

"Bixie," he said, in English, hoping Langlais wouldn't understand. "Lookie what we found in the mud. I reckon it's the Colonel. You'd think at his age he'd know how to land."

"How can I help, Colonel?" Bix said, to Langlais, in poor French. The language gave him fits. The written language always had more letters than were pronounced, and he could never tell which ones to pronounce, and the spoken word carried so many dips and slides that his lips could not always get around them. Fortunately the only requirement to be a legionnaire was the ability to understand basic military commands, not to carry on a conversation.

"I'm going to miss all the action," Langlais grumbled. "I'll have to fly out leaving the men to fight without me. Find Bigeard, tell him I'm coming."

"Yes, sir," said Bix. "I think he's still at his headquarters in the town." He pointed south. "He was going to move to the west of the runway but I don't think he's gone yet." Bix saluted and jogged off.

"Be quick, you bastard," said Crème Brulee.

Bix, out of breath, reported to Colonel Bigeard. As usual, he was busy issuing orders over the radios and had just driven in on his collapsible motor scooter. Smoke rose from the exhaust pipe. His aides jotted notes and dashed in and out of the headquarters. He finally looked at Bix and nodded his head.

"Sir, I must report that Colonel Langlais has landed badly," he said. "He may have broken his ankle." Bigeard almost smiled.

"My old friend Pierre will be embarrassed and pissing mad," he said. "He needs to be humbled. Corporal," he said to a soldier nearby, "find a Thai pony, an ugly one, and let this man take it to the Colonel." Again he nodded as Bix saluted and stepped outside.

"Wait here," said the corporal. "Ponies are everywhere." Bix picked mud from between the cleats of his combat boots. Within minutes the corporal returned with a small, bushy, dirty, and unkempt pony with sad bewildered eyes. Bix led him back to Langlais. The paratroopers help lift Langlais aboard. Although a short man, his legs almost touched the ground from the back of the pony. Bix started to lead the horse back to Bigeard. Langlais cussed him away, tossing his arms out causing the horse to shy, and trotted off toward headquarters.

"Tom Mix," said Crème Brulee. "The Colonel was on that horse like a hobo on scrapple." He pointed to the other paratroop. "You know, my favorite cowboy hero is a little guy named Bob Steele. Not many folks remember him. This is Percy Smith, an Aussie, just transferred in from the south. Claims to be a real fightin' man but he don't look none too tough to me."

"G'day," said Smith, offering his hand.

"Why the Legion?" said Bix. Most soldiers would never ask, respecting a man's privacy. Legionnaires enlisted from everywhere, especially from Spain and Germany, and for every reason: lost loves, escaped criminals, men looking for adventure, and many ex-soldiers who knew no other life. After being defeated by Franco, a horde of Spaniards had enlisted. Germans did the same thing, especially the S.S. trying to avoid prosecution for war crimes. The Legion asked no questions and expected nothing except loyalty and the willingness to die. Since many of the legionnaires were dead men anyway, they often surrendered their lives willingly.

"The name," said Smith. "Come from the town of Wiangaree, south of Brisbane. No place for an Aussie to be named Percy, a damned English name and a queer one, at that. I had to fight constantly."

"Just don't forget and call the alligator-snapper Percy," said Crème Brulee.

"I don't know that I approve," said Richard Mategriffin, standing behind them. He slapped Smith on the ass and had no problem reminding everyone that he was English or that he enjoyed the company of men over women.

The passage to manhood in England has always traveled through homosexuality. At a young age boys are constantly separated from girls. They seldom play together during the early years when they find girls intolerable. In school they are separated out of necessity believing that neither boys nor girls can think with their counterparts in the same classroom. When the idea and interest of learning about girls finally arrives, the boys have been sent to boarding houses or "all boys" schools. Their sexual interests come to the front one evening in the shower and they discover that, while soaping their penises, they cannot stop until they explode in the greatest sensation they have ever felt. It feels so good they cannot stand it. This leads to an interest in the milky flesh of other boys until, filled with courage, a boy confesses the joys he has experienced with himself and that he would like to try it with another. The other boys also confess and, out of curiosity, decide to play with one another. Buggering soon follows.

Because they have no experience with women, they are clumsy in conversation with them and the young women often find them offensive. They return to the joys of their friends, people who understand them. From there it is a short walk to enlistment into the Royal Navy.

That is how Richard Mategriffin remembered being raised. The affairs he had with women had been unsatisfying. They were not tight enough and never knew when to push or to pull, slow down or speed up. A man knew exactly what to do with another man and when. This proclivity toward men never influenced his decision to join the French Foreign Legion. Militaries around the world housed homosexuals and they were often the most diligent of soldiers. Even the great Greek Spartans insisted their soldiers take another mate because they fought harder when fighting for a lover. Women were a necessary sideline used for reproduction. Men preferred the company of men. The other soldiers in the outfit understood his sexual preference but no one cared as long as he did his job. They often found him ridiculously funny because of his honesty and because he was so physically awkward.

Bix gave them the lay of the land as they walked toward the bivouac of le BEP and Captain Pierre Tourret's 8th Parachute Assault Battalion. Men worked everywhere digging trenches, filling sandbags, posting barbed wire. Equipment drops had started and chutes of food, medical supplies, and ammunition for drop zone Octavia seemed to be falling all over the valley. Airmen shoved tons of rolled barbed wire from the back of planes. Without chutes, they bounced on rice fields, streams, the river, the brush and the elephant grass. Soldiers constantly watched the sky so as not to be crushed by falling objects.

Two hours later, Bix watched General Gilles putt across the valley on a folding motor scooter. He wanted to check on every position, make any small adjustments needed, view the morale of the men. Bix and his friends were detailed to start digging entrenchments with the rest of le BEP.

"Knowles must have had trouble with the drop," he said. He did not like being in a fight without him.

"I reckon he'll be along," said Crème Brulee. "He's too tough to die."

"He must be some bloke," said Smith, throwing a shovelful of dirt over his shoulder. "I have heard him mentioned several times."

"Damned near a legend," said Crème Brulee. "Ain't none better."

"This isn't our job," said Bix, kicking at the dirt. "We're Legionnaires, we don't dig holes like rabbits, we fight."

Many of the legionnaires felt the same way. The days of digging holes into the ground had long since passed. Modern warfare consisted of movement.

"Temporary, I'd say." Crème Brulee leaned on his shovel and stuck a cigarette between his lips. None of the fighting forces liked manual labor, especially the Legion. They almost refused to fight defensively and when forced into it they were sadly in need of training. They would rather pout than defend themselves. They had been told they would be on the offense attacking the Communists in the area, protecting the Laos and Cambodian border from invasion, and using Dien Bien Phu as a staging post for resupply. "They want to keep us busy, that's all. Idleness leads to drink then drunkenness, then fighting one another, then whoring."

"All the things we like," said Brulee. The officers don't figure it's right for a man to do what comes natural to him and to be happy. Misery makes a soldier what he is and legionnaires are about the most miserable lot of folks anyone can find. If it weren't for the French bordellos we couldn't even get laid. No respectable woman ever had dinner with one of us and ain't likely to in the future."

"You don't always need a woman," said Mategriffin.

"Don't reckon I trust a man from a country that names its food faggots, bangers, and spotted dick," said Brulee. He knew that Mategriffin was one of the toughest and most reliable soldiers in the outfit.

The sky was dotted with supply airplanes flying in circles and dropping equipment. A dropping bulldozer required 9,000 square feet of canopy to land safely, a beautiful sight. Bix learned later that one of the bulldozers had broken loose from its pallet and drilled itself nine or ten feet into the ground when it hit. Smoke from the valley reached skyward as soldiers cleared away brush from the airfield and the small hills, marked for strongpoints, around the surrounding areas.

Heinrich Knowles appeared about two hours later carrying his heavy load. Another man walked with him. Bix saw him first and pointed. Knowles dropped the gear and offered his hand.

"The drop's been over for hours," said Bix. Knowles breathed hard. The man with him was a Vietnamese, a Viet Minh in ragged black silk pajamas rather than his uniform. His head bowed low although he looked up with his eyes.

"I was put in charge of several prisoners, P.I.M.s." Knowles took a pull from his canteen and offered it to the prisoner who was not bound in any way. "This is Quang. He had the day off when a shell knocked him unconscious by the drop zone. I kept him as a souvenir and put his friends with different units. He seemed the most healthy and he's willing to work."

"Why, he's a right cute little feller," said Crème Brulee, bowing low then handing him his shovel before lighting up a cigarette. "I reckon I know just the spot he can start digging." He handed Quang the lit cigarette. Prisoners seldom caused any trouble and were often used for manual labor, even in important security places.

"We can all stop digging soon," said Knowles. "We're going to form up tomorrow and begin some hunting expeditions. The engineers and the P.I.M.s can do the dirty work."

The men returned to their area and sat on boxes, talking and laughing, as Quang worked. He dug; he fetched water and wine, and brought them warm food. The French believed warm food was essential to maintain health and morale and they served it as often as possible.

Bix smiled at his luck as the others talked. He had found his grand adventure at last, a desperate battle to destroy the Viet Minh and free the country, not that it made any difference to him. He carried no political cognition, no understanding of government or its workings. He fought for the Legion, for his buddies, for excitement and glory, not for France. The romance had not worn off as it would later, replaced by torn bodies, suffering, and the knowledge that everything in the world remained mutable, especially soldiers. The Legion signified his country as it did for all legionnaires. The Legion offered an escape, a chance to redeem one's life from previous poor decisions; it represented ultimate freedom, the opportunity to spare or to take life without repercussions. He watched the night burning with flares and listened to the occasional shellfire in the distance. Life felt good.

Chapter 23

Chau worked his way through the jungle, the leaves dripping wet, the water plop-
ping onto the mud, his shoes gummed and slippery. He moved ducking and dodging,
jumping and wading. He should have brought a soldier with him, Luat especially, but
he did not want anyone to slow his progress, not that Luat was slow. He was the fittest
man Chau had ever known. Because his village was along the route, if he moved fast
enough he might stay the night with his wife and daughter and he wanted to visit
them alone. He rested every half hour for several minutes, just enough time to catch
his breath, to watch the rain drip from the leaves, the bugs crawl through the mud,
the snakes to wiggle the fallen leaves.

He never realized how much he loved the highlands, the greens, the damp, the sun,
the fog that fell each night and rose each morning like a theater curtain announcing
a new play. Streams, rivers, and waterfalls cascading from great heights flowed everywhere. Water pushed through the moss from natural springs and spouted as if from
crystal clear fountains, much different from the mud flowing rivers in the flatlands
dragging along entire hillsides, ripped and bleeding, to the sea. In the sky, birds flew
endless patterns, monkeys, tigers, and buffalo roamed the jungles, snakes slithered
everywhere, on the ground, under the ground, resting like limbs in trees. This land
belonged to the Vietnamese, to their simple lives, their communities, their farming,
and their many religious beliefs. Chau trotted until almost dusk when he heard something down the trail. He quietly moved into the brush, high above the path, and
waited. Viet Minh and French with their allies both used the trail and caution was
essential.

French allies, the Thai, Meo, and Nung tribesmen who lived in these hills, had always
been trouble and they considered the Vietnamese their enemies. The Vietnamese had

always treated them badly and they were happy to fight for the French where they felt better treated. They were strictly guerilla units who knew the highlands well, could live off the land, and fought unmercifully. They took prisoners for questioning only before torturing and beheading them. The Viet Minh treated them likewise. Montagnard officers led them advised mostly by French NCOs of exceptional courage. Only a special soldier could live for months in the hills. The French did everything with the partisans: eat, sleep, train, even learned their language and customs. They often married the native women. The French refused to allow them too much latitude for fear they might become too strong and decide to turn on them. They were the only forces causing any damage to the Viet Minh.

A line of ponies emerged from the trail, tails slapping at flies. Meo tribesmen, wearing silver adornments and holding machine guns rode astride them. One man had a radio strapped to his horse. Beautiful white dogs trotted at their feet. The Meo raised the white dogs for show and companionship, rather than for food. About twenty men passed, probably a scouting party. A brown severed head dangled from a pole carried by one of them. The French would want to know what Viet Minh units waited in the hills. Chau remained quiet hoping the dogs would not discover him. He watched them disappear into the jungle.

He walked until after midnight eating only a handful of sticky rice he carried in a bag. The jungles and forests no longer frightened him. He was aware of every bit of sunlight shining through the trees or drops of rain bouncing from heavy leaves. He crawled off near a creek, making a nest to sleep. How easily he drifted off in the jungle, so much differently than when he had first arrived. He thought of Marie and their nights together in the bushes, her curled under his arm like a warm puppy. He snuggled into the leaves listening to the jewelry of water wash over the rocks.

The sound of digging and muffled voices awakened him the following morning and he cautiously parted the brush to look. Vietnamese were building a bridge across the small creek just under the surface of the water. They always built their bridges slightly below water so French aircraft could not detect them. A Party supervisor, at first surprised, greeted Chau as he walked slowly to the water's edge.

"Lieutenant," said the supervisor. He looked over Chau's shoulder to see if anyone was behind him. "This trail can be dangerous traveling alone."

"I saw partisans yesterday," said Chau. "They rode ponies and had white dogs. I think it is more dangerous for you than for me. Hiding this number of men must be difficult?"

"We are all mostly peasants," he said. "You can not tell us from anyone else." Chau handed the man some paperwork. He read it carefully, neatly folding the papers into their original shape, and handed them back. "You look tired and worn out. Let me get you something to eat. You are doing important work for the country." He motioned to a small man with one hand who went to a steaming pot.

"What are you doing?" said Chau.

"The orders have been sent from General Giap and Ho Chi Minh. The motto is 'All to the Front.' Uncle Ho has asked for 50,000 workers to widen the Dien Bien Phu–Tuan Giao track. There may be 100,000 working. Who can count? We are making it usable for trucks, supplies, and soldiers - a tough job. There are over 100 streams along the trail; most of them must be bridged in a very short time. Then roads must be cut into the sides of hills and run along the valleys. I understand another five roads are being built around the valley of Dien Bien Phu to haul and position artillery, but that is a rumor. We don't get told everything. We only know we are assigned a certain amount of trail to repair and make suitable."

Chau eagerly drank the rice and fish soup. Something hot in the morning helped a man to function for the day. He never thought the French could be beaten, too modern, too strong. He was starting to see another side, starting to cut from the illusion of truth and come to the truth that to win any war you needed ambition and determination. Foraging in the hills and jungles gave the Viet Minh an advantage over the French who had to carry, or parachute, in supplies. The Communists traveled for weeks on a handful of rice and gathered additional food on the trail and from the villages. They drank the water without becoming sick although they still boiled it whenever possible. The French were unable to function more than a few days before being resupplied. Trucks and airplanes, both useless in a guerrilla war where holding ground had no purpose, did not encumber the Viet Minh, yet the French could not function without them. The Viet Minh traveled, like the fog, when and where they liked.

"It's a beautiful trail," said Chau, looking to the canopy of trees overhead. Two men each holding the end of a rope started climbing toward the sky on opposite trees. He knew it was an old trick they used to hide the trails from airplane surveillance by bending the tops of trees and tying them together. No observation pilots could see through to the trail. "Thank you, brother, for the breakfast," he said, with a slight nod. "I have a long way to go. Be assured I will report your good work to the General and understand that we may finally have the French where we can beat them with their own arrogance."

"Be careful, Lieutenant. The country is full of danger. Snakes lie everywhere."

Chau walked away with the tapping of shovels fading to the rear. He often thought of his father, his summer double-breasted European suit, cropped hair, glasses he wore only to read, his apparent sincerity with the French, his decency to the servants and to others, a smile on his face, a face innocent of corruption, sincere, loyal, cloaking the ability to lie and to cheat, the daggers of hate disguised by fisted eyes of glassy energy and heated coal. "Befriend your enemy," he had said. "It is often your best weapon." Chau still had doubts. Did he make the correct decision? He was no true Communist and from what he knew of Stalin's Communism it appeared backwards and cruel, but much of what was written by Marx and Engels made sense. Russia was the wrong place for Communism. It was designed to replace a wealthy industrialized nation, not a poor one. Trotsky said that installing a Communist regime in a poor country would result in a dictatorship. The rich earned their wealth off the labors of the working class in every society, in every form of government. The less they paid the workers, the more wealthy they became, often leaving the workers in poverty. Without strong unions the workers would never be able to rise. Unless workers demanded equality they would always be doormats. Communism seemed the way to help the common person yet those in power seemed just as corrupt as any others, just as rich. Democracy was a good idea but capitalism bred greed and corruption. Eventually the greed would topple a country because there is no limit to greed. Gluttony only lead to more gluttony be it money, power, possessions, or food. Around the world he had seen some people eat themselves to death while others died of starvation. They wanted happiness and never understood that the more they had, the more unhappy they were. Happiness and contentment come from the inside, not the outside. Even a child might think that if he only had a new toy he would be happy then, after receiving it, realize that after a day or two, he is still not happy so he looks for something else. Food, clothes, a home, a family, some work, a pleasant community, are all anyone needed for contentment. Excess brings egress to happiness as the importance of life becomes the morning fog that eventually lifts and is gone.

Political ideologies did not interest Chau, only the freeing of his country. Governments had little effect on the people, anyway. As long as common people paid their taxes they lived the same regardless of the leaders. Farmers and shopkeepers fighting for different governments always returned to being farmers and shopkeepers after the revolt and any freedoms they thought gained became no more than they had before.Chau just wanted it over, wanted to live a quiet life with Au and to raise his family. He wanted Vietnam to be run by Vietnamese. Ho Chi Minh seemed a good man. In a practical sense it mattered little who ran the country.

He felt part of the forest as he walked, part of everything in the world, the universe, as if he were just one small dot of an enormous living breathing painting, and everything else in the universe and beyond, another spot of the same painting all blended together yet discernable, everything individual, alone, but a part of something mysterious too great to comprehend, something impossible, a contradiction, known yet unknown. The idea could not be understood. It was beyond words and comprehension as all important things are. The painting contained no edges, no start, no finish, it just was.

Home was not far ahead, the village peaceful and quiet. Perhaps they had been working on the trail? Someone had been digging where he walked, widening the path. He arrived just before the mountains ate the sun, was just grasping at the orange rays and sucking them into the green. No one seemed to be about, not unusual. Lives succumbed to darkness and rose with light, the opposite of Viet Minh soldiers who became people of the night. The French had no eyes for shadows, no ability to fight without light. They brought their own lanterns, fired them into the air or dropped them from airplanes, bits of bright candles flickering with tails of smoke toward the ground, more useless tools to the Viet Minh who had no such devices. Night increased their vision, their valor, their ability to fight. After thousands of years of war Vietnamese had become nocturnal, skittering about the dark after their prey.

Not to frighten any one, Chau sounded before entering the house. Lac Long Quan sat on the floor before an oil lamp. The light flickered against his face. He rose and embraced Chau. "It is good to see you, my son," he said. "Welcome home."

"Yes," said Chau. "And you. Where is Au and baby Sung?" He was anxious to see them.

"Gone," said Lac Long Quan. He noticed the fear in Chau's face. "No," he said. "Gone across the way at Madam Kin's. We heard you might be coming and I have waited in case you arrived. News moves quickly in the hills."

"Madam Kin, the healer?"

"We've been hit with fever." He scratched at his chin. "Sit awhile and we will talk of what has happened. Au has left some soup, dried fish, and she insists that you eat and rest before she returns. She lives for you and for Sung. I know you are anxious but sit. Impatience seldom leads to good."

Chau crossed his legs and sat as Lac Long Quan lighted his pipe from the lantern. There was no reason to rush him. He spoke when he spoke and no sooner. Chau understood patience as a part of wisdom.

"You wife is very strong," he said. "Each day she has been working on the road as Uncle Ho has requested. You have probably seen the improvements during your walk. Everything for the front. She knows that by helping the trail she is helping you. She wishes to make you proud. It is her expression of love. Now her worries have doubled because the child is sick with fever. Madam Kin has been treating her. She has not improved as yet, nor has she worsened. The baby does not know which world she wants to be in, this one or the next, and she is waiting to decide. Several people have died, the very old and the very young. That is nature's way. We come into the world from what is; we return to the next world to what is. These things are beyond our control. Life and death are two sides of the same coin. If she should live, then she will live, if not, then not. It is not for Madam Kin to decide, nor for us."

"And Au?" said Chau. "You say she is fine."

"She worries only about you, and now the baby. She has received great praise for her work on the road, a hero of the people. Although she is the smallest, she works the hardest, not because of the party but because of you. Because she is so small she is not required to do the difficult work but she insists."

"Why does she worry about me? My job is perfectly safe and sometimes I feel like a coward for not fighting."

"She wants you to be proud of her, not shame you. For this she works too hard but it has done her no harm. She is as strong as any vine."

As Lac Long Quan drew on the pipe, Au entered, stopped, put her hands to her face and dropped to her knees. Chau stood and ran to her tiny body. He lifted her and placed her to his body as if they were one. He felt her warmth against him, gently ran his hands over her body before cradling her head back, kissed her cheeks and felt her tears against his lips. When he turned, Lac Long Quan had vanished.

"I love you," she said, knowing the words were inadequate to express her feelings, that they only hinted at her true emotions, something beyond words, beyond devotion, feelings so strong as to live beyond human experience.

"You are crying?" Chau looked into her weeping eyes and spread her tears with his fingers then tasted the salt with his lips. "Each moment I think of you, always of you. Nothing can destroy that love."

"I am ashamed. I have let Sung get sick and I cannot help her," she said, "and I cry for joy and happiness at seeing you and to release the sorrow I have felt in your absence."

"What you can do for Sung is to love her. With enough love she will decide to stay with us."

"Madam Kin watches over her. She remains the same, a good sign, so tiny and beautiful and strong. She does not cry at her discomfort." She took Chau's hand and led him to their room. "I am anxious to feel all of you against me, to forget our troubles for a short time, to lie quietly and talk of nonsense and of spring and of you growing old and fat and playing with your grandchildren." Chau stated to unclothe.

"And you?" he said. "Will you not also get old and fat?"

"I will defy time," she said. "A spell will be cast on you and in your mind I will always be like this regardless of how hideous and putrid I become. I will be a vision and whenever you close you eyes you will remember me as on this night."

Chau lay on the bed and watched her remove her clothes. Just her shadow was seen, tiny yet shapely and he could sense her small and perfect breasts, the warmth of her kiss, the invitation between her legs. She placed her body on his and they became one, a dot, two hearts beating as one, their heart beating as part of all hearts, a part of the grand painting.

Chau left early that morning, after holding Sung, and promised to return soon. Sung's condition had not changed as Au walked with him to the trail before continuing her work to widen it for supplies and trucks and guns. He felt her eyes watching his back as he walked away.

He reached Giap's camp several days later, a small encampment with few guards present, several bamboo huts, a nearby stream. A bamboo awning held canvass over a large table. A guard announced his presence and Giap, a serious-looking man with a hint of devilment behind his eyes, short, rounder than most Vietnamese, welcomed him.

"You have come a long distance, nephew," he said. "I heard word of your travels and was hoping you would appear before we left for Dien Bien Phu."

"I wanted something to report," said Chau. "The valley is full of activity." Two chairs were brought to the table and he took the seat offered him and welcomed a cup of green tea.

"The morale of the troops concerns me most," said Giap, placing his arms on the table. "I have heard the men are holding up well but, to save face, commanders always tell me that. Without truth decisions are difficult to make. From you I expect the truth, good, or bad."

"In this case they are correct," said Chau. "The men seem anxious for a fight. The French caught us by surprise when they dropped from the sky and in return they were surprised to find us. There is every indication that they thought the valley was deserted of soldiers. The men quickly formed scattered defenses since the paratroopers seemed everywhere and disorganized. It is impossible to drop them in a single place and, to our advantage, they always get scattered. As the French formed up so did we and we fought our way back into the hills with few casualties. Some of our equipment was abandoned in the valley, nothing more. We have now formed in the hills. That devil, Bigeard, leads the paratroopers and, if he has not started already, he will soon be launching attacks and making our lives miserable. Still, our men, filled with enthusiasm, eagerly wait for them. They all understand of the great possibilities ahead as they look down into this large bowl."

"Quite correct," said Giap. "The French started almost immediately to launch attacks into the hills but have been stopped each time. They are surprised at our strength and will soon be confused. They are losing more men than they expected and have abandoned Lai Cho in an attempt to bring the garrison to Dien Bien Phu. I think we have an opportunity here, the one we have been waiting for, the chance to finally soundly beat them and drive the French from our country. All the suffering could have been avoided if only they had been willing to work together with us, rather than act as conquerers. In the end we will become friends and still work together. But that is too much moralizing. Troops from all…." He stopped and smiled. "We will talk later. A committee meeting is scheduled for this afternoon. Until then, eat and rest. The next assignment will demand much of you."

With a full stomach Chau fell asleep quickly and did not dream. A soldier awakened him for the meeting. His body felt stiff and he unrolled it slowly. Forty men, officers and political leaders, sat on the ground facing Giap's headquarters and a large map hung from a bamboo crossbar. When Giap stepped forward the group clapped in unison, their hands perfectly aligned. Chau sat cross-legged toward the back as Giap returned the applause.

"All for the front," he said. "This is our battle cry. This will be the final battle to drive out the foreigners." He stood with his hands behind his back. "I made a mistake at Na San that cost us face and many good men. I learned much from the battle but the loss was strictly my responsibility. I will not make the mistake again. At the moment we are not certain of the French plans. They may stay and build a large base to hold the area and to use for constant harassment; or they may strike at us several times and then quickly withdraw. Then again, they may just wish for us to bring many of our forces here so they can strike us quickly elsewhere. They are landing a great deal of material so we suspect they may be building a permanent base. If that is true we may have a possibility. But we cannot be hasty. We must strike the enemy effectives, eliminate them one by one, and only strike when victory is certain. We must strike surely and advance cautiously. All effort will be put into this battle. "

Europeans seldom took responsibility for any mistakes and were filled with justifications for lost opportunities and if anyone did take responsibility it was only because those responsible pushed it onto the lesser ranks. The Viet Minh insisted on truth and the admission of mistakes. There was no other way to learn. Often meetings were called so each leader could confess his blunders and offer solutions to the errors and take advice from others be they generals or privates.

"I offered my resignation to Uncle Ho," he continued. "But he, and the committee, refused to accept it." He turned to the side and took a step before turning back. "We are in the process of containing the French here, at Dien Bien Phu." He lifted a pointer and jabbed it onto the map. "We have learned that the French plan is to use this base as a means to raid into the hills and stop our movements there. They have brought their most elite fighting troops, excellent and dangerous soldiers. As a caution, should they decide to stay we will fortify these hills..." he drew a circle around the valley "... to keep them contained. All our efforts must go into this battle. We went into Na San with too few troops, too little preparation, and too soon. Those mistakes will not be repeated. After they are trapped in the valley we will begin to devastate them. The key to the battle is right here." An aide folded over another map showing the valley with the known

strongpoints marked to date. Giap pointed out the airstrip.

"The enemy must be supplied from the airstrip. The road has already been cut off. Because we did not destroy the strip at Na San, they think this one will be no problem to keep open. This airstrip will be destroyed, and destroyed as soon as we are prepared. The enemy will quickly start to starve and once they realize they are trapped, the men will become demoralized. Even the Foreign Legionnaire Paratroops will become discouraged. The 308, 312, 351, 316, 304, and 148th Divisions have been alerted and are on the move toward the valley." He smiled at the group. "If we give our all, victory will be ours." He offered his hand to the group. "General Quoan will supply more information."

A very thin and fragile man walked to the map as the sound of clapping pushed him forward. A thin string of whiskers hung from the bottom of his chin. He placed the end of the pointer on the hills surrounding the valley.

"The enemy thinks we cannot supply artillery to our troops. Unlike the massive French we are a weak and puny people incapable of strenuous deeds like bringing guns to the hills." He appeared to enjoy his own sarcasm. "We might position a few guns, no more, nothing to cause more than an annoyance to the French. We will not be capable of supplying them with ammunition beyond a few rounds. The enemy also believes our artillery crews are clumsy and fire slowly and inaccurately. They gave no credence to the fact we have recently been trained by the Chinese and have been supplied with many American artillery pieces captured in Korea. Their arrogance has left them blind. Our strength will come as a shock and they will be confused. Everything they believe will become false."

The general stopped to drink some water. A monkey screeched in the distance. Another chattered back.

"Our guns are on the move being pulled by Russian trucks from the Chinese border and other parts of our country. We will place several hundred of them, including anti-aircraft guns, on hills to surround the enemy." He pointed to the map. "The enemy has learned to fight from past European battles, the information then placed into training manuals and passed to each new army. European wars between large conventional armies are all they know. They have fought like that here because, regardless of how often they lose, they are unable to look at themselves critically and make adjustments. Such tactics, they believe, will win in the end. Any loss only means they needed more men, more equipment. When they get them they always spend them in the same foolish ways."

He stopped for another drink and to pull on his whiskers. Hair on a soldier's face was unusual and generally not tolerated for health reasons. The general crossed his arms.

"For protection, artillery has always been placed behind hills and the shells fired over the tops. Spotters relay information back so guns can be adjusted for more accurate fire. The enemy will attempt to destroy us there, and will fail because we will not be there. We plan to place our weapons on the facing sides of the hills into protecting caves presently being dug. The guns will emerge to fire and then return when finished. There is no need for spotters. Each artillery crew can fire into the valley and adjust fire as needed. Before the attack we will continue to drop a few rounds into the camps. The enemy will consider this harassing fire. What we will actually be doing is registering fire to prepare for the final battle."

General Giap started the clapping, a satisfied smile on his face, as General Quoan bowed slightly. Chau's back was hurting after so much sitting. Sitting cross-legged on the ground still felt foreign to him. The monkeys started sounding off again and Chau saw one of them swing to an adjacent tree and pull the tail of the other.

"Colonel Gai will finish the plan before we open up the meeting to suggestions and criticisms. All options must be discussed and analyzed to assure victory."

Colonel Gai limped on the wooden pole strapped to the stump of his leg. He was also thin but tall with a dignified and sincere look. The northern sector map was flipped up again.

"We have already started the work on widening the road to Dien Bien Phu. The major road is from here, New Nam Quan, near the northern border with China. Russia has given us many Molotova two-and-a-half ton trucks to aid in our fight for freedom. The trucks will begin the journey over road 13-B to the Red River then down road 41 to our supply depot at Tuan Giao. Of course there will be many detours and side roads that must be widened or built. The Government Front Supply Commission is hard at work on this and the 551st Engineer Regiment is helping the people with the project."

The Colonel followed the route with the pointer. Even on the map it seemed a very long way, about 500 miles. Heads started to shake with doubt in the crowd.

"The last fifty miles from the depot to the front is the most difficult since there are only trails and several unusable roads. From there the people will transport all goods by foot, horse, wagon, or bicycle, as the trucks return for another load. The heavy guns are our biggest concern. They must also be pulled by the people and dragged up the mountains. If it takes ten, twenty, or 100 people to get them up the mountains and into their positions, we will get them there, an inch at a time. We are presently gathering rice from the villages and recruiting new soldiers for the final battle."

General Giap thanked the colonel and offered a break so the men could stretch and discuss any problems and solutions to those problems.

Chau realized how far he had come as he leaned against a tree and smoked a terrible French Gauloises cigarette, not an American Chesterfield. He had promised himself to look into every decision made by himself, the French, and the Viet Minh. Gathering rice translated to stealing as much as possible and leaving the farmers near starvation. Recruiting soldiers was no different. Most soldiers were keen on fighting the French for many of the same reasons all soldiers join the military, a chance to get away from home, the thrill and glory of war, to alter the present course of history. Any true belief in political agendas fell far to the bottom of the list, if at all. Men and women who refused to go were often beaten and kidnapped and villages told they would be destroyed if they did not supply enough recruits. The French used this deplorable behavior as another reason they should stay and pacify the country. Chau found it no different than the draft used by all countries to take men away from home and force them into fighting for political causes in which they did not believe. None of this bothered Chau. He felt no need to change the world. Whatever happened, happened. All he could do was to follow his conscience and attempt to live within the nature of life. He had come to realize that his time on earth did not constitute a beginning and an end; rather it was a small section of a continuing band of nature and that his birth started a timeless time before his birth and his death would follow, after his death, a timeless road ahead.

He finished the cigarette as an aide stepped to his side. "General Giap would like to see you," he said. "An interesting assignment awaits."

Chapter 24

Like any good military man General Gilles offered encouragement before all missions and never revealed the fact that he considered most of them a waste of men and firepower. They were being sent to die for an operation doomed to fail. Earlier, in opposition to Operation Castor, he reminded General Navarre about his concerns and offered his report regarding previous similar missions. The Viet Minh would destroy any small French units sent beyond the ten-kilometer limit of protecting artillery fire from any base. Perhaps elite paratroop units like le BEP, of which there were far too few, might venture deeper into enemy territory but not without serious losses. The country belonged to the Viet Minh and only large-scale operations might be successful, too large for a base like Dien Bien Phu. The command post officers, those agreeing and those disagreeing, knew of General Gilles' opposition to such operations – and he was the man most capable of having an opinion - but said nothing about his doubts to most unit officers. There were careers to be considered and opposition to any plans was not healthy. They agreed to try their best to succeed. If the operation did not go well they would compile and document a record of defeats and present it to Generals Navarre and Cogny in hopes they would change their minds, evacuate the troops and abandoned the entire operation. Failure always carried options; success took care of itself.

Decisions in the camp caused much consternation between the officers and men. General Cogny had assured Gilles that Dien Bien Phu would only be a staging point for major attacks, the only reason Gilles accepted the mission, and then only if Cogny relieved him of command as soon as possible after a qualified replacement could be found. Yet, the base must be fortified as a defensive outpost in order to protect the runway just in case the aggressiveness did not go as well as planned. The French military never forgot what happened in WW1 with defensive fighting: mud, misery, and stalemate, things they had wished to avoid. Since then they refused to train for any kind of static defense knowing it would lead to the same situation. Aggression and movement were tactics of success, not digging holes and living like rats under the dirt. But, for the sake of the runway, it must be done. Digging trenches and holes lowered the morale of the soldiers. Regardless, General Gilles set them to work, picks and shovels in hand.

Digging for the command structures began immediately at the destroyed village of Muong Thanh west of the Nam Yum River and to the south end of the runway. This area, code named Claudine, gave access to the runway and to the Pavie Track, a small road, to the west. The 8th Shock of Captain Tourret built camp south of the runway, not far from le BEP. With flat terrain in the area they could move quickly wherever needed to repulse attacks and launch attacks of their own. Attack and counterattack, along with le BEP, were their jobs.

A long corridor ran through HQ and connected with the lesser underground command units. General Gilles' replacement would be Colonel de Castries and he wanted him to be comfortable for the pounding he knew was to come. To improve the living conditions of the HQ underground shelter, engineers covered the red dirt walls with rattan mats. The mats also diverted falling dirt from the radios and dispatches. The engineers chiseled various rooms into the walls of the corridor: intelligence, briefing room, offices, air command headquarters, and rooms for HQ officers and secretaries. Engineers built another headquarters for Lieutenant Colonel Gaucher and one for Lieutenant Colonel Langlais and his GAP 2 staff. De Castries had insisted on a special dining room and even a bathtub. Gilles saw that everything was in place. The engineers dug pits nearby for the arriving ten tanks as protection from artillery when not engaged.

Almost as soon as the digging had started, Major Andre Sudrat, commander of the engineers met with General Gilles.

"Sit," said Gilles. His aide brought them a bottle of wine. He was still in an above ground bunker waiting for HQ to be finished. His narrow vision seemed natural by now and he rubbed a finger above the glass eye being careful not to pop it out. "By the look on your face I suspect the worst."

"Properly fortifying our positions is impossible," said Sudrat, his shoulders slumped in frustration like a flag lowered too soon. General Gilles, as if he already knew, nodded his head in agreement.

"It's always that way," said the General. "Your job is to make the best of a bad situation."

"To protect us from artillery rounds, especially 105's, the formula is basic and has not changed since the First World War," said Sudrat. "A bunker requires a wooden row of tree trunks not less than six inches thick and supported by braces from the ground no more than six feet apart. Three feet of dirt covers the logs followed by another row of six-inch logs then two rows of sandbags. A bursting layer, to detonate the shells upon striking requires a layer of stone, metal, or concrete. Without this layer of protection the shells go right through and explode inside. We have no stone, no metal, and no concrete. It can't be done correctly."

"None in the area?" said Gilles. "No quarries?"

"Nothing," said Sudrat. "You have given me the task of protecting the surrounding strongpoints and I have surveyed them all. Each shelter and machine gun emplacement must be built correctly on all the defense areas to be effective and protected. Using all the trees we can cut still leaves us far short of just basic protection and we still have no bursting layers of stone and such. Plus, our 12 battalions need 34,000 tons of additional material just to survive."

"And that must be flown in?" said Gilles, sipping wine and tapping out a cigarette. He had been a soldier for too long to get excited over the lack of material. No army ever had enough, not enough building materials, not enough ammunition or weapons, not enough food, not enough medical materials or doctors, not enough troops. The only thing in abundance for any army was the lack of everything.

"There is no other way to get it here," said Major Sudrat. He started to fidget. "I have worked it all out on paper." He handed the paper to General Gilles. "We would need 12,000 sorties, or five months of continuous building materials flown in by the entire air wing of all Indochina - no other supplies, no food, no medical materials, no ammunition, just building materials."

"Didn't Cogny's personal engineer, Colonel Legendre, agree the base could be protected without difficulty?" Sudrat nodded but was careful not to criticize. "I see," continued Gilles. "What has been promised?"

"We can expect about 4,000 tons a day, most of that, barbed wire and metal planking for the runway. We're also due another five bulldozers, 20 tons of metal arches and about 130 tons of planks. I requested iron railing for shell bursting layers but so far have been refused." He leaned back and ran his fingers through his thinning hair.

"That certainly leaves us vulnerable," said Gilles. He disliked dealing with such figures, especially since he was leaving. Too many details and he did not believe in entrenching, anyway. Leave it to de Castries when he arrives. Sudrat was to stay on with de Castries, the one to be stuck in this stinking hole, and he can work out his own problems of defense. He poured Sudrat another glass of wine. "What about locally? We can set the men to scrounging."

An orderly entered and handed Gilles a paper. He glanced at it, scrawled a signature on the bottom and handed it back. Sudrat sipped at the wine. "Of course. They have already been given the task and they are ready to revolt. They refuse my orders. They won't work, not even to protect themselves. Some units are refusing to do any manual labor at all, claiming they are an aggressive force not a passive one, that they are soldiers not sewer rats. The units on the outposts must build their own protection since we don't have enough engineers to cover everything so they are having a tough time of it. I've explained that we haven't enough engineers to go around but they don't seem to care. They say if they have to die on the defense they will die in the open like men, not in the dirt like pigs." Sudrat shrugged his shoulders. "We can remove about 2,500 boards and planks by dismantling nearby villages and logging trees. That's only going to turn the natives against us. We have plenty of sandbags and no shortage of dirt but the men have to do the building."

"Soldiers never get enough of anything including building materials and complaints," said Gilles, starting to become annoyed. He knew the accepted requirements for infantry disbursements like he knew about the protection from artillery rounds. A proper defense entailed one battalion to cover every 1,500 yards. Since the valley was 11 miles long and three miles wide, he needed 50 battalions to defend it properly. He had 12, not even close to the requirement, an almost laughable number. "We must make do with what we have," he said. "Perhaps your new commander will bring good news and more supplies." He stood and placed his arm around Sudrat's shoulder. "If soldiers didn't complain, they wouldn't be soldiers." Sudrat stood on Gilles' blind side and he could barely distinguish his outline. "You'll do your best and we'll have a drink in Hanoi when this is over. You'll not be blamed for any shortages, that I promise." He liked Sudrat and hoped they had that drink. He doubted it. He had little hope that Sudrat, or anyone else, would get out, not if Giap decided to pounce.

No desk officer, General Gilles refused to sit around and he wanted to check the positions and the entrenching work. He took Lieutenant Lee Florence and Sergeant Henri Genthe with him. They walked to the first sites before loading into a jeep for the outer strong-points. Soldiers piled sandbags around circular dugouts on the first artillery pits straddling the Pavie Track. The men worked in shorts, bare-chested, slouch hats protecting them from the sun. He noticed artillery commander, Colonel Charles Piroth, smiling and laughing as always, while encouraging his men. They always responded to his joviality and not only liked him, but especially younger recruits loved him as they would have loved a father. At the age of 48 he remained active and, like most of the officers, remained fearless. His dark eyebrows and large ears complemented his round face. Upon seeing General Gilles he walked toward him and saluted with his right arm, the only arm he had. Germans had blown his left arm off to the shoulder yet he refused to leave the service. The salute to Gilles, his personal sign of respect, was not necessary; he was proud of his only arm and exercised it whenever possible.

"Charles," said Gilles, returning the salute and offering his hand, "how is the work?"

"Work is work," he said. "The boys have pitched in wonderfully. As artillerymen they are used to digging, not like the infantry who prefer walking about the jungle and would rather get wounded or killed than hold a shovel." He laughed and motioned to the men digging tunnels to store shells and laying sandbags. "There will not be a Communist anywhere on these hills after we finish with them. I've brought my best men."

"And how many pieces?" Gilles watched him carefully. Behind Piroth's consistent joy laid a man of great sensitivity wrapped in a deeper layer of sadness suspected by only a few. Depression supported his laughter and General Gilles, who understood about the lives of soldiers, wondered when he would break. No man could carry that much sorrow and Piroth viewed every French death as his failed responsibility.

"When all units arrive we will mount about 50 mortars, 105's and 155's. We are also digging in on Dominique 3, east of the river and two more units south of the runway. With the circular gun pits we can aim our fire, for interlacing support, in any direction and mount a tremendous barrage. We are not limited to one field of fire."

"That keeps the men and guns pretty exposed," said Gilles.

"Bah! The yellow bastards won't get a round off before we destroy them. They can't get any guns into those hills, anyway, and if they did they couldn't supply them. No, my boys, and the camp, are perfectly safe, count on it."

Gilles wished him luck and moved on, thankful he was not in one of the pits. From the hills, the pits resembled bull's eyes and, being in the open, might become killing zones. Traditionally placing guns behind hills and firing over them offered some protection. He thought of asking Piroth to rethink his emplacements but changed his mind. It was the best way to mount the most effective fire and there was no other place to put them. Fortunately the Viet Minh were terrible artillerymen, always slow and inaccurate. Besides, like Piroth had said, there was no way to get any significant artillery into the hills and what few pieces Giap did get there could not be supplied longer than a day or two. He might be able to continue a dribble of harassing fire, nothing more. The guns should be fine.

General Gilles crossed his arms and viewed his domain. The entire valley was alive with activity, tents everywhere, fires from burning brush smoking the sky, dug-outs being deepened and roofed over with local timber, soldiers stacking rectangular sandbag walls to protect the fighter aircraft that were to be stationed in the valley, an increasing number of vehicles including heavy-duty trucks and jeeps, an airplane control tower going up beside the runway, hundreds of radio antennas springing from mounds of earth and bunkers like bug feelers, fire and steam from cooking pots, secure emplacements for the water purification machines and generators, a mass of scurrying soldiers building a deep protective hospital, huge ammo dumps and supply centers, and coils of spiraling barbed wire accordioned in what appeared to be a random fashion growing throughout the camp and hills like wild wisteria.

"It always seems a miracle," said Sergeant Genthe. "Within days we can build a complete functioning city, offices, apartments, hospitals, roads, restaurants, motor repair shops, water systems, anything we need." He squatted down and placed his arms on his knees. An arm surveyed the area. "Our own empire. And yet…"

"Our own giant slum, you mean. You can have it," said Lieutenant Florence.

"Aren't you making the Army a career?" said Genthe.

"As an army lawyer," said Florence. "They have other plans for me at the moment. I'm not much of a soldier."

"Ask the General. You're the perfect man for the job."

"Courage," said General Gilles. "That's all it takes to inspire men. Let others do the planning. Stand without fear in the fire of battle and your men will stand with you. I have seen you do that many times."

"I was frozen stiff," said the lieutenant.

"It all counts," said Gilles. "I see in the distance that Sub Lieutenant Leonard is stocking the ammo dump. We'll need plenty of firepower."

"You seem worried," said Florence. Sergeant Genthe stood as they both looked at the general. He seldom released any expression, no sign of good or of bad.

"Not at all," he said. "Every battle is a concern. They usually turn out all right."

"We would all feel better if you stayed," said Genthe. "The men fight for you."

"They will fight for de Castries. He is descended from a long line of soldiers, a handful of generals, a field marshal. Some of them served under Lafayette in the United States."

"Yes," said Sergeant Genthe, turning up his nose. "He's an aristocrat. Rank in such officers is always suspicious."

"I know him," said Lieutenant Florence. "He rose without the help of his blue-blood and entered the military as a cavalryman, rather than through the military academy, and rose to Sergeant before going to the officer's academy. I understand he is popular with the women." He winked.

"A true Frenchman," said Sergeant Genthe, as they started to walk back to the jeep. General Gilles continued to light one cigarette after another leaving a trail of smoking butts in his wake.

"He holds two horseback championships," continued Florence. "Working with a commando unit in the beginning of the last war, he spent much of his time securing Germans for interrogation." Some gunfire was ignored in the distance. Sergeant Genthe tripped over a box but quickly regained his balance. "Later, assigned his own armored unit, he fought for three days against the Germans in a hopeless situation, with his 60 men, all refusing to surrender until ammunition ran out and he was wounded. After three attempts he finally escaped the P.O.W. camp with several others and made it all the way back to France from Germany and joined the Free French in Africa."

"Death bothers him," said General Gilles.

"What?" said Sergeant Genthe.

"It's been rumored," said Florence.

"He won't look at people suffering," said Gilles. "That doesn't discount his courage,

240

it is just a strange trait in a soldier."

"For a second time he was wounded in Italy," said Florence. "Then, in Indochina, the Viet Minh almost finished him off in an ambush that crushed both his legs. After a short stay back home he returned here. I served with him in the Red River Delta."

"How did you do there?" said Gilles. "Attempt to hide?"

Lieutenant Florence chuckled. "I stood quietly, calm and confidently during any action, ready to crap my pants and afraid to speak."

Sergeant Genthe laughed loudly and said, "A born French leader." General Gilles said nothing, showed no reaction other than to blow out a cloud of smoke and wondered about his troops in the hills.

"Let's drive to Beatrice," said Gilles.

Not all of the strongpoints had been finalized. The general plan was to surround the HQ, the attacking forces, and the airport, with a series of independent forts or strongpoints. During a visit from General Cogny they had decided to build a fort to the east of HQ on Hill 506, soon named Beatrice. The choice was a risky one but better than hills 781 and 1066. They surpassed Beatrice in size and height but could be easily cut off and overrun because of their distance from the main camp and because they sat in the jungle giving the Viet Minh unlimited cover to maneuver without being seen. Cogny felt that if the Communists took the hills and managed to hoist artillery onto the heights they could not supply them beyond a few random shots. This was not a worry to the French. There was no way they could get the heavy pieces up there anyway and Piroth would destroy them if they did.

Sergeant Genthe drove the jeep over a bridge crossing the Nam Yum River as they left HQ. Barbed wire lay everywhere on the three Elaine strongpoints being built east of the river. The barbed wire took on no logical formations although the bunkers did. Road 41 cut through the emplacements and moved north to pass just below Beatrice. From Beatrice the entire valley could be seen. It also overlooked and protected the road, a possible route of supply. Captain LaSalle escorted General Gilles and his men around the entrenchments.

"We are entrenching on the three hills that constitute the position," he said, as Gilles offered him a cigarette. "Because the hills form a triangle we can support one another with interlocking fire and protect the command bunker in the center. We should be fine so long as we have enough supplies."

Gilles crossed his arms and looked completely around. He reached out his arm and Lieutenant Florence handed him the binoculars. He could see almost the entire camp and fortifications from here. To the northeast sat another hill they had been calling "The Torpedo Boat" because of its shape. That would also need to be fortified to keep away any enemy artillery. The higher mountains were far enough away to not be a problem,

"What of all this foliage?" he said, pointing to the tangle of brush reaching almost to the barbed wire on the hills. "The Viets could be on you in this stuff before you even noticed."

"And run directly into our guns? We decided the most important thing for now is to get the defenses built. We are arranging the wire in such a way as to funnel the Viet Minh into certain killing zones surrounded by automatic weapons bunkers. We are building communications trenches between the hills so we can travel from one to another without injury. Of course we have lines of slit trenches in strategic areas to hold off any attacks. We will clear out the brush as soon as possible."

"Well done, Captain," said Gilles. "The entire operation depends on holing this position. You must not give it up. Giap's boys can see everything from here so it must be held. I would say the position is in good hands."

La Salle started to beam and rock back on his combat boots. He had blond hair and looked younger than most captains.

"May I offer you some wine, perhaps something to eat?" he said.

"We have much to do today," said Gilles. "I'll make a note of it for my next visit. This feels like a good spot to sit under the sun and contemplate the world."

Like a star-struck schoolboy, Captain La Salle almost waved to him as he left. Instead, he clapped his hands together and giggled.

They drove back across the center of the fortifications. A bulldozer pushed black smoke from the stack with heavier clouds of smoke filling the air when strain tightened the engine, scooped up great mounds of dirt to sink the hospital as low into the ground as possible. There was no worse fate for a wounded soldier than to be injured or killed while in the hospital. The hospital must be the safest place in the compound. Shirtless soldiers stretched miles of barbed wire, erected a hundred telephone wires spider-webbing from the C.P. and in all directions. They moved north on the Pavie Track through clouds of smoke from soldiers burning brush with flame throwers. Small gray flakes of ash drifted into the jeep causing General Gilles' good eye to water. At the Torpedo Boat they watched several engineers marking out emplacements should the hill be added to the defense. At Isabelle and Wieme, five miles south from the C.P., General Gilles surveyed the flat low land. These two strongpoints could supply supporting fire to the main camp but Gilles realized that, because it was so low and flat, it might suffer from flooding if they were still there when the rains started to fall in late March.

He was not at all satisfied with the general layout of the overall defensive positions. The Communists had almost overrun him at Na San, had, in fact, broken through the outer perimeter. Na San was much smaller than Dien Bien Phu therefore easier to defend. All the strong-points there were connected with trenches so reinforcements and counterattacks easily pushed into positions while under cover. Dien Bien Phu was simply too large to defend adequately. He had constantly stated his objections but had been voted down by the other officers. There was no reason to bring it up again. All he could do was to prepare the base as best he could and much of that preparation dealt with defense because he felt that, rather than a staging base for aggressive assaults, they might get trapped there. He would be gone soon enough. Let the big shots worry about it. They knew how he felt.

Chapter 25

The paratroopers started the primary mission of the outpost, searching for, and disrupting the Viet Minh, while the remainder of the garrison built entrenchments to secure the base. Weapons in hands, on the hunt, the drama and excitement of killing or being killed, the adrenaline rush sharpening a man's emotions to a razor's edge – the steel on the verge of cutting the emotions out altogether, Bix and his friends were back in their element.

Crème Brulee had doubts. His emotions had often run contrary to what the others felt. The war had gotten dangerous and, unlike the rest, the Legion was not his home or his country. Kentucky, poor as it is, was good enough for him. Legion training had almost killed him and he found no joy or excitement in being hunted down to be killed. In Vietnam the dope was good as were the women and not even the heat and humidity bothered him - as a Southern boy he was used to that - but not knowing if he would live through each day became a bothersome proposition. He might not have even joined if he did not need to desperately leave Alaska for killing the three men who had raped him.

He had returned to their hotel and caught them in their sleep. They had not even bothered to lock the door and he had caved in the heads of the first two with the axe before the third one opened his drunken eyes. Joining the Legion just to use a joke name was ridiculous, even for him.

"Where's Knowles?" said Smith. "What we are doing, Mate, going into the bush, or not?"

"I don't reckon anyone knows," said Crème Brulee. "Bix, you suppose we're going into the bush? A nice squirrel stew would be right nice for dinner tonight. Imagine those buggers bubbling in thick gravy, their little feet reaching for the sky. Ya got to have a shit-load of them for a meal or you end up with thin mud."

"Have you ever seen a squirrel in this country?" said Bix. He felt a bit annoyed. He dusted off his .30 caliber carbine, an American product and just right for jungle fighting. He slid the clip in and out several times. "It's too soon for them to have a plan. Until then we'll probably patrol the roads before venturing into the bush. You've been here as long as I have."

"It's hotter here than in Sydney," said Smith, wiping his forehead.

"I hear they got some big deserts in that country," said Crème Brulee. "What's folks grow there?"

"Sand, mostly. Sand, heat, snakes, and every kind of animal that can kill you. I'm safer away from that mob and I get paid for it."

"Do any work there?" said Crème Brulee.

"Was a digger – coal mines. That's no life for any man. Work ten hours a day just to buy food and beer. A good woman won't have you."

"I wonder when the bordello will arrive?" said Crème Brulee. "They was just whore houses back home. I never knew what a bordello was until I got here and picked up on some education." They all worked on their rifles and smoked. "I spect they'll have a nice assortment of African Blacks. I'm partial to the darker meats. They's a lot more pretty than washed out white women." He looked up. "I love them Africans."

"Oh?" said Smith. "Ubangi?"

"As often as I can," said Crème Brulee. "Here comes the Sarge now."

Knowles always looked good in any uniform and, like all the Germans, kept his sparkling clean, in direct contrast to the regular French volunteers. After all these years (soldier years, living under constant stress, in battle conditions, and outside, as compared to civilian years) he still looked handsome, perhaps the most handsome man in the outfit. He had a dignity unknown to most men.

"So what we doing Sarge?" said Crème Brulee.

Knowles also tapped out a cigarette, surveyed the area before lighting it and crouching down on a piece of tree trunk. "Sitting," he said. The cigarettes were smashed and he stuck a flattened one between his lips. It drooped. He put the pack back into his tunic.

"I reckon you know what I mean. We heading to the bush?"

"Are you carrying extra ammunition and food?" he said. Two birds flew overhead diving at one another as they moved. "That is probably the wrong question to ask since you steal more food than any man in the outfit."

"A hillbilly trait," said Crème Brulee. "Food ain't so easy to come by back home less you got a job, and most of us hill folks ain't interested in no work, anyway. I once knew a man plowing a field in the sun and this wet salty stuff started leaking out of his forehead and the rest of his body. I ain't seen that kind of stuff until I got here. Well, he done caught pew-moanya and died. I swore that would never happen to me."

Crème Brulee was taking a chance. Knowles, in a bad mood, was like a bull with hemorrhoids and should not be prodded.

"Bix told me you have a lass who runs the bordello," said Smith. Bix tensed and eyed Knowles from the side. Knowles' and Nicole's love affair was legendary in the Legion. She ran an efficient bordello but no one could pry her legs apart at any price except Knowles.

"We have been together many years." A smile pulled up one side of his mouth and his attitude seemed to change. He drew in the cigarette smoke and blew it out slowly like the air brakes on a train.

"How did you get tied up with a whore?" said Smith, "I mean a workingwoman. I don't know how to ask the question politely?" said Smith. He coughed slightly as if he had smelled his own crap and was afraid someone else might have also smelled it.

"Nicole," said Knowles, looking toward one of the towering mountains too close to the camp. Even now the Viet Minh were digging into the area. If nothing else, they were tenacious.

"Anyone can tell you the story," said Bix. "Maybe the Sergeant doesn't want to say."

"Sure he does," said Crème Brulee. "The Sarge tells the story good as anybody and I heard him tell it lots of times."

Knowles thought for a minute before starting then gave the shortest version he could while still hitting the important points. He chuckled at the end of the story snorting a deep gutterance that chilled Percy Smith. He lowered his head, afraid to look at the sergeant, afraid of what he might see there: longing, despair, anger, maybe even the most traumatic emotion of all, indifference.

"We found each other later," said Knowles, "after the war. We will never be apart again." Equivocation found no place in the statement.

"I don't recon I could live without a good woman," said Crème Brulee. "Having my balls whacked off gives me the fan-tags, though. My stomach gets to knotting all up just thinking about it. Guess I don't get the humor in it."

"They make a cute bauble but little more. They are not missed once they are gone."

"What's you gonna do if you ever find him, the guy what whacked them off?" Crème Brulee smiled, a look of evil anticipation on his face. A cackle of gunfire sounded in the distance as the column started to rise.

"It's off to the war," said Knowles. "Allez," he called to the men nearby as they moved off.

In the French Foreign Legion sergeants and corporals carry a great deal of weight almost on a par with the lesser officers. Rank comes slowly so many of the men can spend their entire enlistments as privates. Those rising above that rank have shown great fortitude, bravery, inspiration, and knowledge. Because of his experience as a German officer Knowles rose quickly up the ranks and was respected by the men and officers alike. He had taught more than one new officer how to become a leader. The assignment for this day was not necessarily difficult. Viet Minh had been spotted in the village of Hong Ban Lon to the west. His job was to drive them out.

As the men trudged north on the Pavie Track fighting the brush, Viet Minh artillery rounds, mostly from heavy mortars, occasionally hit the valley. They had been landing since the first day of occupation, just enough to be annoying, and causing little damage. Most soldiers never took cover because they did not hear the first round until it burst and they knew no others would follow in any order. Some mortar rounds could be heard before they landed, but, because there was so much open space in the valley, exploded harmlessly.

The Pavie Track left them covered in dust as they cut west down a trail. Bix almost jumped into a tree when a green and blue-striped snake slithered in front of his boot. He hated snakes of all kinds and they always stopped his heart before it continued beating faster to make up time. He never knew why he hated them. They had never bitten or injured him in any way. Just seeing a garden snake gave him fits and the shits for the next two days. Crème Brulee saw him jump and started to crawl through the grass with his bayonet jabbing into the ground. Smith kicked him in the ass to keep him moving.

In the heat the bugs were not as thick as usual. They, and the mosquitoes, loved to feast on new men, to get their fresh blood. The longer a man stayed in the jungle the less likely he was to get bitten. Crème Brulee pushed through a tangle of gnats in a shady spot mostly ignoring them. He watched Bix's boots make half circles in the dirt from the toes. Bix, a man of slight build, had small feet. Crème Brulee watched the back of his pack sway slightly from side to side. An unhooked canvass strap bobbed slightly with each step. He always kept his bayonet attached to one side of the back so it could be easily reached. Crème Brulee liked his bayonet at the side. It was more likely to catch in the brush on the pack. Bix carried only one canteen because water was so plentiful in the area. He alternated between slinging his rifle and holding it in his hands.

Crème Brulee felt uncomfortable in the valley, too claustrophobic, too dark, too mysterious. Good things were not likely to happen here and he much preferred the Delta. The 100 villages in the valley, bunched together, would have made a decent sized city. That was not the Vietnamese way. Cities were too difficult to manage and they liked their fields around them so they could have a smoke in the evenings and enjoy the satisfaction of watching their fields of hard work grow and change throughout the two seasons – drought and monsoons.

Desertion in the French Foreign Legion was almost mandatory and Brulee had thought of it many times, more now than ever. He wanted out and he missed the cool green of the Appalachians where soft air breezed over the tree tops; catching and torturing snakes and frogs by pulling off their skins with pliers and watching them jump and squirm when he set them free to die; gutting hogs, tying their legs together then lowering them head first into a vat of boiling water to loosen their bristles and always naming them Barbeque or Pork-chop so as not to forget their purpose as food, not pets; fishing the black water for catfish and crawdads, the clear water for bass; laying the young Baptist women in the bushes after church and humping like crazy, not from the sex but because they were trying to keep their clothes from staining; big plates of salted and buttered grits and pork sausage gravy flooding an army of fresh biscuits. His mind continued to wander when Sergeant Knowles called a rest halt.

"Don't become targets on a champ de tir," he said, as he motioned the patrol to keep to the side of the clearing. He made certain he spoke to each soldier, especially the new men, as he worked his way toward Bix and his group.

"Smith," he said. "When we spot the village I want you to pick another man and reconnoiter to the left. DeJohn will do the same to the right. There is nothing worse than going into a situation blindly. Brulee," he said. "You look dejected. Perhaps you also wish to go."

"He's filled with worries these days," said Bix.

"Remember the Legion code d'honneur," said Knowles. "We must live by it."

"I ain't so sure I can," said Crème Brulee. "They sound like a mess of words to me, words that might get me killed."

"Of course they'll get you killed," said Knowles. "Why do you think you're here?"

Knowles squatted Vietnamese style. With some practice soldiers realized how comfortable the squat is. Legs become a chair and travel with them everywhere.

"Throughout life doubts enter every man," he said. "Doubts here can cost the lives of your comrades. Imagine your friends Smith or Bix maimed or killed because for a moment you had reservations. This is the world's best fighting unit because we believe in the Legion. Legio patria nostra, the Legion is our country - not France, not Europe, no government or military. We fight for the Legion and only for the Legion."

"Still sounds like horseshit to me," said Brulee. "You know me to be an honest man so I ain't gonna lie about it and I know you won't bust me out because of it. Those sayings are used to get folks killed before they get things figured out." He drew two circles in the dirt with his finger, one larger than the other.

"Quit moping," said Smith. "You're giving our mates the creeps."

"All you need is a girlfriend to stiffen you up, old chap," said Mategriffin. "Or a boyfriend."

"Not from a Limey corn-holer like you," said Crème Brulee. "Look at the facts, we're down in the bottom of this here little circle. This bigger circle is higher and surrounds all of us. Nothing surrounds it. Them folks can come and go as they please, in and out, round about. Anything they want comes to them." He scratched a straight line inside the smaller circle. "If they get settled in, we can't go nowhere. Folks can't come to us except on this little line. If it falls apart we're in it deep." He looked at everyone looking at him.

"For some people the slogans are all crap," said Knowles. "You're the one with the balls. The fact is, we are led by the finest officers in the world: General Gilles, sporting one eye; Colonel Langlais with a broken ankle; General Cogny crippled and using a cane; Colonel de Castries, who also uses a cane; and Colonel Piroth with only one arm. I understand the tank commander will be Captain Hervuet. He has recently broken his arm." He tapped Crème Brulee on the knee. "See, with leaders like that, we are in the best shape possible. What could go wrong?" He chuckled loudly before he left.

"Sometimes I don't think he's right upstairs," said Crème Brulee. "If the officers are that beat-up everyone else must be near death."

"There's no better man than the Sergeant," said Bix. "He's just trying to cheer you up. Nothing controls life and death, nothing. It just happens."

"He don't care if he gets killed or not," said Crème Brulee. "That's ok for him but what about us? I ain't ready to die."

"Then you had better fight damn hard," said Smith, starting to stand. "Let's go."

"Sometimes I reckon I'm in this mess all by myself."

"If you need me you know where to find me," said Mategriffin.

"Bastards," Crème Brulee mumbled. "You all ain't nothing but a bunch of sick bastards."

Knowles stopped the patrol in early afternoon after the point man, Sangree, reported seeing the village. Everyone knelt on the ground, weapons at the ready. Knowles followed Sangree to the edge of a clearing. Regardless of such dangers as mines and booby-traps, Sangree always took the point. He felt safer in front in case of an ambush because the Viet Minh let the first few soldiers pass before firing. The only time they didn't was if they arranged the ambush in an L formation, soldiers along the trail and at a ninety-degree angle across it. The men at the end of the line were also fairly safe. The ones in the middle caught hell. Knowles unfolded the map on the ground and oriented his compass with the contour lines and matched the lines with the surrounding hills and clearings. He sent for Smith and deJohn. They had both chosen a comrade and started their reconnaissance, disappearing into the jungle. The patrol remained diligent waiting for the report. Smith and Mategriffin returned first.

"It's difficult to know," he said to Knowles. "We went completely to the south, there." He pointed to where the clearing circled around to the edge of the huts and the jungle started climbing the hill. "We could find no path into the foliage and couldn't get through without chopping down the forest. It is as thick as a brick wall. We saw several soldiers relaxing, some smoking, others sleeping. Because of the color of the smoke I thought they might be smoking opium. That should make it easy. This area is one of the greatest for opium, just ask Brulee. No one was on guard nor did they seem concerned. The peasants were doing what peasants do."

"Any artillery or machine guns?" said Knowles.

"Not that we saw. The only rifles we saw were surplus Russian Mossin Nagant bolt actions. And a few M-1's. This bunch is not well equipped."

Knowles surveyed the map again and placed an X toward the village on the south side. Within ten minutes deJohn and his friend returned from the north with almost the same report.

"There is a mound by the trees. Good cover, here on the map." He pointed to the spot.

Knowles nodded his head. "We will place our two machine guns on these X's to interlock fire into the village. Two riflemen will support the south gun, no more. I don't want to split our forces, just keep the Communists from escaping to that side. The rest will move to the north." He tapped the map. "How long is the mound?"

"All the way to the edge of the village like they piled up dirt while working on the field."

"Good. If the force is too great we can redeploy to the long mound and lay down defensive fire. That will give us the better cover. They will have to come into the open to attack. If all goes well we will push them back to the jungle. If it is thick enough and without trails they will be pinned and we can cut them down. I hate to go in without knowing what is there. You say there was no way through the brush?"

"Not that we could see. We couldn't push through," said deJohn. "The undergrowth is like a curtain of steel."

"These Viets are like snakes," said Mategriffin. "They can get through anything."

"You're starting to sound like Crème Brulee," said Smith. "Better to be like his friend, Bix. He has no complaints."

"Let's hope the brush is thick all the way around," said Knowles. "They are not likely to stay in a place with no exit so I wonder."

"For an old Sergeant, you worry about us too much," said Sangree.

"That is how one gets to be an old Sergeant," said Knowles, smiling at them all.

At the edge of the clearing Knowles sent one team south with Smith, wishing them luck. The rest deployed to the north. Bix checked his carbine. DeJohn fumbled to load a round in his French MAS 36.

"Why don't you use your Thompson," said Bix. "That thing is going to get you killed."

"It's from my country and I like it and can shoot farther and more accurately than with the Thompson."

"That's news to everyone else," said Crème Brulee. "Most folks can't hit a cow in the ass at ten feet with that thing."

DeJohn shrugged and looked away holding the rifle close. He loved its design, the lovely turned back bolt, the gentle kick. The peep-sight was a miserable feature but even the American equipment used peep-sights. Not the Germans. They used a decent sight, a tight lovely V that caressed the front sight resting on the forehead of the enemy.

Sergeant Knowles motioned them forward. Because there was no cover near the village there was no place to be hide. By starting from the far right where the foliage began he had lessened the distance they had to travel. They moved ahead slowly, half crouched. They had almost reached the village when the first shots zipped by, some cracking the air, the others flicking up dirt. The legionnaires quickened their pace, half dropping to their knees to give supporting fire, the others moving ten or fifteen yards ahead before dropping to give supporting fire for the first group as they moved up. They leap-frogged forward. Knowles stood knowing that at times like this a decent leader had no other function except encouragement.

Within minutes they had reached the first houses. Resistance had been light and none of his men had been hit. He stepped over the body of a Viet Minh shot through the throat, the blood running through his fingers and him looking as if he had strangled himself, his eyes almost bursting from his skull. Using the houses for cover they moved ahead. The older soldiers seemed indifferent to cover while the newer soldiers carefully protected themselves.

Suddenly a fusillade of tremendous fire screamed from the rear of the village. This was not a village of a few resting Viet Minh but no less than a fully armed company.

"Plaqze au sol!" Knowles shouted, with his German accent. He ran to several newer troops who appeared to be frozen. "You are the best bonshommes," he said. "You are Legionnaires. Now is the time to prove it." Knowles understood that even the best trained soldiers have difficulty their first time in battle. Men could not be prepared for such terror except with experience where their fear eventually turned to concern, then anger, then indifference. " Allez," he said, giving them a small shove.

Knowles understood there was no hope in winning this fight, but, his job was to attempt victory. They pushed slowly ahead, bullets flinging everywhere. The machine guns had moved forward to the action and found the best field of fire they could. The guns clacked in steady rhythm. Viet Minh machine guns responded, followed by mortar rounds that started to chew up the huts. Two legionnaires fell dead to the ground and he noticed

deJohn holding his forearm, blood dripping between the fingers.

Bix moved ahead. He had been in enough minor fights to deny any emotions. He felt no anger, no fear, no joy, nothing. He strongly believed that when a person's time was up, it was up. When any gunfire sounded his mind went completely blank except for one thing at a time – move ahead – shoot – duck – look – shoot again – keep the man in his sights, the single man in his sight regardless of how many others there were. When he fell, sight on another. Move ahead – load weapon – duck – stop friend's bleeding – etc. No bullet had his name on it until it was time.

During his first fight understanding the scenario confused him. He expected to be afraid and expected to be upset afterwards but nothing happened. He faced battle as calmly as a priest faced an altar boy. He seemed to be a natural soldier and at first he wondered if there was something wrong with him. Was he a cold-blooded killer, a man with no emotions? He had always felt himself a compassionate person, kind and respectful of others, always willing to give a helping hand. It was just in war that he felt nothing except the excitement of action.

Crème Brulee's advance had become more and more cautious. At the sound of fire everything crammed into his head, home, life, family, friends, sex, food, dope, everything jumbled up and crowded together. Not only did every bullet have his name on it but it had the name of his complete family, all acquaintances, his dog, his address and phone number and his hourly schedule, even his favorite radio stations.

"Merdique," Knowles mumbled to himself. "Bix – deJohn, fall back to the machine guns and give us protective fire." He could see what the others had not, the trails through the brush that led to the village filling with Viet Minh. They appeared to be everywhere and he saw a group starting to move to the south side and work their way into a flanking position. Knowles ordered a defensive retreat. The fallen legionnaires were dragged back to the long mound. The machine gun, along with Smith, stayed in the village to cover the others before running for their lives and barely escaping complete slaughter as the Viet Minh started across the clearing. Now it was the Legion's turn to splay the field with fire. The Viet Minh charged murderously head-on across the field, void of fear and never slowing. They fired toward the bank as they fell one after another, bullets kicking up dirt around the soldiers and Knowles.

"Druxman," he said, to the radioman. "Have you raised the artillery?" Druxman, frustrated, banged the receiver against his hand. "Ne vous inquietez pas les gars," Knowles calmly said to the men giving them encouragement. Druxman handed him the receiver to the radio as he called in artillery. The spotting round of white phosphorus landed far and to the south. They were at the limits of fire but the rounds might help if they landed anyplace close. Again Knowles spoke clearly into the receiver. The rounds started to walk to their point. Knowles continued to adjust fire until the rounds started falling on the field. The radio suddenly blanked out. He knocked the receiver against the ground and tossed it back to Druxman who shrugged. He tapped the men on the shoulders, pointing them back down the trail toward camp. They picked up the dead and wounded and moved out. No legionnaire ever worried about being left behind, wounded or dead. The Viet Minh also carried away their dead but for different reasons. They did not want the French soldiers to know how many of them had been killed. Two hundred yards down the trail Knowles placed the machine gun crew and several soldiers to slow down the attack. The Viet Minh did not follow.

Chapter 26

Brulee was finished. He had decided that enough was enough and he wanted out. Good legionnaires had a fascination with death, almost craved it, walked its prickly edge to see how long they could balance before succumbing to the icy arms of mortality, then taking the fall into darkness with laughter on their lips and open arms willing to greet the great abyss. They were crazy, every damn one of them. Not him. He did not want to be a soldier in the first place. Getting out of the U.S. and hiding for a few years was all he wanted and now he was stuck in a cauldron of death whose ravenous appetite would finish them all before it was over. These forays into the hills were just the beginning of the end. Dien Bien Phu was no staging area for launching attacks against the Viet Minh, as they had been told. The French needed to get out before it was too late. Giap had screwed the valley down so tightly that the French could not move. Every sortie into the hills had ended in disaster. To step away from the safety of the strongpoints meant chaos and possible death. Now, in January, the third month of the occupation and disastrous planning, General Navarre insisted on another bloody incursion just to prove they were surrounded, to be sure they had made a mistake and it was not just their imagination. Brulee would not have it, not this time. He had decided to use the mission as his chance to escape. Quang, his favorite and accommodating prisoner, had drawn him a map. Quang had become indispensable, cooking, washing, digging, smuggling in drugs from the area. Brulee would slip into the jungle and hide until night, then slowly work his way around the valley before creeping his way over the hills and possibly to the Black river. From there he could float on a raft at night back to civilization and book passage out of the country or take a job aboard a tramp steamer and work his way out. Anyone in this country could be bought so getting onto a ship was simply a matter of commerce and he had saved plenty of money and everything in Vietnam was cheap. Even the most expensive bribes sold for pennies.

There was no reason to ask Bix to leave. He had made his decision. He liked the Legion, the order, the excitement. He was bound to stay until, like Fleming, he had earned his own red badge of courage. Bix would not make the Legion his life but he would make a it a major part of his life, books that could be read over and over again. The adventures on the pages piled in his steamer trunk of stories to be removed like Christmas tree lights upon his return to South Dakota, then packed and repacked throughout the remainder of his life. No longer would his greatest tale be about making the winning score in a basketball game with Brule High School or the senior prom where two girls wanted to go with him, or the bumper crop of alfalfa that year when the other farmers had failed. Now he was right where he wanted to be, in the middle of a desperate battle with an elite force that, through bravery and determination, would break out and defeat the enemy. No, Brulee knew he would not leave. War had become his mistress.

And Knowles? A ridiculous thought. War was also his life and besides, he had everything he needed in the valley, food, action, a beautiful woman devoted to him. Where Bix invited a minor wound, Knowles craved death, sought it out knowing that old age would kill him through an unmerciful dwindling of time. He could not fight for much longer. Already in his thirties, like most of the German legionnaires, his fighting days were limited. War is a job for young men. How Colonel Langlais still managed to trudge effortlessly through the jungle surprised everyone. But he was a special case. Leadership drove him on, leadership and arrogance and a wicked and explosive temper, the stamina to be better than every other soldier. Knowles had his limitations. He attempted to keep going, to be an inspiration but Crème Brulee knew it was an act and had seen him tired many times behind his determination, had seen behind the façade that others missed.

How about Druxman? No, he wasn't traveling with any Jew, not that it made any difference to him, it's just that a Jew had no business being in any military. They were supposed to be peaceful and Brulee was afraid that, at the most inopportune time, the time he most needed to be vicious, he might remember he was really a man of peace. He even liked Druxman but he would be a liability because Jews had a bad reputation for getting caught doing anything, good - or bad. Their ability to help one another and become successful, their belief in education, their will to handle money wisely, grated on just about everyone. No one liked a winner. Druxman would not desert anyway. Deep down inside he felt a loyalty to others. Deserting would have eaten at his mind until he became a street drunk. Not even logic would pull him away. Desertion was the right of every legionnaire, a proud heritage carried out through history. There had been times when over half a unit had deserted at a time, but Druxman would claim that times are different. A man had to live with himself. A man had to remain alive to do that.

DeJohn? Brulee knew he was ready to quit but he would not go so far from safety. The thought of hunger in the jungle, wild animals, poisonous snakes, and headhunting mountain tribes, would frighten him off. Brulee knew that DeJohn was basically a coward and that he would eventually find a way to stop fighting, maybe become a cook, in order to save his skin. Until then DeJohn, like most cowards, fought madly to save his own skin. At least Brulee was willing to take a risk to save himself. That seemed smart, if not honorable.

There was always Mategriffin. No, not because he was bi-sexual, what Southern boy wasn't? He was crazy. He also did not care if he lived or died, simple enough, but it did not bother him to take someone else with him.

And Sangree? Such thoughts would have never entered his head. He was a career man, a regular office worker whose time clock had been punched in and would be punched out in another twenty years if he lived that long.

That left just himself and the reason he had not mentioned his plan to anyone, not that they would have reported him, was that he wanted them to think he had died in battle, his body lost forever. Retaining his honor in the face of cowardice appeared somehow important.

General Navarre wanted to know the Viet Minh units in the hills and he wanted Colonel de Castries to get started, to stop dragging his feet. He had informed Colonel Langlais who now had various units waiting to identify or destroy the Viet Minh infantry around strongpoint Beatrice and to find artillery positions outside Dominique. Just before dawn the units had been placed in order alongside road 41 with le BEP in the lead. A company of 8 BPC, (8th Parachute Assault) three companies of III/3 RTA, (Algerian Rifle) and another three companies of III/3 REI (Foreign Legion Infantry) joined them. The men knew this was a large operation, possibly the largest the camp had ever assembled to attack the enemy. A company of V/7 RTA (Algerian Riflemen) hiked across from Gabrielle while two companies of III/13 DBLE (Foreign Legion) came off strongpoint Beatrice. BT 3 (3rd Thai Battalion) made a separate push northwest of Anne-Marie. All in all it seemed an impressive force especially since the units contained sappers, pioneers carrying flamethrowers, an extra company of Thai auxiliaries (rather undependable soldiers) and several tanks, affectionately called Bisons. Each man had four days of rations and all the ammunition they could carry. It looked to Bix like a full-scale invasion, soldiers everywhere, and up ahead someplace, where he always led, Colonel Langlais.

"I've never seen so many men on an operation," said Bix. "What's the deal?"

"It's big," said Crème Brulee. "If we in can't do some ass-kickin' now then we ain't got no chance a-toll."

"Why are you so pessimistic these days?" said Druxman, the shortest man in the outfit. He always resembled an over-packed mule about to collapse. "If this is the worst that happens to us then I can tell you we've got it made. What can happen on a little walk in the jungle? For this you joined to be a soldier and now it's time to fill the agreement."

"You and your agreements," said Crème Brulee. "Reckon you noticed we're in front again?"

"So, what's the complaint? You signed up with the best and now you've got it. For me, it's just another walk in the park. And my complaints? None."

"Not me," said Crème Brulee, carrying his weapon at an angle across his chest. "That damn Bix sweet-talked me into this Legion shit, said the women would get wild for a Legion paratrooper. Women don't go for no legionnaires; they're afraid of us and figure we is all stupid and just a tad bit short of being a common ape. A woman that'd have us we wouldn't want. She's be built like a tank and stink just as bad as some old hog in a holler."

Bix did not respond. He enjoyed the chase and he was on the trail, into the hunt. Action, not killing thrilled him, the excitement, the close calls, the ecstasy and delight of pulling through a tough fight. No greater pleasure existed. He had become so used to death that he needed a regular fix to feel alive, otherwise living seemed no more than incoming and outgoing oxygen, incoming and outgoing nutrients, no sorrow, no ecstasy. "Shoot at me," he thought. "Rake my path with machine gun fire, drop artillery rounds at my feet to return life to me. To the gods of danger grant my wish; place me near death, not in death."

"Fresh air is all about you, beautiful country, decent pay," said Druxman, to Brulee. "What you need is religion to buck you up."

"I got plenty of it." Crème Brulee frowned. "We got folks back home that'll kiss a snake on the lips or the ass just to show they love God; they'll foam at the mouth and dance in circles and talk so many ways ain't no one can understand em. After a meetin' I'd takem girls out back and filled them with the holy spirit till their eyes popped out. I know all about religion."

"You have no idea about it," said Druxman. "What do you want from the world? You work, you slave, you finish out your life."

"You Kikes don't even believe in God."

"Like I said, you have no idea about it. We believe plenty about God and listen to him. We do not believe Jesus is God. We should know; we were there and knew him personally. He was a good Jew and if people truly believed in his teachings they would be good Jews also."

"Folks gone to hell fer saying less." Crème Brulee tripped and cussed. Mud always caked his boots and made it difficult to walk. "No one gets to heaven like that."

"We don't believe in heaven either," said Druxman.

The sun started to heat up the road and the dust rose like powder.

"Don't reckon you believe in much," said Crème Brulee. "You just as well be one of them Bud-hists."

"Would you guys shut up," said someone from behind. "You're all going to hell, anyway."

Rifle and machine gun fire burst from the brush to the east and ahead blocking the path. Chipping up bits of dust and dirt the fire was closer and heavier than expected. Mortar rounds followed. Everyone scattered for cover and returned fire.

"We ain't hardly out the camp," said Brulee, his stomach starting to tighten as bile clawed up his throat. The ground churned in little stitches from machine gun bullets from Druxman, down to Brulee, and on past Bix.

Bix felt the wonderful rush of independence, a heightened glow of freedom as adrenalin marched through his veins pushing his emotional status ever higher and boosting him from mundane complicity to twittering vivacity. The drug caused his feet to twitch, not in fear, but in anxiety wanting more. Electricity sparked up his legs, into his chest, sparked his brain to alert palpitations as his eyes moved from embers to flames. Soon his entire body would become an intense receptacle sensitive to everything that existed. He would rip apart revealing an open wound so profound that even the air burned and all knowledge would be within his grasp. A bright glowing clarity, void of confusion, contradiction, and decision, would free his mind. As long as the opiate of action remained, life and the world, maybe even the universe, was his.

"They're here!" he yelled, for no particular reason except to breathe, to push out the air so he would be forced to draw it back in. He stood and returned fire, slow, steady, one round after another to prolong the experience, the orgasm of action, to savor the inferno within him before the ejaculation fell back into tired lethargy as the action stopped and he once again had to crawl through the brush for another fix.

Knowles grabbed Bix's collar jerking him to the ground. He kicked him on the butt as he moved on to offer encouragement to the others. No one was allowed to jeopardize his life unnecessarily except him. Life offered him no joy, no pleasure, no surprises at rising suns or setting moons. His job was to help save the lives in his unit, to see that the young men might still experience pleasure before dying, have stories to tell in old age to indifferent nurses who never heard of Dien Bien Phu as they drool, crap and piss their pants. Not even war excited him and he found it as mundane as punching a time clock at an auto factory except this time clock started with his first battle and would end with his death. He heard a rumble in the distance.

Tanks were brought in, artillery called, mortars fired, to move the Viet Minh. Progress remained slow. Each time an area cleared allowing the French to shift, the enemy blocked them again. By the end of the day they had suffered too many casualties for too little gain. They continued to advance through the early evening when war blossoms at its most beautiful, a mosaic of brilliant colors. After setting up a defensive perimeter they ate, rested four hours, and started moving again. Tracers scratched through the night as Brulee and Druxman continued their scatting.

"So what happens when yal die?" said Crème Brulee, munching on a loaf of bread he had stuffed in his pocket.

"This is supposed to be a silent movement," Bix, annoyed, reminded them.

"We sound like a herd of tin elephants in a cigar box," said Brulee. "Yal can't even hear us yapping over the noise."

"What, you think they don't know we're here?" said Druxman, taking Brulee's side. "Everything about us they know – everything!"

"Yeah," grumbled several men from behind. "So, shut up!"

Bix continued to walk quietly before the whole unit broke in a chorus of chatter. Everyone was on edge, tired and close to rebellion. One by one the Vietnamese and Thais had been deserting. The Thais had not agreed to fight away from home and felt indignant that the French had taken advantage of them by placing them in this small valley. They often traveled with whole families, especially wives who cooked and cared for them. When a Thai deserted, friends from the same village often went with him taking their entire families. The Thais who stayed fought well but were not dependable. Homesickness might strike them at anytime, then they would disappear into the hills. They seldom deserted during actual combat – no time to think. But when they sat around, they thought too much.

If the Vietnamese were led by decent officers, they fought well. If not they also deserted in great numbers, often joining the Viet Minh. Most had joined the French for the money and when they had saved enough would have deserted anyway and returned to their farms..

"So what happens when you die, where do you go?" Crème Brulee kept at Druxman.

"New York, where we are issued a sewing machine and a life sentence."

"New York?" He kicked at the dirt. "Reckon that's hell enough."

"Chicago if we have been really bad, and no sewing machine," said Druxman. "Our ghosts walk around in dreadlocks, funny hats and long black coats so everyone can mock and ridicule us for eternity. And for what? For being born a peaceful people willing to die rather than to fight or to defend ourselves, or to cause any trouble."

"You ain't never seemed too peaceful to me." In the distance the machine guns sounded like rain on a tin roof; the artillery trotted on hooves across the damp clay.

Druxman, having grown tired of the conversation, ignored him. The two of them were always at each other but he felt confident that Crème Brulee would not leave him during trouble as he would not leave Brulee. The banter only cinched their closeness. Condescending talk and ridicule, given with humor or a tinge of respect, tightened a friendship between them.

During a break Knowles gathered some of the squad together for a talk. He squatted drawing circles aimlessly in the dirt with a twig. He watched the twig travel around and around spinning the circle smaller then larger then back down again.

"We will probably not leave the fortress again," he said. He had difficulty with the French words and spoke slowly. During conversations all the legionnaires constantly interpreted from French into one or more languages. Commands were always given in French. When in groups, they attempted to find a language the majority of them spoke. Fortunately for Bix, it was often English followed by German, Spanish, then French. "These are my own thoughts, but I am sure the command will come to the same conclusion. Too many men are being lost. They may run small patrols for unit positions, nothing more. We are going around hill 781, between the villages of Ban Him Lam and Ban Na Loi then continue northwest to take hill 674. The Tirailleurs of V/7 RTA are already pinned down on the hill. The artillery we are hearing is ours trying to knock off the surrounding Viet Minh. It's been no good. As always, we will have to do it." He stood up and briefly looked around. "I want no heroes. Not this time. Do your job, fight like paratroopers but take no chances. A rougher time is coming and you will need your strength."

"What do you suppose that means?" said Crème Brulee. "A rougher time is coming?"

Again they started to move and again they were stopped. The Viet Minh refused to relinquish any ground so artillery was again called in. The big guns had little effect. Many of the shells hit the treetops detonating harmlessly overhead. Next came the Bearcat fighter/bombers sagging with napalm. The napalm lifted red flames and black gasoline smoke into the air. Load after load scorched the ground. The French unit finally moved ahead and witnessed the lack of effectiveness by the napalm. Another failed beast of destruction was confirmed. Because of the dampness and thickness of the jungle, the napalm had burnt off a few leaves and darkened the trunks of others, but little more. The great piles of black smoke were just great piles of black smoke, a sign of surrender and frustration rather than eager devastation, as the fuel quickly burnt out causing little damage.

All day the force under Langlais trudged through jungle, elephant grass seven or eight feet tall, hacked through tangles of underbrush, labored up and down hills, as the Communists constantly sniped at them. The napalm had left piles of ash and no cover for the units. Because the limbs had dried out they cracked with every touch, the soldiers could not move quietly. The ash covered their boots, clogged their nostrils, scratched their eyes. The III/13th REI crested a hill and were quickly repulsed by screaming bo doi and machine gun fire. They had no choice but to retreat back down the hill. Northwest of hill 781 the Viet Minh completely stopped le BEP.

The Viet Minh suddenly appeared just yards away as the men drove themselves into the ground. Crème Brulee trembled on the earth as if he had been buried alive and could not shake himself free. By sheer will he wished his body deeply into the dirt but he remained on the surface, bullets snipping his tunic. When he opened his eyes he had three bullet holes through the material of his right sleeve. All had missed his flesh leaving just the impression of heat. Some might have called it luck; he called it his final warning to get out of the war and Vietnam. He noticed Bix and Druxman crawling to some bushes ahead. DeJohn circled to the left. The legionnaires fanned out and attempted to advance. The only defense they knew was to attack or to counterattack. Bits of leaves fell to the ground like snowflakes. Machine guns rattled and mortar rounds started chewing up the ground into a merciless harrow. The Viet Minh were protected from well dug trenches and bunkers. Brulee saw camouflaged communication wires, like stripes of ivy or wisteria, webbing from the main bunker. The Viet Minh immediately charged leaving the legionnaires no choice except to retreat. The soldiers fought fiercely as they moved backwards in typical retreat mode: a squad or platoon withdrawing twenty feet before kneeling and offering covering fire as the front line moved back twenty feet behind them. The action repeated until the unit found a decent place for a stand and put an organized defense into place.

Sweat ran down Crème Brulee's chest. His entire uniform wept with moisture holding his body together in one gooey mess. For a moment his mind left his body, drifted in peaceful repose above his head as he went deaf, numb, and blind. Winter in Kentucky always came on the memory of summer and he remembered how the air there surrounded him like the morning mist rising from harvested cornfields, cool, carrying the dew, the dew cradling the aroma of damp earth, manure, vegetation, and the promise of heat. His mind did not return to the valley until he thought of spring. He knew the rains in the Vietnam highlands would soon crack from the sky. A Viet Minh round snapped past his head like an angry bee.

When his chance to retreat came he ran the twenty feet behind the last unit, stopped to rest, then kept going, first crawling backwards on his stomach, then up to his knees, then to his feet. Everyone was too busy to notice him. He finally stopped to catch his breath again and knelt, his shoulders rising and lowering like a bellows. He could hear the noise of the desperate battle but not see it because of the brush. Because the gunfire continued to grow louder he knew the unit was still retreating so he moved farther along. He needed to get off the trail or be run over. His hands started to shake. The quiver moved through his entire body. He fumbled in his pocket and dumped a small amount of heroin into his mouth, a very ineffective way to take it but the best he could do at the moment. He waited for the pain to subside. A small trail ran off to the west. In a crouch he worked his way under the canopy of brush. West was the best way to go, over the hills toward Laos or Cambodia, then home. The thought caused him to grin.

He crossed a stream of mud and fought off the deluge of gnats and bugs spinning around him and sticking to his face. He finally stood and ran, his left arm out and at an angle to deflect the foliage and tree branches. The freedom flowed over him like a protective hand; but the hand was a lie and slapped him hard as he ran straight into a Viet Minh knocking him flat on the dirt. The Viet Minh soldier looked like a child, surprised and frightened, his eyes jerking like two aggies in a marble game. His M-1 carbine looked like a Civil War Springfield and overpowered him and his pith helmet slanted over his forehead. Crème Brulee looked at him and up where, just emerging from the brush, a line of Viet Minh started to emerge. They seemed as surprised as the boy. From habit, Brulee raised his rifle and fired a shot at the enemy in the brush. He turned and ran back like a pig at a barbecue splashing up mud from the depression. Twice he stopped to fire rounds behind him. He knew the Viet Minh would move slowly until they discovered what they were facing. They seldom took chances. He pulled out a grenade, extracted the pin and tossed it over his head without looking. The grenade hit a tree limb and bounced back. From the corner of his eye he saw it pass and land behind him. He jumped over the grenade and dove for a depression in the ground. The explosion splattered dirt and burning metal everywhere. A piece of shrapnel burned through his thigh. He rolled to his side and continued to fire. The heroin helped ease the pain and allowed him to function. He dug in as deeply as possible, locked his toes into the mud, fired into the brush.

Three legionnaires moving to reinforce le BEP jumped to his side and joined in the fire fight before realizing they saw nothing, not even moving brush.

"Bonhomme! What is the problem?"

"Plaquez au sol," said Brulee, telling them to get down. "The jungle's full of slopes. I been attempting to hold em off. Get some help." He thought hard to come up with an explanation why he was behind the unit but an explanation seemed unnecessary. "I remembered this here small trail and I reckoned they's the type what might attempt to flank us. I stumbled on the whole pack and been fightin' em off by myself."

"We see nothing," one of them said.

"What's this look like to you?" He pointed to his leg.

The soldiers squatted down and looked at him like he was crazy. He appeared badly shaken, his hands quivering. Blood colored the bullet hole in his pants. They glanced at one another and shrugged. Several Viet Minh burst through the brush and almost swamped them as Crème Brulee fired, knocking them back. The legionnaires immediately sprang to action, the will and ability to fight trained into them. Fortunately the trail allowed no more than three Viet Minh to pass at a time. He knew that others would be looking for another way to get through. Without help they would soon be extinguished.

"Get the fuck out of here," he yelled. "Get help." After several more shouted words one of the legionnaires ran for help as the others squirmed into the ground. Brulee tossed another grenade. The blast tore away some brush and he saw a torn and smoking tunic fly into the air. The two soldiers fired methodically, no hurry, no anxious moments. They might as well have been at the firing range shooting paper targets. Brulee remained agitated more than scared; he fired as quickly as he could pull the trigger. Sweat blurred his eyes and left them burning. He felt he would crap his pants.

He refused to die on that patch of dirt in the jungle and left to rot, unknown and un-remembered to the world, to fertilize more grass that would be eaten by water buffalo and eventually crapped out. He almost chuckled when he thought, "what a shitty way to go." It might have been fitting but it did not seem fair.

Artillery continued to churn up the ground before the retreating unit and more Bearcats swooped in with napalm. A shell landed short and killed two legionnaires. A panting legionnaire informed a sergeant about the flanking move by the Viet Minh and that his friends and another soldier were attempting to hold them off. The ser-geant sent a squad to the rear to help repel them. They immediately took up positions in the brush on the other side of the small clearing placing the machine gun directly in the center. Bix and his friends retreated to join them. The only way to kill the Viet Minh was to get them into the open. Crème Brulee and the legionnaires moved back across the clearing. As the Viet Minh started to break into the open, the machine gun opened up cutting them down unmercifully. The survivors crept back into the woods and did not return.

The artillery rounds dwindled; the planes left; the small arms quieted; and soon the unit appeared on their return to camp and safety. They were a bedraggled crew, dirty, covered with fresh mud, uniforms torn, the wounded limping along, all faces con-torted by defeat and the realization they had accomplished nothing. Le BEP had al-ways held the greatest arrogance and confidence yet even they had sunk into remorse at the failure. The march back seemed like weeks rather than hours. The Viet Minh followed with harassing fire and continued to cause causalities. The legionnaires of-fered little defense and had almost lost all faith, had accepted their fate as an animal, in the jaws of another, finally goes slack, eyes staring blankly, content to be eaten. Officers and NCOs split their units off as they entered the wire and led them to their particular areas to commiserate their losses with wine and whisky and wait out the days it would take before the battle became a part of unit history and their confidence might rise to the pitch of laughter and boasting.

"That was something," said Druxman, to Brulee. "For you, I'm grateful. Everyone's talking. You might have saved the entire operation."

Crème Brulee sat on an ammo box chair outside their bunker and propped up his leg. Bix untied the rag around his leg, unrolled the bloody bandage the medic had applied, and checked the wound. The wound was minor, little more than a scrape that had dug a little deeper into the flesh than usual. Quang, his bayonet stuffed into his belt, looked it over carefully. He dashed off to get some water. Brulee took great pains to reveal his pain and viewed the cut as a major wound, something near amputation. Bix washed it with fresh water, applied salve, and rewrapped it with fresh gauze.

"You act like it was blown off," said deJohn. "I've seen bigger scrapes on kids in a playground."

"You Frenchies don't know nothing about pain," he said. "A Limey splained the whole thing to me. A Frenchman came up to his grandad and asked why the Brits wore red uniforms. He said they wore em in case they got shot. The blood blended in with the uniforms and the men would not be frightened. The Frenchman thunk about it a while and replied that he reckoned that's why the French wore brown pants."

"As if I hadn't heard that one a hundred times."

Bix patted Crème Brulee on the shoulder. "We are not used to having a hero in our midst. I, for one, want to thank you. We never would have gotten through without your help. Had they come up behind us it would have been all over."

DeJohn slid into the bunker and emerged with a canteen cup. He handed it to Crème Brulee. Brulee eyed him suspiciously before taking a sip. He choked and coughed, threw his head back and blew out a stream of fire.

"Whop!" he said. "That's real moonshine. It done lit up my tonsil like a firefly and the ashes be burning a hole in my stomach."

"That's for everyone," said deJohn. "Leave it to you to suck the whole thing down."

"To live healthy you gots to drink plenty of fruits." He tipped the cup to deJohn.

"Always he gets greedy," said Druxman. "No manners ever came his way. He acts like he's important, like he is really something." Druxman pulled the cup away and tasted the aluminum rim before the whisky entered his mouth. As his eyes cleared he saw several people walking his way. Lieutenant Wise and Sergeant Knowles approached. Wise resembled a boy in boarding school and seemed out of place in his tunic, drooping and covered with mud.

"Stay where you are men," he said. The men had no intention of standing or acting professional in any way. Druxman offered him the canteen. With a smile he declined. "Word has come down that you have committed a remarkable feat of bravery, Private Brulee. How is the leg?"

"Reckon I can carry on, Sir" he said, making certain he flinched as he moved it. It ain't going to hold me up fer long and I'll be right back at them monkeys soon enough." deJohn and Druxman looked at one another and almost laughed.

"Perhaps you tell me what happened? I have had versions from other legionnaires who were there."

"Them boys came along eventually, after I'd been holding out a while," he said. "See, I knowed they was a small trail back behind us cause we passed it and since we were getting hit so hard from the front, I reckoned they wouldn't let an opportunity go by to get us from there. I ran back that-a-way to see if they was going to flank us. I went alone case if I was wrong I wouldn't be taking no soldiers from the real fight. I don't know much about tactics but I know how to shoot a turkey from the side when he don't expect it. I didn't see nothing so's I went down the trail a piece. After crossing a water run they come upon me. I let them have it just to let them know they was fighting a Legionnaire. I fought backward til I got my tail to the clearing to make a stand. I hoped someone might come along afore I was kilt. Sure enough them other fellas showed up. That's about it. Nothing special. I couldn't have done it alone without them other fellas coming along right there at the end when I finally had the situation under control."

"Nothing special?" said the lieutenant. "Expect to hear from someone tomorrow. And let me salute you for your bravery." He saluted sharply. Before they turned and left, Knowles leaned over and whispered to Brulee, "It's dangerous to try and leave on your own."

"I reckon you know who you're dealing with now," he said, to no one in particular, and wondering what Knowles meant by his comment.

Crème Brulee was summoned the following afternoon. He was still sleeping when two sergeants appeared. He had relived the incident several times during the night and sweat soaked his T-shirt.

"Wear your best uniform," one of them said.

He attempted to move. The whisky had swelled in his head and started to drain as he sat causing him to sway. The dug-out was empty of his friends. What a party they had had last night. Other soldiers had drifted by to congratulate him and to offer food and drinks. Only Knowles had not appeared but he did not begrudge him that. The bordello had arrived and he knew he was with Nicole and what man would not have exchanged a hero's party for her. He had only one clean uniform that he slept on to keep it smooth. He slid into it on wobbly legs and tried to iron out the wrinkles with his hands. He had forgotten to shave so he poured water into his helmet, soaped up his chin, and scraped the razor across the whiskers pulling out as many as he cut. He felt the razor nick and jab over each whisker and he dreamed of the days when he had a hot water shave with a new blade. He had thought nothing of it then, did not realize the joy of simple luxuries: fresh tobacco, a comb, clean water, sheets on a feather bed, a magazine, a piece of hot apple pie. He wiped the scratches of blood on his chin with the back of his hand as they left for the command bunker.

A row of le BEP legionnaires stood at attention before Colonel de Castries' bunker. Bix, deJohn, Druxman, and Knowles stood stiffly in formation. A lieutenant told him to stand before the line. Moments later Guiraud, Langlais, and de Castries emerged from underground. Crème Brulee saluted and the officers returned the salute. Guiraud read an official statement regarding the heroic actions performed by Crème Brulee. Langlais said, "In such troubling times you have given the Legion inspiration, as you have the entire operation. Without thought for your own safety, you exemplified the nature of a Legion paratrooper." He asked Crème Brulee to step forward one step. De Castries pinned the Crouix de Guerre onto Brulee's tunic, kissed him on each cheek. "This award," he said, "could not wait. You are a man of action and all France salutes you. Your achievements are the ones most admired by French soldiers the world over. With men like you, defeat for us is not an option." They saluted again before returning to their bunker. The lieutenant released the men.

"After all them kisses I thought he might ask me to his place for a drink," Brulee said. Many of the men slapped him on the back as they left.

Brulee fingered the medal, rolled it around his fingers as the others patted him on the back and wished him the best of luck. His shock was soon replaced with a grin. He started to believe he was a hero, a man of iron backbone, determination, a tactical genius, a person to be admired. He had not tried to desert, after all. Yes, getting out might have entered his mind, but only as a glancing thought. He knew he had changed his mind about leaving even before he had confronted the Viet Minh. What an award, what a hero! One thing he knew for certain – that medal would be clasped tightly in his hand when he finally did desert.

Chapter 27

"We should have taken the high ground," said Bix, grumbling. The rain had gone, come, and gone again. Thick clods of red clay clung to his boots making them clumsy and heavy. The smell of cordite drifted over the compound and smoke from cooking fires hung like a thin fog. He could see almost all the strongpoints crouching lower than the surrounding hills held by the Viet Minh. Several strongpoints smoked from artillery hits. Bix pushed away from the muddy bank and tried to web his end of barbed wire to a metal post. The wire rose up and hissed under his tug.

"Now you're a General," said Druxman. "The mountains have no airstrip, our one great advantage. At the moment, we suffer some racket, but the little yellow bastards cannot maintain this kind of fire for long. Who is to supply them? For us, we have everything except peace and quiet."

"Still..." said Bix. He was not entirely convinced they held the better position and something false rumbled in Druxman's voice. "There something basic about taking the high ground? The worst soldiers know that." He had read that somewhere. "Even General Custer had made a final attempt to top a hill before being cut down by the Sioux and Cheyenne."

"How did that work out for him?" said Druxman.

"If he had been faster things might have been different," said Bix

"You're starting to be a real worrier," said Crème Brulee, taking a break from the work. "My grandfather, who fought in World War I at the battle of Chateaubriant, said there ain't nothing a man can do in war 'cept forge ahead and try an keep his eyes open."

"Sure," said Bix. "Chateaubriant... Of course, you are the big hero."

"Yessur. He took on a little mustard gas there. Had a small cough the rest of his life."

He smiled at Druxman.

"I don't trust you to shoot straight," said Bix. "Why do I ask, you say? Why am I worried? Lately I see you're a little shaky."

"I can shoot the foreskins off a Jew at a thousand yards."

"We Jews have no foreskins," said Druxman.

"Not any more," said Crème Brulee.

"Would I have chosen the wrong army twice?" said Knowles, as he walked up to inspect the work. He sounded bitter, the words coming out like wood chips. "Soon, that one–armed Frog, Colonel Piroth, will put his big guns to use and blast the yellow bastards from the hills." He did not believe it. No amount of artillery could destroy the guns. Piroth and his counter-battery fire had been useless.

Another shell, wobbling the earth under Bix, landed on the airstrip. They landed intermittently, sometimes one an hour, sometimes ten. Colonel Piroth, commander of the artillery, had lost his arm to the Germans in the last war. Now, Knowles depended on him to pull them from this fix.

"He's done a right poor job today," said Crème Brulee.

Bix chuckled at the joke, at the attempt to make them laugh without angering Knowles who was often solemn but seldom surly. The barbed wire tore at his tunic. Knowles had often said that laughter makes death bearable. He made plenty of jokes himself, always with a straight face. They had both been laughing for weeks. Bix might have laughed to hide his fear, to show Knowles, who had spent his youth fighting Russians on the Eastern Front during the Big War, that he was a man unafraid of death - except that he was a man afraid one minute, unafraid the next. He never knew where his guts were although generally the war did not faze him. Regardless of how hard he tried he could not be wounded, not the slightest scratch. His life seemed blessed with safety and it often made him angry.

Knowles lifted the wire over his head revealing the blood type tattoo under his arm that marked him as a former S.S. soldier. The ink lay behind a layer of scar tissue thick and blurry like a bathroom window, as if Knowles had attempted to cut away his past but had given up.

One of Captain Hervouet's Bisons, an M-24 Chaffee light tank, one of ten in the valley, rumbled through the Center of Resistance, mud clinging to the tracks. The rain was not consistent but the monsoon season would arrive soon when an ocean of water would darken the sky. Bix climbed a pile of dirt and surveyed the handywork of the soldiers. Since November, 1953, when he had dropped with the first wave, the French forces in Indochina had prepared the valley of Dien Bien Phu for war. The French offered the Viet Minh, never eager to fight in large numbers, a bouquet to entice them into a large battle. The plan was simple: establish a force deep in Viet Minh territory, a force small and inviting yet skilled enough to defeat any full scale attack. That was how Bix saw it. Now that they were no longer an aggressive force, they were bait. The camp was never strong enough to be a mooring point for aggressive action like they had been told. Any fool could have seen that. No, the trick now was to entice the Viets into a large battle.

Bix removed his hat and fingered the sweat from his hair. Hot sweat dripped over him as cold chills ran through him. Knowles continued to fight with the wire and the lower barbs nipped small bits of dirt into the air. The camp had come a long way - from a simple valley growing rice and drugs, to a small impenetrable fortress.

Tractors had gouged the red clay pushing up great mounds of dirt, grinding out dug–outs, machine gun pits and command posts. Trucks and tanks flattened roads while soldiers webbed the compound perimeters with barbed wire. The surrounding hills, Gabrielle, Beatrice, Huguette, Francoise, Claudine, Dominique and Elaine, were fortified into the valley's main defense. Isabelle and Weim, five miles to the south and alone, appeared to be added as an afterthought.

Another shell, far to the east, lifted a single tree. The hills were covered with a cotton of foliage and enemy forces remained unseen. No vegetation remained on the Center of Resistance. Bix flipped Knowles a pack of cigarettes. When he knelt to retrieve the pack, a sharp pain knifed through his knee. He was getting too old for war. Yet war, fighting, were the only things he knew. Because he never expected to live this long, he needed the rush of nearby death, the sweet smell of life among the dead. He needed to support the young men with his knowledge. After the last war, what remained for him in Germany? Factory work? Farming? Lumber or steel mills? Not for a soldier. He refused to become a jolly old pretzel maker serving arrogant tourists: ignorant Americans, snooty British trotting about in shorts, or the nasty, unkempt French. But lately, he had been feeling melancholy, a little wrinkled inside.

Knowles needed to avoid any signs of love, compassion, all tender feelings while around his men; only in this way could a soldier survive and be an inspiration. What he required was a fix of hard adrenaline, hot buttery adrenaline to keep him a leader. None of the men believed his act. They never knew a kinder man, or respected one more. He fingered the woman's locket, blue with silver trim that hung around his neck. The locket was the cause of his melancholy. He flipped the lid open and stared at the browning picture of an old woman, whose name he did not know. He had pulled it from the hands of a Russian soldier he had killed in the snow. He did know why he kept it but he did. Only a week ago he had pressed the locket between his hands and, almost as a surprise, had started to cry. Maybe he was breaking down like many of his own men had done in the last war. "Old age comes quickly to soldiers," he thought, "and then they are finished."

He shoved the locket back into his shirt and rolled a cigarette between his fingers. Morning rains left the red clay damp. All week the sky had cracked apart, rain pouring one minute, sun the next. The war was being fought in a steam bath as huge blankets of mist rose after each deluge. The secret to surviving any conflict was to ignore everything except the job at hand. Bitching about the weather would not dry up the sky. The French position also concerned him. The French commanders, strutting like new cocks in a hen yard, treated the Vietnamese like inferior soldiers. Knowles understood too well the kind of trouble underestimation caused. The Russians were not quite soldiers, either, a race of piggish animals. How quickly that view had changed. He refused to worry the younger soldiers about his doubts and attempted to keep on the positive side.

"They are French," said Knowles, attempting to justify their military actions, or lack of actions. "To them, everything is an art. After wine, perhaps a loaf of bread; eventually they get down to business. Of course, there will be arguing, an attempt to throw one another out of command, several votes and protests. Then they will move. And all will be fine."

"We've fired plenty of artillery rounds back at them" said Bix. He looked like a kid standing there, all bones, his tunic hanging almost off his shoulders, hips pushed forward looking anxious, confused and worried like the first man, or the last, in line at a whore house.

"The Legion celebrates defeat," said Knowles. "You can roll them over, but they always return. Only a Frenchman understands. Our job is to drink with them when the thing is finished and boast of the glory, even if the glory is defeat."

Two Bearcat fighters dipped low over the road to Beatrice, unloading bombs of napalm in the jungle forest beside a strongpoint. Great heaps of yellow fire with a top-knot of black smoke rolled toward the sky. "That's the difference," said Knowles. He leaned back and pointed. "The sky is our salvation. You can not win without aircraft." He flipped the pack of cigarettes back to Bix who caught them in mid air. What a lie!

"I don't reckon Piroth's hit a damn thing except dirt with all his boasts," said Brulee. "He done knocked down enough trees in the hills to start his own logging company."

Bix felt reassured Knowles was lying about the outcome. Brulee made much more sense, a frightening thought in itself. Everyone knew that the high command had borrowed military and civilian aircraft, months ago, from all of Indochina just to land the forces and equipment into the valley. It was reported that "Earthquake" McGoon, a legendary American pilot, was flying missions. Any fool could see the conditions of the parachutes that were dropped: patched, torn, many of them used over fifty times and totally unreliable. Now, the silk was used to wrap the dead for burial. Transport planes landed daily and still there were not enough supplies.

"I don't like it," mumbled Bix. He waited anxiously and unsure of himself, waited for Knowles to unwind a string of knowledge and guidance. Anyone who had survived the Russian campaign knew something about war.

"Look how far we've come," said Knowles. He swung his arm in a wide arch.

Friendly Vietnamese, newly formed into fighting units, and Moroccans, had worked to complete the torn airfield. Metal sheets covered the landing strip and at the end of the field, spread like thick fingers on a fan, walls of sandbags protected the Bearcat fighters. In the open, the control tower rose like a fat water tank directing flights of transport aircraft that landed in an endless stream.

They pounded out a formidable defense that only slowly reassured Bix of any chance of victory. They were not supposed to be attacked, anyway. The Viet Minh never fought major battles. His optimism rose and sank on a daily basis. The hospital, the command posts of Colonel de Castries and Colonel Langlais, the paratroop units used in counterattacks, the supply depots, the heavy artillery emplacements and the air field all formed the hub of a giant wheel, called the Center of Resistance. How many enemy could even wade through the thick underbrush or low lying swamps to get here? The Algerians had worked the valley erecting artillery emplacements. Engineer units had notched various headquarters bunkers deeply underground, covered the rooms with layers of logs, dirt, sandbags and metal. Red cross flags secured several hospitals. Boxes of shells and equipment had been parachuted daily from the skies augmenting equipment from transports on the field. Long trails of trucks kicked up piles of red dust while hauling ammunition and food down the spokes of the wheel to nearby strongpoints. Tanks and supplies moved daily between the valley and the five miles to Isabelle.

Barbed wire fenced the airstrip, roads, dugouts and the banks of the Nam Yum River. Thousands of rounds of artillery shells lay in great heaps in the center of camp. Drums of fuel teetered atop one another and ammunition and food soared from the ground like tall fat buildings. The hum of the water purifying machines sounded reassuring. Ten thousand soldiers loyal to France lined the valley and surrounding strongpoints. Yet Bix knew that even as the Fort was being built, enemy trenches had started to encircle the airstrip and the other strongpoints. Legionnaires, with the support of tanks, ran daily clearing sweeps. He had been on enough of them to understand how tightly they were being squeezed. Day and night encounters occurred in the foothills and small arms fire sounded in the distance. Heavy shells often flashed against the night as French artillerymen supported nearby fire-fights and the Viet Minh tested their guns by returning fire on possible targets.

"Help with this wire," said Knowles, to Brulee, sitting on the ground and drinking a canteen of water. "The yellow bastards are falling into our trap, nothing more." Crème Brulee seemed to work less and less as time went on.

Bix wanted be more like Knowles, more confident and sure of himself. Everyone liked Knowles, respected him for his fighting knowledge, and soldiers often called him the Kraut as a sign of respect and affection. Many of the older legionnaires were ex-German soldiers. Knowles seemed to enjoy tight situations and sometimes he grinned and joked about eating the flesh of babies. No one believed him. He might have been the most caring, sympathetic soldier they had ever met. In a fight he was fearless. After telling these stories, he always leaned over and winked at Bix. He often enjoyed singing military songs with the other German legionnaires.

"What difference does all this work make?" said Brulee. "We put up the wire, they blow it back down; we dig a trench, they cover it back up; we bulldoze the airfield, they blow it full of holes. It's like trying to fill a barrel with water that has no bottom." Knowles gave him an icy stare. "Ya, ya, I'm going to do it, to follow orders, I'm just saying it don't make no sense, it's all fur nothing."

"Complain, complain, complain," said Druxman. "Does the Sergeant ask much? Does he ride your ass? I ask you, does the barrel have sides with or without water?"

"What does that mean?"

"It means to start stringing some wire," said Druxman. "It's the sides we've got to worry about. Always you have to make it difficult. Who cares if it gets filled with water so long as we can hide in it, hide in it behind the sides."

"I can work as hard as any man," said Brulee, tripping face down into the mud and wire as he started to help. He rolled over and tried to free himself. "By God, help get my ass out of here," he yelled, but they had difficulty hearing him over their laughter.

Bix watched Knowles roll his hands around the wire, two tight–skinned monsters with knotted knuckles. His fingers easily straddled the lids of ammo boxes and he used them to furrow through his thinning blond hair. Bix had no difficulty imagining Knowles standing tall for inspection in his Waffen S.S. uniform: fair skin, ivory teeth, blue eyes like newly painted sign boards advertising the Master Race. But in this light, fighting with the barbed wire – work, as a sergeant, he was not required to do - and after so much drudgery, Knowles appeared less perfect, more like a middle-aged trolley-man. Exhaustion had rounded his shoulders and his teeth, yellow from smoking, pushed, like rough stones, through his cracked and parted lips. His uniform, usually spotless and pressed, now wrinkled and hanging with sweat, was torn where a button should have been and the leather from his boot tops flapped when he walked – a bad day. He generally appeared spotless, his clothes crisp, his face clean-shaven. Seldom did he sink to the slovenly level of the men who were not required to dress properly as long as they were working.

"Colonel Gaucher will hold Beatrice," said Bix, as another puff of smoke rose from the side of the strongpoint. The sight of the valley had started to increase his confidence. Beatrice expected an attack that night. "He's a good man," he reassured himself. "If he can't hold, no one can."

"He's the best," said Crème Brulee.

"No - better," said Druxman.

"What's one Colonel, more or less, in this place?" Knowles spit into the dirt. "They'll hold because they are the 13th Legionnaires – German legionnaires – and they have a reputation for holding." He wanted to remind them that they were required to fight with or without officers. In an actual battle legionnaires were practically autonomous.

"That's where they'll hit?" said Bix, referring to Beatrice.

"What, you think they'll run right into the valley?" said Druxman. "Nibble at the edges, that's what rats do."

"I mean, why one of the strongest points we have and held by one of our strongest units?" said Bix. They all looked toward Knowles. He never looked up.

Knowles usually emphasized the word "German," sometimes with praise, many times with contempt and scorn. He seemed indifferent this time when he mentioned them. Bix often had difficulty understanding Knowles because he frequently chose both sides of an argument. He argued the benefits of war in one sentence, and the disgust of war, in the next. Bix realized that Knowles was in another place, not this war, not this valley, but someplace Bix could not go. Knowles sometimes called the Vietnamese "Red Russian Bastards" or "Nazi Pricks." Yet, behind his various attitudes there remained a respect for the enemy that Bix did not fully appreciate, or understand.

"Reckon they want to teach us a lesson," said Brulee. "If they can put a scare up there on Beatrice it could shake up everyone."

"Scare everyone?" said Druxman. "I don't feel scared. When the 13th kicks their ass they'll all want to go home and take their chicken faces with them."

"It seems like a lot of trouble and pretty risky," said Bix. "Why do Langlais and de Castries think it's coming tonight?"

Knowles continued to string the barbed wire and remained quiet letting them talk to relieve their anxiety.

"Trouble with the army is ignorance and apathy," said Brulee. "Fact is I don't know and I don't care. If the Viets come tonight then they come."

"The forty beds of the hospital are about full, even after regular evacuation flights," said Bix, watching a corpsman step outside a bunker for a breather. The man leaned against a barrel, rapped his finger against his watch, nodded to Bix. Blood covered his apron and boots. He pissed on the ground before ducking back inside. The main hospital had been dug deep into the ground and covered with a protecting roof of thick planks and dirt. Like the legs of an upturned spider, radio antenna protruded from the clay. Rolls of barbed wire formed a crown of thorns. Knowles and his work detail were trying to finish the last strands of wire around the entrance. They had helped the engineers build the entire hospital to make sure it was the one place totally safe, aside from the bordello. Bix had installed one of the two X-ray machines. Knowles and Smith had worked on the rifle and machine gun slits. Increasing casualties continued to roll into the compound. After stabilization they were flown out. Any fear most of the injured felt about being wounded was over-ridden by their fear of showing fear. He had seen no terror on the face of any casualty. The beds were slowly being filled because the wounded were being created more quickly than they could be flown out.

"Will we reinforce them?" said Bix, nodding toward Beatrice. His knowledge of war did not venture far beyond any immediate task. Everything else seemed too large, too complicated. Only recently, when he jumped into the valley with the first forces, had he seen his first death up close. Four months of training in Algeria had brought him to this place. He felt he was a good soldier, never questioned orders, never concerned himself with anything unseen. Knowing that his officers understood the situation was satisfaction enough for him. But something about not taking the high ground unsettled him.

"You lookin to get kilt?" said Crème Brulee. "All them strongpoints ain't nothing but worms on a fish hook. Trouble is them hooks ain't attached to nothing. That big mudcat in them hills gonna swallow it whole and nothing no one can do about it."

Bix blocked out Brulee and thought of Nicole, at the Legion Bordello. He had never seen a more beautiful woman. Had she been his first sexual encounter he would have never gone to another woman. A pretty thought, indeed but just a thought. She was not a whore but a businesswoman who showed as much kindness to her girls as Knowles did to his men. Bix often felt resentful toward Knowles because he belonged to her and she belonged to him. He was not sure why, maybe because she always treated the old sergeant with such tenderness, the gentle kisses, the touching of hands like ordinary lovers. Knowles, drunk, something that seldom happened, called an evening in Hanoi with Bix the night of the cherub and had celebrated the occasion by having Nicole sit on his lap, her head leaned gently against his head, her hand cradling his chin as if he were a baby and not a tough soldier. Her eyes laughed at him and he wanted to slap her because he could never have her; no one could have her except Knowles. He probably thought of her more than Knowles did.

"They are ringed tight on the hill." Knowles pointed toward Beatrice with his thumb. "Take one of these." He offered Bix a pack of French cigarettes, a terrible smoke in any situation.

"French cigarettes smoke like dust," he said, waving them away.

"I reckon you'll be smoking dog turds before this battle is over," said Brulee, with a laugh. "Lucky you have me to look after you."

Bix listened to the way Knowles spoke French, always more formal than himself. Bix smiled, as his confidence returned. No one could beat this little army. They were, after all, the French Foreign Legion, the toughest fighting force in the world. And they were paratroopers – the best of the best.

"When this battle is over, I'm going to give you a whole carton of King-Size Cavaliers," said Bix.

"Yesterday it took a battalion of legionnaires and two tanks to break through for water," Knowles continued. "If the grand show comes tonight, my German comrades will fight alone. All the fighting – all the glory. There are more 'Yellow Nazis here than we suspect." Any insults he gave the Viet Minh always sounded like praise.

"The 13th will hold," said Bix. Again his confidence grew. Knowles appeared to wane. Bix brushed off the thoughts of earlier setbacks they had suffered on patrols.

The sorties into the hills had become few and fewer as the Viets grew stronger until the French were virtually locked into the valley. The thought that "our" trap had become "their" trap had never occurred to Bix. Still, they attempted to keep the Viet Minh dislodged from the surrounding hills, but lately whenever the paratroop patrols ventured close, the Viets Minh caught them in deadly cross-fires. Only a week ago an attempt to take hill 781 from the enemy had failed. The Viet Minh were deeply entrenched, not just on the hill but also around road 41, and they had almost completely surrounded Beatrice.

"Lately, shells make me flinch," said Knowles, when one landed nearby. "A poor response for a soldier."

"Bad nerves?" said Brulee

"You're too tough," said Bix, not wanting to believe he was growing soft, "like an old piece of leather." He knew Knowles was kidding - must be kidding. He had never seen him afraid of anything and everyone knew the story about Knowles receiving a leg wound in the Red River Delta. Because his unit had been "yellowed" up with Vietnamese, Knowles jabbed a bayonet into the wound to annoy them, to show them what men Germany produced. When he jiggled the bayonet, his foot jumped. Several Vietnamese became sick and turned away at the sight. Knowles had dug the blade in deeper, just to watch them flinch.

"They will attack today," said Knowles, as if predicting a rainstorm.

Bix reached for his watch, remembered he had left it in their tiny quarters. There was plenty of daylight left. Artillery rounds had pocked the compound. The airstrip had been under constant fire for several days now. A shell exploded beside the remains of a Flying Boxcar that had been hit two days earlier.

"Looks to me like they're already here," said Druxman. The sparsity of casualties produced by shelling amazed him.

"Wait until tonight," said Knowles, "when Beatrice catches everything. Such a grand show and the killing should be easy for the 13th and their machine gun emplacements." He touched the locket around his neck. "You..." he said, waving an arm toward Bix, "...you should have stayed home with your mother like all good boys."

"And miss this?" said Bix, forcing a grin. Knowles often called him a boy, and sometimes muffin or pumpkin. He liked the safety Knowles supplied, nothing overt, just a feeling of being watched over and cared for. At such times he felt like a kid, a boy on the football field with a parent in the stands. During times of fighting Bix was a man, a soldier as good as any of them. Only men survived in the Legion.

More puffs of smoke rose from Beatrice. Dirt erupted into the air and powdered its sides. Everywhere Bix looked, men worked, oblivious to the danger. Heavy mortar crews stacked shells, grave-diggers scooped out beds in the cemetery behind the hospital, cooking fires rose from small trenches. On Beatrice, the 13th Foreign Legion

Half-Brigade was deeply entrenched. They were the best of the Legion, impossible to dislodge. They were also working, preparing for the battle.

A jeep slid to a stop beside the hospital entrance and Jean Lachen, assigned to the 1st

Colonial Parachute Battalion, dismounted. Like all paratroop units, Lachen's was held in reserve.

"We'll need our rest tonight," he said, climbing over the embankment after Bix called to him. He squatted against a sandbag, a small man from a French border town, always full of good cheer, always eager to fight. His face was red as if someone had slapped him. "The Colonel has placed us on alert in preparation for the grand show."

Lachen referred to Lieutenant Colonel Langlais, commander of all the paratroop units.

" You French worry too much," said Knowles, offering him a cigarette.

"Not enough when it comes to a grand show," said Lachen. "I shake with fear and excitement at the thought of a battle. Reports of the enemy are numerous. Already their artillery has deafened me." He plugged his ears, made a grotesque face.

"What harm are they?," said Knowles, "except for lifting an occasional bit of runway stripping. Put some iron in your backbone."

Lachen drank from his canteen and kicked a pile of clay with his boot. He offered the canteen to Bix. It was filled with wine that, almost more vital than ammunition to the French, was flown in daily. Lachen, as Bix knew, was far from being a coward. He had dropped into the valley with him in the first wave five months before. The wine tasted sweet and he took a big swallow.

"We've come a long way, you and I," said Lachen. "The day we fell into the valley, it was one man killed..." he twirled his arms around him, "... and now..."

Bix remembered the drop. He grinned and drank again from the canteen. He passed the canteen to Knowles and listened to a distant shell crack the earth. The Viet Minh had finally fallen into the trap. Ordinarily they would not fight in any great numbers. This time was different. The French carrot had lured them in. He caught another glimpse of Beatrice being lightly shelled as they continued to pass around the canteen. The artillery rounds hitting the Center of Resistance lessened. The Viet Minh were right where the French wanted them.

"Maybe the shelling's going to stop," said Bix. "I would hate to have them get away after all this work."

"They're running short of ammunition," said Knowles. "We had better clean our weapons, get some rest, prepare for the counterattack on Beatrice. I must check on the other men in a few minutes and get them ready."

Knowles used a model '44 MAS automatic, which he kept spotless. Bix's M-1 carbine, a weapon Knowles disdained, also remained in good order.

"You'll be a veteran soon," said Lachen, smiling at Bix and pointing to the wound on his own arm. Guilt and resentment burned in Bix yet he also felt shy and ashamed. He wanted his own wound, his own scar to exhibit back home. "We must keep an eye on him. He won't understand the enemy until the enemy has entered his body." He pinched Bix's cheek. "For now, his pink, virgin flesh is a comfort on cold nights." Bix drew back and spit onto the clay.

"The battle won't be tonight," said Bix. "We're too strong for them. They never fight when we are strong." Anxiously, he looked at the hill again and, for only a moment, wondered why he was fighting anyone. The thought had not occurred to him before and even now it entered as only a feeling, a gentle twinge below the neck. He had only wanted an adventure.

"One last drink," said Lachen. He held the canteen above his head. "If the fight is off, I'll see you at the bordello. Until then, keep Bix away from any sharp objects. We wouldn't wish him to injure himself."

Brulee had returned to his spot on the ground, bits of blood leaking from the scratches and barb bites caused by falling into the wire.

"It's on for tonight," Knowles grinned. When he laughed deep and long, Bix knew it was true.

"I'm not worried," said Bix. When he reached for his carbine, the weapon slid down the bank and into the mud.

Chapter 28

After leaving the meeting with General Giap, Chau stood in the town of Mu Nam Quan, for his next assignment, facing the border of China and watched the big Russian 2 ½ ton trucks drive through. Crudely built, they smoked and rattled, thick heavy chunks of machinery that lumbered without the grace of most machinery, including military machinery, from other nations. Many had been loaded to bursting and the frames hunched low over the axels. Hundreds of them would eventually drive to Tuan Giao, 50 miles from the battle at Dien Bien Phu, haul food, supplies, ammunition, and pull guns, American and Japanese artillery pieces and anti-aircraft guns. The trucks would travel down provincial road 13-B to the Red River, then road 41 to the supply depot at Tuan Giao. Peasants retrieved the supplies and carried them the remainder of the way on their backs, by bicycle, and pulled the big guns, dismantling some of them, by hand. All operations were overseen by the Government Front Supply Commission and the 551st Engineer Regiment, spread along the route, kept up the work building and rebuilding bridges and sections of roads. Again, Chau was to be the eyes of Uncle Ho and General Giap.

The health of the troops was the biggest concern for the Viet Minh leaders. Illness was often more deadly than combat. He was to make sure that all commanders were following the new health and hygiene instructions. All drinking water was to be boiled; feet were to be washed in warm salt water each day; clean and dry socks were to be worn after each washing; all soldiers were to be fed at least one hot meal containing meat and vegetables each day; a minimum of 6 hours of sleep a day was mandatory; uniforms were to be washed and changed every two days.

"You look happy, brother" said Lieutenant Luat, Chau's aide who met him at the border.

"I never thought it possible" said Chau. "Such a small poor country with so much equipment, so much energy to fight."

"Our friends, China and Russia, believe in freedom," said Luat, a small grin on his face. "Without them our outlook might appear dismal."

"You are an educated man, Luat. Our freedom cannot be the only reason they are helping us."

"Living too long as a Frenchman has made you cynical," said Luat. "You suspect every gift. Just accept that we are getting help."

"So you don't think that China will eventually want to take over Vietnam?"

"Of course they will," said Luat. "But I am not cynical about it. They have invaded us every two weeks for 10,000 years. No one helps anyone unless they want something in return. China views us as part of China, as they do all the world; they always have and always will. When they get their chance they will spring upon us again as they have done so many times before. And we will fight them back as we have done so many times before. Then, another country will invade us and China will help us resist them then China will attack us and we will beat them off and so it continues for eternity."

"But why?" said Chau.

"It gives us something to do," said Luat, as he yelled to a passing truck. "All China wants is the land next to theirs. We have chosen to keep ours and to be content."

Chau and Luat climbed into the truck. Along with the driver the three men fit in the cab comfortably. Chau wanted to ride the entire route to the battle site. It would also give him a chance to visit Au and the baby again. She seemed to him like a tiny piece of soft pliable porcelain, so delicate, so fragile. Her frailty was a façade. She was as tough as iron with a strong will and tough ideas. Each day she worked on improving the roads, usually with the baby strapped to her back. She insisted on leaving the country in the hands of the Vietnamese and their baby. If she could give her nothing else, she could give her that.

Chau watched the truck dash rattle, so different from the elaborate dash of the Studebaker that belonged to Bix in the United States. He remembered those good times, another world, another life. What had become of him and of Steve and crazy Neal? Perhaps they were all married by now, all had families. Did they ever go to Alaska to fish? They would never have joined the French Foreign Legion, just an illusion, a bit of fancy dreamed of by boys. Everyone wanted an adventure, no one followed through.

The transmission ground in monotonous growls for several days. The men on all the trucks, especially in the cabs, were beaten unmercifully about by the crude roads: dips, holes, fallen trees, wandering ruts pulling the wheels from side to side. One by one the trucks broke down, smoked to a halt; axels broke, piston rods shattered, bearings froze, electrical systems sparked out, tires flattened, brake lines leaked fluid like opened veins, mirrors busted and twisted, fuel pumps locked, generators blazed, valves bent, gear teeth ground in chunks, clutch plates wore to smooth smoking glass, tie rods twisted, springs cracked and leveled, radiators boiled, fan belts snapped like bull whips, and a clatter of other annoyances, to the glory of Communist industry, plagued them all.

The truck pulled to the side of the road, in a lucky place where there was room beside the convoy, and the men piled out to help another stranded truck. A front tire was flat. The two men from the truck had gone into the bush to retrieve a tree trunk. Another truck slowed and a Russian stuck his head from the window.

"A flat?" he said in broken Vietnamese.

"Nothing more," replied Luat.

The Russian looked disgruntled and said, "Baaah," as he drove away. Luat did not like the Russians and found them loud, crude, and dirty.

"I would as soon be without their help," he said.

"You said you would welcome help wherever it came," said Chau.

"The thought of them moving into our country, after this mess is finished, is disgusting. We are better off with the French. They at least exhibit some sophistication. The Russians are filthy and stupid."

The men from the truck emerged with their tree trunk and laid it beside a pile of other logs. They stacked the logs on top of one another three feet in front of the tire then laid down a three foot ramp of bamboo poles from it to the flat tire. The driver drove the truck up the stack of logs. Another stack of logs was placed under the axel. The men used a third pile of logs as a fulcrum and the tree trunk as a lever. They pushed down on the trunk. When the tire lifted slightly off its ramp another piece of wood was placed on the stack under the axel and the axel was lowered so the tire could be removed. In this way the wheel had only to be lifted inches, instead of feet, before the ramp was kicked down and the wheel removed.

Are you getting enough sleep?" said Chau to the men.

"We sleep well," said the driver. "We have it better than those who must walk carrying heavy loads and pushing bicycles."

"And there are those who have it better than you," said Chau. "And those who have it worse than the people walking." He offered them all a cigarette. The large tire was awkward and removing the tube was dangerous work. It was laid on the ground, the stem removed then a wedge-tipped bar was jabbed into an iron ring that held the tire onto the rim. The ring was carefully pried up. They often snapped off like exploding shrapnel and injured, or even killed, someone. "Do you remember to wash your feet each day and to change your clothes?" The driver look up, slightly annoyed, as if Chau were crazy.

"Of course, Uncle. We are not pigs."

"My apologies if I have offended you. My concern is that you stay healthy. A sick soldier is no use to the cause of freedom."

"We are not sure about the salt," said the driver.

"The salt?"

"How much to put into the water," he said "We were not told."

"Do the best you can."

"The government is not always efficient with instructions."

"Yes," said Chau. "The government is not always efficient with anything."

This seemed to amuse them, as Chau had hoped, and they warmed to his questions as he asked them about their families. The trucks continued to rumble past. Neither the start of the convoy nor the finish could be seen.

"The government has a lot on their minds," he said. "Our job is to stay healthy and to keep a positive attitude. Our very survival depends on it."

"May I have another cigarette?" said the driver, reaching out his hand. Chau noticed an unopened pack in his tunic pocket.

After repairing the tire and bolting it back to the axel the ramp was resurrected, the axel lifted a few inches and a piece of bamboo placed on the top of the ramp. The tire was lowered and the truck was backed up then driven away. They preferred using this method rather than relying on the Russian jacks, when any were supplied, because they were often dangerous and faulty.

Everywhere along the route people worked, digging, hauling dirt and rocks, carrying mud, trees, and lumber on their shoulders. French aircraft constantly swooped down in strafing attacks upon them and bombing runs tore up the roads and bridges. As soon as the bombers left the people went back to work filling in the holes and re-building the bridges. The main road branched into smaller roads then back into the main road. Often the main road acted as a decoy while the supplies skirted, covered with vast amounts of foliage, through the jungle. Cooking fires blended with morning and evening mists to help conceal the workers. Along the route Chau visited Au and their daughter, Sung.

He entered his village toward the evening. Au was washing beside the house, the baby close beside her. When she saw Chau she ran to embrace him. She constantly longed for him when he was away. She knew that without him and Sung she could not have continued.

"My husband," she said, crying into his chest. "You have returned."

"Always you state the obvious," he said, trying to make a joke. He became serious. "My heart is yours and only beats when you are around." He held her at arm's length. She was beautiful, so delicate, so fine, such a strange combination of tough determination and frailness, so easy to love. He lifted the necklace from around her neck and held it in his palm, the necklace he had gotten from his father and that she always wore . "You have mud on your face." Au replaced the necklace.

"I have been working on the nearby road. Just yesterday the French bombed out a section I had just helped build. They are on us constantly." She wiped her cheek with the back of her hand.

"They only make noise and have stopped no supplies," he said. "My baby daughter is wiggling."

"She knows you are here." Au placed her into Chau's arms.

"Such a precious flower," he said. Her tiny toes slipped from under the blanket and Chau felt each one of them between his fingers. All babies seemed a mystery to him, first inside a woman and covered with moisture, unable to breathe, totally helpless then, into the cold air, forced to breathe and to eat and to pee and poop, and totally dependent on others.

"Someday she will have her own country," said Au.

"She has her own country now," said Chau. "The French will not accept they are beaten. I must leave in the morning. At least by the afternoon. A big fight is coming and I must be there."

"And I must fight here," said Au, continuing to wash her face.

"Leave it," said Chau. "Even the dirt makes you beautiful."

Men from the village gathered that evening as Nguyen Thu served bia hoi, (fresh brewed beer) and ruou, the local wine. Dead snakes floated in the jug of wine. A tuoc lao (water pipe) was passed around. Many young men remained in the village and had not been placed with the military. Most talk concerned the war.

"Is the war going well?" said Truong Vu. Truong had recently purchased a Russian Zorki camera. He wanted to be a photographer with the Viet Minh and was thinking of leaving with Chau to join the military at Dien Bien Phu. Chau was not sure how to answer.

"A struggle is always a struggle," said Chau. "Everything must go into this battle. A victory might secure our freedom and, with any luck, we will never have to fight again."

"What then," said Dao Thang? "Will it make any difference to those in the villages who wins the war?"

"Every man wishes to run his own house," said Quan, "even if he does not stay there. What man would not prefer to run his house badly than to live in a well-run house owned by another? The house operates regardless of the master but the affection is different."

"I have been to Dien Bien Phu," said Dao Thang. He pinched up his face. "If I re-member correctly it is a dirty little border town of no significance."

"The importance is what we give it," said Chau. "At the moment the French find it vital. We must take it from them to convince them to leave. How is life in the village?" He wanted to talk of something other than the war.

"I want to leave with you," said Truong Vu. "I have a Russian camera and I have learned to develop film. If this is the last battle I must photograph it."

"There is never a last battle," said Quan. "Someone will wish to replace the French, like the Americans."

Chau puffed on the tuoc lao. The smoke felt cool and refreshing. He listened to the sounds of the night, the chattering bugs and birds.

"You have been to America?" said Truong Vu. "Will they want our country?"

"They are a good people," said Chau. "They help the French because they are old friends, no other reason. Sometimes one must help another even if you do not agree with them. Americans believe in freedom so they must understand that we deserve our own freedom, under the influence of no one, free to have our own government, our own lives. Only a very stupid nation would attempt to govern Vietnam. The Americans are not a stupid people." Chau saw Au standing just inside the door. "I must go and prepare for tomorrow's journey."

"When are you leaving?" said Dao Thang.

"Perhaps in the afternoon. Leaving the village and one's family is always difficult. I want to be sure that everyone is safe and happy before I go."

"What could happen to us here?' said Dao Thang. "We are of no importance to any-one."

Au walked Chau to the bed. He held her gently and slipped the clothes from her. He started to remove the necklace again. She never took it off. He inspected every part of her body with his hands and lips, every curve, every slope, every hair before laying her down. She lay back and he cupped the mounds of her breasts feeling their suppleness, the soft gentle flesh, the hard nipples. He worked his lips over her lips, let them roam around her neck, tasted the sweetness of her flesh - the very fruit of his existence – held her nipples, first one, then the other, in his mouth, kissed her all the way to her ankles then back up to the warm flesh inside her thighs. He parted her legs with his palms, parted her bush with his thumbs, placed his tongue into her body and tasted her as he would have tasted a delicate fruit. Their lovemaking was gentle as they floated on a gently rolling sea, all tender undulations and melted caramel. He held her head, the most sacred part of a body, during the act, so he might quietly and softly kiss each part of her face. He let his juices flow into hers and mix into one. Marie had taught him well the art of lovemaking. Au cradled into his arm after the act and Chau forgot about all the problems of the world, the struggle, the fighting, the war. This was his only world, the world of Au, Sung and him and a small village in a valley of rice and good people and contented animals.

"Would you like more?" said Au, nodding to the empty bowl at breakfast.

Chau ate a slice of watermelon followed by a piece of pineapple and looked into her glowing eyes. The pho tasted especially nice.

"I have a long way to walk today," he said. A hint of daylight shown between the mountains and the sky. "First I must check on the construction." He saw the dark figures carrying shovels and picks leaving the village for the job on the road. The sound of bombers droned overhead. "The French are starting early."

"There seems to be more and more of them each day," said Au.

"The road is too near the village," said Chau. "It is dangerous living here."

"The French do not bother us," said Au. "They usually fly farther to the east."

"You must stay home today, take care of our baby. Your work is important but I want to carry with me the image of you and Sung playing on the floor of the house, no troubles, no worries."

"I enjoy the work," said Au. "It brings honor to the family, honor to you."

"Not this morning. The bombers are angry today. Work this afternoon, after I have gone. I want to know that you are safe in the village. You bring me honor by living."

Chau wished that Luat had accompanied him to the village but he had gone ahead. He was good company, honest almost to a fault, and kept a level head when Chau occasionally lost his. Returning to Dien Bien Phu alone would make for a long and quiet walk.

Chau stopped outside the village and watched the construction. The farmers moved soil using baskets and dug into the earth with bamboo picks. Trees were cut with primitive axes, often forged from bronze. To widen the road trunks of bamboo and other trees were laid horizontally beside the existing road, covered with elephant grass, limbs and mud. What few rocks that were available were crushed into gravel and spread on top the mud.

Everyone worked at a relaxed and steady pace. A young boy and girl carried a bucket of water between them, each one holding a side of the handle, and offered drinks with a tin ladle. The men worked bare-chested, sweat dripping down their chests and over their silk pants. Most of them were bare-footed, some in sandals, several lucky ones wearing canvas and rubber legionnaire boots. A Viet Minh engineer eyed Chau cautiously as he gave instructions. The children offered Chau a ladle of water. The cool metal felt good and tasty on his lips.

In the distance he heard the faint reverberations of airplane engines, the steady drone of fuel crackling through pistons, the props whipping and pulling their way through air. The noise grew quickly and soon the bombers appeared. With the animal instincts that understood danger, that felt doom inside a chest, that bent and twisted muscles and quickened the heart and breathing, the rough wire that surfaced through war, everyone scrambled for cover understanding that these bombers were not passing over but had, in fact, found their target.

The sky darkened with periods that elongated and fattened as they fell. The earth felt as if it lifted to meet the bombs, shuttered and jerked like a shaken and beaten rug, sledgehammer blows cracking through the air and breaking the heavens with a cacophony of noise so intense that it tore at the body and mercifully brought on deafness. The attack probably lasted less than a minute. When Chau lifted his head to view the destruction he saw only the heads of all the workers staring in disbelief. The bombs had completely missed the road. He could not believe their luck. He rose to his knees, leaned backwards and started to laugh.

Someone screamed. He looked toward the voice. In the distance great clouds of black smoke rose from the village. Chau half stood, looked one way then the other, unable to move. "It can't be," he thought. He ran toward the smoke, pushed his way through the disbelieving workers bent and weeping, frozen in their tears.

The village had vanished, replaced with smoke, charcoal, fire, twisted poles, a land of churned and scorched earth, an open pustule oozing molten bodies, seared flesh, bits of empty humans and animals in a grand and ludicrous puzzle that was once life. For several hours he lifted the twisted bamboo, stomped through the coals. He could not even find his house, did not recognize where it once sat on the land. On his hands and knees he sifted through the ashes and dirt, the warmth turning to cold. Occasionally he reached into lumps of raw meat or lifted a bone or an arm. His hands became scoops, his fingers sieves, as he tilled the soil hoping for a harvest of life, only to find the crop had failed.

Tears watered the land as he watched the living scrounging the earth hunched like gargoyles or bent in permanent prayer their clasped shaking hands pulling the breath from their bodies. Again Chau scratched at the land. His fingers caught on the necklace his father had given him and that he had given Au, the one she refused to ever remove. Nearby he clasped a small lump of dough. He brushed the mud off the tiny mass until it became a foot, the foot of a baby, the foot he recognized as Sung's. Shock had gripped him and he bent his head to the ground, the foot and necklace clutched to his chest. The pain of loss devastated him, ripped him open letting the air blow through, the dust, the ash, the smoke, the souls of the dead, all the sorrows of the world. As the sun continued to rise and his tears dried the evil wind blowing through him was slowly replaced with warmth, the smells of a promising earth, the aroma of fruit and rice and vegetables and as the wind trickled from the mountains it started to suture his chest and heal it over without even leaving a scar. What he thought to be death was, after all, just death, just another form of what is, an incident in all life, a transformation of one thing to another that amounted to all things that were, in the end, the single thing.

Chau walked to a tree near the rice paddy and dug a small hole. He placed the foot and the necklace inside and covered them with dirt smoothing it over with his fingers. He did not look for Quan. It made no difference. He was either in this world or the next as were all people. He took one final look at the village. The people were digging graves and clearing away debris. Some of them had started to erect new poles to support new houses. Cooking fires had been started. Some children were playing with bamboo poles. Several men had started to return to the road and finish the work.

Chapter 29

Lieutenant-Colonel Gaucher, commander of Mobile Group 9 and the central sector of the base, stood on Beatrice looking over the fortifications. From here he could observe the entire valley, including his command post on Claudine. To the northwest stood Gabrielle, a vital strongpoint as was Beatrice, protecting the airfield. The Nam Yum River wandered through the valley to the west of road 41 and the central headquarters of Colonel de Castries, the hospital, and the airfield. Strongpoints Elaine, Huguette, Claudine, and Dominique helped circle the valley. Beatrice stood farthest east at the foot of the mountains. He thought it an interesting joke that the strongpoints had been named after the mistresses of Colonel de Castries, a bit of whimsy belaying the hard facts of battle.

From the beginning he had opposed the operation. It was sheer madness to attempt to fortify a valley and expect to supply it from the air. The high command saw it differently. They viewed the valley as a perfect position, protected by mountains, that no army could penetrate with any large assaults. The ridges along Route 41 and the valley, properly fortified, could prevent any small forces that managed to filter in. Colonel Gaucher knew that if General Giap managed to get parts of his army entrenched on the hills, especially any artillery, the French would be in for a beating. Well, the Viet Minh had gotten through and so had their artillery. He had continued to complain to Colonel Langlais about the vulnerability of his position on Gabrielle. They stood alone and too far from the main camp to be reinforced. Langlais downplayed his concerns and reminded him that his forces were the best in the Legion. Colonel Charles Piroth assured him that he would use his guns to knock out any attacking Viet Minh and their artillery should they attempt an attack.

Colonel Gaucher had no faith in Piroth. He viewed his bold and boastful talk as annoying arrogance and very distasteful. Gaucher had been in too many battles to believe the bragging of other officers. The ones who talked the most were often the ones most ineffective.

"Still concerned, I see," said Major Vadot, placing his arms together. "Major Pegot is a good officer and works well with the legionnaires. They respect him. The position can not be in better hands."

"It is not Pegot I am worried about," said Gaucher. Beatrice was under his command. He had just walked over the defenses with Pegot making last minute changes. "I never believed in heroic last stands or the silly French belief that there is glory in defeat. The enemy is coming tonight and we are going to catch hell." He surveyed the valley. He saw his own headquarters at Caludine. "It looks peaceful down there, even with the occasionally shelling; yes, very peaceful. We should get back to the command bunker. All we can do now is wait and plan for a counterattack if needed. Pegot is a good commander and I should not like anything to happen to him." He took a last look at the position as if to assure himself. "I choose him personally for the position."

Smith and Bix wandered through the sudden silence of the valley as they walked to the supply depot for extra medical supplies. The shelling had stopped. Not a hostile sound anywhere. The lack of noise left a feeling of cold around Bix, not a physical cold but the emptiness of being left abandoned. Colonel Langlais, water rolling off the hair on his chest and into a wet V, stood under a shower and lathered with soap. The Colonel and Smith had identical bodies; stiff, wiry like those of a middleweight boxer. Langlais was approaching forty, and was as totally devoted to his men as they were to him. Bix remembered that the original jump into the valley broke Langlais' ankle and he had returned to action before the bones healed. As the ankle mended, he had commanded from a pony, his head springing from the jerks of the trotting horse like that of a freshly released jack-in-the-box. The Colonel's bouts with liquor were legendary and legionnaires told and retold of his exploits in the Sahara Desert against bands of pillaging Arabs. There was no better commander in all Indochina, except for Bigeard, and the men fought as hard for Langlais as they did for themselves.

"He's a tough SOB," said Bix. "What is it makes a man fight his whole life? I like it but I don't think I can do it for too long. Staying in physical shape is too much work."

"Are you serious, mate?" said Smith. "Do you think you'll be content driving a tractor or cooking in a pub after this? The only thing that satisfies action is more action. We're bigger junkies than Crème Brulee and must be fed to survive. You're better off dead than returning home to become a school master. Look at Knowles. Do you think he can quit? Neither can the Colonel."

Smith started to make a joke about the Colonel when the sky darkened and the first shells lifted the outposts in flaming smoking volcanic eruptions tossing them

286

into the air. Like a swarm of startled bees, the enemy rounds engulfed Gabrielle and Beatrice gobbling them up in smoke and fire. They blackened the sky as the outposts sizzled in clouds of cacophonous fire and ash.

"Bastards," was the only words Smith uttered before perdition engulfed them both. Geysers of dirt ripped the air; barbed wire suddenly strung and tore sky; jeep parts and equipment broke from the ground and returned to earth like small change tossed into a jar. Bix hit the ground with such force his ribs felt cracked. Colonel Langlais, covered with soap, dashed naked across the compound, his towel flying like the cape of a retreating super hero, soap still clinging to his body. Smith snaked behind a small berm. The earth undulated like a dirty sea: unstable, quivering under the typhoon of explosions.

"Where..." Bix started to ask. Talking was useless. He covered his ears, tried to hear the words echoing in his skull. Smith lay sprinkled with dirt, one arm over his head, the other stretched to his side, his legs spread like a V, the proper prone rifle position. A nearby shell helped mash them both into the ground and Bix's head felt swollen, his neck going limp.

His head dropped back into the dirt and, out of habit, he took inventory, wiggling toes, twisting legs, rocking his body, making sure everything worked. Breathing deeply, he smelled the richness of the soil damp where the dust had been knocked away. Sweat trickled down his neck like condensation from a cold shot glass and his face, around the clipped whiskers, burned. He sought stability from the earth, a chance to clear his head, pop back the eyes that had ballooned with both fright and fatigue. The earth, unrelenting, continued to sway, gently at times, knocking at others, the air overhead billowing like a shaken blanket. Time snatched the hands of a clock twisting them long and short and Bix regained his senses either quickly or at some length, he could not remember which.

Under his chest, the ground became muddied. The shelling on the valley started to lessen and the earth rippled periodically. With head still heavy, neck weak, he managed to rise to his elbows. From the valley, French artillery laid down a fierce counter barrage. In the distance, Beatrice had disappeared under clouds of black smoke.

Ahead, Smith still lay flat and motionless. Quietly, Bix spoke a few words, heard them crackle in his ears.

"Let's break for the dugout," he said. "We can make it."

Fear made running alone impossible. His idea to help Smith was a chance to help himself. Smith refused to answer. Bix crawled ahead, reached for his boot.

"You with me?" he said. Smith's foot jerked.

A battery of French 105's sounded to the right, tongues of dragons spitting from the barrels. Bix worked up to one knee. His face flushed, his balance faltered; the clouded sky twirled to meet the spinning earth and he almost toppled over. A battle was no time to be sick. Lowering his head he again regained his direction and straightened himself up.

Because the world looked translucent, tilted, he decided to move slowly. He knelt beside Smith. Maybe he was hurt, unconscious, or dazed. He grabbed an arm and ran his fingers through Smith's hair. Another Viet Minh round whistled in. Bix ducked. The shell hit hard and he jerked ahead trying to drag Smith along. The arm slipped away from his body.

Bix drew up to his knees and, with clenched fists, he started to run, to seek protection. He had been shelled before but never to this extent. Explosions ripped his entire world apart as the sky became earth. His eardrums pushed against his brain, his eyes blew from their sockets, his nose sucked in the molten metal of scattered blast furnaces. Smith was safer on the ground. Too many shells scrambled the earth and too much open space lay ahead to move him safely. Bix attempted to screw himself back into the dirt. His head throbbed - and the air, God, the air - smells of cordite and shit, burnt flesh, rotting cadavers upended from their graves, diesel fuel and oil, rotten food, stinking clothes, fresh blood, the air thick and translucent with fear terror and unmitigated dread as if Dante's Inferno had developed an even lower level horror and revulsion where redemption was not an option. He stumbled ahead, as if in water, eyes open and burning from chlorine, lungs sealed tight for protection.

The daze continued, his world, the valley, spinning. Bix sloped against the side of a shell crater before sliding to its bottom where the earth remained warm from the blast. His ears clogged again and the clangor of battle sounded blunt like the steady thudding on a soggy drum. He wondered about Knowles and deJohn. Where the Hell was deJohn anyway? And Smith? Did Smith make it? Did he roll into a ditch or under a piece of twisted wreckage? The clouds darkened, bunched together like dirty pillows. Rain started to fall. Bix tried to stagger from the hole but slid back, unconscious, into a deep sleep of daisy fields and grazing cows.

When he awoke, the rain had stopped and moisture rose in a fine mist from the dirt. His body, especially his arm, felt heavy. The earth rocked evenly and what he took for lightning - pleasant flashes cleaving sky, a warm spring night - was the fracture of artillery on Beatrice. The battle, not over yet, had shifted to the strongpoint. He pulled at the arm but his fingers felt tied and he relaxed, unable to rise. A nearby 105 fired and Bix heard the brass tinkle of an ejected shell casing clank against a pile of spent rounds. He tried lifting his arm again. Maybe a shell had taken it off. He had heard of such things, limbs snipped away leaving only the feeling of empty space. His arm moved like the tired limb of a dreaming man.

Slowly, Bix lifted his arm. From the end of it, tangled in his fingers, Smith stared down at him. Bix started to smile, pleased Smith was there to help him. The head moved from side to side. Bix cleared his eyes, focused on Smith, attempted a smile. No smile returned. Smith's severed head dangled, almost floated bloodless, a gloss blue color with lips like two raw pork sausages. Bursts of the heavy guns refracted from his eyes and the head swayed from the strands of hair caught around Bix's fingers.

The air escaped Bix's lungs. He struck at the face, again and again to get it off. The head tumbled to the ground and landed upright, polite, still facing him, the eyes without surprise or amazement like other dead eyes he had seen. His breath continued to jerk in short strokes and he touched his own head, ran a finger from ear to ear, blinked his eyes. Death was no dream or mystery, just a head, Smith's head. Bix looked away, toward the hills, toward the smoking strongpoint, and grabbed at his twisting stomach.

Beatrice had become a smoking ball. There would be a counterattack, but not now in such a deluge of destruction. Looking back at Smith, Bix suddenly felt lucky to be alive. His mind cleared, his hearing returned, and, oblivious to the falling shells, he stretched out and gathered Smith's head, careful not to look into the eyes. He carried the head, always away from his body, back to the dugout. The hole was dark and he stood at the entrance waiting for his eyes to adjust.

"Bring any wine or schnapps?" said Knowles. "I was about ready to send out a search team."

"You're telling us you brought no matzo balls," chuckled Druxman, exchanging humor for fear.

Bix heard his voice clearly and decided that if anyone knew what to do with Smith, it wasn't Druxman but Knowles.

"Wine?" said Knowles, lifting a bottle. "We've almost finished this one but were careful to save some for you and Smith."

"Where is deJohn?" said Bix. He wanted no surprises from him. DeJohn always appeared frighteningly sensible yet slightly unstable.

"Probably drunk," said Knowles. "That's the way with the French."

Knowles did not sound anxious, not worried about the battle.

"We got caught in it," said Bix, standing in the opening, the head behind his back. The dugout smelt like an old canvas shoe. The shelling had taken his senses and he remained dazed. He knew the madness would pass.

"You brought us something, maybe a loaf of bread?" said Druxman. "Food, drink, a tender French whore? Sure, for me you bring nothing but heartache."

"Smith," said Bix. "I brought Smith."

"Like we need Smith," said Druxman. "Such bony Aussie boys can't get home alone? They always need help."

Bix rotated Smith's head to his side. The lantern was not lit and Druxman tried to see what he held.

"What is this, a gift from God?" said Druxman.

"Smith," replied Bix. "It's Smith, what's left of him."

Knowles flipped his lighter bringing the flame close to Smith's face. In the light Knowles looked older today, tired, like he fought one war too many. He cupped the flame closer to Smith. Druxman also pulled closer. Bix felt like a cat bringing a dead bird to the doorstep. Nothing ever surprised Knowles, not even this. Bix looked toward the back of the hole. Barely visible, under Smith's cot, he saw the rows of ammo boxes of opium Brulee had been gathering. Maybe Smith was right. Why live a pauper's life? Taking the opium he had gathered was no different than mining any kind of wealth and opium offered more pleasure than most.

"He's lost weight?" said Knowles, the light flickering across Smith's face. He spoke quietly with his lips almost closed.

"We were escaping the barrage," said Bix.

"You were slow," said Knowles

"Starting a collection, are you," said Druxman. "Is deJohn in your pocket?"

"I didn't bring it here as a joke," said Bix, frustrated and a bit annoyed. "I didn't know what to do with him, leave him in the dirt, or what?"

"There is no 'him'," said Druxman.

Knowles placed a poncho over the opening and lighted the lantern. The glow cast a dull sheen around the dugout, a luster on Smith's face. Bix placed the head on a crate near the opening where he often smoked. The head rocked to the side. The dugout was tight: four cots, cubes for small equipment notched into the walls, a candle beside each cot. The tops of ammunition boxes held stray rounds, cigarette butts, canteen cups, and cards. Although he never finished the pieces, Smith had carved a chess board onto a wooden lid.

"What about Smith?" said Bix.

Knowles lit two cigarettes and handed them to Bix and Druxman. All three of them sat on a single cot staring at Smith, one minute alive, the next, dead. They watched as if he might come alive again.

'Leave him for now," said Knowles.

"So, he can't take care of himself?" said Druxman. "At least we don't have to wipe his ass."

"He's gone quickly from Smith to it," thought Bix. "Maybe that is all we are, all waiting to become its?"

"He might look good on a pole out front, a symbol to other Australians," said Druxman. "Would we want to waste an opportunity like this, the chance for some fun?"

"It seemed wrong to leave him on the dirt," said Bix. "I didn't know what to do. It seemed wrong to just leave him there."

His hands started to shake and he hid one in his pocket. He wasn't afraid. He didn't know what he felt. Without success, he tried to turn away. Smith looked discolored, misshapen like a beginning artist's work molded in clay and placed too near the fireplace.

"Perhaps there is some fun with this, some real fun" said Druxman, a bit of dark mischief seeping into his voice. He had seen enough death in his life to find it amusing and, for a soldier to remain sane he must sometimes go crazy. "We can't have more flies and a home all stunk up but if we clean him quickly, oil him before he dries, he may last for some time."

Knowles said nothing, just sat smoking after turning out the lantern. Maybe he was crazy. Bix could not tell. What distinguished a crazy soldier from a sane one? Madness lies beyond the limits of flesh.

"Bury him," said Bix. "If we keep him we will be cursed."

"We'll have to prong out the eyes," said Druxman. "The eyes never keep. Bringing him here was the right thing. A soldier, like a cow turd, remains useful even after he's dropped. Brulee would agree. If you're afraid, let us have the fun. What's accomplished if he is buried? Nothing. He feeds the worms. Let the burial detail cover his body but an old friend's head is good for more than that."

"I'm not afraid of anything," said Bix. "It just doesn't seem right."

Druxman acted as if Smith was a pretty Christmas present, something to bring joy and wonder into the world. Another figure blocked the opening.

"Bix!" The voice, yelling over the sounds of the artillery, belonged to Jean Lachen. He did not fully enter the hole.

"Crap," said Bix. "We have our own troubles."

"I've brought wine," said Lachen. He tossed the canteen to Knowles. Even in the dark, Knowles caught it. "It's hell out there, the worst rainstorm I've ever seen. Where did they get the heavy guns and the rounds to supply them? I swear they have more artillery than us and Piroth hasn't silenced a single one." Knowles passed the canteen to Druxman. "The radios at the C.P. are unstable and Bix and me are ordered as runners."

"They asked for me? said Bix.

"Me, and someone else," said Lachen. "You're someone else."

"For me, I am truly sorry," said Druxman. "No one should run around on such a night. Watch that you don't catch cold."

"A fine party," said Lachen. " I suppose the rest of the paratroopers will stand by for a counterattack?"

"No word yet," said Sergeant Knowles.

"We better get over there," said Lachen. He turned to leave then jumped back tripping onto an empty cot. "Merde! What the hell is that?" Smith stared at him from beside the opening.

"So soon gone and already you don't recognize your old friend, Smith?" said Druxman.

"You think that's funny?" He slid from the hole amid laughter, Bix following close behind.

Bix and Lachen dashed through the glimmering night. Beatrice continued to blaze like a torch. The low clouds, the rumble, gave the impression of a distant thunder storm or a ship, sunk to its boilers, lights blinking out, on, out, signal flares clawing the sky. Tracers and artillery slit clouds with scratches of gold. Even the roll of guns sounded distant like an eager parade, pawing behind tall buildings, waiting for the cue to march. Never had Bix witnessed such extravagance, such beauty, such deathly aptitude. Virtually all the enemy guns had turned on Beatrice now and Bix was certain if the battle continued there would be no hill left by morning.

"Hurry," said Lachen. "The Colonel can be a tyrant. Such a masterpiece." He indicated the fight for Beatrice. The flares fluttered like lighted streamers over the side of a sinking ship. "Just like the bastards to attack on the 13th."

The thin passages and close rooms of the command post were a shambles: lights had burst from the oppressive halls, narrow walls had partially collapsed, wires twisted overhead, dirt floors crowded with papers, and men massed into small rooms or cubicles. The area reeked of cigarette smoke and a haze enveloped the ground like mustard gas in the Western Front trenches.

"My God," said Bix. "We have stepped into hell."

"I'll report to the Colonel," said Lachen, ducking as another round landed overhead scattering a layer of fine dust from the ceiling.

Bix lit a cigarette, adding smoke to the thick air, and crouched under a string of twisted communication wires. A few rounds still hit the valley. Most of the Viet guns peened Beatrice. Three officers played cards. One man read an old Life magazine featuring the Legion in the valley on the cover, his eyes squinting over the pages. Everyone else seemed occupied.

"We're to stick around," said Lachen, when he returned. "Communications are restored but the Colonel doesn't want to take any chances. A counterattack might be called at any minute."

"What do you think?" said Bix.

"Look here," said Lachen. He jerked his tunic from his pants and revealed a blanched stomach rippling with fine muscles. "My life is this, the life of a soldier. Nothing gets in unless I get out."

"Knowles will be ready," said Bix. He knew he would be waiting, rod and oil in hand, cleaning his rifle one last time. Or maybe Smith had become a problem and Knowles had decided to bury him. Knowles liked fighting but in a different way than Lachen. Everything with Knowles was an obsession. Lachen wanted something else, something Bix did not understand.

"Look," said Lachen. He tramped over the debris to a middle room. The beams had collapsed and splintered. One light, still working, hung from a twisted cord. Table legs protruded up from the floor. "A direct hit. The explosion buried Colonel Langlais and his entire staff. His luck held true but the whole staff is still covered with dirt and cuts. such luck can't hold forever."

"Camel drivers are always lucky," said Bix, referring to the Colonel's days in the Camel Corps.

"Luck and more luck," said Lachen. "Look in the dirt beside that shadow. They told me that another shell, mute this time, a total dud, followed the first and dug into the ground without going off."

Stepping over a beam, Bix knelt beside the shell. Like Lachen said, the shell apparently entered the roof and lodged into the wall. It might have been a Japanese shell. The Viet Minh had much of their abandoned ordinance. They were all poorly made and the shells were unreliable.

"The shell is an old Arab score," Lachen continued.

"And not luck?" said Bix. He knelt and fingered the dirt.

"Of course." Lachen also moved in close. "The shell is the score, a good score. Everyone knows the story. After a small desert battle, the Colonel inspected his men. A prisoner lay face down on the sand, a camel rider about to execute him. The Colonel stepped in and stopped the killing."

"In the desert?" said Bix. Lachen always told good stories. What a good man gets from the military is a reputation. Officers need one more than enlisted men. A reputation goes a long way in winning a battle. "With the Mehariste?"

"Where else?"

"In the desert?" said Bix, again. The shell looked imposing.

"Where else do you find camel riders," said Lachen. "They were about out of water but the Colonel turned the man over and let him drink from his own canteen. The Arab was forever grateful."

"And there was only one Arab?"

"Sure" said Lachen. "The Colonel ordered the guy's brains blown out – that's what a soldier does - but not before fulfilling his request for water. He thanked the Colonel, then went happily to Allah, accepted his death like it was nothing."

"Luck runs pretty thin here," said Bix. "There won't be many shells landing like this one. The Japanese can't make anything worthwhile, never will."

"Not many like this one, that's for sure," repeated Lachen

"I mean really," said Bix. "I have yet to be afraid in the war. It sounds stupid and I am not saying it to sound brave. I understand that almost all soldiers are afraid but I am not. Is that wrong?"

"Forget it," said Lachen.

"Do you think I'm crazy?" said Bix.

Bix thought of Smith and his stomach turned. Death played odd hands. Some people blinked out quickly, others left a piece at a time. Smith's head disgusted him but it had not made him afraid of his own death. Lachen motioned him across the debris and into the main room next to the radio.

"It's been a long night, Mon Due," said Lachen, to the radio operator. The operator listened intently into the headset.

"I'm afraid there's more to come," he replied. He did not look up. One hand curled around his headset and he stared blankly at a jumble of brown wires hissing from a metal plate. The radio whirred and cackled for all to hear.

Lachen shrugged his shoulders. He and Bix slid to the floor next to the wall. The room, disordered and dense, convulsed with command officers. Overhead, the bare light bulbs swayed. Colonel Langlais, along with his staff, looked reticent as they continued to outline the situation. Arms waved over charts. Smoke oppressed the lights and added to the feeling of swampiness, the feeling of stalled air. Bix listened to the radio battle on Beatrice as if it were a radio opera.

"It's a tough one," said Lachen.

"Yes," the radio operator said. "There is much confusion and things do not go well."

Lachen doubled his legs and chewed on a stick. Colonel Langlais glanced at the operator, at Bix, and turned away. His temper was infamous and Bix did not need a scolding. Staying awake without talking was difficult but Bix remained quiet and picked dirt from under his fingernails.

"Things sounded bleak when the radio was out," said the operator. His thin body looked too fragile to support his large head. He seemed willing to talk. "Major Pegot and his entire staff are dead. For a time there was no command on Beatrice. Colonel Gaucher is directing the battle from his C.P. The hill was in chaos but now he has established communications with the individual companies."

"Pegot," said Lachen. "I can't believe it!"

The radio operator drank from his canteen cup. Age covered his eyes and flakes of dry skin curled from his lips.

"Now, the legionnaires are cutting down the enemy." He winked at his own news and coughed.

"Get me Piroth," said Langlais. He grabbed the radio receiver. "Piroth? Where the hell is the artillery?" God Dammit! "I don't give a shit about your petty apologies. Knock those fucking guns off. I'm sick-and-tired of your excuses. Backup your big talk with results. Now get on those guns!" Langlais tossed back the receiver and walked into the hall.

The radio operator continued to talk. His voice pinched out slowly like a radio losing power and Bix's eyes, heavy with smoke and exhaustion, dimmed from lack of energy. The sleep was not the sleep of men but of soldiers as if he had lain in a mass confessional, words, mumbles, even the radios echoing off cathedral walls, bunker lights dim through his divided eye lids like dawn through church windows, the voice of Colonel Langlais like the voice of a truly sorry priest offering hope, advice, yet knowing in his heart the world is Godless. In Bix's conscience, that part of the mind that is no dream, the words of the radio battle played out.

coffee

hell tonight no end to the shells and me with a wife

the 13th will hold if only until morning

damn this dirt yes

give us your position

where is the colonel no response he must get there

command from the hill

no radio no damn radio

does he have something to eat

I remember but no that was Paris and she had tits to here and smelled German ha
ha

the bastards and the guns where did they get them

the goddamnedfuckingguns

piss outside if you must

they're dead all dead

she could milk you dry, that one, without even moving

de Castries on the line

no

all of them

then we will control from here

more wine

and those tits I tell you blond huge ha ha

Gaucher is dead the entire command wiped out

they will hold

both arms gone chest opened like a banana

any return message

we will take over establish contact with each company

hurry things are tight

and the thighs on her could crush your head

overrunningeverything

Communists

the water is no damn good

fighting in and out in and out and the noise the screaming with each thrust ha ha
ha

he is in the hospital but too late try another channel

Colonel de Castries yes we heard Gaucher died in the arms of the chaplain but just
as dead anyway they will lay him down now and

when she was in that position she could make it dance and

yours too haha

badly yesbadly thingsaregoingbadly Pegot and his staff and now Gaucher no arms
chest opened wide and
you could slide it right up to the hilt ha ha
a smoke give me a smoke
no unified command
is there any food move 10th company here and pinch from there
the radio
another channel 9th company responding
responding to every advance I could make ha ha
is there another Sergeant there
yes
still responding and the 11th ammunition almost exhausted
Piroth call Piroth they want it on them another barrage on their heads
drive the round deep and the screams hahaha
9th company around the command post dug in
no response not the 9th and the 10th damn goddamnthosebastards
11th company reporting Viets everywhere Kubiak reporting Sergeant Kubiak 9th
company holding on
sir no counterattack
sir
yes
there can be no counterattack until morning
 and an ass like two melons in a cotton bag ha ha
Kubiak wants it on their heads no other way
try them again
come in come in
no response
hand to hand
raise them again
try again
no response
no response
radio dead
raise them
radio dead
raise them over
finished
and when she was finished she was truly finished
ha ha ha ha

The silence forced Bix's eyes open as if his ears needed vision to hear. His collar had poked a dent into his chin and he flicked the collar away with a finger. A straight-line buzz emerged from the radio. A cork popped from a bottle and a staff officer poured wine for everyone.

"It's over?" said Bix.

"Kaput," said Lachen. "You missed all the fun. Major Pegot got it first so Gaucher was trying to direct the battle from his command post on Claudine. He called some officers, including Major Vadot, into his command bunker so they could decide on a new commander. Vadot curled onto a bunk to make room for everyone. As they were about ready to decide on a commander, they suffered a direct hit. It opened Gaucher like a can of sardines and he died in the hospital. Both his aides were killed. Major Vadot was saved because he was on the bunk and it folded up over him." Lachen held out his canteen cup for the wine. "C'est la guerre," said Lachen "The Viets are one up on us now."

"Up for sure." said Bix. "Now they can see everything we do."

Lachen swirled the wine inside the cup, held it from the bottom with both hands, and tipped the cup to his mouth. Colonel Langlais, shoulders slumped, ducked from the room and into the darkness.

Bix and Lachen stumbled into the passageway, sat against the wall, and there, amidst the decreasing thunder of artillery, nestled their heads together and slept.

Chapter 30

Captain. Chau liked the sound – Captain Chau. The promotion had filled him with pride and every attempt, including not mentioning it, not even alluding to it, was made to stay humble. It did not work. Au would have been proud but he tried not to think of her and Sung. All sorrow lay in the past. There was only now. Being a captain added nothing monetarily – no one in the government, including soldiers, were paid – nor did it add to his power - he was under the orders of both Ho Chi Minh and General Giap. He felt that regular soldiers, bo doi, might seek him out for advice, might view him as an experienced soldier, a man of the world who had spent his life selfishly gathering wisdom for no other reason than to pass it along to them so that they might rise in stature in their villages. He attempted to rein in his joy, to remember that arrogance followed pride and they always led to disaster, but found it difficult to pursue in practice, the reality at war with the ideal. In a day or two he would simply be grateful for the promotion; his suppressed arrogance would have dissipated by then and it was better to have it fade out rather than to last forever.

He looked over the defenses of the French Foreign Legion Paratroopers on Ban Him Lan, known to the French as Beatrice. They had cleaned the three small hills completely of vegetation and their bunkers and trenches resembled a spotless downtown street. The barbed wire twirled about, spiky dark in black curls, like streamers tossed off a departing ship. The legionnaires moved about without fear sorting sandbags and arranging firing positions knowing that an attack was coming. Chau could almost feel their confidence, a brick of wind, a solid breeze knocking over everything in its path before shattering against the hillsides. The Legion 13th battalion had never lost a battle, the reason General Giap had chosen it for destruction at the start of the siege. A full effort must be made to take the hills therefore destroying confidence in the remaining soldiers, sapping their will to fight. Giap did not necessarily want the hill for any strategic reasons. The French had wanted it since because their strategy was defined in complementary and solid ground. Strategy for Giap lay within the mind and emotions. Victory was mental, not physical. Firm western military thinking found virtue in area, in ground, in physical conquest. Eastern thinking found no interest in soil. Once a soldier had taken a piece of ground he had only dirt beneath him, dirt that could be retaken; but take a piece of the heart or mind and eventually the subject will die or go mad and there was nothing left to retake. Europeans equated acreage with victory; Vietnamese could claim victory without moving their feet. Let the French hold all the land in Vietnam and they would still lose, they would still own nothing but dirt. A country built on material products could not stand against one built on ideals.

Although the defenses built on Ban Him Lam looked strong the French had made a terrible mistake. They had not only cleared away all the obstacles within their fields of fire – although they had not excavated far enough into the jungle and the bo doi of the 312th Infantry Division had already dug trenches to within 100 yards of their positions - they had stripped the entire defense system clean leaving everything exposed. The artillery could not possibly miss and the bo doi knew every single bunker to attack. They stood out like a rock on a parade ground. Only conceit could have had the buoyancy to leave every thing exposed and still have the arrogance to think they were invincible.

Chau had spent the morning helping to move up a number of 75mm howitzers, relics abandoned by the Japanese along with the often faulty ammunition. Every gunner clearly saw the bald hills of Beatrice and, to get the range, they occasionally dropped a round causing the legionnaires to duck and scatter although doing little damage. Many of the rounds, old and poorly built, refused to detonate. The Japanese made nothing reliable.

Chau and his orderly, Luat, helped place one of many 57mm recoilless rifles behind some brush. Again, the gunners could adjust their own fire without spotters by watching the rounds land. All the ground remained open, everything visible, everything vulnerable.

"It looks good, comrades, very good." He offered them all a cigarette. "They will get a surprise tonight when they are overrun. Thirteen is an unlucky number and March 13 will stay in their minds forever."

"Has nothing changed about the time of the barrage?" said a boy of about fifteen, his uniform, khaki and clean, hanging on him like a burial shroud. Excitement and anxiety surrounded his body like a virgin on his wedding night.

"It will go off as planned," said Chau. "This will be our final victory and Vietnam will finally be for the Vietnamese, for you and your family."

The boy forced a shaky grin under his down-turned eyes as did the other soldiers standing around the weapon, arms crossed and listening intently and waiting for the sun to drop like a checkered flag bringing on the race and the rush of battle.

"Are you staying with the artillery?" said a man, much older than Chau, his blackened teeth chipped, part of his ear missing from an accident or from battle.

"I prefer a closer look," said Chau. His aide, Luat, shot a curious look at him. "Of course, I have no weapon so am useless as a soldier. I am the eyes of the General, nothing more and basically a coward." He started to laugh. "I intend to leave the fighting with the real soldiers, like you," he said, as he placed his hand on the shoulder of the boy. "You will have a long life remembering this great day of glory and the victory that will be ours. Nothing can ever take that from you."

He and Luat moved down a trail toward the encroachment trenches past soldiers relaxing and laughing. Chau thought how incongruous it seemed to always hear the most laughter from men just prior to an encounter with death as if one was needed to balance the other for the occurrence to take place or perhaps the laughter acted as a catalyst to push a man forward and the more laughter he carried, the more he prodded others to smile and join him, his shoulders bouncing with guffaws, the more distance he trudged into darkness. He had heard in the United States that laughter is the best medicine. The medicine was often deadly, perhaps an overdose because it came with no instructions.

"I did not know you were going toward the trenches," said Luat. "The General wants you safe at all times. You are his eyes and ears."

"Are you afraid?"

"I suffer from back and stomach problems," said Luat.

"I did not know this."

"Yes, a yellow streak down my back and no guts," said Luat.

"I cannot use those keen senses of mine unless I am near the soldiers," said Chau. "What good is a bullet that does not fit a rifle?"

Luat shook his head. He seldom understood Chau's strange metaphors, yet was always worried for his safety. He had never met a more concerned honest or brave man. Chau looked after him as much as he looked after Chau. Chau stopped to talk to the soldiers along the way, to sample their spirits. A layer of frightened afterbirth lay at the foot of their newly born excitement. It was not just national pride at stake; it was a chance to return home to friends and families, to resume a destiny that was hardly a destiny at all since it appeared to be never changing, never ending from the beginning of time until the end.

"General Giap has been effective from the start of his strategic direction," said Chau, answering a question from a soldier. Knowing the general personally felt rewarding and gave him a chance to pass along information not known or understood by many bo doi. "Think of what you have been doing over the last few years because of him. He has had the People's Army, you brave soldiers, destroy enemy effectives whenever possible. This type of action has allowed him to build this great army of trained soldiers. Not long ago you would not have known how to hold a rifle or to work in unison as a team, as brothers, as the family of a nation."

"Attacking the enemy at every possibility would have been a disaster. We would have been worn away to nothing. He knew we must strike to win, strike when success was certain and the chance to wipe out the enemy was great. This was his plan from the beginning although he admits he has occasionally miscalculated. After every successful battle we grew stronger while the French grew weaker. Do you all understand?"

"Yes," they said, almost unanimously, appearing to hang onto Chau's every word, Chau, the former rich Francophile turned patriot and revolutionary. He had learned to tell his stories simply and well.

"The General and the Party Central Committee have always understood the French to be stronger and better equipped than us so we have always attacked where they were weak, exposed, and we could concentrate troops and firepower. This did not happen often so we continued to harass them. Time is nothing to us. The trick was to harass them enough that they would decide to break up their concentrations and spread them around in an effort to catch us. But we have always been faster than them."

He looked into each of their eyes, all staring back intently, knowing that many would not return.

"Because the French had a large concentration in the Bac Bo delta, we continued to jab him with a stick. Then when we started operations toward Laos, he broke his forces and sent part of them here so that they might strike us offensively, something at which they are masters, from this impenetrable position. He also spread his forces to Luang Prabang, Muong Sai, Seno, Pleiku, and again, here. We have pushed the legionnaires from the hills and into the valley. They are now forced to fight defensively, something they do poorly. So tonight, you will show your strength, show what it means to be Vietnamese fighting for your own country rather than paid mercenaries with nothing at stake except your lives."

Chau felt satisfied with his talk, his easy and clear speech, his ability to communicate with the people. He had become very well rounded, able to effortlessly float between peasants and the elite. It was difficult to remember his privileged life of wealth, parties, women and how naive he was, able to view a position from only one side and unable to disassociate propaganda from fact. Believing the Viet Minh and the Communists would have been just as silly as believing the French democracies. They were both right and both wrong. How much better it would have been to have worked together, melded the best of both parts into a system that better equalized the lives in every country by giving the workers a stake in their labors and still leave room for controlled greed and ambition, not a chance for the rich to become infinitely wealthy, but allow them to grow with a cap on their earnings. Chau smiled at his own thoughts. Perhaps he would start his own revolution using his own political doctrine.

"A fine speech," said Lieutenant Luat. "The men feel comfortable around you rather than the Communist spies. They know you look out for their best interests and do not have them punished and beaten for being afraid or contrary."

"Beating a tired mule will not make him less tired," said Chau. "A short rest, some food and water will have him back to pulling more effectively and for longer periods of time. Ridiculing, shaming, and persecuting the men are not good for the country or for the party."

"Without coercion we might not have an army," said Luit. "Many of the men needed to be beaten and threatened with death before they would fight."

"Yes, yes. Perhaps you are right," said Chau. "Except for invasions of their homelands, the French give their soldiers the option of fighting or not, so they will not infringe on their freedoms. Does it worry you that we might not have the same freedoms when this is finished?"

"Freedom is the same for all," said Luat. "As long as a person stays within the law, he is free. Anyway, it is an illusion. Freedom has no definition. We are all bound by something."

"So you claim the amount of freedom people have is decided by the laws? Interesting. I must give it more thought. I like that you feel comfortable talking with me. You are a man of ideas." Chau turned and looked at him. "Be careful about calling the Communist committee members spies. They are mostly uneducated and have little sense of humor."

"Like the French," said Luat, "many of them suffer from arrogance."

They continued to walk the trails through the brush slowly moving down onto the valley where six assault battalions were forming positions and waiting. In the distance the band played "March to the Front," one of many songs of encouragement and inspiration. The band, always filled with brave and kindly men, could always be heard near the front and fought as fiercely as any other soldiers. The bo doi were being read messages from General Giap, their generals, and by Ho Chi Minh reminding them of their duty, that freedom and glory awaited them and that after this battle no other country will ever attempt to invade Vietnam again. The French gunners started interdiction fire on the approach trenches yet the soldiers stood solid.

Chau walked between the nervous concerned faces of the men tapping several of them on the shoulder attempting to build their confidence. Sometimes a simple touch or a smile carries a great deal of power and he used them to his best ability although he did not feel the least bit confident attacking the 13th Foreign Legion Demi-Brigade. Chau had studied them as he had studied all the French units and top officers in the valley. They had been formed in 1940 to help defend Finland against the Russians but Finland capitulated before they were dispatched. They were all seasoned soldiers, some of the best legionnaires available. Most of them had already served for five years and the NCOs were ten-year veterans. The commander, Raoul Magrin-Verenery, had been wounded 17 times in battle – either very lucky or very unlucky but in either case extremely brave and at a time when many commanders stayed well protected, always stood fearlessly at the front of his men, impervious to fear on the outside although the inside may have had crouching stomachs, knotted intestines, collapsing lungs. A great leader can suppress his true feelings with a façade of calm and determination.

The brigade was instead sent to Norway where they disembarked from English torpedo boats at Bjerkvik, often sinking over their heads since the boats were unable to get very close to shore. They immediately took the surrounding high ground, a lesson they had apparently forgotten in the Vietnamese valley, and forced the Germans from Bjerkvik. With the English they moved on Narvik and landed in the middle of the German positions. The English quickly withdrew leaving the legionnaires stranded and giving them no choice except to fight on alone, which they did, so well that the Allies returned to join them. Lieutenant- Colonel Magrin-Vernery, true to form, stayed at the front pointing out enemy positions with his walking stick. They soon found themselves at Bir Hakeim in Libya in a pocket of resistance facing Rommel and his Afrika Korps and helped to stop the Germans at Tobruk.

After the war they made their appearance, and furthered their reputation, in Vietnam in an effort to take Hoa Binh – ironically a Vietnamese name meaning peace – that the Viet Minh had held for two years. The legionnaires held a vital position on a hill at Xon-Pheo and were not to surrender it at any costs. The Viet Minh 88th Infantry Regiment attacked on the night January 9th and overran 5th Company. The legionnaires soon lost many of its officers and NCOs and had almost run out of ammunition. The remaining soldiers fixed bayonets and, with grenades, counterattacked sending the Viet Minh running and killing over 700. Now, Chau watched them preparing for the attack. Major Gaucher had recently commanded them and now Major Paul Pegot held the reins and would expect his men to hold at all costs.

The first to attack would be the Volunteers of Death, ready to surrender their lives for their country. They tried to conceal their concern by laughing and smoking contentedly, probably their last smoke since the next smoke they were likely to see would be that from hot metal smoldering through their own open wounds. Satchel charges, like the briefcases of businessmen waiting at bus stops, sat at some feet. Theirs was the business of killing.

Chau offered them more cigarettes and congratulated them on their decision to possibly die. They were to open the barbed wire with bamboo Bangalore torpedoes. There was no way to execute their mission except to crawl through the minefields, remove those they found under intense artillery and mortar fire, or explode the others with their bodies. Either way chances of getting to the barbed wire remained slim. Chau moved back and sat with another group. A soldier offered him some water.

"You look thirsty, brother," said the soldier, crouching with several other soldiers. "Water is very important in times of stress."

Chau nodded his head and tipped back the canteen.

"He is always too worried about others to take care of himself," said Lieutenant Luat.

"Nothing can change what will happen," said the soldier. "I am Deputy Platoon Commander Hoi. I know how he feels. Responsibility is always a heavy weight. Too much weight can drown a man."

"Thank you," said Chau, returning the canteen. "Your men must respect you." The men sitting around all nodded and some grunted approval. "The sun is starting to hide behind the mountains."

"I think it does not want to look," said Nguyen Huu Oanh, standing beside Hoi. He adjusted the flag that was used to mark positions taken by the Viet Minh so other soldiers knew which ones to bypass and which ones to attack.

"Oanh is from a small village and takes great faith in the sun and the moon." Hoi handed him the canteen. "You have also forgotten to drink."

"Why does it not want to look? Is it afraid?" said Chau.

"The sun brings everything to life in the morning and puts it all to sleep in the evening," he said. "Many men who sleep tonight will not be awakened in the morning. He waits to remind the moon to take them into the night sky to shine forever. The moon is forgetful and often unreliable. Sometimes only part of him crosses the night, sometimes more. A man forgotten sleeps in darkness forever."

"Ha," laughed Hoi. "Oanh is a religious philosopher of one and we are much amused with his ideas. There is no better, or peculiar, soldier in the unit. Of all people who deserve to be a star it is he."

Beatrice suddenly erupted into noise, flame, fire, smoke, broken bodies and body parts, some trailing ten feet of guts as the cavities emptied. The 351st Heavy Division had launched into action. The Viet Minh soldiers ducked at the surprise they knew was coming but had forgotten it would actually arrive, the sudden shock ceasing all conversation knowing that within an hour they must charge though the rifle and machine gun fire, angry grenades, a field of explosions from falling shells and minefields, knowing their last day in this form could extinguish forever leaving wives and family remembering them through altars of smoking incense. Gabrielle, Dominique, and Isabelle also exploded from artillery. Giap and his generals had done their planning well. Shelling the other positions solved two problems: the French might be confused as to which strongpoint would be attacked, rather than those used as a diversionary operation; and the big guns and mortars might be silenced and left unable to support Beatrice.

The bo doi sat in silence for almost an hour, the time of laughter replaced with contemplation, short breaths like an exhausted boxer with more rounds to complete, chests void of any organs, no lungs, no heart, nothing except the echo of a departed metronomed heart pumping through expanded veins and arteries, the elastic tunnels strained to breaking, stressed to the cracked boundaries of endurance, the vigor of potential escape slamming against the lean skin causing actual pain. Chau spent considerable time watching the back of the head of a soldier. The head seemed motionless, sweat dripping from the band of his pith helmet and down under his tunic leaving an ever-widening spot of wet on his back. One ear appeared to be larger than the other and slightly misshapen, the lobe long and fat, several strands of hair protruding across the top like a toothbrush tipped onto its side. Chau looked back to his boots, canvas topped Foreign Legion boots with rubber soles. He preferred boots to sandals because he needed to travel great distances and, having been raised with shoes, he had never gotten used to sandals. The French boots remained cool rugged and practical. Their deep cleats held dry ground well but clogged up in mud. When wet, the canvas dried quickly. Chau retrieved a short stick and used it as a pointer as he drew the outline of the boots onto the dirt then stuck the end into each eye, up one side, down the other. He did this repeatedly until everything, soldiers and smaller equipment, started to move forward. He had not heard nor seen any signal beyond the movement of the soldiers.

He let the soldiers pass, run down their protective trenches, confused about his role. He had no orders except to monitor their feelings, to witness how they performed under the stress. He had placed them in column A before they left and would probably place them in column B when they returned. To understand them he must experience battle. Shells landed all around him but he wanted a better look, a better feel. He stood and started to move forward. Lieutenant Luat grabbed his shoulder.

"Where are you going?" he said, over the noise.

"I must get closer," said Chau, holding on to his helmet to keep it on his head.

"It is too dangerous."

"I will be safe."

"Not you – me! What happens to you is your business," said Luat. "It is too dangerous for me. I cannot feel your pain but I am quite certain mine is monstrous." He smiled as Chau turned to move forward. "If something happens to you I will be given a real job. Have some pity."

The trenches were remarkably deep and well dug, the sides almost sculpted and void of shovel marks. There appeared to be no rocks anywhere just damp red clay and dirt. Chau needed to stoop just slightly to be completely protected by any small arms fire. No place was safe from the big guns and the approach trenches had been targeted by all the artillery in the main French camp. The other strongpoints were unable to offer much supporting fire because of their bombardment by the Viet Minh. Chau moved to the foot of the wire and into a side trench of about ten feet giving him a decent view of a hill. Already the Volunteers of Death had cleared much of the barbed wire leaving a wake of mangled and torn bodies. The bo doi were swarming through in mass, many of them falling from the deadly machine gun fire rattling from protected positions, the red/yellow light of tracers staining the night with thin veins that retired abruptly into the chests of the Viet Minh. The barrels of the machine guns started to glow red from constant use and became easily spotted in the dark. Lieutenant Luat had little inclination to watch and kneeled deep in the trench, his back against the clay, a cigarette shaking from between his lips as he watched flares dropped from a circling C-47 quivering overhead in the darkness.

The bloody mayhem continued through most of the night as the Viet Minh slowly worked their way up the positions, planting flags to mark their territory. Everywhere throughout the valley chaos danced as an ammunition dump blew, a pile of napalm and aviation fuel near the airstrip vomited into the air, Viet Minh attacking from every direction. So many dead piled upon the battlefield that the Communists called a truce at 2200 hours to allow both sides to clear away the dead and wounded. The battle then continued as the sun rose revealing a scorched landscape of death. Nguyen Huu Oanh, protected by Hoi, planted the Communist flag marking the end of the battle. Sporadic gunfire still sounded in small pockets as the legionnaires surrendered their lives with great reluctance. Bo doi led French prisoners, gaunt bits of bloodless gray, from the hills and back toward the hills.

"Captain Chau?" said a runner with three other soldiers. Chau looked at him and attempted to return to the world from the one he had been visiting, a world of clangorous resonance, haunted images, an emotionless place of hollow people blending with the night. "You are to choose a prisoner to send to the French division headquarters. Bring him to us and we will take over from there."

Chau and Luat found a gathering of prisoners, totally beaten, barely men, more like vacuous bits of flesh. Chau walked amongst them and decided to find someone wounded who would benefit from the Legion hospital. He approached a tall thin soldier bleeding from several wounds. He seemed more alert than most of them in spite of his wounds.

"A tough night," said Chau, in perfect French. "Do not be disgraced by the loss. I never witnessed men fight so gallantly. Can I get you anything?"

"Water, please," he said. Luat quickly produced a canteen. The man carried no signs of rank but because of his bearing Chau suspected him of being an officer. Removing signs of rank was standard procedure with soldiers in battle. Officers were easy targets and the love of snipers.

"I am Captain Chau. You are lucky to have survived. What can you tell me of your experiences? Nothing official, nothing you feel will be of military value. I am interested in your bad luck, nothing more."

The other legionnaires watched and listened to the exchange. He eyed Chau cautiously not fully understanding what he wanted or why he wanted it. Something inside of him wanted to tell part of his story, even to the enemy.

"I am Lieutenant Turpin. There is little to tell. I was wounded and reported to the aid post, shot with morphine and bandaged. The drug caused me to sleep. I awoke completely alone after the battle had finished. Some fire continued in pockets but we had clearly lost. The strongpoint had been overrun and I attempted to stagger off the hill when a search team of Viet Minh found me and brought me here. There is nothing else to say."

"Are you able to walk back into the valley?" said Chau. He looked at Chau with confusion. "We need someone to deliver a message to Colonel de Castries."

"Yes," said Turpin, attempting to conceal his good fortune but doing a poor job as one part of his frowning lips attempted to control the side of his smiling lips and leaving his face slightly contorted as if he had been slapped silly. The sudden glint in his eyes would have surrendered his attitude, anyway.

"Take another drink of water and go with these men," said Chau. "They will not harm you. We want no more of killing today. Perhaps this will end it all."

Chau shook Turpin's hand and sent him away with the soldiers before walking back to the strongpoint where bo doi traveled between the hills and the Viet Minh lines carrying useful equipment, wounded soldiers and bodies. Chau decided to survey the French positions.

"You may stay here if you like," he said to Luat. "I understand your aversion to pain."

"It would cause me more pain to stay than to go," he said. "Perhaps the shock of misery will replace my reticence for injury once and for all. My mother wishes to see me alive again."

They worked their way along an approach trench then up over the end of the dirt. The exit had been widened to allow a conglomeration of troops to exit. A profusion of smells started to flow over Chau, an odd congress of odors mostly unrecognizable. As he moved forward, the smells came into focus from the plowed earth, the smells of opened bodies, torn entrails, shit, rotten food, decaying corpses, piss, red and black blood, all swirling in the sweet stench of cordite. Decay and destruction greeted his walk: bloated bodies already beginning to turn black in the morning sun and swarming with enormous blue and black flies, rolls of bloody bandages often holding bits of meat, a landscape of shell craters, collapsed bunkers, empty shell casings, field radios crushed like the vehicles of an auto collision, helmets, body parts, smoking chest cavities, missing faces. A plowed field seeded by at least 500 Viet Minh dead as hundreds of wounded soldiers limped through the fresh turned soil, drove Chau on, a visual delight causing him to look at all the destruction, no, forcing him to look, something inside pulling him toward destruction, the need to see and to understand filling a vast pit of wanting. Sweat dribbled from his forehead as he finally sat, unable to take another step into purgatory, unable to speak for several minutes. Luat offered him a lit cigarette knowing he could not light it himself. Chau breathed the smoke in deeply, blew it out slowly not pushing it away from his face but letting the smoke curl into and past his nose in an effort to eradicate the smells of death.

"I never thought…" he started to say.

"It is a grand mess," said Luat. "If man can create this in times of war think what he can accomplish in times of peace."

"My wife and daughter were killed."

"I know," said Luat.

"Too much peace, not war, causes this," said Chau, looking over the destruction. The earth seemed to moan as bodies, refusing to die, tweaked the dirt. "The world becomes off-balanced and must be righted through blight. It has always been so, drought followed by rains, famine followed by plenty, poverty by riches and riches by poverty. The cycle is never ending."

"I hope to live long enough to see the rich part," said Luat.

A small movement caught Chau's eye, a soldier being bandaged by another soldier. Something seemed familiar about him. He walked in that direction and looked at the man, small, quivering with fear, eyes of terror. Chau knelt beside him.

"Yes," he said.

"He will be fine," said the medic. "I already sewed up the wound with silk thread. Most of his injuries are right there." He pointed to the man's head. "Inside. He continues to blubber about his family."

"Who are you?" Chau asked. The man just shook and stared. Chau poured water over his head. "I know you. Who are you?" The man looked into Chau's eyes and started to cry. "It seems a long time ago that I knew you," he continued. "In what village do you live?" The man held his hands to his face from embarrassment.

"You had a woman with you and I gave you food," he said, his voice quivering. The tears leaked mud through his fingers.

Chapter 31

Although Bix dreamed of romance, the touch on his shoulder was not Nicole's. He crawled from the silky covers of sleep and into the abyss of Knowles' untuned voice.

"Have you become a rug for Colonel Langlais?" said Knowles. He towered over Bix like a dark stone.

The passage of the command post tangled into view, dimly, one memo at a time, wires overhead (the bulb now motionless) casting shadows across Knowles' sharp-boned face. The shelling had stopped.

"The sun will be out soon," said Knowles. "If all goes well, we'll be in the thick of it before breakfast."

"A counterattack on Beatrice? Are you alone?" said Bix. His back ached from twisted inactivity, from the dead sleep that had kept him motionless.

"Where would a man find a trusted friend in this mess?" said Knowles.

"DeJohn?" said Bix. "Has he returned?" Knowles lifted him by the tunic. Lachen had tumbled off his shoulder during sleep. He twitched, growled on the ground like a dog having dreams, his legs jerking.

"Beatrice." Knowles kicked Lachen's boot.

"Beatrice?" said Bix.

"They sent him to Beatrice on some mission while we worked the barbed wire. A sergeant caught him sitting around and now he's gone, probably blown to bits." Because Knowles did not laugh, Bix knew he was angry. "I wished to be there cutting down the yellow bastards. What does a Frenchman know about fighting? Drink wine, retreat, make love, surrender, it's all the same to a Frenchman. But fight…?"

Lachen tipped out his left foot. The boot, buckle unlatched, laces loose, etched a line on the wall which he erased with his back when he sat too far off center.

"Maybe he made it. It's possible. And Smith?" said Bix. He was not sure he wanted an answer. He had once witnessed Knowles ease a fuzzy caterpillar from the road and onto the dirt with his bayonet. He pushed the bug into the safety of the brush. He had also seen Knowles crush the skull of a cat with his rifle butt for whining too much.

"He's safe," said Knowles. "He has been put to bed and he looks well, considering his health."

"DeJohn?"

"Smith. There is no hope for deJohn."

"Then he's buried?" said Bix. He scratched his knee. The dirt walls were damp and his body slipped against itself knocking his ribs together.

"Under blankets, not dirt" said Knowles. "In war it's better to have something than nothing. What goes into the ground rots in the ground, no place for Smith."

Knowles pushed Bix down the hall. Bix felt groggy, unsure of Knowles' remarks. He reached back to wake Lachen but Knowles shoved him away.

"Druxman cleaned Smith like a fish," said Knowles; "rinsed him thoroughly, replaced his eyes with something appropriate. If he still stinks we will bury him until he dries."

"What he's doing is unholy," said Bix, surprised at his own remark. He held no religious concepts, no moral or ethical ideas about the dead. A heavy dark hung over the camp, not just the sky, but also a feeling, and Bix looked to the east for signs of light. He stumbled momentarily, knocking Knowles on the shoulder. The 13th, Gaucher's 13th, one of the toughest units in all Vietnam, an unbeatable unit completely wiped out. Their deaths weighed down the entire camp. Soldiers could not come to grips with it, refused to believe it, knew their information was wrong. If the 13th could be beaten in a single attack, what of the rest of them?

"Smith was a friend," said Knowles, breathing deeply the morning air and helping to right Bix as he walked. Even Knowles was not sure of the game Druxman was playing. He only knew that the head was not Smith, the person, and for Bix to understand that, the head must be used, preferably in a simple and gross fashion. The new men needed to face death to lose their fear, to understand that a man's head is not the man. The more bizarre the use of the head, the higher Druxman's status as a soldier and also the higher that of Knowles for letting him use it. He would rather have buried the head and forgotten it but he needed the status of a strong leader to help the other soldiers. To help them retain their sanity, everything about war must be made ludicrous, a grand joke, a mystic fog of unreality. Only then would they be bold. Nothing killed a soldier faster than caution.

"Not often does one run across such a weapon," he continued. "We'll place him in hot sand for three days, until cured, then decide how best to use him. You don't toss out a comrade like spoilt meat. Druxman understands that, so must you. A soldier lives forever."

In March, French Indochina has no dawn, just a stroke of gray perched on the horizon. Shades of blue, possibly strokes of pink drift by flatly. The colors, never lingering, are briefly tossed into the air followed almost immediately by daylight. Bix waited for the gray in the east.

Knowles had made up his mind about Druxman and Smith. He helped Bix to a pile of sandbags. Bix decided it made no difference how Smith was handled except in the eyes of a court martial for Druxman. Smith was dead. Bix would dispose of him while Knowles was away and no one would be the wiser.

As he rested, his thoughts turned to Beatrice. The idea of a counterattack did not appeal to him even though he felt the sense to get even with the murderous Viet Minh. He was tired and stiff. Why did a soldier always have to fight when he was tired? He walked to the dugout and refused to look toward the strongpoint. In his worn condition the thought of fighting seemed inhuman, suicidal. After radio contact on Beatrice was lost they had heard nothing; no stragglers returned, no special signals, no sign of any French life. If deJohn fought on the hill, as Knowles had said, he was surely dead or captured. In either case he was finished. Because the companionship of a lost friend was not replaceable, Bix's worry turned to Nicole.

That in a war, a man can love any woman, is a lie. The erotic appeal brought by war is there, the contrast of love and war that is no contrast, just a position, a thrust, a conquest, one more object to be sliced and eaten like a piece of fruit. Bix understood the feelings of animal lust, the need to procreate, to continue, but they were not the feelings that picked at him. Smith had been an expert on war-love. Sex was his constant topic. For him, a woman was something to bayonet, pierce, an act beyond the tender sensation of a woman's flesh housing a man's flesh. War gives soldiers the need to procreate; death is constant, life must be seeded. For Smith, the act of sex was like smoking a cigarette. He was quick to mash out the flame when it burnt low.

Knowles, when he spoke of it at all, spoke harshly of sex and usually in past tense, mostly relating to Russians. He hated, despised, and loathed them. Russians were barbarians, inhuman creatures to be crushed under the treads of German Panzers. Women were not exempt from his feelings and more than once he spoke of a young Russian girl who, out of gratitude at being rescued from rapists by Knowles, succumbed to his advances. Behind a bush she dropped to her knees, unlatched his pants, and went to work. He held her head; his eyes rolled back, his body waiting to burst. An incoming shell exploded as he came, killing the girl and almost tearing off his leg. Knowles always cut the story there saying only that it was "a great wedding of pained ecstasy and a pleasure to suffer." Only about Nicole was he kind. Their love had become legend, a love others could feel while in their presence. She was all Bix wanted but, even if Knowles were killed, she would still refuse him.

To Bix, Nicole was everything desirable. Amid the horror, devastation, guilt of war, she lay like a polished unsoiled jewel. Delicate, tender, careful, he had watched her take an hour just to peel, core, section, and eat an apple. Brutality lay outside her door, affection, inside. Bix loved what was her, not her body but the other thing, that bit of nothing: weightless, formless, massless, refusing the conformity of words. He loved beyond flesh like a schoolboy prayed beyond concepts. When he tried to explain it to Knowles he always said, "You don't love her. You are confused. You want to hurt me because you know I will not hurt you, because you can talk to me about my lover and it makes you feel good to do it. Your prick loves her like any man's prick loves a woman. Try another woman and you will see. Someday something unexplainable will happen and you will want to be with a woman with or without sex, then you will understand love."

She was too old to be a whore, older than he, twice as tough in her gentle ways. Dark hair, cropped near her face, was fingered with red and she had eyes the size of grapes, only brown. When she smiled a thin scar appeared on her chin and in that smile only the top row of teeth shone. Her unwrinkled neck sloped to a back molded like fine China. Her hands butterflied when she spoke, each dainty finger articulating and punctuating the words as they sucked out the sweet nectar. Bix could have loved them alone: her fingers, skating across his chest, felt like those of a child swirling short-lived images on a fogged window. At other times they were a tickle of friendly spiders. She was not plump like the Moroccans and Algerians, or tiny, unreal, like the Vietnamese, but hinted of a ballerina with one dance, from her past, still lingering. Grace was hers. Compassion was hers. The ridge on her nose, angular features and uneven teeth made her all the more beautiful.

 Bix remembered her every feature as dawn started to break and they reached the dugout. All artillery fire, all noise had ceased in the valley. He smelled coffee and the wet fresh morning as he stepped into the hole to clean his carbine and prepare for the attack. Smith was not there and he decided not to ask Knowles any more questions about him.

After C-rations of canned peaches and wine, the unit formed near the airfield. Engineers, through the shelling, had worked all night on the runway welding back torn metal strips, making a small usable line for landing supplies. Few people understood how tough they were, always at the head of the line chopping and building roads and bridges so the fighting units could move. The enemy had rendered the airstrip useless, had knocked it out on the first day and it was up to them, under shelling, to make it usable again. The tanks of Captain Hervouet had already formed. He resembled a university professor: thin, pale, thick glasses. His head and shoulders popped from the turret and he drank from a dented cup, his lips curling up into a smile from the heat of the coffee. Some paratroopers looked pensive, others anxious, still others, eager. Knowles shifted from one foot to another. Crème Brulee and Druxman tore a cigar in half and started chewing the tobacco. Although the sun had risen, the sky remained dark and so low that the surrounding hills, Viet-Minh hills, went topless in the gloom. Everyone waited.

In the distance, toward the remains of Beatrice, dragged a small column of men, a dot, a line, the column growing from the ground as it approached. Bix, Knowles, and the rest of the relief unit, split apart like the Red Sea as the Beatrice survivors passed between. Sergeant Kubiak led the survivors of the 13th, many of them half naked, wounded, bootless. Torn limbs hung at their sides or clutched splintered weapons. A limp, stumble, carried by will, determination, or a thick rod of bamboo, several wounded men walked alone. Others, where even will had not survived or whose bodies or minds had fractured in the night, were helped by stronger legionnaires. A shell had torn away the leg of one man. His boot, strapped on the stump, dripped blood and dangled above the ground. His torn trousers waved like defeated flags. Two legionnaires, helping carry another comrade, used an M-1 threaded through his arms. The wounded man's legs trailed in the dirt and his outstretched arms were belted to the rifle in crucifixion. Two dog tags swayed from his neck like tin tombstones. A soldier, completely naked, kept laughing and spitting into the air, howled, laughed and spit again and again. The survivors no longer resembled men, not because of appearances, but because of their overwhelming sense of emptiness. What constituted a man had deserted.

With one arm drawn up, his hand open as if holding air, his tunic in rags and his carbine tracking the dirt, deJohn, gaunt, alone, eyes void, traveled not just down the road, but in a place that retained no tracks, an inner place few people had gone and from which even fewer returned. Knowles reached out for him.

"So now the fun is over," said Knowles. DeJohn's bent arm dropped to his side. He looked suspended from Knowles' hand, blood across his chest, (although Bix saw no wounds,) tunic undone, left pocket torn and flapped over, his top two buttons replaced with triangular rips. DeJohn remained silent. "We take our eyes away from you for just a minute and you run off to become a hero, said Knowles. The women will refuse to leave you alone now and greedy bastard that you are, you'll have them all."

DeJohn fell to his knees, clutched at Knowles' legs, and started to weep. For a moment Knowles held his head and when the time was right he said, "Yes, yes, it's all over now, my friend, and you must get back to the work at hand." He lifted deJohn to his feet.

Bix offered his canteen. Knowles poured the water on his cap and dabbed deJohn's face as if it were a scraped knee.

"You look all beat to hell," said Crème Brulee. "What happened up there?"

"Yes," said deJohn, more from convention than reality. "I suppose the fun is over." He managed a small chuckle as he wiped his eyes. "I guess we showed them." He meant more than he said. He was not responding to a question from a question from Crème Brulee but making him, and the rest of them, some kind of a conviction, promising them something Bix did not fully understand.

They carried deJohn to the shade of a tank. Friends and medics fished other soldiers from the line. Of the seven hundred or more legionnaires that had occupied Beatrice fewer than one hundred had returned. Knowles lit a cigarette, drew twice, blowing the smoke across deJohn's face, before screwing the butt between deJohn's lips. Knowles sat on his haunches Vietnamese style. For a moment deJohn sat unaware of the cigarette. He had no presence in the world.

"You think he's telling us it's bad?" said Druxman. "For us he says nothing, leaving us in the dark. We could use some help here."

For deJohn, joining the Legion had been redemptive. His father, a man of wealth and a French officer during World War II, had laid down his arms before the advancing Germans. Along with the rest of his unit, he was returned home, a fine chateau on a country estate which soon became a German headquarters. For him, the war was over and as he gained the confidence of the enemy he was allowed more freedom.

Riding a bicycle into town became his daily routine and often, his four-year-old daughter, a favorite child, accompanied him. Because he was wealthy, had been an officer, surrendered, or because Germans had occupied his chateau, (no one will ever know) an animosity grew up within the town's people. One afternoon, he and his daughter did not return from their afternoon ride. Two days later, the father, the daughter, arms welded in death around one another, were found in a nearby well. DeJohn wanted to make it all right, prove the family was righteous and courageous in war, and loyal to France and her ideals.

DeJohn remained a mystery to Bix. He had once witnessed deJohn, finger at his lips indicating silence, dip his prick in a glass of cold tea before offering the drink to a soldier with whom he was feuding. When the soldier asked for another glass, deJohn refused, claiming the tea was no good. Two days later, deJohn was beaten while defending the same soldier in a bar.

The cigarette smoke eventually surprised deJohn's lungs and he coughed to life. His body was frail and his hands were pretty like a woman's, his neck thin, his face in every way French and noble.

"Just their numbers made me blind," said deJohn, his voice mystic, airy, not yet a part of conversation. "

"First, the pounding from the artillery," he continued; "then the hills, moving, alive like yellow ants. There were not enough bullets in the entire world to kill them all. Nothing remains. The trench system destroyed, bunkers blown to craters, dugouts opened like wounds." The words came without inflection like the voice of a monotone professor giving a lecture on potatoes.

"You've made it through," said Bix. "Who gives a shit about the rest?"

Knowles poured water into his cupped hand and dribbled it onto deJohn's head brushing his fingers through his hair, careful not to let the water run over his face.

"War's a strange thing," said deJohn.

"A little terror makes you stronger," said Knowles. "Talk about the hurt, then go on;

there is no other course." He emptied the water over deJohn's shoulders.

"They won't stop," said deJohn. "Not until they've killed us all. Sergeant Kubiak gathered us together like sheep. He knew there would be no counterattack, not at night." He finished the cigarette and Knowles placed another one between deJohn's fingers. "We slipped into the jungle, hid, and waited for morning."

"Kubiak is a tough one," said Knowles. "You can do worse than be with him. No one loves his ass more, or the asses of his men, than he does and he will do what it takes to save them."

It appeared to Bix as if deJohn talked to be talking. The story was interesting enough but deJohn was not aware of anyone. He fingered a button, poked at the button with a broken fingernail.

"If we tried to return here last night we might have been mistaken for the enemy," said deJohn. "In darkness, strange things happen, unexpected things like friends killing friends."

The end of the story marked his return to the world and, as he flicked the cigarette away, he said, "C'est la guerre." He had talked himself back into the world of soldiers.

Bix knew that everything would be fine. He would continue because deJohn would continue.

Before any of the survivors could rest they were divided, the wounded taken to the hospital, the rest, including deJohn, re-armed for the counterattack. He offered no complaint and Knowles placed him at his side.

The units formed, moved northwest along Road 41. The air felt warm like a wet towel. Bix checked his carbine which began to feel inadequate and undependable. The rifle had no range and little stopping power. Fortunately, he rationalized, the Viets were small. The bolt was clean. He patted the stock, as he would have patted an old friend. Knowles rested his arm on deJohn's shoulder and was telling him jokes about a French priest and a German barmaid. DeJohn's look, the weight on his delicate frame, the abstract eyes, the cigarette between his lips, which had burnt out since before the move, revealed he heard nothing. Bix again became worried. DeJohn had slipped away again, had dipped into another world when he needed to be very much in this one. A soldier needed his senses about him to stay alive. Even Bix, who knew he could not be injured, needed to be aware of everything about him.

The unit did not travel far before enemy shots stung the air. Bix jumped to the ground, crawled to a clump of brush and kept low. When he looked back, Knowles was pulling deJohn to cover. Knowles almost knocked him into a ditch. DeJohn squatted there, the rifle, like a walking stick, across his bent knees. Bix aimed his weapon toward the oncoming fire and released a round making sure the carbine worked. Tanks and trucks rumbled from behind him. The ground was flat, covered with tall elephant grass, and marshy, only the red road cutting ahead, a link between him and the enemy. Crème Brulee walked ahead firing as he moved. Bix jerked him down.

"You crazy?" he said. "Those bastards can shoot."

"I just figured it out." He sat on the dirt, not interested in cover. "Like you, I reckon I can't be killed either. Ain't no Viet Minh bullet or shell is ever goin' to touch me."

"You're dreaming," said Bix. "Anyone can be killed, even you. Be careful you don't get a shiv up your guts."

The words did not apply to him, not the invincible one, the one soldier that could not be killed.

"His will is gone," said Knowles, dropping into a crouch beside Bix and Brulee.

"You can never see them," said Bix, referring to the Viet Minh. "You can never get a clear shot at them."

"We going, or what?" called Druxman. He was watching deJohn. "What do I do with him?"

"Quang's fixing us some special victuals fur when we get back," said Crème Brulee. "I got him widening out the dugout a bit too. Seems to me, all we got to do is kill a few folks then go back for some eats."

"You shouldn't have given Quang your bayonet," said Bix. "You might need it."

"Reckon he needs he it moren me what with all the cookin' and diggin' and such. A good knife's handy to have."

"Watch he don't use it on you," said Bix. "Isn't that right, Sarge."

No one enjoyed killing Communists more than Knowles. Not even night stopped him. Yet he seemed to have no hatred in him. They could have been paper targets and he would have been just as happy. He just wanted to shoot something. Bix pointed toward deJohn.

"He's surrendered inside - finished," said Knowles.

"Sometimes they come back," said Crème Brulee. "Just needs a little time."

"I never know to shoot high or low," said Bix. "If they would just show themselves and fight like soldiers."

"Reckon they aren't that stupid," said Brulee.

"Well, you're the Sergeant," Druxman yelled. "We going to sit here all day?"

DeJohn continued to sit, oblivious to the action. Insanity in war was an illness, something that struck like a cold. Some men recovered, some men succumbed. The world turned upside down and everything that once made sense became absurd. There was no solid ground. The illness either passed or became fatal. Of all the things Bix might have decided, holding on to his sanity was a promise he was going to keep.

"For the French, one skirmish and it's over," said Knowles. "That's why we beat those Frogs so often." He drew his weapon to his shoulder and fired very cautiously. A bullet snapped the ground between them. "Bastard," he said, and fired back. His ejected shell flipped into Bix's shirt causing him to jump up from the burn and to jiggle the casing lose.

"You're going to fry me," he said, falling back to the ground.

Where his neck sloped to the shoulder the flesh was burnt and started to swell. When Knowles shot again, Bix ducked and moved to his other side. Knowles never moved when he was busy and was content to burn Bix alive without so much as an apology.

"Communists are legal game," said Knowles. "First Jews, then Russians -- now Communists. It's easier for you to think of them like game, fat pigs for the roasting fires."

"Did you say Jews?" said Druxman.

"Damn," said Bix, trying not to listen to Knowles' chatter. Talking during tense situations never felt natural. Knowles often talked incessantly during combat as if language sent his bullets straight for the mark. Other times he said nothing.

"Don't think of them as people," said Knowles. "People give you bad dreams, make you think. You'll never be more than a tender green Pumpkin like that, never a soldier. Think of them as targets."

"Shut up, for Christ's sake," said Bix, taking a bold move with Knowles. He fired three more rounds. "I'm a good soldier, a damn good soldier." The tanks started moving down the road shaking the earth under them.

"Communists are things," said Knowles. "You can't dream about things like you can people. You don't see them when you look."

"I swear," said Bix. "You've gone nuts."

Knowles' streak of sentiment started to annoy Bix. Philosophy never interested him and he began to think he had placed his faith in the wrong soldier.

"Bastard," said Knowles. Two reports sounded from his weapon and he raised his arm in a cheer. "Through the neck. Did you see him kick like a fish? Let your mouth go, keep your mind on killing, that's the secret." He winked at Bix. "You have much to learn," he continued. "When the ground moves it's not the ground but the enemy. Get away a shot and watch the earth buckle." He jerked Bix's shoulder down. "And you with your ass in the air; you'll never get to be an old man."

"I'm not afraid."

"Dead men aren't."

The lead tank jerked to a halt rocking on its tracks, dust rolling up from the ground. DeJohn had not moved except to pinch his chin, jerk up a shoot of grass to roll between his fingers as the gunfire ceased. The fighting had caused Bix to think about the opium Smith had under his cot. He and Crème Brulee had been collecting it since they had landed in the valley. Quang often slipped into the nearby villages to gather it. Any chance at becoming rich made Bix nervous and excited, yet he did not want to be faced with any moral issues beyond killing.

"Look there," said Knowles, pointing at a solitary figure carrying a white flag. "It's Lieutenant Turpin," he mumbled.

"It is?" said deJohn. He was back on his feet and standing with the group. He squinted and yelled out. "It's Lieutenant Turpin from 11th Company."

Turpin staggered forward, feet uneven, weaving from side to side like men do in a dream. Blood ran from a bandage covering his head, his arm slung down from a dirty cloth, clothes torn and covered with blood.

"Careful," said Knowles. "This is no time to play it safe."

Knowles worked himself closer to the ground and placed his chin on the spine of the gunstock. He looked very intense and his eyes darted from side to side like those of a lizard. He had witnessed too many tricks in his day and trusted no one. In tough times, a man might try anything. Turpin, stumbling, almost fell into the arms of several men. They pulled him to the shady side of a tank where officers soon assembled.

"What's it all about?" said Bix. Any noise ceased. Another sergeant was summoned.

"Our hedgehog at Na San was different," said Knowles. "The little yellow bastards came on and on and we cut them down like cattle. Now this. It's all very strange."

At Na San, the earlier battle commanded by Guilles, the French had laid a trap similar to the one they thought they had laid at Dien Bien Phu. The Viet Minh, eager for a victory, had charged straight into the waiting guns in an effort to overpower the French. The bodies had piled up like stacked bags of sand.

For a minute Knowles relaxed, drank from the canteen. He unbuttoned his pants and tried to piss without getting soiled. He had been castrated but his penis remained intact with just a scar, fat and white, that followed its length. The wound was a terrible one, one he never spoke about and always attempted to hide by pissing away from the sight of the others. He joined the group with Turpin.

The sergeant returned and huddled the squad together for an explanation. The Viet Minh 312th Division had captured Turpin. He had been released with a dispatch from the Viet Minh commander offering a truce, a chance for the French to retrieve their wounded from Beatrice. Accepting a truce required confirmation from the Colonel.

"Will he agree?" said Bix.

"He's trapped," said Knowles. "In war, any appearance of good always turns out bad. If de Castries refuses to accept the wounded, no one will fight for fear they will be abandoned. If he does agree it gives the Viets time to solidify their positions on the hill and dig in for good. They also know that the sight of the wounded men can be demoralizing."

Knowles had brought a small loaf of hard bread and he offered a piece to deJohn. DeJohn remained quiet. Bix wondered what swirls of madness, or peace, held him. Madness was not always easy to detect in war.

The sun broke through the clouds and Bix laid back against his pack. The smell of soil, canvas, diesel from the tanks, and gunpowder drifted through the air. Such times were lovely, precious time made more valuable by the circumstances and, as heat from the sun covered his face, he started to drift off watching the red-yellow light pressing against his closed eyelids.

"Not me," said Knowles, the growl in his voice waking Bix. "My job is to kill the bastards not retrieve them."

A sergeant, tall, bent at the neck, round shouldered, looked at deJohn and shook his head. Knowles said something to him. The sergeant jerked a shoulder, continued down the line.

"What is it?" said Bix.

"De Castries has accepted the truce," said Knowles, "and wants volunteers to search among the dead, retrieve what scraps of life are there."

"It's better than sitting here," said Bix. He hated the burden of every day soldiering, the endless lines, the waiting, the regimen. Retrieving the dead seemed heroic enough to look impressive and still be safe.

"Merdique," said Knowles. He spit and tossed his head. Down the line, the other sergeant was having little luck. "Viets are unmerciful bastards, heartless. I knew they were up to something. The screw turns and the Communists are on top."

"There must be wounded," said Bix. He imagined himself in their place, bleeding, abandoned, left to the enemy. Knowles gave him a queer look like a dog hearing a new sound. "We can help," said Bix.

"Like we're helping deJohn here?" said Druxman. "What good is he, Sarge?"

"Time is all he needs. Tomorrow will be better," said Knowles. He squeezed deJohn's shoulder. DeJohn did not respond. Since recognizing the lieutenant he had slipped back into solitude.

"These bastards are using an old trick and the Frogs are falling for it. They learned nothing from the last war." Knowles dug at his boots with his bayonet slicing out chunks of red clay from off the sole. "Listen," he said; "the Viet Minh know the airstrip is destroyed. Tremendous effort will be needed to keep it open and already several guns are zeroed in on the field. The Viets make an offer; retrieve your wounded, they say. It sounds very generous and humanitarian. What an offer! You must think like a soldier to understand the real meaning. We bring in our wounded. Their pitiful, beaten, dying looks play on our minds. Our doctors become overworked, medical supplies run short, more and more personnel are eaten up caring for the sick. The game never ends unless we don't play. If not, we'll be swamped with wounded – no way to get them out."

Knowles looked straight at Bix as if he were a simpleton.

"See how the cancer works?" he said. "And if we don't take our soldiers back? – that too gets around. Who will fight knowing they will not be retrieved if he gets wounded? Going to the Viet Minh is certain death. We all know that. They have no doctors, no medical supplies."

Bix thought about what Knowles was saying. Simple requests always grew complicated with a little thought.

"And the Viet Minh?" said Bix.

"They won't take back their own. You'll see. Every Viet Minh knows he won't be taken back. They don't expect anything unless it comes from us. We get our dead and wounded and theirs, too. Options that appear good on the surface seldom turn out good in a war."

"This sun makes me lazy," said Bix, still looking for a reason to volunteer, to be of some use. "Going up there has got to be better than just sitting here."

"We gonna wait here all day?" said Brulee. "I'd go too cept someone's got to look after deJohn."

"Of course you'll go," Knowles said to Bix. "No need for excuses. You're a green Pumpkin, too decent for soldiering. Leave, satisfy your curiosity, get a look at what can happen. I'll tend to what has already happened." Knowles handed another chunk of bread to deJohn. It fell beside the first one.

Bix's joints had turned stiff from sitting all night and hurt when bent, and sleep had sneaked into his walk. He stumbled with each step. Knowles never volunteered for anything involving peace. In fact, he never volunteered for anything. If a handful of men were needed to attack a division, he would be the first to go but not if he had to volunteer. The care he showed deJohn baffled Bix. He put it out of his mind, chalked such sentiment up to old age, a soldier, childless, unmarried, looking after his flock. Knowles could have the opium, retire to Germany, live well, remember the old times, the old causes. Knowles would never take the good life. Bix turned back once, watched Knowles lift the bread to deJohn's lips and realized that Knowles never intended to leave the valley, the fight. Knowles had entered the valley to help others, to see that they were looked after, to repent any past sins. Bix shook his head. Nothing seemed right anymore. But no, his mind wandered. Knowles wanted to live more than any of them. Bix's imagination was simply making peace with itself.

At 0900, the rescue team started out. Bix climbed into a two-and-a-half ton truck with a dozen volunteers. Knowles kept Bix's carbine. A Red Cross flag billowed from a jeep clearing the road ahead. Captain Demany, the 3/13th's doctor, and Father Tringuand rode in the jeep. An ambulance followed the truck. Bix continued to nod from lack of sleep. The truck kicked red dust onto the bed.

The team was an open target, easy marks for the Viets. What were a dozen more legionnaires to the number they had already killed? A bump jerked Bix awake. Sergeant Kubiak had asked to return and rode in the jeep. What peace of mind could he find on the torn hills? Bix wondered if Kubiak would crack. Maybe he carried a concealed weapon, was waiting for a chance to spring on a Viet and cut him down. Strange ideas enter a man's mind in war. Bix's head was still not clear. Communists were slowly leveling the other French strongpoints; French artillery sat in the dead open; all French positions were void of vegetation and easy targets; the Viet Minh had all Indochina in which to hide. The truce only applied to Beatrice, not the rest of the valley. The French stood out like a sore on the earth. The life of a mercenary offered little payment except a quick pulse and Bix tried not to think about what now appeared to be very serious mistakes on the side of the French. The high officers knew what they were doing and that was all that counted. It was not for him to judge but he could not help himself.

The road to Beatrice looked empty, no Viet Minh, no big guns and Bix wondered where they were. Ahead the Viets had erected a roadblock. The jeep halted and officers dismounted, stood at attention, gave smart salutes out of respect which were answered by the Viet Minh officers behind the blockade. After a short conference where they were given the conditions of the truce, the team dismounted from the truck, moved up the slope of Beatrice.

The hill already stank of rotten meat. Beatrice had taken a beastly pounding and resembled the battlefields of World War I, the earth peened in, shell craters filled with water, bodies hanging and twisted from curls of barbed wire, the air buzzing with enormous black and green flies. The entire landscape had been surgically altered, ripped, torn, covered with blood. Strings of barbed wire sutured earth and air together. Of the elaborate trench systems, bunkers, dugouts and gun emplacements, nothing remained.

Chunks of flesh sprouted from the cultivated earth; legs, arms, the side of a face, all protruded from the clay. Bix walked carefully, knowing that the ground blanketed over 600 dead comrades. The rush of blood, the fear, the sacred walk through a graveyard that he had done as a kid returned to him as he waited for ghosts to spring from the soil. He knew, like Crème Brulee, that he would never die, not then, not as a kid, and not now, not as a man. He would eventually get his wound and leave the Legion with honor. Other men might become cold slabs of granite buried under wicked trees bending under a moon that snatched life from the old, the infirm, but not him.

The battlefield was different. He stopped to examine a stomach torn open like a split cabbage and lined with neat rows of clutching black fingers that had made a desperate attempt to hold life in. Bix bent to the side and puked. Life was a lie. Yesterday, this stomach, these fingers, did not admit to death. What were they now? Something he might become? He pressed his hands against his stomach. He cupped a hand over his nose to pinch off the terrible stench of death. The Viet Minh, who had already cleaned the hills of their dead, did not accompany the rescue team and let them work quietly and without disruption. They had coveted all usable weapons, ammunition and equipment and nothing usable or of military value remained. Bix attempted to check every body as if with his touch, finger against finger, he might bring them back to life.

Distinguishing the living from the dead proved difficult. One soldier after another was tipped over and checked for vital signs. The air had left them stiff, looking up with strange eyes, the same eyes as Smith's, intent, distant. Bix tugged at all partially buried limbs hoping to find life at the other end. He jerked at a leg that flew from the dirt and slapped him in the forehead with its cracked bone.

Father Tringuand knelt over a legionnaire and administered last rites. The young soldier, bleeding from the side and the neck, looked blankly at the Father until the service was complete. He started to convulse kicking his legs and body out, and out again, slapping at his gagging heart. Spittle flowed from his mouth as Father Tringuand tried to hold his head. He was finished. "Legionnaires fight even God," Bix thought.

When the search ended, only eight legionnaires, including the one who died in the Father's arms, were found. The harvest was not a good one and Bix sat on the hill and took a last look down Road 41 and back into the valley. From here, the entire position could be seen.

The rescue truck drove past "le Bep" and Bix watched Knowles still carrying his carbine. Knowles waved, stuck the weapon between his legs and pumped it in false masturbation. Bix yelled to meet him at the hospital. DeJohn walked quietly like a man emerging from a movie theater and trying to adjust to the light. Soldiers lowered the wounded from the truck and carried them into the dim recesses of the hospital. Quarters were cramped; the rooms and hallways stuffed with previously wounded soldiers and litters. Bamboo mats lined the walls to prevent the dirt from falling. Major Grauwin, chief doctor of the hospital, personally examined the newly wounded. Ordinarily a strong man with bold features and a bald head, he looked very tired, almost exhausted, and the fight had just begun.

"You've had some success at least," said Lachen. Bix turned as Lachen moved around a shelf of plasma. "Let's have a drink," he said, and held up his canteen.

"What about the counterattack?" said Bix.

Lachen motioned him through a tight corridor. Outside the Viet Minh had started their shelling again and the ground returned to its regular lazy shake.

"They sent me for blood, six liters," said Lachen. They sat on an empty cot below a machine gun slit. A gray spider had webbed over a corner of the opening.

"Knowles has my carbine," said Bix. Lachen appeared as exuberant as ever, glowing, effervescent, a symphonic smile covering his face.

"Blood is short," said Lachen. "I went to the air strip to pick it up. Everything's a mess. We needed something small, a plane that could drop through the clouds quickly, drop off the blood, and get away just as fast. No way. They said that nothing could get in. Even the landing tower is blown to shit."

"How about some bombers to clear away the hills?" said Bix. He decided not to mention puking on the hill. The taste of bile clung to his teeth like dried cement.

"Not for blood," said Lachen. "A De Havilland fell through the clouds." He flew his hand like a toy from over his head to his lap. "The single engine idled back like this," he sputtered with his lips, "and the little beauty fell quickly from the sky and across a small piece of runway that was not badly damaged; a great job of flying and I have never seen such courage. We waited behind some sandbags with Colonel de Castries' secretary and four badly wounded soldiers."

"That's a load," said Bix. The wine helped mask the taste of the puke.

Lachen poured more wine into the canteen cup and they shared another drink. The wine quickly started to annoy Bix like a good glass of water annoys a man living in rainy country.

"It flew in beautifully," said Lachen. Again he mimicked the plane with his hand and dropped it from overhead in a wide swoop. "Immediately we drove the ambulance onto the field, exchanged the liters of blood for the wounded and the secretary, a real beauty. The plane snarled away in minutes." He swooped his hand skyward.

Knowles approached from down the corridor. He stooped more than usual, his legs heavy and without the quick jerky step of most soldiers. Bix guessed him to be between thirty and thirty-five but he moved like a man of fifty. Perhaps this was one war too many. Without speaking, he handed Bix the carbine and they all went to the hospital mess to eat.

They gathered a handful of cheese and bread and sat in an outside trench beside a brown-skinned Moroccan who had been wounded in the side. Like Lachen he was good-natured and not concerned about the wound which had been neatly dressed. He fingered his heavy beard and spit bits of food from between his black teeth. Thick mud floored the trench and stuck to their boots.

"They're shelling the airstrip again," said Knowles.

"And why not," said the Moroccan, with a chuckle. "We have at least six Bearcats in the pits and they don't wish them to get away. Besides, the advantage is presently theirs. That will change, once we get our heads about us."

Lachen leaned in close and said, "tell me friend, I see you're with the artillery. Is there a chance to silence their guns?" Lachen pointed his chin toward the hills.

"Ha," said the Moroccan. "Look around. We have no cover. No camouflage. No protection. We can't destroy what we can't find. Last night alone we lost a third of our guns."

"A third?" said Lachen, in disbelief. He emitted a small whistle from between his lips. "Still, things could turn out."

"It's a good way to pass the time," said Knowles. He tapped his boot on the mud making a small puddle. He offered the Moroccan more coffee.

"My piece was blown from under me, blasted to bits," said the Moroccan. "I yelped to Allah to save my manhood. There is still a night or two of fun left in me." He twiddled his eyebrows and winked. "The American howitzers are badly designed. The hydraulic recoil mechanisms are easily destroyed. A few bits of metal enters and kaput."

"At least a good sign from Allah," said Lachen, squeezing himself between the legs. He peered over the side of the trench. "Earlier I watched reinforcements fall like confetti on the drop zones. They were the 5th Vietnamese Parachute Battalion, the 'Batwan'. The Communists started gunning them down immediately and many of the little fellows died before they hit the ground." Lachen's voice quieted and for the first time, his smile left. "How did they get such fire power?"

"It's a mystery," said the Moroccan. "We are starting to think the guns are placed on the near sides of the hills rather than the reverse. If so, we still can't find them."

"These are not boys we're playing with," said Knowles.

"And the bombings?" said Lachen.

"Useless, of course," laughed Knowles. "We're in a fine mess. For months we have bombed the far sides of hills trying to find the guns. We'll never find them now and there is nothing more useless in war than aircraft. They never did a thing to Germany except kill civilians causing us to fight even harder. During the last months of the war we were producing more material than at any other time. An airplane is nothing more than a very expensive piece of artillery."

"That's not what our government says," said Bix, annoyed.

"All governments lie," said Knowles. "Yours more than most."

"Unfortunately," said the Moroccan. "And, as you say, they are so well concealed we cannot find them. But it's the ammunition that's the greatest mystery." He drank slowly from the cup and spit a small stream of coffee on the ground. "Our barrage against the Viets last night cost us 6,000 rounds - 6,000 rounds in one night! Think of what the Viets have spent? How are they getting supplies? The counterattack for Beatrice was called off because we don't have the rounds to support such madness."

"The strongpoint is blown to shit, anyway," said Bix. "It's of no use to us now."

"Yes," said the Moroccan. "Gabrielle will catch it tonight, you'll see, and we'll need every available round for support."

There was a moment of silence and Bix thought of Nicole. One little jewel in such hell was all a man could ask. There was time to see her, to make love, but he felt too dirty and tired. Nicole had class and sophistication and out of respect he wanted to wash first before visiting. It was a dream, anyway. She would not have him. She would not have any man except Knowles.

"Look quick," said Lachen. He pointed over the trench rim toward the airstrip. Three Bearcat fighters rumbled down the field revving their engines. In a moment they shot away. "A little luck shines on us."

"At least something small can use the airstrip," said the Moroccan.

"Not for long," said Lachen.

"They're off to Cat-Bi airport at Haiphong for safety," said Knowles. "We'll catch it now."

As Bix returned to the dugout, the artillery fire on the airstrip tripled. He crawled into the dark and, without finding Smith, curled onto his cot. He wondered what Knowles had done with him. Light from exploding rounds flickered across the dugout opening. The trembling earth ironed out his knots and he quickly fell asleep.

Chapter 32

Bix awoke, his eyes adjusting slowly to the dim light. He stiffened and sat, blood draining from his head, making him dizzy. DeJohn, resting on his cot, stretched his legs. His head remained in the dark away from the dugout entrance. Bix could not tell if he was asleep. His feet crossed, his hands curled under his head, his chest moved slowly up and down. They had only slept for several hours.

"Get up you lazy sot," said Knowles, a large grin on his face, cleanly shaven, washed blond hair thin in front, forced his way into the dugout trying not to dirty his clean uniform. His huge hands gripped Bix's shoulders.

"What?" said Bix. "Another counterattack?" He rubbed his eyes like a child does, his hands in curled balls. "I thought they called it off."

"Coffee. We may have another fun and difficult night," said Knowles. "The Communists are zeroed in on Gabrielle, blowing it all to shit like Beatrice."

Bix rubbed his eyes as the ground shook. A soldier learns to sleep under guns and shaking earth and often has difficulty sleeping when the noise and movement stops.

"How long have I been sleeping?"

"A lifetime. Drink this." Knowles handed Bix the hot coffee.

The coffee was thick and strong, European style. It had taken Bix time to get used to it, especially when the French made it, but he could now at least get it down. The rush it gave him was needed.

"Sergeant!" Someone called through the opening. "It's Lieutenant Floss with an assignment."

Bix listened to them talking. Nothing sounded good as the words rolled into the dugout, mumbles, shouts, calmness...

"Even better than I thought. We're going to carry ammunition," said Knowles, clapping his arms against his sides as he sat down.

"Where?" It made no difference to Bix, just a question, a way to hear his voice.

"Gabrielle."

It sounded dangerous. Lately, days had become unstable and precious and Bix wanted to be left out of anything risky, not out of fear, but until he got some rest. He craved dangerous assignments but only if he were well rested. His hands shook from lack of sleep.

"I'm tired," said Bix. "How can they expect a soldier to fight without any sleep? And some food, some hot food."

"The arrangements are made, the orders issued," said Knowles. "While you were picking through the dead, the Lieutenant said to be prepared."

"So you shaved and put on fresh clothes?" said Bix.

Knowles would want to look his best at his own death.

"A man fights better when he carries pride with him," he said. "A bath, a clean uniform, a shave, increases a man's fighting ability ten fold. Anything less and you are already beaten."

"Can't you leave me out of these things until I get some sleep?" said Bix. DeJohn uncrossed his feet and dropped one arm to his side. "I don't mind fighting I just want to do it when I am awake. My stomach is sick."

"A soldier needs the rush of action," said Knowles. "I plan to give you all my expertise as a soldier, not unlike taking one's nephew to a whore house."

"You've screwed me often enough," said Bix. "Leave me alone."

"We're taking supplies to Gabrielle," said Knowles. "The Lieutenant said I was his best Sergeant and I was to pick my best man. Do you want me to choose Druxman or deJohn? Get your ass in gear."

Bix's chest jerked and he felt instantly nauseated. He drew in several deep breaths, took them silently so Knowles would not notice.

"Life at its fullest," said Knowles. "Sleeping is time wasted. There, on the hill, we'll come alive. Gabrielle will catch hell tonight and we'll be there dancing."

"We're just taking the ammo, then returning, right?"

Bix felt the fear creep into him, a fear caused by tiredness. He had thought a great deal after his experience on Beatrice and he was beginning to doubt his decision about being in the Legion. The grand adventure was growing thin. He was not used to fear, had not yet experienced it. Not just the tiredness made him sick, the fear had, just a trickle of fear, just enough to remind him it was there. He had nothing against the Viet Minh. What he expected to be an adventure was growing into horrifying drudgery. Who needed adventure if it required work? He glanced under Smith's bunk; saw the rows of ammo boxes filled with heroin.

"I plan to get out of here," he said. "Crème Brulee and me are going to live good when we get home. Where is he, anyway?"

"Bah," said Knowles. He turned his back. "I should have sacked him long ago. It was a mistake to let him continue with the drugs. I thought he would be dead soon enough,"

"I saw what happened on Beatrice," said Bix. "You weren't there. Gabrielle won't be any different."

Knowles turned quickly, knelt before him and shot a finger as if reprimanding a child.

"I've seen more death than all the wars you'll ever encounter," he said. "Bodies stacked on bodies in Russia, as far as you could see, millions of them. After the war they talked of Jews, the slaughter, the air filled with smoke from all those deaths. What are six million Jews compared with twenty million Russians? No one talks of that." Knowles shifted his weight. A shell landed close to the dugout and shook the cot. "You Americans were big heroes. Bah. The Western Front was only a sideline compared to Russia, and killing Americans was no more difficult than this..." He snapped his fingers and spit. "But Russians, that was something else! In the winter we killed them to use their frozen bodies to fill potholes and we stacked them like walls to protect our cannons. Summer melted them down and filled the air with a filthy stink. Still they came on, masses and hordes of them, oblivious to our guns. And the civilians? Butchers. They would rather starve themselves than feed a hungry German. I tell you there were not enough bullets to kill them all. They fought like madmen, every one, women, children, soldiers."

Bix listened intently. Knowles slumped to the cot beside deJohn, tapped out a French cigarette and tossed the pack to Bix.

"Yes, we treated them just as badly. A squad of German soldiers had taken a young girl from a nearby farmhouse and held her against a tree. When I arrived she looked terribly frightened but made no sound. Her underclothes lay on a nearby plant and the soldiers holding her had lifted her dress and kicked her legs apart. To the delight of the others, a corporal had taken his bayonet and was prying apart her bush."

Bix lit a cigarette. French cigarettes always tasted bad and he choked. Knowles rested his elbows on his knees. Knowles told the story differently each time, sometimes saving the woman, sometimes not.

"I had authority then," he continued, "and stepped into their little party and broke it up. Like all good German soldiers, they snapped to attention and without grumbling clicked their heels together and left quietly. I felt sorry for them because I understood the need for a woman in war. War and women go together. The French, by bringing them along in their bordellos, avoid such mischief. They are quite civilized in some ways."

Knowles slid closer to deJohn. DeJohn recrossed his feet. Bix knew he was awake by the stiffness in his legs.

"There she was, the Russian girl, her hair in two long braids, and me, with the same needs as all soldiers, a need for affection, something tender, my rod throbbing in my trousers. She looked pensive but grateful and I took her hand and lead her behind some brush. She tensed as I pushed her down on her knees."

Another shell rocked the dugout and sprinkles of dirt powdered down. Bix brushed dirt from a piece of dried bread and tore half for Knowles. He waved it away.

"My prick started its last swell. She snapped her head forward, all the way to my abdomen and folded her arms around my legs. She pulled back, started to unfasten my trousers. I reached for my side arm, pulled it gently away from the holster. I stuck the barrel of the pistol into her ear like the cold finger of a lover and pulled the trigger. There was nothing else I could do. The men would have gotten to her soon enough and eventually killed her anyway. This seemed more human. Was it a mistake? Should I have let her blow me and then turned her loose? It was what it was. A man does what he thinks is right at the time and cannot reflect about it later."

Knowles drew long on the cigarette and flicked it to the ground. The dugout felt cool, comfortable.

"Bad luck," said Bix, realizing too late that he should have said nothing. He never knew if Knowles was telling the truth or just trying to make a point. "You talk too much about pricks."

"You can't kill them all," said deJohn. His voice startled Bix.

"Not Russians," said Knowles. "I'm done with them. Not Russians or Communists or Jews or people. They just keep coming." deJohn did not roll over. "Communists," Knowles continued. "At least I can kill as many as possible before I'm done. You, de-John, you're already finished." Knowles squeezed deJohn's leg. "It's your decision. If the fighting for you is over, then it is over, but you will never again live as a man unless you get to your feet."

"I have no share in life anymore," said deJohn. "I will continue to fight - my own way."

Bix could still not see his face. The words rumbled in the dark behind Knowles. Bix looked at the ammo boxes, tried to straighten things out in his mind. Killing people no longer interested him, if it ever did, and he wondered what deJohn would do?

"I can fix everything," Bix finally said. He reached under Smith's cot and retrieved an ammo box filled with opium. He crouched on his haunches with the box between his legs. "With this, half of my share," he said to Knowles, "You can return to Germany, sit around the fireplace, tell war stories to your friends, become a country gentleman, grow old with dignity."

Bix felt elated by his gift and his quick thinking. Knowles looked at him queerly his head cocked to one side.

"DeJohn," said Bix. "For Christ's sake sit up! Look at the box." Knowles moved to the side, slid to one knee as deJohn rolled to his arm. "You take the other half. With this you can return to France, put your father's estate in order, buy the whole damn town if you like."

The heat of excitement rushed over him and Bix panted like a happy puppy.

"If ammo boxes were gold," said Knowles. He kicked the box over, the dope spilling onto the mud, some of it powder but most of it rolled black balls. "Such crap, such big ideas. I thought more of you, Muffin. You are a pumpkin that has gone bad."

"Crème Brulee knows what to do with it," said Bix, looking from one face to the other. His hands lifted the box and he tried to scoop in the contents. The refined powder was mixed with the gummy black raw drug and he had difficulty getting it all in. He snapped the latch and cradled the box.

"He shoves it in his veins," said Knowles. Bix had kept out a ball of dope and rolled it around on his palm. "He'll be dead with the stuff before this is over. I should have him arrested, have all of you arrested. I would do it if you weren't all going to be killed."

"Our fortune," said Bix. DeJohn leaned over the cot, balancing himself with two fingers against the floor. "We only have to make it through this battle, escape this valley."

"Escape?" Knowles squinted in confusion. "Escape? No one is getting out of here unless you forget this crap and fight, fight like you have never fought before."

"Opium," said Bix. "Crème Brulee has filled this ammo box and he is still getting more. We're not living in a dugout, we're living in a gold mine."

"Opium?" DeJohn repeated. He reached out for the ball of dope.

"Smith and Brulee collected it all," said Bix. "Quang has been smuggling it through the lines for them. They were going to get away and be through with the war. We can do the same." He clapped his hand around Knowles wrist.

Knowles snatched the ball from deJohn's hand and tossed it out the door. He had never heard of anything so stupid and he wondered why he even bothered with such an unethical kid, such a green pumpkin. Bix grabbed his wrist again.

"Show some pride," Knowles continued. He pulled Bix's hand away. "I expected more from you."

Bix felt foolish and ashamed.

"What more is there?" he said. The shelling outside was beginning to get on his nerves and the smile, which he tried to maintain, seemed ridiculous. "We just have to get it out, survive a few more days until the Viets have run out of steam. Quang can help us get away." He tried to redeem himself.

"Quang?" said Knowles. "Do not be fooled. He is Vietnamese and will always be Vietnamese regardless of how he acts. The first chance he gets he'll kill us all. No other people in the world can so easily shake your hand while cutting your throat. Have you learned nothing?"

Knowles positioned himself against the top cot. The foolish feeling stayed with Bix and he wanted to get rid of it.

"You're not so damn righteous," he said. "All you've ever done is kill people."

"Listen, Pumpkin," said Knowles. He patted Bix's head as if he were a small boy who had unknowingly committed a crime. "You have nothing here except grief. If you want to save yourself, if you want to save your friend Crème Brulee, burn it."

"Opium," said Bix. "Don't you understand?" He started jerking ammo boxes from under the cot and stacking them at his feet. "Crème Brulee is going to fill them all. We can make a fortune, all go home and forget about this place." He pleaded with Knowles to understand.

"You can't buy your way out of war," said Knowles. "When you signed on you signed with your life. An honorable man will carry out that contract, even if it means his own death. The interest on this kind of loan continues to grow. War allows no withdrawals. You have a chance to live through this mess, to continue your life with your own story to tell but only if you fight. That's the real gold. With that stuff, you've got nothing." Knowles nodded to the boxes. "I'm going to check on Smith. Forget this stupid idea. A man who is dishonest in one thing is dishonest in all things."

"You're nothing but a god-damned killer," said Bix. "I'm keeping it all, me and Brulee, and you can get screwed. I'll take Nicole and you won't have shit."

For a minute, Knowles blocked out the light as he left. The strength left Bix's shoulders. DeJohn had said nothing. Bix thought of Nicole, of giving her all the money, seeing that she was happy. Bix could take her to America or live in comfort in Europe. The world was hers; they had only to live through the siege. His efforts turned to de-John.

"DeJohn," said Bix. "Don't you understand what we have here? For you the war is over."

"What's money to a Frenchman?" he said. "I'm going to the cliffs at Dominique to think."

An increasing camp of internal deserters had dug in beside the river by Strongpoint Dominique. Many Vietnamese prisoners, including Quang, were also there. There was talk from the command of executing the deserters but nothing had materialized. As it was with most French and their ideas of freedom, they simply left them alone. They were shelled along with everyone else. For them the war was over and they refused to fight.

"He needs time," Bix thought. "He will come around."

Like a boy leaving home for the first time, deJohn gathered his pack and, cinching up his belt, left the dugout. Bix carefully stacked the ammo boxes back under the cot. There was no reason to toss out a fortune until he thought things over. He grabbed his carbine. In the distance deJohn screamed his name.

Outside, beside a row of tangled barbed wire, Knowles hunched over his knees. DeJohn, swaying from side to side, hands clasped almost in prayer, looked down, his chest heaving. He stumbled back dragging the pack at his side. His breath continued to come quickly and terror had wrenched the side of his face into a half snarl. Knowles reached out for him. DeJohn turned, dragged the pack several more feet leaving a furrow in the dirt. The pack slipped down his arm and, eyes wide like two headlights, he ran madly toward the Nam Yum River.

Bix smelled death, a sweet rotten odor.

He moved closer to Knowles' shoulder. There, at Knowles' feet, in a small uncovered pit, lay Smith's head. He looked worse than ghastly. Dirt clung to the slick blue-black skin; the empty cheeks sunk like a fallen cake. Stiff tufts of wire, once called hair, sprang from his head; ears had turned to shriveled toast. His neck, jagged, rigid points of skin, seethed with maggots. But the eyes surprised Bix most and caused him to step back. Druxman had driven two empty .50 caliber shells into the sockets. The brass protruded about an inch and the primers, dimpled by the firing pin, gave the impression of two tiny empty cold pupils staring blankly, coldly, skyward. Knowles brushed at the maggots. Several hung on his arm.

"Not yet, you bastards," he said. One by one he flicked them off with a finger.

"Get rid of it," said Bix. He held his nose. His head swirled and he thought he would puke again.

"Needs more time in the oven," said Knowles. "Another day or two in this sand should tighten him up." Knowles lifted the head by the hair and pointed the face toward Bix.

"The eyes..." said Bix.

"Beauties," said Knowles. "A stroke of genius. Leave it to a Jew to have good taste. I didn't know the bastard had it in him, a real eye for art. Notice how perfectly the casings fit." He gave the brass a small shake. "In a day or two you won't be able to pry them out with a bayonet."

"He's mad," said Bix.

"Twenty millimeter would have been too large," said Knowles, "thirty caliber, too small. Nothing else would fit."

"Give him some respect." As a gentle plea, Bix placed a hand on Knowles' shoulder. "I want to go to Gabrielle. I was wrong."

How could Druxman, so crazy, make sense so much of the time? Maybe all soldiers were mad, or going mad, or were just carrying, as standard equipment, a different perspective, a view unique to war. Knowles lifted Smith closer.

"Look," he said. With one hand, Knowles held the back of Bix's head, and with the other, Smith's. Smith's brass eyes, dimpled firing pins for pupils, stared directly into Bix's. "Our friend is going to save us all." He nodded at Smith. "When you understand that this is not Smith, when you realize, truly know this is only a thing, a piece of nothing like all the other things of the world, then you will survive; and I don't mean survive here." He pointed to the ground, "I mean survive here." He slapped Bix's chest and jerked his head from side to side as if shaking sand down an hourglass.

Knowles placed Smith back into the pit and kicked sand over him. When Smith was covered, Knowles rolled barbed wire across the spot.

"Because deJohn understands nothing," said Knowles, "he's gone insane. Not you Pumpkin, my little muffin; not me. Druxman must have soaked Smith in diesel fuel to protect the skin. He'll dry in a few days. Let the maggots have their part. Enough will be left for us later." He cradled his arm around Bix's shoulder and directed him toward the waiting truck. "Once you understand the significance of the head, you will be able to return home and be finished with war. For now, we have Communists to kill."

Knowles and Bix heaved boxes of ammunition onto the truck. The shelling on the Center of Resistance had remained slow but constant: craters of dirt tossed into the air, pieces of equipment shredded like tin foil, barbed wire bent and tangled. Already Bix was learning to live with the confusion. What mattered was the life before him, the solitary life within his grasp. Trying to understand his situation as a whole was madness.

Much was destroyed while he had slept. The airstrip, on which so much depended, looked completely ruined. The last three Bearcat fighters had been blown apart and the control tower, legs shattered, lay in a twisted heap. In just two days their great advantage had been lost. Unless something was done to the runway, any new supplies would have to be dropped by parachute. Bix listened carefully for shells falling close. The air tingled before they hit.

The hot muggy weather continued and he relished a swim in the Nam Yum River to cool down. His tunic stuck to his chest, his legs felt clammy. Tight air made it impossible to clear his head.

Gabrielle contained enough ammunition to sustain four days of non-stop fighting. The French expected a very large attack. Sergeant Soldati, another legionnaire, and a certified Czechoslovakian doctor, was going with them. Why he joined the Legion as a common soldier remained a mystery. Legionnaires never pried into the lives of others. The French had a shortage of doctors. He would be the third one to serve on Gabrielle within the week.

The truck rattled down the Pavie Track through the Center of Resistance, north through the valley, and past the western edge of Gabrielle. Artillery had chewed the road into lumpy puddles. A round or two still whistled in, more as aggravation than a serious threat. The truck crossed a small marsh and began to bog down in the clay. The men unloaded and pushed the truck with other soldiers waiting nearby. Bix was still not sure what Knowles wanted to teach him. Death? He seemed to know plenty about that. Life? That lesson was taking longer. Love? He knew he loved Nicole, what more did he need to know? Perhaps he did not understand the essence of what Knowles wanted him to learn. Maybe he was just a crazy old Kraut, as crazy as Druxman, looking for a place to die.

The sky broke apart and rain poured down. The men sank in the mud while pushing the truck through a puddle. A shell landed nearby and threw dirt into Bix's mouth. Knowles laughed wildly and beat his chest toward the enemy. "Come and get us, you pricks," he said. Bix was glad his chest was so large and he thought of using it for cover if the situation became desperate. A chest like that could stop many rounds before deflating. The truck spun from the mud, the sun reappeared, and they were again on their way.

Gabrielle was not a strongpoint but an impenetrable fortress. The defensive works were beautifully built, every gun emplacement a masterpiece, every mortar pit spotless. All vegetation had been cleared away. The strongpoint had won the defense competition held by Colonel de Castries, a tactic he used to get the men to work. The hill, home of the 5th Battalion 7th Algerian Rifles, looked solid, impregnable, and was the only strongpoint with two complete lines of defense. Algerians fancied themselves better soldiers than the legionnaires and a healthy competition remained between them. They partied as well as they fought. The cash prize won in the defense competition was spent in one night, a festive dinner and blowout to which they invited Colonel de Castries and his staff.

Bix helped unload the supplies into a bunker. The Algerians were a confident, festive bunch, and the impending battle had not deflated their humor. Like pit bulls they were eager to tear at the enemy. The legionnaires had not held on Beatrice but the Algerians would hold Gabrielle. They tried to rib Knowles and Bix and laughed about the legionnaires on Beatrice, although the laughter on that matter was humorless and a grudging admiration sounded between the guffaws.

"We've come to show you how to fight," Knowles yelled to a mortar crew.

"Who taught you on Beatrice?" one of them replied. His yellow teeth and broad grin wrinkled his wide face. Knowles was not amused and he turned to piss. The Algerians watched him closely and laughed claiming he had a lack of equipment. The one with the yellow teeth regained his composure and, unwilling to relinquish his attack said, "I see it was not your fault. You legionnaires are undergunned."

Bix, not knowing how Knowles would take the comment, slowly lowered a box of ammunition, never taking his flashing eyes from the man with the yellow teeth. He looked back to Knowles.

"An unfortunate date with a snapping turtle," Knowles replied.

"Let us offer you something better," said the man.

The Algerians, appreciating Knowles' pleasant counter-attack, chuckled and motioned them over for wine.

"It takes more guts than I have to be a mortarman," said Knowles. "I enjoy a good fight but standing in the open has always appeared madness."

"That is why the French use Algerians. We are, after all, expendable. Maybe after this war we will demand our own freedom."

Knowles and Bix had passed the ritual. Bix, anxious to leave Gabrielle, fidgeted and made quick conversation. Knowles dallied; decided they should view the fortifications. Bix knew Knowles wanted to remain on the hill. Bix also wanted to fight, but with his own unit and, after some rest.

There were so many soldiers on Gabrielle, they almost bumped against each other. The area reminded Bix of a city block at lunch hour. Men had scalped the hill bare, no signs of vegetation anywhere. Because of the lack of approaching cover, Bix could not imagine any Viets advancing without being cut down. Line after line of soldiers crouched shoulder to shoulder. Above, heavy mortar emplacements lined the peak. To the south stood an eight tube battery of 120mm mortars and to the north, well entrenched, a battery of 81mm tubes. Add to this the supporting guns from the Center of Resistance, and the surrounding strongpoints, and Gabrielle added up to an explosive mass of fire power.

The 416th, an auxiliary company of Thai soldiers, were also dug in, but the command expected them to contribute little to the defense. From Lai Chau, they had hacked their way through the jungle. Sniped and attacked the entire way, they were utterly demoralized. Some of them huddled in trenches, their heads low, their eyes hidden. The rest scratched along the trench rims, eyes wide in anticipation of the coming battle. They seldom fought well while away from home.

The Algerians, however, looked eager for a fight. They had served in Indochina since 1951 and had always distinguished themselves. With a legendary reputation of courage, they were recently equipped with new weapons and uniforms which they kept unusually clean. Because they had never failed a mission, they had been assigned to Gabrielle. No better soldiers fought anywhere else in the world. Not even the defeat of Beatrice dampened their fighting spirit.

Bix and Knowles completed the rounds as mess personnel distributed a hot meal to everyone. The hill itself did not interest Knowles; he wanted to know the location of the defenses, the extra supplies, food, and weapons. Supply was the key to any battle. He understood how helpless a soldier felt when confronted with an empty weapon or an empty stomach. Bix was still anxious to leave and his mutterings started to annoy Knowles. "If you do not want to fight," he said, "you should have stayed home." What did a kid want with war, anyway? Some fun? Some adventure? Sure. Mostly he wanted the same thing any kid wants: a sense of belonging, a chance to prove himself among men. Knowles insisted they stay to eat. He knew the Viet Minh were nocturnal warriors and would attack soon. Bix refused to leave him, especially with trouble brewing. He trailed in his wake as Knowles moved to the mess on the top of the hill. Food did not interest Knowles; he wanted to know more about the position, the commanders, the defense, all the questions a young soldier would not ask. Bix trudged behind him through a narrow communications trench.

The mess sergeant, an unusually thin man, older than most soldiers, had a face deeply wrinkled with worry. He offered them mess kits and made conversation easily. Knowles pumped him unmercifully for information, occasionally slapping Bix on the knee. Bix felt the moisture from the sandbag creep against his buttocks. From his position he could see the other soldiers relaxing below him, some even sleeping. The hill smelled of human waste and diesel fuel.

Major de Mecquenem controlled the strongpoint. His tour of duty was finished and his replacement, Major Kah, had arrived on 2nd March. De Mecquenem refused to relinquish command until Major Kah was thoroughly versed on Gabrielle's defenses. Bix thought it odd, but noble, that he did not leave when given the chance. Now, with the airfield closed, de Mecquenem's chances of leaving were slim. Colonel Piroth, the joyful artillery commander of the valley, had recently assured both majors that not a single enemy shell would hit Gabrielle. He had been mistaken about everything else and Bix wondered about this guarantee. Earlier de Mecquenem and Kah had verified the positions of their men with the artillery and the artillery registered on a valley north of the strongpoint, and on approach trenches dug by the Viets.

There was little to do now except eat and wait. Knowles would never leave without a fight. He loved stories of war and his eyes lit, anxious to be part of the action, the adventure. Bix tried to stop fidgeting. All he wanted to do was to lie down and sleep.

Bix was tired - any thrill or adventure - finished. War had become hard dirty work, exhausting and endless. When he enlisted in the Legion he never expected to kill anyone. The idea that France was at war seemed almost a surprise. He wanted to be part of a group, to fit in with someone, to excel at something physical, to be good at what he did, to have his great adventure, receive a small wound, and bring home a medal. All those things, except the wound and the medal, had been accomplished. He loved the tight feel of comrades, the sharing, the unexpressed love they felt for one another. The excitement, racing-heart rush of battle, was beyond thrilling. Being alive at the end of a fight made the emotions, the senses, tingle with the exuberance, the delight, of life. But he took no pleasure in killing and the sexual arousal it caused only added to his confusion.

Knowles started to look anxious and excited about the coming battle. He ate sporadically and fiddled with the bolt on his MAS and checked the clips. Except during a battle, he always loaded them one round short to relieve any extra tension from the clip springs. From his belt he removed a German 98 Mauser bayonet, a favorite weapon of his. He drew the blade across a fingernail slicing a thin curl. He had honed the edge to almost over sharp. Knowles, using the knife, had once gathered the largest ear collection in le BEP. The fascination did not last and he sacrificed them in a burning barrel several months ago.

After all the rain, the food tasted exceptionally good and Bix ate slowly letting his stomach warm. Simple pleasures amplified during combat. Every whiff of air became a curtain call, every temperature change, every drink of water, every extra minute caused life to tingle.

Seeking a dryer place to sit, Bix moved to a box of grenades and finished the last bite of food, sopping up the juices with a crust of bread. The coffee, rich and hot, burnt his knees through the canteen cup. Almost all the equipment was American. A small group of French and Algerians gathered. The jokes, the laughter, came quickly. Knowles, who had an endless supply of smokes, passed around the tobacco. The smell of hard cigarettes mixed well with the hard men and their conversation.

"Those were good times," said Sergeant Rouzic, a small Frenchman with cold eyes and mousey good looks. "Pierrot treated us all well."

"Germans have no gangsters," said Knowles. "Perhaps I can be the first when I return."

"In peace there is only one excitement," said Rouzic, winking.

Bix had heard of Rouzic. Rumors, legends, any tale of heroism quickly circulated through the valley. In France, Rouzic drove the get-away car for Pierrot-le-Fou, an infamous post war gangster. Rouzic related many of his exciting escapes. When the police moved too close to his employer, Rouzic made good his freedom by enlisting in the Army.

"Keep a tight hold on your position," said Knowles to him, as Rouzic left to return to 2nd company. "A good man," said Knowles to Bix. "We would do well to find him if things get tough."

"Don't you mean when things get tough?" said Bix. "It will be dark soon and then we won't get away."

Bix felt fat and comfortable and ready for a nap. The other soldiers drifted off to their positions. Maybe Bix had given the Viets too much credit. Only an occasional round landed near Gabrielle. The attack on Beatrice had sapped their strength and they also needed a rest.

"These are good men," said Bix, to Knowles, no longer angry with him for keeping them on the position.

"Of course," said Knowles. "Only age slows us down." A tingle of sadness dripped from his voice like a man commenting on an old girlfriend's recent wedding.

"You're not so old," said Bix, trying to cheer him. "Just be cool, that's what we say in the States."

"Most of the German legionnaires are old," said Knowles. "We've come from an-other time and keep hanging on, refusing to admit when it's over."

"You're the strongest soldiers here," said Bix "Experience counts for something."

"Age changes men," said Knowles. "Already there is talk of de Castries burrowed deep in his bunker unwilling to come out. Such deplorable behavior does not happen to a young man. It isn't good for morale. Soldiers expect the best from their officers. Langlais, now there is a good one, a soldier to the end."

"I'm glad I'm with you," said Bix. The comment was unexpected and a little flush of embarrassment colored him.

In a trench below them, several soldiers had started a card game. Coins flashed on top a crate and the chatter grew louder.

"There's always talk about officers when situations turn to hell," said Knowles. "Besides, Langlais commands all the paratroops and he's never let down his men. And le BEP's Major Guiraud is just as tough."

"Maybe we should leave," said Bix. He stared at the sky.

"Yes," said Knowles.

"In a minute," said Bix, changing his mind. He saw that Knowles needed the rest. "Let's have another smoke. Maybe I can pay someone to shoot at you to liven you up."

"I'm fine, little Pumpkin," said Knowles, his voice more cheerful. "Look, you've placed your weapon in the dirt and have mud jammed in the front sight. Making a soldier of you is proving difficult."

"Hopeless," said Bix. He thought of bringing up the dope again. Money could not cure old age but it could make it bearable. Any mention of the dope would throw Knowles back in an unpredictable mood. Maybe the church, or some charity could use the proceeds from any sales. He thought how swell it would feel if he did something really good with the money.

The incoming barrage whistled in too quietly to awaken Bix from his philanthropic dreaming until the first round blew him off the box. His dreams tumbled into smoke, his canteen cup flipped in the air, coffee rained everywhere, and immersion heaters from the mess rolled down the hill like runaway tin tires. The fight was on! Bix toppled hard on his face, reached for his weapon, looked for Knowles. The canteen cup lay beside the carbine, a large hole, jagged, sharp edged, blown through its side, coffee dripping from the opening. The entire strongpoint had erupted in a volcanic explosion of enemy shells. Dirt covered his back.

"1800 hours," Knowles yelled through the noise. "The little Yellow Bastards are right on time."

"Damn you, Knowles; damn you," said Bix.

Knowles crawled to his side and placed his arm across Bix's back. A cigarette still hung from between his lips. His teeth, when he grinned, looked more yellow than ever. The mortar rounds came from Ban Na Ten, a short distance away. Bix wondered what had happened to Piroth's artillery. Piroth made too many promises. Much of the success of the camp was based on his predictions. The Algerian and legionnaire mortar crews on Gabrielle started to return mortar fire. Knowles pointed to a series of slit trenches to the south. He jerked Bix to his feet and together they dashed for protection.

The trench was thin, just enough room for them to squeeze in. Bix, panting hard, dug his shoulder against the dirt. Waiting was the worst part of any battle and, at the moment, there was nothing else to do. The artillery would soften things up, break down morale, cause soldiers to lay low. The shock waves would follow, row after row of infantrymen. The very ground on which Bix depended for stability shuddered so violently he could not scramble to his knees. Chunks of hot iron from the bursting shells cut the air above his head leaving trails of thin smoke. Knowles handed him a twig and pointed to the sights on his carbine. Mud had caked them over. Bix felt light-headed. He cleaned away the mud from his carbine, drew back the bolt and checked the barrel. The Viet Minh preferred a good pounding before an attack. Their commander, General Giap, was quick to learn from previous mistakes when he did not use enough artillery. Knowles was all smiles and a little mud hung from his lip that he attempted to wipe away with his tongue.

"You got your wish," said Bix.

"We're in the thick of it now," said Knowles. "The best place to be. Now is the time to feel alive."

"Prick. You're never content?" said Bix.

"Anticipation is murder," said Knowles. "All stress flies away in battle, the world becomes calm, the head clear. Equivocation refuses to exist during a fight."

"My nerves have had it," Bix admitted. Knowles was right. The world always fell into line when situations became intense. "We could be dancing at the bordello right now."

"Women are better after a fight!" said Knowles.

Bix ventured a look over the trench. Soldiers were so tightly packed on the hill that every round caused damage. None of the bunkers or dugouts was designed to sustain a prolonged artillery attack.

"We're in deep this time," he said.

Mounds of dirt spit from the earth. A foot, torn at the ankle, flew from a trench. Someone screamed, a high-pitched wail like that of a skinned cat.

"These will become the best times of your life," said Knowles. From inside his tunic he pulled a long loaf of French bread. "Once you've been a warrior, nothing else will do."

Knowles twisted off a piece of the bread and threw it to Bix. Like cigarettes, Knowles seemed to have an endless supply of bread. The bread fell on his lap. Bix had no appetite, was still full from dinner. Sometimes it seemed that war was nothing except bread and cigarettes. He picked at the flaking crust. Knowles had grown ravenous and shoved great heaps of bread into his mouth.

"When will they attack?" said Bix.

"General Giap is a crafty one," said Knowles. "He will have learned from Na San where the little bastards kept attacking, to no avail. He will be more cautious this time and wait until we have suffered a good pounding."

"Some history professor," said Bix. They all knew of General Giap's previous profession in academia. Bix picked at the inside of the bread making a small tunnel. Giap was no soldier at all. Any history teacher Bix could think of had been a bore: mousey little males who did not date, or was the basketball coach. They usually had thin, monotone, sleepy-time voices and read a great deal from the textbook. Sleeping in their class was accepted, almost encouraged, and if they did not coach basketball, they coached football and coached it badly.

"He doesn't make the same mistakes twice," said Knowles. "The French have years of military training at the best institutions. He has the ability to think."

"Why the hell aren't we winning?" said Bix. He yelled his question above the noise.

"Because we know too much," said Knowles. "The French do not easily change their minds. Winning the last war always puts the military at a disadvantage. Because tactics worked then, they try and use them now. The loser changes his tactics. The only way to win the next war is to lose the last one."

"We can beat them," said Bix, trying to convince himself. "It's a matter of will."

Watching Beatrice being torn apart was not confidence building. Lachen had informed him of the intelligence reports. They estimated the Communists had fifty thousand combat troops on the surrounding hills and over two hundred artillery pieces, maybe more. Some said closer to 300. The French had only sixty big guns that were being rapidly destroyed. Bix would not have believed the reports if he were not sitting on the hill under the full weight of the Viet Minh guns.

In an hour, the Viets opened up with more batteries of 105's. Algerians and French worked their way back and forth through the trench. Knowles and Bix moved farther south and crowded into a small dugout. Many rounds fell around them but most of the pounding hit the north slope of Gabrielle where 4th Company was trying to survive. The attack would come there where they were weakest. The 5th Parachute Battalion guns, from Strongpoint Elaine, joined in the fight against the Viet Minh.

The noise was making Bix deaf. He tried to think of the rocking earth as a cradle putting him to sleep. He had not thought of God since being in the valley and he did not think of him now. God was a comforting illusion for children wishing to know who made the stars and where Uncle Elmo went after he died. Men needed no explanations. Bix knew where soldiers went when they died. A piece of one flew past as he sat there.

Wounded soldiers filed through the trench past the dugout. Bix and Knowles had been lucky, not a scratch. A soldier fell at the opening of the dugout. Knowles was quick to drag him in. His name was Fleury and he had made his way from 4th Company. Things were bad there. Fleury bled badly from a chest wound. Knowles tried to reattach the dressing that had worked itself loose. Pink bubbles of blood foamed from the wound with each breath - a ruptured lung. Ordinarily such wounds offered little blood. He would not last, yet Fleury felt the need to convey information as if it were a grand secret, something he could offer in payment for Knowles' help. Knowles gave him water; Bix handed him the crust of bread he still carried.

Fleury said the north front was weakening. The Viet Minh had destroyed the heavy weapons bunkers of 4th Company and the 4th's commander, Lieutenant Moreau, had been killed, the command post destroyed. Communications were spotty and leadership, almost ruined.

Fleury asked for a cigarette. Knowles fished through his tunic. He lit the cigarette and drew several breaths to keep the cigarette burning before placing it between Fleury's lips. Fleury captured a long draft of air. By the light of a westering sun Bix watched the smoke rise from the hole in Fleury's chest, smolder like a low fog through the dressing on Fleury's chest and disappear toward the beams overhead. Fleury did not exhale and, when Knowles removed the cigarette, Bix realized Fleury was dead. Smoke continued to rise through the wound.

Knowles finished the butt, each puff lighting his face the color of dull red neon, a face tired, deeply creased.

The 5th Foreign Legion Regiment operated the 120mm mortars on the rise above. They made an inviting target and were soon under heavy fire.

When Knowles placed Fleury's body outside, rolled him over the trench, Bix thought of Rouzic. He should have taken his chances with Pierrot-le-Fou and the French police. The Viets were more determined. There was little to do now and Bix closed his eyes and attempted to sleep through the barrage battering the position. As long as they did not sustain a direct hit, they were fine. He covered his ears, wished he were home again, held back the empty feelings of mistake, regret - of remembering. One tear trickled down his nose and he was asleep and dreaming of charging a Viet Minh trench.

Knowles, who never appeared to sleep, waked him at midnight. Blue white light from flares, dropped from an overhead C-47, flickered into the dugout.

"We're on for an attack," said Knowles. He bobbed his head in and out of the dugout several times.

"Let the Algerians do their own fighting," said Bix. "I'm tired."

He wanted a convenient war, one fought during regular daylight hours. The Algerians claimed to be the equals of any legionnaire, let them prove it. But Knowles was ready to fight and Bix could not deny him at least one good battle. While Bix oriented himself, Knowles danced around like a puppy waiting for a treat.

Bix felt like someone had sat on his head. He tried to shake off the weight. Light from the flares burned his eyes and he crawled tenderly into the open slit trench and looked around. The shelling continued to eat the earth. The Viet Minh must have lobbed in hundreds of rounds, maybe thousands. Harsh light from the flares, unnatural, colorless and bright, covered the position and beyond. Tossed and tangled barbed wire glinted against the night. A brocade of bodies and torn earth piled everywhere. Red yellow tracers stitched down the position. Shells flickered against the dark, bright bursts, sudden light like a broken electric transformer. With each blaze of light, heat ruptured the air, tore across the trench.

Dirt flew against his forehead and Bix tasted the sweat dribbling from between his lips, bitter and salty. He crouched low in the trench. His body was soaked. In the light he saw the 120mm mortar positions of the Legion. Completely destroyed. Legionnaires hung from barbed wire like old laundry or lay crumpled like bags of garbage piled on the opened earth. The hill looked worse than Beatrice. A dark Algerian worked his way down the trench.

"4th Company is surrounded and needs rescuing," he said. His face ran with sweat. "We're getting the word out through runners. Communications have been destroyed and we can find no officers alive." He dropped to one knee and ducked at the sound of an incoming round. His dark eyes shone brightly through the dirt on his face.

"We need directions to get there," said Knowles. "We're with le BEP." He pulled the Algerian's head close when he spoke.

"Most of the commanders are finished," said the Algerian. "Our last communications with the Center of Resistance were to hold out. Langlais is sending help. Sergeant Rouzic is leading the rescue of 4th company with a platoon from 2nd Company. Sergeant Major Lebut is taking one from the 416th."

Bix smiled when he learned that Rouzic was still alive.

"Our old friend," said Knowles. "He could have lived comfortably in prison instead of being a hero. There is more to a man than what the law says."

"Everyone knows what a scoundrel Rouzic is," said the Algerian. Dirt flew across the trench. "No braver nor better man ever lived."

"We feared they would break through the north," said Knowles. "That's where it seemed the weakest."

"A rough go there," said the Algerian. "They outnumber us at least eight to one, maybe more, and have infiltrated 4th Company enough to cut them off leaving them disorganized. We start in twenty minutes." The Algerian gave a quick nod and disappeared into the next trench.

The small unit Knowles and Bix joined trudged through the rubble toward the crest of the hill. The going was extremely slow. Destruction lay everywhere and, because there was little solid ground left, walking became as difficult as trying to move through sand. Bix stumbled and fell across the fortress top. Although one side of the hill to the other was only a short distance, they rested frequently, mud clogging their boots and weighing them down. Shells and bullets continued to eat up the ground and they found what cover was available, a berm here, a pile of concrete there, some fallen trees that had been cut but not yet used.

The unit worked to a small crest on the north slope. Below lay a Sargasso of destruction. A sea of Viet Minh and Algerians engaged in hand-to-hand fighting. Under the flickering light of flares, rifle barrels glowed like sticks of burning wood. Men piled upon men. Rouzic, standing and motioning with his arm, urged the unit on.

Knowles fired the first shot. In one quick motion, throwing the MAS from waist to shoulder, dropping to one knee, taking careful aim, he pulled the trigger sending a coffin round square into the forehead of a Viet Minh. Even in the artificial light his marksmanship remained remarkable. The rest of the unit joined in the fight drawing attention to their arrival.

A bullet kicked dirt into Bix's eyes. "Just bad luck," he thought. But he knew he was in trouble when another round landed near. Soldiers blocked out war and fear by concentrating on their work. He hoped they were stray shots but feared a Viet had him in his sights. If he did, he would follow him, until reaching the target, to the exclusion of all other targets. Bix had to get him first but his eye watered from the dirt. He rubbed his eye, realized it was a mistake, then pulled at the eyelid like a window drape.

Another shot winged past. Bix rolled to the side. Damn! They were not stray shots. The Viet had a bead on him. His heart pounded. He rolled into a depression and held his eye apart, let the tears wash the lens clean. The Viet would never give up until he was dead. Bix's stomach started to cramp. His ears closed until the racket of war became a muffle of underwater sounds. Rouzic was a blur as he again motioned them forward. To stand now was certain death. Getting to his feet Bix lunged ahead, tripped on the body of a dead Algerian, and tumbled forward as a round splintered the butt of his carbine. Another flare twinkled over the landscape. A Viet, flinging his weapon to the side, dropped. Sergeant Rouzic pointed to the Viet. Bix realized he was safe. Rouzic had killed his would-be assassin.

Knowles had disappeared. Protecting Bix was his job and Bix felt betrayed and embarrassed. Bix finally saw him ahead removing the ears of a Viet. A tug, two quick slices with his bayonet, and they came away. A new collection? Bix yelled to him and he placed the bloody ears, like antlers, on his head and rocked from side to side with his tongue out. This was no time for games and, when Bix reached him, he slapped him on the head. Knowles tossed the ears to the ground and they continued down the hill and nestled behind a bank.

"A sense of humor is a good thing," said Knowles.

"They're everywhere," said Bix. The Viets did not charge in a human wave but moved in groups and pockets.

"They fight like tigers," said Knowles. He breathed hard, his shoulders rising and lowering like the pump of a bellows. "Colonel Piroth has finally blasted their approaches with artillery - about time, too. How else are they getting through?" The ground below Gabrielle was ripped apart, covered with Viet Minh bodies.

"Knowles," said Bix. He did not finish. He wanted to confess his momentary fear, to admit that inside his fighting body lay a boy who wanted to return home, that he once felt no fear but something, he did not know what, had changed.

"The little bastards have a reason to fight," said Knowles. "When the will gives way, so does the ground."

"What about us?" said Bix. "What's our reason?"

"The joy of it all," said Knowles. "Any cause we carry is imagined. We fight for the adventure, the excitement; we fight for the Legion."

Bix checked his ammunition, tried to think why he was fighting, why he had joined the Legion. He had no causes. Thoughts about fighting communism were ridiculous. The French had invaded Vietnam a long time ago, put her under French rule. That much he learned from some cynical Algerians who said the French did the same to them. The Viets wanted their country returned and they were determined to get it. It was too much to think about. Besides, the Legion was his country and that was all he needed to know. He didn't even know what a Communist was.

"Our mortars should have devastated them," said Bix.

"The tubes are destroyed, blown to crap," said Knowles. "Have you forgotten?"

On Beatrice, the Communists stormed the hills in mass. They were more cautious here and infiltrated in smaller groups. Even so the ground was layered with their dead. The unit with Rouzic moved forward again. The farther ahead they pushed the deeper the dead became until they had no choice but to walk on them.

Flares scratched the landscape like a drawing in pen and ink: stark, basic, colorless. The little Thai soldiers from the 416 all deserted to the nearby hills. They faded away when things got tough. After what they had gone through, Bix could not blame them. They were tired of war, of killing, and wanted to be home with their families. They had agreed to defend their mountains, not this.

Finally, with determination and angry fighting, the French joined the surviving Algerians of 4th Company. They had not lost their spirit and remained tough and determined to continue fighting. Third Platoon was breached and Rouzic ordered the men to take up positions to fill the gap as the fighting slacked.

Ammunition started to run low. Two boxes sat at Bix's feet; both for the M-1 Grand. The rounds would not fit his carbine or Knowles' MAS. Everyone was having the same problem, too many different weapons needing different rounds. Bix checked his pouch. Only three full clips remained, 60 rounds.

"I'm running low," he said to Knowles, pointing at his weapon. The Viet Minh bullet had splintered the carbine stock and the rough wood scraped against his cheek leaving red scratches along his face. Knowles surveyed the trench and behind, up the hill.

"I've plenty," he said. Knowles remained conservative with his ammunition. He fired rounds slowly, carefully, as if still using a bolt action Mauser. "Let me look…"

"This hill must be littered with carbine rounds," said Bix.

Bix scampered down the trench picking over the dead. Most of the Viets used Russian and Chinese weapons so he concentrated on the dead French forces. The flares came in spurts, the landscape turning from light to dark. Each time a new flare ignited, he caught glimpses of Viet Minh ducking low, motionless, waiting.

A moment of light revealed the edge of an ammo box. The box lay half buried in the clay, a torn body close beside, a severed arm clutching the box handle. He hoped the box was packed with .30 caliber carbine rounds. A flare, its tail dying slowly, gently flickered out. In the dark, he dashed to the box and placed the carbine against the corpse. The severed arm, the hand, the fingers, gripped the rope handle. The heat was unbearable and sweat dripped on the hand as he pulled the wrist, prying the fingers loose.

Overhead another flare, like a struck match, fizzled to life and cast light on a Viet standing threateningly over Bix. He was a child, a small boy, with wet fear in his eyes. His helmet was too large for his head, tipped at an angle over his face.

Smooth, unwrinkled, colorless, his face was like molded cheese. Bix clutched the severed arm by the wrist like a baseball bat. The boy's mouth dropped and he fumbled with the bolt on his weapon and tried to swing the barrel toward Bix. Bix sprang like a back alley thug banging the boy's head with the severed arm. The blow knocked him to the side and Bix pummeled him twice more until the weapon fell, barrel first, and, dazed, the boy tumbled over backwards. The boy squirmed as Bix jumped to his chest. Then he stopped, lay motionless. In the light of the flare dancing in his eyes, he looked about to cry. He was pretty, like a girl, lost and alone and for a moment. Bix imagined himself holding his hand, helping him find his way back home. The thought caused Bix confusion and embarrassment and he stopped.

The rapture was brief. The boy had worked a bayonet from his boot.

Instinctively Bix blocked most of the blow. Only the very tip penetrated his tunic. Bix clutched the arm with both hands, then, holding the wrist with just one hand, he smashed the boy square in the nose with the other. Blood and snot gushed out and the boy gnashed his teeth together, pinched his eyes and became a rabid snarling dog. Bix hit him again, wrenched the knife free and plunged it into the boy's chest. The knife entered at an angle deflected by a rib that Bix felt scrape along the blade. Bix leaned back, watched the boy breathe through the opening, blood foaming through the wound. The boy's eyes opened, surprised. Suddenly Bix hated him. He was not a lost boy but, because he was making Bix kill him, an ugly, cruel and sadistic creature.

Bix's shoulders heaved. An erection throbbed between his legs. He had heard the stories of the battlefield harlot, an invisible beauty calling for death, and from death, re-birth. Bix plunged the knife in again and again, the blade sucking through the flesh. Ribs cracked. Blood gushed. The boy moaned and convulsed. His neck twisted as his legs quivered erratically. His head flopped like a landed fish shitting guts from its mouth. Bix beat the boy out of shame at his own pleasure, and for truth and loyalty and because he despised himself for detesting the boy. Blood plunged into the air in a grand symphony of crimson. Bix wanted out, out of the mess, the killing. He wanted home and quiet and Nicole and solitude.

In exhaustion he rolled to the side, his pants filled with ejaculate, overcome with the joyous shame and confusion of the killing. He placed his hand on the boy's chest below the neck. The endless shells, shaking earth, rumbled through. Bix leaned on his elbow and looked into the boy's eyes. Whatever made up the boy, was not there. Only emptiness remained. The flare burnt out. Bix kissed the boy gently on the lips.

From the trench, Sergeant Rouzic yelled for more ammunition. Bix jerked away from the dead Viet Minh boy, aware again of the situation. Rouzic's voice slapped him from a deep dream of confusion and back to the battle. M-1 rounds filled the ammo box, nothing he could use. Bix dragged them to Rouzic who carried a MAT sub-machine gun. Two Algerians carried M-1s and quickly gathered the box. Knowles, his pockets bulging with French rounds, had found a bottle of cognac. He shared the bottle with those nearby. Clearly, everyone enjoyed the respite except the Viets.

Colonel Piroth continued to pound the Viets with his 105's and 155's. The Communist dead continued to pile up and many of their comrades used the bodies for protection. Twice the thin French line engaged in hand-to-hand fighting, their number slowly diminishing. With his ammunition depleted, Rouzic tossed away his weapon and looted an SKS from one of the Viets who had died in the trench.

When all looked bleak, when Bix contemplated surrender, when even Knowles looked beaten, the Viet Minh guns stopped completely; the surge of flesh, soldier upon soldier, stopped. The field became void of any living enemy. Colonel Piroth's guns also ceased. The silence caught everyone by surprise.

"What is it?" said Bix, his mouth dry, half open.

"Another trick," said Knowles. He shrugged his shoulders. "Don't be taken in."

"They must be out of ammunition."

Rouzic was not easily fooled either and he gathered the men together and formed a stronger defense line placing machine guns in three positions and sending several men to scrounge more ammunition. This time Knowles went and took two others with him. They crawled over the dead Viet Minh that covered the hill.

Bix crawled from the trench to a shell crater, scratched the hole deeper in the loose dirt, and relieved himself cleaning up with a scrap of tunic torn from a dead soldier.

Crawling back to the trench, Bix thought of Knowles. His war was with the Communists. He felt that if Germany had been left alone, no one would be fighting Communists now. Bix imagined him almost freezing in Russia, going snow blind, how bodies did not stink on the Eastern Front in winter. War was different there yet the same.

Bix waited in the trench for the sun. The Viet Minh were demons but usually crawled back into their holes at the sight of light. Where was Knowles? Bix wore him like a coat of armor and felt naked without him.

0330 hours. Hell returned. The earth cracked apart with hundreds of artillery rounds. Intense. Determined. The Viet Minh swarmed through their own artillery fire, tan uniforms everywhere, the hill seething with enemy, alive like maggots on dead meat.

Knowles, delivered like a letter by the barrage, hopped into the hole, breathless, covered with wet clay, sweat, dirt. Wide and thin his nostrils flared like a winded horse, chest heaving, a neck of veins throbbing. He lay with his legs sloped up the wall of the trench. A shell landed ten feet to the front and scattered dirt covered them both. A direct hit was the only way to score any damage as long as they remained protected. The noise, the shaking earth, played on everyone's nerves. The French could not keep their heads down forever without the Viets overrunning them.

Knowles had found very little ammunition, two clips for Bix, three for him, several '06 rounds. What he brought back was another M-1 Grand, a sniper rifle with a sniper scope. Knowles laid a cloth over the barrel of his MAS and leaned it against the trench. The other men had found a box of MAS 36 ammunition and a box of grenades.

"A marvelous toy," said Knowles, pointing to the rifle. He cradled the weapon on the edge of the trench. The Viets were so close, Bix could have hit them with stones. He watched Knowles lift the barrel of the sniper rifle for a long shot, ease back on the trigger, smile when, several seconds later, the round hit.

"What the hell are you doing?" said Bix. He quickly fired at a Viet about to jump into the trench. The Viet toppled over backwards, his gun discharging in the air.

Knowles pouted as if Bix had reprehended him for playing with a favorite toy. He liked a challenge.

"Shoots well," he said. "There is no challenge in shooting them up close."

"Why worry about your hand when your throat is being cut? You can club them to death from here," said Bix. Knowles annoyed him, made him anxious. Knowles enjoyed games. Bix liked watching the sun rise, creatures stirred to life from the light, the blanket of red across a sky when morning rose. He waited for it now. Night also fascinated him, the sky blossomed with stars, air heavy with dark, but it was morning he wanted now. He wanted out. Bix wanted to live.

Knowles grabbed the barrel of the Garand and tossed it over the trench. "My God," Bix thought, "he was going to pout, to sit in the hole and pout!"

"OK," said Knowles. "Just this once." He started to fire the MAS, carefully like a skilled craftsman driving nails.

Rouzic, realizing the position was hopeless, rallied the remaining men. Soon they were fighting to the north, the west, and the east. The Viets broke through behind them and charged over the ridge. Surrounded, Bix fired in two directions, and Knowles fired in the other two. Then came the surprise. Artillery from Colonel Piroth started to fall on them, all over the strongpoint. Their last working radio took a direct hit and died. There was no way to contact Piroth, to redirect the fire. They danced in a fire of French and Viet Minh rounds. Bix thought the strongpoint had been deserted, that they were the last holdouts. Too much small arms fire sounded for that to be true. Piroth's artillery continued to fall short. The situation seemed overwhelming and Bix, almost ready to toss his hands into the air to surrender, tried to stand. His hands simply would not rise. The French artillery fire was murderous. Instead of running, Bix squirmed even deeper in the trench. Between explosions he jumped up and fired quick bursts at anything that moved. As the sun started to rise, he again ran short of ammunition.

0600 hours. The Viets broke through pushing the French toward the crest of Gabrielle. Reluctantly, stubbornly, they fought to hold every inch. From the northwest the Viet Minh rolled over 4th Company as Rouzic's unit tried to help them hold the heights. One by one the Viets destroyed the French machine guns. Still Bix fought, the fear now gone, only adrenaline and the feeling of invincibility remaining. He was in the groove, the beat of war where the world came into focus and made perfect sense. The Viets breached the hill, mauled them, shoved the French down the hill on the northeast side, down toward 1st Company. There seemed no escape, no hope. They fell back, kept going, saved what was left. Like dead men, fear had vanished. There is nothing to fear about the inevitable. They fought well, recklessly, determinedly, slaughtered Viets by the hundreds, who fought equally well, if not more viciously.

Another hour passed. The Viets outflanked them again leaving them cut off. Rouzic gathered the unit together for another withdrawal, a chance to push through a small opening. Second Company, to the south, might still be fighting, might still be intact. Only seven of Rouzic's men remained. Dead Communists carpeted the ground. There were just too many of them. When the unit moved south they were quickly ambushed. They tried southeast, farther down Gabrielle. No good and again they were blocked.

Knowles offered his plan. They would again cross the crest of the hill, traveling southwest, turn south on the other side, and approach 2nd Company from the west. Rouzic disagreed with the idea but did not hold them back. He understood the tight situation, mustered a handshake and said "Au revoir." The rest of them would try south again.

With just the two of them, Knowles and Bix, the going was easier. They moved slowly, carefully, sometimes in spurts, bobbing then crawling. Bix picked through the bodies like a corpse rat to uncover more ammunition. Knowles also resupplied. They zipped here and there, jumped to a trench, rested a moment in a bunker, lay in a shell hole where Bix rocked from side to side like the pendulum of a clock. Time became forever.

Five minutes? An hour? What did time matter? It took as long as it took to reach the southern crest of Gabrielle. They remained on the crest long enough to catch their breath. The sky was thick with clouds. Rain fell. The sky cleared. The sky clouded. Rain fell again and the sky cleared. No supplies would drop today. And where was the counterattack Bix had heard about all night? He had fought hard holding waiting for it. Sometimes the military pulled such tricks, got hopes up so men would fight on when they had no intentions of sending help.

The battle was turning into a strange one. Where, especially, were the Commanders? There was not even a general in the Center of Resistance, not one anywhere in the valley. Rank had given way to experience and to personalities. Men followed whomever they thought knew best. Units fought, not as a whole with other units, but for themselves. The Legion fought for the Legion. Other troops went their own way.

Bix and Knowles started down the hill. Movement ahead. Knowles stopped, motionless like a squirrel on a limb when he's been spotted. He started to raise his hands. Finally, Bix thought, the battle is over, the rest of our days spent behind bamboo bars. Knowles yelped at someone up ahead.

"You dirty bastards," he said. "We've come for a new supply of condoms." He laughed with relief, something Bix had never heard from him before.

Knowles had great eyes. There, crouched low behind mounds of dirt, were the remnants of the Heavy Mortar Company legionnaires.

"We've been screwing Communists all night," Knowles continued, speaking German, "and we need more protection."

The hill resembled a giant sore, pocked, split, oozing chunks of flesh. A huge stink covered everything. Heat brought flesh to rot quickly.

Two legionnaires, Pusch and Zimmermann, welcomed them to their hole and offered them a smoke. The action had again momentarily slacked. The mortars were all knocked out and they had armed themselves with automatic weapons.

"It's good to get away from the other side of the hill," said Knowles. "Our own artillery has been killing us."

"You expected perfection?" said Zimmermann.

"Is it finished there?" said Pusch. He and Zimmermann, both good-natured soldiers, looked hard toward the other hill. Humor always rose during desperate situations. Mud, and burnt powder from the mortar rounds covered Pusch's face. His tunic was tied around his waist.

"The little yellow bastards covered over us like a blanket," said Knowles. "The bastards don't know when they've had enough."

"We've got plenty of extra rounds," said Zimmermann. He noticed Bix's empty pouches. "We spent the night with the mortars, mostly trying to pound them back in shape after being dented from exploding shells. They came straight for us with their guns. It's those damn hills." Zimmermann indicated the enemy hills towering over them. "They see everything we do, every movement we make. Can't take a piss without them knowing."" He brushed dirt from a heavy plank revealing different boxes of ammunition buried beneath. Bix stuffed clips in every available place.

"There's no challenge to the killing," said Knowles. "Point in any direction and shoot. No skill involved. Anyone could do it, even an American."

Knowles was still annoyed about the sniper rifle. Bix felt the barbs on his voice.

Only Knowles could have gotten them across the crest of Gabrielle. Out of gratitude, Bix remained silent.

"I like the long shots," he said. "Pick off their buttons at a thousand yards."

"Those days are finished," said Zimmermann. He held up his grease gun. "The idea today is to spray the air with bullets and hope someone runs into them."

"A waste of rounds," said Knowles. "A poor country like France can't throw her money away. Why do you think the Viets use so many bolt-action rifles? To make every shot count." Knowles was leaning forward, sounding very serious.

"So long as the Americans are paying the bill," Pusch said, "what does it matter how many rounds the French shoot up?"

Knowles looked around the hole as if he were about to reveal a grand secret.

"No country helps another without wanting a say in her life," he said. "The more the help, the bigger the say."

"Then, of course, we're safe," said Zimmermann. His eyes almost twinkled. "France never listens to anyone."

Bix kept watch, wondering when the Viet Minh would again attack. Pusch gathered broken ammo boxes and started a small cooking fire for coffee. Bix enjoyed the intensity of a small battle but this fight had been over-done. His stomach churned as if being eaten by large white grubs. The fight was far from over and he watched the Viet Minh re-grouping all around them. Legionnaires always remained calm and he hoped they would not realize that, for a moment, he had become a coward.

"What news of a counterattack?" said Knowles. Bix turned as Pusch pointed to the next hole.

"Lieutenant Clergé is waiting it out in that pile of dirt that used to be a bunker," he said. "I think we have the only working radio and Clergé has been in contact with the Center of Resistance." Zimmermann bent low to blow on the fire. Knowles filled two canteen cups with water. The legionnaires were a regular supply depot. "Captain Hervouet and his squadron of Bisons are on their way. They are supporting the 5th Vietnamese Parachute Battalion and a company of your friends from le BEP."

"The 5th is a bad choice for a counterattack," Knowles interrupted. "They have only just arrived and don't understand the situation or the terrain."

Knowles always knew more than he said.

"Le BEP made it most of the way," said Pusch. "The 5th has been held up at the ford of Ban Ke' Phai, under heavy attack. Of course, le BEP has returned to rescue them so they can turn around and rescue us."

The Viet Minh on the hill moved closer and the remaining legionnaires of the Heavy Mortars started to return fire. Zimmermann and Pusch leaned against the hole. Knowles finished his coffee. Lieutenant Clergé called to Zimmermann and several others. A few minutes later, Zimmermann returned with the bad news.

"The rescue attempt has been called off," said Zimmermann. "The Lieutenant is disappointed but there are just too many Viets and not enough men for the counter-attack. We'll have to fight down the strongpoint to 2nd Co. then work our way south to the rescue force."

"Wait," said Knowles. "One drink before we go." They raised the canteen cups. The coffee had hardly dissolved, the water only luke warm, but it tasted great. Bix and Knowles shared a cup and Zimmermann and Pusch shared a cup. Then it was back to work.

Lieutenant Clergé emerged from his bunker and attempted to lead them down the hill. The Viets had the escape blocked. By the sounds of gunfire, there remained other pockets of French soldiers. They were again surrounded. Zimmermann and Pusch had carried a box of grenades with them. They crouched low, opened the lid, shoved grenades in their belts, hung them from their pockets, cradled them in their arms. Knowles understood and jerked his thumb in the air for good luck.

Like two crazy wild laughing beasts, Zimmermann and Pusch forged ahead, danc-ing, throwing grenades as if tossing flowers. The clownish heroism caught the Viets by surprise and, like Moses parting the Red Sea, a gap opened in the lines. With Lieu-tenant Clergé in the lead, they all funneled through.

When they stopped to regroup on the other side, only fifteen soldiers remained. Lieutenant Clergé was determined to get them through. He was a fine, handsome, young man and did well by his men. One man carried the radio close to him. The Viet Minh, thinking the French troops were already defeated, stormed them in assault waves. The scene reminded Bix of stories he read as a kid of Confederate soldiers charging during the Civil War, or of the Banzai attacks of the Japanese. They were soon surrounded again.

The radio hissed on weakly but Lieutenant Clergé got through and called in more fire support. The Viets rushed like mad men. The legionnaires fought steadily, pro-duction line killing, unemotional, another day's work. Lieutenant Clergé wanted even more artillery support. He tried the radio again but the batteries had gone dead.

Between assault waves, Knowles looked to the valley with binoculars he had found nearby. "Look," he said, and pointed toward the fog. Bix saw the tiny figures, the Bisons and legionnaires of the rescue force moving toward the foot of Gabrielle. "We have only to hold out a little longer. They have come after all."

"You two come with me," said Lieutenant Clergé, indicating Knowles and Bix. "We need batteries for the radio. There's a set at the old position."

He ordered the rest of the men to hold as best they could indicating that he would return soon. Bix was not anxious to leave the safety of the others. He found comfort in the ditch and safety with the men.

"What's the difference if we die at one position or another?" said Knowles.

"The radio will help," said Bix, trying to convince himself of the batteries' impor-tance. And he did convince himself. The radio meant contact with the rest of the world and proved he was still alive. With the radio came life.

Because the Viets had concentrated on the other legionnaires, crawling to the old position was not difficult. Bix worked his way through the mud. Knowles stopped him, pointed back down the hill. A huge wave of Viet Minh engulfed the legionnaires, swarmed over them like a wriggling blanket. From the human mass, Zimmermann, Pusch, and an Algerian, rose from the dead, grenades again flinging from their arms, automatic weapons full ablaze. They built a bridge of dead Viets and traversed the shell craters and barbed wire by jumping on the bodies. "What luck!" Bix thought. They disappeared over the bank. It was good to be blessed in battle and Bix was quite certain they had been very evil men because God did not want them. He vowed to be more of a rake in the future.

At the destroyed bunker, Lieutenant Clergé dug through the dirt and found the radio batteries. He scraped away the mud. As they crawled to a new position, Lieutenant Clergé installed the batteries. Bix shoved a sandbag in front of him and pointed his carbine toward the Viets. Knowles helped Lieutenant Clergé with the radio then moved beside Bix. The Viets had spotted them. Bix rolled his eyes, felt almost euphoric. Nothing mattered anymore. He had burned up his allotment of terror and for the first time since the siege on Gabrielle started, he was truly not afraid.

Before Lieutenant Clergé could radio a message, a shell landed at his feet blowing him over. He was shaken, covered in dirt, but unharmed. The radio however, was destroyed. All that work for nothing and now they were completely cut off.

Artillery rounds severed the earth. The Communists massed for a huge charge. There were not enough bullets in all of French Indochina to destroy them and Bix was beside himself with laughter. The whole thing appeared terribly ridiculous, Bix - killing people he rather liked - them - a human wall wanting a dirty piece of hill - him - trying to protect the hole in which he crouched - them - wanting a position from which they could watch the French wipe their ass - the French - determined to remain in a valley, a country, where everyone hated them, trying to teach people French who wanted to speak Vietnamese, teaching them French history, French culture, French cuisine. Vietnamese were not French, would never be French.

The arrogance of the situation put Bix in stitches. The French demanded that the world operate by their standards, follow their economics, their political system. By helping them, Bix was a Frenchman too. France was a shambles, economically and politically. The politicians made laws favoring themselves, were untrustworthy, took graft whenever possible, spent money on military arms and not culture, built enemies and not friends. Bix wanted to be back in America where things ran smoothly.

Bix continued to laugh. The mass of human flesh surrounding him was hideous and hilarious. He was a cartoon character banging himself over the head with a club. They could not hurt him. If he lost an arm, it would return in the next scene; if his head was crushed he had only to hold his nose and blow it back up. He released his weapon, wiggled his tongue, gave the Bronx cheer, and stuck his thumbs in his ears and waved with his middle fingers. He stood up and started to twirl.

Three artillery rounds landed directly before him. Knowles, acting quickly, jumped up. The shells stunned the Viets, blew a hole through the barbed wire. Knowles snatched Bix's carbine, grabbed his tunic by the shoulder, hauled him through the passageway of Viets and wire. Lieutenant Clergé followed and turned down a side trench. Bix and Knowles stumbled into a deep trench, crawled a hundred yards, tumbled over an embankment, and rolled right into the perimeter of the 2nd Company remains. Second Company had just completed their retreat. As easily as jumping up, Knowles had saved Bix's life. He jabbed Bix in the stomach with the carbine. Bix's senses returned. His neck was sore and chafed, blood ran from his nose, and his hands shook violently.

With the remnants of 2nd Company, they fought to the foot of Gabrielle and into the lines of the rescue force. Because the enemy fire had stalled the rescue force, the outcome did not seem exceptionally bright. Full daylight lighted the area making the retreat hell. A Bison flamed. Medics patched the arm of Captain Lulu Martin of le BEP. It was then that Bix realized Knowles and he were not even scratched.

Martin was a good commander. Bad leaders did not last in the Legion. He made a joke when Bix and Knowles reported, said he had come all this way just to get the two of them off the strongpoint. He seldom lost his sense of humor although he looked concerned about the present situation. He had kept his legionnaires tight behind the Bisons and crossed the ford to the foot of Gabrielle. The 5th Vietnamese Parachute Battalion, under Major Botella, had frozen. Major Seguin-Pazzis, who had taken command of the paratroopers now that Colonel Langlais commanded the Central Sector, ran the rescue operation. He dodged about rallying the men, refused to let them linger. Getting surrounded in the open would mean disaster.

The artillery was called in to dislodge the Viets from around the ford. The Viets appeared impervious to heavy fire. Nothing worked on them. A sea of clouds hung overhead indicating no air support. Captain Hervouet issued orders to hook to the damaged Bison. Men latched a heavy chain to the tank. Twice bullets zipped off the Bison's side almost wounding Bix. Finally under way, the ragged force fought their way back to camp. The lead tank revved its engine and its tracks clawed the earth leaving a trail of perfect, rectangular, bricks.

The force rescued very few men. Not even Majors Kah and de Mecquenem had escaped. Sadly, Bix learned that Kah had his leg blown off and the fate of de Mecquenem was unknown although they suspected he had been captured.

Arriving at the ford, Captain Martin found the rest of the rescuers still pinned down. The little Vietnamese paratroopers shook with fear. The Viets loyal to France always appeared to fight poorly while the Viet Minh fought with determination.

Martin crossed the ford and rallied the little yellow paratroopers. Between explosions they were dragged and kicked. Bix prodded a small group of them awake telling them they would be killed if they did not move. In an instant they were up and running only to be hit by a 155 round that landed among them. Although rummy from lack of sleep, he felt some responsibility for them. He found one of the paratroopers riddled with splinters. The paratrooper looked through him toward the clouds. Below the elbow, his arm was almost blown away and hung by hinges of flesh. There was little time to tend wounds but Bix managed to wrap the arm in a tourniquet using cloth and a stick. He pulled the man's wrist and with his bayonet finished the amputation tossing the arm into the brush. After throwing the soldier over his shoulder, they were off.

Bix's back was wet with sweat and blood. He plodded ahead, half asleep, eyes cracked slightly. Shells burst all around, their whining pop orchestrating the screams from the wounded. Bix became a musical note waltzing through a symphony of death. He swayed with the rhythm of killing, the timpani of muffled shells, the shrill staccato of machine guns accented with the offbeat pop of small arms fire. In the end, he knew, they would all fade out.

By 0900 the unit staggered into the strongpoints of Ann-Marie and Huguette that crossed north of the airfield. Bix's little yellow paratrooper still breathed and he dumped him on one of the waiting stretchers. "Au revoir," he said. There was little chance he would survive unless he could be airlifted out. Bix flopped beside the stretcher, leaned back, breathing hard. Gabrielle burned in the distance.

Knowles poured water on Bix's head.

"You fought well, Pumpkin. We have survived."

Bix grinned, then fell asleep.

Chapter 33

"It must be the slopes! The yellow bastards refuse to counterattack!" Colonel Langlais never hid his emotions just let them run over anyone near. "They've got no guts." Colonel de Castries had placed him in charge of the entire central sector hours after the death of Colonel Gaucher. Gaucher had not been able to get a clear handle of the situation on Beatrice and now there was the added problem with Gabrielle. Communications had almost been severed.

The commander of Beatrice, Pegot, had been killed just the night before. Gaucher called for an immediate meeting in his office to find a replacement. Major Vadot, Major Martinelli, and the aides, Lieutenants Bailly and Brettevilly, all attempted to crowd into the small office. To allow them to fit, Vadot crawled onto Gaucher's bunk. The earth continued to shake and dirt fell from the ceiling. A shell vaulted down the airshaft and exploded into red-hot bits of steel when it hit a roof pillar. The concussion alone almost knocked out Vadot, his world becoming white, red, then black and dark. Only the bunk saved him. Unable to hear and covered with cuts, he worked his way to his feet and checked on his fellow officers. The smoke and dust still swirled in the sudden calmness as if in reverence to the incident. Vadot felt his way around until he found someone's head and attempted to lift it. The head was unattached. Both the aides had been killed instantly; Martinelli was bleeding badly, seriously wounded. Vadot felt better after seeing Gaucher's head move indicating he was still alive. He crowded in closer, for the blast had shrunk the office with supporting logs and dirt rather than expand it, ready to administer aid when he realized it was too late. The first thing he noticed was Gaucher's crushed and twisted legs followed by the ripped open chest. Both his arms were torn off, yet, miraculously, he remained awake. The ubiquitous Father Trinquand soon arrived as Vadot and the medics tended to Gaucher.

"I am here, my son," he said, placing a hand on his bloody shoulder. "You'll be in the hospital in no time," he tried to assure him but Gaucher had been a soldier too long and knew there was no hope. He looked at Vadot, then into Father Trinquand's eyes.

"Please wipe my face," he said. Trinquand wet a cloth and cleaned his face. "I would also like one final drink." He died before the ambulance jeep reached the hospital.

The death of Gaucher was not the only problem for the central command. Unlike Vadot, who immediately returned to his command, the constant shelling drove Colonel Keller, de Castries chief-of-staff officer, into madness. His nervous breakdown was complete and he mumbled and drooled while sitting on the dirt floor.

Langlais spent the night watching Beatrice succumb to the jaws of the Viet Minh and trying to decide if he should launch a counterattack with the 8th shock and le BEP. He decided against it, but now he needed seasoned soldiers for a counterattack on Gabrielle, not inexperienced slopes, but real soldiers. He had no other choice. Only the

Vietnamese Fifth Bawuan, under Captain Botella, tired and disoriented after their arrival hours earlier, was available in any numbers.

"You must find someone else, for the counterattack," said Major Hubert Seguin-Pazzis. "It is not my sector." The official commander of the northern sector, including Beatrice and Gabrielle, was now Colonel Trancart. He was the most familiar with the ground but Langlais, confused about the chain of command, had not contacted him and placed Major Seguin-Pazzis in command over Colonel Trancart. He then called Maurice Guiraud, commander of le BEP.

"Guiraud – Langlais here. Report to Seguin-Pazzis for instructions on the counter-attack on Gabrielle. Alert your two best companies, from le BEP, for the attack. Yes, yes," he appeared agitated and chewed on a cigarette as he talked. "No, just the two companies We might need the others should the bastards hit us in another place. I want you to move immediately before the sun starts to rise. That gives you about an hour to work out the details with Seguin-Pazzis. The Batwan will join you as soon as possible."

He slammed down the receiver. An aide handed him another cup of coffee. "They are not reliable," said the aide, meaning the French Vietnamese.

"No, of course not," said Colonel Langlais. "I have no choice. They will have to do." He paced back and forth, nervous energy eating him up. He was an aggressive com-mander and after any attack he always ordered a counterattack. All the commanders agreed he was the right man for the job. Colonel de Castries seemed unable to make any decisions. "Contact Botella and get them moving."

"Botella's 5th BPVV dropped into the valley less than 14 hours ago," said Seguin-Pazzis, when he entered the command post. "They lugged all their equipment, in the rain, several miles to Elaine 4 then spent hours digging in only to attempt some sleep while under constant shellfire. Now you want them roused, loaded with their equipment, sent across the entire camp, and expect them to fight when they get to Gabrielle?"

"If I tell you to move, " shouted Langlais, "I expect you to move, not to question my orders."

Seguin-Pazzis notified Botella then returned to working out his plan. At the age of 40 he was fearless and thorough and not nearly as reckless as some of the more passionate officers. He accepted no surprises as he worked on the operations orders. He expected complete loyalty from his men and it often seemed to them that he was the most intelligent officer in the valley. Tall, lanky, handsome, a cavalryman of great pride, he always contemplated any situation through a cloud of smoke from his pipe. Working on the orders was proving difficult because the company officers scattered across Gabrielle - Gendre, Antoine Botella and Clerget, were giving him contradictory information. Artillery destroyed most of the radios on the strongpoint and, of those remaining, damage caused them to work poorly or sporadically. Farther communication possibilities were growing thin with each minute. The various companies were not in contact with one another and each one appeared to be fighting a separate war rather than as a concerted effort. The most consistent reports said the Viet Minh had blocked the rescue route so the best he could do was to coordinate an attack to clear them away before moving on to Gabrielle. Botella's unit was not the correct one. Even when rested they did not fight well. Le BEP and the 8th assault were the counterattack units.

Langlais walked to Colonel de Castries C.P.. De Castries was having breakfast. He sat at a single table spread with a white linen tablecloth. The silver lay on napkins and an orderly placed a cheese omelet before him, perfectly cooked to retain its fluff and moistness, and a hot cup of thick coffee. Langlais could not believe either his audacity or his calmness. He knew de Castries to be a good and efficient officer and, try as he did, he could not dislike him. Aristocracy, sophistication and wealth glowed from de Castries. He always remained fearless under fire. Yet, he had not left the safety of his dugout for over a week and there was every indication that he had no intention of stepping outside until the battle was won.

"I have placed Seguin-Pazzis in charge of the Beatrice mission," said Langlais. "Guiraud has already left with two companies of le BEP."

"Coffee, Colonel?" said de Castries.

"There is much to do before sunlight. Have you radioed for more reinforcements?"

"Yes, yes. Your old friend Bruno and his boys," said de Castries. "Although, for the Americans, the cavalry always arrives at the last minute, it is seldom true for the French. Sometimes it is best to sit and think rather than to get overly excited." He placed a small bite of omelet into his mouth followed by a sip of coffee.

356

"Seguin-Pazzis expects to receive orders from you before he gets to Gabrielle," said Langalis. His small frame tensed and he could feel his fists tightening. "You really must start to make some decisions, Colonel. We were at a loss waiting for your orders at Beatrice. Counterattack? Yes or No? We can't afford such indecisions in the future." Langlais tried to remain calm and still make his point.

"Placing you in charge of the northern section was the right choice," said de Castries. "You are a fighter and this battle requires fighters. I am a man of movement. I need room to maneuver - tanks and artillery. I attempted to refuse this assignment for that reason but I had no choice. Now, we must make the best of the situation."

Langlais saluted and returned to his C.P. but not before stepping outside and watching the artillery flashes landing against many of the outposts. Apparently the Viet Minh were massing near Ann-Marie and Dominique. It wasn't that he did not want to use all his paratroops and assault troops against Beatrice but that he might need them to shore up another position. Perhaps Giap was attempting to fein rather than to attack the other positions but there was no way to tell. He did not want to squander his best troops, especially his beloved paratroops. They were the pride of the military world, the best of the best. Paratroops perfectly understood what it meant to die but he was in no hurry to kill them needlessly. It was like owning a racecar and preferring to look at it rather than to drive it for fear it might get dented or wear down too quickly and replacement parts could prove difficult. His best troops were needed for the big race. The two companies of le BEP he sent with Guiraud seemed about right. Rather than just fighting, their courage might provide inspiration for Botella's Vietnamese; show them the kind of guts required for this fight.

Artillery commander Colonel Piroth met him underground. Piroth was depressed and had wandered from one gun position to the next. A kind man, he offered reassuring words to his gunners. But was he able to stop the Viet Minh guns as he had promised.

"What is it this time?" growled Langlais.

"I just wanted to apologize for the inefficiency," he said. "I take the blame for the fiasco, for all of it, full responsibility." He did not lift his head and looked at the floor. Tears rolled down his cheeks.

"Don't apologize to me; apologize to the dead legionnaires on Beatrice, and now Gabrielle," said Colonel Langlais. "You shot off your mouth; you said the Viets would not get more than one round off before your "glorious" gunners destroyed them. How many have you silenced? Not one! Get out of my sight. Go and try to stop at least one gun! You haven't lost an arm, you've lost your guts."

Piroth held the empty sleeve of his missing arm as tears continued to trickle down his cheeks. He left for his C.P. on the other side of the river. As often happened with Langlais, he realized that he had gone too far. Piroth was suffering a deep depression. He simply could not find a single Viet Minh gun although he had all his best men working on it. Langlais sent for Father Trinquand.

"Keep an eye on Piroth," he said. "I haven't time to baby-sit. Give him whatever comfort you can. I was harsh with him but I have no time to apologize. He will understand it was just an outburst due to my frustration and I do not hold him responsible for the situation. He is a good soldier. I will talk to him later."

Guiraud gathered his troops and moved down the side of the runway. The trail was tricky, filled with twisted barbed wire and torn equipment, but he had traveled down it many times, as had most of his troops. Artillery rounds continued to fall near the runway and the soldiers made haste to reach the ford across a stream near Ban Khe Phai. Guiraud stopped his legionnaires near a small floating bridge. They immediately formed a defensive line.

"We must wait," he said, to Lieutenant Glass, who stood dripping wet, rivulets of water running off the brow of his bush hat, his nose, and his chin. "Hervouet should be here soon with his tanks."

"I'll take a patrol across the stream to see what's ahead," said Glass. "Anything is better than drowning here."

"Be careful." Guiraud felt the ground start to twitch. The first hint of morning gray started to push over the black on the horizon. "Send Captain Tospa here before you go."

The tanks slowly emerged from the dark. An artillery round landed near the lead machine sending mud and shrapnel sparks off the side. The tank stopped suddenly, rocking on its tracks, beside Guiraud. Captain Hervouet, his dark eyes covered with youth, peered from behind his glasses, earphones strapped over the beret covering his light-colored hair, emerged from the hatch with the constant smile he never realized he sported.

"You'll break another arm," Guiraud shouted at him.

Hervouet raised both arms to show he had no casts. Another six tanks spaced themselves back and to the sides of Hervouet. Gunfire sounded toward Ban Khe Phai as Captain Tospa joined them with a radio and a corporal.

"What do you make of it?" shouted Hervouet.

"That crafty old school teacher Giap has blocked the way to Beatrice," said Guiraud. "I've sent out a unit to determine the strength." He turned to Tospa. "What news on the radio?"

"It's spotty," he said, wiping a trickle of blood on his forearm caused by scraping a broken branch. "We're in that dead zone time." For a period each day the atmospheric conditions interfered with all radio communications. "What I gather is that our two companies are not enough to secure the strongpoint. I think we are supposed to wait for Botella's outfit but we are still trying to confirm. First they said proceed, then they said stop, then they said nothing."

Guiraud crossed his arms and held his chin with one hand. If he had to wait he wanted to do it on the other side of the ford.

"Let me know when you find out more," he said to Captain Tospa. "What do you make of it from up there?"

Hervouet drew out his binoculars and scanned the area ahead. He saw rifle flashes in the distance but they quickly diminished.

"It's still too dim to see. I think your patrol is returning. There seems to be mostly rice paddies on the other side of the stream all the way up to Gabrielle. Plenty of artillery flashes on the strongpoint."

"I'll have some coffee sent over while we wait for Lieutenant Glass," said Guiraud. "He won't be long."

The coffee had just reached Hervouet and his men when Glass, covered with mud, reported. In excellent physical shape, he still panted.

"The Viet Minh are strongly dug in at Ban Khe Phai," he said. "Nothing we can't handle, probably a battalion, but it will still be a fight." An orderly handed him a hot cup of coffee. He waved it away. "The Bisons (tanks) will be a help."

"Oui. Tell Hervouet to cut us a path in ten minutes. I'll get things moving here. Any casualties?"

"Only Dinkens, a superficial round through his ass. The harassment he is getting hurts more than the wound."

Guiraud instructed the unit officers to prepare to pull out. He felt the tingle, the adrenaline rush of a fight, flow through his body, electrify his mind bringing it to a point of incredible sharpness and clarity. Because of his junkie's rush of action he was a soldier and constantly in anxious wait for the next fix. He saw a jeep drawing close. It stopped beside him and Major Seguin-Pazzis, tall and lanky, a pipe almost grown from his lips, jumped out, his eyes taking in the scenario before him as if it were his duty, his obligation, to paint every detail into his mind: the tall brush beside the muddy gray stream, the floating footbridge, the soldiers just starting to move into position to advance squashing out their cigarettes and taking a last sip of water so as to not die thirsty. The length of his stride, farther and quicker than the stride of most soldiers, caused his aides to shuffle.

"What is the situation?" he said, offering his hand to Guiraud, standing and eager to see him. The orderly handed him the coffee Lieutenant Glass had refused.

"They're entrenched in the village, Hubert," said Guiraud. "We're going across in a few minutes to secure the other side."

"That's good. Botella is coming with his unit and I am afraid they are too worn out and too new to help. They would never be able to fight their way across unless you had already done so."

"I suppose it's the best we are going to get."

"Major!" Captain Tospa shouted to Seguin-Pazzis. He held up the receiver of the radio. Seguin-Pazzis took the phone and listened to a static voice creeping over the airwaves with barely the energy to vibrate the internal wire. "Say again," he said, and then, "Say again." The soldiers were just about to move when he told Guiraud, "We are to reinforce Gabrielle."

"I thought they said, no?"

"So now it's yes." He shrugged his shoulders.

Artillery shells started falling all around the French soldiers. The tanks chewed up the mud in the stream as the water attempted to wash them off. The tracks slid up the bank causing the tanks to slip from side to side looking for firm ground before sloshing through the mud churning under the still raining sky. Legion paratroopers are fearless and these, especially so. This group consisted of a large number of German soldiers, many from the S.S. who joined the Legion to avoid persecution by the allies for atrocities that most of them, especially the Waffen S.S. soldiers, had not committed except through association. Sharp sunken faces distinguished them, sun driven through their barbed wire bodies, bodies ten years older than most other legionnaires, soldiers who did not fear death. They almost welcomed death by the Viet Minh, preferable to one by Russians.

The legionnaires fell in behind the tanks for protection, occasionally plunging to the ground to fire toward the enemy then resurrecting themselves to catch the cover of the tanks. Lieutenant Boisbouvier, of 4th Company, led the way. Filled with confidence and conviction, he moved with determination, his men following. Not to be outdone, Lieutenant Bertrand pushed his platoon forward followed by Lieutenant Martin's 3rd Company. Lieutenant Domingo shouted encouragement to his 4th Company. He stood clearly in the open, a smile on his face, mud covering his boots and pants, his arm pointing toward the village. He spun to the side and dropped to his knees, shot through the leg. Angry and cussing he stood up and dropped his pants to his ankles as the medical officer, Lieutenant Rondy, dressed the wound. As soon as Rondy finished Domingo hobbled back to the head of his company and, standing in the open, continued to push them ahead.

Most of the artillery rounds exploded harmlessly in the rice paddies, smothered with water and mud. Unfortunately for Sergeant Chief Guntz, who guided his tank from the opening of the turret, a shell landed close enough to kill him instantly and damage his tank, Smolensk. The Viet Minh fought with determination but the legionnaires broke through into the village and scattered them. Seguin-Pazzis received a new radio message from the Center of Resistance. The rescue unit was ordered to stop, not refortify the strongpoint but to wait and pick up survivors. The order seemed puzzling to both Seguin-Pazzis and to Guiraud who felt they could hold the hill if only they were allowed to get there. The perimeter of Gabrielle's strongpoint sat just 600 yards away. Seguin-Pazzis could not get verification on the message. Now, as artillery rounds fell, they waited for Botella and any additional orders. New orders arrived. The C.P. stated that Seguin-Pazzis could either reinforce Gabrielle or retreat with the survivors. Again he looked to Guiraud.

"Impossible," he said, frustrated. "Three different sets of orders for one mission and all within an hour. Now we can attack and move onto the hill or wait and pick up survivors, it's our choice."

"Such orders are the sign of a good officer," said Guiraud, smiling, because the mission had become absurd, and resting his hand on Seguin-Pazzis' shoulder he said, "They take no responsibility because they have left the decision to you. And you cannot be blamed for anything because you have been given permission to do as you please."

"Then let's take the strongpoint."

Orders were given to move out. About 200 yards from the hill, retreating Algerians met them. Guiraud called a group of them over.

"Sergeant," he said. "Why are you retreating? Is Gabrielle lost?" Seguin-Pazzis stepped over to listen.

"Orders, sir," he said. There was no fear in his eyes, just disappointment.

"Orders; what orders?"

"We were told to hold the positions until you arrived for support. Later, we were told to retreat. You were coming to take us from the hill and cover our retreat."

"Who gave the orders?"

"The radios were working badly but Captain Gendre managed to intercept the orders coming to you. He said you were coming to support the retreat. He tried to get confirmation but could not get through."

"Was the position impossible to hold? Could you have held on?" said Seguin-Pazzis.

"Possibly," said the sergeant. "We were not beaten and were surprised they were pulling us off. With reinforcements we could have held."

Seguin-Pazzis ordered the paratroops forward to save the position, but they did not get far before another 200 Algerians and several officers staggered off the hill. Through his binoculars, Guiraud saw Viet Minh swarming over the position. Gabrielle was lost.

Nothing had gone right for Botella and his Vietnamese. His troops were groggy, soaking wet, sleep weary, slow to react. They had started out about forty-five minutes before sunrise but had made little progress. Since they had not been in the valley, they were to receive guides to lead them through the rubble and around the runway, but they never showed so they stumbled around in the dark, bursts of light exploding into the night, until they found the runway. The fire was so intense that they crawled into the drainage ditch beside the field dug by the Japanese in the last war. Officers and NCOs constantly chided the hesitant soldiers as if herding reluctant donkeys to the slaughterhouse. The race across the fields and through the protection of Anne-Marie moved as slowly. Outdistancing the remaining unit, Captain Gaven's 3rd Company, parts of 2nd and Headquarters Company, finally reached the legionnaires. The small bundles of muddy men breathed heavily, rain dripping over their helmets, their only discernable features being huge grins glowing like billboards advertising espret-de-core. They were paratroopers and proud of it. They crouched with the legionnaires and waited.

After starting to move, a soldier from 2nd Company froze at the crossing. His fear raced down the line and everyone halted. The remaining unit reached the stream as more rifle fire from the Viet Minh, who had moved positions, ripped through the brush. The Vietnamese soldiers refused to cross the water. Before he could get them moving, Botella saw tanks, loaded with Algerian wounded, moving south toward the Center of Resistance. The fight was over and he had missed it all.

Chapter 34

Block by block a wariness had built around Chau and, as it rose, left no windows, no cracks, no way for air to seep in, no circulation. The enormity of the operation, the tons of munitions, the thousands of deaths, was more than he could comprehend. The sacrifices of blocks held him tightly. No amount of screaming would release him, no banging, no clawing of fingernails to pinhole the smallest opening of air. All of the fallen young men, all of their families, wailing at their loss, were too great a price to pay for any country. What happened to people sitting down over tea to discuss their differences and find a solution? Silly. A damn lie! No such time ever existed. The preoccupation of man has always been war. Talk, if any, had usually led to war and what had war ever accomplished? Nothing. There had always been a Vietnam and there would always be a Vietnam regardless of who occupied the country. It was the same everywhere. Germany was always Germany; France, France; Ireland, Ireland; Spain, Spain. A nation resided inside a people, not outside. Governments were a superficial wound. Man had not advanced since his arrival. He still clubbed his meat to death and cheered at dangerous sports urging teams to kill one another. Sit together and work out solutions to problems; use the money saved on war for peace?

Chau fell asleep after the battle of Beatrice on a toppled layer of elephant grass knowing that Gabrielle was next. He thought of Au and the baby. A child and her care was special. Perhaps they would have raised her in the village, taught her the basics of community life, the importance of respect for her elders, the satisfaction of work. The idea of a further education, even university, was more difficult to contemplate. Communists remained skeptical of a liberal education. A technical education was acceptable, but sniffing around in literature, philosophy, and religion, served no purpose except for the potential of revolt. Even some of the religions, the Taoists especially, frowned upon a formal education feeling it removed people from the natural state with nature. What good was an education except to cause misery? The more one knew the more miserable he became. In Chau's travels he had often heard the saying "Ignorance is bliss." It seemed a true statement. The less one knew the happier he was unless he realized he knew nothing, then he was equally as miserable as the educated. Who cares how many angles can sit on the head of a pin? Who cares if there are any angels or gods or even reality? If you think it is there then it is. Even though he could not justify it, he could not dismiss the idea or value of a university education. Such thoughts might present problems if the Communists prevailed. Ho Chi Minh and Giap were both very educated men as were many of the people in their organization. Perhaps they would retain the idea of an education. They had sent teachers to villages to educate people in reading.

Could he be happy for the remainder of his life in a small village? Perhaps. With Au and the baby it seemed like a wonderful vacation at a quiet mountain spa. Would he have eventually become restless? Obviously the teachings of Quan had not stuck with him, not in a practical way. Understanding the teachings and doing them were difficult. Perhaps he had been too long in the cities, had traveled too much, met too many different people. Contemplating himself and existence for his remaining years seemed unlikely. Were the modern world and the ancient one even compatible? "The misery of modern life can become a habit and preferable to simple pleasure," he thought. But all that was in the past, another life. A memory is not real.

Chau awoke in a puddle of drool that dribbled from his mouth and onto the hat lying under his head on the grass. He was alone. The drool soaked his palm as he wiped it from his lips. Every joint in his body ached, felt swollen and fused together. He had difficulty focusing his eyes and twice he coughed phlegm from his throat and spit globs of green mucus onto the ground. Rain had soaked his clothes. Water saturated French skin leaving them sick. Vietnamese were waterproof, the water running off unnoticed. Even their clothes dried faster than the garments of the French.

Soldiers moved rapidly through the brush. Occasional shells still thudded on the valley floor and small arms fire plodded through the air in the distance. Beatrice had been a great battle, a great and terriblevictory. Rows upon rows of attacking Viet Men were cut to shreds and piled deeply on top one another. Such losses could not be sustained for long nor would the men tolerate it in every battle. Frontal assaults seemed poor tactics against a modern army yet it often appeared the only strategy ever used by Giap. The men would soon be discouraged, might even refuse to fight. Right now they floated between the doorway of elation, having won a great victory, and despondency over so many losses. Chau offered encouragement to the passing bo doi who smiled or looked dewildered. He saw Lieutenant Luat squatting beside the trail drinking tea with Kuim.

"I see we're still at it," said Chau, looking toward Gabrielle. Luat poured him a cup of tea. The heat warmed his hands and throat. Kuim stood and bowed. "Not necessary," said Chau. "We work together in my unit."

"I work to keep the Captain happy," said Luat. "You work to keep me happy." Chau was not interested in his humor at the moment. "The Generals are transferring troops to Gabrielle, not many but some." Luat handed Chau his binoculars.

Chau stood and swept the valley toward Gabrielle. Three Russian trucks and a squad of men traveled at the far end toward Gabrielle. French artillery opened up on them. The accurate fire destroyed them in minutes leaving a jumble of iron, and tires spewing fire and black smoke into the air.

"You fed and housed us on our journey to find the village of Khe Hieu?" Chau said to Kuim. "I remember the kindness of you and your family. Why have you decided to join the Communist movement?" Kuim held his head low as if afraid to talk. "Talk, I am part of no organization."

"The Viet Minh came into our village," he said softly. "They lined up all the people and asked for volunteers to save Vietnam from the foreign invaders. No one stepped forward. They asked again saying people must fight for their land and for freedom. Hinh, the blacksmith, said, 'we are all working here. No one can be spared.' A soldier raised his rifle and shot him. He fell forward onto the dirt. The blood ran from under his chest and puddled into a pool at his side." His voice quivered. He sipped his tea. "Some soldiers grabbed several of us and laughed as they said 'We knew there would be volunteers.' They said that Uncle Ho wished to thank us for our sacrifices. They took our rice and we left for training in China to become soldiers. They guarded us like prisoners for days until they thought we could be trusted. Then, they tried to become our friends. All day long they schooled us on the Communist way of government and why we must fight for our country. At night I remembered my wife crying as we left." He began to cry, quietly, the tears dribbling down his cheeks.

"You will see her soon enough," said Luat. "This battle will eliminate the French and you can return home a free man, hero, able to hold your head high. Chau will look after you as he looks after everyone. He knows everything about the French because he is French, just looks Vietnamese. They will fight to the last man because they cannot believe they are losing. Their lack of respect will finish them off. And after them? Who would be stupid enough as to invade us again?"

"Your backbone has been weakened by your loss of family and village," said Chau. "You must strengthen before you return home. You are safe with us, but remember your sorrow is in the past. Think not of a former life and you will start to heal, will learn to walk again. There is only today, only this minute. You fought in the most dangerous attack ever staged by us and you survived. Living or dying is not in your hands. Do not be miserable. Live pleasantly each day and you will eventually find yourself at home and ready for the biggest fight of your life – growing old." Chau was pleased with the wise advice he gave and at how impassive and impressive he sounded.

Kuim tried to clear his head. He had felt like a coward since he was taken from the village. The Viet Minh would have killed him had he not come. He wanted to live for his wife, for his family. The Viet Minh had abducted more than his body; they had removed part of his soul, a piece of what made him Kuim. He showed he was no coward during the attack. He remained at the front lines as men fell around him. The brutality had mesmerized him and he showed no fear just a quiet curiosity that rooted him to the trench floor. Combat sent electricity through him yet, when it finished, he had no juice left, not a single spark. The thrill was replaced with tears. Resisting the Communists would have been foolish.

"We will go to Doc lap but not participate in the battle," said Chau. "I must see how the soldiers feel, if their energy continues. The General will rest after this, give the men a chance to relax and savor their victory, time to re-supply. After this fight against Doc lap – the French call it Gabrielle - you may visit your village. Luat will fill out the papers. After three days home you must return and fret no more, knowing that you are in good hands. The Lieutenant will travel with me to check the supply lines and the attitude of the workers." Kuim's tears started to dry and he raised his head and smiled. "Luat," said Chau, "if you wish to visit a village for several days, let me know. I can go alone."

"No one will have me," he said. "You are my only family."

"You are a poor man, indeed."

"I think not," said Luat. "You have never asked to borrow money."

"It is foolish to ask for what does not exist," said Chau. "Perhaps we can find you some gentle company along the way, someone fat enough to keep you warm at night, and provide shade for you during the day."

"I would be content with a thin women to warm my feet."

They moved across the valley at the northern end of Doc lap beside other troops massing for the attack. The strongpoint made the same mistakes as all the others. The Moroccans shaved the hill clean of any vegetation so all positions were easily spotted. Bunkers and dugouts became easy targets. Their openings were cleanly brushed smooth and several of them had log walkways framed with wood. The trenches were not dug deep enough to protect a standing man and few of them were connected so the French soldiers had to traverse long open spaces to communicate with one another and to relocate. Even the barbed wire was sparse for a defense of so many soldiers. They did not take the time to build the strongpoint properly. There seemed no excuse for such a mistake. The French, of all the armies in the world, should have known how to prepare proper trenches for defense. They were experts in the First World War and certainly must have documented the techniques.

An occasional artillery round kicked up dirt yet most of the Algerian soldiers still sat on the rims of the trenches or continued to string barbed wire. More artillery than that used on Ban Him Lam would pound the hill before the attack. The Viet Minh sappers had dug more trenches closer to the positions.

Like finding a choice location for a fireworks show, the men seated themselves on a small outlay of rocks with a clear view of the valley. Kuim went for food as they waited. Luat started a small fire and boiled water for tea. Chau witnessed battle first hand at Ban Him Lam. He needed no more excitement at the moment and wondered at the bravery of the few bo doi who would join this battle just a day after the last one. The main attacking forces would be People's Army Regiments 86 and 102. Again, soldiers would die on both sides. Death leaves a hole the following morning that usually fills in by evening. Chau found it difficult to sit and tried to walk off his restlessness by talking to the troops as they passed. An aura of tenseness and assurance surrounded them. He noticed a soldier pulling a strange looking gun.

"What is this," he said, as the man approached. His friends started to laugh.

"My cannon," he said. He looked too thin and small for such a weapon. "I built it myself." Chau looked over the weapon carefully.

"Your cannon?" he said. "What is your name and what kind of beast is it?"

"I am Pham Van Tuy and this is my 75mm cannon. It works very well but I must be close to the target because it is not accurate at long distances."

"How close?"

"About three meters," laughed a soldier.

"Why build such a thing?" said Chau. "The Chinese and Russians give us plenty of guns."

"I built it before their help and have used it in many battles. My friends carry the ammunition and I work the cannon."

"It is a remarkable piece," said Chau. "You are an inspiration to the cause of freedom. Use it well tonight." Without thinking, Chau offered his hand.

Tuy held it softly not understanding that Europeans shook hands as a contest of strength, personality, and dominance. Chau was careful not to crush the hands of the gentler Vietnamese who used handshakes to indicate calm, tranquility, and peace.

Chau awoke later as if from a long dream, a world transparent, shimmering, the images elusive, sweet at one moment, bitter the next, where flowers grew from the clouds and rivers, like liquid glass, ran uphill to be eaten by the sun, only to open his eyes to the flashes of artillery. He rose onto one arm.

"Have I been sleeping long?" said Chau.

"All night and half the day," said Lieutenant Luat. "Such sleep is unhealthy. Sweat has covered your whole body and you have missed the battle."

Chau shook his head and watched the world rattle behind his eyes before coming into focus.

"Kuim?" he said.

"He went for water and never returned," said Luat, shrugging his shoulders. "I asked several soldiers passing this way but they knew nothing. I described him but all Vietnamese look the same to all other Vietnamese." He smiled and winked at Chau. "What can you say? He is a slight bony brown man with sunken cheeks, a bewildered frightened face, black hair and slanted eyes. That narrows it down to 50,000 soldiers in the valley. You don't suppose he returned home? Love of a family is a powerful thing."

Some soldiers were coming off the hills of Gabrielle, quietly stumbling along, uniforms torn or burnt or bloodstained, all bent under the weight of weapons and victory. In the distance Gabrielle smoked, as had Beatrice, and occasional weapons fire sounded as Viet Minh cleared out small pockets of Algerian soldiers.

"We'll get some food and make inquiries of the men, make ourselves useful," said Chau. "I imagine there will be some rest before any further attacks. No soldiers can keep up this pace. Then, we'll report to General Giap."

In spite of the victory, the soldiers were weary, beaten down, finally demoralized. Many claimed the losses they suffered were too great. The bolder ones said that they would refuse to participate in any further such attacks. All out frontal charges required no tactics and they felt that officers, even General Giap, could devise a safer and easier road to victory. Because the French were trapped, there was no hurry.

Chau inspected one of the many anti-aircraft crews surrounding the valley. Unlike the infantry, their spirits remained high and they were pleased, almost elated, grins stretched ear to ear and bubbly with boasting at their successes, something they had not suspected. Their surprise at accuracy was overwhelming. Every French pilot risked death any time he flew near the valley and every approach to the airstrip was like tossing a rock through a shower and hoping it would not get wet. Already, smoking aircraft littered the valley and surrounding hills.

Chau also visited several artillery emplacements dug deeply into the hillsides where the cannons were pushed into the open, fired, then shoved back into their protective cocoons.

"They look very secure," he said, to a captain.

"No French rounds have even come close," he said. "They cannot find us yet we see every movement they make and we make them suffer dearly."

"The men seem to be in good spirits." Chau watched the men grinning broadly and twitching nervously from leg to leg not quite trusting the reason for his visit.

"They live to fight," said the captain.

Chau and Luat checked out the cave, dug deeply and with a precision not needed in times of war. Three walls had been scraped smooth and sleeping areas notched into the dirt and lined with grass mats, an unneeded layer of thick logs propped against the ceiling for extra protection. Various tin pans were piled upside down near a cooking stove where tea leaves, a small bunch, green and limp, was boiling. Washed clothes hung on limbs outside to dry and two men were busy washing themselves from a bucket. As Chau inspected the emplacement a number of coolies arrived carrying ammunition and supplies, an equal number of women as men and carrying the same heavy and awkward loads: shells in wooden boxes or bundled together with rope, food and clothing, fuel for cooking. The only things not delivered were medical supplies, as scarce as surgeons – the Viet Minh had only one for the entire battle although they had several poorly-trained general practitioners.

Giap was as concerned about the food as he was about the ammunition. Supply crews consumed three bags of rice for every bag delivered. It took a tremendous number of coolies to keep a steady supply coming. He insisted on a single line of focus – everything for the front – no deviation. Everything on the last 50 miles of the supply route was hauled on foot or bicycle. Even the cannons, some intact and others dismantled and reassembled later, had been pulled up the mountains and placed in positions by sheer determination and manpower. Over 40% of his forces were now engaged in the battle compared to just 4% of the French. Much depended on this battle, perhaps the survival of the Vietnamese as a free and independent nation.

"You are doing a good job, comrades," he said. "Just a word of caution; the battle is a long way from being won. If the French find you, keep up your good spirits and do not get over confident. Arrogance is destroying them; we do not wish it to destroy you."

Chau decided to check on the main hospital as they moved deeper into the jungle, the trees and foliage smelling wet and musty.

"Your observations?" he said, to Luat.

"Let them have fun," he said. "It has been many years since they have had such pride." He pulled a twig from a tree and placed the end into his mouth.

"The infantry are not so happy," said Chau.

"Their victory has been very costly," said Luat. "General Giap will make adjustments; he always does. Being a teacher is natural for him."

"Meaning?"

"He is eager to learn. He analyzes each encounter, separates the good from the bad, what works and does not work, and always does it objectively. Such a quality is unusual in a leader. He seldom makes the same mistake twice."

Wounded soldiers lay about under makeshift shelters while the doctor worked inside a small cave. There were no shortages of nurses, petite and kind women comforting the men as best they could, a kind word to one, a drink of fresh water to another, cold towels across the foreheads of others, a little pho or tea, concern showing behind their smiling soothing eyes. Chau spoke to soldiers and nurses offering his own kind words and encouragement.

They continued toward Muong Phang, a small village surrounded by Thai stilt houses. General Giap had established his headquarters nearby in a cave. They managed to catch a ride on a Russian truck that skidded its way across the mud and dropped them near the village. People waited to load wounded soldiers onto the truck.

"Sometimes it seems they can do anything," said Chau, watching the villagers. Vietnamese still seemed like "they's" to him and not "we's," some kind of foreign people he still did not understand.

"We have been fighting forever," said Luat. "It has become a way of life."

"It's the lack of doubt that surprises me," said Chau. He scratched at his arm as they walked.

"Not arrogance?" said Luat.

"Something else I can't understand. Even if supplies are hauled 500 miles and canons dragged up mountains they never doubt themselves. No one says 'impossible, it can't be done.' No one says anything; they just do it."

"Perhaps we are stupid?" said Luat. "Not smart enough to understand the impossible."

They came to an encampment of soldiers, cooking fires rising into the mist, clothes being washed, weapons cleaned, card and dice games in progress. Before reaching headquarters Chau offered his credentials to a guard who escorted them the rest of the way. A woman soldier, tall and slender, attractive but not overly so, with long pretty fingers, seated them at a table built of bamboo and covered with a mat. She brought tea as they waited. When he entered, Giap looked tired but remained cheerful. He shook hands and hugged Chau.

"I am sorry for your recent loss," said Giap.

It surprised Chau that Giap knew of the deaths of his wife and daughter. The woman soldier stood near Giap.

"They live in my heart," said Chau.

"What news have you brought me?"

The woman poured tea for the general.

"The artillery are in high spirits," said Chau. "They believe they can beat anyone and their pride is showing."

"Of course," said Giap. "High spirits are easily maintained when one remains in a cave. Not so the infantry?"

Chau looked down at the table before continuing. Truth was difficult in any situation.

"They are happy at the victories but are discouraged," he said. "Many are losing confidence and some might refuse to fight. Impossible as it seems, some have even deserted to return home or to fight with the French."

Giap rubbed his chin.

"Blaming them is difficult," he said. "We cannot sustain the losses of continued frontal attacks. They were important to demoralize the French, to convince them they are not invincible. Our first objectives have been reached and now the enemy is afraid and confused. This morning I issued orders to start digging approach trenches. They will reach out like spider webs surrounding the positions and slowly the camp will die. When we attack we will already be upon them. Until then we will continue to drop shells constantly day and night to keep them rattled."

"Yes, the soldiers need a rest from battle," said Chau. "They will feel safe in the trenches."

"What of the positions near Ban…, the ones the French call Anne-Marie?" said Luat. He seldom spoke when Chau was talking with other officers. It was not his place to ask questions.

"A stroke of luck," said Giap, a broad smile coming across his face. "The position was manned with Thai troops. Thinking they would be attacked next they simply left their positions on Ann-Marie 1 and went home. We walked onto the hill. The French reinforced the other hill, Ann-Marie 2. We have decided not to attack at this point. Let them die of loneliness."

"Very satisfying," said Luat, a little embarrassed.

"I understand the Lieutenant is your only aide?" said Giap. "You need another. I am assigning Private Hong to you." He motioned the woman soldier forward. "She will attend to your needs."

"I am happy with the Lieutenant," said Chau. "There is no need for another aide. He is bothersome enough and treats me like a child."

"Nonsense," said Giap. "I must finish a speech for the troops. It's all settled. Hong will show you where to sleep tonight before you leave in the morning."

Chau said nothing as Hong led them to a tent in a small clearing. Luat walked beside her, his arms swaying easily at his sides, a smile on his face, lightness to his steps.

"It is very kind of you to help us," he said. He leaned over and spoke quietly. "The Captain will soften up. Many things are bothering him at the moment, much responsibility, much sadness. I am, however, already softened up."

"I am his aide; we are both his aides," she said. "You will have to find your own aide."

"To reach him it is sometimes best to go through me." He grinned again and his eyebrows, thin as they were, fanned his forehead like two ferns.

"As long as you do not have to go through me, everything should be fine," she said.

Already Luat liked her quick wit, her long body, her deep eyes like black river rocks.

The tent held two American cots with American wool blankets, a lantern, a table and two stools. A book from Balzac, in French, sat on a wooden box beside one bed along with an American military flashlight. Chau sat quickly like a period to Hong's sentence preventing her from lingering like so many modifiers, so many extra words helping to describe him. She stayed anyway straightening the cots, the blankets, then leaving briefly before returning with two bowls of steaming pho. While they ate, she spread a blanket on the ground for her.

"You're staying here?" said Luat, rather anxious.

"I am comrade Chau's aide. What good am I elsewhere?" She picked up the book, sat cross-legged on the blanket, and thumbed through the pages.

"You read French?" said Chau, the first time he had spoken to her. His voice was cold, sarcastic.

"Are you surprised?" she said, not looking up.

"I am surprised you can read at all." The words were hurtful and he felt ashamed and wanted to apologize but it was too soon to befriend another woman although he wanted her touch, her soft flesh against his as if she were his tiny Au, lovely and innocent.

"I have been to university," she said. "The General thought you might enjoy the company of someone intellectual." She glanced at Luat, a slight grin starting at the point of her chin, crawling to the corners of her lips, up past her cheeks, and into her eyes, where it split and glowed like two pinpoints of light.

Chau tossed through the night. He thought too much, worried too much. Too much of his previous French life lived within him, lingered like a sour stomach brought on by rich and delicious food that had decided to overstay its welcome. The smell of eggs and toast brought him into daylight.

"I thought you might enjoy a change from Pho," said Hong. She poured thick deep black coffee into a cup of condensed milk.

"I can always eat Pho," Chau said.

"You are not telling the truth," she said, avoiding his eyes. She placed a knife and fork beside the plate. "We cannot get along if you lie to me."

"Where is my brother, Luat?"

"He is collecting papers from the General's staff. You are to distribute the official speech to units upon your return."

A heavy mist crowded the outside of the tent as he ate. Any French flights for the day would be delayed because of visibility. Rain would probably follow the mist. The valley suffered more rain than in any other part of Vietnam. Chau almost felt sorry for the French for soon they would be rotting in the mud and water.

"I decided to do something useful," said Luat, as he entered and handed Chau a paper. Chau read the paper several times, several phrases sticking with him:

"The enemies' morale is affected, his difficulties are numerous, but do not underestimate him. If we underestimate him, we might lose the battle..." Giap later reinforced the statement. "The first difficulty comes because certain comrades, unaware of the actual situation and the forces involved, show subjectivity and underestimate our adversaries, from which comes a weakening of our combat organization that can easily lead to defeat."

Overconfidence, primarily a European illness, was an affliction generally not suffered by the Viet Minh. The general insisted it not affect his army. Chau wondered what messages of encouragement from French officers were being read to the soldiers?

Chapter 35

Bix leaned against a pile of musty sandbags. After fighting through the roadblocks and making it to Anne-Marie, soldiers loaded into trucks for the return to the main camp. Exhaustion, relief, the sweet pleasure of his own personal world, were the same feelings as on the farm. But in combat all emotions peaked. He had survived the attack on Gabrielle. He felt great, felt relieved and ecstatic about being alive, would fight again knowing the feeling would re-appear and that he was a soldier the equal of any soldier and, once again, he did not fear death.

Knowles rested his arm around Bix's shoulder. His face drooped in tired heaviness, scruffy after just one night and in need of a shave. His crisp clean uniform was a mess. Bix and Knowles waited to load onto the last truck. The earth felt like home and they were reluctant to climb into the truck to leave it too soon. The other trucks pulled away. The Vietnamese of the 5th held their heads low, ashamed to mingle with the European paratroopers because they had not fought with determination, had not fought at all.

Two soldiers, paratroopers from the rescue team, perched in the truck opposite Bix as he and Knowles climbed in. They asked about the battle; one, a Pole from the 1st Battalion 2nd Foreign Legion Regiment; the other, a French sergeant from the 3rd Thai Battalion. Both were in excellent physical shape. Bix sometimes felt like the only soldier in the camp who had not lost a thin layer of baby fat during training.

"They kept coming?" asked the Pole. He pulled at his chin and scratched a long scar, traveling from wrist to elbow. The scar resembled a diseased twig.

"Communists have no sense," said Knowles. "They don't know when they are beaten." His voice sounded like concrete. "They're like an endless supply of easy women; before you know it, they are all over you."

The Frenchman offered them dried meat and coffee. Knowles never liked French civilians. They were a dirty lot, gros pore, like pigs. France blew their stench into the Fatherland. Germany continued to invade them simply to clean house, to give them a bath. Only French soldiers were spared his wrath and contempt. They held certain gentlemanly qualities and carried some sophistication. Besides, soldiers had no nationality and all, even the Viet Minh, were to be admired.

"I don't understand?" said the Pole.

"They fought like the Russians when they pummeled us back into Germany," said Knowles. He chewed on the meat. "Better trained than we expected. Death comes easy to them. They are easy to kill, but, there are too many of them."

"The Thai battalion is a good bunch," said the Frenchman, proud of his unit. His smile was wide. "They will fight well, not like our Viets." His voice sounded confident and Knowles thought well of him to defend his soldiers.

"The Vietnamese paratroopers turned to merdique,." said the Pole.

"A Thai is not a Viet," said the Frenchman. "They hate the Vietnamese."

"You should have seen this Gironne fight," Knowles said, mussing Bix's hair. "He tried to get the Vietnamese paratroopers killed when they attempted to rescue us, then he carried their bodies to safety."

"Gabrielle had the best defenses of any strongpoint," said the Pole. He did not seem interested in joking and it was clear that his confidence had been badly shaken.

"We will continue," said Knowles, an edge coming to his voice.

"There are a finite number of French in this valley," said the Pole. His voice bristled and he dug deeper at the scar. "Look." He pointed at the sky. "There'll be no supplies today, not with those clouds. Without the sky we are finished."

"You are going to cry about a few clouds when the airfield is destroyed anyway," said Knowles. The Frenchman grinned at him. "Every soldier knows you can't count on air support during the rainy season."

"I don't like it," said the Pole. He held a canteen cup in his scarred hand. "You can still hear shots on Gabrielle. Our comrades have been abandoned to die alone."

"It's just the Viets dispatching our wounded," said Knowles, "or an occasional Algerian going under with his teeth bared." His verbal jabs were becoming dangerous. The Pole started to annoy him. "There's the road if you feel like joining the fight. They could use a real man, like you, up there." Knowles placed his hand on Bix's knee.

Bix rocked from side to side, felt the venom start to rise in Knowles.

"The night was a disaster," said the Pole. He became more agitated. "We lost over a thousand troops, a Bison was badly damaged, LuLu Martin's company of legionnaires was cut down by a fourth, Botella's Battalion of yellow paratroopers busted under fire, and the entire garrison has been badly shaken."

"Perhaps you've lost your guts?" said Knowles. He flipped his arm off Bix's knee and slid it to the ground to touch the bayonet handle where it pressed against his leg.

"I'll do my part," said the Pole. The Pole fumbled with a broken tunic button.

"Your part's in your ass," said Knowles. Bix felt Knowles' muscles tense, his fingers strap around the bayonet. He pointed the other hand at the Pole.

"Look," said Bix, jumping to his feet. He pulled Knowles by the shoulder. "We can get off here and walk the rest of the way. Thanks for the hospitality." He dragged Knowles, who walked awkwardly backward, behind him.

Bix awoke in his hole later that day with a stiff body. Finally, some sleep. He felt like an old man must feel after a day scratching in the garden. His uniform was torn and covered with mud and blood. Sleep, like a cat's dry tongue, scratched his eyes causing them to water. He pried the lids apart with the his palms and cradled his head. The earth occasionally shook through a shell's injection. Little had changed except two strongpoints were lost. Smith, deJohn, and Knowles were gone. Most of le BEP was engaged in rebuilding fortifications. Knowles and he had the day off. Having time for recreation in the middle of a battle seemed a little strange to him. He had not slept long and thought of relaxing at the bordello, a few drinks, a warm body.

Outside, rain had fallen and the smell of earth floated on the air. Bix staggered to the water tank and underwent the torture of a coldwater shave. The razor slowly plucked out whiskers, each root pulling through each follicle. The blue blade of the razor cut his face leaving the skin raw and bleeding. He hated to shave but knew he would feel worse if he did not. He chanced a quick bath in the muddy Nam Yum River, rinsed out his clothes while there, changed into a fresh set, and started for the bordello. Deserters lounged along the banks or built caves in the dirt. He had not seen Nicole in almost three weeks and, as Knowles often said, "a man needs a tune-up as often as possible to keep running smoothly."

The calm of a camp under siege had settled in and soldiers worked oblivious to the occasional bursting shells. Outside the Command Post of Colonel Langlais the remains of the 5th Vietnamese Parachute Battalion stood at strict attention suffering a vicious reprimand. Alone, clenched fists at his side, Captain Botella, strutting from side to side like a fiddler crab, ground out every word he uttered, stuttering amidst spittle and fiery breath. Bix never witnessed such mad outrage as that shown by Botella. He was a man insane. Freezing under fire was unforgivable and what the little Vietnamese had done at the ford was a disgrace. Yet Bix understood their fear and dilemma and he felt sorry for their embarrassment now.

Botella stomped from side to side spitting, shouting obscenities, twirling his arms, crunching the men to bits with his voice as his fist smashed into his palm. They were not soldiers but cowardly pigs who stopped to rut in the mud at Ban Ke' Phai. Because of them the rescue of the "MEN" on Gabrielle had been a failure. He could no longer stomach the stench of so many cowards. "Toi!" he said, singling a man. "Putain! Espece d'encule!"

Each word, a blowing powder charge, swelled Botella's neck and head. His face went from red to white and saliva issued from his mouth. Botella called several sergeants to his side, men he trusted. Together they cut through the ranks. Bix no longer heard what Botella said but gathered he was purging every soldier from the ranks whose conduct was not beyond reproach. Officers and men alike were stripped of rank and weapons, then dismissed, on the spot, from the battalion and left to fend for themselves.

The display was wicked, unmerciful, and Bix felt uneasy and a little ashamed as he walked away. The 5th, untried and still shaken from their recent landing, was a poor choice to send on any rescue mission. Their performance was hardly their fault. Becoming a soldier, learning that death was a random beast, took time and at least one difficult battle. They now had their battle. Given another chance the men of the 5th would have fought like devils. Bix hoped their own disgrace would push the remaining unit forward to glory. Death was better than shame. Those who were dismissed would probably join the growing number of prisoners and internal deserters along the banks of the Nam Yum.

"Le BEP" should have been sent," thought Bix. "All of it, not just a part. They are, after all, prepared for counterattacks." Colonel Langlais had command of the central sector. Perhaps he did not wish to bloody his beloved paratroopers. Bix was pleased that such decisions were not his. All he had to do was fight and ask no questions, a simple life for a simple man.

Call it chivalry - or greed - but the two Legion Bordellos were the most secure positions in the valley. Engineers had gouged the playroom deep into the earth and piled twice the required amount of dirt across the thick ceiling beams. "Better not to be caught with our pants down," deJohn, in a quieter moment, once joked. Mostly Vietnamese worked the brothel, several Algerians from the Oulad-Nail tribe of Constantine - beautiful black women - a favorite menu item of Crème Brulee's - and an occasional European. Serving in the bordellos was a tradition with the Oulad-Nail women. They worked as prostitutes to earn their dowry. When they had earned enough, they returned home, married, and became devoted wives and mothers. The French appreciated a soldier's needs and understood sex as a natural act, a very civilized trait, thought Bix. Nicole's bordello was one of two in the camp. Bix had not visited the other.

Dim light hung on the smoke-drenched air of the bordello. The main room was shaped like a rough diamond, not the jewel but the spots on a playing card. One corner of the diamond held the entrance and the bar. Bamboo mats covered the walls and tables crowded the floor. Music played from a distant phonograph and several soldiers danced with girls in a dark tip of the diamond. The bordello was not unlike the small, underground artists clubs Bix had witnessed on his one visit to France: shabby, thick with cigarette smoke, slick women free with sex; people exchanging conversation about money, and employment, for the world of ideas. Soldiers were not unlike such people. Bix pushed between the tables. Soldiers knew what artists knew, only they understood it, felt the mist beyond life that had touched the things that cannot be boxed by words, imprisoned by oil, trapped by music. Artists could only nip at the edges of some reality that combat soldiers understood. Soldiers could not explain what they knew because there was nothing to explain. The reality was in the experience, not in words or music or paint.

Bix did not see Nicole and he found an empty chair with Manuel and Perkins.

"You need some ass too?" said Perkins. Perkins was an American with long legs and delicate fingers like those of a woman. He always turned his head aside when he smoked and pulled at the cigarette, with his thick pink lips, as if licking a sucker. Perkins talked too much and his conversations were limited to sex and baseball. Before Bix answered, Perkins hooked a tiny Vietnamese and pulled her down the passageway to the rooms where a man might relax and enjoy the affections and tender touches of a woman.

"Perkins talks too much," said Bix. He was embarrassed that Perkins was an American. "Those Viet women shop at nearby villages. It would be just like Perkins to pass on information."

"What information?" said Manuel. "That there's a condom shortage? Anything else they already know." Manuel was even older than Knowles, a good tough Spaniard who, as a kid, fought against Franco in the Spanish Civil War and worked as a scout with the Abraham Lincoln Brigade. "If the rubber condition continues, the war will stop. We cannot fight without condoms."

"Have you seen Nicole?" said Bix.

"The old lady of France, the beautiful madam?"

"Not so old," said Bix. Most of the tables were filled and soldiers filed in and out of the back rooms. Nicole was older than the prostitutes.

"Yes, not as old as me. She's with your kraut friend," said Manuel. He pulled at the gray in his beard. "She has something for him as he does for her. I would not be such a fool as to call it love but it is something very near it."

"Knowles?" said Bix, not wanting to believe the obvious. He often spent time with her although Bix did not understand why. A hardened old soldier like him could never love anyone yet they were inseparable. Even when they were apart some connection remained.

"In the back. He takes more time than any of the rest because she is not pressed for time. He is be the only one who can be with her; probably because he can do her no harm." Manuel chuckled at his joke. "I've finished my fun and must return to work.

Don't be hard on Perkins. He fights well, even for an American."

Bix no longer thought of himself as an American. The legionnaires often referred to one another by nationality but mostly as a derogatory joke. They were men brought together by a common language they seldom understood: French, and a common cause: war.

Nicole emerged from the passageway followed by Knowles, his thick hand on her slight shoulder. Her red dress fit closely and Bix knew she wore nothing underneath, no bra, no panties, nothing except flesh, warm and accessible. Nicole was the only happy woman Bix had ever met. Nothing depressed her.

She held Knowles' fingers as they rested on her shoulder. Bix did not like him touching her. Lately Bix had grown possessive, a feeling new to him and one he did not understand. In the beginning, he liked men to like her. She was like a jewel, more valuable, more precious. Her value had increased over time. She was someone everyone wanted and Bix wanted her more than most. Bix tried to avoid being jealous. Too often he had seen it happen, emotions rampant, logic gone astray. Nothing killed a man quicker than a reason to live. Nicole was rapidly becoming his, at least in his mind if not in reality. He knew he could shorten the distance she kept between every man. Although not vain, he understood his handsome looks.

"The Gironne has come to spread his seeds," said Knowles, as the two of them approached.

"Nicole," said Bix. He stood and shyly offered his hand. He did not offer her a kiss although he wanted to give her one to show Knowles he had the ability to take her.

"Yes," she answered, giving him a queer look, a distant look, one almost of confusion.

"It's me," said Bix. He stammered, felt an urge to slap Knowles.

"The green Gironne," said Knowles. "You remember, the boy in love, the boy who wants you, more than any other woman."

"Oui," she said. "The good friend of my Knowles, the one he is making into a man."

"I am a man," Bix said. "The soldier from 'le BEP." He wanted to separate himself from Knowles.

"Of course it's you," she said, smiling. "Lately there have been so many soldiers coming in and out." Nicole cradled his chin, kissed him on the nose like a mother would. Bix drew back embarrassed, angry. He wanted her arms around him. He wanted to kiss her again and again, to stake his territory. "Such a pretty young man," she said. "And so virile. How could I forget the stiffest soldier in all Indochina? You're almost a legend amongst the women."

"Sit down Gironne, and rest from the war," said Knowles. He turned to Nicole. "If he ever gets at you you'll need your strength." He kissed her quite gently on the lips. "Bring us a drink, my lover," he said to Nicole. "Something to oil the gears." He whistled at Nicole when she left.

"I do not appreciate the teasing," said Bix, feeling foolish as soon as he spoke. He leaned close to Knowles and whispered, "Have you got an extra condom? I'm running low."

"There's a shortage," Knowles laughed, pulling sharply away. "I don't think you will need it. She won't have you and the other women are checked for disease. They get more attention by the doctors than do the wounded."

"Why won't she have me?" said Bix. "You keep her away from me, away from every-one."

"She makes her own decisions."

"What whore doesn't take a man?"

"Baah," said Knowles. "Trade any rubbers you find for food or use them on the other women. She only favors me. Women cannot be understood."

Bix wanted to be cruel, then regretted the thoughts he carried. "I have only two condoms left," he said.

"For you, a years supply," said Knowles.

Bix knew when to stop, yet he continued. "She is a whore and she must have me if I pay her," said Bix, like a son turning on his father.

"You are mistaken. Nicole is a business woman," said Knowles. "She treats the women decently, watches for their safety and pays them fairly. She views none of them as whores but as women comforting us in times of need."

"I'm sorry,"said Bix, relaxing. "The noise has made me crazy." Bix felt ashamed at calling her a whore and wondered why he had turned on Knowles.

"When you're old, you won't take sides against friends," said Knowles. "When you know women like I do you'll understand something about living. Here..." Knowles slid a small bottle of Pond's Angel Skin lotion past the candle and across the table. "I saved this for you as a gift to Nicole." He smiled. "This time it will do you no good but in the future remember, a small present is the quickest way into a woman's pants." He mussed Bix's hair. "Even if she's not wearing any."

Bix held the bottle and read the label: "Pond's Angel Skin - Revolutionary New Hand Lotion Scientifically Years Ahead – Pond's extract co. N.Y. - 4 fl oz." The bottle was full and gracefully shaped. "Thanks," he said. He felt more ashamed than ever. "I'll give it to her later."

"Too late," said Knowles.

"Brandy for you both," said Nicole, placing the cups on the table. She saw the jar before Bix could slide it under the table. "What's this?"

"The little pumpkin has brought you a gift," said Knowles. "Go on, give it to her."

"It's nothing," said Bix. He tried to hoard the bottle. "It's really from the Sergeant..."

"Of course it is," said Knowles. He slapped the table and pried the bottle from Bix's hand. He handed it to Nicole. "The bastard placed this little jewel in my charge in case he did not return from Gabrielle. What a joke! Twice, maybe three times, he saved my life. He's a hero. And all because I had his bottle."

"Knowles got us home," said Bix, quietly, shyly.

Nicole weighed the bottle in her hands.

"Don't be modest," said Knowles, pinching Bix's cheek. "You've raised both her nipples with a single shot."

Bix reddened. He could not understand the concept of a whore. The women resembled any other ladies he had seen. They simply closed a curtain, did all the pleasurable things a respectable woman would not do, (so they claimed) and returned the same ladies as before. There was no miraculous change, no visible sign of debauchery, no shame or outrage on their faces, just pleasant smiles as if they had just come from tea.

Nicole, holding the bottle like a jewel, paid no attention to either of them.

"True, I'm good," said Knowles. He leaned back in his chair. "But I can only raise the nipples on cold days."

Nicole caressed the jar like a small baby, held the jar against her face, unscrewed the cap and dabbed a tiny amount on one finger. She smelled the cream, rubbed the lotion onto her lips. She threw her arms around Bix, hugged, kissed him hard. He wanted her to gently pry apart his lips with her tongue.

"It's the most precious gift anyone has ever given me," she said. "I must do something very special for you today." Knowles winked at Bix and jiggled his eyebrows as if they were on a string.

"It's not like you think," Bix protested, wanting more than ever to be with her.

"He's modest." Knowles sipped at the brandy and gargled it down his throat. "Take him on a trip he'll not soon forget, delights he'll remember only in dreams." Knowles rocked back in his chair and drank the rest of the brandy.

"And you, you crusty old fart?" said Nicole. "Have you nothing for your favorite woman?"

"A soldier's gift," said Knowles, "not the gift of a lover punched senseless by stars." Knowles reached back for a knapsack sitting against the wall. He drew the sack near and fumbled with the latches. The latches started to come apart and he dropped the sack under the table, out of sight. "A little lotion is a fine gift from a boy to a woman who wants to keep her virginity. But a man brings you the gift of vengeance."

He motioned for them to come in closer. Knowles flicked out his arm. The severed head of Smith bounced twice across the table, spun, wobbled like a spent top before coming to a stop directly in front of Bix. Bix almost flipped over his chair. Smith was blue, and caked with white powder. The candlelight flickered against the brass eyes.

"Merdique!" said Bix. "Burn that damn thing!" He tried to shield Nicole from the sight. Nicole, unafraid, pushed past him, placed an arm beside each side of the head and bent low as if watching herself in a stream. Her eyes reflected in Smith's brass eyes and appeared to rest on the candle's flames floating there. Knowles had attached a round piece of wood to the neck so the head would sit up.

"Who is this one?" said Nicole, quietly, her voice like a prayer. Bix moved behind her, placed his hands on her hips to let her know he was there.

"It is Smith," said Bix. "Get rid of the hideous thing."

She pushed away his outreached arm.

A crowd started to gather. Nicole turned and nudged Bix away.

"He was a brutal man," she said. "He once beat me for not going in back with him. He was good with the blows; cut me, but never any bruises. Only the pain remained." She leaned even closer. Other legionnaires crowded in. Overhead lamps swayed from side to side from the shelling. "It's a fine gift," said Nicole. "A beautiful gift. Is it truly mine?"

"Of course," said Knowles. "I knew what he had done even though you had said nothing. The Viets got to him before me. I covered him with foot powder because he stinks a bit. I had wished to carry him through the war, make a man of him as I am doing with the pumpkin. I knew he beat you, the scar on your breast, the mark he left in Algeria." Knowles took another drink of brandy. "The Communists saved me the trouble of removing his head. They're good for something, after all."

"He was a good soldier," someone said.

"The best," answered Knowles. "Just not much of a lover."

"Let us keep him," said another legionnaire. "He'll bring us luck."

Nicole crossed her arms and thought while soldiers argued about Smith's merits as a soldier and as a man. The room felt hot to Bix and smelled too much of liquor, cheap perfume, and dank bamboo. He wanted to get back to the war. Being off-duty seemed dangerous.

"You're all good fellows," said Nicole. "I can honestly tell you now that what he thought were his best parts are not here."

"An oversight," said Knowles. "This is all we found."

"What is a gift if not given to those we love?" Nicole continued. She tipped forward, winked at Knowles. "This precious gift I have received, I now give to the men of the Legion. Carry your comrade with you at all times, protect him as you would protect one another. Let my friend Henrich Knowles and his young friend Ben..."

"Bix," Bix corrected her.

"...Bix, treasure this gift for the unit and keep him in good health."

The men cheered as Nicole hoisted the head by the hair, twirled Smith around, and handed him to Knowles. Knowles jabbed his bayonet into the wall. Nicole kissed him. Knowles, using the tangled hair, tied Smith to the bayonet.

What difference did any of it make? Bix thought. They were all a little mad and a madman never notices his affliction. All sanity had fled. Yet he realized something was wrong; the earth had tilted perhaps, birds swam, fish flew, honest men laughed at lies. And death? Death was beauty and, in a world of ugly mayhem, soldiers sought beauty above all else.

Nicole took Knowles by the hand and led him to the dance floor, a small square of wooden planks sprinkled with dust. She felt good, both soft and firm, in his arms. He had already joined the Legion when she found him and she decided she would follow him wherever he went. Sometimes being at a place seemed a mistake, yet she held him tight and he was glad she was here. He worried about her and often became careless. Each time they turned, he noticed Bix watching Smith hanging from the wall.

Knowing he had been vicious to Nicole and Knowles caused Bix to feel less like burying Smith. He grabbed a small black girl and also started to dance. Let the bastard hang on the wall. He was not real, anyway. Nothing was real, maybe Nicole was the only real person in the world. Bix concentrated on pushing his hips against the girl and rubbing his cheek into her hair. The war disappeared, Smith, Knowles, deJohn, all vanished as Nicole led Knowles back to her room.

The small room, chipped from the earth, smelled of mold and flowers. A door of strung beads tinkled after they entered. A small bed nestled against a corner, a basin of water rested on a shelf, two towels hung from a bayonet beside a coat rack. Bamboo mats dressed the floor and a lantern hung overhead casting long shadows. Nicole lit a candle beside the basin and dimmed the lantern. Turning, she pushed her back toward Knowles. He lowered her zipper and the dress slid down. She caught it with a small foot, retrieved it with her hands, stepped from the dress as if emerging from a bath.

Nicole kissed him gently, unlatched his clothes and placed everything on the coat rack. They had been here only an hour before but she could not be without him. She slid a sheet across her and lay, bent legged, on the bed like a painting waiting to be unveiled. Candlelight sketched her features softly in warm yellow. Knowles drew back the sheet, descended to the shadow between her thighs. She was a slender woman and his hand spanned the small of her back. She rose against him, pushing against his hand in a rhythm that transcended battle, placed him in a field of fresh grass warmed by a late afternoon sun where lovers drink wine and chase butterflies. They lay together for almost an hour gently touching one another and whispering their love.

"Get the bastard," someone yelled, as Nicole and Knowles entered the main room. Everything was in chaos and Knowles saw the glint of weapons: bayonets, rifles, pistols. He crouched low, tried to pull Nicole down. A sapper must have gotten through the line. Knowles grabbed his rifle.

"An infiltrator?" said Bix, fumbling with the French word and not understanding what was happening.

"The dance floor. Blast him. Get the little sonofabitch," others yelled.

Knowles worked his way along the wall. A mob gathered around the floor. Several soldiers remained drinking and joking. A legionnaire smashed a chair against the wall, issued the broken legs to others.

"Run him to me," Knowles yelled, crouching on a table, his head low under the ceiling. "I'll crush him with my bare hands."

Bix looked for the Viet Minh, saw nothing but twirling soldiers.

"Knowles," Bix yelled. "My rifle."

Two shots sounded near the dance floor. "Careful where you plant those rounds," said Knowles. He glanced at the enemy and, for the first time, understood the outrage expressed by the others.

Bix fumbled for the weapon, shook Knowles by the leg. "What is it?" he said.

Knowles looked down. "A thieving rat," he said. "A filthy thieving rat. He's stolen a condom."

"A condom?"

"Took it from a man's pack and tried to scurry out with it," someone explained. He waved his arms. "Get him! Get the bastard!"

More shots rang out and a ricochet flashed against the wall.

"That's no reason to kill him," said Bix. "He might be a good soldier that panicked."

"Good man?" Knowles looked strangely at Bix and laughed. "You're mistaken Gironne. Always you think of people. A rat, this is a real rat, a corps rat fat and nasty that's crept in to steal the last of our rations." Knowles turned to the crowd. "Is he dead?"

More commotion. Two legionnaires smashed another table against the floor. "Over there. Quick!" one of them yelled.

"Let the condom go to the man who kills the rat!" someone else yelled.

Now everyone rose from the tables. "Don't let him get away with it."

"Crush the bastard!"

"Over here, over here."

"He's mine."

"Get back, let him into the open!"

Men seethed, spit, rolled like an ocean across the room, bodies splashed high against the walls, rolled back flowing around the furniture. The giant wave sloshed toward Bix.

"He's getting away!"

"There, between your feet!" someone yelled to Knowles.

Knowles flipped from the table, crashed down with one leg like a blunt pike. Bix heard the rat's skull crush beneath Knowles' boot.

"Give us a speech," said a legionnaire. "Such an act of heroism."

Knowles cleared his throat, slid one arm behind his back, tipped up his chin as if it was raised by the finger of a dainty virgin. He waved the condom, still in the package.

"Friends," he started. "I am here today to accept this honor, this treasure. Although the filthy rat has been killed, I expected no reward. It is fitting, however, that this gentle galosh go to me. We face difficult times ahead and a man should keep his feet dry…"

A soldier nudged Bix's ribs, offered him a cigarette. Bix moved toward Nicole. The cigarette was strong and he recognized the brand, another Gaulois, a French weed often used by Lachen. The soldier handed him the pack waving back any thanks Bix offered.

"…But as many of you know," Knowles continued, "I am too much man to be contained in such a small package. The young among us need protection. Even as I have vowed to watch over Smith, an easy task since his needs are few," Knowles looked to a point several feet below Smith's head, "I have also taken an oath to protect the virgins amongst us. To my little Gironne goes the reward." Knowles pulled Bix toward him. Bix's face flushed when Knowles stuffed the condom into his tunic pocket. The men offered a cheer and one soldier spit a stream of beer into the air. "Now," said Knowles. "Will some lady be kind enough to give the Gironne a bobby-pin so his reward doesn't slip off when being used."

Bix tried to hide from the laughter as Captain Bassin stepped forward. He had pushed through the doorway during the speech. "Laisse qa et viens avec moi!" he yelled. "Everyone back to your units! There is still a war on?"

Chapter 36

Colonel Piroth watched the muzzle flashes of his artillery followed by the blips of light sprinkling on the hills. What good did it do now? The battles were over and his guns did nothing except kill legionnaires. His artillery had taken a beating: eight gun crews out of action, six guns totally destroyed. He'd not been able to see the battle objectively? Good men paid the price for his arrogance and pride. Bruno (Bigeard) warned him that the Viets were capable of anything including hauling big guns through jungles and up the mountains and they should not to be underestimated. Piroth almost got into a fight with him and had yelled out, "What you are saying is scandalous! Nobody has the right to praise the enemy!" Bigeard carried the bad habit of giving too much credit to the enemy. They had given the French some trouble, nothing more. Piroth had the best artillery in the world.

When Colonel Berteil, Navarre's Deputy for Operations, a man who thoroughly approved the operations in the valley, suggested better protection for the guns, Piroth had only sloughed him off. Under standard procedures, major earthworks were needed to protect his guns and he needed twice as many of them. French minister and reserve officer in the French Air Force, M. Jacquet, offered all guns he needed from Hanoi. He had only to ask. Piroth had more guns than he needed. How many guns did it take to knock off a few Viet Minh emplacements, anyway? He had 25 105s, four big 155s plus 16 heavy mortars.

All he needed to secure the camp were the guns he had, some experienced forward observers, and the use of the observation planes at the airstrip. He never imagined that his observers would be killed so quickly and that the airstrip would be destroyed making his observation planes useless.

Even de Castries had some doubts about the capability of the French artillery, but he was no artillery officer and had deferred to Piroth. Day after day they flew over the hills looking for any signs of Viet Minh guns. None, as Piroth gloated, were to be seen. Piroth explained why his guns were mostly unprotected. "You see, Colonel, they are arranged for all-azimuth firing. They can be moved in any direction, all 360 degrees. I can then bring full firepower onto any position. If they were dug in and protected they could only be fired in one direction. I would need more guns to be effective." The only concession he made to de Castries was to circle the guns with a thin ring of shoulder high sandbags to offer the men some protection. He did it grudgingly.

He sat on the toppled sandbags around a destroyed 105 and observed the smoldering wreckage. A passing soldier stopped.

"Colonel, you must get under cover," he said. "It is very dangerous here."

"Do you remember when the Viets celebrated Tet by firing their guns?" He spoke quietly, as if to himself. "I gave them hell that day. We sent over 1,650 rounds and the air force dropped another 150 bombs. We thought many of their guns were destroyed. Only later did we discover the destroyed guns were fake, stripped down logs in phony emplacements."

"Come on, Colonel. Let me help you back to the C.P." He tried to lift the Colonel by the arm. "Shells are falling everywhere."

"All is lost."

Outside the C.P. the soldier stopped and handed Colonel Piroth to a paratrooper from the 8th Assault.

"What should I do with him?" he said. He looked the Colonel up and down as if he were a strange and unknown animal.

"Put him inside." He pointed to his head and rolled his eyes. "He needs some rest. Take him to the Colonel, Langlias or de Castries."

"Best to stay clear of Langlais," said the paratrooper. "He's tossing bodies out right and left. I've never seen such an angry dog."

The paratrooper sat Piroth down in Dr. Grauwin's office in the hospital and offered him a smoke.

"Can I get you anything else?" said the paratrooper. "Some wine, perhaps, Colonel. Maybe I can find some whisky."

"I'm sorry," said Piroth. "It's all my fault. I take full responsibility. It's all my fault."

"Nonsense," said the paratrooper. "One must expect these little setbacks in battle. Who knew they had so many guns?"

Piroth smoked quietly and watched the wounded being carried past on stretchers. Dr. Grauwin entered with a bottle of whisky. He poured some into a cup and offered it to Piroth.

"You must not take it so hard," he said.

"We have always had the worst luck," said Piroth.

"Life is that way. Bad times today, good times tomorrow."

"Remember the Thai Binh outpost, the time we were attacked and overrun?" Piroth shook his head. The whisky burned down his throat. "We were lucky to escape," he said.

"Don't confuse bad luck with good," said Dr. Grauwin. "It was bad luck that the Viets attacked the outpost but good luck we got away. And now look at us, together again, both doing our jobs. And pretty little Pauline Bougeade, now de Castries secretary, who got away with us that time. She is a tough one. The kind of luck she carries is a good thing, and all of it here with us now. Everything will turn out fine. Until then, I must get back to work. Rest here as long as you like. Don't leave until I return."

He poured Piroth another shot of whisky then left with the bottle. Piroth felt the earth rumble. He finished the drink and walked through the halls, past the screaming men and the chaos of the command room. Outside the guns still flashed. He walked across the compound and over the Bailey bridge to his room on the other side of the river. His breath came in short strokes and his heart thumped slowly against his chest. He had not eaten for two days, felt no need for food while the soldiers were being massacred. At the age of 48 he had accomplished nothing, had left no mark on history until now. He would be forever remembered as the man who lost the battle of Dien Bien Phu. Such a distinction was more than any man could handle. He removed his hat and ran his hand over his bald head. There was an honorable way out. He lifted a hand grenade from under his cot and held it between his praying hands. How silly the movies were, soldiers always pulling the pins with their teeth. It took a great effort to pull the pins on grenades. The thick cotter pins were shoved through tiny holes then bent on the opposite sides of the rings. No amount of effort could pull them out unless the pins were first straightened with great effort. Then, while twisting on the rings, they came out stiffly and with great effort. Hand grenades with an easy pulling pin would have been a disaster, soldiers constantly going up in smoke. Piroth heard Father Heinrich calling his name.

"Charles, are you there?" said Heinrich. "These halls are so dark." Father Heinrich entered the room with a mess tin of food. He sat on the cot beside Piroth. "And what do you have there?" He lifted the grenade from Piroth's hand and replaced it with the tin of food. "You must have something to eat. Believe in God's merciful grace. Our lives are in his hands. This thing is not the answer." He examined the grenade.

"Why does a priest go to war?" said Piroth.

"You're just upset," Heinrich said. "Eat a little food. God is watching you. What happens is his will, not ours."

"Is it his will that we are here? Didn't the church get us into this mess," said Piroth.

"Try just a bite."

"The church came here to convert these heathens, then called for the government to protect them. Isn't that right? Government protection means the military."

"There is no blame," said Father Heinrich. "We must spread the word of God. That often requires conflict. What are a few exchanged bodies for the eternal soul. In the end it is for the best. Surely you still believe in God?"

"How could he let this happen?" said Piroth. "Do you believe in God, Father? Priests are educated men. Can an educated man believe in God?"

"I believe in the goodness of people." He said. "This is not your fault. You must not blame yourself."

"Men are killers who thrive on war."

"There are no warlike people, only warlike leaders," said Father Heinrich. "Take a bite of food and you will feel better." He tried to lift the plate to Piroth's lips.

"The Colonel will have me court-martialed," said Piroth. "I cannot live in disgrace."

"Nonsense," said Father Heinrich. "The Colonel asked me to look in on you. Yes, he has been harsh, but he is presently overwhelmed. Directing a huge battle is not an easy task. He lashed out because you were there. God forgives all our sins. You made the best decisions possible. That is no sin."

Piroth took a small bite of food, followed by another. He listened as Father Heinrich comforted him. He finished the food. Father Heinrich blessed him and asked him to rest.

"Do you want to take my hand grenade?" said Piroth.

Father Heinrich rolled it on his hand then tossed it onto the cot.

"You keep it," he said. "Suicide is the one sin God will not forgive."

Heinrich reported to Langlais.

"Yes?" said Langlais.

"He is doing much better," said Heinrich. "With God's grace he will recover completely."

They did not hear the exploding hand grenade from across the river. Piroth's batman, a faithful Senegalese, rushed into the C.P. hall in despair and excitement. "Come! Come! You must help the Colonel!"

There, in his room across the river, lay what remained of Colonel Piroth. Colonel Langlais pushed his way in. Piroth's chest was blown apart, his good arm torn away, his face missing. His body smoked from the blast.

"Send for Colonel de Castries," said Langlais. "Everyone stay here. Not a word of this is to be mentioned. Get him wrapped up. I'll be in the command post, but this must remain a secret. The men must not know."

Father Heinrich helped wrap Colonel Piroth in a blanket as Langlais returned to the small briefing room. The job seemed overwhelming, too many breaches to seal, too much shellfire, ammunition worries, not enough troops for counterattacks, low morale. The decimation of officers had destroyed the chain of command. Order must be restored. What he needed was a small respite, some time to gather his thoughts. Fortunately the Viet Minh also needed time and all was quieting. Perhaps they had run low on ammunition, or soldiers? The first problem was Colonel de Castries. He was useless. He must be eliminated, placed in a position without authority. But how best to do it without alarming the troops or the high command? His inability to lead might not have been completely his fault. He had not wanted the command unless it was understood to be an offensive base, room to maneuver, a chance to strike the Viet Minh at every opportunity. In the present situation, he was the wrong man in the wrong place. He knew nothing of defense, of stationary fortifications. Langlais knew little himself but at least he could make decisions, was a man of action. This had turned into a battle for the paratroops and paratroop officers needed to command it. Left in his current position, de Castries remained dumbfounded, stunned as if artillery bursts had removed his senses, knocked his wits completely out. Langlais became ever more agitated at seeing de Castries eating at his perfectly set table, linen tablecloth, candlelight, expensive tableware, and being waited on by servants. At least Langlais had gotten de Castries to order reinforcements, Bigeard and his 6th Colonial paratroops. They were ordered out of the valley to engage in other operations. His return would raise the spirits of the camp. No officer was so respected than he and he would soon be arriving from Hanoi, not a moment too soon.

"How is the leg?" asked Cogny.

"It's a leg," said Bigeard. "A paratrooper expects difficulties."

"No need to hide the truth from you, Bruno." Cogny leaned back in his chair. "The fortress at Dien Bien Phu is suffering difficulties, a terrible situation." He poured Bigeard a glass of cognac. "Beatrice and Gabrielle have fallen. Piroth has done nothing with his artillery and we have lost two crack battalions. Nothing is going right."

Bigeard kneaded his calf. The pain was deep.

"My troops are worn out," Bigeard said. "We have been engaged in every major operation for the last twenty months. Without rest we cannot be effective. Even the best thoroughbred needs time between races."

"I never liked the operation from the beginning," said Cogny. "Navarre put me up to it. What was I to do? I am his subordinate and must obey orders, make the best of his poor decisions. Now we are stuck. I don't see any way out. We have poked in our little finger and must stick it in up to the elbow. It's too late to get out." He tapped his walking stick against the desk. "The whole operation seems poorly led. The messages are garbled and conflicting. The officers seem to be incompetent or inefficient, unable to give me clear and concise information. De Castries babbles on about evacuating his Chief of Staff, Keller, who has broken down, and getting his secretary out. What about the battle? He'll not know what to do without her giving him a sponge bath every night. He is not a buffoon, but I can make nothing of the information he is sending. He sounds like a desperate man."

"Perhaps you should drop into the valley and lead it yourself?" said Bigeard.

"Nonsense," said Cogny. He started to fidget. "I can do more good here. They need to get their heads about them, get organized and put up some resistance. You don't have to go yourself. Stay in Hanoi until your leg heals."

"I always jump with my men."

"Yes, yes. Always the hero. I need you in top form."

"Is there no chance of withdrawal?"

"I suggested that months ago to General Navarre, when we started to be surrounded. We could have gotten out leaving most of Giap's troop caught in the hills, attacked his supply lines on the border of China. He refused to listen. Now look at the mess we are in. I see little hope. Do what you can to pull us out of this mess. There will be a staffing in two hours. Bring any ideas you have."

Major Bigeard inspected his troops, all good and reliable men. The Sixth Parachute Battalion was his special project and he was proud of them, warriors every one. They were worn and tired, but they had always accepted every challenge without complaint. They would accept this one. He walked down the lines with his aides, Captain Maurice Fayette and Lieutenant Renee Blanc. A smile, a handshake, a tap on the shoulder, came easy to him when it concerned his men. He explained the mission ahead, promised to get them leave as soon as possible, spoke of his pride about the unit, said they were men of action and that they were going to find that action at Dien Bien Phu. Each soldier stiffened at his approach, stretched out his chest with satisfaction. Bigeard tried, unsuccessfully, to walk without limping.

The following morning he sat in a C-47 circling the valley. Smoke rose from everywhere and he saw an occasional mushroom burst of exploding shells.

"So, we're back," Bigeard said, to Lieutenant Blanc. "It's a fine mess."

"One we can handle," said Blanc. He adjusted the straps on his parachute. He enjoyed the excitement of battle but never liked the jump. "Where are they dropping us?"

"On drop zone Octavie, near Isabelle. We'll have to make our way back to the Center of Resistance, about five miles."

"As if we're not worn out enough," said Captain Fayette. "I suppose we'll be under fire the whole way?"

"You worry too much," said Lieutenant Blanc.

"Someone has to. The Major isn't going to do it."

"Yes, yes, Maurice," said Bigeard. "Everyone has his place in the military. You are Captain of worry, Renee, of optimism, me, of indifference. One must remain objective about the situation to be effective."

"You are the calmest officer in the military," said Blanc.

Bigeard again landed badly, spraining his ankle. For a moment he lay on the ground watching his paratroops spiral down. The sky looked clean and filled with men. Nothing seemed as spectacular to him as a parachute drop. An exploding artillery round drew him from his reverie. Fayette and Blanc were nowhere to be seen, scattered like paratroopers always were after a drop. Replacements for 1 BEP and the 8th Assault were also dropping. Within minutes, Lieutenant Blanc appeared driving a jeep. He slid to a halt.

"Thought you might need this," he said.

"Give me a hand," said Bigeard. "I've broken my ankle, or badly sprained it." He hobbled to the jeep. "Take me to Colonel Lalande at Isabelle for a briefing. I'll have a doctor look at the ankle there." Another shell landed near the jeep. "Come on come on, let's get moving before we're all killed," he said.

Chapter 37

Bix thought Sangree was fearless. He was not. He had been afraid on many occasions, the dry mouth, shortness of breath, quivering hands, weak legs. He pissed his pants twice and crapped them once. An inability to control one's bodily functions hit them all at least once. People who only read about war in newspapers and magazines never understood what a messy and nasty event it is. Every dead person in pictures was physically complete. More soldiers in war were blown to greasy unrecognizable bits than were shot. Piles of arms, legs, torsos, heads, and ropes of slippery guts littered the forfeited hills around Dien Bien Phu. The stench of an opened body haunted him for days and he could not eat.

"Smoke?" said Bix.

Sangree caught the cigarette between his fingers. He scratched a match across his boot and torched the end of the tobacco. The cigarette started to burn crookedly so he turned it over to even it out as he inhaled. "They say Colonel Piroth killed himself," said Sangree.

"Who?"

"Piroth, the artillery commander." Sangree turned the cigarette in his fingers.

"I mean, who said it?" said Bix.

"It's going around. Castries chief of staff, Keller, has had a breakdown. Anyway, that's what they're saying."

"A man can take just so much abuse before he cracks," said Bix. "It will happen to us all if we stay here long enough. One day you are fine, the next day you are finished. No one expects it. Some men never recover. I heard you turned down two promotions."

"Looking after myself is a full-time job." He had not glanced at Bix.

"I'll buy you a beer at the bordello," said Bix. He liked Sangree but he was not sure why. It might have been the mystic, or a combination of other things. He looked after the other soldiers, helped them out of tight spots, often without emotion as if they had been toy dolls. Whatever was troubling him was so deeply entrenched it might never come out. "Except for the constant shelling, things have quieted down. You should have been here a day or two ago."

"I was. Too many soldiers at the bordello," he said. "They spend most of their time misunderstanding one another in several languages."

"It's not crowded these days. Can I get you something?" Bix wanted to be his friend. Sangree shook his head and looked between his arms at the ground.

"Ever think of love?" said Sangree.

"What?"

"Love. You know, being in love," said Sangree. "I think of it all the time. I want to find a woman I can take care of, one who needs me, one I need."

"Maybe some day," said Bix. "I'm not sure I know what love is." He thought of Nicole, but said nothing.

That night Bix tried, unsuccessfully, to sleep. He was restless and he enjoyed the night-time explosions, the beauty of the flashes, the red hot metal streaking the night like flowering tracers. More replacements would arrive in the morning. He thought of the bordello.

Nicole gathered her girls, her "precious jewels" as she often called them, for a meeting. She acted like a mother hen catering to their every needs, seeing that they were dressed well, given enough to eat, in good health. In return they loved her dearly, confided their innermost secrets, told of their dreams and the soldiers they eventually fell in love with. Even prostitutes feel the need for love, perhaps even more than most women. She found them to be remarkable women, able to differentiate between love and sex so when they fell in love they fell hard and completely.

"How are my precious jewels?" she said. They moved closer like moths to a flame. "This is a tough assignment and I am going to ask for you to make great sacrifices, perhaps even greater than the girls did at Tsinh-Ho." The two women who had traveled deep behind enemy lines at Tsinh-Ho had become a legend with the B.M.C, Bordel Mobile de Campagne. "For those who do not know the story, let me briefly tell it.

"A small platoon defending a supply route was trapped outside Lai-Chau. The airhead at Lai-Chau was surrounded for over a year, as was the platoon. When a B.M.C was airlifted into Lai-Chau to help relieve the suffering of the men and to give them a brief moment of comfort – some more brief than others –" she smiled, "Lieutenant Laurent, the morale officer, felt the platoon in the jungle also needed relaxation. Two young ladies volunteered, packed their finest and most provocative clothing and left with a commando unit for the 30-mile adventure over a demanding jungle path that was constantly under attack from the Viet Minh. They wore jungle boots and military fatigues and hiked through the mud and thorns. forded rivers and streams, all without complaint."

Nicole watched the girls listening intently, even Nimni, the ebony-skinned Oulad-Nail girl, who had heard the story many times.

"The Viet Minh ambushed the commando unit on their return. The girls acted as cool and collected as any seasoned legionnaire and, when weapons became available, joined the fighting. Without their help the unit would not have survived."

"Tell us about the medals," said Nimni, waving her hand in the air like an eager school-girl.

"I am afraid your fate will be much the same as theirs," said Nicole, her head down. "Lieutenant Laurent found their courage so overwhelming that he put them both in for the croix de guerre. The big-shots in Hanoi turned them down but the soldiers had two of them made by a local artist and presented them in a small ceremony. That is what you must remember. It is the soldiers who will never forget you."

Nicole and the girls stood silently for a few minutes as if out of respect for all the people who seldom get recognized. "What are we to do?" said Mowbwi.

The girls started to fidget.

"We are in a tight situation and we might better serve the men who are wounded. There is no place to put them once they are treated and not enough people to care for them. Perhaps we can offer that care? I am going to ask the Doctor. He is a good and a caring man and I am sure he will accept our help. The soldiers are frightened, not just the wounded, but all of them. Everywhere the healthy are worried. What if they get injured? They have no place to go, no way to get out of the valley if they are injured. Their fate is to rot in stinking mud-holes and wait to die of infections. Such thoughts make them afraid to fight. Remind them that you are here and will care for them if they are hurt and also that you need protection if they are well. No man fights harder than when he is protecting a woman."

Later that evening Nicole held Knowles in her arms in the valley and watched the shells burst in bright colors around the compound. Thinking of living in peace and prosperity in France or Germany after the Second World War proved to be a waste of time. For Knowles, there would never be a time without war, never a time to live without fear and excitement. Knowles knew no other life so Nicole had never asked him to take another job, had never put him into a compromising position. Because he would always be at war, she would always remain at his side. He started to stir and unrolled like a rising muffin. He pressed his face into her and mumbled.

"I must return to the men."

"They can do without you for a while." She ran her fingers through his hair. "Let me have you a few minutes longer."

"The dirt must have you soaked you through," he said. "With the rains nothing ever dries out and you have traipsed all through the mud to find me."

"There won't be much work at the bordello if this continues," she said, knowing it would continue and knowing the siege would not turn out well. She never mentioned the possible outcome to Knowles, did not want to worry him unnecessarily. "Business usually increases in dangerous times but it has fallen off because there are not enough soldiers to fight while others get time off to visit."

"I must be with the men." He raised his head and stretched his arms against the night. "They act bravely enough but they are little more than boys playing soldiers. They do not understand this play is for good. Each death comes as a surprise and confuses them."

"You must sneak away to be with me. I am not asking much." She wrapped her arms around him and placed her head on his chest.

"Boys cannot lead themselves. They want advice without the embarrassment of asking."

"I am going to the infirmary to see if the girls can be of any assistance," she said. "We only need a few to work the bordello. The wounded might appreciate a woman's touch in their pain."

She felt a slight chill from the damp and it had started to sprinkle, something unusual in a land where oceans suddenly fell from the sky, not small drops. Dark figures, silhouetted by fires moved in the darkness. Rifle and machine gun fire sounded occasionally, clattered in the distance like hailstones on metal. She shivered on her return to the bordello, unafraid of the dangers of being in the open. Most of the girls sat in the dim light smoking and playing cards. Only two soldiers had flown sorties to the back rooms. Business was unusually slow as it often was when there was too much danger around, or too little.

Her bedroom was no larger than that of the other girls, perhaps even smaller since she never had visitors except Knowles and they held each other so closely she only needed half the bed she had. Rattan against the pictureless walls kept the dirt from falling. She preferred to use the candles and their deceiving magic glow on the nightstand rather than a harsh electric light of truth. She changed into fatigues and buttoned her tunic, tied the laces on her petite U.S. combat boots, placed a scarf around her neck and brushed her hair. She lay back on the bed to rest a moment and fell asleep. She awoke just after dawn and straightened herself again before walking to the infirmary. On the way there a group of men, heating breakfast, offered her coffee and bread. She kindly accepted knowing that as important as sex was to them, they enjoyed the presence and calming effect of women. The roughest of them behaved like gentlemen, never a sour word and always polite.

"It looks like a beautiful morning," she said, as they wiped a box clean and offered her a seat.

"Please, mademoiselle," said the oldest one, directing her to sit. "It's the best we have in such circumstances." The U.S. aluminum canteen cup liner burned her fingers but she was careful not to comment as she searched for the handle.

"Notice how the light hits the clouds," she said.

"Yes, the clouds. We're in for another drenching today. Already there must be a foot of water in the dugouts and trenches."

"Henri is always full of complaints," said the African, his broad grin revealing his good nature. The other men just squatted and stared at Nicole. "In Africa we have the same problems – no water – too much water."

"Are all of you with the regular army?" She pinched off an inch of bread.

"Volunteers, every one," said Henri. "Even Salami."

"Salamay," said the African, correcting him. "Always he makes a joke yet I have already saved him twice."

"That is only because I am so easy to spot in the dark. Salami walks around at night as he pleases."

"Are you all from France?" she said, smiling back. Immediately hands shot into the air as if they were schoolboys who finally knew an answer to a question. "Are you having a good time on this adventure?" They looked questioningly at one another. "I understand how much young men crave excitement."

"Perhaps this time it's overdone," said Henri. "Don't worry, we'll get out of it once we catch our breath."

"I am positive you will save us," said Nicole, as she stood, ready to leave. "And what a grand story you will tell your grandchildren."

When she walked out of hearing range, Henri pulled out his penis and said, "Wouldn't you like to faire l'amour that beautiful little putain. She is the only virgin in the camp (he pointed to a boy still sitting with his mouth open) except for you, Bodine."

She thought she heard faint laughter as she worked herself across the torn ground. Men and their silly ways did not fool or annoy her. Their bodies grew but not their minds. Mentally they remained boys and pretended to be tough and heartless and performed their acts to fool the other actors playing men. The same antics they did as boys, like being respectful to the teacher when being reprimanded, then making faces behind her back, continued through life. Only the language changed as their vocabulary expanded deeper into the mysterious and inviting gutter of adulthood.

Lumps of dead lined up in rows beside the trail, neatly wrapped in parachutes or canvas tent shelters and tied with nylon cords like Christmas packages. Bare-shirted legionnaires dug graves in which to roll them. Other soldiers carried more white cocoons and dumped them on the ground. Jeeps and trucks delivered more bodies as the vehicles slipped and sank into the ground flinging mud from the tires and into the air.

Nicole followed her nose to the infirmary. Smells of shit, piss, blood, entrails, and infection emerged as a shimmering light green mist drifted from the entrance before settling into the approach trench like a stagnant stream. She never smelled such rotten odors and could never have imagined how much more offensive it was to become as the battle continued. As she moved down the trench, the entrance, some distance away, resembled a cave of darkness, a pit into some unforgiving hell. Wounded soldiers sitting in the mud lined the trench, their bloody bandages limp and soggy. Their vacuous eyes appeared to look someplace she could not see, a land of both calm and of fear. Had they been treated or were they waiting for care? She did not ask. There was no reason to comfort them. They would not have heard. A closer look showed they were dead. She continued into the darkness, stumbled and fell onto the goop. Her ankle twisted and she reached back to remove the object, possibly a thick tree limb. She pulled it toward her, repressed the urge to scream when she saw it was a severed leg that had fallen from a pile of limbs stacked in a corner. Her eyes started to adjust to the light. In the distance a dim electric light fluttered and buzzed. Candles were punched into the walls.

The infirmary was a labyrinth of tunnels branching off the main line. A medic adjusted a bandage on the arm of a soldier who winced and moaned.

"Corporal," she said. "May I speak with the doctor?" He looked up for a minute and nodded to acknowledge her presence.

"Not possible, mademoiselle," he said. "He and doctor Gindrey have been operating for several days. I don't think they have the energy for your type of services." He snickered. Nicole placed her hand on the wounded man's head. He quit moaning and a smile crossed his face.

"It must be painful?" she said.

"A scratch, nothing more," said the soldier. He tried to look unconcerned, tried to hold back the pain. "I'll be back at them in no time."

The medic stretched his back. "Perhaps I can get a word to the doctor. Might I inquire what this is about?"

"We might be of value assisting the doctor," she said. "We can change bandages, wash the men, offer them comfort, write letters, listen to their complaints, clean areas, whatever you want. It will lessen some stress for those of you doing the important work."

As she waited she went from soldier to soldier offering a kind word, a gentle touch, an occasional kiss on the forehead. Shells shook the ground and bits of dirt trickled down. A pack of cigarettes lay beside a soldier she noticed was dead. She offered them to other men often lighting them between her lips before passing it to them. A smile from the men, either with their lips or with their eyes, always greeted her. Those who were moaning stopped their noise and attempted to nod their heads as way of greeting. The medic returned and motioned her to follow him. He pointed to a hanging bamboo door. She entered cautiously.

The operating room was sweltering and small. Bamboo mats had been attached to the walls and overhead on the ceiling to stop any falling dirt. A bright operating light swayed with the rhythm of the dancing ground, its glare moving across an arm being severed below the elbow by the doctor. A medic, still in his tunic and wearing his helmet, looked on. The doctor pulled away the forearm and handed it to another medic who dropped it into a large bucket overflowing with other torn limbs: a hand reaching toward the ceiling, a thigh doubled over the rim where the remainder of the leg and foot disappeared into the bucket, the foot under a sheen of blood. Doctor Grauwin stood over the patient, his bald head bent down, sweat dripping from his forehead and off the rims of his glasses. Unlike the others in the room, he worked bare-chested; a thick chest covered with curly hair, and he wore no mask. Without turning to look he said, "A pleasure to meet you, mademoiselle. Pardon me for not kissing your hand but I am rather busy at the moment. I have not had the satisfaction of your company but your reputation for concern with our soldiers and for your employees is well known. I apologize for the situation, for not meeting you in my room, but, as you can see, it could not be helped. I am frozen in this position as the wounded are passed across the table one after the other." He worked with the silk thread as he sutured the stump. "How may I help?"

"It is I and my girls who would like to help." She felt that he had asked her into the room to see if she could handle the gore. "We found ourselves with extra time. Perhaps we can help with the men? Clean them, change dressings, comfort them, whatever you like."

"You are truly an angel. Of course, I cannot have them comforted too much," he said, a bit of seriousness in his voice. "I do not wish to stitch them up a second time," he chuckled. "They cannot think of a better way to die, but it must not be allowed. The presence of a woman can lift a man's spirits and help him to recover faster or allow him to die in peace. There will be much disgusting work. Can your girls handle it as you have standing here?"

"I will see to it," she said, happy she had passed the test.

"Return tomorrow evening about 1800 hours. See Sergeant Blughet for instructions. I will speak with him tonight to make the arrangements."

"You are very kind," she said. "Our concern has always been for the men."

"As I've heard," he said, cutting the last stitch. He did not look up as the patient was removed and another placed onto the table. The doctor moved his chin. Something grey oozed from the bandage on his head. Dr. Grauwin motioned with his hand and the dead soldier was replaced with another.

Chapter 38

"I don't know if I should believe that bull or not," said Crème Brulee, referring to the information passed to the troops from Colonel de Castries. "Sounds down right desperate."

He and Mategriffin stood amongst the severely wounded waiting to be evacuated. A small piece of the airstrip had been repaired, enough for a single hospital aircraft, clearly marked with a Red Cross, to land. De Castries was counting on the humanitarian aspect of the Viet Minh not to fire on the wounded.

"What, dare say, was it all about?" said Mategriffin. "I didn't hear."

"He says we ain't got nothing to worry about," he continued. "Supplies and reinforcements is being dropped in daily as they's being used up. We kinda got caught by surprise but them days is over now that we know what the little yellow bastards is up to."

"I wonder why they have always been called yellow?," said Mategriffin. "They have always looked tan to me. Wasn't the same mistake made with your so-called 'Redskins'? They don't look at all red."

"No," said Crème Brulee, "I don't like this pep talk stuff one bit. It always spells trouble."

Two soldiers, bare chested, helmeted, holding large Red Cross flags, waited to dash toward the landing plane to clear the way for the stretchers. Some of the wounded rested on elbows, eyes anxious, anticipating the arrival of their savior, a rumbling tube of aluminum and gasoline capable of lifting them toward heaven and, with any luck, returning them safely to earth, air conditioning, hot food and clean beds. Soldiers in more pain lay back and grimaced or passed out.

The faint sound of engines thumped from overhead as the stretchers were lifted. The plane dropped through the clouds and drifted toward the short usable strip of runway, the engines idling back, the flaps lowered and trailing water, the wheels touching down and bouncing the plane as it slid to a stop, the side door opened, a nurse and medic kicking boxes to the ground. Soldiers carrying the flags ran to the plane forming a gauntlet through which the stretchers were carried, one end shoved into the open fuselage, the other jammed in like a shell into a breach and disappearing into the darkness. Ambulatory cases thrust past, fighting to fit into the plane, tearing open their wounds, fresh blood dripping through dressings of old blood, fighting for a chance at life even at the destruction of the weaker wounded for even at the end of life the fittest have the best chance of survival.

Brulee and Mategriffin tore back to gather another stretcher and jostled him to the plane. Several men slipped from the plane and attempted to mingle with the soldiers as they helped to lift the wounded through the doorway before working their way along the line to disappear into the hospital dugout.

"I imagine the boss is up to no good," said Mategriffin. He patted the suffering soldier on the shoulder as he eased him into the plane. "They look like replacement officers trying to sneak in."

"Reckon it's what the French do best," said Brulee. "Them Reds ain't going to like it if we're sneaking in officers. They been letting us get away with these red cross flights. I'm guessing things is going to get rough shortly if they find out then, nobody's getting out."

The door of the plane slammed shut as the engines started to roar, the propellers kicking up mud and water that splattered across Brulee's back as he folded over and ran for cover. The plane lumped along picking up speed before lifting into the air and vanishing into the clouds.

"That went well," he said, tapping out a cigarette and offering one to Mategriffin.

"I hear some American bloke is flying in supplies," said Mategriffin. "A hero named Earthquake McGoon."

"Only Earthquake McGoon I know is in the funny papers."

"It's not his real name."

"What is it?" said Brulee.

"How would I know? He's an American hero, not British."

"If he can save our asses, it's all right by me," said Brulee.

"Isn't that the Sergeant's girl?" Mategriffin nodded toward a small figure giving drinks to the next batch of waiting wounded.

"She looks right good even in them fatigues." When Crème Brulee caught her eye she came over and squatted.

"I see you are hard at work," she said. "How is Henrich?"

"Fit, as ever," said Brulee. "I 'spect he's going to win the war just to save you. What's going on here?"

After the medical airplane left, artillery rounds started falling more heavily than before.

"My girls are helping in the hospital," she said. "They are short of personnel."

"What about the rest of us that's suffering?" said Crème Brulee. "We might succumb to a lingering death without them. Nothing's worse than a man dying of a broken heart."

"We wouldn't leave you out," said Nicole. "There are enough girls to help with all the suffering." She patted Brulee on the knee.

"What's with them soldiers that got off the plane? They ran into the hospital. More doctors? They look like officers to me. That ain't right and the history professor won't put up with it for long."

"They wanted directions to the command post," she said. "That's all I know. How long are you going to be helping with the stretchers?"

"We're just temporary," said Brulee. "Easy duty before we go on the offensive. Some replacements are sposed to land today. I'll tell the Sergeant we saw you and you're doing fine."

She returned to the wounded serving the last of the water before going for more.

"I say they're up to no good," said Crème Brulee. "They're using the red cross to sneak in officers."

"Frenchmen," said Mategriffin. "Who knows what goes on inside that command post?"

Crème Brulee watched Major Bigeard, back and arms stiff, teeth clenched, limp toward the Command Dugout supported by a large walking stick.

"He looks sizeable mad," he said.

"They don't come any tougher," said Mategriffin, drawing on the cigarette. "More officers like him and we wouldn't be in this fix."

"More officers like him and we'd all be dead," said Crème Brulee. "A man can be too tough, I reckon. Looks like he means business."

"At least he would be dead with us, unlike Colonel de Castries," said Mategriffin.

Pushing his way into the tunnel, Bigeard drove through the darkness like a river rat, slick, firm and determined. Langlais ordered one of his companies from the Sixth Battalion on a reconnaissance patrol without informing him. Such insolence would be straightened out immediately. He burst into Langlais' command post like a meteor, red hot and flaming. Langlais looked up from his maps.

"You had better guess again if you think you are God!" said Bigeard, shouting, spittle squirting from the corners of his mouth. "No one issues orders to my men except me, understand?" He resembled a mad dog too angry to bark; just offering guttering growls and choking against the leash of authority that kept him just out of reach of his prey.

Langlais stood slowly, fists clenched, two tight rough balls spring-loaded.

"General Cogny says the battle is being run badly," he continued. "He feels the officers are incompetent. I intend to change all that and it can't be done with your interference. All orders to my unit go through me, understand?"

For several moments Langlais stood chest to chest with Bigeard, the two toughest paratroopers in all French Indochina. Finally Langlais spoke quietly, evenly.

"You are a Lorraine; I am a Breton. We both have hard heads. Let's bang them together against this post and we'll soon see whose is the hardest."

They continued to stare at one another then, simultaneously, burst into laughter like comedians overcome at their own jokes. Langlais put his hand affectingly on Bigeard's shoulder and offered him a chair.

"How is the leg, Bruno?" he said. "Yes; in the excitement I overstepped my bounds. It won't happen again."

"Of no importance," said Bigeard. "I do not like to hobble about in front of my men." An aide brought in cups of hot coffee.

"It shows you are with them," said Langlais. "An officer who can fight although injured is an inspiration to his men."

He held up the coffee cup as a toast.

"General Cogny is correct," said Langlais. "Things are going badly and we suffer from lack of leadership and coordination. Colonel de Castries, generally a good brave and intelligent man, seems powerless here, unable to make decisions. He has lost his nerve. Something must be done if we are to prevail."

"I see," said Bigeard, tapping his fingers on the table. "What do you have in mind?"

"I am still trying to work it out. I scheduled a staffing later in the week with the fighting unit officers, mostly the paratroopers, to discuss the problems."

"A meeting with de Castries?"

"No, no. He is the problem." Colonel Langlais crossed his arms and looked toward the ceiling.

Brulee watched Major Bigeard limp back in the direction he had come. He looked more relaxed and his face was not so twisted.

"Whatever it was it musta got worked out," he said.

"Like I said, a good man." Mategriffin wiped his hands on his pants.

"If he got it worked out it means we're in deep shit," said Crème Brulee. "Only thing he knows is fightin' and we can't hide from that."

The faint sound of engines was heard overhead and soon several planes dropped through the clouds. Viet Minh guns filled the air with bullets.

"Looks like more supplies or more replacements," said Mategriffin.

Parachutes started to fill the sky.

"Reckon it's the cavalry," said Crème Brulee. "They always come in the nick of time. I wouldn't want to be dropping through all that lead. Nothing spoils a day more than getting filled with holes."

They sat for another thirty minutes before a captain appeared and give them a new assignment.

"They'll be no more ambulance planes today," he said. "Some of the replacements are for le BEP and they are landing all over the place. Catch one of the trucks and see if you can find any of them and take them back to your outfit."

Crème Brulee had his share of complaints as they left, the thick mud sticking to his feet, the danger of being out in the constant shelling, nothing to eat since breakfast, no woman to love, an itchy crotch, a fungus between his toes, tired of being wet, bad cigarettes, and he was starting to get withdrawal pains and needed a fix. Mategriffin knew of his problem, as they all did, but was unable to talk him into quitting. In his present state he was unreliable as a soldier therefore not much good in their present situation. He could not be disliked so he was tolerated.

They latched onto a retrieval truck and stopped to help out a corporal stuck in a watery shell crater.

"Merde," said the corporal, in perfect French, for he was a Frenchman, often unusual in the Foreign Legion.

"Corporal," said Mategriffin. "Avec moi demerde toi, you must get yourself out of this shit but I don't know how. This is just the beginning."

"You in deep," said Crème Brulee. "What outfit you looking fer?"

The corporal tossed his equipment up the bank. Mategriffin offered him the barrel of his rifle and pulled him from the hole.

"I am a replacement for le BEP," he said, ducking as a shell went overhead. "You get a lot of that?" referring to the round.

"Tain't nothing," said Crème Brulee. "We got at truck that'll take you to the outfit. We been losin' men right fast around these parts. We ain't but a ways behind the command post where they can reach us fast."

A soldier bleeding from the arm was helped to the truck.

"If you were going to land already wounded you might as well have stayed at home," said Mategriffin.

He helped toss the corporal's equipment on to the truck before looking for more strays for le BEP. The drive across the compound revealed the destruction that had already taken place. The neat rows of barbed wire had become twisted and torn vines of thorns; the earth scarred and pocked like giant pustules of disease; upended vehicles smoking and burning; communication wires hanging from torn poles; soldiers moving in slow dreams. The truck dropped the replacements near the company bivouac.

"Sergeant Knowles is the best man in the outfit," said Mategriffin.

"Reckon you'll be assigned to him," said Crème Brulee to the corporal, before dashing into his dugout.

"We just lost a Corporal," said Druxman, who had emerged from the dugout. "Not killed, you understand, just disappeared. A good fellow, too."

Brulee, shaking his arm, a distant look on his face, rejoined the group as Druxman left to inform Knowles about the replacements. Knowles was giving instructions to several soldiers that had arrived the day before. He released them and started walking with Druxman.

"Do I look like an expert?" said Druxman. "No, not an expert but a pretty smart fellow. The Corporal seems capable. He might be a good one to keep. Just my opinion."

The replacements were listening to Mategriffin with their backs to Knowles. As he approached they turned around. The corporal stepped forward and offered his hand. Knowles stopped, unable to lift his arm, his heart banging against his ribs, breath quickening like an exhausted cat, his eyes looking directly into the eyes of the Frenchman. A peculiar birthmark sat on his forehead, the shape of Scotland. Knowles knew he would never forget that face, the very person who had taken his manhood and who had raped Nicole.

"I am Corporal Toan."

Knowles' arm lifted, the granite cracking under the determination to reveal nothing, to show no surprise to the man who did not recognize him. The hands clasped, flesh against flesh, firm grips from both, palm upon palm.

"Sergeant Knowles," said Knowles, his eyes narrowing. "We can use good men."

Their hands released.

"We are waiting to get into the fight," said Toan. "I understand it is a tough situation. Just rumor, or course. We are never told anything."

"A bloody nose, nothing more," said Knowles. "I will make the assignments then inform the Lieutenant. You will stay with me. A good man is difficult to find and I want to keep you close. We'll be clearing the road to Isabelle tomorrow and you will get plenty of fighting there."

Bix, Sangree, and others came straggling up covered in mud and soaking wet. They all looked exhausted.

"These are the new men," said Knowles. "Look sharp, like soldiers, or you will give them the wrong impression."

"What a bitch," said Bix, nodding to the men and sitting on an empty ammo box. "It does no good to send us on patrols to find the enemy – he's everywhere!"

"Get some rest," said Knowles. "You'll be at it again tomorrow."

Knowles had Mategriffin and Druxman take the replacements to their dugouts. He kept Toan with him.

"I recon these boys is tired after their walk," said Crème Brulee. "You fellas take a nice rest and Quang and me'll go fetch some soup."

Quang stood like a tattered scarecrow, a smile on his face, Crème Brulee's bayonet at his side. He carried it everywhere and used it for everything from digging to opening cans. There were almost 2,000 P.I.M.s (prisoners) now under French control. Quang seemed devoted to Brulee almost like a personal servant.

"I'll show you our hole," said Knowles, lifting Toan's equipment bag.

Bix dropped into the dark and onto his cot. Fallen dirt, shaken loose from the artillery bursts, covered the blanket as exhaustion covered him. Since the beginning of the siege there had been little sleep and constant engagements. Le BEP was charged with keeping the road to Isabelle open, a task becoming more dangerous every day. The Viet Minh had established a roadblock at the village of Ban Kho Lai. Each time the French drove them away, they returned almost immediately when the French left, digging in more deeply and more determined to stay and hold the position. Le BEP was being reduced more quickly than its casualties could be replaced.

The only comfort Bix had was his love for Nicole. She become an obsession with him, his reach for her just beyond his grasp. He imagined her in his arms, tenderly embraced, entwined and inseparable like vines. If only she would give him a chance to prove his love before the officers of the Command Post had them all killed.

The morning arrived for Bix like a hot pile of mud he tried, without much success, to climb through. He gathered no additional energy during the night and no recuperative powers pumped new vigor into his system. If anything, he felt worse than the day before like a partially drowned cat taking its first watery breaths after reaching shore. He was dressed, wrinkled muddy pants, wet boots swelling his feet, his fatigue shirt soaked with sweat. Druxman looked energetic and ready to go as he drank his morning coffee.

"There's just enough time to grab some food - bread and jam - before formation," he said. "We leave at 0730. I waited to wake you until the last minute. You seemed to need the sleep."

"I didn't sleep," said Bix. "I wasn't awake, either, but I wasn't asleep. How come you always look so fresh and eager?"

"What, you think I'm one of those old Jews that let the Germans take him to slaughter without a whimper?" he said. "I'm a fighting Jew descended from the mighty army of King David, a warrior, fit and enthusiastic for a fight, a tight ball of muscle, a ham bone that makes the stew…"

"You ain't no Southern Jew chewing on a ham bone," said Brulee, sticking his head into the dark.

"OK, I was stretching it with ham bone," he said. "But I'm still a fighting Jew descended from a great race."

"You best get your ass up," said Brulee to Bix and fiddling with something in his hand. "You got me inta this mess and I ain't going into a fight without you."

"Leave any time you want," said Bix. "No one's stopping you."

He carried nastiness in his voice as if he had swallowed a fly. He was in no mood to listen to his friend. Crème Brulee became nothing more than a junkie, a whining junkie who could not live without a fix. It seemed a sign of weakness to Bix and weak soldiers never won a war. No one could count on him for protection and he became totally unreliable in any situation.

"The Sergeant and new corporal are waiting," said Crème Brulee, tossing him a roll of buttered bread, hard and covered with hairy mold.

Clearing Road 41 to Isabelle became a larger operation than Bix had thought. The array of soldiers seemed to be the entire reserves. Two days earlier the operation cost the French five killed and five wounded. The following day legionnaires from Isabelle, supported by the tank platoons of Lieutenant Preaud and Warrant Officer Carette battled all morning before finally clearing the road late in the afternoon rather than at noon, as expected. Adding to the morale difficulties of the French, Viet Minh commandos, in the early morning, walked right past the guards and blew a giant hole in the middle of the airstrip then escaped without a casualty. No place in the camp seemed safe.

Captain Vieulles led the unit of legionnaires from le BEP and a contingent of Air Force personnel under Captain Charnod. The men were stranded after the aircraft at the base was destroyed so they had been formed into infantry. Although ground fighting was new to them they fought as well as any soldiers new to combat in an effort to prove themselves. Tanks and Algerian riflemen were sent from Isabelle to form a pincer movement. Eighty-eight air force missions were assigned to support the operation. Colonel Langlais wanted to clear the road once and for all.

"What happened to Major Bigeard?" said Bix, thinking he would lead the operation.

He always felt more comfortable with Bigeard in charge. He was a man who knew how to fight and he did it with the safety of his men in mind. They all fought better when he was around.

"He's running another operation," said Ferdinand. "It must be more important than this one."

"Makes me feel better," said Crème Brulee, in a dreamy voice. "I spect to get from this valley alive. Trouble with him is he expects a man to fight. There's no quicker way of gettin' hurt than that."

At first everything went smoothly, little opposition, an easy walk along Road 41. Keeping alert, the men talked and joked quietly like a railroad engineer unattached to the work yet always with his eyes on the gauges.

Suddenly everything changed. Rifle and machine gun fire came zipping like angry wasps from the brush and mortar fire started to eat up the road. The unit came to a halt, pinned down. Bix watched Captain Vieulles continue the business of being a leader. He stood upright, as if soaking up the sun on an early morning, issuing orders through the radio strapped to the back of a very nervous radio-man. He breathed in the smoke from his cigarette, tilted back his head, and blew it out like a low-lying cloud. The French officers often seemed to him like the bravest men he had ever seen. The tanks were brought forward and air strikes called in. He ordered more units from Isabelle to work the backside of the pincer movement. Slowly they started to move.

Knowles and the new corporal moved the men ahead pointing out possible targets, and places to protect themselves, small dips in the ground, thick brush. Bix stayed close to Brulee, watching for any sign of running, any quiver of fear. The fear was evident but he stayed with the rest of the unit. Druxman and Ferdinand continued to fire from his other side.

The shell exploded like a cast iron stove whirlwinding up and out with shards of white hot metal, one piece, obsidian-sharp, as if in the hands of an ancient shaman, cutting cleanly across Druxman's abdomen, his guts folding out and dripping onto the ground, surprise, confusion, and disbelief, on his face as he watched them fall. Crème Brulee, knocked to the ground, cleared the mud from his eyes and saw Bix and Ferdinand rush to Druxman, now on his knees, hands clasped in the air as if praying to the steaming pile of gray goop before him.

Brulee left his rifle on the ground and moved to the group. Airplanes swirled overhead, bombs jabbed the ground, mortar shells rattled the earth, bullets cracked the air, everywhere were shouts and screaming, a great parliament of noisy madness. Through it all came the mousey squeak of Druxman's voice, "Put them back, please put them back."

Bix pulled a dressing from his belt and wrapped it over Druxman's head and around his uninjured eyes to prevent him from seeing his insides, outside.

"Lay back, man," he said, pulling gently on his shoulder and lowering him to the ground.

Ferdinand, another friend of theirs, lifted his legs to keep the blood in his head and help lessen the results of shock. For once Brulee had nothing to say. He knelt beside Druxman, his hands shaking; a gurgling in his throat where some comforting words might have attempted to escape. Mategriffin flagged the attention of a medic working on a nearby soldier.

"You ain't even bleedin'," Crème Brulee finally said, in a failed attempt to sound nonchalant. He placed his hands on Druxman's forehead. It was not a lie. Wounds in the abdomen bleed but slightly since they have no major veins or arteries. If Druxman died it would not be from loss of blood. Brown-green mush oozed from a split in his colon.

"The medic will be right over," said Bix, shooting him with a vial of morphine. "You have all the luck, a cushy rest in the hospital with Nicole and the other nurses, then off to Hanoi for recuperation while the rest of us are stuck here doing your job."

Ferdinand removed his T-shirt and made a pouch to put in the guts and tied it around Druxman's waist. They could not be put back in until they had been washed and the colon repaired. Corporal Toan grabbed Bix by the shoulder and tried to lift him.

"Come on," he said. "All of you keep moving before you're killed."

Bix pushed the hand away, ready to fight, to knock Toan on his ass, to run his bayonet through him. Toan stepped back and looked surprised. Knowles moved in.

"Let's go, Muffin," he said. "The medic is on his way. Your friend will be fine. Your job is not here."

The men, except Brulee, gathered their gear and started to reenter the battle.

"You, too," said Toan, to Crème Brulee and feeling rebuffed at Knowles words and at his ability to get the men moving.

Crème Brulee was finished; Knowles saw it in his face as he had seen it so many times over his lifetime, the vacuous stare into a land few knew, the quivering hand, the calmness in the voice as if the words were flamingos gliding through the sun over a morning lit lake. Brulee kept patting Druxman gently on the chest and saying, "You'll be OK old friend; you'll be OK"

"Leave him," said Knowles, to Toan. "They are both finished."

Toan looked at Knowles, then at Brulee, then back to Knowles.

"Oui," he said. "C'est fini."

The medic arrived as the others left, quickly checked over Druxman, called for a stretcher carried by another soldier.

"You've done a good job," said the medic looking at the wrapping job. "Too many guys want to shove everything back in and make a mess of it. Did you give him any morphine?"

Brulee nodded.

"Help get him onto the stretcher. Where is your partner?" He said to the stretcher-bearer. The man drew a finger across his throat.

The three of them lifted Druxman gently onto the stretcher like a delicate omelet.

"Shouldn't you put a better dressing on him?" said Brulee.

"He's fine. Everything is in short supply. It's not far."

Brulee watched Druxman grimace, his face contorted then relaxing then contorting again.

"How-bout more morphine?" said Brulee. "We only had one vial and I reckon he's in lots of pain."

"One?" said the medic, his face twisting up as he rummaged through his bag. "You're lucky to have that. Such comforts are difficult to find these days and medical supplies are second on the list – first ammunition, then medical supplies, then food. Now, help with the stretcher."

The medic moved to a soldier missing an arm as Crème Brulee and the stretcher-bearer carried Druxman from the fight, leaving their weapons where they had fallen. They placed the stretcher with others inside a waiting ambulance. Crème Brulee started to climb in.

"We'll take it from here," said a medic with the truck.

Brulee shoved him aside and crawled inside with Druxman. The medic realized the situation and knew better than to protest. Brulee continued to rub his hand over Druxman's forehead as he attempted to regain his composure and put Druxman at ease. The ambulance was a Bartok of groans and moans as the symphony rolled over the pitted ground and toward the hospital.

"I reckon I ain't seen any wound so minor since that time my aunt Mertel got a tittie caught in the wringer. She howled like crazy but kept turning the handle crank anyway. Always walked a little lop-sided after that. Had to roll that tittie up in a sock before she put on a bra. Looked like a giant dog's tongue lapping up water whenever she took a bath."

The sounds of the battle started to fade, replaced with constant bursts of artillery shells throughout the camp. "At what point did a man die?" thought Brulee. First he was there, then gone. A person is not in his body when he died, but where is he? What is he? When he killed the three men in Alaska for raping him, chopping them into bits with an axe, he could not find them – their bodies, but not them. It was as if he had not killed them at all, as if the sight of the axe had scared them away leaving their bodies behind. Druxman lay somewhere between his body and himself and he kept his hand on his forehead as if to hold him in.

A line of wounded waited in a trench outside the hospital, all sick, all bewildered. The entrance to the hospital appeared like a giant gaping foul-smelling mouth waiting to swallow its young. The medic pushed his way past many of the wounded and motioned Brulee and Druxman, his arm laying over the side of the stretcher, forward into the hole.

"Priority," he said, to another blood-draped medic.

"Over there, somewhere," said the hospital medic. "You'll have to find room."

They adjusted several stretchers, mashing one against the wall, to fit in Druxman. The room was small and dark and tight. A small figure moved in the distance.

"Hey, you," he said. "Over here."

A petite black woman moved in his direction.

"I am very busy," she said. She knelt down and placed her hand across Druxman's cheek.

"Ain't I been with you at the bordello?" said Brulee. "I remember now, just two weeks ago."

"Yes," she said, not knowing him from any other soldier. "You were that very special one."

"I thought so," he said, standing a little straighter. "It ain't easy for a woman to forget a man like me. I wonder if you can't do something for me?"

"You'll have to wait until I get back to the bordello," she said. "I'm tending to soldiers in a different way today."

"I can understand why you might be anxious to get at me," said Brulee, 'but I was wondering if you couldn't find Nicole and tell her we was here? She knows us, at least she knows our Sergeant, Knowles."

"That's different," she said. She patted Druxman on the shoulder before she left.

Crème Brulee squatted on his haunches. He removed two cigarettes from a pack lying beside a soldier on another stretcher. He did not know if he was sleeping or dead. He lit them both and placed one between the lips of Druxman.

"You ain't in any damn bad shape," he said. "It was all I could do to keep that woman from crawling under the covers with you."

Druxman managed to utter several words, the morphine easing some of his pain. His situation started to enter his mind and he was slowly accepting his fate.

"What's that?" said Brulee. He leaned closer to Druxman's lips.

"I don't have any covers," said Druxman.

"Damned if you don't," said Brulee. "Anyway, I done saved you from a fate worse than death, not the sex but the fact you'd of had to pay her. Parting with a few coins is like driving a stake into the heart of a Jew."

"You're a good friend," said Druxman.

The words caught Brulee by surprise, a statement that marked the finality of life, an admission that all was lost.

"You ain't nothing but a damned old prick," said Brulee, holding Druxman's hand. "I don't want to hear that kind of talk."

He felt the hand go limp, saw the cigarette fall from Druxman's lips. He placed the hand across Druxman's chest, removed the cigarette, gently flicked off the ash, then put it into his pocket. He stood slowly as if lifting a great weight.

Outside another ambulance airplane landed. After learning about officers being smuggled, the Viet Minh no longer held their fire to let the wounded escape. Soldiers rushed casualties to the plane attempting to push them. A hoard of slightly wounded mobbed their way past the stretcher cases. Guards tried to push them back. Crème Brulee suddenly dashed forward and, using the wounded as a ladder, jabbing his boots over their backs, shoulders, and wounds, tried to climb into the plane. A legionnaire guard inside the plane smashed him in the face with his rifle butt. Brulee fell over backward and tumbled onto a pile of wounded as the plane revved its engines and started to rumble away half loaded.

He rolled to his knees and felt the side of his face. His cheekbone felt broken, as did his nose. He joined the crowd of dejected wounded and healthy walking back into the muck and filth. The daze he was in carried him back to his dugout where he entered the darkness and sat on the cot.

"Petit enculé," he mumbled over and over, the only phrase in French he knew well.

He slid out the full ammo box of dope and rested one foot on it. Thinking came hard to him but he made the attempt to concentrate, to sort out the mess in his head. He had to get straight to survive, that was certain, but the illness had already started to buckle him over. Being a heroin addict did not mean having a craving for dope; it meant a fear of not having any dope to deaden the pain of withdrawal. The agony and anguish were more than most addicts could bare, the insidious worm eating its way through every blood vessel, gnawing, chomping, ripping up the guts to bleed internally. He melted the dope in a spoon over a candle and tied off his arm. The needle to the eyedropper was missing so he poked a small hole into the vein with the tip of his bayonet, sucked the juice into the eyedropper, placed it close to the cut and squeezed it in. Blood ran from the arm and over the purple scars. He leaned back against the wall. Perhaps tomorrow he could quit. Yes, tomorrow, when he was stronger.

Quang entered with a bottle of wine. He withdrew the bayonet to open the wine and handed the bottle to Brulee.

"It's time to get out," said Brulee.

"No can leave now," said Quang.

"It's time."

"Viet Minh too tight. Must wait."

"What are y'all going to do?" said Crème Brulee. "You don't have to come with me. Major Coldeboeuf and Lieutenant Patrico is in charge of the prisoners. They's pretty good fellas and will treat you right."

"You me together," said Quang. He replaced the bayonet.

"To the river, then," said Brulee. "We'll go to the river with the other deserters and wait it out. You'll let me know when it's time to make our break? I'm counting on you."

"I stay with you till the end," said Quang.

"Lets go then," said Crème Brulee.

He started toward the opening then stopped. He went back inside and grabbed the ammo box.

Chapter 39

"Earthquake, we've been assigned a crew," said Wallace Buford as he slid onto a bench in the mess hall. The noon sun heated the air to the consistency and color of hot honey and he had difficulty moving.

"Good men?" said Earthquake. His hands, knobby loaves of flesh, were so large that steam appeared to be rising from his fists clutched around the coffee cup. Throughout Asia, pilot James McGovern was called Earthquake McGoon after a Li'l Abner comic strip character who shook the earth when he walked. The earth might not have shook when he walked but, by Vietnamese standards, it certainly moved.

"Some Frenchies and a Malay or Thai. Go figure," said Buford. "Tough to get help in secret."

Earthquake and his copilot Buford could not have been more physically dissimilar. At 260 pounds Earthquake looked too large to be a pilot. His square face and sunken eyes, shaded by bushy awnings, looked almost Neanderthal. His barrel chest had to be tamped into the pilot's cockpit, especially into a fighter. Once strapped down only his arms and hands moved and he had to constantly shake them awake to keep the pinched blood flowing. Claustrophobia had no effect on him and after joining Claire Chennault's 14th Air Force in China, he quickly dispatched four Japanese fighters and destroyed another five on the ground making him an ace. After the war the CIA approached Chennault to start a phony commercial airlines called Civil Air Transport to support American allies, (namely the French) short of aircraft, without breaking any government treaties or raising suspicion to various enemies. He needed men he could trust and Earthquake was on the top on his list. He promised him a job piloting C-119s, known as flying boxcars because of their spaciousness, including the cockpit where Earthquake could kick back and breathe.

"You have a reputation for partying and hard living," said Buford. "A real soldier-of-fortune."

"Overblown," said Earthquake. "There are old pilots and bold pilots but no old/bold pilots. I enjoy a good mission then return home to celebrate. The returning home is the best part."

"I wasn't worried. I'm sure we will work fine together. Just that they said you were an old dog."

"Not what you think, not a killer hound. I don't bite anyone, just sit around all day licking my balls. I hear you're no slouch, either," said Earthquake. He sweated heavily from the heat. "B-24s wasn't it? A pilot with the guts to fly through flack and enemy fighters can pilot with me anytime. Then what?"

"Boxcars in Korea," said Buford. He swatted at a fly. "I decided not to make flying my life and I was studying for an engineer degree at the university."

"So, what happened?" said Earthquake. "Sounds like a pretty good job to me, a chance at a real future. Why here?"

"Three thousand dollars a month. Whew," he said wiping his shirtsleeve against his forehead. "No one makes that kind of money. It's just lucky I saw the ad. I understand the French have gotten themselves into a fix."

"The Frogs are in shit up to their necks," said Earthquake. "The Reds are kicking the crap out of them down some valley in the mountains. Frogs have a big problem with math. They figured they had enough transports to keep their boys supplied but they weren't even close. The Reds are also knocking them out of the sky almost daily. Guess they've shot up over 50 by now; didn't bring them all down but have the French Air Force pilots pretty spooked. Only the French Navy pilots are worth a shit and don't mind coming in close enough to do any good. Thankfully they came crying to Eisenhower for help, putting money in our pockets. You ready to check out the ship?"

The heat shimmied from the tarmac like a string of airy dancers. Everything looked hot, the hangers, the quarters, the airplanes lined in neat rows. The heat burnt blue from the sky leaving it a dull gray. Touching a Quonset hut would burn skin from the hands curling it up like wood chips. Women carrying laundry moved about with cleaning bags, cooks, laborers, and mechanics, all Vietnamese employed by the French. They found most work cheaper to hire out than to do themselves. The Vietnamese appreciated the work and went about their labors with large smiles and good nature while gathering military information for the Viet Minh. Earthquake trudged to the first parked C-119. Heat sparkled off its aluminum skin.

"This thing ready to go?" he said, to Watkins, part of the ground crew. Watkins tried not to laugh. Earthquake was wearing a large Hawaiian shirt and bedroom sippers. He looked like a portable flower garden.

"Couldn't be any better," he said. "These beauties hum like a Hudson and pack a real load. Don't bring it back full of holes. You have that reputation. Flinner fixed your seat."

"Don't worry," said Earthquake. "Living's become a habit with me. Better keep that hat on. Your brains might fry."

Watkins was using his hat to wipe sweat from his forehead. He ran the hat up over his head. Although a young man his hair was already thinning.

"Hotter than hell. The chair is as solid as they come." He replaced the hat. "Let me know if you need any other modifications."

Earthquake tapped him on the shoulder and smiled. It seemed he was always smiling and never had a bad day. Watkins, Flinner, and Whitney were a top-notch ground crew. They could fix anything.

Earthquake climbed into the airplane. Buford followed, his shirt pulling from his pants as he stretched to enter. The inside of the airplane resembled a large cave and could hold twice the load of a C-24. Buford entered the cabin.

"What's this?" he said. A large wicker chair had replaced the pilot's chair.

"That's my baby," said Earthquake, sinking into the chair. The wicker squeaked under the strain. "My ass is just too big for a pilot's chair. Aviation engineers must think all pilots are starving Mexicans."

Buford slid into his seat, jiggled his shoulders, stretched out his legs and worked the pedals. He ran his hands over the controls like a blind man. He pulled back on the wheel and started to make engine noises. Earthquake laughed.

"It's good to be back," he said. "She feels like a woman I once knew."

"Just one?"

"I've always been selective" said Buford. "Love is a risky business. If they don't feel right then I don't go for them. A woman can hook you in to marrying her before you know what's happened so I don't take them to bed unless I think we can get along."

"I prefer these babies, these boxcars," said Earthquake. "The cockpits have more room than the C-24's and there's plenty of room for sandwiches and coffee. A few extra comforts makes a long mission easier."

The heat in the cockpit felt good and clean and if Earthquake sat perfectly still the sweat seemed to draw out his impurities. He leaned his head back and watched dust motes dance on the air. An airplane was his mistress, his life, and his home. He would have been happy to never touch the ground, to spend the remainder of his life floating through the clouds. He did not know the definition of freedom but he imagined it resembled what he felt in the air. They moved to the cargo bay.

"We'll be hauling the heavier stuff," said Earthquake. "Artillery and the like. The valley is almost in Laos so it's a long haul, about as far as we can go and still get back. I've flown over and it's a terrible place. When it isn't fogged in its pouring buckets of water and the clouds hang down like sagging panties. Apparently the Frenchies didn't figure that either. They had an airstrip but that was ripped apart by the Commies. They fixed it several times, just enough to get in a few flights, but it never lasted a day before the Commies shredded it again. They decided to not even bother, too torn up to repair."

"You should know something about Commies," said Buford. His hands gripped an overhead support and he stretched out his body. "That time you got shot down in China flying for Chiang Kai-shek has become a legend."

"They're not bad fellas, those Chinese," said Earthquake. "I didn't get shot down; I ran out of fuel and landed on a dry riverbed. They figured that Chiang Kai-shek was nothing but a gangster and I suppose they were right. They kept me six months and I badgered them the entire time until they turned me loose just to be rid of me. I think they also got tired of feeding me. They never mentioned killing me and I was never worried. People are pretty decent the world over once you get to know them, even if they are the enemy."

They exited the plane and walked toward a briefing room. A small group of children ambushed them, clutching Earthquake's legs. He lifted up the smallest one, a little girl with snot running from her nose. Earthquake wiped it with his handkerchief.

"This is my backup crew," he said. She looked like a doll in his large arms. He knelt down and placed the girl back on the tarmac. From his top pocket he retrieved a handful of hard candies and dealt them to the kids. He pushed them on their behinds to send them away. "They eat more than me. I can hardly keep them in candy."

"The new pilot?" said Kusak, as they entered the building and he offered his hand.

"Wallace Buford," said Earthquake. "Gave up a career on Wall Street to come fly with us."

"Money got yah, did it?"

"I can finish college anytime," said Buford. "This kind of money is almost worth giving your life for."

"Got coffee over here!" said Smitty, another pilot. He poured coffee for everyone, the steam rising from the ceramic cups. Other pilots, all Americans, joined them. "The rest of the crews will be here any minute. The boss is sorting them out."

General chatter floated between them, happenings back home, war experiences, the best restaurants in town. The talk fell to "the" subject: sexual conquests, the primary topic of all male chatter and one that eventually enters into every conversation.

The crews pushed themselves through the door. The pilots formed a line and one-by-one called out their names. They gathered their designated crews and took them aside. Earthquake and Buford had three legionnaires, Maurice, Bannack, and Sterlow.

"We are recovering from wounds received at Dien Bien Phu," said Sterlow. "We were chosen because we all speak English."

"I hear it's pretty tough down there," said Earthquake.

"We were lucky. They lifted us out before the airfield was destroyed. We are perfectly happy flying with you."

Earthquake laughed. "Luck is a funny thing," he said. "No one but a soldier would consider a survivable wound as lucky, or, flying with me." He scratched at the flowers covering his stomach. "You'll be shoving the cargo out of the plane's rear, rather like an enema. I understand you have been receiving instructions?" They all nodded. "Of course the crews, like the co-pilots, will not always fly with the same pilot and you may be assigned differently each day. Tomorrow it's with us. I think we can get to know one another better over beer and whisky. Let's find a better place to talk."

Earthquake knew of a decent beer place off Trang Tien Street. Because most of the chairs or stools sat just inches off the ground, they had built him a special chair where he sat like a king above his vassals. They arrived just as the bia hoa, a special home brew good for only several hours, was finished.

"You Frenchies get yourselves in the damndest messes," said Earthquake.

The waitress brought the beer in a gallon bucket and placed it on the table. The table was sticky with old beer. They dipped their glasses into the bucket. They were the only foreigners in the bar. Venturing many places in Hanoi in the evening was dangerous for the French and their allies. Hanoi was the last place in the north on which they had a grip. The Viet Minh seemed to be everyplace and were slowly working their way through the south. The French managed to hold on to most of the cities but the countryside belonged to the Viet Minh. Earthquake never felt threatened anyplace he went. Life, to him, was what you made it. If you thought you were in a miserable situation, then you were in a miserable situation. If you thought things were good and would turn out, then things were good and would turn out. He never knew a sour day.

"We don't try and make decisions for the higher command," said Maurice. "If they say jump into the valley of Dien Bien Phu, then we jump, that's all." His face pinched together with the bitter taste of the beer.

"I'm here for the money," said Buford. "I can't imagine there's that much in the Legion."

"We join for reasons other than money," said Sterlow.

"What other reasons?" said Maurice. "The pay is fabulous compared to a Vietnamese street vendor. Besides, none of us could hold a job in a decent society."

"It's a real fix," said Earthquake.

"How do you think it will turn out?" said Buford. The beer was warm and gummy and not to his liking.

"Badly, of course," said Maurice. "Such situations always turn out badly for the French. They take great pride in such predicaments and seek out hopeless circumstances, then try and work their way through them. They feel that if we are killing more of the enemy than the enemy is of us, then we are winning – ridiculous! It doesn't works that way. You cannot kill them all. Each day you can claim you have killed 100 of them and only lost 5 of us and hope you are fooling the press and the citizens into thinking the war is almost won - yet, they are still ahead."

A woman walked over and placed her arm around Earthquake. She whispered something in his ear. He patted her on the behind.

"I see you have a friend," said Bannack. "Perhaps there is also one for me?"

"You Frenchies are the world's great lovers, or so I've heard," said Earthquake. "A poor American like me must pay for everything he gets." He stood up from the table. "It seems I'm needed elsewhere."

The woman took his hand and lead him out the back door and down the alley. She looked extremely tiny beside his bulk, like a canoe pulling a tanker down a treacherous stream. They passed an old lady gutting fish, a fruit vendor selling green-skinned oranges, another offering a red fruit with strange arms and white pulp spotted with black seeds that Earthquake liked, but could not remember the name, and buckets of peanuts. In the darkest and most remote part of the alley someone was always selling something.

"I don't have much money on me," he told the woman.

"What you have is enough," she said.

"I am getting to be an old man."

"You are not so old," she said. She stopped and placed both her hands around his, then started off again.

They entered a small gate under a concrete arch. A vine grew up the arch. A pile of trash sat rotting on the dirt. One dim light glowed from a second story window behind a balcony. She led him up the stairs and stopped outside the door.

"You have been good to me," she said.

He placed his meaty hands around her cheeks and drew her to his chest. His arms almost smothered her and her shoulders seemed too fragile to hold the weight of his arms, big firm limbs hanging down her back. She entered the room on silent feet that seemed not to touch the floor, just glided slightly above the surface. She sat on the bed and motioned for Earthquake to sit beside her. He did, sinking deeply and causing her to almost slide onto his lap. He leaned across her to pick up the oil lamp so he coud get a better look at the boy under the covers.

"He looks better today," he said, watching the boy's pale skin and heavy eyes.

"I think so," she said. "The doctor says we need more medicine."

"Of course, of course," said Earthquake.

The woman moved to the floor and sat on her knees, her arms resting on the bed. Earthquake ran his palm across the boy's forehead then placed his hand on her head. He was told it was impolite to touch the head of a Vietnamese, their most sacred part, but she never seemed to mind. He reached into his pocket and handed her ten dollars.

"Let me know if you need more," he said.

Chapter 40

Colonel Langlais waited in his briefing room. Most of the other paratroop officers had arrived. They talked quietly and laughed among themselves. Major Seguin-Pazzis Chief of Staff, Major Bigeard 6th BPC, Major Botella 5th BPVN, Major Guiraud 1st BEP, and Major Tourret 8th Assault, were some of the officers in attendance. When everyone had arrived Langlais discussed his concerns about the battle and offered a solution. De Castries was not informed of the meeting.

"We are in a rough situation," said Langlais. "It will take guts, cunning, and decisive action to get us out." He paced to one side of the table. "So far there has been no organization to our defense, no chance to take the offensive. Everything is chaos. Our troubles stem from Colonel de Castries. He has been unable to move, frozen in his C.P.. With your help I intend to assume control of the battle."

All the officers shuffled on their seats.

"He won't stand for it," said Tourret. A small determined man, he, like the rest of the paratroop officers, was all muscle and determination. "This is nothing less than mutiny and there'll be hell to pay."

"We'll pay with our lives if we do nothing. We paratroopers are the fighting units of the camp," Langlais continued. "I do not wish my men to be badly lead and killed unnecessarily. If we are to survive, we need men of action. We are those men. We have no choice, but to take over."

"Like the Italians?" said Botella.

Langlais looked directly at him in an effort to understand.

"Italians?" he said.

"The Mafia." They all laughed when Botella said, "The Paratroop Mafia. We will become the Paratroop Mafia pitting our will, and our arms against the establishment."

"They are more effective than their own government," said Langlais. "Talk it over before we make a decision,"

"What is there to talk over?" said Bigeard. "It must be done."

"Then let us all go to confront him and show him that we are in agreement, that it's not just my decision. I am known for my hot head," he said. "This is not an irrational decision made by one man."

They pushed their way through the tunnel, carrying their weapons, and into de Castries' area. He was sitting at a table draped with a white tablecloth, a fine cooked duck, golden brown, simmering in its own juices, before him.

"I am afraid there is not enough to go around," he said. His uniform was perfectly clean and pressed. "Is this a social call? I sense some determination and urgency."

"We are here on serious business," said Langlais, standing in his disheveled clothes, a crumpled cigarette dangling from between his lips.

"So, not a social call?" de Castries put down his knife and fork and dabbed his lips with a napkin. "Then, I suppose I should stop eating and listen."

"I am assuming command of the battle," said Langlais. He was careful not say WE are assuming command. The responsibility of the mutiny, if that was what officials were later to describe it, would be totally his.

"I don't understand, Colonel?" said de Castries. He looked confused, his eyes almost blank, waiting to draw in more information from the scene before him.

"We have the greatest respect for you, Colonel," said Langlais, "but this fight is beyond your capability. You seem unable to get a grasp of the situation and are confused and indecisive. The paratroops are the fighting units of this camp so the paratroops will make the decisions about the battle, nothing more complicated than that. Our intent is not to embarrass you, but you are a tank commander in an infantryman's war. As far as the world knows, you will still be in command. You will relay all radio messages to Hanoi and Saigon and keep us supplied. Of course I will inform you of all operations and ask your opinion on my decisions. I still value your judgments and good sense. We are going to my headquarters to work out the details."

De Castries sliced off a piece of the duck and chewed it slowly.

"Then it is decided," he said. "Will you be joining me for bridge tonight?"

"Of course," said Langlais, as he left to start the new organization.

They worked all night to set up a workable organization. Langlais placed himself in charge of the entire defense, with Lemeunier as his deputy. The paratroops decided to divide Dien Bien Phu in half with different officers in charge of each section. The dividing line was the Nam Yum River. Langlais would be directly responsible for the eastern section including the strongpoints of Elaine and Dominique. From Colonel Trancart's headquarters Lieutenant Colonel Voinot would command the western section. Langlais had removed Trancart after blaming him for the losses of Gabrielle and Ann-Marie and placed with him de Castries where he could do no harm. Seguin-

Pazzis commanded Gap 2. Bigeard's new position as deputy for intervention remained the toughest assignment of all, a roll of constant fighting, a position he relished. The tanks and quad 50's remained under the control of Langlais and any counterattacks must be cleared with him.

When they had finished they felt they finally had some control and organization over the situation. A new spirit filled the room. They decided to stay on the offensive to keep the Viet Minh off balance, keep them guessing. It made no difference what General Giap had in mind now – the paratroopers were back in action.

Chapter 41

It was a challenge for Giap to put the next step of his plan into action. Because of the recent success of the troops, many of his generals, excited at the prospects of victory, wanted to continue to attack in an attempt to overrun the French base and shorten the battle. Giap was not fooled. The French were far from beaten and he had been too brutal with the bo doi in an effort to surprise the French, to show them that they were not invincible. Taking such losses would be a mistake and might lead to revolt. His concern now was for the safety of his men. The length of the battle was irrelevant. The idea now was to starve them out, keep up the pressure, surround the strongpoints, let them die a slow and hungry death. Sappers were brought in to dig trenches around every position and, in some cases, completely surround them so they could not be supplied. Don't bother with overrunning them, don't even attack them, just keep the supplies away - the food, the fresh water, the ammunition, keep up the harassment so their nerves are constantly tingled, so they can not sleep, keep them pinned down so they can not even bury their dead and they have to see and smell the mangled rotting corpses, keep them in fear of attack, but never attack unless sure of victory, let them understand that the war for them is over.

Chau looked over the valley with his captured French binoculars, U.S. Army issue. The French no longer buried their dead in neat little rows with marked pure white crosses surrendering to God. They were using a bulldozer to dig deep pits in which to dump the bodies outside the hospitals. In the beginning, all the corpses were brought to this site for neat little burials, a ceremony, an honor guard to send them neatly on their way. Now they buried many of them around the strongpoints where they fell, no time, no equipment, no manpower, no room, to deliver them to the cemetery. Because the graves were scattered and shallow, the bodies, in various states of decomposition, continued to be unearthed from artillery. Even from Chau's vantage point he could smell the bodies.

Luat sat on his haunches staring over the valley. Chau handed him the binoculars. He never learned the patience of the Vietnamese, the ability to sit hour after hour and never suffer boredom. Like most Europeans, Chau was unable to sit for long periods of time without twiddling at something or reading a book. He never saw a Vietnamese read outside of academia, never saw them thumb though dog-eared pages, eyes following words or pictures, their minds drifting over concepts, ideas, other real or imagined worlds.

Luat neatly folded the binocular straps and slid them into the case. He handed it to Hong. She took it with her long carved fingers, fingers that seemed to live outside the rest of her body as if they were their own entity capable of making their own decisions. They curled around the leather case like small snakes capturing a small mouse.

"Don't lose them," said Luat. "My friend made the case from water buffalo skin."

Hong said nothing, placed the case over her shoulder. She watched Chau carefully, so small, so muscular, so handsome, so alone and troubled. He seemed constantly conflicted, often doubting his decisions, nothing obvious, just a sense of hesitation she noticed in his eyes or his voice. No one else ever noticed, she was sure of that, and she never mentioned it.

"Is it the eastern hills?" said Luat.

"Another dangerous fight," said Chau. "The French call them Dominique and Elaine and gave them numbers. They will not easily let them go. Once we have them they are finished. Dominique is the largest one, there…" He pointed to the tallest hill just east of road 41. "They don't have enough men to defend it."

"They don't have enough men to defend anything," said Luat, standing and stretching his legs.

"And still they do," said Hong, quietly.

"Yes, yes," said Luat. "Now we have an expert. Perhaps you can make us a nice pho this afternoon."

"She is right," said Chau. "I heard many jokes about the French Army in the United States. The Americans do not understand how tough and tenacious they are. They have botched their affairs badly in Vietnam, have politically incompetent leaders, but the men fight."

"The Legionaries, yes," he said, "But they are not French."

"The officers are and they die very bravely," said Chau. He ran his finger over his chin as if feeling for whiskers that were not there.

"And easily," said Luat. "We kill them so quickly they will soon be without leaders."

The faint sounds of engines were heard overhead as two dive-bombers broke from the sky and dropped napalm onto one of the hills. Heavy black smoke rose from the jungle. Rows of transports followed as the sky opened with flack from the Vietnamese gunners. Supplies started to parachute to the ground. Some of the supplies floated into the Vietnamese lines.

"They fly too high to be accurate," said Luat. "The pilots have lost their nerve."

"So it seems," said Chau. "No one wants to die, including pilots."

"Don't forget to duck," said Hong.

"You are very funny," said Luat. "The navy pilots appear to keep their guts. I understand they come from an aircraft carrier. I have never seen one but a boat that can hold an airplane must be very large. Will you make the pho?"

"I am Captain Chau's aide," she said. "I take care of him."

"A common soldier like myself also needs tenderness," he said, looking dejected.

"Chau is an important man but are not all men alike, all equal under this government?"

"And women," she reminded him. "They, too, are equal."

Chau started to walk down toward the valley. He enjoyed their banter although he did not participate. The women were not only equal but did most of the work, tending fields, planting, harvesting, working the shops, having children, raising the families, tending the sick and elderly, waiting on the men, working manual labor on the roads, carrying goods, and cooking pho.

The soldiers did not seem to be as enthusiastic as before but they appeared willing enough to execute the job and if not willing, at least able to do it with a little prodding, first verbal humiliation in a effort to shame them before the other soldiers, then physical punishment.

Twice he almost fell in the mud. His head had been swirling for several days and he often felt faint. The men were digging very quickly, dirt flying through the air as if blown from the ground. They dug toward Dominique, the highest hill near the airfield. Within ten days the coolies had dug, with their usual efficiency and determination, almost 60 miles of communications and approach trenches throughout the valley. Soldiers by the thousands waited patiently in the surrounding hills to attack. They did not wait without trepidation and not a day had passed without the French launching small, but fierce, attacks of their own. The French were far from beaten and they refused to sit passively and accept their fate. These five hills would be severely contested and units, as small as they were, were seen moving into them almost daily.

Chau felt pride in the ability of his small country to tackle a modern industrial country. He wondered why the United States did not stop the French from recolonizing Vietnam? They have no love for the French and feel they did nothing to help the other Allies during the big war, but simply capitulated, helped the Germans, and especially the Japanese by letting them walk into Vietnam to use it as a base for their ever-expanding empire. They botched their control of Vietnam badly, were brutal, and were an inefficient and bungling government. Even de Gaulle was nothing but an egotistical blow-hard. The United States felt that, in the name of freedom, all colonies should be abolished. The British certainly did not see it that way and built their empire on the backs of others. From the beginning, they encouraged and helped the French move back into Vietnam. If France could not have colonies then what of their own? So, why did the United States let this happen and why are they helping the French now? It was all a mystery to Chau, but he had no time to think about it now.

During his checks on the supply routes not everything went smoothly. Traveling 500 miles through the jungle was hazardous on even the best roads, much less jungle trails. A bite from a venomous snake meant almost instant death, the victim quivering on the ground, his mouth frothing and lips quivering; people fell from cliffs, tumbling over rocks like dolls, or toppled from bridges or drowned in the rivers, their hands rising from above the rushing water as if waving goodbye; trees fell during high winds crushing and impaling the workers; and many coolies washed away in flash floods, tops and bottoms rolling end-for-end through the water. Sickness also brought them down, malaria and fever making them emaciated and shaking from the cold while burning up. Leeches feasted on them at night leaving exposed flesh covered in blood. Twice tigers attacked, killing one man and scattering the columns.

Chau was squatting as he watched the troops dig and cover the trenches with twigs and, as he started to stand, a white curtain closed across his eyes and he toppled onto the dirt. He passied out and hit the ground, Luat and Hong attempting to catch him. He remained unconscious for almost two weeks, near death. Hong, always at his side, cleaned and washed him, keeping cool cloths on his forehead and rubbing his chest with water. She and Luat attemptied to get liquids down his throat to keep him alive. He slowly opened his eyes one evening to the gentle rumble of artillery explosions and the glow from the lamp in Hong's eyes as she crouched over him.

"I think I fell," he said. He voice sounded scratchy and his throat hurt as he spoke.

"You will be fine," said Hong.

It seemed to Chau that she had always been there, had always been in his life, that she was Marie and Au and all the women he had even known, and that she would always be there. He tried to sit but fell back.

"What is happening?"

"You must rest." Her voice was smooth and quiet. He had listened to her sing several times over the short time he had known her and she had a soothing and melodic sound.

"There is fighting. I must...."

Luat entered with a bowl of pho. Some of it spilled when he realized Chau was awake.

"You have returned," he said, kneeling beside the cot, a luxury item from the Americans. "These holidays leave us concerned. We know you will come back but we never know when. Take some soup."

He tried to hand the bowl and spoon to Chau but Hong took it away, tested the heat with her lips, dipped out the broth and placed it between his lips. He choked as it went down.

"You must try," she said. "Just a little."

"The battle?" he said, between drinks.

"Baaa," said Luat. "The French are stubborn. We knock them from the five hills and they take them back so we knock them off again and they counterattack. Our numbers are overwhelming but they refuse to quit. For such a lazy people they certainly fight when they get angry. But this part of the battle is almost over. We have taken what we have taken and Giap says that is good enough for now. Our losses are too great, the men are getting discouraged, and he will put us to digging again."

"We must not lose heart," said Chau, trying to remain awake.

Hong placed her hands on his chest.

"You must rest," she said. "For your health."

"There is much to do," said Chau, rising to one elbow. "Can I see the fighting from here?"

"Go outside and look around," said Luat, moving his arm in a circle. "The fighting is everywhere. Many of the French are finished. All along the river they have quit, refusing to fight. They are a strange people."

"What do you mean, quit?" said Chau.

"Just that," said Luat, shrugging his shoulders. "They deserted but, having no place to go, they sit beside the river and wait for the battle to end. Very strange."

Chau managed, with the help of Hong who realized he would not rest, to roll his legs off the cot. His head swirled for a moment and he placed it on his hands. Hong rubbed his neck. When he looked up, he said…

"Nothing has been done about it?"

"About what?" said Luat.

"The deserters. The officers allow such behavior?"

"They are too busy defending themselves. There are thousands of them there, a grand parade of cowards."

"Maybe the leaflets have worked."

Leaflets, telling the French forces to quit fighting, were first smuggled into the camps, then fired in shells. They were directed at the colonial forces. The Vietnamese encouraging them to leave, to take up arms against the people oppressing them and their countries, asking them to revolt even as the Viet Minh revolted.

Hong helped Chau to dress. His clothes were washed and neatly pressed. His tiny frame had grown even smaller and Hong helped adjust the clothes as best she could. She cinched his belt as tightly as she could.

"I must re-sew your uniform to make it fit better," she said.

Luat stood with his arms crossed watching the procedure.

"What a silly thing to say," he said. "Just like a woman, always taking the hardest route. Don't make his uniform smaller; make him bigger. We don't want him to look foolish."

Turning to leave Luat tripped over the pho bowl and fell face down onto the mud.

Chapter 42

They were called the rats of the Nam Yum, internal deserters living on the banks of the river, unable to escape but refusing to fight for the French, and Brulee became one. After the death of Druxman, he grabbed Quang, the ammo box of dope, and they went to the river bank where Quang dug a tunnel into the sandy clay with Brulee's bayonet. He never questioned anything Crème Brulee did, just followed faithfully like a good dog follows his master. He refused to work for anyone else and he built a bed from two pallets. A candle holder jabbed into the wall.

Quang was boiling rice when Brulee injected himself with the dope. He no longer did it in secrecy but used the dull needle taped to the end of the eyedropper in the open. A deserter had no use for pride and he could have buggered a prisoner, raped an old lady, tortured a child, without repercussions.

"Brulee, is that you?" said a soldier, his shorts torn and his knee scraped.

"What?" Brulee looked up slowly, as the dope deadened his senses and he looked toward the voice as if he needed glasses for nearsightedness.

"It's me, Mulligan, Stu Mulligan." He reached out his hand, the last bit of civility a deserter possessed.

"You old bastard," said Brulee. "Come on and sit a spell. Quang be making up some lunch. Ain't got much, but you can join us."

"Food is pretty scarce," said Mulligan. "The camp's on half rations and it will soon be going down from there."

"I heard you were with the 8th Assault. Thought I might run into you seeing as how we been working together. What you been doing?"

"A little of this, a little of that," he said. "It all comes out in the end. Never thought I would see you here."

"I'd offer you a smoke 'cept I don't got one," said Brulee. He noticed the crushed pack in Mulligan's tunic pocket.

"Me neither," said Mulligan, glancing toward his pocket. "Everything's pretty scarce these days. It wasn't that long ago we dropped on the caves at Lang Son and gave the bastards a drubbing. The Viets had 500 cartons of Russian cigarettes and Tourret told us to take them all."

"Russian cigarettes?" said Brulee. "Was he trying to kill you for doing a good job?"

Quang poured the soup and rice into tin cans and gave them to the men. He took nothing for himself and Brulee did not offer him any. Quang always got along fine and he looked in no worse shape than the rest of them.

The camp of deserters resembled a garbage heap, jerry cans, empty ammo boxes, torn wood, shell craters, laundry hanging on sticks, and filthy soldiers, all adding to the decor. The men were on their own and scavenged food dropped at night from the fighting soldiers. Almost 4,000 deserters hid in the mud waiting for the battle to end.

"Do you think the Colonel will try and clean us out?" said Mulligan.

"Don't appear so," said Brulee. "It's a wonder, ain't it? All us sitting here refusing to fight and them doing nothing about it. Don't recon there's another army in the world would put up with that."

"Not another one," said Mulligan. He tapped his shoes in the mud. "Say, why don't we team up together? Wouldn't be a bad idea, go out together, look after each other's stuff, that sort of thing. Wouldn't be a bad idea, would it?"

Crème Brulee continued to watch the cigarette bulge in Mulligan's pocket, the thin rectangular outline pressing against the material.

"Don't recon I need no help," said Brulee. "Me and Quang's done OK."

"Sure, but he ain't nothing but a nigger, no matter what you think. You need a white man with you, one you can trust, one who will stick with you for sure."

"You mean like you done stuck with the army, you and me done stuck with the army, that is," said Crème Brulee.

He did not like deserters. They could not be trusted even in the best of times.

"That's different," said Mulligan. "You know it's different. This fight isn't ours and never was. Sticking together is a matter of survival." He noticed Brulee looking at his tunic. He started to pat his chest. "Listen…" He stopped, as if he had made a surprise discovery. "Damn, forgot I had these." He lifted out the cigarette pack. "There're Commie cigs but at least they smoke." He pulled out one for Brulee. He said nothing, just placed it between his lips. Quang lit it for him. "What do you say we give it a try?"

"I'm going out tonight," said Brulee. "Reckon you can tag along if you like but I ain't making no promises. We'll see how it goes."

They did not leave until after midnight and they heard the supply airplanes overhead. The parachutes were barely visible in the dim light. The flack bursts and tracers from the Viet Minh anti-aircraft helped light the night. Lately there was no way to tell where the supplies might land. The pilots took no chances and flew too high to be accurate with their drops and a large percentage of the supplies landed behind the Viet Minh lines. The civilian pilots took greater chances than the military ones and often flew in lower. The soldiers on the ground started to detest the air force pilots and crews, but carried a great respect for the navy pilots, from the aircraft carriers, who seemed always willing to take chances.

Traversing the Center of Resistance seemed to Crème Brulee like crossing no man's land in the First World War. There was great danger. Viet Minh constantly broke into the compound blowing up trucks and other equipment. They moved like ghosts blowing in and out as they pleased. Regardless of how much the French tried, they could not stop or catch them. They almost became accepted, or at least tolerated, like lice and filth, too bothersome to scratch, too much effort to clean up.

Brulee and Mulligan moved from one destroyed vehicle to another, sometimes crawling, often dashing from safety point to safety point, tumbling into shell craters, tripping over boxes, their feet often getting tangled in abandoned parachute lines and harnesses. They now had two enemies, the Viet Minh and the French Forces. Not all the soldiers were as magnanimous as Colonel de Castries and shot deserters, especially when they were stealing food and ammunition. Moving east, they saw several boxes nestled in the barbed wire. As they moved forward, a shot rang out kicking up the dirt. Brulee dropped to one knee and Mulligan pointed his rifle toward the sound. Nothing moved or was heard. When Brulee started to stand another shot nipped at his feet.

"We don't mean no harm," he said, as if he were crossing a farmer's field during hunting season.

"Brulee?" The voice sounded closer than the rifle shot.

"Oui," he replied.

"Merdique," sounded the voice. "Petit encu'le. It's me, Sangree." Like a mole man, Sangree rose from the dirt. He moved cautiously forward keeping his rifle at the ready. "Who's that with you?"

"Stu, Stu Mulligan. You remember him from before. He ain't going to cause no trouble."

"Have him lower his weapon," said Sangree. "If you're one of the rats, he must be one also."

Mulligan seemed hesitant to comply.

"It's OK, Mulligan," said Crème Brulee. "You remember Sangree? He ain't going to shoot us."

Mulligan slowly lowered the weapon.

"You can't be too careful," he said. "We're not bothering anyone."

Sangree approached and offered his hand to Brulee. He eyed Mulligan.

"It's all I got," he said, breaking a cigarette in half. Each man took one.

"I can tell by the smell it a damn Gauloise," said Brulee. "Back in Tennessee the smell of curing tobacco filled the air like nectar. I could lay in a field all day just breathing it in."

"I'm after those boxes," said Sangree. He pointed to the crates. "I can't carry it all so you can have what's left."

"There are two of us," said Mulligan.

Sangree did not respond as he tried to scratch his way through the wire. He noticed some figures in the distance coming his way. He raised his rifle and all three men shot knocking over the figures.

"Them Commies is everywhere," said Brulee. "They got no respect for personal property."

They slung their rifles and fought to get the boxes from the claws of the wire. The barbs chewed at their clothes adding to their tattered appearance. They finally shoved the boxes from the wire. One contained medical supplies; one was filed with Vioginal, a concentrated wine syrup to be mixed with water; and one had emergency field rations. They left a larger box, marked 120mm mortar rounds in the wire because it was too heavy to move. Sangree started to divide the contents. He took all of the medical supplies and as many field rations as he could carry. The rest he gave to Crème Brulee and Mulligan. That seemed to satisfy them since they had no use for medical supplies and they got enough food for several days and the Vioginal, as bad as it was, still helped ease any pain.

"I'll go on ahead," said Mulligan. He gathered as much as he could and left.

"He's a bad one," said Sangree. "Don't trust him."

"Not much to choose from in my neighborhood," said Brulee. "Folks mostly keep to themselves."

"The guys are asking about you, especially Bix," said Sangee. "He's wanted to look you up but we're all pretty busy. He doesn't understand why you don't fight. At least you'll have a chance with us."

"It's not the fighting," said Crème Brulee. "I swear to God I'll never hurt another living creature in my life. If I ever get out of this mess, I'm going to get me one of them mail order preacher certificates and start spreading the gospel."

"Do you want to see something special?" said Sangree, his voice low as if he held a great secret.

"It ain't going to hurt me, is it?"

They gathered up the supplies and walked carefully for twenty minutes to the edge of the compound where a group of civilians were living, mostly families, wives and children, of the Thai soldiers. Sangree motioned for Crème Brulee to sit in a shallow trench.

"What are we supposed to see?" he said.

Sangree pulled out a full pack of Old Gold's and handed three of them to Brulee. Brulee sniffed them under his nose.

"There, look there," said Sangree.

A slight figure appeared to float just over the ground. Artillery bursts lit her golden face. Her dress was made of silken clouds and wind and her hair flowed like water as she started to dance. There was nothing real about her, nothing tangible as she drifted in snake-like movements, her fingers caressing the night. An occasional flare bathed her in a warm glow. She danced for twenty minutes as Brulee and Sangree watched silently.

"What the hell was that?" said Brulee, as she moved back to the compound.

"She is the love of my life, my muse, my sister," Sangree whispered. "I visit her whenever I can."

"So, you have finally found your woman."

"I imagined her my whole life."

"She damn sure ain't no whore," said Brulee.

"She is a ballet dancer, I think."

"A ballet dancer – a ballet dancer, here?" said Brulee, scratching his chin.

"I heard there was ballet troupe in the valley," said Sangree. "Maybe their plane broke down or may be they came from Lai Chou. The king had his own ballet performers. I don't really care. I only know I love her with the kind of love I thought I would never feel again."

"Whyant you go say hi? I don't recon she's the kind that bites. Go on now, over to the camp…" Brulee tried to give him a push on the back.

"No," said Sangree. "For now I want to soak in the love, feel her in my soul, my heart. It's better that way."

"I'd say there ain't nothing better than being inside her pants but then I'm just a hillbilly and if I can't give it a good sniff then I don't believe in it."

"Listen," said Sangree. He grabbed Brulee by the wrist. "You're a good man. I can't always make it by here. After all, some of us must do the fighting. Would you pass by here when you're out scrounging? Just look to make sure she's OK. I know you won't bother her. In spite of all your crassness, you are a sensitive fellow and I know I can trust you to protect her. What do you say?"

"Guess it wouldn't hurt none," he said. "In my arms she'll sleep like a baby".

Chapter 43

Bix had never been so hungry. He was not a big man but it seemed he had shrunk to almost nothing. There was not enough meat on his bones to press against his tunic and his belt had difficulty strangling his pants although they now bunched around his waist like a kitchen curtain.

He was chosen to supply Hugette 6, a small fortification to the north of the airstrip. The Viet Minh surrounded it with trenches and they needed supplies each night, a wasted effort as far as he was concerned. There was no way to save them, to keep the position open. The Viets attacked them each night drawing off their ammunition. There was never enough food, medical supplies, or water. It had to be hauled in each night at great cost. Often 50 men or more (mostly P.I.M.s) were killed with each delivery. Such casualties could not be sustained. The position could not hold; even Bix knew that so why not let it go before men were killed? Then what? With that position gone there was only Hugette 1 left to defend the western part of the airstrip. Of course, why defend the airstrip, anyway. It was completely useless, just a hard flat piece of ground full of holes and twisted metal. If the airstrip was not defended, where would the supplies be dropped? Who cared? They were landing all over the valley, anyway. Why not just surrender? They were doomed, just call it a day, shake hands, go off, have a beer and talk about the game, congratulate the winners and let them praise your guts for stiffing it out as long as you did under such impossible odds.

Bix reassembled his weapon. A soldier was nothing without his rifle and it had to be in perfect working order. This action would not be any different than the counterattack on Hugette 7 when he was unlucky enough to be assigned to Captain Bizard's make-shift force of troops from the 5th BPVN and 1/2 REI from Hugette 1 in an effort to save Lieutenant Spozio and his rag-tag company of legionnaires. If it was not for the three tanks of Sergeant Boussrez, the attack by the 100 men would have been a disaster. Rushing toward the blazing strongpoint they completely surprised the Viets. The sight of the tanks scattered them to the hills. Only Spozio, and thirteen survivors, remained in the last remaining bunker. Not enough soldiers were available to rebuild the position. The attack was for nothing and Colonel Langlais abandoned the strongpoint in the morning. Hugette 6 would come to the same end, engulfed, eaten, swallowed by the insensible appetite of the Viet Minh.

Only the thought of Nicole kept him going, kept him fighting rather than join Crème Brulee along the riverbank. If he could just talk to her, sit her down – one man to one woman – and explain his love, surely she would understand and not resist. Whatever she wanted would be hers, and what he could not supply for lack of money, he would supply emotionally.

"Don't be so slow," said Knowles, entering the dugout. "There are good men waiting for us and we mustn't disappointment them."

"Who is it this time?" said Bix, his voice an indifferent monotone.

"Legionnaires, muffin, legionnaires. They are always worth saving even if there are only 100 of them left. Look what I found…" He held out a tin of pound cake. "You're getting much too thin. Get it down before Sangree gets here. You know what a pig he is."

"And Toan?" Bix scooped out the cake with his bayonet.

"Not this time. He's being held in reserve."

"He seems a good corporal," said Bix. "Plenty of guts."

"Get ready now. We'll rally by Smith."

Smith's head rested on a pole near a disabled truck where he seemed to watch over the compound. The men believed he was good luck.

"You don't like him much, do you?" said Bix.

"Toan?" Knowles straightened his tunic. "Why do you ask?"

"No reason," said Bix. "It's difficult to read you but I keep trying. If I learn to understand you then I can understand any man."

"You're being silly. I have no feelings one way or another about the Corporal," said Knowles. "He does his job well, something we all respect."

"I don't believe you treat any soldier differently from another, except for me," said Bix. "Why is that?"

"You are much like I once was," said Knowles. "Looking for adventure. War can ruin a man if he is not careful. He becomes a part of it and it becomes a vital part of him leaving him wanting more. It is an addiction not unlike that suffered by Brulee. Any chance at a sedentary life is over, no peace, no contentment, never again happy to sit by a stream and smell the hair of a woman. Always there must be action to bring joy - no, not joy - something beyond joy, something essential to life, some essence necessary to a soldier's existence. Hope lies in the realm of the naive yet a person must be ignorant to be happy, something a soldier cannot be. I thought I might help you retain a bit of that but I think it is too late. All I can do now is to help you survive. Now, let's move out. Lieutenant Rastouil and his boys are waiting for us at Hugette 6."

The P.I.M.s were already loaded, mostly with water followed by ammunition then food and medical supplies. Although many of their comrades were recently killed they appeared remarkably calm. They never attempted to escape.

"The 8th Assault just counterattacked from Sparrowhawk the other night," said Sangree, "Captain Desmont's company along with three of Sergeant Ney's tanks. They should have taken extra supplies."

"No radio?" said Bix.

"Why bother?" said Sangree. "Everyone knows where we are." He sounded disgusted. "But of course, it's just there." He pointed to a small hole. "The Sergeant insists I be a pack animal. Sangree is over by Smith and will trade off with me. Mategriffin lucked out and is in reserve."

The small unit moved across the open runway, little worker ants off scurrying to the nest. The artillery bursts never slacked, 24 hours a day in a steady cadence they fell until there was not a level piece of ground anywhere. The men took fire as they moved, trying to protect themselves behind one piece of airplane wreckage then another until they reached the eastern side and dropped into the drainage ditch. They just arrived when the shelling turned to Hugette 6 and they heard the gunfire of an attack. Ferdinand's radio crackled as Knowles took the receiver. His head nodded in affirmation and he calmly took in the information. He started to issue orders.

"Have the prisoners stow their goods in the ditch," he said. "Hugette 6 is again under attack. Lieutenant Bailly is launching a counterattack with part of the 8th Assault and should be here soon. Send the prisoners back. We'll get the supplies later."

When the prisoners left, Bix noticed how few soldiers remained. It was good the P.I.M.s were so complacent; they could have overrun the solders at any minute and returned to their lines. Bix thought how different they were from the Europeans. They didn't think like Europeans, or act like them, of talk like them, or look like them. There were no similarities. Not even the sex was the same. The women mostly lay there indifferent to the whole act and when they moaned and groaned in fake ecstasy it appeared strictly for financial reasons. It was an interesting trade-off: the sex was unemotional but they performed whenever asked. Bix imagined something quite different with Nicole.

Lieutenant Bailly arrived with his unit rather quickly. His company of the 8th Assault consisted of units of the Air Force, now fighting as infantrymen. Pilots, mechanics, radio operators, supply personnel, cooks and clerks, all fought in the company now known as the Special Air Service Company. They did not move out immediately but waited for the tanks of Lieutenant Mengelle and Sergeant Ney. The tanks were met with a heavy barrage of artillery as they all moved toward the northern end of the airfield.

Lieutenants Rastouil and Francois, with fewer than eighty legionnaires were barely holding on to the position after being attacked from three sides. Captain Viard's Intervention Company was sent in to reinforce, but was cut to pieces. The defenders retreated to a single bunker on the southern rim of the strongpoint in an attempt to hold on.

Bailly's force fought their way along the drainage ditch behind the tanks. Unlike last time, the Viet Minh had prepared for the tanks. Land mines were placed between the end of the runway and Hugette 6. Bix was almost blown to bits when one of the tanks, just reaching the corner of the southwestern strongpoint, hit a mine. The Viets dug into the strongpoint with a machine gun. He and Sangree both went flying from the blast. When they recovered their senses, they ran to the burning tank to help rescue the survivors. A soldier pushed from the turret, his chest smoking. Bix and Sangree grabbed his shoulders and pulled him through. The last one out was Sergeant Ney. He staggered to the ground behind the tank.

"C'est fini," he said. Sangree started to bandage his arm. "Conti was a good old girl," he said looking at the tank.

Another blast against metal sounded as Ettligen, the other tank, rocked to its side. Although smoking it continued to move forward firing its 75mm cannon into the Communists.

"They won't be happy until they get Mengelle, too," he said. "Go on; I'll finish the arm and look after the men. You're needed elsewhere."

Bix tapped Sangree on the shoulder and they caught up with Ferdinand, crouched on one knee and holding the radio for Knowles. Bailly split the unit in half sending part into the position while the other kept the Viet Minh mortars at bay. Within an hour they were surrounded again and needed rescuing. Ferdinand had rifled through the Viet dead in an effort to scrounge any cigarettes, food, and water. He had a half-filled canteen, offered some to Bix and Sangree before taking any himself. A round smashed against the mud throwing some into his eyes. Bix lay back his head and poured water into his eyes, mixing with the tears and clearing his vision.

"Don't they ever stop?" said Sangree.

"How are they getting all the ammunition?" said Bix, frustrated at his dwindling rounds. Even his bayonet seemed dull.

"There..." said Ferdinand, pointing toward two running figures. He fired... one, two, three rounds – all misses as they disappeared into the mud.

"You OK?" said Bix.

"My eyes have never been any good," said Ferdinand. "That's why they made me a radio man. If it wasn't for this, I'd still be one." He tossed the fragged radio to the side. The shooting started to subside.

A figure moved over the trench toward where the two figures had disappeared. In an artillery flash they noticed Knowles. He crouched as he moved forward. Suddenly, the two figures jumped up. Two quick rounds from Knowles' gun dropped them and he moved back toward the trench, a killer silhouette. He moved toward the men.

"Le BEP will be here soon," he said, hardly breathing above a pant like an excited puppy.

"Here?" said Sangree. The shooting almost stopped.

"Some new officer named Cledic is on the way, Captain Cledic. Just arrived yesterday. He's coming with a company of light infantry." Sangree offered him the last of the water. Knowles shook it off. "There're coming from Elaine 2."

"With Le BEP?" said Bix.

"Not yet, but they'll have to be put in; no one else can do it. Bigeard will be put on the job and it will all work out."

Again the area burst to life, bullet and machine gun rounds, mortars, recoilless rifles, artillery rounds bursting everywhere and churning up the mud like bubbling water. The relief column fought their way back along the trench until they reached the survivors of the strongpoint. They formed a small perimeter, barely holding on. The Viet Minh were attacking with thousands of men.

In the distance, they saw Cledic and his men almost running, shooting from the hip stopping only to fight briefly hand-to-hand before joining the survivors who now numbered less than twenty.

The fighting lasted until daylight then, just as Knowles predicted, a large counterattack was launched consisting of units of the 6th Parachute Battalion with Vieulles' 1st BEP in reserve. The Viet Minh, under General Le Trong Tan and Colonel Thuy just threw another battalion into the fight, raising the ranks to over 3,000, but they waited too long, too long to overcome the struggling 200 French forces. Now daylight, the French artillery started cutting the Viets to shreds and fighter-bombers darkened the sky. Dead bo doilittered the fields like blown chaff as the Viet Minh retreated. Once again, the French averted disaster against overwhelming odds. For a time the fight seemed to go out of the Viet Minh.

Bix and Sangree crawled from the trench and lay sprawled on the ground, spread eagle as if about to make snow angels. Ferdinand sat on an empty box smoking a cigarette, his last bit of opulence in a devastated place. Dead Viet soldiers seemed to lie everywhere like little lumps of earth, a housing development for maggots. A line of prisoners were marched past on the way to the main camp, frightened bewildered boys about sixteen years old, their legs in a dance of confusion, eyes wide as if they had been sitting for hours just feet from the screen of a drive-in movie, hands and arms shaking.

"What I wouldn't give to lean over, flip on the radio, and listen to an episode of 'Broadway is My Beat'," said Bix. "It always sounded so distant, so exotic to a farm boy from South Dakota."

"Those days are over," said Sangree.

"What about you?" Bix said to Ferdinand. "What do you miss?"

Ferdinand twirled the cigarette between his fingers and said nothing.

"There must be something?" said Sangree.

Ferdinand stood, flipped the cigarette onto the mud, and said "Nothing," as he walked away.

"A problem?" said Sangree. "Maybe he's tired."

"He acts like he's in love," said Bix. "Not happy, but miserable in love like he wants to be with her but he can't. That kind of love."

"It ruins a man," said Sangree. "Who would have him, anyway?"

"Mategriffin," said Bix. They laughed.

On the return to their dugout Bix decided to make a detour. He drifted to the rear of the remaining men and veered toward the bordello. There was someone in the valley a man could be in love with. He decided to make his point with Nicole. The love he felt was a fire in his chest and he would have her at any cost.

The bordello seemed empty, no laughing, drunken soldiers with their accommodating women, no dim and inviting lights, no whisky spilled on the floor or clouds of cigarette smoke or the thick aroma of perfume gardens, rouged cheeks, painted lips, no life at its most joyous time or most miserable. There was no gentle touching or tenderness; there was no crass roughness or animal behavior; there was no soft gentle flesh inviting and warm; there was no rutting, hips pounding against hips; there was no sweet whispers with lips caressing lips; there was no groaning and panting; but mostly there was no love; there was no hate; there was no emotion.

Bix sat at an empty table and placed his head on his arms. "What is to become of me?" he thought. He heard someone enter from a back room. When he looked up he saw Nicole, more petite and slender, more beautiful than ever. She wore military fatigues cut to her size, the size of a Vietnamese soldier.

"We are closed," she said, her voice tired and quiet. She sat at the table. "We have found better ways to serve men."

"I love you," said Bix, unable to say anything else.

"Who are you?" she said. He looked familiar as all soldiers looked familiar.

"You know who I am," said Bix. "I was here not long ago with Sergeant Knowles."

He face brightened and a small smile curled the corners of her lips.

"Yes," she said. "You are the one he calls his little muffin. He is very fond of you and thinks you might amount to something after the war. Tell me…" she reached across and held his hands "…have you seen him lately? Is he OK? He has not been here for over a week."

Bix did not want to talk about Knowles. In fact, he wished he had never heard of him, that he did not exist, that he was not the overwhelming obstacle he was.

"You can come with me to America," he said, refusing to acknowledge Knowles.

Her hands sent a warmth through his arms and into his chest. He wanted her above all things, to hold her, to love her, to possess her.

"And Heinrich?" she said. "How is he?"

"I don't want to talk about the Sergeant." Bix banged the table and stood up, his fists quivering. "It's you I want and it's you I'll have."

He started to move around the table, the fire inside him starting to burn uncontrollably. Nicole slowly rose from the chair and started to back away. Bix lunged at her catching her by the neck and wrenching her to his chest. He pulled her head back by her hair to get at her lips. She tried to fight him off but he was too strong. She pushed her arms against his chest to push his away.

"You'll see," he said. "You'll see."

For a moment she broke free, but he grabbed her again and punched her on the side of her face. He wrestled her to the ground, ripping her tunic open to grab at her breasts. He held his forearm against her throat and started to unfasten her belt and pants. He tried pulling down her pants but he could not get them over her boots. He forced himself between her legs and started to push down his pants. She was gagging from the arm on her neck and spittle dribbled from her mouth. She managed a scream. Bix smiled. He had never experienced the joy of rape before. The pain in his side came as a surprise as he started to guide himself in and he rolled to the floor.

"Grubby little bastard," said Corporal Toan, standing over him. He kicked him again. "Thought you would come by for a sortie did you. You jeune are all alike, filthy animals."

Bix curled up from the pain as Toan helped Nicole stand. He lifted her pants and helped fasten them around her waist. She stood dazed and wobbly.

"The Sergeant sent me to keep an eye on you, wanted to make sure you were safe" said Toan. "A good thing, too. A petit enculé like you doesn't deserve a friend like him. This woman is no whore! If Knowles knew what you were up to you wouldn't last a minute. Now pull up your pants and get out. Vasay! Scram. And never try this again or I will kill you myself."

Bix scrambled out the door, more embarrassed and ashamed than frightened.

Toan sat Nicole in a chair.

"There there, miss," he said. "Let me find you something to drink while you get your head about you. The Sergeant wanted me to say that he would be here tonight. I've never seen a man so silently and surely in love before. I don't know what could have driven two people so close but you are certainly inseparable."

Chapter 44

Earthquake felt the controls of the flying boxcar shake under his grip. He was making a daylight run over Dien Bien Phu – very risky these days when flack pocked the air from the Viet Minh gunners. He was still twenty minutes from the valley but the turbulence rising from the mountains seemed more severe than usual. The fog had started to lift and the jungle formed a blanket of greens below. He never saw such a beautiful country.

"A bit rough today," said Buford, his head shaking.

"It'll be plenty calm tonight when the temperatures even out,"

The two pilots yelled at each other to be heard over the groaning engines.

"Got any more of that coffee?" said Buford, nodding toward a can on the floor.

"What?" said Earthquake, leaning toward him.

"Coffee," said Buford. "Any coffee left?"

Earthquake nodded and handed the can to Buford. Buford filled his cup halfway so the coffee had room to slosh.

"These last few days have been hell," he said. "How many holes have they patched in this crate?"

"This piece of tin flies no matter what," said Earthquake. "Never seen a better ship. Lost half a tail section before you got here. Bit of a rough landing, but it was still a landing."

"I wondered how you got a new ship," said Buford. The coffee spilled down his chin when he tried to drink. "I better check on that gun."

"The boys strapped it down pretty good," said Earthquake. "Maurice is a real stickler for safety. Legionnaires are trained like that."

Buford looked toward the cargo bay. Maurice, Bannack, and Sterlow, sat beside the

105. Sterlow was reading a book while Maurice and Bannack smoked. The gun was strapped in several positions. Stretched in front of it was a large bundle of parachutes supplied by the U.S. The French, unable to retrieve the ones dropped ran out.

"They sure need it," said Buford.

"It's going to Isabelle," said Earthquake. "Although they are under constant attack, they still have a bit of space for drops."

"You couldn't get me down there at any price. I don't mind the action, but I like to get home for a bath and a steak every night. The sleep isn't bad either." He tried the coffee again and again it spilled. "If you don't mind me asking, how long have you had the woman?"

"What woman?" said Earthquake.

"The one you leave with every night."

"You mean Twee?" He grinned. "You know how it is."

"Don't you know it," said Buford.

They saw the little balls of flack in the distance surrounding the airplanes.

"I hear Vietnamese women are really something," said Buford. "Maybe I'll get me one, too. They offer a certain civilizing factor to men."

"Some of the boys are talking about quitting," said Earthquake, starting to feather the engines for the drop. "The place is getting a bit too hot for them and they didn't sign up for this kind of action. What about you?"

"For this kind of pay, I'd eat pig shit."

Earthquake opened the rear door. The crew were unstrapping the canon. Maurice was hooking up the pulleys. The plane almost glided over Isabelle as the men pushed the cannon out. The sudden loss of weight tossed the nose of the plane into the air and for a moment it was almost uncontrollable. Earthquake wrestled it back into line and turned to leave. A shell burst near the fuselage breaking the skin and tossing shrapnel inside. The hot metal sounded like a handful of gravel rattling inside an oil drum.

Buford looked into the hold. Sterlow's arm was bleeding and Maurice was unfolding a bandage. Bannack gave Buford a "thumbs up."

"It's OK," he said to Earthquake.

Earthquake nodded as he passed under a C-47 that was circling the valley.

General Cogny felt the vibrations of the aircraft engines, the shutter of the wings searching for air, the turbulence lift and sink the ship like a car on a roller coaster as they circled. In the valley below, small puffs of smoke twirled up and out like smallpox sores. Beatrice, Gabrielle, and Ann-Marie had long since cooled into defeat. The Hugettes were being overrun. The Center of Resistance had shrunk to little more than the size of a football field. He was lucky to see anything, since the valley remained mostly fogged in.

"They have lost their will to fight," he said. "There can be no other explanation. I have given them the best troops in all Indochina and yet they do nothing. They are making me look bad, very bad. What started as a meche lente has become a raging fire."

The general shivered at the cold. Captain Thomas showed him a bottle of whisky.

"It's a tight situation," he said, pouring the general a glass. "They will get their feet under them, just give them time. No one expected the hell they are going through."

"No one except me," said the general. "From the beginning I said it was a mistake. What did that bastard Navarre know? This country is completely foreign to him and as soon as he arrived he started making important decisions about things he knew nothing about. Even now he has no concept of the situation. A paper-pushing clochard is all he is, a damn putain. I know how it will turn out – a disaster; and who will be to blame? Me, of course, the one who said not to go, from the beginning, the one who said it was a mistake. I will be remembered for the greatest defeat in France's history and yet I am completely innocent. Tell the pilot to circle those hills to the east. Perhaps we might see some guns."

Thomas informed the pilot and the plane circled low over the hills. The sky came alive with anti-aircraft fire, flack creating a colorless fireworks display of smoke.

"Take it up," said Cogny. "He'll get us all killed at this altitude. Let him be a hero on his own time."

The plane slowly lifted. Cogny looked around the fuselage. The plane was filled with radio equipment.

"Are the radios working?"

"Affirmative," said Thomas.

"Get me de Castries. I must get some fire into him or my career is ruined. So far he has been totally incompetent, a waste of time, worthless. He seems to be frozen in his boots."

The whisky started to warm him and his cheeks began to flush. Thomas fumbled with the radio and handed the receiver to Cogny.

"Henri, my friend," he said. "I am above you. How are things down there?"

"We need more ammunition and replacements." De Castries voice cackled through the set. "We are short of everything. You promise reinforcements yet you send us nothing. We must have enough to replace our casualties. We are barely holding on."

"Yes, yes," said Cogny. "It is the complaint of every solder. You are not alone. We are all in this fight together." He sipped at the whisky. "We will get you what you need. Even now everything is being prepared. You are doing a good job, my friend, a good job. When you defeat the Viet Minh you will be remembered as one of France's finest generals."

"Will you be taking us out of here?" said de Castries, urgency in his voice.

"Let's not talk such nonsense," said Cogny. "We have plenty of reinforcements on the way and no shortage of food and ammunition. You must get some forces into the hills and take out some of those anti-aircraft guns. They are playing hell with our pilots and causing them to fly too high. Get those guns out so we can get you the supplies. I know you are showing courage to your men but you must get out and show them more. Keep me informed. Out."

He handed the receiver to Thomas and shook his head.

"I understand our supplies are low," said Thomas; "and the reinforcements?"

"What reinforcements?" said Cogny. "All our men are presently committed in the Delta. This is just a sideshow. Only about four percent of our forces are engaged here. Their loss will hardly be noticed."

"Perhaps you should drop into the valley to boost morale," said Thomas. "The presence of a General in the valley would be worth a brigade."

"Bah, you are the second man who has made such a suggestion. Drop into that pit? You must be crazy. It would be an admission of guilt and indicate that it was my idea all along. I won't give that bastard Navarre the satisfaction."

"Still," said Thomas. "It is unusual for a colonel to lead such a great battle, or so many men."

"I can lead it fine from here. We are presently negotiating with the Americans for help. After all, they approved the plan and would not leave us hanging now."

"What are the chances?"

"When they helped approve this operation, all gloated with pride, they assured us the Viet Minh supply lines could be stopped from the air. Bah! The air force is useless. They stopped nothing. They cannot even supply the camp. Flying around and making a lot of noise is all they are good for. The American strength lies in industrial might, in numbers of equipment, not in tactics. They never had any great generals, any mighty thinkers. What they have is material, greedy merchants of war anxious to produce goods and stuff their pockets with profit. That's what we need. They said they would rescue us, if needed. That was their guarantee, that the plan was a good one." He shook his head and looked disgusted. "What do they know of good plans? Like that prick, Navarre, they know nothing about these people, about this country. If this were their war they would do even worse than us."

"They had better come soon," said Thomas.

"Take us back to Hanoi," said General Cogny, waving his hands. "That paper general will want a report. Well, he can just ask me for it and see if I respond, just see if I respond!"

Chapter 45

"I'll kill the bastard; I'll kill him," said Brulee. He tossed the planks from his tunnel and stood outside on the bank of the river, arms bowed at his sides, fists clenched as if closing off an artery, his neck swollen, a flash-flood of veins rolling under the thin skin, his face a monkey's ass of red and purple, eyes bulged and twirling and flashing like those of a chameleon, nostrils flared, a shotgun blast of spittle flying into the air where not a single deserter paid any attention as they worked on projects in their own world, a world of self-preservation with a population of one.

"God damned them; God damned them," he said, dropping to sit on the mud, the rain draining over his head as if intentionally attempting to cool and calm him, but instead blurring his vision even farther. "What am I to do; what am I to do?" He rolled to his stomach and started kicking his feet and slapping his hands on the mud throwing a complete tantrum. The tears tumbled from his eyes as he rolled to his back.

"You OK boss?" said Quang, kneeling beside him. "I have noodle broth for you."

Brulee knocked the canteen cup from his hands.

"You bastard; you bastard," he said, repeating everything as if the second statement needed to be practiced in order to be understood. "You let them take it, my box of dope, my future; you let them take it."

"No boss," said Quang, leaning back, away from the wrath. "I no take."

"No you, you bloody bastard." Crème Brulee worked himself to his knees and shook his fists. "You bloody wog! Fucking wanker! You simple-minded yeller bastard lost my dope."

"I no take nothing. Just find food."

Brulee's hands started to shake, maybe from anger, maybe from withdrawal or the thought of withdrawal since the lack of heroin should not have bothered him this soon since his last injection. His shoulders slumped in defeat, utter surrender at the situation, a beaten man, total acceptance overcoming him.

"Yes," he said. "Recon it's not you fault."

"Dope is gone?"

"No, it's not gone." He said. "It's just not here. Someone has it." He took a deep breath. "Got any food?"

Quang pointed to the mud where the broth had spilled.

"Here, for you," he said.

He handed Brulee a small waxed packet. Brulee unfolded it carefully, a grin crossing his face.

"I love you, man," he said, eyeing the heroin. "I knowed I could count on you. It ain't much but I reckon it'll do till we can get some more."

"Very difficult," said Quang. "Very dangerous. Many Viet Minh everywhere."

"You can do anything," said Crème Brulee. "My very life depends on you."

Mulligan worked his way around the empty boxes. A gob of shit stuck to his boot. The rain had stopped. Quang was splitting a box with Brulee's bayonet and putting the wood on a small cooking fire where he boiled plants for tea.

"Got any food?" he said to Brulee.

"It's scarcer than hen's teeth," he said. "Quang's cooking up some god-awful tea might last us til tonight."

"If we get something, I'm not sharing it with anyone - anyone but you, that is. We'll starve before we get out of here. Why don't we just surrender, get it over with? The more we fight, the more suffering there is and the outcome will be the same. No one's going to rescue us."

"They say there's a relief force on the way from Laos," said Brulee, no enthusiasm or belief in his voice.

"If you believe that then you're crazier than most people. They've given up on all of us. We won't even make the funny papers when this is over."

The parachute drops started at 2200 hours. Because of the dangers of anti-aircraft fire and flack, there no longer appeared to be any attempts at accuracy although the airstrip seemed the be the general vicinity of most supplies. All goods now landed about half inside and half outside the Center of Resistance. The Viet Minh received so many artillery rounds from the French that they needed fewer of their own supplies and they seemed to have an abundance of never-ending rounds. Retrieving supplies became a hazardous necessity for the French. The Viet Minh staged ambushes near inviting boxes and waited for the starving soldiers.

Brulee and Mulligan did most of their hunting toward the eastern perimeter of the compound where fewer parachutes drifted and fewer Viet Minh waited. What little safety remained was always on their minds. Brulee thought more and more about getting back to Kentucky, maybe get a job in a tavern or shoot for the sky and be a cashier at a cigar bar where he could insult the customers without them knowing it, play the dumb hillbilly game while outsmarting them all. If a man had nothing but amusement left in his life that was a good way to get it? He might even become a preacher. He already knew more about religion than most preachers. Reveling in their ignorance was a favorite pastime. If they brought up something like the creation story, he might ask which of the two stories they were talking about, since there are two. Or, he might ask who killed Goliath, knowing it was not David. He enjoyed arguing that if people followed the teachings of Jesus they would be Jewish, not Christians, who follow the teachings of Paul. He found the possibilities of peace in the U.S. endless.

The thoughts rumbled through his mind and he had difficulty keeping to the current task of staying alive.

Mulligan pointed to a parachute drifting down nearby between several rows of wire. It floated gracefully to the ground. Mulligan dropped to one knee and surveyed the area. The package seemed to be in the clear. They moved closer. Crème Brulee guarded the area as Mulligan pried the box open and found it filled with emergency rations, not tasty but at least filling.

"Grab one end," he said. "We can take the whole thing. It's not that heavy and it'll last for days."

"I'm hoping this'll be over before then," said Brulee, grabbing hold of the rope. "There ain't nothing left of us and it seems the supplies is about over. "They sure ain't sending us any more replacements."

"Let's go." Mulligan pulled on the box as they slogged to get their feet from the mud.

"Maybe I'll go back to the unit," said Crème Brulee. "I ain't been feeling right about this lately."

"Shut up," said Mulligan. "You think they'll welcome you with open arms and forget the whole mess? You made your choice. Any soldier will blow your ass away in a minute without thinking twice."

"I have friends there."

"A man doesn't leave his friends," said Mulligan. "You've got you; nothing else."

Brulee struggled to walk through the mud, his feet sinking deeper and deeper. The rain was incessant, filling the Nam Yum River almost to overflowing. Even his cave was half under water. The entire valley became a giant swamp. Trenches grew to canals and soldiers slept in used water for blankets. The mud dyed their skin red and brown to such a depth, the color could not be removed with any amount of soap and scrubbing as if they had become a part of the valley, not a living entity like rice or grass but something inert – clay, dirt, mud, sand, parts of the earth that forever remained parts of the earth, pounded, plowed, washed about - forever here.

"You'll have to take this," said Crème Brulee, dropping his end of the box. "I've got something to do."

"What do you mean?" said Mulligan. "I can't carry this thing." He let go of his end and sat on the box. "We can carry it back and eat decently for a few days."

"I promised a guy I know – you know him – Sangree – I promised him I would look after someone."

"You can't look after yourself."

The hill at Dominique 1 was burning, another counterattack chewing up the mud and dirt, the shit and bodies from both sides.

"He's got this girl," said Brulee. "I got to look in on her once-in-a-while so's he can sleep nights."

"No one sleeps nights, anymore. Why can't he look after her himself?"

"I reckon he's over on the hill." He nodded toward Dominique. "I ain't doing nothing 'cept stuffing my face." He kicked the box of food. "Just leave it here and wait for me if you can't take it yourself."

Mulligan turned in a circle and said, "Damn."

"It won't take no time afore I'm back."

"I can't take it and I can't leave it here," said Mulligan. "If I stay with it some soldier will shoot me to get his hands on it."

"Maybe we can cover it up," said Brulee. "Set those two jerry-cans on top so's we can find it again. That won't be so hard. We'll run off and give her a look then come right back. Won't take more'n an hour at best."

They worked their way east through empty trenches and over open stretches of ground. Another battle seemed to be taking place toward the northeast, but Brulee no longer remembered which strongpoints were there, not that it mattered. The Viet Minh seemed to be everyplace and no place. Twice they avoided Legion patrols and several units of bo doi. Brulee turned in a trench and stopped, motioning Mulligan to keep low.

"We have to wait here for a spell," he said.

"I'm not going to spend the night here," said Mulligan, placing his rifle on the edge of the trench.

Within minutes a petite figure drifted into view. Mulligan started to raise his rifle and aim but Crème Brulee stopped him.

"That's her," he said, placing his arms on top the trench where he rested his chin as if to watch a theater act. "I just like to watch a spell, then we'll go."

"My God," said Mulligan. "She's beautiful. Let's have some fun with her, a bit of faire l'amore, as the French say."

"Quoi fucking," said Brulee, giving him some French of his own. "This is a real lady and ought not be touched by the likes of us."

"I don't care what you say," said Mulligan, starting to crawl from the trench. "Hey little lady. How about some of the old fuckaroo," he said, as he lunged toward her.

She stopped in amazement, almost frozen at the sight of the unshaven, derelict, filthy,

446

mud-man – inhuman, incoherent, a beast of giant proportions lumbering after its prey. Before she could flee he was on her dragging her onto the mud and ripping at her dress. Brulee hit him behind the head with his rifle butt and Mulligan rolled to the side clenching at his bleeding skull.

"Bastard!" he said. "I'll kill you for that."

"I didn't mean nothing by it," said Brulee, kneeling and holding the woman in one arm. She shivered there like a cold and frightened puppy. "It might be the only promise I ever keep in this hell-hole but ain't no one going to touch her while I'm about."

Mulligan rolled to his knees, still holding his head. The blood ran around the back of his head and over his shoulders. Brulee suddenly dropped to his knees, pulling Mulligan back onto the mud.

"Shut up," he whispered. "A Viet patrol coming this way."

He pointed into the darkness. The shell-bursts silhouetted a dozen flat-helmeted soldiers moving their way. Mulligan grabbed his rifle. They moved in closer as if they knew exactly where they were going. He waited for them to stop or turn or go back but they kept coming. Finally, he fired two quick rounds and started running as Crème Brulee pulled the dancer deeper into him. The Viet Minh moved toward the departing figure. A burst of rifle fire sounded followed by silence, then laughter.

The woman struggled to escape and started to scream, but Brulee clapped his hand tightly around her mouth before the Viet Minh could hear them over their celebrating. As she continued to struggle, Brulee clasped her more tightly. Their only chance of survival was to lie perfectly still and quiet. Who knew what the Viets would do to her if they found her with him. She struggled again and he wrenched her head quickly and violently, enough to quiet her down. He felt her finally relax and he relaxed his grip and let her cuddle there on his chest. It felt good to have a woman with him in such a tense situation. He felt his warm breath reflect off her neck as if they had just finished making love and were now content to stay entwined in each other's arms until they drifted off to sleep. He heard the voices of the Viet Minh fade as they walked back toward their unit.

Crème Brulee, content with finally doing a noble act, pulled back her hair and kissed her dead neck.

Chapter 46

The stench of the hospital almost gagged Nicole. Even though she worked there every day she could not get accustomed to it and she constantly fought back the bile on the verge of rising. The hospital expanded again and again and now held over 500 soldiers, every inch containing festering, torn, rotting, men. Even in the First World War the wounded were taken to the rear to be treated decently and humanly. What kind of men were the Vietnamese who were cruel, so heartless? If they only saw what suffering they had brought on to the soldiers whose fight was over, surely they would have allowed them to leave, to have some solace before death. Death seemed so final, not like some abstract thought that everyone understood but did not believe, so certain, just full throttle into the darkness, a darkness she now saw every day as men cried out for light clinging with bloody fingers to that last dying flame, or closed their eyes in acceptance as if being taken into the arms of a caring lover, content in the embrace, welcoming the mysterious dark and the warm lips they felt would follow.

As cruel as the situation was Colonel Langlais agreed with Giap. If the situation were reversed, he would not have let the Viet Minh wounded leave. A pile of wounded on the other side was more valuable than a fresh brigade on yours.

Nicole worked her way through the darkness and stopped to hold the outstretched hand of a Moroccan. Maggots crawled through the bandage around his face. Only one eye shown through, unblinking, distant. Dr. Grauwin tried to convince the men that the maggots were a good thing, that they only ate dead flesh and were better at cleaning wounds than most surgeons. No one believed it but they appreciated his effort to comfort them.

Mud and water dripped into the caverns and in some places a foot or more of water covered the floor and often the men. It appeared that some were as likely to drown as to die of their wounds. Maggots seethed inches deep on dryer ground and wrapped themselves in discarded bloody bandages. Attempting to feed so many men in such tight compartments seemed impossible, changing dressings, even more so.

Occasionally Nicole stumbled across a regular customer, once vigorous, alive with vital fluids, eager to join flesh-to-flesh, now all little injured boys wanting nothing more than a gentle touch, a last bit of human contact.

She tried to find all her girls, make sure they were OK. The camp would fall, that was inevitable, and she worried what would happen to them. Would they survive? Would the Communists let them go, return them to their homes and families? Probably not. They would, after all, want a bit of fun and cruelty for themselves.

She decided to check on the newest addition to the hospital, a former mess hall near an abandoned artillery battery where Dr. Ernest Hantz set up his surgery. The operating room was small and unventilated and the ceiling and walls were covered with parachutes to keep out the dirt. A bundle of parachutes were piled in a corner where he slept. She found him doing triage in a trench just outside. The soldiers there were all emaciated wrecks bandaged in rags and torn bits of clothing. She knew that one or two of every ten would die before they entered the operating room. Supplies and time were so short that gut wounds were no longer treated, the soldiers given heavy doses of morphine to ease the pain, then left to die.

Hantz examined each patient quickly but carefully. He read the tags attached to their clothing explaining what medications they were given before arriving. A medic followed him with a crayon and wrote numbers on their foreheads to place them in an assembly line for treatment.

"You are very busy today, doctor," said Nicole.

"They keep coming in, a never-ending procession of torn flesh," he said, without looking up. "The rain only added to our problems. Look..." He pointed to an open wound. "Filled with mud. They are all like that, infected even before they get here." He turned to the medic. "Antigangrene and antitetanus shots all around. You know the procedure, Jock."

"I'll get some soap and water," said Nicole, turning to leave.

"You work too hard, young lady," said Hantz. "I see you and your girls everywhere, never resting, never taking a break."

"We spent enough time on our backs to last a lifetime."

Hantz laughed and said, "Yes, get some soap and water. I see you are still in fine shape."

Nicole built a small fire under a bucket of water and waited for it to boil. She leaned against a pile of sandbags and slept for several minutes. Her dreams remained sweet, even in this hell, and she pictured herself fixing dinner for Henrich, waiting for his embrace. When she awoke he was there, placing sticks on the fire.

"You are difficult to find," he said. "The hospital is too big and everywhere I went they said you had just left."

She leaned over and placed her arms around his neck. He looked so very thin and his hair had started to gray. She liked the fact that he was getting older because they were getting older together, growing closer with each year. He held her firmly but did not squeeze her.

"There is so much work," she said. "I don't think it will ever end."

The water just started to boil and he dipped in his canteen cup, took some wet tea from a pouch, and dumped it in the water. It had been used so often that the soggy leaves hardly colored the water.

"It won't be long now," he said. He resisted the urge to say he loved her. Being overly sentimental might frighten her.

"How long?"

"A few days, a week at the most." He offered her the tea. "All the signs are there: medals given out, everyone promoted, just like at Stalingrad. De Castries was made a General." He chuckled. "His stars, with a bottle of champagne, were dropped to the enemy. Such bits of irony and humor do not go unnoticed with the men. They don't even know him since he has not shown himself since the battle began. Langlais is another story, a soldier's soldier, and that Bigeard. The men would follow him into hell."

"Perhaps they already have," said Nicole, straightening Henrich's collar.

She knew how important it was to him to stay neat, even in this mess, and she ran her hands over his sleeves.

"I have washed a fresh set of clothes for you," she said. "You're such a mess your men will think you have gone soft."

"The Communists will be making another play for the Elia's," he said. "We've no one left to defend it."

"There, there," she said. "Drink some of this." She placed the canteen cup to his lips.

"We have around three thousand men still capable of fighting." He drank slowly. "There are about thirty to forty thousand Viets facing us and another fifty thousand support troops left. The odds are not exactly favorable."

"I am sure the Viet Minh will not run away in fright and will try and fight, anyway," she said.

Henrich chuckled at her joke and kissed her.

"I love you very much," he said.

"Have you seen Bix?" he said. "The little muffin I worry about."

"You worry too much about everyone. You must start worrying about yourself."

"He has become withdrawn and talks to no one," said Knowles. "I know he misses his friend, Brulee. Maybe that is the problem. At least his friend is alive."

"What if we get separated?" said Nicole. She did not say it loudly or with any alarm, just a simple statement.

"What do you mean?"

"There will be much confusion at the end," she said. "How will we find each other? Remember the last war? You were not so easy to search out."

"Yes, yes," he said. "First, no matter what happens I will attempt to make it back to the hospital. You must wait for me here, at this spot. Check several times a day. If I am captured – who knows? We will not be together until a peace is signed and arrangements are made. I will return to France and wait every day on the bench by the river opposite the church. It might be years."

He leaned against the sand bags and held her in his arms. In the distance he heard a unit of German legionnaires marching toward the hills and singing: Im Hafen Kehren die legionnaire – beider Schwarzen – Si pfeiffen auf Geld und Ruhm Ehre – Denn Schon bald Kann alles anders sein…

"I must go," he said.

He reached into his tunic and produced a revolver, presented it like a reluctant gift to Nicole as if a consolation prize offered for a failed relationship. She looked at it strangely and did not reach up, her hands trembling, a small breath catching in her chest. Knowles placed the pistol into her hands, folding her fingers around the handle.

"I must tend the wounded," she said.

Chapter 47

The Viet Minh attacked with their usual ferocity. It was not easy to get them moving.
Their losses were so great that they started to refuse to fight. The hills and valley were
covered with thousands of the dead, without appreciable progress. Most of the French
forces fought tirelessly. There was some hope of collapse when many colonial forces
deserted or refused to fight, but the legionnaires and the paratroopers, even the Vietnamese paratroopers, fought like mad dogs clinging to every inch of ground. The elite
troops were diminished by half, or more, yet still they battled, refused to admit defeat.
The Viets were losing heart and General Giap and Ho Chi Minh decided to preach
land reform, a chance for every soldier to own a piece of land, to fire them up and hit
the trenches again. It worked. Giap understood that the final battle must be made and
he decided to attack in all directions with everything he had. If the French could not
be overrun this time his troops may decide to go home.

Chau sat on a ridge overhanging Dominique 1, the highest hill above the Nam Yum.
The key to overrunning the Center of Resistance was Eliane 2, to the south. As important as it was, very few troops held the position because there were no other soldiers available. All the French positions were stretched to their limits and they had
no reserve forces for counterattacks. Chau knew that once the reserves are lost, so is
the battle.

"You think too much," said Luat. "An annoyance left over from living with the
French."

"We'll join the attack on A-1 hill," said Chau.

"Eliane 2?"

"If you're French. We'll go soon."

"At a great distance, I hope," said Luat. "Your job is not to fight. My job is to see that you keep me safe." He pulled a twig from the mud, peeled off the bark, and started chewing the meat. "What do we do with Hong? She will insist on going."

"She is also a soldier," said Chau.

"You don't believe that," said Luat. "We have been together for too long. Regardless of what you say, she is still a woman; and regardless of what you say, you care for her; and regardless of…"

"I am going to ask General Giap for a quieter aide, perhaps one who is mute."

"You don't listen to me, anyway," said Luat. "What's the difference?"

Soldiers seemed to be on the move everywhere, great masses of men and women traveling in every direction. General Giap ordered a three-hour artillery bombardment prior to the attacks on all the strongpoints to soften them up, keep their heads down. The attacks would not be launched until they were finished. He decided to attack Elaine 2 last, well after the others were being overrun, and hoped that any reinforcements the French had left would already be engaged plugging the other gaps and leaving Eliane 2 vunerable. A tunnel was dug under Eliane 2 and stuffed with explosives. Giap counted on blowing the top off the hill before rushing in and finishing the job. After the blast the "Death Volunteers", men willing to sacrifice their lives by strapping twenty pounds of TNT to their chests then charging against the remaining defenses, would attack followed by the infantry. He would launch a new attack every half-hour until they were successful. Once he held Eliane 2 the rest of the camp was doomed. The lower strongpoints were low to the ground and would be easily overcome leaving the Bailey bridge open to them.

"The 224th Battalion is assigned the task of taking the hill," said Chau.

"Isn't that Vu Dinh Ho's unit?" said Luat. "A good commander. Very smart and very tough."

"I think so. At least he commands part of it, maybe just a regiment," said Chau, straightening his pants. "We once shared a bottle of snake wine. It seems a long time ago."

Hong rounded the hill carrying the binoculars. She carefully worked her way down to the two men, picking her steps carefully on the slippery slope.

"The Battalion is moving out," she said.

"So you know about the attack?" said Luat.

"The Captain will want to be in on the final assault. It is only natural. You cannot stop a man from doing his job, even if you want to stay home."

"You seem to think nothing of his life, not to mention mine." Luat slipped as he started back up the hill. "I have yet to find my life-long love and now you send me off for execution."

"Your punishment is to live a very long life," she said.

"And what of the Captain?"

"With you and I protecting him, he shall also live a long life – but a happy one," she said. "Yours will just be long."

Chau asked for the binoculars and scanned the valley one last time.

Bix emerged from his dugout looking very tired, very hungry, and very old. He gave up trying to keep his uniform clean and mud clung to it everywhere especially from his boots to his thighs where the cloth had turned brownish red. Two buttons had torn from his tunic and his dirty chest shown through where a T-shirt once covered the tender white flesh. Bearded stubble covered his face and his teeth had started to yellow. His eyes, rimmed in red raw meat, hung like the sad eyes of a bloodhound and fog lay closely over them as if hovering above a morning field.

Sangree checked his clips and flipped mud from the stock of his rifle. He stood in a small group of men who accepted their fate, quiet for the moment, inspecting their bodies for one last time. Corporal Toan milled among them before Sergeant Knowles appeared wearing a fresh uniform. He said something to all the men inspecting them one by one straightening a collar there, pulling on a button there, a smile, a tap on the cheek, a bit of final advice. Bix looked up at his approach, emotion welling in his throat.

"Sergeant," he said. "I have something to say."

He was not sure what it was - what he could say - but a calmness came over him as if he wanted to make peace with the world, as if he needed to forgive Knowles for something Knowles did not do, but something he had done and was unable to forgive himself. He made a mistake, had mistaken love for lust and had blamed Knowles.

"There is nothing to say," said Knowles. He shook Bix's hand, one man to another.

"It's about Nicole."

"She said you came by looking for me," said Knowles. "I appreciate the concern but a muffin like you has better things to do than worry about an old man."

"It's not that…" Bix fumbled with the words.

"It's only that, nothing more," said Knowles. "Now, we must prepare. Keep close to me when we reach the hill. I need protection. Don't let them cover my face with dirt. I want to die looking at the sky." He chuckled.

"Do you suppose…"

"Yes, of course," said Knowles. "We will be passing the river where the Rats are wallowing. I will call a break near there and you can say goodbye to your friend. Sangree will go with you but you must not stay long, only a few minutes. The history professor will not hold back his troops for long. Once the barrage starts, they will be everywhere."

Sangree walked beside Bix. He had cigarettes and they smoked quietly. Men often joke near danger, the laughter pushing back the fear, knowing they may die, be maimed, might even survive. They seldom joke when death is a certainty. They will still fight, fight hard, fight viciously, fight without hate or animosity firing their weapons, bashing in skulls, slitting throats, all without any personal emotions.

"The sun has come out," said Sangree.

"You must have the last cigarettes in the camp," said Bix.

"The sergeant is certainly a good man."

"I came to war from a farm in South Dakota."

When the unit rested, Bix and Sangree slipped over the bank of the Nam Yum. Sergeant Knowles was careful enough to stop some distance away since many of the legionnaires were less than forgiving toward the deserters. What energy remained might easily be expended on their former comrades. Corporal Toan stayed aware and was ready to step in should there be any trouble.

Bix slid over the bank followed by Sangree. Many of the rats moved toward their weapons, suspicious of anyone who did not look totally defeated. They stumbled over the empty boxes, torn parachutes, dented Jerry cans and artillery casings. A few fires burned. They did not have to go far before they found Crème Brulee chewing on a piece of bamboo, Quang kneeling nearby, a scruffy dog on guard protecting his master. Brulee stood at their approach. They faced each other, hesitant to speak. Brulee finally said:

"Hey…"

"We're going up the hill," said Bix. "Thought you might want to know."

"Sure," he said. "Spect she'll be a hot one up there."

"A bunch of the wounded returned to man gun emplacements, guys with missing legs and arms even." If he expected Brulee to suddenly pick up his weapon and join the hunt, he was mistaken. But he did not expect that kind of response; he expected no response, nothing positive or negative, no sudden act of bravery or of cowardice. Whether he fought or not would make no difference in the outcome of the coming battle.

"Quang can fix up some grass tea fer you fellas," said Brulee. "Won't take but a minute."

"Thanks anyway," said Bix, a little uncomfortable. He took a step back to let Sangree talk.

"Have you seen her?" he said.

"Was by the other day," said Brulee. "Guess she's moving out with the rest."

"It's best," said Sangree.

"Listen, I wrote down the name of the village where she's going," said Brulee. "Just in case."

"Just in case." Sangree offered his hand.

"Well, reckon I'll see you all," said Brulee. He offered his hand to Bix.

Bix wanted to say "Maybe you just want to tag along, not close, just follow behind."

"See you Steve," he said, wanting to say his real name once more, as if saying the word might bring back the past, might erase the war, might return to a field of fresh mown hay and hard dusty work under a hot dry sun with the promise of a cold swim in a stream of glistening pure water followed by crackling stars and pure air.

He and Sangree walked back quietly, slipping as they tried to climb the bank of the river. They looked up at the sound of engines. Supplies fell everywhere, one of the largest operations in months. Unfortunately there was no time or personnel to retrieve them. They were painfully short of ammunition as it piled up on the drop zones. For a moment they continued to watch the parachutes float through the clear sky.

Earthquake and Buford had been in the air for half an hour. They had another half hour before reaching the valley.

"You and Paul Holden are the history makers," he said.

Buford leaned over to hear. Clouds flashed past the windshield.

"Gave me a pucker-factor of 12," said Buford. "I don't want to be the first American killed in this war."

Buford, while flying with Holden, took a round in heavy flack. A piece had wounded Holden, the first CAT pilot injured over Dien Bien Phu.

"You damn near stopped the war single-handed," said Earthquake. "I didn't think any Yanks would fly after that. You had them all scared shitless."

"The only one shitless was me. I thought the plane was going to shake apart but it held together. It's tough to bring one of these babies down."

Earthquake nodded. Although he was tired from flying so many missions – this was his forty-fifth - he always felt more refreshed in the air than on the ground. He never saw so many aggressive planes on the way to a battle: forty-seven B-26 bombers, eighteen Corsairs, sixteen Helldivers, and twenty-six Bearcats. Five four-engine Privateers even joined in the fight and he heard over the radio that the anti-aircraft fire and flack were fairly light as gunners, suddenly targets, decided to keep low. Add to the mix the numerous supply planes – twenty-nine Dakotas and twenty-three Flying Boxcars, and the sky appeared crowded.

Major Guerin's Air Traffic Control Center, inside the valley, was finally working to capacity and the pilots, previously ignoring instructions they felt were too dangerous, were finally following orders.

"She's a bit sluggish," said Buford, pointing to the controls.

"Ten thousand pounds of artillery ammunition is quite a load," said Earthquake. "Feels like I'm packing my ass around." He always seemed to carry a smile and he shot Buford a grin. "The boys are going to have a hell of a time pushing it all off."

Second Lieutenant Jean Arlaux joined the team of kickers. They waited patiently in the cargo hold.

"We're going to have to drop in pretty low to hit the target," said Earthquake. "Too many supplies are falling to the Communists. If the boys are fast, we should get it in one pass. I'll pull the nose up and just let the cargo drop out the back."

Flack bursts started to appear as they approached the valley. They burst like dirty pimples in the air, a cloud of smoke followed by streamers of light. Over the radio, they heard that Arthur Wilson's plane was hit while attempting to drop an artillery piece over Isabelle. Part of his port tail boom was shot away but he was making his way back to Cat Bi airport in Haiphong.

"Sounds like it was close," said Buford.

"Wilson's always been lucky," said Earthquake.

Earthquake took the approach designated by the Air Traffic Control Center. He remained high then started to drop, He loved the feeling of his stomach rising into his chest, the roller coaster of flying. "No other men have such fun," he thought. "A constant carnival ride."

He dove through the clogging bursts of flack as the bursts bottlenecked around the plane. The bursts buffeted the plane knocking it from side to side as his grin widened and he felt the adrenaline rush through his body, tingling his fingers as he strangled the controls. The plane jerked to the left and the engine burst into flames. He tried to pull up while feathering the engine.

"What the hell!" he said. The flames quickly turned to smoke from the leaking oil. "This baby flies fine with one engine, anyway!" he shouted, in an attempt to reassure Buford who remained calm, knowing one engine was all they needed.

Earthquake kept eyeing the engine as he had the kick-off crew dump the load to ease the weight. The plane again shuddered, this time violently as a shell ripped off part of the tail section. Earthquake could no longer retain the altitude and the plane started dropping. They drifted over the hills.

"If we can find a flat spot I can still get her down," he said.

"You're the best pilot I know," said Buford, looking desperately out the window.

The crew in back held on to anything they could find. Shrapnel hit one of them and Arlaux was bandaging him while still holding on to an aluminum bar. He tried to see into the cockpit.

Earthquake fought with the controls, heavy and unmanageable. Buford pointed to a small stream, not much room but maybe just enough. Earthquake tried to wheel the plane over and straighten it out. For a moment it looked good. The controls shook in his hands. He aimed carefully. The wind and trees whipped past the side windows. Then, the wingtip smacked into an outcropping of stone. The plane flipped and burst into flame.

Chau never saw so many planes over the valley. They seldom flew during daylight, except bombers, and this showed how desperate the situation was for the French. The flack was light yet several planes went down or limped across the sky leaving a trail of smoke behind them.

Reports throughout the day were delivered to Chau. The French, revealing their resolve to fight, repulsed some minor attacks early in the day. They were not yet finished. The Viet Minh attempted to storm Eliane 3 without success. Major Guiraud and a small unit of remaining legionnaires stopped larger attempts on Hugette 3 and

Hugette 5 and even probed beyond their positions and cleared out several approach trenches.

He moved closer to Eliane 2 where sappers were loading explosives into the tunnel and soldiers of the 174th Regiment stumbled from the hillside where they were fighting French probes. He worked his way to an observation position where Vu Dinh Ho was issuing orders for units of his 249th Battalion. They were given the honor of taking the strongpoint. He divided his forces sending half to attack up the southwest section of the hill and the other half to entrench along the road and block any reinforcements that might attempt to a rescue.

"I've brought some food," he told Chau. "If the French put up a fight it could be a long night."

"I will join you in a celebration after we take the position," said Chau. "Perhaps something for my aides?"

"Of course," said Ho.

"We will wait for the celebration afterwards," said Hong. "I have brought tea until then."

"Perhaps a little something," said Luat.

Hong shot him a nasty look and said,

"Perhaps a little something later."

"Exactly what I meant," said Luat. "For us it's fighting all the way. Nothing else will suffice."

"You don't plan to go in, do you?" said Ho, eyeing them all suspiciously.

"I wanted a good look from here before we go down," said Chau.

"It won't be long," said Ho. "General Giap ordered us to attack even before we blow the hill."

Elaine 2 resembled a rumpled plowed field. With his binoculars, he watched a paratrooper crawl through the barbed wire and remove a pack off a dead Viet Minh before crawling back to his trench. Other paratroopers appeared to cheer him, as he got closer.

"What is going on there?" said Chau.

Ho moved back to his desk and a captain looked with his binoculars.

"It's very odd," he said. Many of our Volunteers of Death, carrying packs filled with TNT were killed. The French started some kind of game. The bravest ones crawl through the open to take the packs. We don't know why? The TNT does them no good. They are a difficult people to understand."

Chau smiled and looked past the position and toward the valley.

Bix felt his legs might give out from hunger. The hill seemed miles rather than a few hundred yards. All this time in the valley, all this time fighting and not a single scratch, and now he didn't want one not because he was afraid of being wounded but because he knew there was no way out, no real medical help. The slightest nick might lead to an infection followed by gangrene and a lingering painful reeking death. Wounds were fine if they could be treated, sewn up, infections stemmed, a cushy stay in a hospital followed by a medal and adoration by those wishing they had their own wound.

Most of the soldiers were living on Maxiton, a form of Benzedrine, used to keep them awake. Food might be scarce but not speed. It left Bix feeling jumpy, on edge, and a bit shaky, not a good side effect for a man who needed steady hands to sight his rifle.

A jeep headed for the strongpoints pulled up beside them, probably the last vehicle still working. The sides were dented and a shell had torn off the left fender. Colonel Langlais sat in the front seat beside the driver and Bigeard in the back with an armed paratrooper. Neither officer carried a weapon. Langlais stepped down and walked over to the men.

"How is it looking, Sergeant?" he said to Knowles.

"The boys will do fine," he said, offering a salute knowing it was unnecessary.

Bigeard moved from the jeep and over to Bix.

"This one looks mighty thin," he said, shaking his tunic to show how empty it was. "Apparently you haven't been enjoying the roast pig we have sent you last week, or the champagne."

"It's fine, Major," said Bix; "but I am holding out for the duck."

"You legionnaires are always so finicky," he said. "Well, if it's duck you want, then it's duck you shall have; what do you say Colonel?"

"Just as soon as we handle this little matter," said Langlais, as they climbed back into their jeep and stopped again to speak with a group of soldiers coming off Elaine 2. Before they left Sergeant Knowles said,

"On behalf of the men, I just wanted to say what a fine job you and the Major have done."

"We're not out of it yet," said Langlais. "Now, we must be off to capture that duck."

The soldiers were the remnants of the 1/13 Half Brigade under Major Coutant. They were relieved on Elaine 2 by Captain Pouget and were so happy to be off the hill that they practically jumped with joy as they rolled back into the main camp.

Sergeant Knowles reported to Major Pouget. He sat in his bunker built in the basement of the former governor's house, long since blown away by the Viet Minh. The bunker seemed more secure than most Knowles had seen, the roof piled high with logs dirt and more logs, more than six feet in depth. It withstood everything the Veits offered and, inside, remained unscathed. The soldiers dug the trenches to the bunker deeper than on the other positions. The trenches were deep and rimmed with sandbags. A string of well-entrenched bunkers surrounded the position and, in front of them, layers and layers of barbed wire. The destroyed tank, Bazeilles, was slowly sinking in the mud on the southern side of the position. The .50 cal. machine gun remained intact.

"So you and the others are the lucky ones," said Major Pouget, offering his hand. Major Coutant had not left with his men and was helping to explain the defenses. Lieutenant Edme also offered his hand. "What units?"

"A few men from le BEP, two from the 8th parachute, a handful of others, the remnants from various destroyed units," said Knowles. "Most of le BEP is off to the west, in the Hugettes, with Guiraud."

"They just beat off an attack," said Pouget. "If only we had more paratroopers and legionnaires we would not be in this fix. Baaah, wishful thinking." He shook his head. "Langlais says there are no more reinforcements so we are lucky to get you few. We have all the remaining ammunition. Yes, it's falling from the sky but we can't get to it until after this battle. Stay for the briefing. Lieutenant Edme will assign you to your positions. He holds the southern positions where the Communists are most likely to attack. Lieutenant Robin…?"

Lieutenant Robin, a forward artillery observer, did a remarkable job on the strongpoint. He was there three weeks and knew every inch of the hill, all the approach trenches, including Baldy and Phony hills, facing Eliane 2 and presently held by the Viets.

"We can't expect much artillery support," he said. "I marked out some of the most important areas, the ones where the Viets are most likely to attack." He pointed to various spots on the soggy wall map. His fire charts sat on the table. "I must be very stingy with the artillery so do not expect any continuous barrage. There are not enough shells for anything prolonged so they will come in occasional bursts. It's the best we can do."

"What you have will have to be good enough," said Pouget.

Bix thought he was used to the stench of the valley but the smell of the rotting bodies on Eliane 2 almost caused him to gag. Hundreds of bodies, maybe closer to two thousand, lay bloated on the ground and hanging in the wire, black and greasy, pushing through the torn uniforms, maggots dripping out of every crack like syrupy rice dripping from a bag into bubbling lumps of white on the ground. The stench was so great it could almost been seen, a shimmering mass of crooked air hovering over the hill.

"I never thought I would puke until now," said Sangree, burying his nose into the crook of his arm. "The rest of the old gang would be appalled."

Bix thought of their friends, Brulee gone to the rats, Smith's head still hanging outside the bordello, Druxman dead, all the rest wounded, missing, dead, deserted, or scattered to other make-shift units. Le BEP ceased to function as a unit and was almost completely destroyed.

Knowles emerged from the trench and spoke to Toan before addressing the small group. He laid his rifle on a sandbag and lighted a cigarette.

"It seems the little yellow bastards are digging a tunnel," he said. "They expect to blow the top off this hill, a silly idea and you aren't to be concerned. Any explosion so far underground will simply lift you into the air on the dirt and place you back down like a baby in a crib." He took a deep breath of smoke and blew it out slowly through his nose. "We'll be with Lieutenant Edme, a good man. Now, lets grab the last boxes of grenades and find some good positions." He patted the shoulder of each soldier.

Bix and Knowles joined Lieutenants Julien and Paul on the western side of the hill while Sangree and Corporal Toan went with Lieutenant Edme to the northeast below the old governor's house. Knowles struck up a conversation with an old friend, Sergeant Bruni. Bruni and Sergeant Ballait decided to climb inside of the tank, Bazeilles, and use it as a bunker. They got one of the machine guns to work and stuffed the tank with ammunition. Bix joined some men between a machine gun bunker and an open machine -gun emplacement. Anyone attempting to attack from this position would be caught in a murderous crossfire.

As the sun started to set, the sky opened with a torrent of rain. Within minutes the trenches were a foot deep in water. The water slightly stemmed the stench of the corpses but pushed out the maggots at a rapid rate. Following the rain, Viet artillery started to rip the sky apart. Everywhere the French positions came under fire, whole sections of earth lifted into the air, abandoned trucks flipped end for end, the river turned into a cauldron of bubbling liquid. Then, a new sound, as if ravaging banshees attacked the sky, screeching, howling, shrieks of despair and foreboding. The noise ripped Bix's ears as Sergeant Knowles tried to calm his men.

"A simple taste of Russia, boys," said Knowles, "Nothing more. Stalin's Organs, nothing more." The sound was too familiar to him and he remembered when the Russians used the rockets against the Germans on the Russian Front. "All bark and no bite. We're safe from attack until they stop."

Although far more powerful than the artillery shells, the rockets were inaccurate, could only be used over wide areas, not close combat. Knowles kept looking over the hill and wondering what the Viet Minh were preparing.

Chau walked along the reverse slope of Old Baldy. He never saw so many mortars in one place. He understood that the 75mm recoilless rifles were on the other side facing the French. Parts of Regiment 98 were working their way toward the south and preparing to attack.

"Let's give them a chance to make some progress first," said Luat. "There is no reason to be hasty. After all, we are not part of the infantry."

This time Hong agreed.

"We must see how the battle is going," she said. "Only then can you know what to do, where to go."

"I think you have spent too much time with my brother, Luat," said Chau. "I have not seen you this cautious before."

It was as if he saw her for the first time, the French flares lighting her face and burning in her eyes. She was very pretty, not beautiful, but pretty, and her hands and fingers were the most beautiful he had ever seen.

"A man who throws away his life needlessly," she said, "throws away his life needlessly."

Chau and Luat looked quietly at her for a moment, as if attempting to decipher the wisdom in her voice. Luat suddenly burst into laugher.

"What the hell does that mean?" he said.

Chau started to laugh and for a moment he thought he saw Hong blush, although he never saw a Vietnamese blush.

"It is just something I thought," she said.

"You, and not me," said Luat.

The rockets stopped. It was time for the attack and Chau saw the bo doi start for Eliane 2.

In all the combat Bix witnessed in Vietnam he never saw such slaughter. The Viet Minh charged up the hillside, or attempted to, throwing themselves onto the barbed wire as it ripped and tore at their clothes and flesh leaving them both in shreds, tumbling and stumbling over their dead and wounded comrades, forcing their way forward through the rain, as if swimming. Lieutenant Robin had done his work well. The French artillery opened up with devastating accuracy plowing the hillside and planting it with bones and flesh, never to be harvested. The Viet Minh regiment ceased to exist, gone, disappeared, vaporized, evaporated, transformed from men to meat, the heritage of entire families vanished, no children, no wives, no growing old in the comfort of relatives and the love of grandchildren, the reassurance of future generations, nothing left to exist except nothing. And then it stopped.

"They are finished," said Bix. "We did it; we beat them back."

He rolled his back against the trench, then sank down and sat in a foot of water and started to laugh, the laughter mixed with crying as he held his head between his knees. Relief ran through the trench like a flood of goodwill as the remaining soldiers started to joke and the sighs of relief rose like steam.

"Get up, you bastards," said Knowles. "Here they come again."

The Viet Minh artillery opened up from Baldy, over fifty mortars, followed by recoilless rifles and 105's, devastating the hilltop. Again the Viets rushed forward, an endless supply of bodies now attacking three sides of the strongpoint. Bix felt the earth rumble. He looked back to see the hill behind him begin to lift.

Sangree also felt it, the mud jiggling, the ground, along with him, rising in the air as if he were being flung into the air on a giant blanket. The Viets detonated the mine and Lieutenant Edme's company took a great trip high over the valley before landing again. Soldiers rolled everywhere some landing on top the dirt and mud, others under it. Badly shaken, Sangree tried to compose his thoughts, shake loose his battered senses. Soldiers writhed through the mud everywhere.

"Tricky bastards," said Corporal Toan, wiping mud from his face. "Get ready boys, they'll be coming any minute."

Captain Pouget climbed from his command post and looked to where the earth rose before sinking back into a deep depression. He quickly ordered a defense around the depression, machine guns on the rim, legionnaires and paratroops at the ready.

Sangree lay on his stomach and searched toward Phony Mountain waiting for the attack, but nothing happened, no one came, no charging masses, not even a scouting party. The Viet Minh officers blew it, threw away their chance to take the hill while the French were confused. It was the Viet Minh who were disorganized and for a moment Sangree realized they were safe.

"I think Navarre and Cogny went to the other side," said Toan, as he checked his men. "They don't have a clue."

For over an hour everything remained calm on the hill as all fighting again stopped. But this time Bix was not fooled and he remained ready. Another barrage and the Viets attacked.

As Lieutenant Robin stated, the French artillery dwindled to almost nothing, their ammunition running out. When there was none and without it the Viet Minh could not be stopped. Sergeants Bruni and Ballait continued to cut them down but elsewhere the ammunition was running out. Captain Pouget ordered the remaining thirty-five men to work their way toward the top of the hill for a last stand. A mortar round tossed Knowles backwards. Another round buried him with mud as Bix ran toward him. The soldiers worked their way toward the top of the hill leaving Bix exposed.

He ran to Knowles and searched in the mud feeling for any lump of flesh. He touched a body and started digging, flinging dirt and mud as if he were a dog after a bone. He felt Knowles' chest and worked his way to his head. He dug the mud from his face and cleared it from his eyes. He could not feel a pulse, yet, under a flickering flare, saw him open his eyes for a moment as he went from this world to the next.

Sangree, rounded the crest of the hill, grabbed Bix by the shoulder and tried to lift him to his feet.

"Let's go," he said. "There is nothing to be done for him." He tugged, but Bix was reluctant to release his grip. "They are here. Come on."

Bix looked up as the first Viets jumped him. He smashed one in the face with his rifle butt. Sangree, out of ammunition, bayoneted another. They turned to run just as the shell exploded overhead, a white flash, flames, glowing streamers flowering out and above, a shard of molten iron driving into Sangree's skull. As Bix started to crush under the blast, another shell exploded at his feet lifting into the first dying blast. The blasts crushed into his chest squeezing out every atom of oxygen, wrapping his skin around his bones, and ripping off a leg that twisted complete from the socket, and tearing away his arm and tossing it into the air with the rifle still clutched in his hand.

Chau, breathless, worked his way up the hill, through the wire, over the bodies, some still moaning not understanding they were already dead. A legionnaire fired off two quick rounds just missing him before Luat brought him down, a round directly through the head.

"I didn't know you shot so well," said Chau.

"A secret best kept between us," he said. "General Giap might consider such a skill valuable in the infantry."

A handful of French survivors were gathered together and stripped of their weapons. The Viet Minh collected the prisoners' boots, making them walk barefoot.

"This one is alive," said Hong, kneeling over a battered lump of flesh. "They do not die easily. An arm and a leg is missing and yet he still breathes."

"Leave him," said Chau, but as he glanced her way he noticed something familiar about the soldier, more a feeling than what he saw. He stood over the man, then leaned down to brush the dirt from his face. "Quickly, bring a stretcher. Go!"

Luat started to yell at two men carrying an American stretcher, compliments of the latest missed airdrops.

"What is it?" said Hong. "He is not an officer, not anyone important."

"He is my friend. He once saved my life." He asked Luat for some water and tried to pour it into Bix's mouth. Bix remained unconscious. "Take him directly to the surgeon. Tell him that this man must be saved at all costs. He is a priority. If he is not treated right soon, the doctor will have to answer to me."

Bix was carried carefully off the hill as Chau stood and looked into the valley. Hong handed him the binoculars. He watched the Viets storming the lower Hugettes and Elianes. Some troops moved toward the Nam Yum.

Crème Brulee crouched low against the riverbank, the cool wetness caressing his skin like a cloak, thick yet unprotective. The battle swirled about him, a giant merry-go-round with him at the axis unable to grasp the dancing figurines; capable only of watching them move through a space he could not reach nor comprehend, the horses alight prancing, the swans undulating, the elephant thudding over the mud. He wanted to think of his life, tried with every breath to grasp some memory, but he drew a blank, as if he had never existed, a lifetime that had only started this moment and wanted to blink out. Quang crouched with him, unmoved, the bayonet resting in his hand as if waiting to prepare dinner, his face a blank ready to fill with Brulee's words, as if an imaginary creature, a body without life. Quang remained something tangible and comfortable in Brulee's life.

Brulee loaded his rifle and lifted it onto the bank, comfortable, with Quang beside him clutching the bayonet, his knuckles not glowing white, but tense anyway. The Viets moved forward through the mist, figures in tan uniforms, faceless at this distance. Brulee took aim, waited until he noticed their expressions. The ground shook with artillery bursts from the Viet Minh gunners, the French guns either destroyed or out of ammunition. The Viets came on, a solid wall, the faces now visible, blank, uncaring, neither hatred nor animosity nor concern, not even fear or determination on them but something so far from human emotion as to reach indifference or possibly apathy. Even the movement carried no determination beyond inertia; no mighty push forward, no energy. The action carried nothing with it except the ability to drift forward, a mass so strong that it flowed without effort yet moved still as if nothing could stop it, as if it would roll on for the end of time.

A few soldiers remained against the bank, hands quivering, some arms already raised in surrender, skeletal arms protruding from torn sleeves. Skid marks scoured the opposite bank where mud had been pancaked into the air from retreating boots, fear and horror traced into the clay as if an epitaph for cowardice, insane men retreating from the advancing enemy only to crowd into the arms of the advancing enemy opposite where a great circle of Viet Minh closed in upon itself.

Crème Brulee quickly loaded his rifle, the Viet Minh everywhere. He was afraid that if he raised his arms in surrender, he would be shot; that if he attempted to defend himself, he would be shot; that if he did nothing, he would be shot. He leaned against the riverbank and lowered his rifle toward the Communists, the wooden butt warm against his face. Quang leaned in beside him, the bayonet gripped ever more tightly in his hands.

"Recon we can get off a few shots then make a run for it," he said, the words cracking from his chest.

He took careful aim, squeezed the trigger, the recoil biting his shoulder. He had been punched in the back, a dull painless blow. The bayonet pushed through his heart, his lungs, foaming, gurgling. Him, already dead, although his mind not accepting it. For a moment it refused to blank out. He rolled over, slid down the bank. Death slowly pulled closed the curtain. Saw Quang through the mist. His hands mud-bloody. Scrambling through mud. Quivering illusion. Gone.

Quang ran from the advancing Viet Minh across the valley toward the west. The camp seemed deserted, everyone either dead or underground, a giant graveyard of bodies and debris. He stumbled over a grotesque head, the two bullet casings in the skull staring up like eyes, the head on a broken stick, the skin like dried rough leather. He ran past a small woman kneeling in the mud beside the hospital, her hands clasped around a pistol, her face wet with tears, her eyes going between the gun and the smoking hills then back again. He continued to run, barbed wire tearing at his skin.

Chapter 48

Bix floated in a gentle swirl between two worlds, one of life, one of death, his leg drifting past followed by his arm, red clay mixed with the blood the pain deadened by more pain until it was not pain at all, just a hammering weight against his body as if an enormous stone lay upon him, his head too heavy to lift or to even move. It was not as if he did not remember anything but that he remembered so much he was unable to pick out the parts and make them understandable, recognizable bits of information he could pluck from a tree and enjoy at will. The blast tore away all understanding, briefly stripped him clean of knowledge and only now started to rewrite his history, an epistemology scratched with hard chalk on a rough blackboard. Voices scratched at his ears and light wavered like deep water across his eyes as if he were slowly rising from a great depth. He fought against the world of death without knowing he was fighting, without understanding the great battle for life was not one of physicality but the torn silk of spirit splayed against the dark that carried on the fight, no pressure, no great lunges or surges, just hanging as a curtain not to keep the light in but to keep the night out. Figures and images moved like boats bobbing from under water as he grasped for air and tried to surface, the sky always just beyond his reach. The light dimmed as someone leaned over him eclipsing what light there was.

"He's in pretty bad shape," said Luat. "He doesn't know where he wants to be, in this world or the next."

Hong placed a cool wet cloth across Bix's forehead. Blood covered the bandages around the stumps of his leg and arm.

"They'll have to be changed soon," she said. "He should not be bleeding so much."

"Legionnaires have much blood in them," said Chau, "especially American legionnaires. This one has more than most. He is my responsibility and we will do everything we can to keep him safe."

Chau insisted that the only surgeon operate on Bix immediately. It was the only time he had used the letter from General Giap to obtain a favor. The doctor was not pleased working on a French soldier over the Viet Minh and, although Chau knew nothing about amputations, he stayed with an air of knowledge and watched the work being done, occasionally clearing his throat as if to say "yes" or to question or to make sure all was correct. The work went quickly and Bix was moved to the shade of a tree on the hillside.

"You seem to care much about him?" said Luat, making a gently inquiry.

"He saved my life." Chau turned without further explanation and looked over the battlefield.

The morning was bringing about the final defeat of the French, the remaining outposts being overrun in the valley. With the fall of A-1 hill, known to the enemy as Elaine 2, the Viet Minh victory was secured. He wondered if it would mark the end of the war. The fortress was a small one with few French soldiers involved. Their loss was hardly significant beyond pride – a slap in the face, nothing more. The battle was fought off-handedly, piecemeal, not by the soldiers or the garrison, but by the higher command who seemed reluctant to make a full commitment to support the men, expendable men as all soldiers are expendable, not even pawns in a chess game but bits of pawns often chipped away until they can no longer stand while the kings scurry about in an effort to save themselves. Chau suspected the French and Vietnamese would eventually become friends or at least work together for their mutual benefit, something that could have been done without war, yet a war is always needed to understand how useless and unnecessary it is.

"Your friend is very sick," said Hong.

She stood close to Chau and he moved slightly in an effort to touch her, to feel her warmth against him. He longed to be with a woman again, the touch of flesh, a living breathing person, someone he could try and understand yet knowing that no person can understand another person through attempting to climb into another's body, to leave a part of himself there as a marker, a thing indescribable yet a thing just the same as real and tangible as a thought or an idea. Even more than that he wanted to be loved, wanted someone to want him with all his frailties his imperfections and his strengths, wanted this above all else, above all other desires.

"Yes," said Chau. "He is very weak but we must try."

"You are a good man," she said, without shame or embarrassment.

The statement from a Vietnamese woman seemed strange to Chau. Vietnamese, except Luat, never came to the point, never said anything directly, only hinted at statements. A declarative sentence appeared beyond their capability.

"I knew him long ago," said Chau, feeling the need to talk. "I was a Frenchman then and thought I knew many things about the world. I am Vietnamese now and understand nothing about the world except that it goes on and will continue long after I have ceased to exist." He scratched his chin. "He, and his friend, Steve, taught me to laugh."

Hong moved closer to him. Their hands touched. He turned toward her and leaned near.

"He said something," said Luat, coming up behind them.

"Yes," said Chau, looking directly at him.

"I don't know," said Luat. "He is coming around and I know he will be frightened and confused."

"At seeing you?" said Hong.

"I am not nearly so beautiful as Chau," said Luat. "Perhaps the soldier should see Chau's face first?"

"I think so," said Chau. "He might not remember me."

They moved toward the stretcher, past wounded Viet Minh mostly suffering in silence, arms and legs missing, heads bandaged, blood soaking through tunics. The sounds of battle sounded distant, mostly small arms fire popping and sputtering. Bix looked almost white as if his body was bloodless, porcelain and cold. He started to heave, only gas and acid rising from his stomach. The world appeared through gauze as he tried to focus his eyes, distinguish forms and shapes. A face appeared to hover above his.

"Bix," whispered a voice. "Can you hear me? You must return to this world."

Bix tried to speak. He knew the words within him, the sounds and the logical order. Only incoherent scratches emerged, the sound of his own voice confusing him. Nothing that emerged was what he thought would emerge and he remained frustrated at the noise he thought was speech.

"You are safe now, my friend," said Chau. "You are badly injured. I am Chau, your friend."

Bix's mind flitted about the name, a name from years past. He tried to grab the sound as it floated in the air.

"Chau," he whispered, finally something coherent.

"Yes, yes, Chau, your old friend." Chau moved the wet cloth from Bix's forehead replacing it with his warm hand as if some life from him might drain into Bix.

Bix tried to lift his arm and touch Chau but the reach fell short, an unaccustomed length, a missing hand.

"What is it?" said Bix, understanding without knowing.

"Don't worry," said Chau. "The hand is gone, and also a leg. Better to know it now so you can recover without surprises."

Bix tried to comprehend the missing parts and moved both his arms, one lighter than the other and uncontrollable. Both his legs felt painful, one feeling no different than the other, both feeling intact, yet smashed as if having been run over by a truck.

"Are you with the relief column?" said Bix. "Have they come at last?"

Chau looked uncomfortably at his friends. The truth was more than Bix could handle in his present situation. He looked back at Bix.

"You are with me and my friends," said Chau. "We have much to discuss and much time for contemplation as you recover."

"Then there's no hope?" said Bix. "I hear it in your voice. I tried my best to help your country but mostly I came for me."

Chau replaced the cloth on Bix's head and offered him some water.

"I still hear gunfire?" said Bix.

"It is finished," said Chau. "We are on a hillside waiting for the final surrender when all will be at peace and we can start over again."

"Is there anything to see?" said Bix.

"We will move you closer," said Chau.

They moved the stretcher to a small ledge. Chau held Bix's head toward the valley; Hong rested one hand on Chau's shoulder, the other against Luat's back; Luat supported Bix's twisted body, and together they remained connected as Bix watched the final assault and tried to understand the scene before him.

There, in the valley below, where he had hoped to attain his manhood, enjoy the feast of victory, come to the great epiphany of life, he watched the camp heaped with smoke, maggots of tiny Viet Minh crawling through the eaten earth like an undulating carpet of independence, the bones of French soldiers and legionnaires creeping through rags as they emerged from their holes, hands above their heads, and leaving him not with some great wisdom but, as he rolled back onto the stretcher, but with what he thought would be the epistle of his life, now melted into two simple whispered words: "What happened?"

Epilogue

Of the 14,000 French troops eventually involved in the battle at Dien Bien Phu, almost 4,000 refuse to fight becoming internal deserters. Only 5,500 able-bodied combat troops remain during the last weeks of the battle. 10,863 are sent to prison camps of which 3,290 survive. France is finished as a colonial power. The United States assumes her position.

Within months an estimated 100,000 to 300,000 Vietnamese civilians build a 500 mile supply route through the jungles, mountains, and across rivers, from the Chinese border to the battlefield. It remains one of the greatest engineering feats in history. The Viet Minh feed over 50,000 combat troops into the battle. An estimated 25,000 become casualties. Although they never win a single battle against the United States, their experience in combat helps them defeat the world's greatest military power through atrition and determination.